The Great Tales of
SIR ARTHUR
CONAN DOYLE

The Great Tales of
SIR ARTHUR
CONAN DOYLE

MAGPIE/PARRAGON

This edition first published by Magpie Books in 1993

Magpie Books
7 Kensington Church Court
London W8 4SP

A copy of the British Library Data Cataloguing in Data is available
from the British Library

Printed and bound in the EC
by Firmin-Didot (France)
Groupe Hérissey

The Great Tales of

SIR ARTHUR
CONAN DOYLE

CONTENTS

Tales of the Ring

Tales of Pirates

Tales of Blue Water

CONTENTS

Tales of Terror

Tales of Twilight and the Unseen

Tales of Long Ago

TALES OF THE RING

1. *The Croxley Master*

MR. ROBERT MONTGOMERY was seated at his desk, his head upon his hands, in a state of the blackest despondency. Before him was the open ledger with the long columns of Dr. Oldacre's prescriptions. At his elbow lay the wooden tray with the labels in various partitions, the cork box, the lumps of twisted sealing-wax, while in front a rank of empty bottles waited to be filled. But his spirits were too low for work. He sat in silence, with his fine shoulders bowed and his head upon his hands.

Outside, through the grimy surgery window over a foreground of blackened brick and slate, a line of enormous chimneys like Cyclopean pillars upheld the lowering, dun-coloured cloud-bank. For six days in the week they spouted smoke, but to-day the furnace fires were banked, for it was Sunday. Sordid and polluting gloom hung over a district blighted and blasted by the greed of man. There was nothing in the surroundings to cheer a desponding soul, but it was more than his dismal environment which weighed upon the medical assistant.

His trouble was deeper and more personal. The winter session was approaching. He should be back again at the University completing the last year which would give him his medical degree ; but, alas ! he had not the money with which to pay his class fees, nor could he imagine how he could procure it. Sixty pounds were wanted to make his career, and it might have been as

3

many thousands for any chance there seemed to be of his obtaining it.

He was roused from his black meditation by the entrance of Dr. Oldacre himself, a large, clean-shaven, respectable man, with a prim manner and an austere face. He had prospered exceedingly by the support of the local Church interest, and the rule of his life was never by word or action to run a risk of offending the sentiment which had made him. His standard of respectability and of dignity was exceedingly high, and he expected the same from his assistants. His appearance and words were always vaguely benevolent. A sudden impulse came over the despondent student. He would test the reality of this philanthropy.

" I beg your pardon, Dr. Oldacre," said he, rising from his chair ; " I have a great favour to ask of you."

The doctor's appearance was not encouraging. His mouth suddenly tightened, and his eyes fell.

" Yes, Mr. Montgomery ? "

" You are aware, sir, that I need only one more session to complete my course."

" So you have told me."

" It is very important to me, sir."

" Naturally."

" The fees, Dr. Oldacre, would amount to about sixty pounds."

" I am afraid that my duties call me elsewhere, Mr. Montgomery."

" One moment, sir ! I had hoped, sir, that perhaps, if I signed a paper promising you interest upon your money, you would advance this sum to me. I will pay you back, sir, I really will. Or, if you like, I will work it off after I am qualified."

The doctor's lips had thinned into a narrow line. His eyes were raised again, and sparkled indignantly.

" Your request is unreasonable, Mr. Montgomery. I am surprised that you should have made it. Consider, sir, how many thousands of medical students there are

4

in this country. No doubt there are many of them who have a difficulty in finding their fees. Am I to provide for them all? Or why should I make an exception in your favour? I am grieved and disappointed, Mr. Montgomery, that you should have put me into the painful position of having to refuse you." He turned upon his heel, and walked with offended dignity out of the surgery.

The student smiled bitterly, and turned to his work of making up the morning prescriptions. It was poor and unworthy work—work which any weakling might have done as well, and this was a man of exceptional nerve and sinew. But, such as it was, it brought him his board and £1 a week, enough to help him during the summer months and let him save a few pounds towards his winter keep. But those class fees! Where were they to come from? He could not save them out of his scanty wage. Dr. Oldacre would not advance them. He saw no way of earning them. His brains were fairly good, but brains of that quality were a drug in the market. He only excelled in his strength; and where was he to find a customer for that? But the ways of Fate are strange, and his customer was at hand.

"Look y'ere!" said a voice at the door.

Montgomery looked up, for the voice was a loud and rasping one. A young man stood at the entrance—a stocky, bull-necked young miner, in tweed Sunday clothes and an aggressive necktie. He was a sinister-looking figure, with dark, insolent eyes, and the jaw and throat of a bulldog.

"Look y'ere!" said he again. "Why hast thou not sent t' medicine oop as thy master ordered?"

Montgomery had become accustomed to the brutal frankness of the Northern worker. At first it had enraged him, but after a time he had grown callous to it, and accepted it as it was meant. But this was something different. It was insolence—brutal, overbearing insolence, with physical menace behind it.

5

"What name?" he asked coldly.

"Barton. Happen I may give thee cause to mind that name, yoong man. Mak' oop t' wife's medicine this very moment, look ye, or it will be the worse for thee."

Montgomery smiled. A pleasant sense of relief thrilled softly through him. What blessed safety-valve was this through which his jangled nerves might find some outlet. The provocation was so gross, the insult so unprovoked, that he could have none of those qualms which take the edge off a man's mettle. He finished sealing the bottle upon which he was occupied, and he addressed it and placed it carefully in the rack.

"Look here!" said he, turning round to the miner, "your medicine will be made up in its turn and sent down to you. I don't allow folk in the surgery. Wait outside in the waiting-room, if you wish to wait at all."

"Yoong man," said the miner, "thou's got to mak' t' wife's medicine here, and now, and quick, while I wait and watch thee, or else happen thou might need some medicine thysel' before all is over."

"I shouldn't advise you to fasten a quarrel upon me." Montgomery was speaking in the hard, staccato voice of a man who is holding himself in with difficulty. "You'll save trouble if you'll go quietly. If you don't you'll be hurt. Ah, you would? Take it, then!"

The blows were almost simultaneous—a savage swing which whistled past Montgomery's ear and a straight drive which took the workman on the chin. Luck was with the assistant. That single whizzing uppercut, and the way in which it was delivered, warned him that he had a formidable man to deal with. But if he had underrated his antagonist, his antagonist had also underrated him, and had laid himself open to a fatal blow.

The miner's head had come with a crash against the corner of the surgery shelves, and he had dropped heavily on to the ground. There he lay with his bandy legs drawn up and his hands thrown abroad, the blood trickling over the surgery tiles.

" Had enough ? " asked the assistant, breathing fiercely through his nose.

But no answer came. The man was insensible. And then the danger of his position came upon Montgomery, and he turned as white as his antagonist. A Sunday, the immaculate Dr. Oldacre with his pious connection, a savage brawl with a patient ; he would irretrievably lose his situation if the facts came out. It was not much of a situation, but he could not get another without a reference, and Oldacre might refuse him one. Without money for his classes, and without a situation—what was to become of him ? It was absolute ruin.

But perhaps he could escape exposure after all. He seized his insensible adversary, dragged him out into the centre of the room, loosened his collar, and squeezed the surgery sponge over his face. He sat up at last with a gasp and a scowl.

" Domn thee, thou's spoilt my necktie," said he, mopping up the water from his breast.

" I'm sorry I hit you so hard," said Montgomery, apologetically.

" Thou hit me hard ! I could stan' such fly-flappin' all day. 'Twas this here press that cracked my pate for me, and thou art a looky man to be able to boast as thou hast outed me. And now I'd be obliged to thee if thou wilt give me t' wife's medicine."

Montgomery gladly made it up and handed it to the miner.

" You are weak still," said he. " Won't you stay awhile and rest ? "

" T' wife wants her medicine," said the man, and lurched out at the door.

The assistant, looking after him, saw him rolling with an uncertain step down the street, until a friend met him, and they walked on arm-in-arm. The man seemed in his rough Northern fashion to bear no grudge, and so

7

Montgomery's fears left him. There was no reason why the doctor should know anything about it. He wiped the blood from the floor, put the surgery in order, and went on with his interrupted task, hoping that he had come scathless out of a very dangerous business.

Yet all day he was aware of a sense of vague uneasiness which sharpened into dismay when, late in the afternoon, he was informed that three gentlemen had called and were waiting for him in the surgery. A coroner's inquest, a descent of detectives, an invasion of angry relatives— all sorts of possibilities rose to scare him. With tense nerves and a rigid face he went to meet his visitors.

They were a very singular trio. Each was known to him by sight; but what on earth the three could be doing together, and, above all, what they could expect from *him*, was a most inexplicable problem.

The first was Sorley Wilson, the son of the owner of the Nonpareil Coalpit. He was a young blood of twenty, heir to a fortune, a keen sportsman, and down for the Easter Vacation from Magdalene College. He sat now upon the edge of the surgery table, looking in thoughtful silence at Montgomery, and twisting the ends of his small, black, waxed moustache.

The second was Purvis, the publican, owner of the chief beershop, and well known as the local bookmaker. He was a coarse, clean-shaven man, whose fiery face made a singular contrast with his ivory-white bald head. He had shrewd, light-blue eyes with foxy lashes, and he also leaned forward in silence from his chair, a fat, red hand upon either knee, and stared critically at the young assistant.

So did the third visitor, Fawcett, the horse-breaker, who leaned back, his long, thin legs, with their box-cloth riding-gaiters, thrust out in front of him, tapping his protruding teeth with his riding-whip, with anxious thought in every line of his rugged, bony face. Publican, exquisite, and horsebreaker were all three equally silent, equally earnest, and equally critical. Montgomery, seated in the midst of them, looked from one to the other.

" Well, gentlemen ? " he observed, but no answer came. The position was embarrassing.

" No," said the horsebreaker, at last. " No. It's off. It's nowt."

" Stand oop, lad ; let's see thee standin'." It was the publican who spoke.

Montgomery obeyed. He would learn all about it, no doubt, if he were patient. He stood up and turned slowly round, as if in front of his tailor.

" It's off ! It's off ! " cried the horsebreaker. " Why, mon, the Master would break him over his knee."

" Oh, that be hanged for a yarn ! " said the young Cantab. " You can drop out if you like, Fawcett, but I'll see this thing through, if I have to do it alone. I don't hedge a penny. I like the cut of him a great deal better than I liked Ted Barton."

" Look at Barton's shoulders, Mr. Wilson."

" Lumpiness isn't always strength. Give me nerve and fire and breed. That's what wins."

" Ay, sir, you have it theer—you have it theer ! " said the fat, red-faced publican, in a thick, suety voice. " It's the same wi' poops. Get 'em clean-bred an' fine, an' they'll yark the thick 'uns—yark 'em out o' their skins."

" He's ten good pund on the light side," growled the horsebreaker.

" He's a welter weight, anyhow."

" A hundred and thirty."

" A hundred and fifty, if he's an ounce."

" Well, the Master doesn't scale much more than that."

" A hundred and seventy-five."

" That was when he was hog-fat and living high. Work the grease out of him, and I lay there's no great difference between them. Have you been weighed lately, Mr. Montgomery ? "

It was the first direct question which had been asked

him. He had stood in the midst of them, like a horse at a fair, and he was just beginning to wonder whether he was more angry or amused.

" I am just eleven stone," said he.

" I said that he was a welter weight."

" But suppose you was trained ? " said the publican. " Wot then ? "

" I am always in training."

" In a manner of speakin,' no doubt, he *is* always in trainin'," remarked the horsebreaker. " But trainin' for everyday work ain't the same as trainin' with a trainer ; and I dare bet, with all respec' to your opinion, Mr. Wilson, that there's half a stone of tallow on him at this minute."

The young Cantab put his fingers on the assistant's upper arm. Then with his other hand on his wrist he bent the forearm sharply, and felt the biceps, as round and hard as a cricket-ball, spring up under his fingers.

" Feel that ! " said he.

The publican and horsebreaker felt it with an air of reverence.

" Good lad ! He'll do yet ! " cried Purvis.

" Gentlemen," said Montgomery, " I think that you will acknowledge that I have been very patient with you. I have listened to all that you have to say about my personal appearance, and now I must really beg that you will have the goodness to tell me what is the matter."

They all sat down in their serious, business-like way.

" That's easy done, Mr. Montgomery," said the fat-voiced publican. " But before sayin' anything we had to wait and see whether, in a way of speakin', there was any need for us to say anything at all. Mr. Wilson thinks there is. Mr. Fawcett, who has the same right to his opinion, bein' also a backer and one o' the committee, thinks the other way."

" I thought him too light built, and I think so now," said the horsebreaker, still tapping his prominent teeth with the metal head of his riding-whip. " But happen he may pull through ; and he's a fine-made, buirdly young chap, so if you mean to back him, Mr. Wilson——"

" Which I do."

" And you, Purvis ? "

" I ain't one to go back, Fawcett."

" Well, I'll stan' to my share of the purse."

" And well I knew you would," said Purvis, " for it would be somethin' new to find Isaac Fawcett as a spoil-sport. Well, then, we make up the hundred for the stake among us, and the fight stands—always supposin' the young man is willin'."

" Excuse all this rot, Mr. Montgomery," said the University man, in a genial voice. " We've begun at the wrong end, I know, but we'll soon straighten it out, and I hope that you will see your way to falling in with our views. In the first place, you remember the man whom you knocked out this morning ? He is Barton— the famous Ted Barton."

" I'm sure, sir, you may well be proud to have outed him in one round," said the publican. " Why, it took Morris, the ten-stone-six champion, a deal more trouble than that before he put Barton to sleep. You've done a fine performance, sir, and happen you'll do a finer, if you give yourself the chance."

" I never heard of Ted Barton, beyond seeing the name on a medicine label," said the assistant.

" Well, you may take it from me that he's a slaugh-terer," said the horsebreaker. " You've taught him a lesson that he needed, for it was always a word and a blow with him, and the word alone was worth five shillin' in a public court. He won't be so ready now to shake his nief in the face of every one he meets. However, that's neither here nor there."

Montgomery looked at them in bewilderment.

" For goodness' sake, gentlemen, tell me what it is you want me to do ! " he cried.

" We want you to fight Silas Craggs, better known as the Master of Croxley."

"But why?"

"Because Ted Barton was to have fought him next Saturday. He was the champion of the Wilson coal-pits, and the other was the Master of the iron-folk down at the Croxley smelters. We'd matched our man for a purse of a hundred against the Master. But you've queered our man, and he can't face such a battle with a two-inch cut at the back of his head. There's only one thing to be done, sir, and that is for you to take his place. If you can lick Ted Barton you may lick the Master of Croxley; but if you don't we're done, for there's no one else who is in the same street with him in this district. It's twenty rounds, two-ounce gloves, Queensberry rules, and a decision on points if you fight to the finish."

For a moment the absurdity of the thing drove every other thought out of Montgomery's head. But then there came a sudden revulsion. A hundred pounds!— all he wanted to complete his education was lying there ready to his hand if only that hand were strong enough to pick it up. He had thought bitterly that morning that there was no market for his strength, but here was one where his muscle might earn more in an hour than his brains in a year. But a chill of doubt came over him.

"How can I fight for the coal-pits?" said he. "I am not connected with them."

"Eh, lad, but thou art!" cried old Purvis. "We've got it down in writin', and it's clear enough. 'Anyone connected with the coal-pits.' Doctor Oldacre is the coal-pit club doctor; thou art his assistant. What more can they want?"

"Yes, that's right enough," said the Cantab. "It would be a very sporting thing of you, Mr. Montgomery, if you would come to our help when we are in such a hole. Of course, you might not like to take the hundred pounds; but I have no doubt that, in the case of your winning, we could arrange that it should take the form of a watch or piece of plate, or any other shape which might suggest itself to you. You see, you are responsible for our having lost our champion, so we really feel that we have a claim upon you."

" Give me a moment, gentlemen. It is very unexpected. I am afraid the doctor would never consent to my going—in fact, I am sure that he would not."

" But he need never know—not before the fight, at any rate. We are not bound to give the name of our man. So long as he is within the weight limits on the day of the fight, that is all that concerns any one."

The adventure and the profit would either of them have attracted Montgomery. The two combined were irresistible.

" Gentlemen," said he, " I'll do it ! "

The three sprang from their seats. The publican had seized his right hand, the horse-dealer his left, and the Cantab slapped him on the back.

" Good lad ! good lad ! " croaked the publican. " Eh, mon, but if thou yark him, thou'll rise in one day from being just a common doctor to the best-known mon 'twixt here and Bradford. Thou are a witherin' tyke, thou art, and no mistake ; and if thou beat the Master of Croxley, thou'll find all the beer thou want for the rest of thy life waiting for thee at the Four Sacks."

" It is the most sporting thing I ever heard of in my life," said young Wilson. " By George, sir, if you pull it off, you've got the constituency in your pocket, if you care to stand. You know the outhouse in my garden ? "

" Next the road ? "

" Exactly. I turned it into a gymnasium for Ted Barton. You'll find all you want there : clubs, punching-ball, bars, dumb-bells, everything. Then you'll want a sparring partner. Ogilvy has been acting for Barton, but we don't think that he is class enough. Barton bears you no grudge. He's a good-hearted fellow, though cross-grained with strangers. He looked upon you as a stranger this morning, but he says he knows you now. He is quite ready to spar with you for practice, and he will come at any hour you will name."

" Thank you ; I will let you know the hour," said Montgomery ; and so the committee departed jubilant upon their way.

The medical assistant sat for a little time in the surgery turning it over in his mind. He had been trained originally at the University by the man who had been middle-weight champion in his day. It was true that his teacher was long past his prime, slow upon his feet and stiff in his joints, but even so he was still a tough antagonist ; but Montgomery had found at last that he could more than hold his own with him. He had won the University medal, and his teacher, who had trained so many students, was emphatic in his opinion that he had never had one who was in the same class with him. He had been exhorted to go in for the Amateur Championships, but he had no particular ambition in that direction. Once he had put on the gloves with Hammer Tunstall in a booth at a fair, and had fought three rattling rounds, in which he had the worst of it, but had made the prize-fighter stretch himself to the uttermost. There was his whole record, and was it enough to encourage him to stand up to the Master of Croxley ? He had never heard of the Master before, but then he had lost touch of the ring during the last few years of hard work. After all, what did it matter ? If he won, there was the money, which meant so much to him. If he lost, it would only mean a thrashing. He could take punishment without flinching, of that he was certain. If there were only one chance in a hundred of pulling it off, then it was worth his while to attempt it.

Dr. Oldacre, new come from church, with an ostentatious prayer-book in his kid-gloved hand, broke in upon his meditation.

" You don't go to service, I observe, Mr. Montgomery," said he, coldly.

" No, sir ; I have had some business to detain me."

" It is very near to my heart that my household

should set a good example. There are so few educated people in this district that a great responsibility devolves upon us. If we do not live up to the highest, how can we expect these poor workers to do so? It is a dreadful thing to reflect that the parish takes a great deal more interest in an approaching glove-fight than in their religious duties."

" A glove-fight, sir ? " said Montgomery, guiltily.

" I believe that to be the correct term. One of my patients tells me that it is the talk of the district. A local ruffian, a patient of ours, by the way, is matched against a pugilist over at Croxley. I cannot understand why the law does not step in and stop so degrading an exhibition. It is really a prize-fight."

" A glove-fight, you said."

" I am informed that a two-ounce glove is an evasion by which they dodge the law, and make it difficult for the police to interfere. They contend for a sum of money. It seems dreadful and almost incredible—does it not ?— to think that such scenes can be enacted within a few miles of our peaceful home. But you will realize, Mr. Montgomery, that while there are such influences for us to counteract, it is very necessary that we should live up to our highest."

The doctor's sermon would have had more effect if the assistant had not once or twice had occasion to test his highest and come upon it at unexpectedly humble elevations. It is always so particularly easy to " compound for sins we're most inclined to by damning those we have no mind to." In any case, Montgomery felt that of all the men concerned in such a fight—promoters, backers, spectators—it is the actual fighter who holds the strongest and most honourable position. His conscience gave him no concern upon the subject. Endurance and courage are virtues, not vices, and brutality is, at least, better than effeminacy.

There was a little tobacco-shop at the corner of the street, where Montgomery got his bird's-eye and also his local information, for the shopman was a garrulous soul, who knew everything about the affairs of the district. The assistant strolled down there after tea and asked, in a casual way, whether the tobacconist had ever heard of the Master of Croxley.

" Heard of him ! Heard of him ! " the little man could hardly articulate in his astonishment. " Why, sir, he's the first mon o' the district, an' his name's as well known in the West Riding as the winner o' t' Derby. But Lor', sir "—here he stopped and rummaged among a heap of papers. " They are makin' a fuss about him on account o' his fight wi' Ted Barton, and so the *Croxley Herald* has his life an' record, an' here it is, an' thou canst read it for thysel'."

The sheet of the paper which he held up was a lake of print around an islet of illustration. The latter was a coarse wood-cut of a pugilist's head and neck set in a cross-barred jersey. It was a sinister but powerful face, the face of a debauched hero, clean-shaven, strongly eye-browed, keen-eyed, with a huge, aggressive jaw, and an animal dewlap beneath it. The long, obstinate cheeks ran flush up to the narrow, sinister eyes. The mighty neck came down square from the ears and curved out-wards into shoulders, which had lost nothing at the hands of the local artist. Above was written " Silas Craggs," and beneath, " The Master of Croxley."

" Thou'll find all about him there, sir," said the tobacconist. " He's a witherin' tyke, he is, and w're proud to have him in the county. If he hadn't broke his leg he'd have been champion of England."

" Broke his leg, has he ? "

" Yes, and it set badly. They ca' him owd K behind his bock, for thot is how his two legs look. But his arms—well, if they was both stropped to a bench, as the sayin' is, I wonder where the champion of England would be then."

" I'll take this with me," said Montgomery ; and putting the paper into his pocket he returned home.

It was not a cheering record which he read there. The whole history of the Croxley Master was given in full, his many victories, his few defeats.

" Born in 1857," said the provincial biographer, " Silas Craggs, better known in sporting circles as The Master of Croxley, is now in his fortieth year."

" Hang it, I'm only twenty-three," said Montgomery to himself, and read on more cheerfully.

" Having in his youth shown a surprising aptitude for the game, he fought his way up among his comrades, until he became the recognized champion of the district and won the proud title which he still holds. Ambitious of a more than local fame, he secured a patron, and fought his first fight against Jack Barton, of Birmingham, in May, 1880, at the old Loiterers' Club. Craggs, who fought at ten-stone-two at the time, had the better of fifteen rattling rounds, and gained an award on points against the Midlander. Having disposed of James Dunn, of Rotherhithe, Cameron, of Glasgow, and a youth named Fernie, he was thought so highly of by the fancy that he was matched against Ernest Willox, at that time middle-weight champion of the North of England, and defeated him in a hard-fought battle, knocking him out in the tenth round after a punishing contest. At this period it looked as if the very highest honours of the ring were within the reach of the young Yorkshireman, but he was laid upon the shelf by a most unfortunate accident. The kick of a horse broke his thigh, and for a year he was compelled to rest himself. When he returned to his work the fracture had set badly, and his activity was much impaired. It was owing to this that he was defeated in seven rounds by Willox, the man whom he had previously beaten, and afterwards by James Shaw, of London, though the latter acknowledged that he had found the toughest customer of his career. Undismayed by his reverses, the Master adapted the style of his fighting to his physical disabilities, and resumed his career of victory—defeating Norton (the black), Bobby Wilson,

17

and Levi Cohen, the latter a heavy-weight. Conceding two stone, he fought a draw with the famous Billy McQuire, and afterwards, for a purse of fifty pounds, he defeated Sam Hare at the Pelican Club, London. In 1891 a decision was given against him upon a foul when fighting a winning fight against Jim Taylor, the Australian middle-weight, and so mortified was he by the decision, that he withdrew from the ring. Since then he has hardly fought at all save to accommodate any local aspirant who may wish to learn the difference between a bar-room scramble and a scientific contest. The latest of these ambitious souls comes from the Wilson coal-pits, which have undertaken to put up a stake of £100 and back their local champion. There are various rumours afloat as to who their representative is to be, the name of Ted Barton being freely mentioned ; but the betting, which is seven to one on the Master against any untried man, is a fair reflection of the feeling of the community."

Montgomery read it over twice, and it left him with a very serious face. No light matter this, which he had undertaken ; no battle with a rough-and-tumble fighter who presumed upon a local reputation. The man's record showed that he was first class—or nearly so. There were a few points in his favour, and he must make the most of them. There was age—twenty-three against forty. There was an old ring proverb that " Youth will be served," but the annals of the ring offer a great number of exceptions. A hard veteran, full of cool valour and ring-craft, could give ten or fifteen years and a beating to most striplings. He could not rely too much upon his advantage in age. But then there was the lameness ; that must surely count for a great deal. And, lastly, there was the chance that the Master might underrate his opponent, that he might be remiss in his training, and refuse to abandon his usual way of life, if he thought that he had an easy task before him. In a man of his age and habits this seemed very possible. Montgomery prayed that it might be so. Meanwhile, if his opponent were the best man who ever jumped the ropes into a ring, his own duty was clear. He must prepare himself carefully, throw away no chance, and do the very best that he could. But he knew enough to appreciate the difference which exists in boxing, as in every sport, between the amateur and the professional. The coolness, the power of hitting, above all the capability of taking punishment, count for so much. Those specially developed, gutta-percha-like abdominal muscles of the hardened pugilist will take without flinching a blow which would leave another man writhing on the ground. Such things are not to be acquired in a week, but all that could be done in a week should be done.

The medical assistant had a good basis to start from. He was 5 feet 11 inches—tall enough for anything on two legs, as the old ring men used to say—lithe and spare, with the activity of a panther, and a strength which had hardly yet ever found its limitations. His muscular development was finely hard, but his power came rather from that higher nerve-energy which counts for nothing upon a measuring tape. He had the well-curved nose and the widely opened eye which never yet were seen upon the face of a craven, and behind everything he had the driving force, which came from the knowledge that his whole career was at stake upon the contest. The three backers rubbed their hands when they saw him at work punching the ball in the gymnasium next morning; and Fawcett, the horsebreaker, who had written to Leeds to hedge his bets, sent a wire to cancel the letter, and to lay another fifty at the market price of seven to one.

Montgomery's chief difficulty was to find time for his training without any interference from the doctor. His work took him a large part of the day, but as the visiting was done on foot, and considerable distances had to be traversed, it was a training in itself. For the rest, he punched the swinging ball and worked with the dumb-bells for an hour every morning and evening, and boxed twice a day with Ted Barton in the gymnasium, gaining as much profit as could be got from a rushing, two-handed slogger. Barton was full of admiration for his cleverness and quickness, but doubtful about his strength. Hard hitting was the feature of his own style, and he exacted it from others.

" Lord, sir, that's a turble poor poonch for an eleven-stone man ! " he would cry. " Thou wilt have to hit harder than that afore t' Master will know that thou art theer. Ah, thot's better, mon, thot's fine ! " he would add, as his opponent lifted him across the room on the end of a right counter. " Thot's how I likes to feel 'em. Happen thou'lt pull through yet." He chuckled with joy when Montgomery knocked him into a corner. " Eh, mon, thou art comin' along grand. Thou hast fair yarked me off my legs. Do it again, lad, do it again ! "

The only part of Montgomery's training which came within the doctor's observation was his diet, and that puzzled him considerably.

" You will excuse my remarking, Mr. Montgomery, that you are becoming rather particular in your tastes. Such fads are not to be encouraged in one's youth. Why do you eat toast with every meal ? "

" I find that it suits me better than bread, sir."

" It entails unnecessary work upon the cook. I observe, also, that you have turned against potatoes."

" Yes, sir ; I think that I am better without them."

" And you no longer drink your beer ? "

" No, sir."

" These causeless whims and fancies are very much to be deprecated, Mr. Montgomery. Consider how many there are to whom these very potatoes and this very beer would be most acceptable."

" No doubt, sir. But at present I prefer to do without them."

They were sitting alone at lunch, and the assistant

thought that it would be a good opportunity of asking leave for the day of the fight.

"I should be glad if you could let me have leave for Saturday, Doctor Oldacre."

"It is very inconvenient upon so busy a day."

"I should do a double day's work on Friday so as to leave everything in order. I should hope to be back in the evening."

"I am afraid I cannot spare you, Mr. Montgomery."

This was a facer. If he could not get leave he would go without it.

"You will remember, Doctor Oldacre, that when I came to you it was understood that I should have a clear day every month. I have never claimed one. But now there are reasons why I wish to have a holiday upon Saturday."

Doctor Oldacre gave in with a very bad grace.

"Of course, if you insist upon your formal rights, there is no more to be said, Mr. Montgomery, though I feel that it shows a certain indifference to my comfort and the welfare of the practice. Do you still insist?"

"Yes, sir."

"Very good. Have your way."

The doctor was boiling over with anger, but Montgomery was a valuable assistant—steady, capable, and hard working—and he could not afford to lose him. Even if he had been prompted to advance those class fees, for which his assistant had appealed, it would have been against his interests to do so, for he did not wish him to qualify, and he desired him to remain in his subordinate position, in which he worked so hard for so small a wage. There was something in the cool insistence of the young man, a quiet resolution in his voice as he claimed his Saturday, which aroused his curiosity.

"I have no desire to interfere unduly with your affairs, Mr. Montgomery, but were you thinking of having a day in Leeds upon Saturday?"

" No, sir."

" In the country ? "

" Yes, sir."

" You are very wise. You will find a quiet day among the wild flowers a very valuable restorative. Had you thought of any particular direction ? "

" I am going over Croxley way."

" Well, there is no prettier country when once you are past the iron-works. What could be more delightful than to lie upon the Fells, basking in the sunshine, with perhaps some instructive and elevating book as your companion ? I should recommend a visit to the ruins of St. Bridget's Church, a very interesting relic of the early Norman era. By the way, there is one objection which I see to your going to Croxley on Saturday. It is upon that date, as I am informed, that that ruffianly glove-fight takes place. You may find yourself molested by the blackguards whom it will attract."

" I will take my chance of that, sir," said the assistant

On the Friday night, which was the last before the fight, Montgomery's three backers assembled in the gymnasium and inspected their man as he went through some light exercises to keep his muscles supple. He was certainly in splendid condition, his skin shining with health, and his eyes with energy and confidence. The three walked round him and exulted.

" He's simply ripping ! " said the undergraduate. " By Gad, you've come out of it splendidly. You're as hard as a pebble, and fit to fight for your life."

" Happen he's a trifle on the fine side," said the publican. " Runs a bit light at the loins, to my way of thinkin'."

" What weight to-day ? "

" Ten-stone eleven," the assistant answered.

" That's only three pund off in a week's trainin'," said the horsebreaker. " He said right when he said that he was in condition. Well, it's fine stuff all there is of it, but I'm none so sure as there is enough." He kept poking his finger into Montgomery, as if he were one of his horses. " I hear that the Master will scale a hundred and sixty odd at the ring-side."

" But there's some of that which he'd like well to pull off and leave behind wi' his shirt," said Purvis. " I hear they've had a rare job to get him to drop his beer, and if it had not been for that great red-headed wench of his they'd never ha' done it. She fair scratted the face off a potman that had brought him a gallon from t' Chequers. They say the hussy is his sparrin' partner, as well as his sweetheart, and that his poor wife is just breakin' her heart over it. Hullo, young 'un, what do you want ? "

The door of the gymnasium had opened, and a lad about sixteen, grimy and black with soot and iron, stepped into the yellow glare of the oil-lamp. Ted Barton seized him by the collar.

" See here, thou yoong whelp, this is private, and we want noan o' thy spyin' ! "

" But I maun speak to Mr. Wilson."

The young Cantab stepped forward.

" Well, my lad, what is it ? "

" It's aboot t' fight, Mr. Wilson, sir. I wanted to tell your mon somethin' aboot t' Maister."

" We've no time to listen to gossip, my boy. We know all about the Master."

" But thou doant, sir. Nobody knows but me and mother, and we thought as we'd like thy mon to know, sir, for we want him to fair bray him."

" Oh, you want the Master fair brayed, do you ? So do we. Well, what have you to say ? "

" Is this your mon, sir ? "

" Well, suppose it is ? "

" Then it's him I want to tell aboot it. T' Maister is blind o' the left eye."

" Nonsense ! "

" It's true, sir. Not stone blind, but rarely fogged. He keeps it secret, but mother knows, and so do I. If

23

thou slip him on the left side he can't cop thee. Thou'll find it right as I tell thee. And mark him when he sinks his right. 'Tis his best blow, his right upper-cut. T' Maister's finisher, they ca' it at t' works. It's a turble blow, when it do come home."

" Thank you, my boy. This is information worth having about his sight," said Wilson. " How came you to know so much ? Who are you ? "

" I'm his son, sir."

Wilson whistled.

" And who sent you to us ? "

" My mother. I maun get back to her again."

" Take this half-crown."

" No, sir, I don't seek money in comin' here. I do it——"

" For love ? " suggested the publican.

" For hate ! " said the boy, and darted off into the darkness.

" Seems to me t' red-headed wench may do him more harm than good, after all," remarked the publican. " And now, Mr. Montgomery, sir, you've done enough for this evenin', and a nine-hours' sleep is the best trainin' before a battle. Happen this time to-morrow night you'll be safe back again with your one hundred pounds in your pocket."

II

Work was struck at one o'clock at the coal-pits and the iron-works, and the fight was arranged for three. From the Croxley Furnaces, from Wilson's Coal-pits, from the Heartsease Mine, from the Dodd Mills, from the Leverworth Smelters the workmen came trooping, each with his fox-terrier or his lurcher at his heels. Warped with labour and twisted by toil, bent double by week-long work in the cramped coal galleries, or half-blinded with years spent in front of white-hot fluid metal, these men still gilded their harsh and hopeless lives by their devotion to sport. It was their one relief, the only thing which could distract their minds from sordid surroundings, and give them an interest beyond the blackened circle which inclosed them. Literature, art, science, all these things were beyond their horizon ; but the race, the football match, the cricket, the fight, these were things which they could understand, which they could speculate upon in advance and comment upon afterwards. Sometimes brutal, sometimes grotesque, the love of sport is still one of the great agencies which make for the happiness of our people. It lies very deeply in the springs of our nature, and when it has been educated out, a higher, more refined nature may be left, but it will not be of that robust British type which has left its mark so deeply on the world. Every one of these ruddled workers, slouching with his dog at his heels to see something of the fight, was a true unit of his race.

It was a squally May day, with bright sunbursts and driving showers. Montgomery worked all morning in the surgery getting his medicine made up.

" The weather seems so very unsettled, Mr. Montgomery," remarked the doctor, " that I am inclined to think that you had better postpone your little country excursion until a later date."

" I am afraid that I must go to-day, sir."

" I have just had an intimation that Mrs. Potter, at the other side of Angleton, wishes to see me. It is probable that I shall be there all day. It will be extremely inconvenient to leave the house empty so long."

" I am very sorry, sir, but I must go," said the assistant, doggedly.

The doctor saw that it would be useless to argue, and departed in the worst of bad tempers upon his mission. Montgomery felt easier now that he was gone. He went up to his room, and packed his running-shoes, his fighting-drawers, and his cricket-sash into a handbag. When he came down Mr. Wilson was waiting for him in the surgery.

" I hear the doctor has gone."

" Yes ; he is likely to be away all day."

" I don't see that it matters much. It's bound to come to his ears by to-night."

" Yes ; it's serious with me, Mr. Wilson. If I win, it's all right. I don't mind telling you that the hundred pounds will make all the difference to me. But if I lose, I shall lose my situation, for, as you say, I can't keep it secret."

" Never mind. We'll see you through among us. I only wonder the doctor has not heard, for it's all over the country that you are to fight the Croxley Champion. We've had Armitage up about it already. He's the Master's backer, you know. He wasn't sure that you were eligible. The Master said he wanted you whether you were eligible or not. Armitage has money on, and would have made trouble if he could. But I showed him that you came within the conditions of the challenge, and he agreed that it was all right. They think they have a soft thing on."

" Well, I can only do my best," said Montgomery.

They lunched together ; a silent and rather nervous repast, for Montgomery's mind was full of what was before him, and Wilson had himself more money at stake than he cared to lose.

Wilson's carriage and pair were at the door, the horses with blue-and-white rosettes at their ears, which were the colours of the Wilson Coal pits, well known on many a football field. At the avenue gate a crowd of some hundred pitmen and their wives gave a cheer as the carriage passed. To the assistant it all seemed dream like and extraordinary—the strangest experience of his life, but with a thrill of human action and interest in it which made it passionately absorbing. He lay back in the open carriage and saw the fluttering handkerchiefs from the doors and windows of the miners' cottages. Wilson had pinned a blue-and-white rosette upon his coat, and every one knew him as their champion.

"Good luck, sir! good luck to thee!" they shouted from the roadside. He felt that it was like some un-romantic knight riding down to sordid lists, but there was something of chivalry in it all the same. He fought for others as well as for himself. He might fail from want of skill or strength, but deep in his sombre soul he vowed that it should never be for want of heart.

Mr. Fawcett was just mounting into his high-wheeled, spidery dogcart, with his little bit of blood between the shafts. He waved his whip and fell in behind the carriage. They overtook Purvis, the tomato-faced publi-can, upon the road, with his wife in her Sunday bonnet. They also dropped into the procession, and then, as they traversed the seven miles of the high road to Croxley, their two-horsed, rosetted carriage became gradually the nucleus of a comet with a loosely radiating tail. From every side-road came the miners' carts, the humble, ramshackle traps, black and bulging, with their loads of noisy, foul-tongued, open-hearted partisans. They trailed for a long quarter of a mile behind them—cracking, whipping, shouting, galloping, swearing. Horsemen and runners were mixed with the vehicles. And then suddenly a squad of the Sheffield Yeomanry, who were having their annual training in those parts, clattered and jingled out of a field, and rode as an escort to the carriage. Through the dust-clouds round him Mont-gomery saw the gleaming brass helmets, the bright coats, and the tossing heads of the chargers, the delighted brown faces of the troopers. It was more dream-like than ever.

And then, as they approached the monstrous uncouth line of bottle-shaped buildings which marked the smelting-works of Croxley, their long, writhing snake of dust was headed off by another but longer one which wound across their path. The main road into which their own opened was filled by the rushing current of traps. The Wilson contingent halted until the others should get past. The iron-men cheered and groaned, according to their humour, as they whirled past their antagonist. Rough chaff flew back and forwards like iron nuts and splinters of coal. " Brought him up, then ! " " Got t' hearse for to fetch him back ? " " Where's t' owd K-legs ? " " Mon, mon, have thy photograph took— 'twill mind thee of what thou used to look ! " " He fight ?—he's now't but a half-baked doctor ! " " Happen he'll doctor thy Croxley Champion afore he's through wi't."

So they flashed at each other as the one side waited and the other passed. Then there came a rolling murmur swelling into a shout, and a great break with four horses came clattering along, all streaming with salmon-pink ribbons. The driver wore a white hat with pink rosette, and beside him, on the high seat, were a man and a woman—she with her arm round his waist. Montgomery had one glimpse of them as they flashed past : he with a furry cap drawn low over his brow, a great frieze coat, and a pink comforter round his throat ; she brazen, red-headed, bright-coloured, laughing excitedly. The Master, for it was he, turned as he passed, gazed hard at Montgomery, and gave him a menacing, gap-toothed grin. It was a hard, wicked face, blue-jowled and craggy, with long, obstinate cheeks and inexorable eyes. The break behind was full of patrons of the sport—flushed iron-foremen, heads of departments, managers. One was drinking from a metal flask, and raised it to Montgomery as he passed ; and then the crowd thinned, and the Wilson cortège with their dragoons swept in at the rear of the others.

The road led away from Croxley, between curving green hills, gashed and polluted by the searchers for coal and iron. The whole country had been gutted, and vast piles of refuse and mountains of slag suggested the mighty chambers which the labour of man had burrowed beneath. On the left the road curved up to where a huge building, roofless and dismantled, stood crumbling and forlorn, with the light shining through the windowless squares.

" That's the old Arrowsmith's factory. That's where the fight is to be," said Wilson. " How are you feeling now ? "

" Thank you. I was never better in my life," Montgomery answered.

" By Gad, I like your nerve ! " said Wilson, who was himself flushed and uneasy. " You'll give us a fight for our money, come what may. That place on the right is the office, and that has been set aside as the dressing- and weighing-room."

The carriage drove up to it amidst the shouts of the folk upon the hill-side. Lines of empty carriages and traps curved down upon the winding road, and a black crowd surged round the door of the ruined factory. The seats, as a huge placard announced, were five shillings, three shillings, and a shilling, with half-price for dogs. The takings, deducting expenses, were to go to the winner, and it was already evident that a larger stake than a hundred pounds was in question. A babel of voices rose from the door. The workers wished to bring their dogs in free. The men scuffled. The dogs barked. The crowd was a whirling, eddying pool surging with a roar up to the narrow cleft which was its only outlet.

The break, with its salmon-coloured streamers and four reeking horses, stood empty before the door of the office ; Wilson, Purvis, Fawcett, and Montgomery passed in.

There was a large, bare room inside with square, clean patches upon the grimy walls, where pictures and almanacs had once hung. Worn linoleum covered the floor, but there was no furniture save some benches and a deal table with a ewer and a basin upon it. Two of the corners were curtained off. In the middle of the room was a weighing-chair. A hugely fat man, with a salmon tie and a blue waistcoat with birds'-eye spots, came bustling up to them. It was Armitage, the butcher and grazier, well known for miles round as a warm

29

man, and the most liberal patron of sport in the Riding.

" Well, well," he grunted, in a thick, fussy, wheezy voice, " you have come, then. Got your man ? Got your man ? "

" Here he is, fit and well. Mr. Montgomery, let me present you to Mr. Armitage."

" Glad to meet you, sir. Happy to make your acquaintance. I make bold to say, sir, that we of Croxley admire your courage, Mr. Montgomery, and that our only hope is a fair fight and no favour and the best man win. That's our sentiment at Croxley."

" And it is my sentiment also," said the assistant.

" Well, you can't say fairer than that, Mr. Montgomery. You've taken a large contrac' in hand, but a large contrac' may be carried through, sir, as anyone that knows my dealings could testify. The Master is ready to weigh in ! "

" So am I."

" You must weigh in the buff."

Montgomery looked askance at the tall, red-headed woman who was standing gazing out of the window.

" That's all right," said Wilson. " Get behind the curtain and put on your fighting-kit."

He did so, and came out the picture of an athlete, in white, loose drawers, canvas shoes, and the sash of a well-known cricket club round his waist. He was trained to a hair, his skin gleaming like silk, and every muscle rippling down his broad shoulders and along his beautiful arms as he moved them. They bunched into ivory knobs, or slid into long, sinuous curves, as he raised or lowered his hands.

" What thinkest thou o' that ? " asked Ted Barton, his second, of the woman in the window.

She glanced contemptuously at the young athlete.

" It's but a poor kindness thou dost him to put a thread-paper yoong gentleman like yon against a mon as is a mon. Why, my Jock would throttle him wi' one hond lashed behind him."

30

" Happen he may—happen not," said Barton. " I have but twa pund in the world, but it's on him, every penny, and no hedgin'. But here's t' Maister, and rarely fine he do look."

The prize-fighter had come out from his curtain, a squat, formidable figure, monstrous in chest and arms, limping slightly on his distorted leg. His skin had none of the freshness and clearness of Montgomery's, but was dusky and mottled, with one huge mole amid the mat of tangled black hair which thatched his mighty breast. His weight bore no relation to his strength, for those huge shoulders and great arms, with brown, sledge-hammer fists, would have fitted the heaviest man that ever threw his cap into a ring. But his loins and legs were slight in proportion. Montgomery, on the other hand, was as symmetrical as a Greek statue. It would be an encounter between a man who was specially fitted for one sport, and one who was equally capable of any. The two looked curiously at each other: a bulldog, and a high-bred, clean-limbed terrier, each full of spirit.

" How do you do ? "

" How do ? " The Master grinn— again, and his three jagged front teeth gleamed for an instant. The rest had been beaten out of him in twenty years of battle. He spat upon the floor. " We have a rare fine day for't."

" Capital," said Montgomery.

" That's the good feelin' I like," wheezed the fat butcher. " Good lads, both of them !—prime lads !—hard meat an' good bone. There's no ill-feelin'."

" If he downs me, Gawd bless him ! " said the Master.

" An' if we down him, Gawd help him ! " interrupted the woman.

" Haud thy tongue, wench ! " said the Master, impatiently. " Who art thou to put in thy word ? Happen I might draw my hand across thy face."

The woman did not take the threat amiss.

" Wilt have enough for thy hand to do, Jock," said she. " Get quit o' this gradely man afore thou turn on me."

The lovers' quarrel was interrupted by the entrance of a new-comer, a gentleman with a fur-collared overcoat and a very shiny top-hat—a top-hat of a degree of glossiness which is seldom seen five miles from Hyde Park. This hat he wore at the extreme back of his head, so that the lower surface of the brim made a kind of frame for his high, bald forehead, his keen eyes, his rugged and yet kindly face. He bustled in with the quiet air of possession with which the ring-master enters the circus.

" It's Mr. Stapleton, the referee from London," said Wilson. " How do you do, Mr. Stapleton ? I was introduced to you at the big fight at the Corinthian Club, in Piccadilly."

" Ah, I dare say," said the other, shaking hands. " Fact is, I'm introduced to so many that I can't undertake to carry their names. Wilson, is it ? Well, Mr. Wilson, glad to see you. Couldn't get a fly at the station, and that's why I'm late."

" I'm sure, sir," said Armitage, " we should be proud that anyone so well known in the boxing world should come down to our little exhibition."

" Not at all. Not at all. Anything in the interest of boxin'. All ready ? Men weighed ? "

" Weighing now, sir."

" Ah, just as well I should see it done. Seen you before, Craggs. Saw you fight your second battle against Willox. You had beaten him once, but he came back on you. What does the indicator say ?—one hundred and sixty-three pounds—two off for the kit—one hundred and sixty-one. Now, my lad, you jump. My goodness, what colours are you wearing ? "

" The Anonymi Cricket Club."

" What right have you to wear them ? I belong to the club myself."

" So do I."

" You an amateur ? "

" Yes, sir."

" And you are fighting for a money prize? "

" Yes."

" I suppose you know what you are doing. You realize that you're a professional pug from this onwards, and that if ever you fight again——"

" I'll never fight again."

" Happen you won't," said the woman, and the Master turned a terrible eye upon her.

" Well, I suppose you know your own business best. Up you jump. One hundred and fifty-one, minus two, one hundred and forty-nine—twelve pounds' difference. but youth and condition on the other scale. Well, the sooner we get to work the better, for I wish to catch the seven-o'clock express at Hellifield. Twenty three-minute rounds, with one minute intervals, and Queensberry rules. Those are the conditions, are they not ? "

" Yes, sir."

" Very good, then, we may go across."

The two combatants had overcoats thrown over their shoulders, and the whole party, backers, fighters, seconds, and the referee, filed out of the room. A police inspector was waiting for them in the road. He had a notebook in his hand—that terrible weapon which awes even the London cabman.

" I must take your names, gentlemen, in case it should be necessary to proceed for breach of peace."

" You don't mean to stop the fight ? " cried Armitage, in a passion of indignation. " I'm Mr. Armitage, of Croxley, and this is Mr. Wilson, and we'll be responsible that all is fair and as it should be."

" I'll take the names in case it should be necessary to proceed," said the inspector, impassively.

" But you know me well."

" If you was a dook or even a judge it would be all the same," said the inspector. " It's the law, and there's

33

an end. I'll not take upon myself to stop the fight, seeing that gloves are to be used, but I'll take the names of all concerned. Silas Craggs, Robert Montgomery, Edward Barton, James Stapleton of London. Who seconds Silas Craggs?"

"I do," said the woman. "Yes, you can stare, but it's my job, and no one else's. Anastasia's the name—four a's."

"Craggs?"

"Johnson. Anastasia Johnson. If you jug him, you can jug me."

"Who talked of juggin', ye fool?" growled the Master. "Coom on, Mr. Armitage, for I'm fair sick o' this loiterin'."

The inspector fell in with the procession, and proceeded, as they walked up the hill, to bargain in his official capacity for a front seat, where he could safeguard the interests of the law, and in his private capacity to lay out thirty shillings at seven to one with Mr. Armitage.

Through the door they passed, down a narrow lane walled with a dense bank of humanity, up a wooden ladder to a platform, over a rope which was slung waist-high from four corner stakes, and then Montgomery realized that he was in that ring in which his immediate destiny was to be worked out. On the stake at one corner there hung a blue-and-white streamer. Barton led him across, the overcoat dangling loosely from his shoulders, and he sat down on a wooden stool. Barton and another man, both wearing white sweaters, stood beside him. The so-called ring was a square, twenty feet each way. At the opposite angle was the sinister figure of the Master, with his red-headed woman and a rough-faced friend to look after him. At each corner were metal basins, pitchers of water, and sponges.

During the hubbub and uproar of the entrance Montgomery was too bewildered to take things in. But now there was a few minutes' delay, for the referee had lingered behind, and so he looked quietly about him. It was a

sight to haunt him for a lifetime. Wooden seats had
been built in, sloping upwards to the tops of the walls.
Above, instead of a ceiling, a great flight of crows passed
slowly across a square of grey cloud. Right up to the
topmost benches the folk were banked—broadcloth in
front, corduroys and fustian behind ; faces turned
everywhere upon him. The grey reek of the pipes
filled the building, and the air was pungent with the
acrid smell of cheap, strong tobacco. Everywhere
among the human faces were to be seen the heads of
the dogs. They growled and yapped from the back
benches. In that dense mass of humanity one could
hardly pick out individuals, but Montgomery's eyes
caught the brazen gleam of the helmets held upon the
knees of the ten yeomen of his escort. At the very edge
of the platform sat the reporters, five of them : three
locals, and two all the way from London. But where
was the all-important referee ? There was no sign of
him, unless he were in the centre of that angry swirl of
men near the door.

Mr. Stapleton had stopped to examine the gloves
which were to be used, and entered the building after
the combatants. He had started to come down that
narrow lane with the human walls which led to the ring.
But already it had gone abroad that the Wilson champion
was a gentleman, and that another gentleman had been
appointed as referee. A wave of suspicion passed
through the Croxley folk. They would have one of
their own people for a referee. They would not have
a stranger. His path was stopped as he made for the
ring. Excited men flung themselves in front of him ;
they waved their fists in his face and cursed him. A
woman howled vile names in his ear. Somebody struck
at him with an umbrella. " Go thou back to Lunnon.
We want noan o' thee. Go thou back ! " they yelled.

Stapleton with his shiny hat cocked backwards, and
his large, bulging forehead swelling from under it, looked
round him from beneath his bushy brows. He was

in the centre of a savage and dangerous mob. Then he drew his watch from his pocket and held it dial upwards in his palm.

"In three minutes," said he, "I will declare the fight off."

They raged round him. His cool face and that aggressive top-hat irritated them. Grimy hands were raised. But it was difficult, somehow, to strike a man who was so absolutely indifferent.

"In two minutes I declare the fight off."

They exploded into blasphemy. The breath of angry men smoked into his placid face. A gnarled, grimy fist vibrated at the end of his nose. "We tell thee we want noan o' thee. Get thou back where thou com'st from."

"In one minute I declare the fight off."

Then the calm persistence of the man conquered the swaying, mutable, passionate crowd.

"Let him through, mon. Happen there'll be no fight after a'."

"Let him through."

"Bill, thou loomp, let him pass. Dost want the fight declared off?"

"Make room for the referee!—room for the Lunnon referee!"

And half pushed, half carried, he was swept up to the ring. There were two chairs by the side of it, one for him and one for the time-keeper. He sat down, his hands on his knees, his hat at a more wonderful angle than ever, impassive but solemn, with the aspect of one who appreciates his responsibilities.

Mr. Armitage, the portly butcher, made his way into the ring and held up two fat hands, sparkling with rings, as a signal for silence.

"Gentlemen!" he yelled. And then in a crescendo shriek, "Gentlemen!"

"And ladies!" cried somebody, for indeed there was a fair sprinkling of women among the crowd.

"Speak up, owd man!" shouted another. "What price pork chops?" cried somebody at the back. Everybody laughed, and the dogs began to bark. Armitage waved his hands amidst the uproar as if he were conducting an orchestra. At last the babel thinned into silence.

"Gentlemen," he yelled, "the match is between Silas Craggs, whom we call the Master of Croxley, and Robert Montgomery, of the Wilson Coal-pits. The match was to be under eleven eight. When they were weighed just now Craggs weighed eleven seven, and Montgomery ten nine. The conditions of the contest are—the best of twenty three-minute rounds with two-ounce gloves. Should the fight run to its full length it will, of course, be decided upon points. Mr. Stapleton, the well-known London referee, has kindly consented to see fair play. I wish to say that Mr. Wilson and I, the chief backers of the two men, have every confidence in Mr. Stapleton, and that we beg that you accept his rulings without dispute."

He then turned from one combatant to the other, with a wave of his hand.

III

"Montgomery—Craggs!" said he.

A great hush fell over the huge assembly. Even the dogs stopped yapping; one might have thought that the monstrous room was empty. The two men had stood up, the small white gloves over their hands. They advanced from their corners and shook hands: Montgomery gravely, Craggs with a smile. Then they fell into position. The crowd gave a long sigh—the intake of a thousand excited breaths. The referee tilted his chair on to its back legs, and looked moodily critical from the one to the other.

It was strength against activity—that was evident from the first. The Master stood stolidly upon his K-leg. It gave him a tremendous pedestal; one could hardly imagine his being knocked down. And he could pivot round upon it with extraordinary quickness ; but his advance or retreat was ungainly. His frame, however, was so much larger and broader than that of the student, and his brown, massive face looked so resolute and menacing, that the hearts of the Wilson party sank within them. There was one heart, however, which had not done so. It was that of Robert Montgomery.

Any nervousness which he may have had completely passed away now that he had his work before him. Here was something definite—this hard-faced, deformed Hercules to beat, with a career as the price of beating him. He glowed with the joy of action ; it thrilled through his nerves. He faced his man with little in-and-out steps, breaking to the left, breaking to the right, feeling his way, while Craggs, with a dull, malignant eye, pivoted slowly upon his weak leg, his left arm half extended, his right sunk low across the mark. Montgomery led with his left, and then led again, getting lightly home each time. He tried again, but the Master had his counter ready, and Montgomery reeled back from a harder blow than he had given. Anastasia, the woman, gave a shrill cry of encouragement, and her man let fly his right. Montgomery ducked under it, and in an instant the two were in each other's arms.

" Break away ! Break away ! " said the referee.

The Master struck upwards on the break, and shook Montgomery with the blow. Then it was " time." It had been a spirited opening round. The people buzzed into comment and applause. Montgomery was quite fresh, but the hairy chest of the Master was rising and falling. The man passed a sponge over his head, while Anastasia flapped the towel before him. " Good lass ! Good lass ! " cried the crowd, and cheered her.

The men were up again, the Master grimly watchful, Montgomery as alert as a kitten. The Master tried a sudden rush, squattering along with his awkward gait, but coming faster than one would think. The student slipped aside and avoided him. The Master stopped, grinned, and shook his head. Then he motioned with his hand as an invitation to Montgomery to come to him. The student did so and led with his left, but got a swinging right counter in the ribs in exchange. The heavy blow staggered him, and the Master came scrambling in to complete his advantage; but Montgomery, with his greater activity, kept out of danger until the call of " time." A tame round, and the advantage with the Master.

" 'T' Maister's too strong for him," said a smelter to his neighbour.

" Ay; but t'other's a likely lad. Happen we'll see some sport yet. He can joomp rarely."

" But t' Maister can stop and hit rarely. Happen he'll mak' him joomp when he gets his neif upon him."

They were up again, the water glistening upon their faces. Montgomery led instantly and got his right home with a sounding smack upon the Master's forehead. There was a shout from the colliers, and " Silence! Order ! " from the referee. Montgomery avoided the counter and scored with his left. Fresh applause, and the referee upon his feet in indignation. " No comments gentlemen, if *you* please, during the rounds."

" Just bide a bit ! " growled the Master.

" Don't talk—fight ! " said the referee, angrily.

Montgomery rubbed in the point by a flush hit upon the mouth, and the Master shambled back to his corner like an angry bear, having had all the worst of the round.

" Where's that seven to one ? " shouted Purvis, the publican. " I'll take six to one ! "

There were no answers.

" Five to one ! " There were givers at that. Purvis booked them in a tattered notebook.

Montgomery began to feel happy. He lay back with his legs outstretched, his back against the corner-post and one gloved hand upon each rope. What a delicious minute it was between each round. If he could only keep out of harm's way, he must surely wear this man out before the end of twenty rounds. He was so slow that all his strength went for nothing. "You're fightin' a winnin' fight—a winnin' fight," Ted Barton whispered in his ear. "Go canny; tak' no chances; you have him proper."

But the Master was crafty. He had fought so many battles with his maimed limb that he knew how to make the best of it. Warily and slowly he manœuvred round Montgomery, stepping forward and yet again forward until he had imperceptibly backed him into his corner. The student suddenly saw a flash of triumph upon the grim face, and a gleam in the dull, malignant eyes. The Master was upon him. He sprang aside and was on the ropes. The Master smashed in one of his terrible upper-cuts, and Montgomery half broke it with his guard. The student sprang the other way and was against the other converging rope. He was trapped in the angle. The Master sent in another, with a hoggish grunt which spoke of the energy behind it. Montgomery ducked, but got a jab from the left upon the mark. He closed with his man. "Break away! Break away!" cried the referee. Montgomery disengaged and got a swinging blow on the ear as he did so. It had been a damaging round for him, and the Croxley people were shouting their delight.

"Gentlemen, I will *not* have this noise!" Stapleton roared. "I have been accustomed to preside at a well-conducted club, and not at a bear-garden." This little man, with the tilted hat and the bulging forehead, dominated the whole assembly. He was like a headmaster among his boys. He glared round him, and nobody cared to meet his eye.

Anastasia had kissed the Master when he resumed his seat. "Good lass. Do't again!" cried the laughing crowd, and the angry Master shook his glove at her, as she flapped her towel in front of him. Montgomery was weary and a little sore, but not depressed. He had learned something. He would not again be tempted into danger.

For three rounds the honours were fairly equal. The student's hitting was the quicker, the Master's the harder. Profiting by his lesson, Montgomery kept himself in the open, and refused to be herded into a corner. Sometimes the Master succeeded in rushing him to the side-ropes, but the younger man slipped away, or closed, and then disengaged. The monotonous " Break away ! Break away ! " of the referee broke in upon the quick, low patter of rubber-soled shoes, the dull thud of the blows, and the sharp, hissing breath of two tired men.

The ninth round found both of them in fairly good condition. Montgomery's head was still singing from the blow that he had in the corner, and one of his thumbs pained him acutely and seemed to be dislocated. The Master showed no sign of a touch, but his breathing was the more laboured, and a long line of ticks upon the referee's paper showed that the student had a good show of points. But one of this iron-man's blows was worth three of his, and he knew that without the gloves he could not have stood for three rounds against him. All the amateur work that he had done was the merest tapping and flapping when compared to those frightful blows, from arms toughened by the shovel and the crowbar.

It was the tenth round, and the fight was half over. The betting was now only three to one, for the Wilson champion had held his own much better than had been expected. But those who knew the ring-craft as well as the staying-power of the old prize-fighter knew that the odds were still a long way in his favour.

" Have a care of him ! " whispered Barton. as he sent his man up to the scratch. " Have a care ! He'll play thee a trick, if he can."

But Montgomery saw, or imagined he saw, that his antagonist was tiring. He looked jaded and listless, and his hands drooped a little from their position. His own youth and condition were beginning to tell. He sprang in and brought off a fine left-handed lead. The Master's return lacked his usual fire. Again Montgomery led, and again he got home. Then he tried his right upon the mark, and the Master guarded it downwards.

"Too low! Too low! A foul! A foul!" yelled a thousand voices.

The referee rolled his sardonic eyes slowly round. "Seems to me this buildin' is chock-full of referees," said he.

The people laughed and applauded, but their favour was as immaterial to him as their anger.

"No applause, please! This is not a theatre!" he yelled.

Montgomery was very pleased with himself. His adversary was evidently in a bad way. He was piling on his points and establishing a lead. He might as well make hay while the sun shone. The Master was looking all abroad. Montgomery popped one upon his blue jowl and got away without a return. And then the Master suddenly dropped both his hands and began rubbing his thigh. Ah! that was it, was it! He had muscular cramp.

"Go in! Go in!" cried Teddy Barton.

Montgomery sprang wildly forward, and the next instant was lying half senseless, with his neck nearly broken, in the middle of the ring.

The whole round had been a long conspiracy to tempt him within reach of one of those terrible right-hand upper-cuts for which the Master was famous. For this the listless, weary bearing, for this the cramp in the thigh. When Montgomery had sprang in so hotly he had exposed himself to such a blow as neither flesh nor blood could stand. Whizzing up from below with a rigid arm, which put the Master's eleven stone into its force, it struck him under the jaw: he whirled half round, and fell a helpless and half-paralysed mass.

A vague groan and murmur, inarticulate, too excited for words, rose from the great audience. With open mouths and staring eyes they gazed at the twitching and quivering figure.

"Stand back! Stand right back!" shrieked the referee, for the Master was standing over his man ready to give him the *coup-de-grâce* as he rose.

"Stand back, Craggs, this instant!" Stapleton repeated.

The Master sank his hands sulkily and walked backwards to the rope with his ferocious eyes fixed upon his fallen antagonist. The timekeeper called the seconds. If ten of them passed before Montgomery rose to his feet, the fight was ended. Ted Barton wrung his hands and danced about in an agony in his corner.

As if in a dream—a terrible nightmare—the student could hear the voice of the timekeeper—three—four—five—he got up on his hand—six—seven—he was on his knee, sick, swimming, faint, but resolute to rise. Eight— he was up, and the Master was on him like a tiger, lashing savagely at him with both hands. Folk held their breath as they watched those terrible blows, and anticipated the pitiful end—so much more pitiful where a game but helpless man refuses to accept defeat.

Strangely automatic is the human brain. Without volition, without effort, there shot into the memory of this bewildered, staggering, half-stupefied man the one thing which could have saved him—that blind eye of which the Master's son had spoken. It was the same as the other to look at, but Montgomery remembered that he had said that it was the left. He reeled to the left side, half felled by a drive which lit upon his shoulder. The Master pivoted round upon his leg and was at him in an instant.

"Yark him, lad! yark him!" screamed the woman.

"Hold your tongue!" said the referee.

Montgomery slipped on the left again and yet again ; but the Master was too quick and clever for him. He struck round and got him full on the face as he tried once more to break away. Montgomery's knees weakened under him, and he fell with a groan on the floor. This time he knew that he was done. With bitter agony he realized, as he groped blindly with his hands, that he could not possibly raise himself. Far away and muffled he heard, amid the murmurs of the multitude, the fateful voice of the timekeeper counting off the seconds.

" One—two—three—four—five—six——"

" Time ! " said the referee.

Then the pent-up passion of the great assembly broke loose. Croxley gave a deep groan of disappointment. The Wilsons were on their feet, yelling with delight. There was still a chance for them. In four more seconds their man would have been solemnly counted out. But now he had a minute in which to recover. The referee looked round with relaxed features and laughing eyes, He loved this rough game, this school for humble heroes. and it was pleasant to him to intervene as a *deus ex machina* at so dramatic a moment. His chair and his hat were both tilted at an extreme angle ; he and the timekeeper smiled at each other. Ted Barton and the other second had rushed out and thrust an arm each under Montgomery's knee, the other behind his loins, and so carried him back to his stool. His head lolled upon his shoulder, but a douche of cold water sent a shiver through him, and he started and looked round him.

" He's a' right ! " cried the people round. " He's a rare brave lad. Good lad ! Good lad ! " Barton poured some brandy into his mouth. The mists cleared a little, and he realized where he was and what he had to do. But he was still very weak, and he hardly dared to hope that he could survive another round.

" Seconds out of the ring ! " cried the referee. " Time ! "

The Croxley Master sprang eagerly off his stool.

" Keep clear of him ! Go easy for a bit," said Barton ; and Montgomery walked out to meet his man once more.

He had had two lessons—the one when the Master got him into his corner, the other when he had been lured into mixing it up with so powerful an antagonist. Now he would be wary. Another blow would finish him ; he could afford to run no risks. The Master was determined to follow up his advantage, and rushed at him, slogging furiously right and left. But Montgomery was too young and active to be caught. He was strong upon his legs once more, and his wits had all come back to him. It was a gallant sight—the line-of-battle-ship trying to pour its overwhelming broadside into the frigate, and the frigate manœuvring always so as to avoid it. The Master tried all his ring-craft. He coaxed the student up by pretended inactivity ; he rushed at him with furious rushes towards the ropes. For three rounds he exhausted every wile in trying to get at him. Montgomery during all this time was conscious that his strength was minute by minute coming back to him. The spinal jar from an upper-cut is overwhelming, but evanescent. He was losing all sense of it beyond a great stiffness of the neck. For the first round after his downfall he had been content to be entirely on the defensive, only too happy if he could stall off the furious attacks of the Master. In the second he occasionally ventured upon a light counter. In the third he was smacking back merrily where he saw an opening. His people yelled their approval of him at the end of every round. Even the iron-workers cheered him with that fine unselfishness which true sport engenders. To most of them, unspiritual and unimaginative, the sight of this clean-limbed young Apollo, rising above disaster and holding on while consciousness was in him to his appointed task, was the greatest thing their experience had ever known.

But the Master's naturally morose temper became more and more murderous at this postponement of his hopes. Three rounds ago the battle had been in his hands ; now it was all to do over again. Round by round his man was recovering his strength. By the fifteenth he was strong again in wind and limb. But the vigilant Anastasia saw something which encouraged her.

" That bash in t' ribs is telling on him, Jock," she whispered. " Why else should he be gulping t' brandy ? Go in, lad, and thou hast him yet."

Montgomery had suddenly taken the flask from Barton's hand, and had a deep pull at the contents. Then, with his face a little flushed, and with a curious look of purpose, which made the referee stare hard at him, in his eyes, he rose for the sixteenth round.

" Game as a pairtridge ! " cried the publican, as he looked at the hard-set face.

" Mix it oop, lad ; mix it oop ! " cried the iron-men to their Master.

And then a hum of exultation ran through their ranks as they realized that their tougher, harder, stronger man held the vantage, after all.

Neither of the men showed much sign of punishment. Small gloves crush and numb, but they do not cut. One of the Master's eyes was even more flush with his cheek than Nature had made it. Montgomery had two or three livid marks upon his body, and his face was haggard, save for that pink spot which the brandy had brought into either cheek. He rocked a little as he stood opposite his man, and his hands drooped as if he felt the gloves to be an unutterable weight. It was evident that he was spent and desperately weary. If he received one other blow it must surely be fatal to him. If he brought one home, what power could there be behind it, and what chance was there of its harming the colossus in front of him ? It was the crisis of the fight. This round must decide it. " Mix it oop, lad ; mix it oop ! " the iron-men whooped. Even the savage eyes of the referee were unable to restrain the excited crowd.

Now, at last, the chance had come for Montgomery. He had learned a lesson from his more experienced rival. Why should he not play his own game upon him ? He was spent, but not nearly so spent as he pretended. That brandy was to call up his reserves, to let him have strength to take full advantage of the opening when it came. It was thrilling and tingling through his veins, at the very moment when he was lurching and rocking like a beaten man. He acted his part admirably. The Master felt that there was an easy task before him, and rushed in with ungainly activity to finish it once for all. He slap-banged away left and right, boring Montgomery up against the ropes, swinging in his ferocious blows with those animal grunts which told of the vicious energy behind them.

But Montgomery was too cool to fall a victim to any of those murderous upper-cuts. He kept out of harm's way with a rigid guard, an active foot, and a head which was swift to duck. And yet he contrived to present the same appearance of a man who is hopelessly done. The Master, weary from his own shower of blows, and fearing nothing from so weak a man, dropped his hand for an instant, and at that instant Montgomery's right came home.

It was a magnificent blow, straight, clean, crisp, with the force of the loins and the back behind it. And it landed where he had meant it to—upon the exact point of that blue-grained chin. Flesh and blood could not stand such a blow in such a place. Neither valour nor hardihood can save the man to whom it comes. The Master fell backwards, flat, prostrate, striking the ground with so simultaneous a clap that it was like a shutter falling from a wall. A yell which no referee could control broke from the crowded benches as the giant went down. He lay upon his back, his knees a little drawn up, his huge chest panting. He twitched and shook, but could not move. His feet pawed convulsively once or twice. It was no use. He was done. " Eight—nine—ten ! " said the timekeeper, and the roar of a thousand voices, with a deafening clap like the broadside of a ship, told that the Master of Croxley was the Master no more.

Montgomery stood half dazed, looking down at the huge, prostrate figure. He could hardly realize that it was indeed all over. He saw the referee motion towards him with his hand. He heard his name bellowed in triumph from every side. And then he was aware of some one rushing towards him ; he caught a glimpse of a flushed face and an aureole of flying red hair, a glove-less fist struck him between the eyes, and he was on his back in the ring beside his antagonist, while a dozen of his supporters were endeavouring to secure the frantic Anastasia. He heard the angry shouting of the referee, the screaming of the furious woman, and the cries of the mob. Then something seemed to break like an over-stretched banjo-string, and he sank into the deep, deep, mist-girt abyss of unconsciousness.

The dressing was like a thing in a dream, and so was a vision of the Master with the grin of a bulldog upon his face, and his three teeth amiably protruded. He shook Montgomery heartily by the hand.

" I would have been rare pleased to shake thee by the throttle, lad, a short while syne," said he. " But I bear no ill-feelin' again' thee. It was a rare poonch that brought me down—I have not had a better since my second fight wi' Billy Edwards in '89. Happen thou might think o' goin' further wi' this business. If thou dost, and want a trainer, there's not much inside t' ropes as I don't know. Or happen thou might like to try it wi' me old style and bare knuckles. Thou hast but to write to t' ironworks to find me."

But Montgomery disclaimed any such ambition. A canvas bag with his share—one hundred and ninety sovereigns—was handed to him, of which he gave ten to the Master, who also received some share of the gate-money. Then, with young Wilson escorting him on one side, Purvis on the other, and Fawcett carrying his bag behind, he went in triumph to his carriage, and drove amid a long roar, which lined the highway like a hedge for the seven miles, back to his starting-point.

" It's the greatest thing I ever saw in my life. By George, it's ripping ! " cried Wilson, who had been left in a kind of ecstasy by the events of the day. " There's a chap over Barnsley way who fancies himself a bit. Let us spring you on him, and let him see what he can make of you. We'll put up a purse—won't we, Purvis ? You shall never want a backer."

" At his weight," said the publican, " I'm behind him, I am, for twenty rounds, and no age, country, or colour barred."

" So am I ! " cried Fawcett ; " middle-weight champion of the world, that's what he is—here, in the same carriage with us."

But Montgomery was not to be beguiled.

" No ; I have my own work to do now."

" And what may that be ? "

" I'll use this money to get my medical degree."

" Well, we've plenty of doctors, but you're the only man in the Riding that could smack the Croxley Master off his legs. However, I suppose you know your own business best. When you're a doctor, you'd best come down into these parts, and you'll always find a job waiting for you at the Wilson Coal-pits."

Montgomery had returned by devious ways to the surgery. The horses were smoking at the door and the doctor was just back from his long journey. Several patients had called in his absence, and he was in the worst of tempers.

" I suppose I should be glad that you have come back at all, Mr. Montgomery ! " he snarled. " When next you elect to take a holiday, I trust it will not be at so. busy a time."

" I am sorry, sir, that you should have been inconvenienced."

" Yes, sir, I have been exceedingly inconvenienced." Here, for the first time, he looked hard at the assistant. " Good heavens, Mr. Montgomery, what have you been doing with your left eye ? "

It was where Anastasia had lodged her protest.

Montgomery laughed. " It is nothing, sir," said he.

" And you have a livid mark under your jaw. It is, indeed, terrible that my representative should be going about in so disreputable a condition. How did you receive these injuries ? "

" Well, sir, as you know, there was a little glove-fight to-day over at Croxley."

" And you got mixed up with that brutal crowd ? "

" I *was* rather mixed up with them."

" And who assaulted you ? "

" One of the fighters."

" Which of them ? "

" The Master of Croxley."

" Good heavens ! Perhaps you interfered with him ? "

" Well, to tell the truth, I did a little."

" Mr. Montgomery, in such a practice as mine, intimately associated as it is with the highest and most progressive elements of our small community, it is impossible——"

But just then the tentative bray of a cornet-player searching for his keynote jarred upon their ears, and an instant later the Wilson Colliery brass band was in full cry with " See the Conquering Hero Comes," outside the surgery window. There was a banner waving, and a shouting crowd of miners.

" What is it ? What does it mean ? " cried the angry doctor.

" It means, sir, that I have, in the only way which was open to me, earned the money which is necessary for my education. It is my duty, Doctor Oldacre, to warn you that I am about to return to the University, and that you should lose no time in appointing my successor."

2. *The Lord of Falconbridge*

A LEGEND OF THE RING

TOM CRIBB, Champion of England, having finished his active career by his two famous battles with the terrible Molineux, had settled down into the public-house which was known as the Union Arms, at the corner of Panton Street in the Haymarket. Behind the bar of this hostelry there was a green baize door which opened into a large, red-papered parlour, adorned by many sporting prints and by the numerous cups and belts which were the treasured trophies of the famous prize-fighter's victorious career. In this snuggery it was the custom of the Corinthians of the day to assemble in order to discuss, over Tom Cribb's excellent wines, the matches of the past, to await the news of the present, and to arrange new ones for the future. Hither also came his brother pugilists, especially such as were in poverty or distress, for the Champion's generosity was proverbial, and no man of his own trade was ever turned from his door if cheering words or a full meal could mend his condition.

On the morning in question—August 25, 1818—there were but two men in this famous snuggery. One was Cribb himself—all run to flesh since the time seven years before, when, training for his last fight, he had done his forty miles a day with Captain Barclay over the Highland roads. Broad and deep, as well as tall, he was a little short of twenty stone in weight, but his heavy, strong face and lion eyes showed that the spirit of the prize-fighter was not yet altogether overgrown by the fat of the publican. Though it was not eleven o'clock, a great tankard of bitter ale stood upon the table before him, and he was busy cutting up a plug of black tobacco and rubbing the slices into powder between his horny fingers. For all his record of desperate battles, he looked what he was—a good-hearted, respectable householder, law-abiding and kindly, a happy and prosperous man.

His companion, however, was by no means in the same easy circumstances, and his countenance wore a very different expression. He was a tall and well-formed man, some fifteen years younger than the Champion, and recalling in the masterful pose of his face and in the fine spread of his shoulders something of the manly beauty which had distinguished Cribb at his prime. No one looking at his countenance could fail to see that he was a fighting man by profession, and any judge of the fancy, considering his six feet in height, his thirteen stone of solid muscle, and his beautifully graceful build, would admit that he had started his career with advantages which, if they were only backed by the driving-power of a stout heart, must carry him far. Tom Winter, or Spring—as he chose to call himself—had indeed come up from his Herefordshire home with a fine country record of local successes, which had been enhanced by two victories gained over formidable London heavy-weights. Three weeks before, however, he had been defeated by the famous Painter, and the set-back weighed heavily upon the young man's spirits.

" Cheer up, lad," said the Champion, glancing across from under his tufted eyebrows at the disconsolate face of his companion. "Indeed, Tom, you take it over-hard."

The young man groaned, but made no reply.

" Others have been beat before you and lived to be Champions of England. Here I sit with that very title. Was I not beat down Broadwater way by George Nicholls in 1805 ? What then ? I fought on, and here I am. When the big Black came from America it was not George Nicholls they sent for. I say to you—fight on, and by George, I'll see you in my own shoes yet ! "

Tom Spring shook his head. "Never, if I have to fight you to get there, Daddy."

" I can't keep it for ever, Tom. It's beyond all reason. I'm going to lay it down before all London at the Fives Courts next year, and it's to you that I want to hand it. I couldn't train down to it now, lad. My day's done."

" Well, Dad, I'll never bid for it till you choose to stand aside. After that, it is as it may be."

" Well, have a rest, Tom ; wait for your chance, and, meantime, there's always a bed and crust for you here."

Spring struck his clenched fist on his knee. " I know, Daddy ! Ever since I came up from Fownthorpe, you've been as good as a father to me."

" I've an eye for a winner."

" A pretty winner ! Beat in forty rounds by Ned Painter."

" You had beat him first."

" And by the Lord, I will again ! "

" So you will, lad. George Nicholls would never give me another shy. Knew too much, he did. Bought a butcher's shop in Bristol with the money, and there he is to this day."

" Yes, I'll come back on Painter, but I haven't a shilling left. My backers have lost faith in me. If it wasn't for you, Daddy, I'd be in the kennel."

" Have you nothing left, Tom ? "

" Not the price of a meal. I left every penny I had, and my good name as well, in the ring at Kingston. I'm hard put to it to live unless I can get another fight, and who's going to back me now ! "

" Tut, man ! the knowing ones will back you. You're the top of the list, for all Ned Painter. But there are other ways a man may earn a bit. There was a lady in here this morning—nothing flash, boy, a real tip-top out-and-outer with a coronet on her coach—asking after you."

" Asking after me ! A lady ! " The young pugilist stood up with surprise and a certain horror rising in his eyes. " You don't mean, Daddy——"

" I mean nothing but what is honest, my lad. You can lay to that ! "

" You said I could earn a bit ! "

" So, perhaps, you can. Enough, anyhow, to tide you over your bad time. There's something in the wind there. It's to do with fightin'. She asked questions about your height, weight, and my opinion of your prospect. You can lay that my answers did you no harm."

" She ain't making a match, surely ? "

" Well, she seemed to know a tidy bit about it. She asked about George Cooper, and Richmond the Black, and Tom Oliver, always comin' back to you, and wantin' to know if you were not the pick of the bunch. *And* trustworthy. That was the other point. Could she trust you ? Lord, Tom, if you was a fightin' archangel you could hardly live up to the character that I've given you."

A drawer looked in from the bar. " If you please, Mr. Cribb, the lady's carriage is back again."

The Champion laid down his long clay pipe. " This way, lad," said he, plucking his young friend by the sleeve towards the side window. " Look there, now ! Saw you ever a more slap-up carriage ? See, too, the pair of bays—two hundred guineas apiece. Coachman, too, and footman—you'd find 'em hard to beat. There she is now, stepping out of it. Wait here, lad, till I do the honours of my house."

Tom Cribb slipped off, and young Spring remained by the window, tapping the glass nervously with his fingers, for he was a simple-minded country lad with no knowledge of women, and many fears of the traps which await the unwary in a great city. Many stories were afloat of pugilists who had been taken up and cast aside again by wealthy ladies, even as the gladiators were in decadent Rome. It was with some suspicion therefore, and considerable inward trepidation, that he faced round as a tall veiled figure swept into the room. He was much consoled, however, to observe the bulky form of Tom Cribb immediately behind her as a proof that the interview was not to be a private one. When the door was closed, the lady very deliberately removed her gloves. Then with fingers which glittered with diamonds she slowly rolled up and adjusted her heavy veil. Finally, she turned her face upon Spring.

" Is this the man ? " said she.

They stood looking at each other with mutual interest, which warmed in both their faces into mutual admiration. What she saw was as fine a figure of a young man as England could show, none the less attractive for the restrained shyness of his manner and the blush which flushed his cheeks. What he saw was a woman of thirty, tall, dark, queen-like, and imperious, with a lovely face, every line and feature of which told of pride and breed, a woman born to Courts, with the instinct of command strong within her, and yet with all the softer woman's graces to temper and conceal the firmness of her soul. Tom Spring felt as he looked at her that he had never seen nor ever dreamed of anyone so beautiful, and yet he could not shake off the instinct which warned him to be upon his guard. Yes, it was beautiful, this face—beautiful beyond belief. But was it good, was it kind, was it true ? There was some strange subconscious repulsion which mingled with his admiration for her loveliness. As to the lady's thoughts, she had already put away all idea of the young pugilist as a man, and regarded him now with critical eyes as a machine designed for a definite purpose.

" I am glad to meet you, Mr.—Mr. Spring," said she, looking him over with as much deliberation as a dealer who is purchasing a horse. " He is hardly as tall as I was given to understand, Mr. Cribb. You said six feet, I believe ? "

" So he is, ma'am, but he carries it so easy. It's only the beanstalk that looks tall. See here, I'm six foot myself, and our heads are level, except I've lost my fluff."

" What is the chest measurement ? "

" Forty-three inches, ma'am."

" You certainly seem to be a very strong young man. And a game one, too, I hope ? "

Young Spring shrugged his shoulders. ·

" It's not for me to say, ma'am."

" I can speak for that, ma'am," said Cribb. " You read the *Sporting Chronicle* for three weeks ago, ma'am. You'll see how he stood up to Ned Painter until his senses were beat out of him. I waited on him, ma'am, and I know. I could show you my waistcoat now— that would let you guess what punishment he can take."

The lady waved aside the illustration.

" But he was beat," said she coldly. " The man who beat him must be the better man."

" Saving your presence, ma'am, I think not, and out-side Gentleman Jackson my judgment would stand against any in the ring. My lad here has beat Painter once, and will again, if your ladyship could see your way to find the battle-money."

The lady started and looked angrily at the Champion.

" Why do you call me that ? "

" I beg pardon. It was just my way of speaking."

" I order you not to do it again."

" Very good, ma'am."

" I am here incognita. I bind you both upon your honours to make no inquiry as to who I am. If I do not get your firm promise, the matter ends here."

" Very good, ma'am. I'll promise for my own part, and so, I am sure, will Spring. But if I may be so bold, I can't help my drawers and potmen talking with your servants."

" The coachman and footman know just as much about me as you do. But my time is limited, so I must get to business. I think, Mr. Spring, that you are in want of something to do at present ? "

" That is so, ma'am."

" I understand from Mr. Cribb that you are prepared to fight anyone at any weight ? "

" Anything on two legs," cried the Champion.

" Who did you wish me to fight ? " asked the young pugilist.

" That cannot concern you. If you are really ready to fight anyone, then the particular name can be of no importance. I have my reasons for withholding it."

" Very good, ma'am."

" You have been only a few weeks out of training. How long would it take you to get back to your best ? "

" Three weeks or a month."

" Well, then, I will pay your training expenses and two pounds a week over. Here are five pounds as a guarantee. You will fight when I consider that you are ready, and that the circumstances are favourable. If you win your fight, you shall have fifty pounds. Are you satisfied with the terms ? "

" Very handsome, ma'am, I'm sure."

" And remember, Mr. Spring, I choose you, not because you are the best man—for there are two opinions about that—but because I am given to understand that you are a decent man whom I can trust. The terms of this match are to be secret."

" I understand that. I'll say nothing."

" It is a private match. Nothing more. You will begin your training to-morrow."

" Very good, ma'am."

" I will ask Mr. Cribb to train you."

" I'll do that, ma'am, with pleasure. But, by your leave, does he have anything if he loses ? "

A spasm of emotion passed over the woman's face and her hands clenched white with passion:

" If he loses, not a penny, not a penny ! " she cried. " He must not, shall not lose ! "

" Well, ma'am," said Spring, " I've never heard of any such match. But it's true that I am down at heel, and beggars can't be choosers. I'll do just what you say.

I'll train till you give the word, and then I'll fight where you tell me. I hope you'll make it a large ring."

"Yes," said she; "it will be a large ring."

"And how far from London?"

"Within a hundred miles. Have you anything else to say? My time is up."

"I'd like to ask, ma'am," said the Champion, earnestly, "whether I can act as the lad's second when the time comes. I've waited on him the last two fights. Can I give him a knee?"

"No," said the woman, sharply. Without another word she turned and was gone, shutting the door behind her. A few moments later the trim carriage flashed past the window, turned down the crowded Haymarket, and was engulfed in the traffic.

The two men looked at each other in silence.

"Well, blow my dickey, if this don't beat cock-fightin'!" cried Tom Cribb at last. "Anyhow, there's the fiver, lad. But it's a rum go, and no mistake about it."

After due consultation, it was agreed that Tom Spring should go into training at the Castle Inn on Hampstead Heath, so that Cribb could drive over and watch him. Thither Spring went on the day after the interview with his patroness, and he set to work at once with drugs, dumb-bells, and breathers on the common to get himself into condition. It was hard, however, to take the matter seriously, and his good-natured trainer found the same difficulty.

"It's the baccy I miss, Daddy," said the young pugilist, as they sat together on the afternoon of the third day. "Surely there can't be any harm in my havin' a pipe?"

"Well, well, lad, it's against my conscience, but here's my box and there's a yard o' clay," said the Champion. "My word, I don't know what Captain Barclay of Ury would have said if he had seen a man smoke when he was in trainin'! He was the man to work you! He had me down from sixteen to thirteen the second time I fought the Black."

Spring had lit his pipe and was leaning back amid a haze of blue smoke.

" It was easy for you, Daddy, to keep strict trainin' when you knew what was before you. You had your date and your place and your man. You knew that in a month you would jump the ropes with ten thousand folk around you, and carrying maybe a hundred thousand in bets. You knew also the man you had to meet, and you wouldn't give him the better of you. But it's all different with me. For all I know this is just a woman's whim, and will end in nothing. If I was sure it was serious, I'd break this pipe before I would smoke it."

Tom Cribb scratched his head in puzzlement.

" I can make nothing of it, lad, 'cept that her money is good. Come to think of it, how many men on the list could stand up to you for half an hour ? It can't be Stringer, 'cause you've beat him. Then there's Cooper ; but he's up Newcastle way. It can't be him. There's Richmond ; but you wouldn't need to take your coat off to beat him. There's the Gasman ; but he's not twelve stone. And there's Bill Neat of Bristol. That's it, lad. The lady has taken into her head to put you up against either the Gasman or Bill Neat."

" But why not say so ? I'd train hard for the Gasman and harder for Bill Neat, but I'm blowed if I can train with any heart when I'm fightin' nobody in particular and everybody in general, same as now."

There was a sudden interruption to the speculations of the two prize-fighters. The door opened and the lady entered. As her eyes fell upon the two men her dark, handsome face flushed with anger, and she gazed at them silently with an expression of contempt which brought them both to their feet with hangdog faces. There they stood, their long, reeking pipes in their hands, shuffling and downcast, like two great rough mastiffs before an angry mistress.

59

" So ! " said she, stamping her foot furiously. " And this is training ! "

" I'm sure we're very sorry, ma'am," said the abashed Champion. " I didn't think—I never for one moment supposed——"

" That I would come myself to see if you were taking my money on false pretences ? No, I dare say not. You fool ! " she blazed, turning suddenly upon Tom Spring. " You'll be beat. That will be the end of it."

The young man looked up with an angry face.

" I'll trouble you not to call me names, ma'am. I've my self-respect, the same as you. I'll allow that I shouldn't have smoked when I was in trainin'. But I was saying to Tom Cribb here, just before you came in, that if you would give over treatin' us as if we were children, and if you would tell us just who it is you want me to fight, and when, and where, it would be a deal easier for me to take myself in hand."

" It's true, ma'am," said the Champion. " I know it must be either the Gasman or Bill Neat. There's no one else. So give me the office, and I'll promise to have him as fit as a trout on the day."

The lady laughed contemptuously.

" Do you think," said she, " that no one can fight save those who make a living by it ? "

" By George, it's an amateur ! " cried Cribb, in amazement. " But you don't surely ask Tom Spring to train for three weeks to meet a Corinthian ? "

" I will say nothing more of who it is. It is no business of yours," the lady answered fiercely. " All I *do* say is, that if you do not train I will cast you aside and take some one who will. Do not think you can fool me because I am a woman. I have learned the points of the game as well as any man."

" I saw that the very first word you spoke," said Cribb.

" Then don't forget it. I will not warn you again. If I have occasion to find fault I shall choose another man."

" And you won't tell me who I am to fight ? "

" Not a word. But you can take it from me that at your very best it will take you, or any man in England, all your time to master him. Now get back this instant to your work, and never let me find you shirking it again." With imperious eyes she looked the two strong men down, and then, turning on her heel, she swept out of the room.

The Champion whistled as the door closed behind her, and mopped his brow with his red bandanna handkerchief as he looked across at his abashed companion. " My word, lad," said he, " it's earnest from this day on."

" Yes," said Tom Spring, solemnly, " it's earnest from this day on."

In the course of the next fortnight the lady made several surprise visits to see that her champion was being properly prepared for the contest which lay before him. At the most unexpected moments she would burst into the training quarters, but never again had she to complain of any slackness upon his part or that of his trainer. With long bouts of the gloves, with thirty-mile walks, with mile runs at the back of a mailcart with a bit of blood between the shafts, with interminable series of jumps with a skipping-rope, he was sweated down until his trainer was able to proudly proclaim that " the last ounce of tallow is off him, and he is ready to fight for his life." Only once was the lady accompanied by anyone upon these visits of inspection. Upon this occasion a tall young man was her companion. He was graceful in figure, aristocratic in his bearing, and would have been strikingly handsome had it not been for some accident which had shattered his nose and broken all the symmetry of his features. He stood in silence with moody eyes and folded arms, looking at the splendid torso of the prize-fighter as, stripped to the waist, he worked with his dumb-bells.

" Don't you think he will do ? " said the lady.

TALES OF THE RING

The young swell shrugged his shoulders. " I don't like it, *cara mia*. I can't pretend that I like it."

" You must like it, George. I have set my very heart on it."

" It is not English, you know. Lucrezia Borgia and Mediæval Italy. Woman's love and woman's hatred are always the same, but this particular manifestation of it seems to me out of place in nineteenth-century London."

" Is not a lesson needed ? "

" Yes, yes ; but one would think there were other ways."

" You tried another way. What did you get out of that ? "

The young man smiled rather grimly, as he turned up his cuff and looked at a puckered hole in his wrist.

" Not much, certainly," said he.

" You've tried and failed."

" Yes, I must admit it."

" What else is there ? The law ? "

" Good gracious, no ! "

" Then it is my turn, George, and I won't be balked."

" I don't think anyone is capable of balking you, *cara mia*. Certainly I, for one, should never dream of trying. But I don't feel as if I could co-operate."

" I never asked you to."

" No, you certainly never did. You are perfectly capable of doing it alone. I think, with your leave, if you have quite done with your prize-fighter, we will drive back to London. I would not for the world miss Goldoni in the Opera."

So they drifted away ; he, frivolous and dilettante, she with her face as set as Fate, leaving the fighting men to their business.

And now the day came when Cribb was able to announce to his employer that his man was as fit as science could make him.

" I can do no more, ma'am. He's fit to fight for a kingdom. Another week would see him stale."

62

The lady looked Spring over with the eye of a connoisseur.

" I think he does you credit," she said at last. " To-day is Tuesday. He will fight the day after to-morrow."

" Very good, ma'am. Where shall he go ? "

" I will tell you exactly, and you will please take careful note of all that I say. You, Mr. Cribb, will take your man down to the Golden Cross Inn at Charing Cross by nine o'clock on Wednesday morning. He will take the Brighton coach as far as Tunbridge Wells, where he will alight at the Royal Oak Arms. There he will take such refreshment as you advise before a fight. He will wait at the Royal Oak Arms until he receives a message by word, or by letter, brought him by a groom in a mulberry livery. This message will give him his final instructions."

" And I am not to come ? "

" No," said the lady.

" But surely, ma'am," he pleaded, " I may come as far as Tunbridge Wells ? It's hard on a man to train a cove for a fight and then to leave him."

" It can't be helped. You are too well known. Your arrival would spread all over the town, and my plans might suffer. It is quite out of the question that you should come."

" Well, I'll do what you tell me, but it's main hard."

" I suppose," said Spring, " you would have me bring my fightin' shorts and my spiked shoes ? "

" No ; you will kindly bring nothing whatever which may point to your trade. I would have you wear just those clothes in which I saw you first, such clothes as any mechanic or artisan might be expected to wear."

Tom Cribb's blank face had assumed an expression of absolute despair.

" No second, no clothes, no shoes—it don't seem regular. I give you my word, ma'am, I feel ashamed to be mixed up in such a fight. I don't know as you can call the thing a fight where there is no second. It's just a scramble—nothing more. I've gone too far to wash my hands of it now, but I wish I had never touched it."

In spite of all professional misgivings on the part of the Champion and his pupil, the imperious will of the woman prevailed, and everything was carried out exactly as she had directed. At nine o'clock Tom Spring found himself upon the box-seat of the Brighton coach, and waved his hand in good-bye to burly Tom Cribb, who stood, the admired of a ring of waiters and ostlers, upon the doorstep of the Golden Cross. It was in the pleasant season when summer is mellowing into autumn, and the first golden patches are seen amid the beeches and the ferns. The young country-bred lad breathed more freely when he had left the weary streets of Southwark and Lewisham behind him, and he watched with delight the glorious prospect as the coach, whirled along by six dapple greys, passed by the classic grounds of Knowle, or after crossing Riverside Hill skirted the vast expanse of the Weald of Kent. Past Tonbridge School went the coach, and on through Southborough, until it wound down a steep, curving road with strange outcrops of sandstone beside it, and halted before a great hostelry, bearing the name which had been given him in his directions. He descended, entered the coffee-room, and ordered the underdone steak which his trainer had recommended. Hardly had he finished it when a servant with a mulberry coat and a peculiarly expressionless face entered the apartment.

" Beg your pardon, sir, are you Mr. Spring—Mr. Thomas Spring, of London ? "

" That is my name, young man."

" Then the instructions which I had to give you are that you wait for one hour after your meal. After that time you will find me in a phaeton at the door, and I will drive you in the right direction."

The young pugilist had never been daunted by any experience which had befallen him in the ring. The rough encouragement of his backers, the surge and shouting of the multitude, and the sight of his opponent had always cheered his stout heart and excited him to prove himself worthy of being the centre of such a scene. But this loneliness and uncertainty were deadly. He flung himself down on the horsehair couch and tried to doze, but his mind was too restless and excited. Finally he rose, and paced up and down the empty room. Suddenly he was aware of a great rubicund face which surveyed him from round the angle of the door. Its owner, seeing that he was observed, pushed forward into the room.

" I beg pardon, sir," said he, " but surely I have the honour of talking to Mr. Thomas Spring ? "

" At your service," said the young man.

" Bless me ! I am vastly honoured to have you under my roof ! Cordery is my name, sir, landlord of this old-fashioned inn. I thought that my eyes could not deceive me. I am a patron of the ring, sir, in my own humble way, and was present at Mousley in September last, when you beat Jack Stringer of Rawcliffe. A very fine fight, sir, and very handsomely fought, if I may make bold to say so. I have a right to an opinion, sir, for there's never been a fight for many a year in Kent or Sussex that you wouldn't find Joe Cordery at the ringside. Ask Mr. Gregson at the Chop-house in Holborn, and he'll tell you about old Joe Cordery. By the way, Mr. Spring, I suppose it is not business that has brought you down into these parts ? Anyone can see with half an eye that you are trained to a hair. I'd take it very kindly if you would give me the office."

It crossed Spring's mind that if he were frank with the landlord it was more than likely that he would receive more information than he could give. He was a man of his word, however, and he remembered his promise to his employer.

" Just a quiet day in the country, Mr. Cordery. That's all."

" Dear me ! I had hoped there was a mill in the wind. I've a nose for these things, Mr. Spring, and I thought I had a whiff of it. But, of course, you should know best. Perhaps you will drive round with me this afternoon and view the hop-gardens—just the right time of year, sir."

Tom Spring was not very skilled in deception, and his stammering excuses may not have been very convincing to the landlord, or finally persuaded him that his original supposition was wrong. In the midst of the conversation, however, the waiter entered with the news that a phaeton was waiting at the door. The inn-keeper's eyes shone with suspicion and eagerness.

" I thought you said you knew no one in these parts, Mr. Spring ? "

" Just one kind friend, Mr. Cordery, and he has sent his gig for me. It's likely that I will take the night coach to town. But I'll look in after an hour or two and have a dish of tea with you."

Outside the mulberry servant was sitting behind a fine black horse in a phaeton, which had two seats in front and two behind. Tom Spring was about to climb up beside him, when the servant whispered that his directions were that he should sit behind. Then the phaeton whirled away, while the excited landlord, more convinced than ever that there was something in the wind, rushed into his stable-yard with shrieks to his ostlers, and in a very few minutes was in hot pursuit, waiting at every cross-road until he could hear tidings of a black horse and a mulberry livery.

The phaeton meanwhile drove in the direction of Crowborough. Some miles out it turned from the high road into a narrow lane spanned by a tawny arch of beech trees. Through this golden tunnel a lady was walking, tall and graceful, her back to the phaeton. As it came abreast of her she stood aside and looked up, while the coachman pulled up the horse.

" I trust that you are at your best," said she, looking very earnestly at the prize-fighter. " How do you feel ? "

" Pretty tidy, ma'am, I thank you."

"I will get up beside you, Johnson. We have some way to go. You will drive through the Lower Warren, and then take the lane which skirts the Gravel Hanger. I will tell you where to stop. Go slowly, for we are not due for twenty minutes."

Feeling as if the whole business was some extraordinary dream, the young pugilist passed through a network of secluded lanes, until the phaeton drew up at a wicket gate which led into a plantation of firs, choked with a thick undergrowth. Here the lady descended and beckoned Spring to alight.

"Wait down the lane," said she to the coachman. "We shall be some little time. Now, Mr. Spring, will you kindly follow me? I have written a letter which makes an appointment."

She passed swiftly through the plantation by a tortuous path, then over a stile, and past another wood, loud with the deep chuckling of pheasants. At the farther side was a fine rolling park, studded with oak trees, and stretching away to a splendid Elizabethan mansion, with balustraded terraces athwart its front. Across the park, and making for the wood, a solitary figure was walking.

The lady gripped the prize-fighter by the wrist. "That is your man," said she.

They were standing under the shadow of the trees, so that he was very visible to them, while they were out of his sight. Tom Spring looked hard at the man, who was still some hundreds of yards away. He was a tall, powerful fellow, clad in a blue coat with gilt buttons, which gleamed in the sun. He had white corded breeches and riding-boots. He walked with a vigorous step, and with every few strides he struck his leg with a dog-whip which hung from his wrist. There was a great suggestion of purpose and of energy in the man's appearance and bearing.

"Why, he's a gentleman!" said Spring. "Look 'ere, ma'am, this is all a bit out of my line. I've nothing against the man, and he can mean me no harm. What am I to do with him ? "

" Fight him ! Smash him ! That is what you are here for."

Tom Spring turned on his heel with disgust. " I'm here to fight, ma'am, but not to smash a man who has no thought of fighting. It's off."

" You don't like the look of him," hissed the woman. " You have met your master."

" That is as may be. It is no job for me."

The woman's face was white with vexation and anger. " You fool ! " she cried. " Is all to go wrong at the last minute ? There are fifty pounds—here they are in this paper—would you refuse them ? "

" It's a cowardly business. I won't do it."

" Cowardly ? You are giving the man two stone, and he can beat any amateur in England."

The young pugilist felt relieved. After all, if he could fairly earn that fifty pounds, a good deal depended upon his winning it. If he could only be sure that this was a worthy and willing antagonist !

" How do you know he is so good ? " he asked.

" I ought to know. I am his wife."

As she spoke she turned, and was gone like a flash among the bushes. The man was quite close now, and Tom Spring's scruples weakened as he looked at him. He was a powerful, broad-chested fellow, about thirty, with a heavy, brutal face, great thatched eyebrows, and a hard-set mouth. He could not be less than fifteen stone in weight, and he carried himself like a trained athlete. As he swung along he suddenly caught a glimpse of Spring among the trees, and he at once quickened his pace and sprang over the stile which separated them.

" Halloa ! " said he, halting a few yards from him, and staring him up and down. " Who the devil are you, and where the devil did you come from, and what the devil are you doing on my property ? "

His manner was even more offensive than his words. It brought a flush of anger to Spring's cheeks.

" See here, mister," said he, " civil words is cheap. You've no call to speak to me like that."

" You infernal rascal ! " cried the other. " I'll show you the way out of that plantation with the toe of my boot. Do you dare to stand there on my land and talk back at me ? " He advanced with a menacing face and his dog-whip half raised. " Well, are you going ? " he cried, as he swung it into the air.

Tom Spring jumped back to avoid the threatened blow. " Go slow, mister," said he. " It's only fair that you should know where you are. I'm Spring, the prize-fighter. Maybe you have heard my name."

" I thought you were a rascal of that breed," said the man. " I've had the handling of one or two of you gentry before, and I never found one that could stand up to me for five minutes. Maybe you would like to try ? "

" If you hit me with that dog-whip, mister——"

" There, then ! " He gave the young man a vicious cut across the shoulder. " Will that help you to fight ? "

" I came here to fight," said Tom Spring, licking his dry lips. " You can drop that whip, mister, for I *will* fight. I'm a trained man and ready. But you would have it. Don't blame me."

The man was stripping the blue coat from his broad shoulders. There was a sprigged satin vest beneath it, and they were hung together on an alder branch.

" Trained, are you ? " he muttered. " By the Lord, I'll train you before I am through ! "

Any fears that Tom Spring may have had lest he should be taking some unfair advantage were set at rest by the man's assured manner and by the splendid physique, which became more apparent as he discarded a black satin tie, with a great ruby glowing in its centre, and threw aside the white collar which cramped his thick muscular neck. He then, very deliberately, undid a pair of gold sleeve-links, and, rolling up his shirt-sleeves, disclosed two hairy and muscular arms, which would have served as a model for a sculptor.

" Come nearer the stile," said he, when he had finished. " There is more room."

The prize-fighter had kept pace with the preparations of his formidable antagonist. His own hat, coat, and vest hung suspended upon a bush. He advanced now into the open space which the other had indicated.

" Ruffianing or fighting ? " asked the amateur, coolly.

" Fighting."

" Very good," said the other. " Put up your hands, Spring. Try it out."

They were standing facing one another in a grassy ring intersected by the path at the outlet of the wood. The insolent and overbearing look had passed away from the amateur's face, but a grim half-smile was on his lips and his eyes shone fiercely from under his tufted brows. From the way in which he stood it was very clear that he was a past-master at the game. Tom Spring, as he paced lightly to right and left, looking for an opening, became suddenly aware that neither with Stringer nor with the redoubtable Painter himself had he ever faced a more business-like opponent. The amateur's left was well forward, his guard low, his body leaning back from the haunches, and his head well out of danger. Spring tried a light lead at the mark, and another at the face, but in an instant his adversary was on to him with a shower of sledge-hammer blows which it took him all his time to avoid. He sprang back, but there was no getting away from that whirlwind of muscle and bone. A heavy blow beat down his guard, a second landed on his shoulder, and over went the prize-fighter with the other on the top of him. Both sprang to their feet, glared at each other, and fell into position once more.

There could be no doubt that the amateur was not only heavier, but also the harder and stronger man. Twice again he rushed Spring down, once by the weight of his blows, and once by closing and hurling him on to his

THE LORD OF FALCONBRIDGE

back. Such falls might have shaken the fight out of a
less game man, but to Tom Spring they were but incidents
in his daily trade. Though bruised and winded he was
always up again in an instant. Blood was trickling from
his mouth, but his steadfast blue eyes told of the unshaken
spirit within.

He was accustomed now to his opponent's rushing
tactics, and he was ready for them. The fourth round
was the same as to attack, but it was very different in
defence. Up to now the young man had given way and
been fought down. This time he stood his ground. As
his opponent rushed in he met him with a tremendous
straight hit from his left hand, delivered with the full
force of his body, and doubled in effect by the momentum
of the charge. So stunning was the concussion that the
pugilist himself recoiled from it across the grassy ring.
The amateur staggered back and leaned his shoulder on
a tree-trunk, his hand up to his face.

" You'd best drop it," said Spring. " You'll get
pepper if you don't."

The other gave an inarticulate curse, and spat out a
mouthful of blood.

" Come on ! " said he.

Even now the pugilist found that he had no light task
before him. Warned by his misadventure, the heavier
man no longer tried to win the battle at a rush, nor to
beat down an accomplished boxer as he would a country
hawbuck at a village fair. He fought with his head and
his feet as well as with his hands. Spring had to admit
in his heart that, trained to the ring, this man must have
been a match for the best. His guard was strong, his
counter was like lightning, he took punishment like a
man of iron, and when he could safely close he always
brought his lighter antagonist to the ground with a
shattering fall. But the one stunning blow which he had
courted before he was taught respect for his adversary
weighed heavily on him all the time. His senses had lost
something of their quickness and his blows of their sting.

He was fighting, too, against a man who, of all the boxers who have made their names great, was the safest, the coolest, the least likely to give anything away, or lose an advantage gained. Slowly, gradually, round by round, he was worn down by his cool, quick-stepping, sharp-hitting antagonist. At last he stood exhausted, breathing hoarsely, his face, what could be seen of it, purple with his exertions. He had reached the limit of human endurance. His opponent stood waiting for him, bruised and beaten, but as cool, as ready, as dangerous as ever.

" You'd best drop it, I tell you," said he. " You're done."

But the other's manhood would not have it so. With a snarl of fury he cast his science to the winds, and rushed madly to slogging with both hands. For a moment Spring was overborne. Then he side-stepped swiftly ; there was the crash of his blow, and the amateur tossed up his arms and fell all asprawl, his great limbs outstretched, his disfigured face to the sky.

For a moment Tom Spring stood looking down at his unconscious opponent. The next he felt a soft, warm hand upon his bare arm. The woman was at his elbow.

" Now is your time ! " she cried, her dark eyes aflame. " Go in ! Smash him ! "

Spring shook her off with a cry of disgust, but she was back in an instant.

" I'll make it seventy-five pounds—— "

" The fight's over, ma'am. I can't touch him."

" A hundred pounds—a clear hundred ! I have it here in my bodice. Would you refuse a hundred ? "

He turned on his heel. She darted past him, and tried to kick at the face of the prostrate man. Spring dragged her roughly away, before she could do him a mischief.

" Stand clear ! " he cried, giving her a shake. " You should take shame to hit a fallen man."

With a groan the injured man turned on his side. Then he slowly sat up and passed his wet hand over his face. Finally, he staggered to his feet.

" Well," he said, shrugging his broad shoulders, " it was a fair fight. I've no complaint to make. I was Jackson's favourite pupil, but I give you best." Suddenly his eyes lit upon the furious face of the woman. " Halloa, Betty ! " he cried. " So I have you to thank. I might have guessed it when I had your letter."

" Yes, my lord," said she, with a mock curtsy. " You have me to thank. Your little wife managed it all. I lay behind those bushes, and I saw you beaten like a hound. You haven't had all that I had planned for you, but I think it will be some little time before any woman loves you for the sake of your appearance. Do you remember the words, my lord ? Do you remember the words ? "

He stood stunned for a moment. Then he snatched his whip from the ground, and looked at her from under his heavy brows.

" I believe you're the devil ! " he cried.

" I wonder what the governess will think ? " said she.

He flared into furious rage and rushed at her with his whip. Tom Spring threw himself before him with his arms out.

" It won't do, sir ; I can't stand by."

The man glared at his wife over the prize-fighter's shoulder.

" So it's for dear George's sake ! " he said, with a bitter laugh. " But poor, broken-nosed George seems to have gone to the wall. Taken up with a prize-fighter, eh ? Found a fancy man for yourself ! "

" You liar ! " she gasped.

" Ha, my lady, that stings your pride, does it ? Well, you shall stand together in the dock for trespass and assault. What a picture—great Lord, what a picture ! "

" You wouldn't, John ! "

" Wouldn't I, by—— ! You stay there three minutes and see if I wouldn't." He seized his clothes from the bush, and staggered off as swiftly as he could across the field, blowing a whistle as he ran.

"Quick! quick," cried the woman. "There's not an instant to lose." Her face was livid, and she was shivering and panting with apprehension. "He'll raise the country. It would be awful—awful!"

She ran swiftly down the tortuous path, Spring following after her and dressing as he went. In a field to the right a gamekeeper, his gun in his hand, was hurrying towards the whistling. Two labourers, loading hay, had stopped their work and were looking about them, their pitchforks in their hands. But the path was empty, and the phaeton awaited them, the horse cropping the grass by the lane-side, the driver half asleep on his perch. The woman sprang swiftly in and motioned Spring to stand by the wheel.

"There is your fifty pounds," she said, handing him a paper. "You were a fool not to turn it into a hundred when you had the chance. I've done with you now."

"But where am I to go?" asked the prize-fighter, gazing around him at the winding lanes.

"To the devil!" said she. "Drive on, Johnson!"

The phaeton whirled down the road and vanished round a curve. Tom Spring was alone.

Everywhere over the countryside he heard shoutings and whistlings. It was clear that so long as she escaped the indignity of sharing his fate his employer was perfectly indifferent as to whether he got into trouble or not. Tom Spring began to feel indifferent himself. He was weary to death, his head was aching from the blows and falls which he had received, and his feelings were raw from the treatment which he had undergone. He walked slowly some few yards down the lane, but had no idea which way to turn to reach Tunbridge Wells. In the distance he heard the baying of dogs, and he guessed that they were being set upon his track. In that case he could not hope to escape them, and might just as well await them where he was. He picked out a heavy stake from the hedge, and he sat down moodily waiting, in a very dangerous temper, for what might befall him.

But it was a friend and not a foe who came first into sight. Round the corner of the lane flew a small dog-cart, with a fast-trotting chestnut cob between the shafts. In it was seated the rubicund landlord of the Royal Oak, his whip going, his face continually flying round to glance behind him.

" Jump in, Mr. Spring, jump in ! " he cried, as he reined up. " They're all coming, dogs and men ! Come on ! Now, hud up, Ginger ! " Not another word did he say until two miles of lanes had been left behind them at racing speed and they were back in safety upon the Brighton road. Then he let the reins hang loose on the pony's back, and he slapped Tom Spring with his fat hand upon the shoulder.

" Splendid ! " he cried, his great red face shining with ecstasy. " Oh, Lord ! but it was beautiful ! "

" What ! " cried Spring. " You saw the fight ? "

" Every round of it ! By George ! to think that I should have lived to have had such a fight all to myself ! Oh, but it was grand," he cried, in a frenzy of delight, " to see his lordship go down like a pithed ox and her ladyship clapping her hands behind the bush ! I guessed there was something in the wind, and I followed you all the way. When you stopped, I tethered little Ginger in a grove, and I crept after you through the wood. It's as well I did, for the whole parish was up ! "

But Tom Spring was sitting gazing at him in blank amazement.

" His lordship ! " he gasped.

" No less, my boy. Lord Falconbridge, Chairman of the Bench, Deputy Lieutenant of the County, Peer of the Realm—that's your man."

" Good Lord ! "

" And you didn't know ? It's as well, for maybe you wouldn't have whacked it in as hard if you had ; and, mind you, if you hadn't, he'd have beat you. There's not a man in this county could stand up to him. He takes the poachers and gipsies two and three at a

75

time. He's the terror of the place. But you did him
—did him fair. Oh man, it was fine ! "

Tom Spring was too much dazed by what he heard
to do more than sit and wonder. It was not until he
had got back to the comforts of the inn, and after a bath
had partaken of a solid meal, that he sent for Mr. Cordery
the landlord. To him he confided the whole train of
events which had led up to his remarkable experience,
and he begged him to throw such light as he could upon
it. Cordery listened with keen interest and many chuckles
to the story. Finally he left the room and returned with
a frayed newspaper in his hand, which he smoothed out
upon his knee.

" It's the *Pantiles Gazette*, Mr. Spring, as gossiping
a rag as ever was printed. I expect there will be a fine
column in it if ever it gets its prying nose into this day's
doings. However, we are mum and her ladyship is
mum, and, my word ! his lordship is mum, though he
did, in his passion, raise the hue and cry on you. Here
it is, Mr. Spring, and I'll read it to you while you smoke
your pipe. It's dated July of last year, and it goes like
this :—

" ' FRACAS IN HIGH LIFE.—It is an open secret that
the differences which have for some years been known
to exist between Lord F—— and his beautiful wife have
come to a head during the last few days. His lordship's
devotion to sport, and also, as it is whispered, some attentions which he has shown to a humbler member of his
household, have, it is said, long alienated Lady F——'s
affection. Of late she has sought consolation and friendship with a gentleman whom we will designate as Sir
George W——n. Sir George, who is a famous lady-
killer, and as well-proportioned a man as any in England,
took kindly to the task of consoling the disconsolate fair.
The upshot, however, was vastly unfortunate, both for
the lady's feelings and for the gentleman's beauty. The
two friends were surprised in a rendezvous near the house

by Lord F—— himself at the head of a party of his servants. Lord F—— then and there, in spite of the shrieks of the lady, availed himself of his strength and skill to administer such punishment to the unfortunate Lothario as would, in his own parting words, prevent any woman from loving him again for the sake of his appearance. Lady F—— has left his lordship and betaken herself to London, where, no doubt, she is now engaged in nursing the damaged Apollo. It is confidently expected that a duel will result from the affair, but no particulars have reached us up to the hour of going to press.' "

The landlord laid down the paper. " You've been moving in high life, Mr. Thomas Spring," said he.

The pugilist passed his hand over his battered face. " Well, Mr. Cordery," said he, " low life is good enough for me."

3. *The Fall of Lord Barrymore*

THERE are few social historians of those days who have not told of the long and fierce struggle between those two famous bucks, Sir Charles Tregellis and Lord Barrymore, for the Lordship of the Kingdom of St. James, a struggle which divided the whole of fashionable London into two opposing camps. It has been chronicled also how the peer retired suddenly and the commoner resumed his great career without a rival. Only here, however, one can read the real and remarkable reason for this sudden eclipse of a star.

It was one morning in the days of this famous struggle that Sir Charles Tregellis was performing his very complicated toilet, and Ambrose, his valet, was helping him to attain that pitch of perfection which had long gained him the reputation of being the best-dressed man in town. Suddenly Sir Charles paused, his *coup d'archet* half-executed, the final beauty of his neck-cloth half-achieved, while he listened with surprise and indignation upon his large, comely, fresh-complexioned face. Below, the decorous hum of Jermyn Street had been broken by the sharp, staccato, metallic beating of a door-knocker.

"I begin to think that this uproar must be at our door," said Sir Charles, as one who thinks aloud. "For five minutes it has come and gone; yet Perkins has his orders."

At a gesture from his master Ambrose stepped out upon the balcony and craned his discreet head over it. From the street below came a voice, drawling but clear.

"You would oblige me vastly, fellow, if you would do me the favour to open this door," said the voice.

"Who is it? What is it?" asked the scandalized Sir Charles, with his arrested elbow still pointing upwards.

Ambrose had returned with as much surprise upon his dark face as the etiquette of his position would allow him to show.

"It is a young gentleman, Sir Charles."

"A young gentleman? There is no one in London who is not aware that I do not show before midday. Do you know the person? Have you seen him before?"

"I have not seen him, sir, but he is very like someone I could name."

"Like someone? Like whom?"

"With all respect, Sir Charles, I could for a moment have believed that it was yourself when I looked down. A smaller man, sir, and a youth; but the voice, the face, the bearing——"

"It must be that young cub Vereker, my brother's ne'er-do-weel," muttered Sir Charles, continuing his toilet. "I have heard that there are points in which he resembles me. He wrote from Oxford that he would come, and I answered that I would not see him. Yet he ventures to insist. The fellow needs a lesson! Ambrose, ring for Perkins."

A large footman entered with an outraged expression upon his face.

" I cannot have this uproar at the door, Perkins ! "

" If you please, the young gentleman won't go away, sir."

" Won't go away ? It is your duty to see that he goes away. Have you not your orders ? Didn't you tell him that I am not seen before midday ? "

" I said so, sir. He would have pushed his way in, for all I could say, so I slammed the door in his face."

" Very right, Perkins."

" But now, sir, he is making such a din that all the folk are at the windows. There is a crowd gathering in the street, sir."

From below came the crack-crack-crack of the knocker, ever rising in insistence, with a chorus of laughter and encouraging comments from the spectators. Sir Charles flushed with anger. There must be some limit to such impertinence.

" My clouded amber cane is in the corner," said he. " Take it with you, Perkins. I give you a free hand. A stripe or two may bring the young rascal to reason."

The large Perkins smiled and departed. The door was heard to open below and the knocker was at rest. A few moments later there followed a prolonged howl and a noise as of a beaten carpet. Sir Charles listened with a smile which gradually faded from his good-humoured face.

" The fellow must not overdo it," he muttered. " I would not do the lad an injury, whatever his deserts may be. Ambrose, run out on the balcony and call him off. This has gone far enough."

But before the valet could move there came a swift patter of agile feet upon the stairs, and a handsome youth, dressed in the height of fashion, was standing framed in the open doorway. The pose, the face, above all the curious, mischievous dancing light in the large blue eyes, all spoke of the famous Tregellis blood. Even such was

Sir Charles when, twenty years before, he had by virtue of his spirit and audacity, in one short season taken a place in London from which Brummell himself had afterwards vainly struggled to depose him. The youth faced the angry features of his uncle with an air of debonair amusement, and he held towards him, upon his outstretched palms, the broken fragments of an amber cane.

" I much fear, sir," said he, " that in correcting your fellow I have had the misfortune to injure what can only have been your property. I am vastly concerned that it should have occurred."

Sir Charles stared with intolerant eyes at this impertinent apparition. The other looked back in a laughable parody of his senior's manner. As Ambrose had remarked after his inspection from the balcony, the two were very alike, save that the younger was smaller, finer cut, and the more nervously alive of the two.

" You are my nephew, Vereker Tregellis ? " asked Sir Charles.

" Yours to command, sir."

" I hear bad reports of you from Oxford."

" Yes, sir, I understand that the reports *are* bad."

" Nothing could be worse."

" So I have been told."

" Why are you here, sir ? "

" That I might see my famous uncle."

" So you made a tumult in his street, forced his door, and beat his footman ? "

" Yes, sir."

" You had my letter ? "

" Yes, sir."

" You were told that I was not receiving ? "

" Yes, sir."

" I can remember no such exhibition of impertinence."

The young man smiled and rubbed his hands in satisfaction.

" There is an impertinence which is redeemed by

wit," said Sir Charles, severely. " There is another which is the mere boorishness of the clodhopper. As you grow older and wiser you may discern the difference."

" You are very right, sir," said the young man, warmly. " The finer shades of impertinence are infinitely subtle, and only experience and the society of one who is a recognized master "—here he bowed to his uncle—" can enable one to excel."

Sir Charles was notoriously touchy in temper for the first hour after his morning chocolate. He allowed himself to show it.

" I cannot congratulate my brother upon his son," said he. " I had hoped for something more worthy of our traditions."

" Perhaps, sir, upon a longer acquaintance——"

" The chance is too small to justify the very irksome experience. I must ask you, sir, to bring to a close a visit which never should have been made."

The young man smiled affably, but gave no sign of departure.

" May I ask, sir," said he, in an easy conversational fashion, " whether you can recall Principal Munro, of my college ? "

" No, sir, I cannot," his uncle answered, sharply.

" Naturally you would not burden your memory to such an extent, but he still remembers you. In some conversation with him yesterday he did me the honour to say that I brought you back to his recollection by what he was pleased to call the mingled levity and obstinacy of my character. The levity seems to have already impressed you. I am now reduced to showing you the obstinacy." He sat down in a chair near the door and folded his arms, still beaming pleasantly at his uncle.

" Oh, you won't go ? " asked Sir Charles, grimly.

" No, sir ; I will stay."

"Ambrose, step down and call a couple of chairmen."

" I should not advise it, sir. They will be hurt."

" I will put you out with my own hands."

" That, sir, you can always do. As my uncle, I could scarce resist you. But, short of throwing me down the stair, I do not see how you can avoid giving me half an hour of your attention."

Sir Charles smiled. He could not help it. There was so much that was reminiscent of his own arrogant and eventful youth in the bearing of this youngster. He was mollified, too, by the defiance of menials and quick submission to himself. He turned to the glass and signed to Ambrose to continue his duties.

" I must ask you to await the conclusion of my toilet," said he. " Then we shall see how far you can justify such an intrusion."

When the valet had at last left the room Sir Charles turned his attention once more to his scapegrace nephew, who had viewed the details of the famous buck's toilet with the face of an acolyte assisting at a mystery.

" Now, sir," said the older man, " speak, and speak to the point, for I can assure you that I have many more important matters which claim my attention. The Prince is waiting for me at the present instant at Carlton House. Be as brief as you can. What is it that you want ? "

" A thousand pounds."

" Really ! Nothing more ? " Sir Charles had turned acid again.

" Yes, sir ; an introduction to Mr. Brinsley Sheridan, whom I know to be your friend."

" And why to him ? "

" Because I am told that he controls Drury Lane Theatre, and I have a fancy to be an actor. My friends assure me that I have a pretty talent that way."

" I can see you clearly, sir, in Charles Surface, or any other part where a foppish insolence is the essential. The less you acted, the better you would be. But it is absurd to suppose that I could help you to such a career. I could not justify it to your father. Return to Oxford at once, and continue your studies."

" Impossible ! "

" And pray, sir, what is the impediment ? "

" I think I may have mentioned to you that I had an interview yesterday with the Principal. He ended it by remarking that the authorities of the University could tolerate me no more."

" Sent down ? "

" Yes, sir."

" And this is the fruit, no doubt, of a long series of rascalities."

" Something of the sort, sir, I admit."

In spite of himself, Sir Charles began once more to relax in his severity towards this handsome young scapegrace. His absolute frankness disarmed criticism. It was in a more gracious voice that the older man continued the conversation.

" Why do you want this large sum of money ? " he asked.

" To pay my college debts before I go, sir."

" Your father is not a rich man."

" No, sir. I could not apply to him for that reason."

" So you come to me, who am a stranger ! "

" No, sir, no ! You are my uncle, and, if I may say so, my ideal and my model."

" You flatter me, my good Vereker. But if you think you can flatter me out of a thousand pounds, you mistake your man. I will give you no money."

" Of course, sir, if you can't——"

" I did not say I can't. I say I won't."

" If you can, sir, I think you will."

Sir Charles smiled, and flicked his sleeve with his lace handkerchief.

" I find you vastly entertaining," said he. " Pray continue your conversation. Why do you think that I will give you so large a sum of money ? "

" The reason that I think so," continued the younger man, " is that I can do you a service which will seem to you worth a thousand pounds."

Sir Charles raised his eyebrows in surprise.

" Is this blackmail ? " he inquired.

Vereker Tregellis flushed.

" Sir," said he, with a pleasing sternness, " you surprise me. You should know the blood of which I come too well to suppose that I would attempt such a thing."

" I am relieved to hear that there are limits to what you consider to be justifiable. I must confess that I had seen none in your conduct up to now. But you say that you can do me a service which will be worth a thousand pounds to me ? "

" Yes, sir."

" And pray, sir, what may this service be ? "

" To make Lord Barrymore the laughing-stock of the town."

Sir Charles, in spite of himself, lost for an instant the absolute serenity of his self-control. He started, and his face expressed his surprise. By what devilish instinct did this raw undergraduate find the one chink in his armour ? Deep in his heart, unacknowledged to anyone, there was the will to pay many a thousand pounds to the man who would bring ridicule upon this his most dangerous rival, who was challenging his supremacy in fashionable London.

" Did you come from Oxford with this precious project ? " he asked, after a pause.

" No, sir. I chanced to see the man himself last night, and I conceived an ill-will to him, and would do him a mischief."

" Where did you see him ? "

" I spent the evening, sir, at the Vauxhall Gardens."

" No doubt you would," interpolated his uncle.

" My Lord Barrymore was there. He was attended by one who was dressed as a clergyman, but who was, as I am told, none other than Hooper the Tinman, who acts as his bully and thrashes all who may offend him. Together they passed down the central path,

insulting the women and browbeating the men. They
actually hustled me. I was offended, sir—so much so
that I nearly took the matter in hand then and there."

" It is as well that you did not. The prize-fighter
would have beaten you."

" Perhaps so, sir—and also, perhaps not."

" Ah, you add pugilism to your elegant accomplish-
ments ? "

The young man laughed pleasantly.

" William Ball is the only professor of my Alma Mater
who has ever had occasion to compliment me, sir. He
is better known as the Oxford Pet. I think, with all
modesty, that I could hold him for a dozen rounds. But
last night I suffered the annoyance without protest, for
since it is said that the same scene is enacted every
evening, there is always time to act."

" And how would you act, may I ask ? "

." That, sir, I should prefer to keep to myself ; but
my aim, as I say, would be to make Lord Barrymore a
laughing-stock to all London."

Sir Charles cogitated for a moment.

" Pray, sir," said he, " why did you imagine that any
humiliation to Lord Barrymore would be pleasing to
me ? "

" Even in the provinces we know something of what
passes in polite circles. Your antagonism to this man
is to be found in every column of fashionable gossip.
The town is divided between you. It is impossible that
any public slight upon him should be unpleasing to
you."

Sir Charles smiled.

" You are a shrewd reasoner," said he. " We will
suppose for the instant that you are right. Can you give
me no hint what means you would adopt to attain this
very desirable end ? "

" I would merely make the remark, sir, that many
women have been wronged by this fellow. That is a
matter of common knowledge. If one of these damsels

were to upbraid him in public in such a fashion that the sympathy of the bystanders should be with her, then I can imagine, if she were sufficiently persistent, that his lordship's position might become an unenviable one."

" And you know such a woman ? "

" I think, sir, that I do."

" Well, my good Vereker, if any such attempt is in your mind, I see no reason why I should stand between Lord Barrymore and the angry fair. As to whether the result is worth a thousand pounds, I can make no promise."

" You shall yourself be the judge, sir."

" I will be an exacting judge, nephew."

" Very good, sir ; I should not desire otherwise. If things go as I hope, his lordship will not show face in St. James's Street for a year to come. I will now, if I may, give you your instructions."

" My instructions ! What do you mean ? I have nothing to do with the matter."

" You are the judge, sir, and therefore must be present."

" I can play no part."

" No, sir. I would not ask you to do more than be a witness."

" What, then, are my instructions, as you are pleased to call them ? "

" You will come to the Gardens to-night, uncle, at nine o'clock precisely. You will walk down the centre path, and you will seat yourself upon one of the rustic seats which are beside the statue of Aphrodite. You will wait and you will observe."

" Very good ; I will do so. I begin to perceive, nephew, that the breed of Tregellis has not yet lost some of the points which have made it famous."

It was at the stroke of nine that night when Sir Charles, throwing his reins to the groom, descended from his high yellow phaeton, which forthwith turned to take its place in the long line of fashionable carriages waiting for their owners. As he entered the gate of the Gardens, the centre at that time of the dissipation and revelry of London, he turned up the collar of his driving-cape and drew his hat over his eyes, for he had no desire to be personally associated with what might well prove to be a public scandal. In spite of his attempted disguise, however, there was that in his walk and his carriage which caused many an eye to be turned after him as he passed and many a hand to be raised in salute. Sir Charles walked on, and, seating himself upon the rustic bench in front of the famous statue, which was in the very middle of the Gardens, he waited in amused suspense to see the next act in this comedy.

From the pavilion, whence the paths radiated, there came the strains of the band of the Foot Guards, and by the many-coloured lamps twinkling from every tree Sir Charles could see the confused whirl of the dancers. Suddenly the music stopped. The quadrilles were at an end.

An instant afterwards the central path by which he sat was thronged by the revellers. In a many-coloured crowd, stocked and cravated with all the bravery of buff and plum-colour and blue, the bucks of the town passed and repassed with their high-waisted, straight-skirted, be-bonneted ladies upon their arms.

It was not a decorous assembly. Many of the men, flushed and noisy, had come straight from their potations. The women, too, were loud and aggressive. Now and then, with a rush and a swirl, amid a chorus of screams from the girls and good-humoured laughter from their escorts, some band of high-blooded, noisy youths would break their way across the moving throng. It was no place for the prim or demure, and there was a spirit of good-nature and merriment among the crowd which condoned the wildest liberty.

And yet there were some limits to what could be tolerated even by so Bohemian an assembly. A murmur of anger followed in the wake of two roisterers who were making their way down the path. It would, perhaps, be fairer to say one roisterer; for of the two it was only the first who carried himself with such insolence, although it was the second who ensured that he could do it with impunity.

The leader was a very tall, hatchet-faced man, dressed in the very height of fashion, whose evil, handsome features were flushed with wine and arrogance. He shouldered his way roughly through the crowd, peering with an abominable smile into the faces of the women, and occasionally, where the weakness of the escort invited an insult, stretching out his hand and caressing the cheek or neck of some passing girl, laughing loudly as she winced away from his touch.

Close at his heels walked his hired attendant, whom, out of insolent caprice and with a desire to show his contempt for the prejudices of others, he had dressed as a rough country clergyman. This fellow slouched along with frowning brows and surly, challenging eyes, like some faithful, hideous human bulldog, his knotted hands protruding from his rusty cassock, his great underhung jaw turning slowly from right to left as he menaced the crowd with his sinister gaze. Already a close observer might have marked upon his face a heaviness and looseness of feature, the first signs of that physical decay which in a very few years was to stretch him, a helpless wreck, too weak to utter his own name, upon the causeway of the London streets. At present, however, he was still an unbeaten man, the terror of the Ring, and as his ill-omened face was seen behind his infamous master many a half-raised cane was lowered and many a hot word was checked, while the whisper of " Hooper ! 'Ware Bully Hooper ! " warned all who were aggrieved that it might be best to pocket their injuries lest some even worse thing should befall them. Many a maimed and disfigured man had carried away from Vauxhall the handiwork of the Tinman and his patron.

Moving in insolent slowness through the crowd, the

bully and his master had just come opposite to the bench upon which sat Sir Charles Tregellis. At this place the path opened up into a circular space, brilliantly illuminated and surrounded by rustic seats. From one of these an elderly, ringleted woman, deeply veiled, rose suddenly and barred the path of the swaggering nobleman. Her voice sounded clear and strident above the babel of tongues, which hushed suddenly that their owners might hear it.

"Marry her, my lord! I entreat you to marry her! Oh, surely you will marry my poor Amelia!" said the voice.

Lord Barrymore stood aghast. From all sides folk were closing in and heads were peering over shoulders. He tried to push on, but the lady barred his way and two palms pressed upon his beruffled front.

"Surely, surely you would not desert her! Take the advice of that good, kind clergyman behind you!" wailed the voice. "Oh, be a man of honour and marry her!"

The elderly lady thrust out her hand and drew forward a lumpish-looking young woman, who sobbed and mopped her eyes with her handkerchief.

"The plague take you!" roared his lordship, in a fury. "Who is the wench? I vow that I never clapped eyes on either of you in my life!"

"It is my niece Amelia," cried the lady, "your own loving Amelia! Oh, my lord, can you pretend that you have forgotten poor, trusting Amelia, of Woodbine Cottage at Lichfield?"

"I never set foot in Lichfield in my life!" cried the peer. "You are two impostors who should be whipped at the cart's tail."

"Oh, wicked! Oh, Amelia!" screamed the lady, in a voice that resounded through the Gardens. "Oh, my darling, try to soften his hard heart; pray him that he make an honest woman of you at last."

With a lurch the stout young woman fell forward and

embraced Lord Barrymore with the hug of a bear. He would have raised his cane, but his arms were pinned to his sides.

"Hooper! Hooper!" screamed the furious peer, craning his neck in horror, for the girl seemed to be trying to kiss him.

But the bruiser, as he ran forward, found himself entangled with the old lady.

"Out o' the way, marm," he cried. "Out o' the way, I say!" and pushed her violently aside.

"Oh, you rude, rude man!" she shrieked, springing back in front of him. "He hustled me, good people; you saw him hustle me! A clergyman, but no gentleman! What! you would treat a lady so—you would do it again? Oh, I could slap, slap, slap you!"

And with each repetition of the word, with extraordinary swiftness, her open palm rang upon the prize-fighter's cheek.

The crowd buzzed with amazement and delight.

"Hooper! Hooper!" cried Lord Barrymore once more, for he was still struggling in the ever-closer embrace of the unwieldy and amorous Amelia.

The bully again pushed forward to the aid of his patron, but again the elderly lady confronted him, her head back, her left arm extended, her whole attitude, to his amazement, that of an expert boxer.

The prize-fighter's brutal nature was roused. Woman or no woman, he would show the murmuring crowd what it meant to cross the path of the Tinman. She had struck him. She must take the consequence. No one should square up to him with impunity. He swung his right with a curse. The bonnet instantly ducked under his arm, and a line of razor-like knuckles left an open cut under his eye.

Amid wild cries of delight and encouragement from the dense circle of spectators, the lady danced round the sham clergyman, dodging his ponderous blows, slipping under his arms, and smacking back at him most successfully. Once she tripped and fell over her own skirt, but was up and at him again in an instant.

" You vulgar fellow ! " she shrieked. " Would you strike a helpless woman ! Take that ! Oh, you rude and ill-bred man ! "

Bully Hooper was cowed for the first time in his life by the extraordinary thing that he was fighting. The creature was as elusive as a shadow, and yet the blood was dripping down his chin from the effects of the blows. He shrank back with an amazed face from so uncanny an antagonist. And in the moment that he did so his spell was for ever broken. Only success could hold it. A check was fatal. In all the crowd there was scarce one who was not nursing some grievance against master or man, and waiting for that moment of weakness in which to revenge it.

With a growl of rage the circle closed in. There was an eddy of furious, struggling men, with Lord Barry-more's thin, flushed face and Hooper's bulldog jaw in the centre of it. A moment after they were both upon the ground, and a dozen sticks were rising and falling above them.

" Let me up ! You're killing me ! For God's sake let me up ! " cried a crackling voice.

Hooper fought mute, like the bulldog he was, till his senses were beaten out of him.

Bruised, kicked, and mauled, never did their worst victim come so badly from the Gardens as the bully and his patron that night. But worse than the ache of wounds for Lord Barrymore was the smart of the mind as he thought how every club and drawing-room in London would laugh for a week to come at the tale of his Amelia and her aunt.

Sir Charles had stood, rocking with laughter, upon the bench which overlooked the scene. When at last he made his way back through the crowds to his yellow phaeton, he was not entirely surprised to find that the back seat was already occupied by two giggling females, who were exchanging most unladylike repartees with the attendant grooms.

" You young rascals ! " he remarked, over his shoulder, as he gathered up his reins.

The two females tittered loudly.

" Uncle Charles ! " cried the elder, " may I present Mr. Jack Jarvis, of Brasenose College ? I think, uncle, you should take us somewhere to sup, for it has been a vastly fatiguing performance. To-morrow I will do myself the honour to call, at your convenience, and will venture to bring with me the receipt for one thousand pounds."

4. *The Crime of the Brigadier*

IN all the great hosts of France there was only one officer towards whom the English of Wellington's Army retained a deep, steady, and unchangeable hatred. There were plunderers among the French, and men of violence, gamblers, duellists, and *roués*. All these could be forgiven, for others of their kidney were to be found among the ranks of the English. But one officer of Massena's force had committed a crime which was unspeakable, unheard of, abominable ; only to be alluded to with curses late in the evening, when a second bottle had loosened the tongues of men. The news of it was carried back to England, and country gentlemen who knew little of the details of the war grew crimson with passion when they heard of it, and yeomen of the shires raised freckled fists to Heaven and swore. And yet who should be the doer of this dreadful deed but our friend the Brigadier, Etienne Gerard, of the Hussars of Conflans, gay-riding, plume-tossing, débonnaire, the darling of the ladies and of the six brigades of light cavalry.

But the strange part of it is that this gallant gentleman did this hateful thing, and made himself the most unpopular man in the Peninsula, without ever knowing that he had done a crime for which there is hardly a name amid all the resources of our language. He died of old age, and never once in that imperturbable self-confidence which adorned or disfigured his character knew that so many thousand Englishmen would gladly have hanged him with their own hands. On the contrary, he numbered this adventure among those other exploits which he has given to the world, and many a time he chuckled and hugged himself as he narrated it to the eager circle who gathered round him in that humble café where, between his dinner and his dominoes, he would tell, amid tears and laughter, of that inconceivable Napoleonic past when France, like an angel of wrath, rose up, splendid and terrible, before a cowering continent. Let us listen to him as he tells the story in his own way and from his own point of view.

You must know, my friends, said he, that it was towards the end of the year eighteen hundred and ten that I and Massena and the others pushed Wellington backwards until we had hoped to drive him and his army into the Tagus. But when we were still twenty-five miles from Lisbon we found that we were betrayed, for what had this Englishman done but build an enormous line of works and forts at a place called Torres Vedras, so that even we were unable to get through them! They lay across the whole Peninsula, and our army was so far from home that we did not dare to risk a reverse, and we had already learned at Busaco that it was no child's play to fight against these people. What could we do, then, but sit down in front of these lines and blockade them to the best of our power? There we remained for six months, amid such anxieties that Massena said afterwards that he had not one hair which was not white upon his body. For my own part, I did not worry much about our situation, but I looked after our horses, who were in great need of rest and green fodder. For the rest, we drank the wine of the country and passed the time as best we might. There was a lady at Santarem—but my lips are sealed. It is the part of a gallant man to say nothing, though he may indicate that he could say a great deal.

One day Massena sent for me, and I found him in his tent with a great plan pinned upon the table. He looked at me in silence with that single piercing eye of his, and I felt by his expression that the matter was serious. He was nervous and ill at ease, but my bearing seemed to reassure him. It is good to be in contact with brave men.

" Colonel Etienne Gerard," said he, " I have always heard that you are a very gallant and enterprising officer."

It was not for me to confirm such a report, and yet it would be folly to deny it, so I clinked my spurs together and saluted.

" You are also an excellent rider."

I admitted it.

" And the best swordsman in the six brigades of light cavalry."

Massena was famous for the accuracy of his information.

" Now," said he, " if you will look at this plan you will have no difficulty in understanding what it is that I wish you to do. These are the lines of Torres Vedras. You will perceive that they cover a vast space, and you will realize that the English can only hold a position here and there. Once through the lines you have twenty-five miles of open country which lie between them and Lisbon. It is very important to me to learn how Wellington's troops are distributed throughout that space, and it is my wish that you should go and ascertain."

His words turned me cold.

" Sir," said I, " it is impossible that a colonel of light cavalry should condescend to act as a spy."

He laughed and clapped me on the shoulder.

" You would not be a Hussar if you were not a hothead," said he. " If you will listen you will understand that I have not asked you to act as a spy. What do you think of that horse ? "

He had conducted me to the opening of his tent, and there was a Chasseur who led up and down a most admirable creature. He was a dapple grey, not very tall—a little over fifteen hands perhaps—but with the short head and splendid arch of the neck which comes with the Arab blood. His shoulders and haunches were so muscular, and yet his legs so fine, that it thrilled me with joy just to gaze upon him. A fine horse or a beautiful woman, I cannot look at them unmoved, even now when seventy winters have chilled my blood. You can think how it was in the year '10.

" This," said Massena, " is Voltigeur, the swiftest horse in our army. What I desire is that you should start to-night, ride round the lines upon the flank, make your way across the enemy's rear, and return upon the other flank, bringing me news of his dispositions. You will wear a uniform, and will, therefore, if captured, be safe from the death of a spy. It is probable that you will get through the lines unchallenged, for the posts are very scattered. Once through, in daylight you can outride anything which you meet, and if you keep off the roads you may escape entirely unnoticed. If you have not reported yourself by to-morrow night, I will understand that you are taken, and I will offer them Colonel Petrie in exchange."

Ah, how my heart swelled with pride and joy as I sprang into the saddle and galloped this grand horse up and down to show the Marshal the mastery which I had of him ! He was magnificent—we were both magnificent, for Massena clapped his hands and cried out in his delight. It was not I, but he, who said that a gallant beast deserves a gallant rider. Then, when for the third time, with my panache flying and my dolman streaming behind me, I thundered past him, I saw upon his hard old face that he had no longer any doubt

that he had chosen the man for his purpose. I drew
my sabre, raised the hilt to my lips in salute, and galloped
on to my own quarters. Already the news had spread
that I had been chosen for a mission, and my little rascals
came swarming out of their tents to cheer me. Ah ! it
brings the tears to my old eyes when I think how proud
they were of their Colonel. And I was proud of them
also. They deserved a dashing leader.

The night promised to be a stormy one, which was
very much to my liking. It was my desire to keep my
departure most secret, for it was evident that if the
English heard that I had been detached from the army
they would naturally conclude that something important
was about to happen. My horse was taken, therefore,
beyond the picket line, as if for watering, and I followed
and mounted him there. I had a map, a compass,
and a paper of instructions from the Marshal, and with
these in the bosom of my tunic and my sabre at my
side, I set out upon my adventure.

A thin rain was falling and there was no moon, so
you may imagine that it was not very cheerful. But
my heart was light at the thought of the honour which
had been done me and the glory which awaited me.
This exploit should be one more in that brilliant series
which was to change my sabre into a bâton. Ah, how
we dreamed, we foolish fellows, young, and drunk with
success ! Could I have foreseen that night as I rode,
the chosen man of sixty thousand, that I should spend
my life planting cabbages on a hundred francs a month !
Oh, my youth, my hopes, my comrades ! But the wheel
turns and never stops. Forgive me, my friends, for
an old man has his weakness.

My route, then, lay across the face of the high ground
of Torres Vedras, then over a streamlet, past a farm-
house which had been burned down and was now only
a landmark, then through a forest of young cork oaks,
and so to the monastery of San Antonio, which marked
the left of the English position. Here I turned south

and rode quietly over the downs, for it was at this point that Massena thought that it would be most easy for me to find my way unobserved through the position. I went very slowly, for it was so dark that I could not see my hand in front of me. In such cases I leave my bridle loose and let my horse pick its own way. Voltigeur went confidently forward, and I was very content to sit upon his back and to peer about me, avoiding every light. For three hours we advanced in this cautious way, until it seemed to me that I must have left all danger behind me. I then pushed on more briskly, for I wished to be in the rear of the whole army by daybreak. There are many vineyards in these parts which in winter become open plains, and a horseman finds few difficulties in his way.

But Massena had underrated the cunning of these English, for it appears that there was not one line of defence, but three, and it was the third, which was the most formidable, through which I was at that instant passing. As I rode, elated at my own success, a lantern flashed suddenly before me, and I saw the glint of polished gun-barrels and the gleam of a red coat.

" Who goes there ? " cried a voice—such a voice ! I swerved to the right and rode like a madman, but a dozen squirts of fire came out of the darkness, and the bullets whizzed all round my ears. That was no new sound to me, my friends, though I will not talk like a foolish conscript and say that I have ever liked it. But at least it had never kept me from thinking clearly, and so I knew that there was nothing for it but to gallop hard, and try my luck elsewhere. I rode round the English picket, and then, as I heard nothing more of them, I concluded rightly that I had at last come through their defences. For five miles I rode south, striking a tinder from time to time to look at my pocket compass. And then in an instant—I feel the pang once more as my memory brings back the moment—my horse, without a sob or stagger, fell stone dead beneath me !

I had not known it, but one of the bullets from that infernal picket had passed through his body. The gallant creature had never winced nor weakened, but had gone while life was in him. One instant I was secure on the swiftest, most graceful horse in Massena's army. The next he lay upon his side, worth only the price of his hide, and I stood there that most helpless, most ungainly of creatures, a dismounted Hussar. What could I do with my boots, my spurs, my trailing sabre? I was far inside the enemy's lines. How could I hope to get back again? I am not ashamed to say that I, Etienne Gerard, sat upon my dead horse and sank my face in my hands in my despair. Already the first streaks were whitening the east. In half an hour it would be light. That I should have won my way past every obstacle and then at this last instant be left at the mercy of my enemies, my mission ruined, and myself a prisoner— was it not enough to break a soldier's heart?

But courage, my friends! We have these moments of weakness, the bravest of us; but I have a spirit like a slip of steel, for the more you bend it the higher it springs. One spasm of despair, and then a brain of ice and a heart of fire. All was not yet lost. I who had come through so many hazards would come through this one also. I rose from my horse and considered what had best be done.

And first of all it was certain that I could not get back. Long before I could pass the lines it would be broad daylight. I must hide myself for the day, and then devote the next night to my escape. I took the saddle, holsters, and bridle from poor Voltigeur, and I concealed them among some bushes, so that no one finding him could know that he was a French horse. Then, leaving him lying there, I wandered on in search of some place where I might be safe for the day. In every direction I could see camp-fires upon the sides of the hills, and already figures had begun to move around them. I must hide quickly, or I was lost.

But where was I to hide? It was a vineyard in which I found myself, the poles of the vines still standing, but the plants gone. There was no cover there. Besides, I should want some food and water before another night had come. I hurried wildly onwards through the waning darkness, trusting that chance would be my friend. And I was not disappointed. Chance is a woman, my friends, and she has her eye always upon a gallant Hussar.

Well, then, as I stumbled through the vineyard, something loomed in front of me, and I came upon a great square house with another long, low building upon one side of it. Three roads met there, and it was easy to see that this was the posada, or wine-shop. There was no light in the windows, and everything was dark and silent, but, of course, I knew that such comfortable quarters were certainly occupied, and probably by some-one of importance. I have learned, however, that the nearer the danger may really be the safer the place, and so I was by no means inclined to trust myself away from this shelter. The low building was evidently the stable, and into this I crept, for the door was unlatched. The place was full of bullocks and sheep, gathered there, no doubt, to be out of the clutches of marauders. A ladder led to a loft, and up this I climbed, and concealed myself very snugly among some bales of hay upon the top. This loft had a small open window, and I was able to look down upon the front of the inn and also upon the road. There I crouched and waited to see what would happen.

It was soon evident that I had not been mistaken when I had thought that this might be the quarters of some person of importance. Shortly after daybreak an English light dragoon arrived with a despatch, and from then onwards the place was in a turmoil, officers continually riding up and away. Always the same name was upon their lips: " Sir Stapleton—Sir Stapleton." It was hard for me to lie there with a dry moustache and watch the great flagons which were brought out by the landlord to these English officers. But it amused me to look at their fresh-coloured, clean-shaven, careless faces, and to wonder what they would think if they knew that so celebrated a person was lying so near to them. And then, as I lay and watched, I saw a sight which filled me with surprise.

It is incredible the insolence of these English! What do you suppose Milord Wellington had done when he found that Massena had blockaded him and that he could not move his army? I might give you many guesses. You might say that he had raged, that he had despaired, that he had brought his troops together and spoken to them about glory and the fatherland before leading them to one last battle. No, Milord did none of these things. But he sent a fleet ship to England to bring him a number of fox-dogs, and he with his officers settled himself down to chase the fox. It is true what I tell you. Behind the lines of Torres Vedras these mad Englishmen made the fox-chase three days in the week. We had heard of it in the camp, and now I was myself to see that it was true.

For, along the road which I have described, there came these very dogs, thirty or forty of them, white and brown, each with its tail at the same angle, like the bayonets of the Old Guard. My faith, but it was a pretty sight! And behind and amidst them there rode three men with peaked caps and red coats, whom I understood to be the hunters. After them came many horsemen with uniforms of various kinds, stringing along the roads in twos and threes, talking together and laughing. They did not seem to be going above a trot, and it appeared to me that it must indeed be a slow fox which they hoped to catch. However, it was their affair, not mine, and soon they had all passed my window and were out of sight. I waited and I watched, ready for any chance which might offer.

Presently an officer, in a blue uniform not unlike that of our flying artillery, came cantering down the road—an elderly, stout man he was, with grey side-whiskers. He stopped and began to talk with an orderly officer of dragoons, who waited outside the inn, and it was then that I learned the advantage of the English which had been taught me. I could hear and understand all that was said.

" Where is the meet ? " :said the officer, and I thought that he was hungering for his bifstek. But the other answered him that it was near Altara, so I saw that it was a place of which he spoke.

" You are late, Sir George," said the orderly.

" Yes, I had a court-martial. Has Sir Stapleton Cotton gone ? "

At this moment a window opened, and a handsome young man in a very splendid uniform looked out of it.

" Holloa, Murray ! " said he. " These cursed papers keep me, but I will be at your heels."

" Very good, Cotton. I am late already, so I will ride on."

" You might order my groom to bring round my horse," said the young general at the window to the orderly below, while the other went on down the road.

The orderly rode away to some outlying stable, and then in a few minutes there came a smart English groom with a cockade in his hat, leading by the bridle a horse —and, oh, my friends, you have never known the perfection to which a horse can attain until you have seen a first-class English hunter. He was superb : tall, broad, strong, and yet as graceful and agile as a deer. Coal black he was in colour, and his neck, and his shoulder, and his quarters, and his fetlocks—how can I describe him all to you ? The sun shone upon him as on polished ebony, and he raised his hoofs in a little, playful dance so lightly and prettily, while he tossed his mane and whinnied with impatience. Never have I seen such a mixture of strength and beauty and grace. I had often wondered how the English Hussars had managed to ride over the Chasseurs of the Guards in the affair at Astorga, but I wondered no longer when I saw the English horses.

There was a ring for fastening bridles at the door of the inn, and the groom tied the horse there while he entered the house. In an instant I had seen the chance which Fate had brought to me. Were I in that saddle I should be better off than when I started. Even Voltigeur could not compare with this magnificent creature. To think is to act with me. In one instant I was down the ladder and at the door of the stable. The next I was out and the bridle was in my hand. I bounded into the saddle. Somebody, the master or the man, shouted wildly behind me. What cared I for his shouts! I touched the horse with my spurs, and he bounded forward with such a spring that only a rider like myself could have sat him. I gave him his head and let him go—it did not matter to me where, so long as we left this inn far behind us. He thundered away across the vineyards, and in a very few minutes I had placed miles between myself and my pursuers. They could no longer tell, in that wild country, in which direction I had gone. I knew that I was safe, and so, riding to the top of a small hill, I drew my pencil and note-book from my pocket and proceeded to make plans of those camps which I could see, and to draw the outline of the country.

He was a dear creature upon whom I sat, but it was not easy to draw upon his back, for every now and then his two ears would cock, and he would start and quiver with impatience. At first I could not understand this trick of his, but soon I observed that he only did it when a peculiar noise—" yoy, yoy, yoy "—came from somewhere among the oak woods beneath us. And then suddenly this strange cry changed into a most terrible screaming, with the frantic blowing of a horn. Instantly he went mad—this horse. His eyes blazed. His mane bristled. He bounded from the earth and bounded again, twisting and turning in a frenzy. My pencil flew one way and my note-book another. And then, as I looked down into the valley, an extraordinary sight met my eyes. The hunt was streaming down it. The fox I could not see, but the dogs were in full cry, their noses down, their tails up, so close together that they might have been one great yellow and white moving carpet. And behind them rode the horsemen—my faith, what a sight ! Consider every type which a great army could show : some in hunting dress, but the most in uniforms ; blue dragoons, red dragoons, red-trousered hussars, green riflemen, artillery men, gold-slashed lancers, and most of all red, red, red, for the infantry officers ride as hard as the cavalry. Such a crowd, some well mounted, some ill, but all flying along as best they might, the subaltern as good as the general, jostling and pushing, spurring and driving, with every thought thrown to the winds save that they should have the blood of this absurd fox ! Truly, they are an extraordinary people, the English !

But I had little time to watch the hunt or to marvel at these islanders, for of all the mad creatures the very horse upon which I sat was the maddest. You understand that he was himself a hunter, and that the crying of these dogs was to him what the call of a cavalry trumpet in the street yonder would be to me. It thrilled him. It drove him wild. Again and again he bounded into the air, and then, seizing the bit between his teeth, he plunged down the slope and galloped after the dogs. I swore and tugged, and pulled, but I was powerless. This English General rode his horse with a snaffle only, and the beast had a mouth of iron. It was useless to pull him back. One might as well try to keep a Grenadier from a wine bottle. I gave it up in despair, and, settling down in the saddle, I prepared for the worst which could befall.

What a creature he was ! Never have I felt such a horse between my knees. His great haunches gathered under him with every stride, and he shot forward ever faster and faster, stretched like a greyhound, while the wind beat in my face and whistled past my ears. I was wearing our undress jacket, a uniform simple and dark in itself—though some figures give distinction to any uniform—and I had taken the precaution to remove the long panache from my busby. The result was that, amidst the mixture of costumes in the hunt, there was no reason why mine should attract attention, or why these men, whose thoughts were all with the chase, should give any heed to me. The idea that a French officer might be riding with them was too absurd to enter their minds. I laughed as I rode, for, indeed, amid all the danger, there was something of comic in the situation.

I have said that the hunters were very unequally mounted, and so, at the end of a few miles, instead of being one body of men, like a charging regiment, they were scattered over a considerable space, the better riders well up to the dogs and the others trailing away behind. Now, I was as good a rider as any, and my horse was the best of them all, and so you can imagine that it was not long before he carried me to the front. And when I saw the dogs streaming over the open, and the red-coated huntsman behind them, and only seven or eight horsemen between us, then it was that the strangest thing of all happened, for I, too, went mad—I, Etienne Gerard ! In a moment it came upon me, this spirit of sport, this desire to excel, this hatred of the fox. Accursed animal, should he then defy us ? Vile robber, his hour was come ! Ah, it is a great feeling, this feeling of sport, my friends, this desire to trample the fox under the hoofs of your horse. I have made the fox-chase with the English. I have also, as I may tell you some day, fought the box-fight with the Bustler, of Bristol. And I say to you that this sport is a wonderful thing—full of interest as well as madness.

The farther we went the faster galloped my horse, and soon there were but three men as near the dogs as I was. All thought of fear of discovery had vanished.

My brain throbbed, my blood ran hot—only one thing upon earth seemed worth living for, and that was to overtake this infernal fox. I passed one of the horsemen —a Hussar like myself. There were only two in front of me now : the one in a black coat, the other the blue artilleryman whom I had seen at the inn. His grey whiskers streamed in the wind, but he rode magnificently. For a mile or more we kept in this order, and then, as we galloped up a steep slope, my lighter weight brought me to the front. I passed them both, and when I reached the crown I was riding level with the little, hard-faced English huntsman. In front of us were the dogs, and then, a hundred paces beyond them, was a brown wisp of a thing, the fox itself, stretched to the uttermost. The sight of him fired my blood. " Aha, we have you, then, assassin ! " I cried, and shouted my encouragement to the huntsman. I waved my hand to show him that there was one upon whom he could rely.

And now there were only dogs between me and my prey. These dogs, whose duty it is to point out the game, were now rather a hindrance than a help to us, for it was hard to know how to pass them. The hunts-man felt the difficulty as much as I, for he rode behind them, and could make no progress towards the fox. He was a swift rider, but wanting in enterprise. For my part, I felt that it would be unworthy of the Hussars of Conflans if I could not overcome such a difficulty as this. Was Etienne Gerard to be stopped by a herd of fox-dogs ? It was absurd. I gave a shout and spurred my horse.

" Hold hard, sir ! Hold hard ! " cried the huntsman. He was uneasy for me, this good old man, but I reassured him by a wave and a smile. The dogs opened in front of me. One or two may have been hurt, but what would you have ? The egg must be broken for the omelette. I could hear the huntsman shouting his congratulations behind me. One more effort, and the dogs were all behind me. Only the fox was in front.

Ah, the joy and pride of that moment. To know that I had beaten the English at their own sport. Here were three hundred all thirsting for the life of this animal, and yet it was I who was about to take it. I thought of my comrades of the light cavalry brigade, of my mother, of the Emperor, of France. I had brought honour to each and all. Every instant brought me nearer to the fox. The moment for action had arrived, so I unsheathed my sabre. I waved it in the air, and the brave English all shouted behind me.

Only then did I understand how difficult is this fox-chase, for one may cut again and again at the creature and never strike him once. He is small, and turns quickly from a blow. At every cut I heard those shouts of encouragement from behind me, and they spurred me to yet another effort. And then, at last the supreme moment of my triumph arrived. In the very act of turning I caught him fair with such another back-handed cut as that with which I killed the aide-de-camp of the Emperor of Russia. He flew into two pieces, his head one way and his tail another. I looked back and waved the blood-stained sabre in the air. For the moment I was exalted—superb !

Ah ! how I should have loved to have waited to have received the congratulations of these generous enemies. There were fifty of them in sight, and not one who was not waving his hand and shouting. They are not really such a phlegmatic race, the English. A gallant deed in war or in sport will always warm their hearts. As to the old huntsman, he was the nearest to me, and I could see with my own eyes how overcome he was by what he had seen. He was like a man paralysed—his mouth open, his hand, with outspread fingers, raised in the air. For a moment my inclination was to return and to embrace him. But already the call of duty was sounding in my ears, and these English, in spite of all the fraternity which exists among sportsmen, would certainly have made me prisoner. There was no hope for my mission now, and I had done all that I could do. I could see the lines of Massena's camp no very great distance off, for, by a lucky chance, the chase had taken us in that direction. I turned from the dead fox, saluted with my sabre, and galloped away.

But they would not leave me so easily, these gallant huntsmen. I was the fox now, and the chase swept bravely over the plain. It was only at the moment when I started for the camp that they could have known that I was a Frenchman, and now the whole swarm of them were at my heels. We were within gunshot of our pickets before they would halt, and then they stood in knots and would not go away, but shouted and waved their hands at me. No, I will not think that it was in enmity. Rather would I fancy that a glow of admiration filled their breasts, and that their one desire was to embrace the stranger who had carried himself so gallantly and well.

5. *The King of the Foxes*

IT was after a hunting dinner, and there were as many scarlet coats as black ones round the table. The conversation over the cigars had turned, therefore, in the direction of horses and horsemen, with reminiscences of phenomenal runs where foxes had led the pack from end to end of a county, and been overtaken at last by two or three limping hounds and a huntsman on foot, while every rider in the field had been pounded. As the port circulated the runs became longer and more apocryphal, until we had the whips inquiring their way and failing to understand the dialect of the people who answered them. The foxes, too, became more eccentric, and we had foxes up pollard willows, foxes which were dragged by the tail out of horses' mangers, and foxes which had raced through an open front door and gone to ground in a lady's bonnet-box. The master had told one or two tall reminiscences, and when he cleared his throat for another we were all curious, for he was a bit of an artist in his way and produced his effects in a *crescendo* fashion. His face, wore the earnest, practical, severely accurate expression which heralded some of his finest efforts.

" It was before I was master," said he. " Sir Charles Adair had the hounds at that time, and then afterwards they passed to old Lathom, and then to me. It may possibly have been just after Lathom took them over, but my strong impression is that it was in Adair's time. That would be early in the seventies—about seventy-two, I should say.

" The man I mean has moved to another part of the country, but I dare say that some of you can remember him. Danbury was the name—Walter Danbury, or Wat Danbury, as the people used to call him. He was the son of old Joe Danbury, of High Ascombe, and when his father died he came into a very good thing, for his only brother was drowned when the *Magna Charta* foundered, so he inherited the whole estate. It was but a few hundred acres, but it was good arable land, and those were the great days of farming. Besides, it was freehold, and a yeoman farmer without a mortgage was a warmish man before the great fall in wheat came. Foreign wheat and barbed wire—those are the two curses of this country, for the one spoils the farmer's work and the other spoils his play.

" This young Wat Danbury was a very fine fellow, a keen rider, and thorough sportsman, but his head was a little turned at having come, when so young, into a comfortable fortune, and he went the pace for a year or two. The lad had no vice in him, but there was a hard-drinking set in the neighbourhood at that time, and Danbury got drawn in among them ; and, being an amiable fellow who liked to do what his friends were doing, he very soon took to drinking a great deal more than was good for him. As a rule, a man who takes his exercise may drink as much as he likes in the evening,

and do himself no very great harm, if he will leave it
alone during the day. Danbury had too many friends
for that, however, and it really looked as if the poor
chap was going to the bad, when a very curious thing
happened which pulled him up with such a sudden jerk
that he never put his hand upon the neck of a whisky
bottle again.

" He had a peculiarity which I have noticed in a good
many other men, that though he was always playing
tricks with his own health, he was none the less very
anxious about it, and was extremely fidgety if ever he
had any trivial symptom. Being a tough, open-air
fellow, who was always as hard as a nail, it was seldom
that there was anything amiss with him ; but at last
the drink began to tell, and he woke one morning with
his hands shaking and all his nerves tingling like over-
stretched fiddle-strings. He had been dining at some
very wet house the night before, and the wine had,
perhaps, been more plentiful than choice ; at any rate,
there he was, with a tongue like a bath-towel and a
head that ticked like an eight-day clock. He was very
alarmed at his own condition, and he sent for Doctor
Middleton, of Ascombe, the father of the man who
practises there now.

" Middleton had been a great friend of old Danbury's,
and he was very sorry to see his son going to the devil ;
so he improved the occasion by taking his case very
seriously, and lecturing him upon the danger of his
ways. He shook his head and talked about the possibility
of *delirium tremens*, or even of mania, if he continued to
lead such a life. Wat Danbury was horribly frightened.

" ' Do you think I am going to get anything of the
sort ? ' he wailed.

" ' Well, really, I don't know,' said the doctor, gravely.
' I cannot undertake to say that you are out of danger.
Your system is very much out of order. At any time
during the day you might have those grave symptoms
of which I warn you.'

" ' You think I shall be safe by evening ? '

" ' If you drink nothing during the day, and have no nervous symptoms before evening, I think you may consider yourself safe,' the doctor answered. A little fright would, he thought, do his patient good, so he made the most of the matter.

" ' What symptoms may I expect ? ' asked Danbury.

" ' It generally takes the form of optical delusions.'

" ' I see specks floating all about.'

" ' That is mere biliousness,' said the doctor soothingly, for he saw that the lad was highly strung and he did not wish to overdo it. ' I dare say that you will have no symptoms of the kind, but when they do come they usually take the shape of insects, or reptiles, or curious animals.'

" ' And if I see anything of the kind ? '

" ' If you do, you will at once send for me ; ' and so, with a promise of medicine, the doctor departed.

" Young Wat Danbury rose and dressed and moped about the room feeling very miserable and unstrung, with a vision of the County Asylum for ever in his mind. He had the doctor's word for it that if he could get through to evening in safety he would be all right ; but it is not very exhilarating to be waiting for symptoms, and to keep on glancing at your bootjack to see whether it is still a bootjack or whether it has begun to develop antennæ and legs. At last he could stand it no longer, and an overpowering longing for the fresh air and the green grass came over him. Why should he stay indoors when the Ascombe Hunt was meeting within half a mile of him ? If he was going to have these delusions which the doctor talked of, he would not have them the sooner nor the worse because he was on horseback in the open. He was sure, too, it would ease his aching head. And so it came about that in ten minutes he was in his hunting-kit, and in ten more he was riding out of his stable-yard with his roan mare Matilda between his knees. He was a little unsteady in his saddle just at

first, but the farther he went the better he felt, until
by the time he reached the meet his head was almost
clear, and there was nothing troubling him except those
haunting words of the doctor's about the possibility of
delusions any time before nightfall.

" But soon he forgot that also, for as he came up the
hounds were thrown off, and they drew the Gravel
Hanger and afterwards the Hickory Copse. It was just
the morning for a scent—no wind to blow it away, no
water to wash it out, and just damp enough to make it
cling. There was a field of forty, all keen men and good
riders, so when they came to the Black Hanger they knew
that there would be some sport, for that's a cover which
never draws blank. The woods were thicker in those
days than now, and the foxes were thicker also, and
that great dark oak-grove was swarming with them. The
only difficulty was to make them break, for it is, as you
know, a very close country, and you must coax them out
into the open before you can hope for a run.

" When they came to the Black Hanger the field took
their positions along the cover-side wherever they thought
that they were most likely to get a good start. Some
went in with the hounds, some clustered at the ends of
the drives, and some kept outside in the hope of the
fox breaking in that direction. Young Wat Danbury
knew the country like the palm of his hand, so he made
for a place where several drives intersected, and there
he waited. He had a feeling that the faster and the
farther he galloped the better he should be, and so he
was chafing to be off. His mare, too, was in the height
of fettle and one of the fastest goers in the county. Wat
was a splendid light-weight rider—under ten stone with
his saddle—and the mare was a powerful creature, all
quarters and shoulders, fit to carry a lifeguardsman ;
and so it was no wonder that there was hardly a man
in the field who could hope to stay with him. There
he waited and listened to the shouting of the huntsman
and the whips, catching a glimpse now and then in the

darkness of the wood of a whisking tail, or the gleam of a white-and-tan side amongst the underwood. It was a well-trained pack, and there was not so much as a whine to tell you that forty hounds were working all round you.

" And then suddenly there came one long-drawn yell from one of them, and it was taken up by another, and another, until within a few seconds the whole pack was giving tongue together and running on a hot scent. Danbury saw them stream across one of the drives and disappear upon the other side, and an instant later the three red coats of the hunt-servants flashed after them upon the same line. He might have made a shorter cut down one of the other drives, but he was afraid of heading the fox, so he followed the lead of the huntsman. Right through the wood they went in a bee-line, galloping with their faces brushed by their horses' manes as they stooped under the branches. It's ugly going, as you know, with the roots all wriggling about in the darkness, but you can take a risk when you catch an occasional glimpse of the pack running with a breast-high scent ; so in and out they dodged, until the wood began to thin at the edges, and they found themselves in the long bottom where the river runs. It is clear going there upon grassland, and the hounds were running very strong about two hundred yards ahead, keeping parallel with the stream. The field, who had come round the wood instead of going through, were coming hard over the fields upon the left ; but Danbury, with the hunt-servants, had a clear lead, and they never lost it. Two of the field got on terms with them : Parson Geddes on a big seventeen-hand bay which he used to ride in those days, and Squire Foley, who rode as a featherweight, and made his hunters out of cast thoroughbreds from the New-market sales ; but the others never had a look-in from start to finish, for there was no check and no pulling, and it was clear cross-country racing from start to finish. If you had drawn a line right across the map with a pencil you couldn't go straighter than that fox ran, heading for the South Downs and the sea ; and the hounds ran as surely as if they were running to view, and yet from the beginning no one ever saw the fox, and there was never a hallo forrard to tell them that he had been spied. This, however, is not so surprising, for if you've been over that line of country you will know that there are not very many people about.

" There were six of them then in the front row : Parson Geddes, Squire Foley, the huntsman, two whips, and Wat Danbury, who had forgotten all. about his head and the doctor by this time, and had not a thought for anything but the run. All six were galloping just as hard as they could lay hoofs to the ground. One of the whips dropped back, however, as some of the hounds were tailing off, and that brought them down to five. Then Foley's thoroughbred strained herself, as these slim-legged, dainty-fetlocked thoroughbreds will do when the going is rough, and he had to take a back seat. But the other four were still going strong, and they did four or five miles down the river flat at a rasping pace. It had been a wet winter, and the waters had been out a little time before, so there was a deal of sliding and splashing ; but by the time they came to the bridge the whole field was out of sight, and these four had the hunt to themselves.

" The fox had crossed the bridge—for foxes do not care to swim a chilly river any more than humans do—and from that point he had streaked away southward as hard as he could tear. It is broken country, rolling heaths, down one slope and up another, and it's hard to say whether the up or down is the more trying for the horses. This sort of switchback work is all right for a cobby, short-backed, short-legged little horse, but it is killing work for a big, long-striding hunter such as one wants in the Midlands. Anyhow, it was too much for Parson Geddes' seventeen-hand bay, and, though he tried the Irish trick—for he was a rare keen sportsman

—of running up the hills by his horse's head, it was all to no use, and he had to give it up. So then there was only the huntsman, the whip, and Wat Danbury—all going strong.

" But the country got worse and worse, and the hills were steeper and more thickly covered in heather and bracken. The horses were over their hocks all the time, and the place was pitted with rabbit-holes ; but the hounds were still streaming along, and the riders could not afford to pick their steps. As they raced down one slope, the hounds were always flowing up the opposite one, until it looked like that game where the one figure in falling makes the other one rise. But never a glimpse did they get of the fox, although they knew very well that he must be only a very short way ahead for the scent to lie so strong. And then Wat Danbury heard a crash and a thud at his elbow, and looking round he saw a pair of white cords and top-boots kicking out of a tussock of brambles. The whip's horse had stumbled, and the whip was out of the running. Danbury and the hunts-man eased down for an instant ; and then, seeing the man staggering to his feet all right, they turned and settled into their saddles once more.

" Joe Clarke, the huntsman, was a famous old rider, known for five counties round ; but he reckoned upon his second horse, and the second horses had all been left many miles behind. However, the one he was riding was good enough for anything with such a horseman upon his back, and he was going as well as when he started. As to Wat Danbury, he was going better. With every stride his own feelings improved, and the mind of the rider has its influence upon the mind of the horse. The stout little roan was gathering its muscular limbs under it and stretching to the gallop as if it were steel and whalebone instead of flesh and blood. Wat had never come to the end of its powers yet, and to-day he had such a chance of testing them as he had never had before.

" There was a pasture country beyond the heather

slopes, and for several miles the two riders were either
losing ground as they fumbled with their crop-handles
at the bars of gates, or gaining it again as they galloped
over the fields. Those were the days before this accursed
wire came into the country, and you could generally
break a hedge where you could not fly it, so they did
not trouble the gates more than they could help. Then
they were down in a hard lane, where they had to slacken
their pace, and through a farm where a man came shouting
excitedly after them ; but they had no time to stop and
listen to him, for the hounds were on some ploughland,
only two fields ahead. It was sloping upwards, that
ploughland, and the horses were over their fetlocks in
the red, soft soil. When they reached the top they
were blowing badly, but a grand valley sloped before
them, leading up to the open country of the South
Downs. Between, there lay a belt of pinewoods, into
which the hounds were streaming, running now in a
long straggling line and shedding one here and one there
as they ran. You could see the white-and-tan dots here
and there where the limpers were tailing away. But half
the pack were still going well, though the pace and distance had both been tremendous—two clear hours now
without a check.

" There was a drive through the pinewood—one of
those green, slightly-rutted drives where a horse can
get the last yard out of itself, for the ground is hard
enough to give him clean going and yet springy enough
to help him. Wat Danbury got alongside of the huntsman and they galloped together with their stirrup-irons
touching, and the hounds within a hundred yards of
them.

" ' We have it all to ourselves,' said he.

" ' Yes, sir, we've shook off the lot of 'em this time,'
said old Joe Clarke. ' If we get this fox it's worth while
'aving 'im skinned an' stuffed, for 'e's a curiosity, 'e is.'

" ' It's the fastest run I ever had in my life ! ' cried
Danbury.

" ' And the fastest that ever I 'ad, an' that means more,' said the old huntsman. ' But what licks me is that we've never 'ad a look at the beast. 'E must leave an amazin' scent be'ind 'im when these 'ounds can follow 'm like this, and yet none of us have seen 'im when we've 'ad a clear 'alf-mile view in front of us.'

" ' I expect we'll have a view of him presently,' said Danbury ; and in his mind he added, ' at least, I shall,' for the huntsman's horse was gasping as it ran, and the white foam was pouring down it like the side of a washing-tub.

" They had followed the hounds on to one of the side tracks which led out of the main drive, and that divided into a smaller track still, where the branches switched across their faces as they went and there was barely room for one horse at a time. Wat Danbury took the lead, and he heard the huntsman's horse clumping along heavily behind him, while his own mare was going with less spring than when she had started. She answered to a touch of his crop or spur, however, and he felt that there was something still left to draw upon. And then he looked up, and there was a heavy wooden stile at the end of the narrow track, with a lane of stiff young saplings leading down to it, which was far too thick to break through. The hounds were running clear upon the grassland on the other side, and you were bound either to get over that stile or lose sight of them, for the pace was too hot to let you go round.

" Well, Wat Danbury was not the lad to flinch, and at it he went full split, like a man who means what he is doing. She rose gallantly to it, rapped it hard with her front hoof, shook him on to her withers, recovered herself, and was over. Wat had hardly got back into his saddle when there was a clatter behind him like the fall of a woodstack, and there was the top bar in splinters, the horse on its belly, and the huntsman on hands and knees half a dozen yards in front of him. Wat pulled up for an instant, for the fall was a smasher ; but he saw

old Joe spring to his feet and get to his horse's bridle.
The horse staggered up, but the moment it put one foot
in front of the other Wat saw that it was hopelessly lame
—a slipped shoulder and a six weeks' job. There was
nothing he could do, and Joe was shouting to him not
to lose the hounds, so off he went again, the one solitary
survivor of the whole hunt. When a man finds himself
there, he can retire from fox-hunting, for he has tasted
the highest which it has to offer. I remember once when
I was out with the Royal Surrey—but I'll tell you that
story afterwards.

" The pack, or what was left of them, had got a bit
ahead during this time ; but he had a clear view of them
on the downland, and the mare seemed full of pride at
being the only one left, for she was stepping out rarely
and tossing her head as she went. There were two
miles over the green shoulder of a hill, a rattle down a
stony, deep-rutted country lane, where the mare stumbled
and nearly came down, a jump over a five-foot brook, a
cut through a hazel copse, another dose of heavy ploughland, a couple of gates to open, and then the green,
unbroken Downs beyond. ' Well,' said Wat Danbury
to himself, ' I'll see this fox run into or I shall see it
drowned, for it's all clear going now between this and
the chalk cliffs which line the sea.'

" But he was wrong in that, as he speedily discovered.
In all the little hollows of the Downs at that part there
are plantations of fir-woods, some of which have grown
to a good size. You do not see them until you come upon
the edge of the valleys in which they lie. Danbury
was galloping hard over the short-springy turf when he
came over the lip of one of these depressions, and there
was the dark clump of wood lying in front of and beneath
him. There were only a dozen hounds still running,
and they were just disappearing among the trees. The
sunlight was shining straight upon the long, olive-green
slopes which curved down towards this wood, and Danbury, who had the eyes of a hawk, swept them over this

great expanse ; but there was nothing moving upon it.
A few sheep were grazing far up on the right, but there
was no othersight of any living creature.   He was certain
then that he was very near to the end, for either the fox
must have gone to ground in the wood or the hounds'
noses must be at his very brush.   The mare seemed
to know also what that great empty sweep of countryside
meant, for she quickened her stride, and a few minutes
afterwards Danbury was galloping into the fir-wood.

" He had come from bright sunshine, but the wood
was very closely planted, and so dim that he could hardly
see to right or to left out of the narrow path down which
he was riding.   You know what a solemn, churchyardy
sort of place a fir-wood is.   I suppose it is the absence
of any undergrowth, and the fact that the trees never
move at all.   At any rate a kind of chill suddenly struck
Wat Danbury, and it flashed through his mind that there
had been some very singular points about this run—its
length and its straightness, and the fact that from the
first find no one had ever caught a glimpse of the creature.
Some silly talk which had been going round the country
about the king of the foxes—a sort of demon fox, so fast
that it could outrun any pack, and so fierce that they could
do nothing with it if they overtook it—suddenly came
back into his mind, and it did not seem so laughable
now in the dim fir-wood as it had done when the story
had been told over the wine and cigars.   The nervousness
wnich had been on him in the morning, and which he
had hoped that he had shaken off, swept over him again
in an overpowering wave.   He had been so proud of
being alone, and yet he would have given ten pounds
now to have had Joe Clarke's homely face beside him.
And then, just at that moment, there broke out from
the thickest part of the wood the most frantic hullaballoo
that ever he had heard in his life.   The hounds had run
into their fox.

" Well, you know, or you ought to know, what your
duty is in such a case.   You have to be whip, huntsman,

and everything else if you are the first man up. You get in among the hounds, lash them off, and keep the brush and pads from being destroyed. Of course, Wat Danbury knew all about that, and he tried to force his mare through the trees to the place where all this hideous screaming and howling came from, but the wood was so thick that it was impossible to ride it. He sprang off, therefore, left the mare standing, and broke his way through as best he could with his hunting-lash ready over his shoulder. But as he ran forward he felt his flesh go cold and creepy all over. He had heard hounds run into foxes many times before, but he had never heard such sounds as these. They were not the cries of triumph, but of fear. Every now and then came a shrill yelp of mortal agony. Holding his breath, he ran on until he broke through the interlacing branches and found himself in a little clearing with the hounds all crowding round a patch of tangled bramble at the farther end.

"When he first caught sight of them the hounds were standing in a half-circle round this bramble-patch with their backs bristling and their jaws gaping. In front of the brambles lay one of them with his throat torn out, all crimson and white-and-tan. Wat came running out into the clearing, and at the sight of him the hounds took heart again, and one of them sprang with a growl into the bushes. At the same instant a creature the size of a donkey jumped on to its feet, a huge grey head, with monstrous glistening fangs, and tapering fox jaws, shot out from among the branches, and the hound was thrown several feet into the air, and fell howling among the cover. Then there was a clashing snap like a rat-trap closing, and the howls sharpened into a scream and then were still.

"Danbury had been on the look-out for symptoms all day, and now he had found them. He looked once more at the thicket, saw a pair of savage red eyes fixed upon him, and fairly took to his heels. It might only be a passing delusion, or it might be a permanent mania of which the doctor had spoken, but, anyhow, the thing to do was to get back to bed and to quiet, and to hope for the best. He forgot the hounds, the hunt, and everything else in his desperate fears for his own reason. He sprang upon his mare, galloped her madly over the downs, and only stopped when he found himself at a country station. There he left his mare at the inn, and made back for home as quickly as steam would take him. It was evening before he got there, shivering with apprehension and seeing those red eyes and savage teeth at every turn. He went straight to bed and sent for Dr. Middleton.

" ' I've got 'em, doctor,' said he. ' It came about exactly as you said—strange creatures, optical delusions, and everything. All I ask you now is to save my reason.'

" The doctor listened to his story and was shocked as he heard it.

" ' It appears to be a very clear case,' said he. ' This must be a lesson to you for life.'

" ' Never a drop again if I only come safely through this,' cried Wat Danbury.

" ' Well, my dear boy, if you will stick to that it may prove a blessing in disguise. But the difficulty in this case is to know where fact ends and fancy begins. You see, it is not as if there was only one delusion. There have been several. The dead dogs, for example, must have been one as well as the creature in the bush.'

" ' I saw it all as clearly as I see you.'

" ' One of the characteristics of this form of delirium is that what you see is even clearer than reality. I was wondering whether the whole run was not a delusion also.'

" Wat Danbury pointed to his hunting-boots still lying upon the floor, flecked with the splashings of two counties.

" ' Hum ! that looks very real, certainly. No doubt, in your weak state, you over-exerted yourself and so brought this attack upon yourself. Well, whatever the cause, our treatment is clear. You will take the soothing mixture which I will send to you, and we shall put two leeches upon your temples to-night to relieve any congestion of the brain.'

" So Wat Danbury spent the night in tossing about and reflecting what a sensitive thing this machinery of ours is, and how very foolish it is to play tricks with what is so easily put out of gear and so difficult to mend. And so he repeated and repeated his oath that this first lesson should be his last, and that from that time forward he would be a sober, hard-working yeoman as his father had been before him. So he lay, tossing and still repentant, when his door flew open in the morning and in rushed the doctor with a newspaper crumpled up in his hand.

" ' My dear boy,' he cried. ' I owe you a thousand apologies. You're the most ill-used lad and I the greatest numskull in the county. Listen to this ! ' And he sat down upon the side of the bed, flattened out his paper upon his knee, and began to read.

" The paragraph was headed, ' Disaster to the Ascombe Hounds,' and it went on to say that four of the hounds, shockingly torn and mangled, had been found in Winton Fir Wood upon the South Downs. The run had been so severe that half the pack were lamed ; but the four found in the wood were actually dead, although the cause of their extraordinary injuries was still unknown. ' So you see,' said the doctor, looking up, ' that I was wrong when I put the dead hounds among the delusions.'

" ' But the cause ? ' cried Wat.

" ' Well, I think we may guess the cause from an item which has been inserted just as the paper went to press. " Late last night, Mr. Brown, of Smither's Farm, to the east of Hastings, perceived what he imagined to be an enormous dog worrying one of his sheep. He shot the creature, which proves to be a grey Siberian wolf of the variety known as *Lupus Giganticus*. It is supposed to have escaped from some travelling menagerie." '

" That's the story, gentlemen, and Wat Danbury stuck to his good resolutions, for the fright which he had cured him of all wish to run such a risk again ; and he never touches anything stronger than lime-juice—at least, he hadn't before he left this part of the country, five years ago next Lady Day."

6. *The Bully of Brocas Court*

THAT year—it was in 1878—the South Midland Yeomanry were out near Luton, and the real question which appealed to every man in the great camp was not how to prepare for a possible European war, but the far more vital one how to get a man who could stand up for ten rounds to Farrier-Sergeant Burton. Slogger Burton was a fine upstanding fourteen stone of bone and brawn, with a smack in either hand which would leave any ordinary mortal senseless. A match must be found for him somewhere or his head would outgrow his dragoon helmet. Therefore Sir Fred. Milburn, better known as Mumbles, was dispatched to London to find if among the fancy there was no one who would make a journey in order to take down the number of the bold dragoon.

They were bad days, those, in the prize-ring. The old knuckle-fighting had died out in scandal and disgrace, smothered by the pestilent crowd of betting men and ruffians of all sorts who hung upon the edge of the movement and brought disgrace and ruin upon the decent fighting men, who were often humble heroes whose gallantry has never been surpassed. An honest sportsman who desired to see a fight was usually set upon by villains, against whom he had no redress, since he was himself engaged on what was technically an illegal action. He was stripped in the open street, his purse taken, and his head split open if he ventured to resist. The ring-side could only be reached by men who were prepared to fight their way there with cudgels and hunting-crops. No wonder that the classic sport was attended now by those only who had nothing to lose.

On the other hand, the era of the reserved building and the legal glove-fight had not yet arisen, and the cult was in a strange intermediate condition. It was impossible to regulate it, and equally impossible to abolish it, since nothing appeals more directly and powerfully to the average Briton. Therefore there were scrambling contests in stableyards and barns, hurried visits to France, secret meetings at dawn in wild parts of the country, and all manner of evasions and experiments. The men themselves became as unsatisfactory as their surroundings. There could be no honest open contest, and the loudest bragger talked his way to the top of the list. Only across the Atlantic had the huge figure of John Lawrence Sullivan appeared, who was destined to be the last of the earlier system and the first of the later one.

Things being in this condition, the sporting Yeomanry Captain found it no easy matter among the boxing saloons and sporting pubs of London to find a man who could be relied upon to give a good account of the huge Farrier-Sergeant. Heavy-weights were at a premium. Finally his choice fell upon Alf Stevens of Kentish Town, an excellent rising middle-weight who had never yet known defeat and had indeed some claims to the championship. His professional experience and craft would surely make up for the three stone of weight which separated him from the formidable dragoon. It was in this hope that Sir Fred. Milburn engaged him, and proceeded to convey him in his dog-cart behind a pair of spanking greys to the camp of the Yeomen. They were to start one evening, drive up the Great North Road, sleep at St. Albans, and finish their journey next day.

The prize-fighter met the sporting Baronet at the Golden Cross, where Bates, the little groom, was standing at the head of the spirited horses. Stevens, a pale-faced, clean-cut young fellow, mounted beside his employer and waved his hand to a little knot of fighting men, rough, collarless, reefer-coated fellows who had gathered to bid their comrade good-bye. " Good luck, Alf ! " came in a hoarse chorus as the boy released the horses' heads and sprang in behind, while the high dog-cart swung swiftly round the curve into Trafalgar Square.

Sir Frederick was so busy steering among the traffic in Oxford Street and the Edgware Road that he had little thought for anything else, but when he got into the edges of the country near Hendon, and the hedges had at last taken the place of that endless panorama of brick dwellings, he let his horses go easy with a loose rein while he turned his attention to the young man at his side. He had found him by correspondence and recommendation, so that he had some curiosity now in looking him over. Twilight was already falling and the light dim, but what the Baronet saw pleased him well. The man was a fighter every inch, clean-cut, deep-chested, with the long straight cheek and deep-set eye which goes with an obstinate courage. Above all, he was a man who had never yet met his master and was still upheld by the deep sustaining confidence which is never quite the same after a single defeat. The Baronet chuckled as he realized what a surprise packet was being carried north for the Farrier-Sergeant.

" I suppose you are in some sort of training, Stevens ? " he remarked, turning to his companion.

" Yes, sir ; I am fit to fight for my life."

" So I should judge by the look of you."

" I live regular all the time, sir, but I was matched against Mike Connor for this last week-end and scaled down to eleven four. Then he paid forfeit, and here I am at the top of my form."

" That's lucky. You'll need it all against a man who has a pull of three stone and four inches."

The young man smiled.

" I have given greater odds than that, sir."

" I dare say. But he's a game man as well."

" Well, sir, one can but do one's best."

The Baronet liked the modest but assured tone of the young pugilist. Suddenly an amusing thought struck him, and he burst out laughing.

" By Jove ! " he cried. " What a lark if the Bully is out to-night ! "

Alf Stevens pricked up his ears.

" Who might he be, sir ? "

" Well, that's what the folk are asking. Some say they've seen him, and some say he's a fairy-tale, but there's good evidence that he is a real man with a pair of rare good fists that leave their marks behind him."

" And where might he live ? "

" On this very road. It's between Finchley and Elstree, as I've heard. There are two chaps, and they come out on nights when the moon is at full and challenge the passers-by to fight in the old style. One fights and the other picks up. By George ! the fellow *can* fight, too, by all accounts. Chaps have been found in the morning with their faces all cut to ribbons to show that the Bully had been at work upon them."

Alf Stevens was full of interest.

" I've always wanted to try an old-style battle, sir, but it never chanced to come my way. I believe it would suit me better than the gloves."

" Then you won't refuse the Bully ? "

" Refuse him ! I'd go ten mile to meet him."

" By George ! it would be great ! " cried the Baronet. " Well, the moon is at the full, and the place should be about here."

" If he's as good as you say," Stevens remarked, " he should be known in the ring, unless he is just an amateur who amuses himself like that."

" Some think he's an ostler, or maybe a racing man from the training stables over yonder. Where there are horses there is boxing. If you can believe the accounts, there is something a bit queer and outlandish about the fellow. Hi! Look out, damn you, look out!"

The Baronet's voice had risen to a sudden screech of surprise and of anger. At this point the road dips down into a hollow, heavily shaded by trees, so that at night it arches across like the mouth of a tunnel. At the foot of the slope there stand two great stone pillars, which, as viewed by daylight, are lichen-stained and weathered, with heraldic devices on each which are so mutilated by time that they are mere protuberances of stone. An iron gate of elegant design, hanging loosely upon rusted hinges, proclaims both the past glories and the present decay of Brocas Old Hall, which lies at the end of the weed-encumbered avenue. It was from the shadow of this ancient gateway that an active figure had sprung suddenly into the centre of the road and had, with great dexterity, held up the horses, who ramped and pawed as they were forced back upon their haunches.

"Here, Rowe, you 'old the tits, will ye?" cried a high strident voice. "I've a little word to say to this 'ere slap-up Corinthian before 'e goes any farther."

A second man had emerged from the shadows and without a word took hold of the horses' heads. He was a short, thick fellow, dressed in a curious brown many-caped overcoat, which came to his knees, with gaiters and boots beneath it. He wore no hat, and those in the dog-cart had a view, as he came in front of the side-lamps, of a surly red face with an ill-fitting lower lip clean shaven, and a high black cravat swathed tightly under the chin. As he gripped the leathers his more active comrade sprang forward and rested a bony hand upon the side of the splashboard while he looked keenly up with a pair of fierce blue eyes at the faces of the two travellers, the light beating full upon his own features. He wore a hat low upon his brow, but in spite of its shadow both the Baronet and the pugilist could see enough to shrink from him, for it was an evil face, evil but very formidable, stern, craggy, high-nosed, and fierce, with an inexorable mouth which bespoke a nature which would neither ask for mercy nor grant it. As to his age, one could only say for certain that a man with such a face was young enough to have all his virility and old enough to have experienced all the wickedness of life. The cold, savage eyes took a deliberate survey, first of the Baronet and then of the young man beside him.

"Aye, Rowe, it's a slap-up Corinthian, same as I said," he remarked over his shoulder to his companion. "But this other is a likely chap. If 'e isn't a millin' cove 'e ought to be. Any'ow, we'll try 'im out."

"Look here," said the Baronet, "I don't know who you are, except that you are a damned impertinent fellow. I'd put the lash of my whip across your face for two pins!"

"Stow that gammon, gov'nor! It ain't safe to speak to me like that."

"I've heard of you and your ways!" cried the angry soldier. "I'll teach you to stop my horses on the Queen's high road! You've got the wrong men this time, my fine fellow, as you will soon learn."

"That's as it may be," said the stranger. "May'ap, master, we may all learn something before we part. One or other of you 'as got to get down and put up your 'ands before you get any farther."

Stevens had instantly sprung down into the road.

"If you want a fight you've come to the right shop," said he; "it's my trade, so don't say I took you unawares."

The stranger gave a cry of satisfaction.

"Blow my dickey!" he shouted. "It *is* a millin' cove, Joe, same as I said. No more chaw-bacons for us, but the real thing. Well, young man, you've met your master to-night. Happen you never 'eard what Lord Longmore said o' me? 'A man must be made special to beat you,' says 'e. That's wot Lord Longmore said."

"That was before the Bull came along," growled the man in front, speaking for the first time.

" Stow your chaffing, Joe ! A little more about the Bull and you and me will quarrel. 'E bested me once, but it's all betters and no takers that I glut 'im if ever we meet again. Well, young man, what d'ye think of me ? "

" I think you've got your share of cheek."

" Cheek. Wot's that ? "

" Impudence, bluff—gas, if you like."

The last word had a surprising effect upon the stranger. He smote his leg with his hand and broke out into a high neighing laugh, in which he was joined by his gruff companion.

" You've said the right word, my beauty," cried the latter, " ' Gas ' is the word and no error. Well, there's a good moon, but the clouds are comin' up. We had best use the light while we can."

Whilst this conversation had been going on the Baronet had been looking with an ever-growing amazement at the attire of the stranger. A good deal of it confirmed his belief that he was connected with some stables, though making every allowance for this his appearance was very eccentric and old-fashioned. Upon his head he wore a yellowish-white top-hat of long-haired beaver, such as is still affected by some drivers of four-in-hands, with a bell crown and a curling brim. His dress consisted of a short-waisted swallow-tail coat, snuff-coloured, with steel buttons. It opened in front to show a vest of striped silk, while his legs were encased in buff knee-breeches with blue stockings and low shoes. The figure was angular and hard, with a great suggestion of wiry activity. This Bully of Brocas was clearly a very great character, and the young dragoon officer chuckled as he thought what a glorious story he would carry back to the mess of this queer old-world figure and the thrashing which he was about to receive from the famous London boxer.

Billy, the little groom, had taken charge of the horses, who were shivering and sweating.

" This way ! " said the stout man, turning towards

the gate. It was a sinister place, black and weird, with the crumbling pillars and the heavy arching trees. Neither the Baronet nor the pugilist liked the look of it.

" Where are you going, then ? "

" This is no place for a fight," said the stout man. " We've got as pretty a place as ever you saw inside the gate here. You couldn't beat it on Molesey Hurst."

" The road is good enough for me," said Stevens.

" The road is good enough for two Johnny Raws," said the man with the beaver hat. " It ain't good enough for two slap-up millin' coves like you an' me. You ain't afeard, are you ? "

" Not of you or ten like you," said Stevens, stoutly.

" Well, then, come with me and do it as it ought to be done."

Sir Frederic and Stevens exchanged glances.

" I'm game," said the pugilist.

" Come on, then."

The little party of four passed through the gateway. Behind them in the darkness the horses stamped and reared, while the voice of the boy could be heard as he vainly tried to soothe them. After walking fifty yards up the grass-grown drive the guide turned to the right through a thick belt of trees, and they came out upon a circular plot of grass, white and clear in the moonlight. It had a raised bank, and on the farther side was one of those little pillared stone summer-houses beloved by the early Georgians.

" What did I tell you ? " cried the stout man, triumphantly. " Could you do better than this within twenty mile of town ? It was made for it. Now, Tom, get to work upon him, and show us what you can do."

It had all become like an extraordinary dream. The strange men, their odd dress, their queer speech, the moonlit circle of grass, and the pillared summer-house all wove themselves into one fantastic whole. It was only the sight of Alf Stevens's ill-fitting tweed suit, and his homely English face surmounting it, which brought the Baronet back to the workaday world. The thin stranger had taken off his beaver hat, his swallow-tailed coat, his silk waistcoat, and finally his shirt had been drawn over his head by his second. Stevens in a cool and leisurely fashion kept pace with the preparations of his antagonist. Then the two fighting men turned upon each other.

But as they did so Stevens gave an exclamation of surprise and horror. The removal of the beaver hat had disclosed a horrible mutilation of the head of his antagonist. The whole upper forehead had fallen in, and there seemed to be a broad red weal between his close-cropped hair and his heavy brows.

"Good Lord," cried the young pugilist. "What's amiss with the man?"

The question seemed to rouse a cold fury in his antagonist.

"You look out for your own head, master," said he. "You'll find enough to do, I'm thinkin', without talkin' about mine."

This retort drew a shout of hoarse laughter from his second. "Well said, my Tommy!" he cried. "It's Lombard Street to a China orange on the one and only."

The man whom he called Tom was standing with his hands up in the centre of the natural ring. He looked a big man in his clothes, but he seemed bigger in the buff, and his barrel chest, sloping shoulders, and loosely-slung muscular arms were all ideal for the game. His grim eyes gleamed fiercely beneath his misshapen brows, and his lips were set in a fixed hard smile, more menacing than a scowl. The pugilist confessed, as he approached him, that he had never seen a more formidable figure. But his bold heart rose to the fact that he had never yet found the man who could master him, and that it was hardly credible that he would appear as an old-fashioned stranger on a country road. Therefore, with an answering smile, he took up his position and raised his hands.

But what followed was entirely beyond his experience.

The stranger feinted quickly with his left, and sent in a swinging hit with his right, so quick and hard that Stevens had barely time to avoid it and to counter with a short jab as his opponent rushed in upon him. Next instant the man's bony arms were round him, and the pugilist was hurled into the air in a whirling cross-buttock, coming down with a heavy thud upon the grass. The stranger stood back and folded his arms while Stevens scrambled to his feet with a red flush of anger upon his cheeks.

"Look here," he cried. "What sort of game is this?"

"We claim foul!" the Baronet shouted.

"Foul be damned! As clean a throw as ever I saw!" said the stout man. "What rules do you fight under?"

"Queensberry, of course."

"I never heard of it. It's London prize-ring with us."

"Come on, then!" cried Stevens, furiously. "I can wrestle as well as another. You won't get me napping again."

Nor did he. The next time that the stranger rushed in Stevens caught him in as strong a grip, and after swinging and swaying they came down together in a dog-fall. Three times this occurred, and each time the stranger walked across to his friend and seated himself upon the grassy bank before he recommenced.

"What d'ye make of him?" the Baronet asked, in one of these pauses.

Stevens was bleeding from the ear, but otherwise showed no sign of damage.

"He knows a lot," said the pugilist. "I don't know where he learned it, but he's had a deal of practice somewhere. He's as strong as a lion and as hard as a board, for all his queer face."

"Keep him at out-fighting. I think you are his master there."

"I'm not so sure that I'm his master anywhere, but I'll try my best."

It was a desperate fight, and as round followed round it became clear, even to the amazed Baronet, that the middle-weight champion had met his match. The stranger had a clever draw and a rush which, with his springing hits, made him a most dangerous foe. His head and body seemed insensible to blows, and the horribly malignant smile never for one instant flickered from his lips. He hit very hard with fists like flints, and his blows whizzed up from every angle. He had one particularly deadly lead, an uppercut at the jaw, which again and again nearly came home, until at last it did actually fly past the guard and brought Stevens to the ground. The stout man gave a whoop of triumph.

" The whisker hit, by George ! It's a horse to a hen on my Tommy ! Another like that, lad, and you have him beat."

" I say, Stevens, this is going too far," said the Baronet, as he supported his weary man. " What will the regiment say if I bring you up all knocked to pieces in a bye-battle ! Shake hands with this fellow and give him best, or you'll not be fit for your job."

" Give him best ? Not I ! " cried Stevens, angrily. " I'll knock that damned smile off his ugly mug before I've done."

" What about the Sergeant ? "

" I'd rather go back to London and never see the Sergeant than have my number taken down by this chap."

" Well, 'ad enough ? " his opponent asked, in a sneering voice, as he moved from his seat on the bank.

For answer young Stevens sprang forward and rushed at his man with all the strength that was left to him. By the fury of his onset he drove him back, and for a long minute had all the better of the exchanges. But this iron fighter seemed never to tire. His step was as quick and his blow as hard as ever when this long rally had ended. Stevens had eased up from pure exhaustion. But his opponent did not ease up. He came back on him with a shower of furious blows which beat down the weary guard of the pugilist. Alf Stevens was at the end of his strength and would in another instant have sunk to the ground but for a singular intervention.

It has been said that in their approach to the ring the party had passed through a grove of trees. Out of these there came a peculiar shrill cry, a cry of agony, which might be from a child or from some small woodland creature in distress. It was inarticulate, high-pitched, and inexpressibly melancholy. At the sound the stranger, who had knocked Stevens on to his knees, staggered back and looked round him with an expression of helpless horror upon his face. The smile had left his lips and there only remained the loose-lipped weakness of a man in the last extremity of terror.

" It's after me again, mate ! " he cried.

" Stick it out, Tom ! You have him nearly beat ! It can't hurt you."

" It can 'urt me ! It will 'urt me ! " screamed the fighting man. " My God ! I can't face it ! Ah, I see it ! I see it ! "

With a scream of fear he turned and bounded off into the brushwood. His companion, swearing loudly, picked up the pile of clothes and darted after him, the dark shadows swallowing up their flying figures.

Stevens, half-senselessly, had staggered back and lay upon the grassy bank, his head pillowed upon the chest of the young Baronet, who was holding his flask of brandy to his lips. As they sat there they were both aware that the cries had become louder and shriller. Then from among the bushes there ran a small white terrier, nosing about as if following a trail and yelping most piteously. It squattered across the grassy sward, taking no notice of the two young men. Then it also vanished into the shadows. As it did so the two spectators sprang to their feet and ran as hard as they could tear for the gateway and the trap. Terror had seized them—a panic terror far above reason or control. Shivering and shaking, they threw themselves into the dog-cart, and it was not until the willing horses had put two good miles between that ill-omened hollow and themselves that they at last ventured to speak.

" Did you ever see such a dog ? " asked the Baronet.

" No," cried Stevens. " And, please God, I never may again."

Late that night the two travellers broke their journey at the Swan Inn, near Harpenden Common. The landlord was an old acquaintance of the Baronet's, and gladly joined him in a glass of port after supper. A famous old sport was Mr. Joe Horner, of the Swan, and he would talk by the hour of the legends of the ring, whether new or old. The name of Alf Stevens was well known to him, and he looked at him with the deepest interest.

" Why, sir, you have surely been fighting," said he. " I hadn't read of any engagement in the papers."

" Enough said of that," Stevens answered, in a surly voice.

" Well, no offence ! I suppose "—his smiling face became suddenly very serious—" I suppose you didn't, by chance, see anything of him they call the Bully of Brocas as you came north ? "

" Well, what if we did ? "

The landlord was tense with excitement.

" It was him that nearly killed Bob Meadows. It was at the very gate of Brocas Old Hall that he stopped him. Another man was with him. Bob was game to the marrow, but he was found hit to pieces on the lawn inside the gate where the summer-house stands."

The Baronet nodded.

" Ah, you've been there ! " cried the landlord.

" Well, we may as well make a clean breast of it," said the Baronet, looking at Stevens. " We have been there, and we met the man you speak of—an ugly customer he is, too ! "

" Tell me ! " said the landlord, in a voice that sank

THE BULLY OF BROCAS COURT

to a whisper. " Is it true what Bob Meadows says, that the men are dressed like our grandfathers, and that the fighting man has his head all caved in ? "

" Well, he was old-fashioned, certainly, and his head was the queerest ever I saw."

" God in Heaven ! " cried the landlord. " Do you know, sir, that Tom Hickman, the famous prize-fighter, together with his pal, Joe Rowe, a silversmith of the City, met his death at that very point in the year 1822, when he was drunk, and tried to drive on the wrong side of a wagon ? Both were killed and the wheel of the wagon crushed in Hickman's forehead."

" Hickman ! Hickman ! " said the Baronet. " Not the gasman ? "

" Yes, sir, they called him Gas. He won his fights with what they called the ' whisker hit,' and no one could stand against him until Neate—him that they called the Bristol Bull—brought him down."

Stevens had risen from the table as white as cheese.

" Let's get out of this, sir. I want fresh air. Let us get on our way."

The landlord clapped him on the back.

" Cheer up, lad ! You've held him off, anyhow, and that's more than anyone else has ever done. Sit down and have another glass of wine, for if a man in England has earned it this night it is you. There's many a debt you would pay if you gave the Gasman a welting, whether dead or alive. Do you know what he did in this very room ? "

The two travellers looked round with startled eyes at the lofty room, stone-flagged and oak-panelled, with great open grate at the farther end.

" Yes, in this very room. I had it from old Squire Scotter, who was here that very night. It was the day when Shelton beat Josh Hudson out St. Albans way, and Gas had won a pocketful of money on the fight. He and his pal Rowe came in here upon their way, and he was mad-raging drunk. The folk fairly shrunk into the corners and under the tables, for he was stalkin' round with the great kitchen poker in his hand, and there was murder behind the smile upon his face. He was like that when the drink was in him—cruel, reckless, and a terror to the world. Well, what think you that he did at last with the poker? There was a little dog, a terrier as I've heard, coiled up before the fire, for it was a bitter December night. The Gasman broke its back with one blow of the poker. Then he burst out laughin', flung a curse or two at the folk that shrunk away from him, and so out to his high gig that was waiting outside. The next we heard was that he was carried down to Finchley with his head ground to a jelly by the wagon wheel. Yes, they do say the little dog with its bleeding skin and its broken back has been seen since then, crawlin' and yelpin' about Brocas Corner, as if it were lookin' for the swine that killed it. So you see, Mr. Stevens, you were fightin' for more than yourself when you put it across the Gasman."

"Maybe so," said the young prize-fighter, "but I want no more fights like that. The Farrier-Sergeant is good enough for me, sir, and if it is the same to you, we'll take a railway train back to town."

TALES OF PIRATES

13. *Captain Sharkey : How the Governor of Saint Kitt's came Home*

WHEN the great wars of the Spanish Succession had been brought to an end by the Treaty of Utrecht, the vast number of privateers which had been fitted out by the contending parties found their occupation gone. Some took to the more peaceful but less lucrative ways of ordinary commerce, others were absorbed into the fishing-fleets, and a few of the more reckless hoisted the Jolly Roger at the mizzen and the bloody flag at the main, declaring a private war upon their own account against the whole human race.

With mixed crews, recruited from every nation, they scoured the seas, disappearing occasionally to careen in some lonely inlet, or putting in for a debauch at some outlying port, where they dazzled the inhabitants by their lavishness and horrified them by their brutalities.

On the Coromandel Coast, at Madagascar, in the African waters, and above all in the West Indian and American seas, the pirates were a constant menace. With an insolent luxury they would regulate their depredations by the comfort of the seasons, harrying New England in the summer and dropping south again to the tropical islands in the winter.

They were the more to be dreaded because they had none of that discipline and restraint which made their predecessors, the Buccaneers, both formidable and respectable. These Ishmaels of the sea rendered an account to no man, and treated their prisoners according to the drunken whim of the moment. Flashes of grotesque generosity alternated with longer stretches of inconceivable ferocity, and the skipper who fell into their hands might find himself dismissed with his cargo, after serving as boon companion in some hideous debauch, or might sit at his cabin table with his own nose and his lips served up with pepper and salt in front of him. It took a stout seaman in those days to ply his calling in the Caribbean Gulf.

Such a man was Captain John Scarrow, of the ship *Morning Star*, and yet he breathed a long sigh of relief when he heard the splash of the falling anchor and swung at his moorings within a hundred yards of the guns of the citadel of Basseterre. St. Kitt's was his final port of call, and early next morning his bowsprit would be pointed for Old England. He had had enough of those robber-haunted seas. Ever since he had left Maracaibo upon the Main, with his full lading of sugar and red pepper, he had winced at every topsail which glimmered over the violet edge of the tropical sea. He had coasted up the Windward Islands, touching here and there, and assailed continually by stories of villainy and outrage.

Captain Sharkey, of the 20-gun pirate barque, *Happy Delivery*, had passed down the coast, and had littered it with gutted vessels and with murdered men. Dreadful anecdotes were current of his grim pleasantries and of his inflexible ferocity. From the Bahamas to the Main his coal-black barque, with the ambiguous name, had been freighted with death and many things which are worse than death. So nervous was Captain Scarrow, with his new full-rigged ship and her full and valuable lading, that he struck out to the west as far as Bird's Island to be out of the usual track of commerce. And yet even in those solitary waters he had been unable to shake off sinister traces of Captain Sharkey.

One morning they had raised a single skiff adrift upon the face of the ocean. Its only occupant was a delirious seaman, who yelled hoarsely as they hoisted him aboard, and showed a dried-up tongue like a black and wrinkled fungus at the back of his mouth. Water and nursing soon transformed him into the strongest and smartest sailor on the ship. He was from Marblehead, in New England, it seemed, and was the sole survivor of a schooner which had been scuttled by the dreadful Sharkey.

For a week Hiram Evanson, for that was his name, had been adrift beneath a tropical sun. Sharkey had ordered the mangled remains of his late captain to be thrown into the boat, " as provisions for the voyage," but the seaman had at once committed them to the deep, lest the temptation should be more than he could bear. He had lived upon his own huge frame, until, at the last moment, the *Morning Star* had found him in that madness which is the precursor of such a death. It was no bad find for Captain Scarrow, for, with a short-handed crew, such a seaman as this big New Englander was a prize worth having. He vowed that he was the only man whom Captain Sharkey had ever placed under an obligation.

Now that they lay under the guns of Basseterre, all danger from the pirate was at an end, and yet the thought of him lay heavily upon the seaman's mind as he watched the agent's boat shooting out from the custom-house quay.

" I'll lay you a wager, Morgan," said he to the first mate, " that the agent will speak of Sharkey in the first hundred words that pass his lips."

" Well, captain, I'll have you a silver dollar, and chance it," said the rough old Bristol man beside him.

The negro rowers shot the boat alongside, and the linen-clad steersman sprang up the ladder.

" Welcome, Captain Scarrow ! " he cried. " Have you heard about Sharkey."

The captain grinned at the mate.

" What devilry has he been up to now ? " he asked.

" Devilry ! You've not heard, then ! Why, we've got him safe under lock and key here at Basseterre. He was tried last Wednesday, and he is to be hanged to-morrow morning."

Captain and mate gave a shout of joy, which an instant later was taken up by the crew. Discipline was forgotten as they scrambled up through the break of the poop to hear the news. The New Englander was in the front of them with a radiant face turned up to heaven, for he came of the Puritan stock.

" Sharkey to be hanged ! " he cried. " You don't know, Master Agent, if they lack a hangman, do you ? "

" Stand back ! " cried the mate, whose outraged sense of discipline was even stronger than his interest at the news. " I'll pay that dollar, Captain Scarrow, with the lightest heart that ever I paid a wager yet. How came the villain to be taken ? "

" Why, as to that, he became more than his own comrades could abide, and they took such a horror of him that they would not have him on the ship. So they marooned him upon the Little Mangles to the south of the Mysteriosa Bank, and there he was found by a Portobello trader, who brought him in. There was talk of sending him to Jamaica to be tried, but our good little governor, Sir Charles Ewan, would not hear of it. ' He's my meat,' said he, ' and I claim the cooking of it.' If you can stay till to-morrow morning at ten, you'll see the joint swinging."

" I wish I could," said the captain, wistfully, " but I am sadly behind time now. I should start with the evening tide."

" That you can't do," said the agent with decision. " The Governor is going back with you."

" The Governor ! "

" Yes. He's had a dispatch from Government to return without delay. The fly-boat that brought it has gone on to Virginia. So Sir Charles has been waiting for you, as I told him you were due before the rains."

" Well, well ! " cried the captain, in some perplexity, " I'm a plain seaman, and I don't know much of governors and baronets and their ways. I don't remember that I ever so much as spoke to one. But if it's in King George's service, and he asks a cast in the *Morning Star* as far as London, I'll do what I can for him. There's my own cabin he can have and welcome. As to the cooking, it's lobscouse and salmagundy six days in the week ; but he can bring his own cook aboard with him if he thinks our galley too rough for his taste."

" You need not trouble your mind, Captain Scarrow," said the agent. " Sir Charles is in weak health just now, only clear of a quartan ague, and it is likely he will keep his cabin most of the voyage. Dr. Larousse said that he would have sunk had the hanging of Sharkey not put fresh life into him. He has a great spirit in him, though, and you must not blame him if he is somewhat short in his speech."

" He may say what he likes and do what he likes so long as he does not come athwart my hawse when I am working the ship," said the captain. " He is Governor of St. Kitt's, but I am Governor of the *Morning Star*. And, by his leave, I must weigh with the first tide, for I owe a duty to my employer, just as he does to King George."

" He can scarce be ready to-night, for he has many things to set in order before he leaves."

" The early morning tide, then."

" Very good. I shall send his things aboard to-night, and he will follow them to-morrow early if I can prevail upon him to leave St. Kitt's without seeing Sharkey do the rogue's hornpipe. His own orders were instant, so it may be that he will come at once. It is likely that Dr. Larousse may attend him upon the journey."

Left to themselves, the captain and mate made the best preparations which they could for their illustrious passenger. The largest cabin was turned out and adorned in his honour, and orders were given by which barrels of fruit and some cases of wine should be brought off to vary the plain food of an ocean-going trader. In the evening the Governor's baggage began to arrive—great ironbound ant-proof trunks, and official tin packing-cases, with other strange-shaped packages, which suggested the cocked hat or the sword within. And then there came a note, with a heraldic device upon the big red seal, to say that Sir Charles Ewan made his compliments to Captain Scarrow, and that he hoped to be with him in the morning as early as his duties and his infirmities would permit.

He was as good as his word, for the first grey of dawn had hardly begun to deepen into pink when he was brought alongside, and climbed with some difficulty up the ladder. The captain had heard that the Governor was an eccentric, but he was hardly prepared for the curious figure who came limping feebly down his quarter-deck, his steps supported by a thick bamboo cane. He wore a Ramillies wig, all twisted into little tails like a poodle's coat, and cut so low across the brow that the large green glasses which covered his eyes looked as if they were hung from it. A fierce beak of a nose, very long and very thin, cut the air in front of him. His ague had caused him to swathe his throat and chin with a broad linen cravat, and he wore a loose damask powdering-gown secured by a cord round the waist. As he advanced he carried his masterful nose high in the air, but his head turned slowly from side to side in the helpless manner of the purblind, and he called in a high, querulous voice for the captain.

" You have my things ? " he asked.

" Yes, Sir Charles."

" Have you wine aboard ? "

" I have ordered five cases, sir ? "

" And tobacco ? "

" There is a keg of Trinidad."

" You play a hand at piquet ? "

" Passably well, sir."

" Then up anchor, and to sea ! "

There was a fresh westerly wind, so by the time the sun was fairly through the morning haze, the ship was hull down from the islands. The decrepit Governor still limped the deck, with one guiding hand upon the quarter-rail.

"You are on Government service now, captain," said he. "They are counting the days till I come to Westminster, I promise you. Have you all that she will carry?"

"Every inch, Sir Charles?"

"Keep her so if you blow the sails out of her. I fear, Captain Scarrow, that you will find a blind and broken man a poor companion for your voyage."

"I am honoured in enjoying your Excellency's society," said the captain. "But I am sorry that your eyes should be so afflicted."

"Yes, indeed. It is the cursed glare of the sun on the white streets of Basseterre which has gone far to burn them out."

"I had heard also that you had been plagued by a quartan ague."

"Yes; I have had a pyrexy, which has reduced me much."

"We had set aside a cabin for your surgeon."

"Ah, the rascal! There was no budging him, for he has a snug business amongst the merchants. But hark!"

He raised his ring-covered hand in the air. From far astern there came the low deep thunder of cannon.

"It is from the island!" cried the captain in astonishment. "Can it be a signal for us to put back?"

The Governor laughed.

"You have heard that Sharkey, the pirate, is to be hanged this morning. I ordered the batteries to salute when the rascal was kicking his last, so that I might know of it out at sea. There's an end of Sharkey!"

"There's an end of Sharkey!" cried the captain; and the crew took up the cry as they gathered in little knots upon the deck and stared back at the low, purple line of the vanishing land.

It was a cheering omen for their start across the Western Ocean, and the invalid Governor found himself a popular man on board, for it was generally understood that but for his insistence upon an immediate trial and sentence, the villain might have played upon some more venal judge and so escaped. At dinner that day Sir Charles gave many anecdotes of the deceased pirate ; and so affable was he, and so skilful in adapting his conversation to men of lower degree, that captain, mate, and Governor smoked their long pipes and drank their claret as three good comrades should.

" And what figure did Sharkey cut in the dock ? " asked the captain.

" He is a man of some presence," said the Governor.

" I had always understood that he was an ugly, sneering devil," remarked the mate.

" Well, I dare say he could look ugly upon occasions," said the Governor.

" I have heard a New Bedford whaleman say that he could not forget his eyes," said Captain Scarrow. " They were of the lightest filmy blue, with red-rimmed lids. Was that not so, Sir Charles ? "

" Alas, my own eyes will not permit me to know much of those of others ! But I remember now that the Adjutant-General said that he had such an eye as you describe, and added that the jury were so foolish as to be visibly discomposed when it was turned upon them. It is well for them that he is dead, for he was a man who would never forget an injury, and if he had laid hands upon any one of them he would have stuffed him with straw and hung him for a figure-head."

The idea seemed to amuse the Governor, for he broke suddenly into a high, neighing laugh, and the two seamen laughed also, but not so heartily, for they remembered that Sharkey was not the last pirate who sailed the western seas, and that as grotesque a fate might come to be their own. Another bottle was broached to drink to a pleasant voyage, and the Governor would drink just

146

one other on the top of it, so that the seamen were glad at last to stagger off—the one to his watch and the other to his bunk. But when after his four hours' spell the mate came down again, he was amazed to see the Governor in his Ramillies wig, his glasses, and his powdering-gown still seated sedately at the lonely table with his reeking pipe and six black bottles by his side.

"I have drunk with the Governor of St. Kitt's when he was sick," said he, "and God forbid that I should ever try to keep pace with him when he is well."

The voyage of the *Morning Star* was a successful one, and in about three weeks she was at the mouth of the British Channel. From the first day the infirm Governor had begun to recover his strength, and before they were half-way across the Atlantic he was, save only for his eyes, as well as any man upon the ship. Those who uphold the nourishing qualities of wine might point to him in triumph, for never a night passed that he did not repeat the performance of his first one. And yet he would be out upon deck in the early morning as fresh and brisk as the best of them, peering about with his weak eyes, and asking questions about the sails and the rigging, for he was anxious to learn the ways of the sea. And he made up for the deficiency of his eyes by obtaining leave from the captain that the New England seaman—he who had been cast away in the boat—should lead him about, and above all that he should sit beside him when he played cards and count the number of the pips, for unaided he could not tell the king from the knave.

It was natural that this Evanson should do the Governor willing service, since the one was the victim of the vile Sharkey, and the other was his avenger. One could see that it was a pleasure to the big American to lend his arm to the invalid, and at night he would stand with all respect behind his chair in the cabin and lay his great stub-nailed forefinger upon the card which he should play. Between them there was little in the pockets either of Captain Scarrow or of Morgan, the first mate, by the time they sighted the Lizard.

And it was not long before they found that all they had heard of the high temper of Sir Charles Ewan fell short of the mark. At a sign of opposition or a word of argument his chin would shoot out from his cravat, his masterful nose would be cocked at a higher and more insolent angle, and his bamboo cane would whistle up over his shoulder. He cracked it once over the head of the carpenter when the man had accidentally jostled him upon the deck. Once, too, when there was some grumbling and talk of a mutiny over the state of the provisions, he was of opinion that they should not wait for the dogs to rise, but that they should march forward and set upon them until they had trounced the devilment out of them. " Give me a knife and a bucket ! " he cried with an oath, and could hardly be withheld from setting forth alone to deal with the spokesman of the seamen.

Captain Scarrow had to remind him that though he might be only answerable to himself at St. Kitt's, killing became murder upon the high seas. In politics he was, as became his official position, a stout prop of the House of Hanover, and he swore in his cups that he had never met a Jacobite without pistolling him where he stood. Yet for all his vapouring and his violence he was so good a companion, with such a stream of strange anecdote and reminiscence, that Scarrow and Morgan had never known a voyage pass so pleasantly.

And then at length came the last day, when, after passing the island, they had struck land again at the high white cliffs at Beachy Head. As evening fell the ship lay rolling in an oily calm, a league off from Winchelsea, with the long dark snout of Dungeness jutting out in front of her. Next morning they would pick up their pilot at the Foreland, and Sir Charles might meet the king's ministers at Westminster before the evening. The boatswain had the watch, and the three friends were met for a last turn of cards in the cabin, the faithful American still serving as eyes to the Governor. There was a good stake upon the table, for the sailors had tried on this last night to win their losses back from their passenger. Suddenly he threw his cards down, and swept all the money into the pocket of his long-flapped silken waist-coat.

" The game's mine ! " said he.

" Heh, Sir Charles, not so fast ! " cried Captain Scarrow ; " you have not played out the hand, and we are not the losers."

" Sink you for a liar ! " said the Governor. " I tell you that I *have* played out the hand, and that you *are* a loser." He whipped off his wig and his glasses as he spoke, and there was a high, bald forehead, and a pair of shifty blue eyes with the red rims of a bull terrier.

" Good God ! " cried the mate. " It's Sharkey ! "

The two sailors sprang from their seats, but the big American castaway had put his huge back against the cabin door, and he held a pistol in each of his hands. The passenger had also laid a pistol upon the scattered cards in front of him, and he burst into his high, neighing laugh.

" Captain Sharkey is the name, gentlemen," said he, " and this is Roaring Ned Galloway, the quartermaster of the *Happy Delivery*. We made it hot, and so they marooned us : me on a dry Tortuga cay, and him in an oarless boat. You dogs—you poor, fond, water-hearted dogs—we hold you at the end of our pistols ! "

" You may shoot, or you may not ! " cried Scarrow, striking his hand upon the breast of his frieze jacket. " If it's my last breath, Sharkey, I tell you that you are a bloody rogue and miscreant, with a halter and hell-fire in store for you ! "

" There's a man of spirit, and one of my own kidney, and he's going to make a very pretty death of it ! " cried Sharkey. " There's no one aft save the man at the wheel, so you may keep your breath, for you'll need it soon. Is the dinghy astern, Ned ? "

"Ay, ay, captain!"

"And the other boats scuttled?"

"I bored them all in three places."

"Then we shall have to leave you, Captain Scarrow. You look as if you hadn't quite got your bearings yet. Is there anything you'd like to ask me?"

"I believe you're the devil himself!" cried the captain. "Where is the Governor of St. Kitt's?"

"When last I saw him his Excellency was in bed with his throat cut. When I broke prison I learnt from my friends—for Captain Sharkey has those who love him in every port—that the Governor was starting for Europe under a master who had never seen him. I climbed his verandah and I paid him the little debt that I owed him. Then I came aboard you with such of his things as I had need of, and a pair of glasses to hide these tell-tale eyes of mine, and I have ruffled it as a governor should. Now, Ned, you can get to work upon them."

"Help! Help! Watch ahoy!" yelled the mate; but the butt of the pirate's pistol crashed down on to his head, and he dropped like a pithed ox. Scarrow rushed for the door, but the sentinel clapped his hand over his mouth, and threw his other arm round his waist.

"No use, Master Scarrow," said Sharkey. "Let us see you go down on your knees and beg for your life."

"I'll see you——" cried Scarrow, shaking his mouth clear.

"Twist his arm round, Ned. Now will you?"

"No; not if you twist it off."

"Put an inch of your knife into him."

"You may put six inches, and then I won't."

"Sink me, but I like his spirit!" cried Sharkey. "Put your knife in your pocket, Ned. You've saved your skin, Scarrow, and it's a pity so stout a man should not take to the only trade where a pretty fellow can pick up a living. You must be born for no common death, Scarrow, since you have lain at my mercy and lived to tell the story. Tie him up, Ned."

" To the stove, captain ? "

" Tut, tut ! there's a fire in the stove. None of your rover tricks, Ned Galloway, unless they are called for, or I'll let you know which of us two is captain and which is quartermaster. Make him fast to the table."

" Nay, I thought you meant to roast him ! " said the quartermaster. " You surely do not mean to let him go ? "

" If you and I were marooned on a Bahama cay, Ned Galloway, it is still for me to command and for you to obey. Sink you for a villain, do you dare to question my orders ? "

" Nay, nay, Captain Sharkey, not so hot, sir ! " said the quartermaster, and, lifting Scarrow like a child, he laid him on the table. With the quick dexterity of a seaman, he tied his spreadeagled hands and feet with a rope which was passed underneath, and gagged him securely with the long cravat which used to adorn the chin of the Governor of St. Kitt's.

" Now, Captain Scarrow, we must take our leave of you," said the pirate. " If I had half a dozen of my brisk boys at my heels I should have had your cargo and your ship, but Roaring Ned could not find a foremast hand with the spirit of a mouse. I see there are some small craft about, and we shall get one of them. When Captain Sharkey has a boat he can get a smack, when he has a smack he can get a brig, when he has a brig he can get a barque, and when he has a barque he'll soon have a full-rigged ship of his own—so make haste into London town, or I may be coming back, after all, for the *Morning Star*."

Captain Scarrow heard the key turn in the lock as they left the cabin. Then, as he strained at his bonds, he heard their footsteps pass up the companion and along the quarter-deck to where the dinghy hung in the stern. Then, still struggling and writhing, he heard the creak of the falls and the splash of the boat in the water. In a mad fury he tore and dragged at his ropes, until at last, with flayed wrists and ankles, he rolled from the table, sprang over the dead mate, kicked his way through the closed door, and rushed hatless on to the deck.

"Ahoy! Peterson, Armitage, Wilson!" he screamed. "Cutlasses and pistols! Clear away the long-boat! Clear away the gig! Sharkey, the pirate, is in yonder dinghy. Whistle up the larboard watch, bo'sun, and tumble into the boats all hands."

Down splashed the long-boat and down splashed the gig, but in an instant the coxswains and crews were swarming up the falls on to the deck once more. "The boats are scuttled!" they cried. "They are leaking like a sieve."

The captain gave a bitter curse. He had been beaten and outwitted at every point. Above was a cloudless, starlit sky, with neither wind nor the promise of it. The sails flapped idly in the moonlight. Far away lay a fishing-smack, with the men clustering over their net.

Close to them was the little dinghy, dipping and lifting over the shining swell.

"They are dead men!" cried the captain. "A shout all together, boys, to warn them of their danger."

But it was too late.

At that very moment the dinghy shot into the shadow of the fishing-boat. There were two rapid pistol-shots, a scream, and then another pistol-shot, followed by silence. The clustering fishermen had disappeared. And then, suddenly, as the first puffs of a land-breeze came out from the Sussex shore, the boom swung out, the mainsail filled, and the little craft crept out with her nose to the Atlantic.

14. *The Dealings of Captain Sharkey with Stephen Craddock*

CAREENING was a very necessary operation for the old pirate. On his superior speed he depended both for overhauling the trader and escaping the man-of-war. But it was impossible to retain his sailing qualities unless he periodically—once a year, at the least—cleared his vessel's bottom from the long, trailing plants and crusting barnacles which gather so rapidly in the tropical seas.

For this purpose he lightened his vessel, thrust her into some narrow inlet where she would be left high and dry at low water, fastened blocks and tackles to her masts to pull her over on to her bilge, and then scraped her thoroughly from rudder-post to cutwater.

During the weeks which were thus occupied the ship was, of course, defenceless ; but, on the other hand, she was unapproachable by anything heavier than an empty hull, and the place for careening was chosen with an eye to secrecy, so that there was no great danger.

So secure did the captains feel, that it was not uncommon for them, at such times, to leave their ships under a sufficient guard and to start off in the long-boat, either upon a sporting expedition or, more frequently, upon a visit to some outlying town, where they turned the heads of the women by their swaggering gallantry, or broached pipes of wine in the market square, with a threat to pistol all who would not drink with them.

Sometimes they would even appear in cities of the size of Charleston, and walk the streets with their clattering sidearms—an open scandal to the whole law-abiding colony. Such visits were not always paid with impunity. It was one of them, for example, which provoked Lieutenant Maynard to hack off Blackbeard's head, and to spear it upon the end of his bowsprit. But, as a rule, the pirate ruffled and bullied and drabbed without let or hindrance, until it was time for him to go back to his ship once more.

There was one pirate, however, who never crossed even the skirts of civilization, and that was the sinister Sharkey, of the barque *Happy Delivery*. It may have been from his morose and solitary temper, or, as is more probable, that he knew that his name upon the coast was such that outraged humanity would, against all odds, have thrown themselves upon him, but never once did he show his face in a settlement.

When his ship was laid up he would leave her under the charge of Ned Galloway—her New England quartermaster—and would take long voyages in his boat, sometimes, it was said, for the purpose of burying his share of the plunder, and sometimes to shoot the wild oxen of Hispaniola, which, when dressed and barbecued, provided provisions for his next voyage. In the latter case the barque would come round to some prearranged spot to pick him up and take on board what he had shot.

There had always been a hope in the islands that Sharkey might be taken on one of these occasions; and at last there came news to Kingston which seemed to justify an attempt upon him. It was brought by an elderly logwood-cutter who had fallen into the pirate's hands, and in some freak of drunken benevolence had been allowed to get away with nothing worse than a slit nose and a drubbing. His account was recent and definite. The *Happy Delivery* was careening at Torbec on the south-west of Hispaniola. Sharkey, with four men, was buccaneering on the outlying island of La Vache. The blood of a hundred murdered crews was calling out for vengeance, and now at last it seemed as if it might not call in vain.

Sir Edward Compton, the high-nosed, red-faced Governor, sitting in solemn conclave with the commandant and the head of the council, was sorely puzzled in his mind as to how he should use his chance. There was no man-of-war nearer than Jamestown, and she was a clumsy old fly-boat, which could neither overhaul the pirate on the seas, nor reach her in a shallow inlet. There were forts and artillerymen both at Kingston and Port Royal, but no soldiers available for an expedition.

A private venture might be fitted out—and there were many who had a blood-feud with Sharkey—but what could a private venture do? The pirates were numerous and desperate. As to taking Sharkey and his four companions, that, of course, would be easy if they could get at them ; but how were they to get at them on a large well-wooded island like La Vache, full of wild hills and impenetrable jungles ? A reward was offered to whoever could find a solution, and that brought a man to the front who had a singular plan, and was himself prepared to carry it out.

Stephen Craddock had been that most formidable person, the Puritan gone wrong. Sprung from a decent Salem family, his ill-doing seemed to be a recoil from the austerity of their religion, and he brought to vice all the physical strength and energy with which the virtues of his ancestors had endowed him. He was ingenious, fearless, and exceedingly tenacious of purpose, so that when he was still young his name became notorious upon the American coast.

He was the same Craddock who was tried for his life in Virginia for the slaying of the Seminole Chief, and, though he escaped, it was well known that he had corrupted the witnesses and bribed the judge.

Afterwards, as a slaver, and even, as it was hinted, as a pirate, he had left an evil name behind him in the Bight of Benin. Finally he had returned to Jamaica with a considerable fortune, and had settled down to a life of sombre dissipation. This was the man, gaunt, austere, and dangerous, who now waited upon the Governor with a plan for the extirpation of Sharkey.

Sir Edward received him with little enthusiasm, for in spite of some rumours of conversion and reformation, he had always regarded him as an infected sheep who might taint the whole of his little flock. Craddock saw the Governor's mistrust under his thin veil of formal and restrained courtesy.

" You've no call to fear me, sir," said he ; " I'm a changed man from what you've known. I've seen the light again, of late, after losing sight of it for many a black year. It was through the ministration of the Rev. John Simons, of our own people. Sir, if your spirit

155

should be in need of quickening, you would find a very sweet savour in his discourse."

The Governor cocked his Episcopalian nose at him. "You came here to speak of Sharkey, Master Craddock," said he.

"The man Sharkey is a vessel of wrath," said Craddock. "His wicked horn has been exalted over long, and it is borne in upon me that if I can cut him off and utterly destroy him, it will be a goodly deed, and one which may atone for many backslidings in the past. A plan has been given to me whereby I may encompass his destruction."

The Governor was keenly interested, for there was a grim and practical air about the man's freckled face which showed that he was in earnest. After all, he was a seaman and a fighter, and, if it were true that he was eager to atone for his past, no better man could be chosen for the business.

"This will be a dangerous task, Master Craddock," said he.

"If I meet my death at it, it may be that it will cleanse the memory of an ill-spent life. I have much to atone for."

The Governor did not see his way to contradict him. "What was your plan?" he asked.

"You have heard that Sharkey's barque, the *Happy Delivery*, came from this very port of Kingston?"

"It belonged to Mr. Codrington, and it was taken by Sharkey, who scuttled his own sloop and moved into her because she was faster," said Sir Edward.

"Yes; but it may be that you have never heard that Mr. Codrington has a sister ship, the *White Rose*, which lies even now in the harbour, and which is so like the pirate, that, if it were not for a white paint line, none could tell them apart."

"Ah! and what of that?" asked the Governor keenly, with the air of one who is just on the edge of an idea.

" By the help of it this man shall be delivered into our hands."

" And how ? "

" I will paint out the streak upon the *White Rose*, and make it in all things like the *Happy Delivery*. Then I will set sail for the Island of La Vache, where this man is slaying the wild oxen. When he sees me he will surely mistake me for his own vessel which he is awaiting, and he will come on board to his own undoing."

It was a simple plan, and yet it seemed to the Governor that it might be effective. Without hesitation he gave Craddock permission to carry it out, and to take any steps he liked in order to further the object which he had in view. Sir Edward was not very sanguine, for many attempts had been made upon Sharkey, and their results had shown that he was as cunning as he was ruthless. But this gaunt Puritan with the evil record was cunning and ruthless also.

The contest of wits between two such men as Sharkey and Craddock appealed to the Governor's acute sense of sport, and though he was inwardly convinced that the chances were against him, he backed his man with the same loyalty which he would have shown to his horse or his cock.

Haste was, above all things, necessary, for upon any day the careening might be finished, and the pirates out at sea once more. But there was not very much to do, and there were many willing hands to do it, so the second day saw the *White Rose* beating out for the open sea. There were many seamen in the port who knew the lines and rig of the pirate barque, and not one of them could see the slightest difference in this counterfeit. Her white side line had been painted out, her masts and yards were smoked, to give them the dingy appearance of the weather-beaten rover, and a large diamond shaped patch was let into her foretopsail.

Her crew were volunteers, many of them being men who had sailed with Stephen Craddock before—the mate,

Joshua Hird, an old slaver, had been his accomplice in many voyages, and came now at the bidding of his chief.

The avenging barque sped across the Caribbean Sea, and, at the sight of that patched topsail, the little craft which they met flew left and right like frightened trout in a pool. On the fourth evening Point Abacou bore five miles to the north and east of them.

On the fifth they were at anchor in the Bay of Tortoises at the Island of La Vache, where Sharkey and his four men had been hunting. It was a well-wooded place, with the palms and underwood growing down to the thin crescent of silver sand which skirted the shore. They had hoisted the black flag and the red pennant, but no answer came from the shore. Craddock strained his eyes, hoping every instant to see a boat shoot out to them with Sharkey seated in the sheets. But the night passed away, and a day and yet another night, without any sign of the men whom they were endeavouring to trap. It looked as if they were already gone.

On the second morning Craddock went ashore in search of some proof whether Sharkey and his men were still upon the island. What he found reassured him greatly. Close to the shore was a boucan of green wood, such as was used for preserving the meat, and a great store of barbecued strips of ox-flesh was hung upon lines all round it. The pirate ship had not taken off her provisions, and therefore the hunters were still upon the island.

Why had they not shown themselves? Was it that they had detected that this was not their own ship? Or was it that they were hunting in the interior of the island, and were not on the lookout for a ship yet? Craddock was still hesitating between the two alternatives, when a Carib Indian came down with information. The pirates were in the island, he said, and their camp was a day's march from the sea. They had stolen his wife, and the marks of their stripes were still pink upon his

brown back. Their enemies were his friends, and he
would lead them to where they lay.

Craddock could not have asked for anything better;
so early next morning, with a small party armed to the
teeth, he set off under the guidance of the Carib. All
day they struggled through brushwood and clambered
over rocks, pushing their way farther and farther into
the desolate heart of the island. Here and there they
found traces of the hunters, the bones of a slain ox,
or the marks of feet in a morass, and once, towards
evening, it seemed to some of them that they heard the
distant rattle of guns.

That night they spent under the trees, and pushed on
again with the earliest light. About noon they came to
the huts of bark, which, the Carib told them, were the
camp of the hunters, but they were silent and deserted.
No doubt their occupants were away at the hunt and
would return in the evening, so Craddock and his men
lay in ambush in the brushwood around them. But no
one came, and another night was spent in the forest.
Nothing more could be done, and it seemed to Craddock
that after the two days' absence it was time that he
returned to his ship once more.

The return journey was less difficult, as they had
already blazed a path for themselves. Before evening
they found themselves once more at the Bay of Palms,
and saw their ship riding at anchor where they had left
her. Their boat and oars had been hauled up among
the bushes, so they launched it and pulled out to the
barque.

" No luck, then ! " cried Joshua Hird, the mate, looking
down with a pale face from the poop.

" His camp was empty, but he may come down to
us yet," said Craddock, with his hand on the ladder.

Somebody upon deck began to laugh. " I think,"
said the mate, " that these men had better stay in the
boat."

" Why so ? "

" If you will come aboard, sir, you will understand it."
He spoke in a curious hesitating fashion.

The blood flushed to Craddock's gaunt face.

" How is this, Master Hird ? " he cried, springing up
the side. " What mean you by giving orders to my
boat's crew ? "

But as he passed over the bulwarks, with one foot upon
the deck and one knee upon the rail, a tow-bearded man,
whom he had never before observed aboard his vessel,
grabbed suddenly at his pistol. Craddock clutched at
the fellow's wrist, but at the same instant his mate
snatched the cutlass from his side.

What roguery is this ? " shouted Craddock, looking
furiously around him. But the crew stood in little knots
about the deck, laughing and whispering amongst themselves without showing any desire to go to his assistance.
Even in that hurried glance Craddock noticed that they
were dressed in the most singular manner, with long
riding-coats, full-skirted velvet gowns and coloured
ribands at their knees, more like men of fashion than
seamen.

As he looked at their grotesque figures he struck his
brow with his clenched fist to be sure that he was awake.
The deck seemed to be much dirtier than when he had
left it, and there were strange, sun-blackened faces turned
upon him from every side. Not one of them did he
know save only Joshua Hird. Had the ship been captured in his absence ? Were these Sharkey's men who
were around him ? At the thought he broke furiously
away and tried to climb over to his boat, but a dozen
hands were on him in an instant, and he was pushed aft
through the open door of his own cabin.

And it was all different from the cabin which he had
left. The floor was different, the ceiling was different,
the furniture was different. His had been plain and
austere. This was sumptuous and yet dirty, hung with
rare velvet curtains splashed with wine-stains, and panelled
with costly woods which were pocked with pistol-marks.

SHARKEY AND STEPHEN CRADDOCK

On the table was a great chart of the Caribbean Sea, and beside it, with compasses in his hand, sat a clean-shaven, pale-faced man with a fur cap and a claret-coloured coat of damask. Craddock turned white under his freckles as he looked upon the long, thin, high-nostrilled nose and the red-rimmed eyes which were turned upon him with the fixed, humorous gaze of the master player who has left his opponent without a move.

" Sharkey ? " cried Craddock.

Sharkey's thin lips opened and he broke into his high, sniggering laugh.

" You fool ! " he cried, and, leaning over, he stabbed Craddock's shoulder again and again with his compasses. " You poor, dull-witted fool, would you match yourself against me ? "

It was not the pain of the wounds, but it was the contempt in Sharkey's voice which turned Craddock into a savage madman. He flew at the pirate, roaring with rage, striking, kicking, writhing, and foaming. It took six men to drag him down on to the floor amidst the splintered remains of the table—and not one of the six who did not bear the prisoner's mark upon him. But Sharkey still surveyed him with the same contemptuous eye. From outside there came the crash of breaking wood and the clamour of startled voices.

" What is that ? " asked Sharkey.

" They have stove the boat with cold shot, and the men are in the water."

" Let them stay there," said the pirate. " Now, Craddock, you know where you are. You are aboard my ship the *Happy Delivery*, and you lie at my mercy. I knew you for a stout seaman, you rogue, before you took to this long-shore canting. Your hands then were no cleaner than my own. Will you sign articles, as your mate has done, and join us, or shall I heave you over to follow your ship's company ? "

" Where is my ship ? " asked Craddock.

" Scuttled in the bay."

161

"And the hands?"

"In the bay, too."

"Then, I'm for the bay also."

"Hock him and heave him over." said Sharkey.

Many rough hands had dragged Craddock out upon deck, and Galloway, the quartermaster, had already drawn his hanger to cripple him, when Sharkey came hurrying from his cabin with an eager face.

"We can do better with the hound!" he cried. "Sink me if it is not a rare plan. Throw him into the sail-room with the irons on, and do you come here, quartermaster, that I may tell you what I have in my mind."

So Craddock, bruised and wounded in soul and body, was thrown into the dark sail-room, so fettered that he could not stir hand or foot, but his northern blood was running strong in his veins, and his grim spirit aspired only to make such an ending as might go some way towards atoning for the evil of his life. All night he lay in the curve of the bilge listening to the rush of the water and the straining of the timbers which told him that the ship was at sea, and driving fast. In the early morning someone came crawling to him in the darkness over the heaps of sails.

"Here's rum and biscuits," said the voice of his late mate. "It's at the risk of my life, Master Craddock, that I bring them to you."

"It was you who trapped me and caught me as in a snare!" cried Craddock. "How shall you answer for what you have done?"

"What I did I did with the point of a knife betwixt my blade-bones."

"God forgive you for a coward, Joshua Hird. How came you into their hands?"

"Why, Master Craddock, the pirate ship came back from its careening upon the very day that you left us. They laid us aboard, and, short-handed as we were, with the best of the men ashore with you, we could offer but a poor defence. Some were cut down, and they were the happiest. The others were killed afterwards. As to me, I saved my life by signing on with them."

"And they scuttled my ship?"

"They scuttled her, and then Sharkey and his men, who had been watching us from the brushwood, came off to the ship. His mainyard had been cracked and fished last voyage, so he had suspicions of us, seeing that ours was whole. Then he thought of laying the same trap for you which you had set for him."

Craddock groaned.

"How came I not to see that fished mainyard?" he muttered. "But whither are we bound?"

"We are running north and west."

"North and west! Then we are heading back towards Jamaica."

"With an eight-knot wind."

"Have you heard what they mean to do with me?"

"I have not heard. If you would but sign the articles——"

"Enough, Joshua Hird! I have risked my soul too often."

"As you wish! I have done what I could. Farewell!"

All that night and the next day the *Happy Delivery* ran before the easterly trades, and Stephen Craddock lay in the dark of the sail-room working patiently at his wrist-irons. One he had slipped off at the cost of a row of broken and bleeding knuckles, but, do what he would, he could not free the other, and his ankles were securely fastened.

From hour to hour he heard the swish of the water, and knew that the barque must be driving with all set in front of the trade-wind. In that case they must be nearly back again to Jamaica by now. What plan could Sharkey have in his head, and what use did he hope to make of him? Craddock set his teeth, and vowed that if he had once been a villain from choice he would, at least, never be one by compulsion.

On the second morning Craddock became aware that sail had been reduced in the vessel, and that she was tacking slowly, with a light breeze on her beam. The varying slope of the sail-room and the sounds from the deck told his practised senses exactly what she was doing. The short reaches showed him that she was manœuvring near shore, and making for some definite point. If so, she must have reached Jamaica. But what could she be doing there ?

And then suddenly there was a burst of hearty cheering from the deck, and then the crash of a gun above his head, and then the answering booming of guns from far over the water. Craddock sat up and strained his ears. Was the ship in action ? Only the one gun had been fired, and though many had answered there were none of the crashings which told of a shot coming home.

Then, if it was not an action, it must be a salute. But who would salute Sharkey, the pirate ? It could only be another pirate ship which would do so. So Craddock lay back again with a groan, and continued to work at the manacle which still held his right wrist.

But suddenly there came the shuffling of steps outside, and he had hardly time to wrap the loose links round his free hand, when the door was unbolted and two pirates came in.

" Got your hammer, carpenter ? " asked one, whom Craddock recognized as the big quartermaster. " Knock off his leg shackles, then. Better leave the bracelets— he's safer with them on."

With hammer and chisel the carpenter loosened the irons.

" What are you going to do with me ? " asked Craddock.

" Come on deck and you'll see."

The sailor seized him by the arm and dragged him roughly to the foot of the companion. Above him was a square of blue sky cut across by the mizzen gaff with the colours flying at the peak. But it was the sight of those colours which struck the breath from Stephen

164

Craddock's lips. For there were two of them, and the British ensign was flying above the Jolly Roger—the honest flag above that of the rogue.

For an instant Craddock stopped in amazement, but a brutal push from the pirates behind drove him up the companion ladder. As he stepped out upon deck, his eyes turned up to the main, and there again were the British colours flying above the red pennant, and all the shrouds and rigging were garlanded with streamers.

Had the ship been taken, then ? But that was impossible, for there were the pirates clustering in swarms along the port bulwarks, and waving their hats joyously in the air. Most prominent of all was the renegade mate, standing on the fo'c'sle head, and gesticulating wildly. Craddock looked over the side to see what they were cheering at, and then in a flash he saw how critical was the moment.

On the port bow, and about a mile off, lay the white houses and forts of Port Royal, with flags breaking out everywhere over their roofs. Right ahead was the opening of the palisades leading to the town of Kingston. Not more than a quarter of a mile off was a small sloop working out against the very slight wind. The British ensign was at her peak, and her rigging was all decorated. On her deck could be seen a dense crowd of people cheering and waving their hats, and the gleam of scarlet told that there were officers of the garrison among them.

In an instant, with the quick perception of a man of action, Craddock saw through it all. Sharkey, with that diabolical cunning and audacity which were among his main characteristics, was simulating the part which Craddock would himself have played, had he come back victorious. It was in *his* honour that the salutes were firing and the flags flying. It was to welcome *him* that this ship with the Governor, the commandant, and the chiefs of the island was approaching. In another ten minutes they would all be under the guns of the *Happy*

Delivery, and Sharkey would have won the greatest stake that ever a pirate played for yet.

" Bring him forward," cried the pirate captain, as Craddock appeared between the carpenter and the quartermaster. " Keep the ports closed, but clear away the port guns, and stand by for a broadside. Another two cable lengths and we have them."

" They are edging away," said the boatswain. " I think they smell us."

" That's soon set right," said Sharkey, turning his filmy eyes upon Craddock. " Stand there, you—right there, where they can recognize you, with your hand on the guy, and wave your hat to them. Quick, or your brains will be over your coat. Put an inch of your knife into him, Ned. Now, will you wave your hat ? Try him again, then. Hey, shoot him ! stop him ! "

But it was too late. Relying upon the manacles, the quartermaster had taken his hands for a moment off Craddock's arm. In that instant he had flung off the carpenter and, amid a spatter of pistol bullets, had sprung the bulwarks and was swimming for his life. He had been hit and hit again, but it takes many pistols to kill a resolute and powerful man who has his mind set upon doing something before he dies. He was a strong swimmer, and, in spite of the red trail which he left in the water behind him, he was rapidly increasing his distance from the pirate.

" Give me a musket ! " cried Sharkey, with a savage oath.

He was a famous shot, and his iron nerves never failed him in an emergency. The dark head appearing on the crest of a roller, and then swooping down on the other side, was already half-way to the sloop. Sharkey dwelt long upon his aim before he fired. With the crack of the gun the swimmer reared himself up in the water, waved his hands in a gesture of warning, and roared out in a voice which rang over the bay. Then, as the sloop swung round her head-sails, and the pirate fired an impotent broadside, Stephen Craddock, smiling grimly in his death agony, sank slowly down to that golden couch which glimmered far beneath him.

15. *The Blighting of Sharkey*

SHARKEY, the abominable Sharkey, was out again. After two years of the Coromandel coast, his black barque of death, the *Happy Delivery*, was prowling off the Spanish Main, while trader and fisher flew for dear life at the menace of that patched fore-topsail, rising slowly over the violet rim of the tropical sea.

As the birds cower when the shadow of the hawk falls athwart the field, or as the jungle folk crouch and shiver when the coughing cry of the tiger is heard in the night-time, so through all the busy world of ships, from the whalers of Nantucket to the tobacco ships of Charleston, and from the Spanish supply ships of Cadiz to the sugar merchants of the Main, there spread the rumour of the black curse of the ocean.

Some hugged the shore, ready to make for the nearest port, while others struck far out beyond the known lines of commerce, but none were so stout-hearted that they did not breathe more freely when their passengers and cargoes were safe under the guns of some mothering fort.

Through all the islands there ran tales of charred derelicts at sea, of sudden glares seen afar in the night-time, and of withered bodies stretched upon the sand of waterless Bahama Keys. All the old signs were there to show that Sharkey was at his bloody game once more.

These fair waters and yellow-rimmed palm-nodding islands are the traditional home of the sea rover. First it was the gentleman adventurer, the man of family and honour, who fought as a patriot, though he was ready to take his payment in Spanish plunder.

Then, within a century, his debonair figure had passed to make room for the buccaneers, robbers pure and simple, yet with some organized code of their own, commanded by notable chieftains, and taking in hand great concerted enterprises.

They, too, passed with their fleets and their sacking of cities, to make room for the worst of all, the lonely, outcast pirate, the bloody Ishmael of the seas, at war with the whole human race. This was the vile brood which the early eighteenth century had spawned forth, and of them all there was none who could compare in audacity, wickedness, and evil repute with the unutterable Sharkey.

It was early in May, in the year 1720, that the *Happy Delivery* lay with her fore-yard aback some five leagues west of the Windward Passage, waiting to see what rich, helpless craft the trade-wind might bring down to her.

Three days she had lain there, a sinister black speck, in the centre of the great sapphire circle of the ocean. Far to the south-east the low blue hills of Hispaniola showed up on the skyline.

Hour by hour as he waited without avail, Sharkey's savage temper had risen, for his arrogant spirit chafed against any contradiction, even from Fate itself. To his quartermaster, Ned Galloway, he had said that night, with his odious neighing laugh, that the crew of the next captured vessel should answer to him for having kept him waiting so long.

The cabin of the pirate barque was a good-sized room, hung with much tarnished finery, and presenting a strange medley of luxury and disorder. The panelling of carved and polished sandal-wood was blotched with foul smudges and chipped with bullet-marks fired in some drunken revelry.

Rich velvets and laces were heaped upon the brocaded settees, while metal-work and pictures of great price filled every niche and corner, for anything which caught the pirate's fancy in the sack of a hundred vessels was thrown haphazard into his chamber. A rich, soft carpet covered the floor, but it was mottled with wine-stains and charred with burned tobacco.

Above, a great brass hanging-lamp threw a brilliant yellow light upon this singular apartment, and upon the two men who sat in their shirt-sleeves with the wine between them, and the cards in their hands, deep in a game of piquet. Both were smoking long pipes, and the thin blue reek filled the cabin and floated through the skylight above them, which, half opened, disclosed a slip of deep violet sky spangled with great silver stars.

Ned Galloway, the quartermaster, was a huge New England wastrel, the one rotten branch upon a goodly Puritan family tree. His robust limbs and giant frame were the heritage of a long line of God-fearing ancestors, while his black savage heart was all his own. Bearded to the temples, with fierce blue eyes, a tangled lion's mane of coarse, dark hair, and huge gold rings in his ears, he was the idol of the women in every waterside hell from the Tortugas to Maracaibo on the Main. A red cap, a blue silken shirt, brown velvet breeches with gaudy knee-ribbons, and high sea-boots made up the costume of the rover Hercules.

A very different figure was Captain John Sharkey. His thin, drawn, clean-shaven face was corpse-like in its pallor, and all the suns of the Indies could but turn it to a more deathly parchment tint. He was part bald, with a few lank locks of tow-like hair, and a steep, narrow forehead. His thin nose jutted sharply forth, and near-set on either side of it were those filmy blue eyes, red-rimmed like those of a white bull-terrier, from which strong men winced away in fear and loathing. His bony hands, with long, thin fingers which quivered ceaselessly like the antennæ of an insect, were toying constantly with the cards and the heap of gold moidores which lay before him. His dress was of some sober drab material, but, indeed, the men who looked upon that fearsome face had little thought for the costume of its owner.

The game was brought to a sudden interruption, for the cabin door was swung rudely open, and two rough fellows—Israel Martin, the boatswain, and Red Foley,

the gunner—rushed into the cabin. In an instant Sharkey
was on his feet with a pistol in either hand and murder
in his eyes.

" Sink you for villains ! " he cried. " I see well that
if I do not shoot one of you from time to time you will
forget the man I am. What mean you by entering my
cabin as though it were a Wapping alehouse ? "

" Nay, Captain Sharkey," said Martin, with a sullen
frown upon his brick-red face, " it is even such talk as
this which has set us by the ears. We have had enough
of it."

" And more than enough," said Red Foley, the gunner.
" There be no mates aboard a pirate craft, and so the
boatswain, the gunner, and the quartermaster are the
officers."

" Did I gainsay it ? " asked Sharkey with an oath.

" You have miscalled us and mishandled us before
the men, and we scarce know at this moment why we
should risk our lives in fighting for the cabin and against
the fo'c'sle."

Sharkey saw that something serious was in the wind.
He laid down his pistols and leaned back in his chair with
a flash of his yellow fangs.

" Nay, this is sad talk," said he, " that two stout
fellows who have emptied many a bottle and cut many
a throat with me, should now fall out over nothing. I
know you to be roaring boys who would go with me against
the devil himself if I bid you. Let the steward bring
cups and drown all unkindness between us."

" It is no time for drinking, Captain Sharkey," said
Martin. " The men are holding council round the main-
mast, and may be aft at any minute. They mean mischief,
Captain Sharkey, and we have come to warn you."

Sharkey sprang for the brass-handled sword which
hung from the wall.

" Sink them for rascals ! " he cried. " When I have
gutted one or two of them they may hear reason."

But the others barred his frantic way to the door.

" There are forty of them under the lead of Sweetlocks, the master," said Martin, " and on the open deck they would surely cut you to pieces. Here within the cabin it may be that we can hold them off at the points of our pistols."

He had hardly spoken when there came the tread of many heavy feet upon the deck. Then there was a pause with no sound but the gentle lapping of the water against the sides of the pirate vessel. Finally, a crashing blow as from a pistol-butt fell upon the door, and an instant afterwards Sweetlocks himself, a tall, dark man, with a deep red birth-mark blazing upon his cheek, strode into the cabin. His swaggering air sank somewhat as he looked into those pale and filmy eyes.

" Captain Sharkey," said he, " I come as spokesman of the crew."

" So I have heard, Sweetlocks," said the captain, softly. " I may live to rip you the length of your vest for this night's work."

" That is as it may be, Captain Sharkey," the master answered, " but if you will look up you will see that I have those at my back who will not see me mishandled."

" Cursed if we do ! " growled a deep voice from above, and glancing upwards the officers in the cabin were aware of a line of fierce, bearded, sun-blackened faces looking down at them through the open skylight.

" Well, what would you have ? " asked Sharkey. " Put it in words, man, and let us have an end of it."

" The men think," said Sweetlocks, " that you are the devil himself, and that there will be no luck for them whilst they sail the sea in such company. Time was when we did our two or three craft a day, and every man had women and dollars to his liking, but now for a long week we have not raised a sail, and save for three beggarly sloops, have taken never a vessel since we passed the Bahama Bank. Also, they know that you killed Jack Bartholomew, the carpenter, by beating his head in with a bucket, so that each of us goes in fear of his

life. Also, the rum has given out, and we are hard put
to it for liquor. Also, you sit in your cabin whilst it is
in the articles that you should drink and roar with the
crew. For all these reasons it has been this day in
general meeting decreed——"

Sharkey had stealthily cocked a pistol under the table,
so it may have been as well for the mutinous master that
he never reached the end of his discourse, for even as
he came to it there was a swift patter of feet upon the
deck, and a ship lad, wild with his tidings, rushed into
the room.

"A craft!" he yelled. "A great craft, and close
aboard us!"

In a flash the quarrel was forgotten, and the pirates
were rushing to quarters. Sure enough, surging slowly
down before the gentle trade-wind, a great full-rigged
ship, with all sail set, was close beside them.

It was clear that she had come from afar and knew
nothing of the ways of the Caribbean Sea, for she made
no effort to avoid the low, dark craft which lay so close
upon her bow, but blundered on as if her mere size
would avail her.

So daring was she, that for an instant the rovers, as
they flew to loose the tackles of their guns, and hoisted
their battle-lanterns, believed that a man-of-war had
caught them napping.

But at the sight of her bulging, portless sides and
merchant rig a shout of exultation broke from amongst
them, and in an instant they had swung round their fore-
yard, and darting alongside they had grappled with her
and flung a spray of shrieking, cursing ruffians upon her
deck.

Half a dozen seamen of the night-watch were cut
down where they stood, the mate was felled by Sharkey
and tossed overboard by Ned Galloway, and before the
sleepers had time to sit up in their berths, the vessel
was in the hands of the pirates.

The prize proved to be the full-rigged ship *Portobello*

—Captain Hardy, master—bound from London to Kingston in Jamaica, with a cargo of cotton goods and hoop-iron.

Having secured their prisoners, all huddled together in a dazed, distracted group, the pirates spread over the vessel in search of plunder, handing all that was found to the giant quartermaster, who in turn passed it over the side of the *Happy Delivery* and laid it under guard at the foot of her mainmast.

The cargo was useless, but there were a thousand guineas in the ship's strong-box, and there were some eight or ten passengers, three of them wealthy Jamaica merchants, all bringing home well-filled boxes from their London visit.

When all the plunder was gathered, the passengers and crew were dragged to the waist, and under the cold smile of Sharkey each in turn was thrown over the side —Sweetlocks standing by the rail and ham-stringing them with his cutlass as they passed over, lest some strong swimmer should rise in judgment against them. A portly, grey-haired woman, the wife of one of the planters, was among the captives, but she also was thrust screaming and clutching over the side.

" Mercy, you hussy ! " neighed Sharkey, " you are surely a good twenty years too old for that."

The captain of the *Portobello*, a hale, blue-eyed greybeard, was the last upon the deck. He stood, a thickset resolute figure, in the glare of the lanterns, while Sharkey bowed and smirked before him.

" One skipper should show courtesy to another," said he, " and sink me if Captain Sharkey would be behind in good manners ! I have held you to the last, as you see, where a brave man should be ; so now, my bully, you have seen the end of them, and may step over with an easy mind."

" So I shall, Captain Sharkey," said the old seaman, " for I have done my duty so far as my power lay. But before I go over I would say a word in your ear."

" If it be to soften me, you may save your breath. You have kept us waiting here for three days, and curse me if one of you shall live ! "

" Nay, it is to tell you what you should know. You have not yet found what is the true treasure aboard of this ship."

" Not found it ? Sink me, but I will slice your liver, Captain Hardy, if you do not make good your words ! Where is this treasure you speak of ? "

" It is not a treasure of gold, but it is a fair maid, which may be no less welcome."

" Where is she, then ? And why was she not with the others ? "

" I will tell you why she was not with the others. She is the only daughter of the Count and Countess Ramirez, who are amongst those whom you have murdered. Her name is Inez Ramirez, and she is of the best blood of Spain, her father being Governor of Chagre, to which he was now bound. It chanced that she was found to have formed an attachment, as maids will, to one far beneath her in rank aboard this ship ; so her parents, being people of great power, whose word is not to be gainsaid, constrained me to confine her close in a special cabin aft of my own. Here she was held straitly, all food being carried to her, and she allowed to see no one. This I tell you as a last gift, though why I should make it to you I do not know, for indeed you are a most bloody rascal, and it comforts me in dying to think that you will surely be gallow's-meat in this world, and hell's-meat in the next."

At the words he ran to the rail, and vaulted over into the darkness, praying as he sank into the depths of the sea, that the betrayal of this maid might not be counted too heavily against his soul.

The body of Captain Hardy had not yet settled upon the sand forty fathoms deep before the pirates had rushed along the cabin gangway. There, sure enough, at the farther end, was a barred door, overlooked in their previous search. There was no key, but they beat it in with their gunstocks, whilst shriek after shriek came from within. In the light of their outstretched lanterns they saw a young woman, in the very prime and fullness of her youth, crouching in a corner, her unkempt hair hanging to the ground, her dark eyes glaring with fear, her lovely form straining away in horror from this inrush of savage blood-stained men. Rough hands seized her, she was jerked to her feet, and dragged with scream on scream to where John Sharkey awaited her. He held the light long and fondly to her face, then, laughing loudly, he bent forward and left his red handprint upon her cheek.

" 'Tis the Rovers' brand, lass, that he marks his ewes. Take her to the cabin and use her well. Now, hearties, get her under water, and out to our luck once more."

Within an hour the good ship *Portobello* had settled down to her doom, till she lay beside her murdered passengers upon the Caribbean sand, while the pirate barque, her deck littered with plunder, was heading northward in search of another victim.

There was a carouse that night in the cabin of the *Happy Delivery*, at which three men drank deep. They were the captain, the quartermaster, and Baldy Stable, the surgeon, a man who had held the first practice in Charleston, until, misusing a patient, he fled from justice, and took his skill over to the pirates. A bloated fat man he was, with a creased neck and a great shining scalp, which gave him his name. Sharkey had put for the moment all thought of the mutiny out of his head, knowing that no animal is fierce when it is over-fed, and that whilst the plunder of the great ship was new to them he need fear no trouble from his crew. He gave himself up, therefore, to the wine and the riot, shouting and roaring with his boon companions. All three were flushed and mad, ripe for any devilment, when the thought of the woman crossed the pirate's evil mind. He yelled to the negro steward that he should bring her on the instant.

Inez Ramirez had now realized it all—the death of her father and mother, and her own position in the hands of their murderers. Yet calmness had come with the knowledge, and there was no sign of terror in her proud, dark face as she was led into the cabin, but rather a strange, firm set of the mouth and an exultant gleam of the eyes, like one who sees great hopes in the future. She smiled at the pirate captain as he rose and seized her by the waist.

" 'Fore God ! this is a lass of spirit," cried Sharkey ; passing his arm round her. " She was born to be a Rover's bride. Come, my bird, and drink to our better friendship."

" Article Six ! " hiccoughed the doctor. " All *bona robas* in common."

" Aye ! we hold you to that, Captain Sharkey," said Galloway. " It is so writ in Article Six."

" I will cut the man into ounces who comes betwixt us ! " cried Sharkey, as he turned his fish-like eyes from one to the other. " Nay, lass, the man is not born that will take you from John Sharkey. Sit here upon my knee, and place your arm round me so. Sink me, if she has not learned to love me at sight ! Tell me, my pretty, why you were so mishandled and laid in the bilboes aboard yonder craft ? "

The woman shook her head and smiled. " No Inglese —no Inglese," she lisped. She had drunk off the bumper of wine which Sharkey held to her, and her dark eyes gleamed more brightly than before. Sitting on Sharkey's knee, her arm encircled his neck, and her hand toyed with his hair, his ear, his cheek. Even the strange quartermaster and the hardened surgeon felt a horror as they watched her, but Sharkey laughed in his joy. " Curse me, if she is not a lass of metal ! " he cried, as he pressed her to him and kissed her unresisting lips.

But a strange intent look of interest had come into the surgeon's eyes as he watched her, and his face set rigidly, as if a fearsome thought had entered his mind. There stole a grey pallor over his bull face, mottling all the red of the tropics and the flush of the wine.

" Look at her hand, Captain Sharkey ! " he cried. " For the Lord's sake, look at her hand ! "

Sharkey stared down at the hand which had fondled him. It was of a strange dead pallor, with a yellow shiny web betwixt the fingers. All over it was a white fluffy dust, like the flour of a new-baked loaf. It lay thick on Sharkey's neck and cheek. With a cry of disgust he flung the woman from his lap ; but in an instant, with a wild-cat bound, and a scream of triumphant malice, she had sprung at the surgeon, who vanished yelling under the table. One of her clawing hands grasped Galloway by the beard, but he tore himself away, and snatching a pike, held her off from him as she gibbered and mowed with the blazing eyes of a maniac.

The black steward had run in on the sudden turmoil, and among them they forced the mad creature back into a cabin and turned the key upon her. Then the three sank panting into their chairs and looked with eyes of horror upon each other. The same word was in the mind of each, but Galloway was the first to speak it.

" A leper ! " he cried. " She has us all, curse her ! "

" Not me," said the surgeon ; " she never laid her finger on me."

" For that matter," cried Galloway, " it was but my beard that she touched. I will have every hair of it off before morning."

" Dolts that we were ! " the surgeon shouted, beating his head with his hand. " Tainted or no, we shall never know a moment's peace till the year is up and the time of danger past. 'Fore God, that merchant skipper has left his mark on us, and pretty fools we were to think that such a maid would be quarantined for the cause he gave. It is easy to see now that her corruption broke forth in the journey, and that save throwing her over they had no choice but to board her up until they should come to some port with a lazarette."

Sharkey had sat leaning back in his chair with a ghastly face while he listened to the surgeon's words. He mopped himself with his red handkerchief, and wiped away the fatal dust with which he was smeared.

"What of me ?" he croaked. "What say you, Baldy Stable ? Is there a chance for me ? Curse you for a villain ! speak out, or I will drub you within an inch of your life, and that inch also ! Is there a chance for me, I say ! "

But the surgeon shook his head. "Captain Sharkey," said he, "it would be an ill deed to speak you false. The taint is on you. No man on whom the leper scales have rested is ever clean again."

Sharkey's head fell forward on his chest, and he sat motionless, stricken by this great and sudden horror, looking with his smouldering eyes into his fearsome future. Softly the mate and the surgeon rose from their places, and stealing out from the poisoned air of the cabin, came forth into the freshness of the early dawn, with the soft, scent-laden breeze in their faces and the first red feathers of cloud catching the earliest gleam of the rising sun as it shot its golden rays over the palm-clad ridges of distant Hispaniola.

That morning a second council of the Rovers was held at the base of the mainmast, and a deputation chosen to see the captain. They were approaching the after-cabins when Sharkey came forth, the old devil in his eyes, and his bandolier with a pair of pistols over his shoulder.

"Sink you all for villains !" he cried. "Would you dare to cross my hawse ? Stand out, Sweetlocks, and I will lay you open ! Here, Galloway, Martin, Foley, stand by me and lash the dogs to their kennel ! "

But his officers had deserted him, and there was none to come to his aid. There was a rush of the pirates. One was shot through the body, but an instant afterwards Sharkey had been seized and was triced to his own mainmast. His filmy eyes looked round from face

178

to face, and there was none who felt the happier for having met them.

"Captain Sharkey," said Sweetlocks, "you have mishandled many of us, and you have now pistolled John Masters, besides killing Bartholomew, the carpenter, by braining him with a bucket. All this might have been forgiven you, in that you have been our leader for years, and that we have signed articles to serve under you while the voyage lasts. But now we have heard of this *bona roba* on board, and we know that you are poisoned to the marrow, and that while you rot there will be no safety for any of us, but that we shall all be turned into filth and corruption. Therefore, John Sharkey, we Rovers of the *Happy Delivery*, in council assembled, have decreed that while there be yet time, before the plague spreads, you shall be set adrift in a boat to find such a fate as Fortune may be pleased to send you."

John Sharkey said nothing, but slowly circling his head, he cursed them all with his baleful gaze. The ship's dinghy had been lowered, and he, with his hands still tied, was dropped into it on the bight of a rope.

"Cast her off!" cried Sweetlocks.

"Nay, hold hard a moment, Master Sweetlocks!" shouted one of the crew. "What of the wench? Is she to bide aboard and poison us all?"

"Send her off with her mate!" cried another, and the Rovers roared their approval. Driven forth at the end of pikes, the girl was pushed towards the boat. With all the spirit of Spain in her rotting body she flashed triumphant glances at her captors.

"Perros! Perros Ingleses! Lepero, Lepero!" she cried in exultation, as they thrust her over into the boat.

"Good luck, captain! God speed you on your honeymoon!" cried a chorus of mocking voices, as the painter was unloosed, and the *Happy Delivery*, running full before the trade-wind, left the little boat astern, a tiny dot upon the vast expanse of the lonely sea.

* * * * *

Extract from the log of H.M. 50-gun ship *Hecate* in her cruise off the American Main.

" *Jan.* 26, 1721.—This day, the junk having become unfit for food, and five of the crew down with scurvy, I ordered that we send two boats ashore at the nor'western point of Hispaniola, to seek for fresh fruit, and perchance shoot some of the wild oxen with which the island abounds.

" 7 *p.m.*—The boats have returned with good store of green stuff and two bullocks. Mr. Woodruff, the master, reports that near the landing-place at the edge of the forest was found the skeleton of a woman, clad in European dress, of such sort as to show that she may have been a person of quality. Her head had been crushed by a great stone which lay beside her. Hard by was a grass hut, and signs that a man had dwelt therein for some time, as was shown by charred wood, bones and other traces. There is a rumour upon the coast that Sharkey, the bloody pirate, was marooned in these parts last year, but whether he has made his way into the interior, or whether he has been picked up by some craft, there is no means of knowing. If he be once again afloat, then I pray that God send him under our guns."

16: *How Copley Banks slew Captain Sharkey*

THE Buccaneers were something higher than a mere band of marauders. They were a floating republic, with laws, usages, and discipline of their own. In their endless and remorseless quarrel with the Spaniards they had some semblance of right upon their side. Their bloody harryings of the cities of the Main were not more barbarous than the inroads of Spain upon the Netherlands—or upon the Caribs in these same American lands.

The chief of the Buccaneers, were he English or French, a Morgan or a Granmont, was still a responsible person, whose country might countenance him, or even praise him, so long as he refrained from any deed which might shock the leathery seventeenth-century conscience too outrageously. Some of them were touched with religion, and it is still remembered how Sawkins threw the dice overboard upon the Sabbath, and Daniel pistolled a man before the altar for irreverence.

But there came a day when the fleets of the Buccaneers no longer mustered at the Tortugas, and the solitary and outlawed pirate took their place. Yet even with him the tradition of restraint and of discipline still lingered; and among the early pirates, the Avorys, the Englands, and the Robertses, there remained some respect for human sentiment. They were more dangerous to the merchant than to the seaman.

But they in turn were replaced by more savage and desperate men, who frankly recognized that they would get no quarter in their war with the human race, and who swore that they would give as little as they got. Of their histories we know little that is trustworthy. They wrote no memoirs and left no trace, save an occasional blackened and bloodstained derelict adrift upon the face of the Atlantic. Their deeds could only be surmised from the long roll of ships which never made their port.

Searching the records of history, it is only here and there in an old-world trial that the veil that shrouds them seems for an instant to be lifted, and we catch a glimpse of some amazing and grotesque brutality behind. Such was the breed of Ned Low, of Gow the Scotchman, and of the infamous Sharkey, whose coal-black barque, the *Happy Delivery*, was known from the Newfoundland Banks to the mouths of the Orinoco as the dark fore-runner of misery and of death.

There were many men, both among the islands and on the Main, who had a blood feud with Sharkey, but not one who had suffered more bitterly than Copley

Banks, of Kingston. Banks had been one of the leading sugar merchants of the West Indies. He was a man of position, a member of the Council, the husband of a Percival, and the cousin of the Governor of Virginia. His two sons had been sent to London to be educated, and their mother had gone over to bring them back. On their return voyage the ship, the *Duchess of Cornwall*, fell into the hands of Sharkey, and the whole family met with an infamous death.

Copley Banks said little when he heard the news, but he sank into a morose and enduring melancholy. He neglected his business, avoided his friends, and spent much of his time in the low taverns of the fishermen and seamen. There, amidst riot and devilry, he sat silently puffing at his pipe, with a set face and a smouldering eye. It was generally supposed that his misfortunes had shaken his wits, and his old friends looked at him askance, for the company which he kept was enough to bar him from honest men.

From time to time there came rumours of Sharkey over the sea. Sometimes it was from some schooner which had seen a great flame upon the horizon, and approaching to offer help to the burning ship, had fled away at the sight of the sleek, black barque, lurking like a wolf near a mangled sheep. Sometimes it was a frightened trader, which had come tearing in with her canvas curved like a lady's bodice, because she had seen a patched fore-topsail rising slowly above the violet water-line. Sometimes it was from a Coaster, which had found a waterless Bahama cay littered with sun-dried bodies.

Once there came a man who had been mate of a Guinea-man, and who had escaped from the pirate's hands. He could not speak—for reasons which Sharkey could best supply—but he could write, and he did write, to the very great interest of Copley Banks. For hours they sat together over the map, and the dumb man pointed here and there to outlying reefs and tortuous inlets, while his companion sat smoking in silence, with his unvarying face and his fiery eyes.

One morning, some two years after his misfortune, Mr. Copley Banks strode into his own office with his old air of energy and alertness. The manager stared at him in surprise, for it was months since he had shown any interest in business.

" Good morning, Mr. Banks ! " said he.

" Good morning, Freeman. I see that *Ruffling Harry* is in the Bay."

" Yes, sir ; she clears for the Windward Islands on Wednesday."

" I have other plans for her, Freeman. I have determined upon a slaving venture to Whydah."

" But her cargo is ready, sir."

" Then it must come out again, Freeman. My mind is made up, and the *Ruffling Harry* must go slaving to Whydah."

All argument and persuasion were vain, so the manager had dolefully to clear the ship once more.

And then Copley Banks began to make preparations for his African voyage. It appeared that he relied upon force rather than barter for the filling of his hold, for he carried none of those showy trinkets which savages love, but the brig was fitted with eight nine-pounder guns and racks full of muskets and cutlasses. The after sailroom next the cabin was transformed into a powder magazine, and she carried as many round shot as a wellfound privateer. Water and provisions were shipped for a long voyage.

But the preparation of his ship's company was most surprising. It made Freeman, the manager, realize that there was truth in the rumour that his master had taken leave of his senses. For, under one pretext or another, he began to dismiss the old and tried hands, who had served the firm for years, and in their place he embarked the scum of the port—men whose reputations were so vile that the lowest crimp would have been ashamed to furnish them.

There was Birthmark Sweetlocks, who was known to have been present at the killing of the logwood cutters, so that his hideous scarlet disfigurement was put down by the fanciful as being a red afterglow from that great crime. He was first mate, and under him was Israel Martin, a little sun-wilted fellow who had served with Howell Davies at the taking of Cape Coast Castle.

The crew were chosen from amongst those whom Banks had met and known in their own infamous haunts, and his own table-steward was a haggard-faced man, who gobbled at you when he tried to talk. His beard had been shaved, and it was impossible to recognize him as the same man whom Sharkey had placed under the knife, and who had escaped to tell his experiences to Copley Banks.

These doings were not unnoticed, nor yet uncommented upon in the town of Kingston. The Commandant of the troops—Major Harvey, of the Artillery—made serious representations to the Governor.

" She is not a trader, but a small warship," said he. " I think it would be as well to arrest Copley Banks and to seize the vessel."

" What do you suspect ? " asked the Governor, who was a slow-witted man, broken down with fevers and port wine.

" I suspect," said the soldier, " that it is Stede Bonnet over again."

Now, Stede Bonnet was a planter of high reputation and religious character, who, from some sudden and overpowering freshet of wildness in his blood, had given up everything in order to start off pirating in the Caribbean Sea. The example was a recent one, and it had caused the utmost consternation in the islands. Governors had before now been accused of being in league with pirates, and of receiving commissions upon their plunder, so that any want of vigilance was open to a sinister construction.

" Well, Major Harvey," said he, " I am vastly sorry

to do anything which may offend my friend Copley Banks, for many a time have my knees been under his mahogany, but in face of what you say there is no choice for me but to order you to board the vessel and to satisfy yourself as to her character and destination."

So at one in the morning Major Harvey, with a launchful of his soldiers, paid a surprise visit to the *Ruffling Harry*, with the result that they picked up nothing more solid than a hempen cable floating at the moorings. It had been slipped by the brig, whose owner had scented danger. She had already passed the Palisades, and was beating out against the north-east trades on a course for the Windward Passage.

When upon the next morning the brig had left Morant Point a mere haze upon the Southern horizon, the men were called aft, and Copley Banks revealed his plans to them. He had chosen them, he said, as brisk boys and lads of spirit, who would rather run some risk upon the sea than starve for a living upon the shore. King's ships were few and weak, and they could master any trader who might come their way. Others had done well at the business, and with a handy, well-found vessel, there was no reason why they should not turn their tarry jackets into velvet coats. If they were prepared to sail under the black flag, he was ready to command them ; but if any wished to withdraw, they might have the gig and row back to Jamaica.

Four men out of six-and-forty asked for their discharge, went over the ship's side into the boat, and rowed away amidst the jeers and howlings of the crew. The rest assembled aft, and drew up the articles of their association. A square of black tarpaulin had the white skull painted upon it, and was hoisted amidst cheering at the main.

Officers were elected, and the limits of their authority fixed. Copley Banks was chosen captain, but, as there are no mates upon a pirate craft, Birthmark Sweetlocks became quartermaster, and Israel Martin the boatswain.

There was no difficulty in knowing what was the custom of the brotherhood, for half the men àt least had served upon pirates before. Food should be the same for all, and no man should interfere with another man's drink ! The captain should have a cabin, but all hands should be welcome to enter it when they chose.

All should share and share alike, save only the captain, quartermaster, boatswain, carpenter, and master-gunner, who had from a quarter to a whole share extra. He who saw a prize first should have the best weapon taken out of her. He who boarded her first should have the richest suit of clothes aboard of her. Every man might treat his own prisoner, be it man or woman, after his own fashion. If a man flinched from his gun, the quarter-master should pistol him. These were some of the rules which the crew of the *Ruffling Harry* subscribed by putting forty-two crosses at the foot of the paper upon which they had been drawn.

So a new rover was afloat upon the seas, and her name before a year was over became as well known as that of the *Happy Delivery*. From the Bahamas to the Leewards, and from the Leewards to the Windwards, Copley Banks became the rival of Sharkey and the terror of traders. For a long time the barque and the brig never met, which was the more singular, as the *Ruffling Harry* was for ever looking in at Sharkey's resorts ; but at last one day, when she was passing down the inlet of Coxon's Hole, at the east end of Cuba, with the intention of careening, there was the *Happy Delivery*, with her blocks and tackle-falls already rigged for the same purpose.

Copley Banks fired a shotted salute and hoisted the green trumpeter ensign, as the custom was among gentlemen of the sea. Then he dropped his boat and went aboard.

Captain Sharkey was not a man of a genial mood, nor had he any kindly sympathy for those who were of the same trade as himself. Copley Banks found him seated astride upon one of the after guns, with his New England

quartermaster, Ned Galloway, and a crowd of roaring
ruffians standing about him. Yet none of them roared
with quite such assurance when Sharkey's pale face and
filmy blue eyes were turned upon him.

He was in his shirt-sleeves, with his cambric frills
breaking through his open red satin long-flapped vest.
The scorching sun seemed to have no power upon his
fleshless frame, for he wore a low fur cap, as though it
had been winter. A many-coloured band of silk passed
across his body and supported a short murderous sword,
while his broad, brass-buckled belt was stuffed with
pistols.

"Sink you for a poacher!" he cried, as Copley Banks
passed over the bulwarks. "I will drub you within an
inch of your life, and that inch also! What mean you
by fishing in my waters?"

Copley Banks looked at him, and his eyes were like
those of a traveller who sees his home at last.

"I am glad that we are of one mind," said he, "for
I am myself of opinion that the seas are not large enough
for the two of us. But if you will take your sword and
pistols and come upon a sand-bank with me, then the
world will be rid of a damned villain whichever way it
goes."

"Now this is talking!" cried Sharkey, jumping off
the gun and holding out his hand. "I have not met
many who could look John Sharkey in the eyes and speak
with a full breath. May the devil seize me if I do not
choose you as a consort! But if you play me false, then
I will come aboard of you and gut you upon your own
poop."

"And I pledge you the same!" said Copley Banks,
and so the two pirates became sworn comrades to each
other.

That summer they went north as far as the Newfoundland Banks, and harried the New York traders and the
whale-ships from New England. It was Copley Banks
who captured the Liverpool ship, *House of Hanover*, but

it was Sharkey who fastened her master to the windlass and pelted him to death with empty claret-bottles.

Together they engaged the King's ship *Royal Fortune*, which had been sent in search of them, and beat her off after a night action of five hours, the drunken, raving crews fighting naked in the light of the battle-lanterns, with a bucket of rum and a pannikin laid by the tackles of every gun. They ran to Topsail Inlet in North Carolina to refit, and then in the spring they were at the Grand Caicos, ready for a long cruise down the West Indies.

By this time Sharkey and Copley Banks had become very excellent friends, for Sharkey loved a whole-hearted villain, and he loved a man of metal, and it seemed to him that the two met in the captain of the *Ruffling Harry*. It was long before he gave his confidence to him, for cold suspicion lay deep in his character. Never once would he trust himself outside his own ship and away from his own men.

But Copley Banks came often on board the *Happy Delivery*, and joined Sharkey in many of his morose debauches, so that at last any lingering misgivings of the latter were set at rest. He knew nothing of the evil that he had done to his new boon companion, for of his many victims how could he remember the woman and the two boys whom he had slain with such levity so long ago ! When, therefore, he received a challenge to himself and to his quartermaster for a carouse upon the last evening of their stay at the Caicos Bank, he saw no reason to refuse.

A well-found passenger ship had been rifled the week before, so their fare was of the best, and after supper five of them drank deeply together. There were the two captains, Birthmark Sweetlocks, Ned Galloway, and Israel Martin, the old buccaneersman. To wait upon them was the dumb steward, whose head Sharkey split with his glass, because he had been too slow in the filling of it.

The quartermaster had slipped Sharkey's pistols away from him, for it was an old joke with him to fire them cross-handed under the table, and see who was the luckiest man. It was a pleasantry which had cost his boatswain his leg, so now, when the table was cleared, they would coax Sharkey's weapons away from him on the excuse of the heat, and lay them out of his reach.

The captain's cabin of the *Ruffling Harry* was in a deck-house upon the poop, and a stern-chaser gun was mounted at the back of it. Round shot were racked round the wall, and three great hogsheads of powder made a stand for dishes and for bottles. In this grim room the five pirates sang and roared and drank, while the silent steward still filled up their glasses, and passed the box and the candle round for their tobacco-pipes. Hour after hour the talk became fouler, the voices hoarser, the curses and shoutings more incoherent, until three of the five had closed their bloodshot eyes, and dropped their swimming heads upon the table.

Copley Banks and Sharkey were left face to face, the one because he had drunk the least, the other because no amount of liquor would ever shake his iron nerve or warm his sluggish blood. Behind him stood the watchful steward, for ever filling up his waning glass. From without came the low lapping of the tide, and from over the water a sailor's chanty from the barque.

In the windless tropical night the words came clearly to their ears :

" A trader sailed from Stepney Town,
Wake her up ! Shake her up ! Try her with the mainsail !
A trader sailed from Stepney Town
With a keg full of gold and a velvet gown.
Ho, the bully Rover Jack,
Waiting with his yard aback
Out upon the Lowland Sea."

The two boon companions sat listening in silence. Then Copley Banks glanced at the steward, and the man took a coil of rope from the shot-rack behind him.

"Captain Sharkey," said Copley Banks, "do you remember the *Duchess of Cornwall*, hailing from London, which you took and sank three years ago off the Statira Shoal ? "

"Curse me if I can bear their names in mind," said Sharkey. "We did as many as ten ships a week about that time."

"There were a mother and two sons among the passengers. Maybe that will bring it back to your mind."

Captain Sharkey leant back in thought, with his huge thin beak of a nose jutting upwards. Then he burst suddenly into a high treble, neighing laugh. He remembered it, he said, and he added details to prove it.

"But burn me if it had not slipped from my mind ! " he cried. "How came you to think of it ? "

"It was of interest to me," said Copley Banks, "for the woman was my wife and the lads were my only sons."

Sharkey stared across at his companion, and saw that the smouldering fire which lurked always in his eyes had burned up into a lurid flame. He read their menace, and he clapped his hands to his empty belt. Then he turned to seize a weapon, but the bight of a rope was cast round him, and in an instant his arms were bound to his side. He fought like a wild cat and screamed for help.

"Ned ! " he yelled. "Ned ! Wake up ! Here's damned villainy ! Help, Ned, help ! "

But the three men were far too deeply sunk in their swinish sleep for any voice to wake them. Round and round went the rope, until Sharkey was swathed like a mummy from ankle to neck. They propped him stiff and helpless against a powder barrel, and they gagged him with a handkerchief, but his filmy, red-rimmed eyes still looked curses at them. The dumb man chattered in his exultation, and Sharkey winced for the first time when he saw the empty mouth before him. He understood that vengeance, slow and patient, had dogged him long, and clutched him at last.

The two captors had their plans all arranged, and they were somewhat elaborate.

First of all they stove the heads of two of the great powder barrels, and they heaped the contents out upon the table and floor. They piled it round and under the three drunken men, until each sprawled in a heap of it. Then they carried Sharkey to the gun and they triced him sitting over the port-hole, with his body about a foot from the muzzle. Wriggle as he would he could not move an inch either to right or left, and the dumb man trussed him up with a sailor's cunning, so that there was no chance that he should work free.

" Now, you bloody devil," said Copley Banks, softly, " you must listen to what I have to say to you, for they are the last words that you will hear. You are my man now, and I have bought you at a price, for I have given all that a man can give here below, and I have given my soul as well.

" To reach you I have had to sink to your level. For two years I strove against it, hoping that some other way might come, but I learnt that there was no other way. I've robbed and I have murdered—worse still, I have laughed and lived with you—and all for the one end. And now my time has come, and you will die as I would have you die, seeing the shadow creeping slowly upon you and the devil waiting for you in the shadow."

Sharkey could hear the hoarse voices of his rovers singing their chanty over the water.

" Where is the trader of Stepney Town ?
Wake her up ! Shake her up ! Every stick a-bending !
Where is the trader of Stepney Town ?
His gold's on the capstan, his blood's on his gown.
All for bully Rover Jack,
Reaching on the weather tack
Right across the Lowland Sea."

The words came clear to his ear, and just outside he

could hear two men pacing backwards and forwards upon the deck. And yet he was helpless, staring down the mouth of the nine-pounder, unable to move an inch or to utter so much as a groan. Again there came the burst of voices from the deck of the barque.

" So it's up and it's over to Stornoway Bay,
Pack it on ! Crack it on ! Try her with the stun-sails !
It's off on a bowline to Stornoway Bay,
Where the liquor is good and the lasses are gay,
Waiting for their bully Jack,
Watching for him sailing back,
Right across the Lowland Sea."

To the dying pirate the jovial words and rollicking tune made his own fate seem the harsher, but there was no softening in his venomous blue eyes. Copley Banks had brushed away the priming of the gun, and had sprinkled fresh powder over the touch-hole. Then he had taken up the candle and cut it to the length of about an inch. This he placed upon the loose powder at the breach of the gun. Then he scattered powder thickly over the floor beneath, so that when the candle fell at the recoil it must explode the huge pile in which the three drunkards were wallowing.

" You've made others look death in the face, Sharkey," said he ; " now it has come to be your own turn. You and these swine here shall go together ! " He lit the candle-end as he spoke, and blew out the other lights upon the table. Then he passed out with the dumb man, and locked the cabin door upon the outer side. But before he closed it he took an exultant look backwards and received one last curse from those unconquerable eyes. In the single dim circle of light that ivory-white face, with the gleam of moisture upon the high, bald forehead, was the last that was ever seen of Sharkey.

There was a skiff alongside, and in it Copley Banks and the dumb steward made their way to the beach, and looked back upon the brig riding in the moonlight just outside the shadow of the palm trees. They waited and waited, watching that dim light which shone through the stern port. And then at last there came the dull thud of a gun, and an instant later the shattering crash of the explosion. The long, sleek, black barque, the sweep of white sand, and the fringe of nodding, feathery palm trees sprang into dazzling light and back into darkness again. Voices screamed and called upon the bay.

Then Copley Banks, his heart singing within him, touched his companion upon the shoulder, and they plunged together into the lonely jungle of the Caicos.

17. *The " Slapping Sal "*

IT was in the days when France's power was already broken upon the seas, and when more of her three-deckers lay rotting in the Medway than were to be found in Brest harbour. But her frigates and corvettes still scoured the ocean, closely followed ever by those of her rival. At the uttermost ends of the earth these dainty vessels, with sweet names of girls or of flowers, mangled and shattered each other for the honour of the four yards of bunting which flapped from the end of their gaffs.

It had blown hard in the night, but the wind had dropped with the dawning, and now the rising sun tinted the fringe of the storm-wrack as it dwindled into the west and glinted on the endless crests of the long, green waves. To north and south and west lay a skyline which was unbroken save by the spout of foam when two of the great Atlantic seas dashed each other into spray. To the east was a rocky island, jutting out into craggy points, with a few scattered clumps of palm trees and a pennant of mist streaming out from the bare, conical hill which capped it. A heavy surf beat upon the shore, and, at a safe distance from it, the British 32-gun frigate *Leda*, Captain A. P. Johnson, raised her black, glistening side upon the crest of a wave, or swooped down into an emerald valley, dipping away to the nor'ard under easy sail. On her snow-white quarter-deck stood a stiff little brown-faced man, who swept the horizon with his glass.

" Mr. Wharton ! " he cried, with a voice like a rusty hinge.

A thin, knock-kneed officer shambled across the poop to him.

" Yes, sir."

" I've opened the sealed orders, Mr. Wharton."

A glimmer of curiosity shone upon the meagre features of the first lieutenant. The *Leda* had sailed with her consort, the *Dido*, from Antigua the week before, and the admiral's orders had been contained in a sealed envelope.

" We were to open them on reaching the deserted island of Sombriero, lying in north latitude eighteen, thirty-six, west longitude sixty-three, twenty-eight. Sombriero bore four miles to the north-east from our port-bow when the gale cleared, Mr. Wharton."

The lieutenant bowed stiffly.. He and the captain had been bosom friends from childhood. They had gone to school together, joined the navy together, fought again and again together, and married into each other's families, but so long as their feet were on the poop the iron discipline of the service struck all that was human out of them and left only the superior and the subordinate. Captain Johnson took from his pocket a blue paper, which crackled as he unfolded it.

" The 32-gun frigates *Leda* and *Dido* (Captains A. P. Johnson and James Munro) are to cruise from the point at which these instructions are read to the mouth of the Caribbean Sea, in the hope of encountering the French frigate *La Gloire* (48), which has recently harassed our merchant ships in that quarter. H.M. frigates are also directed to hunt down the piratical craft known sometimes as the *Slapping Sal* and sometimes as the *Hairy Hudson*, which has plundered the British ships as per margin, inflicting barbarities upon their crews. She is a small brig, carrying ten light guns, with one twenty-

THE " SLAPPING SAL "

four pound carronade forward.   She was last seen upon
the 23rd ult. to the north-east of the island of Sombriero.
"(Signed) JAMES MONTGOMERY
"(*Rear-Admiral*).
" H.M.S. *Colossus*, Antigua."

" We appear to have lost our consort," said Captain
Johnson, folding up his instructions and again sweeping
the horizon with his glass. " She drew away after we
reefed down.   It would be a pity if we met this heavy
Frenchman without the *Dido*, Mr. Wharton.   Eh ? "

The lieutenant twinkled and smiled.

" She has eighteen-pounders on the main and twelves
on the poop, sir," said the captain. " She carries four
hundred to our two hundred and thirty-one.   Captain
de Milon is the smartest man in the French service.
Oh, Bobby boy, I'd give my hopes of my flag to rub
my side up against her ! " He turned on his heel,
ashamed of his momentary lapse. " Mr. Wharton,"
said he, looking back sternly over his shoulder, " get
those square sails shaken out and bear away a point
more to the west."

" A brig on the port-bow," came a voice from the
forecastle.

" A brig on the port-bow," said the lieutenant.

The captain sprang upon the bulwarks and held on
by the mizzen-shrouds, a strange little figure with flying
skirts and puckered eyes.   The lean lieutenant craned
his neck and whispered to Smeaton, the second, while
officers and men came popping up from below and
clustered along the weather-rail, shading their eyes with
their hands—for the tropical sun was already clear of
the palm trees.   The strange brig lay at anchor in the
throat of a curving estuary, and it was already obvious
that she could not get out without passing under the
guns of the frigate.   A long, rocky point to the north
of her held her in.

" Keep her as she goes, Mr. Wharton," said the

195

captain. " Hardly worth while our clearing for action, Mr. Smeaton, but the men can stand by the guns in case she tries to pass us. Cast loose the bow-chasers and send the small-arm men to the forecastle."

A British crew went to its quarters in those days with the quiet serenity of men on their daily routine. In a few minutes, without fuss or sound, the sailors were knotted round their guns, the marines were drawn up and leaning on their muskets, and the frigate's bowsprit pointed straight for her little victim.

" Is it the *Slapping Sal*, sir ? "

" I have no doubt of it, Mr. Wharton."

" They don't seem to like the look of us, sir. They've cut their cable and are clapping on sail."

It was evident that the brig meant struggling for her freedom. One little patch of canvas fluttered out above another, and her people could be seen working like madmen in the rigging. She made no attempt to pass her antagonist, but headed up the estuary. The captain rubbed his hands.

" She's making for shoal water, Mr. Wharton, and we shall have to cut her out, sir. She's a footy little brig, but I should have thought a fore-and-after would have been more handy."

" It was a mutiny, sir."

" Ah, indeed ! "

" Yes, sir, I heard of it at Manilla : a bad business, sir. Captain and two mates murdered. This Hudson, or Hairy Hudson as they call him, led the mutiny. He's a Londoner, sir, and a cruel villain as ever walked."

" His next walk will be to Execution Dock, Mr. Wharton. She seems heavily manned. I wish I could take twenty topmen out of her, but that would be enough to corrupt the crew of the ark, Mr. Wharton."

Both officers were looking through their glasses at the brig. Suddenly the lieutenant showed his teeth in a grin, while the captain flushed a deeper red.

" That's Hairy Hudson on the after-rail, sir."

" The low, impertinent blackguard ! He'll play some other antics before we are done with him. Could you reach him with the long eighteen, Mr. Smeaton ? "

" Another cable length will do it, sir."

The brig yawed as they spoke, and as she came round a spurt of smoke whiffed out from her quarter. It was a pure piece of bravado, for the gun could scarce carry half-way. Then with a jaunty swing the little ship came into the wind again, and shot round a fresh curve in the winding channel.

" The water's shoaling rapidly, sir," repeated the second lieutenant.

" There's six fathoms by the chart."

" Four by the lead, sir."

" When we clear this point we shall see how we lie. Ha ! I thought as much ! Lay her to, Mr. Wharton. Now we have got her at our mercy ! "

The frigate was quite out of sight of the sea now at the head of this river-like estuary. As she came round the curve the two shores were seen to converge at a point about a mile distant. In the angle, as near shore as she could get, the brig was lying with her broadside towards her pursuer and a wisp of black cloth streaming from her mizzen. The lean lieutenant, who had re-appeared upon deck with a cutlass strapped to his side and two pistols rammed into his belt, peered curiously at the ensign.

" Is it the Jolly Roger, sir ? " he asked.

But the captain was furious.

" He may hang where his breeches are hanging before I have done with him ! " said he. " What boats will you want, Mr. Wharton ? "

" We should do it with the launch and the jolly-boat."

" Take four and make a clean job of it. Pipe away the crews at once, and I'll work her in and help you with the long eighteens."

With a rattle of ropes and a creaking of blocks the four

boats splashed into the water. Their crews clustered thickly into them : bare-footed sailors, stolid marines, laughing middies, and in the sheets of each the senior officers with their stern schoolmaster faces. The captain, his elbows on the binnacle, still watched the distant brig. Her crew were tricing up the boarding-netting, dragging round the starboard guns, knocking new port-holes for them, and making every preparation for a desperate resistance. In the thick of it all a huge man, bearded to the eyes, with a red nightcap upon his head, was straining and stooping and hauling. The captain watched him with a sour smile, and then snapping up his glass he turned upon his heel. For an instant he stood staring.

" Call back the boats ! " he cried in his thin, creaking voice. " Clear away for action there ! Cast loose those main-deck guns. Brace back the yards, Mr. Smeaton, and stand by to go about when she has weigh enough."

Round the curve of the estuary was coming a huge vessel. Her great yellow bowsprit and white-winged figure-head were jutting out from the cluster of palm trees, while high above them towered three immense masts with the tricolour flag floating superbly from the mizzen. Round she came, the deep-blue water cream-ing under her fore foot, until her long, curving, black side, her line of shining copper beneath and of snow-white hammocks above, and the thick clusters of men who peered over her bulwarks were all in full view. Her lower yards were slung, her ports triced up, and her guns run out all ready for action. Lying behind one of the promontories of the island, the lookout men of the *Gloire* upon the shore had seen the *cul de sac* into which the British frigate was headed, so that Captain de Milon had served the *Leda* as Captain Johnson had the *Slapping Sal*.

But the splendid discipline of the British service was at its best in such a crisis. The boats flew back ; their crews clustered aboard, they were swung up at the davits and the fall-ropes made fast. Hammocks were brought up and stowed, bulkheads sent down, ports and magazines opened, the fires put out in the galley, and the drums beat to quarters. Swarms of men set the head-sails and brought the frigate round, while the gun-crews threw off their jackets and shirts, tightened their belts, and ran out their eighteen-pounders, peering through the open port-holes at the stately Frenchman. The wind was very light. Hardly a ripple showed itself upon the clear blue water, but the sails blew gently out as the breeze came over the wooded banks. The French-man had gone about also, and both ships were now heading slowly for the sea under fore-and-aft canvas, the *Gloire* a hundred yards in advance. She luffed up to cross the *Leda's* bows, but the British ship came round also, and the two rippled slowly on in such a silence that the ringing of ramrods as the French marines drove home their charges clanged quite loudly upon the ear.

" Not much sea-room, Mr. Wharton," remarked the captain.

" I have fought actions in less, sir."

" We must keep our distance and trust to our gun-nery. She is very heavily manned, and if she got along-side we might find ourselves in trouble."

" I see the shakos of soldiers aboard of her."

" Two companies of light infantry from Martinique. Now we have her ! Hard-a-port, and let her have it as we cross her stern ! "

The keen eye of the little commander had seen the surface ripple, which told of a passing breeze. He had used it to dart across the big Frenchman and to rake her with every gun as he passed. But, once past her, the *Leda* had to come back into the wind to keep out of shoal water. The manœuvre brought her on to the starboard side of the Frenchman, and the trim little frigate seemed to heel right over under the crashing broadside which burst from the gaping ports. A moment

later her topmen were swarming aloft to set her topsails
and royals, and she strove to cross the *Gloire's* bows
and rake her again. The French captain, however,
brought his frigate's head round, and the two rode side
by side within easy pistol-shot, pouring broadsides into
each other in one of those murderous duels which, could
they all be recorded, would mottle our charts with blood.

In that heavy tropical air, with so faint a breeze, the
smoke formed a thick bank round the two vessels, from
which the topmasts only protruded. Neither could see
anything of its enemy save the throbs of fire in the darkness, and the guns were sponged and trained and fired
into a dense wall of vapour. On the poop and the forecastle the marines, in two little red lines, were pouring
in their volleys, but neither they nor the seamen-gunners
could see what effect their fire was having. Nor,
indeed, could they tell how far they were suffering themselves, for, standing at a gun, one could but hazily see
that upon the right and the left. But above the roar of
the cannon came the sharper sound of the piping shot, the
crashing of riven planks, and the occasional heavy thud
as spar or block came hurtling on to the deck. The
lieutenants paced up and down the line of guns, while
Captain Johnson fanned the smoke away with his cocked-
hat and peered eagerly out.

"This is rare, Bobby!" said he, as the lieutenant
joined him. Then, suddenly restraining himself, "What
have we lost, Mr. Wharton?"

"Our main topsail yard and our gaff, sir."

"Where's the flag?"

"Gone overboard, sir."

"They'll think we've struck! Lash a boat's ensign
on the starboard arm of the mizzen cross-jackyard."

"Yes, sir."

A round-shot dashed the binnacle to pieces between
them. A second knocked two marines into a bloody,
palpitating mash. For a moment the smoke rose, and
the English captain saw that his adversary's heavier

metal was producing a horrible effect. The *Leda* was a shattered wreck. Her deck was strewed with corpses. Several of her port-holes were knocked into one, and one of her eighteen-pounder guns had been thrown right back on to her breech, and pointed straight up to the sky. The thin line of marines still loaded and fired, but half the guns were silent, and their crews were piled thickly round them.

" Stand by to repel boarders ! " yelled the captain.

" Cutlasses, lads, cutlasses ! " roared Wharton.

" Hold your volley till they touch ! " cried the captain of marines.

The huge loom of the Frenchman was seen bursting through the smoke. Thick clusters of boarders hung upon her sides and shrouds. A final broadside leapt from her ports, and the mainmast of the *Leda*, snapping short off a few feet above the deck, spun into the air and crashed down upon the port guns, killing ten men and putting the whole battery out of action. An instant later the two ships scraped together, and the starboard bower anchor of the *Gloire* caught the mizzen-chains of the *Leda* upon the port side. With a yell the black swarm of boarders steadied themselves for a spring.

But their feet were never to reach that blood-stained deck. From somewhere there came a well-aimed whiff of grape, and another, and another. The English marines and seamen, waiting with cutlass and musket behind the silent guns, saw with amazement the dark masses thinning and shredding away. At the same time the port broadside of the Frenchman burst into a roar.

" Clear away the wreck ! " roared the captain. " What the devil are they firing at ? "

" Get the guns clear ! " panted the lieutenant. " We'll do them yet, boys ! "

The wreckage was torn and hacked and splintered until first one gun and then another roared into action again. The Frenchman's anchor had been cut away, and the *Leda* had worked herself free from that fatal hug. But now, suddenly, there was a scurry up the shrouds of the *Gloire*, and a hundred Englishmen were shouting themselves hoarse: " They're running ! They're running ! They're running ! "

And it was true. The Frenchman had ceased to fire, and was intent only upon clapping on every sail that he could carry. But that shouting hundred could not claim it all as their own. As the smoke cleared it was not difficult to see the reason. The ships had gained the mouth of the estuary during the fight, and there, about four miles out to sea, was the *Leda's* consort bearing down under full sail to the sound of the guns. Captain de Milon had done his part for one day, and presently the *Gloire* was drawing off swiftly to the north, while the *Dido* was bowling along at her skirts, rattling away with her bow-chasers, until a headland hid them both from view.

But the *Leda* lay sorely stricken, with her mainmast gone, her bulwarks shattered, her mizzen-topmast and gaff shot away, her sails like a beggar's rags, and a hundred of her crew dead and wounded. Close beside her a mass of wreckage floated upon the waves. It was the stern-post of a mangled vessel, and across it, in white letters on a black ground, was painted, " *The Slapping Sal*."

" By the Lord ! it was the brig that saved us ! " cried Mr. Wharton. " Hudson brought her into action with the Frenchman, and was blown out of the water by a broadside ! "

The little captain turned on his heel and paced up and down the deck. Already his crew were plugging the shot-holes, knotting and splicing and mending. When he came back, the lieutenant saw a softening of the stern lines about his eyes and mouth.

" Are they all gone ? "

" Every man. They must have sunk with the wreck."

The two officers looked down at the sinister name,

and at the stump of wreckage which floated in the discoloured water. Something black washed to and fro beside a splintered gaff and a tangle of halliards. It was the outrageous ensign, and near it a scarlet cap was floating.

"He was a villain, but he was a Briton!" said the captain, at last. "He lived like a dog, but, by God, he died like a man!"

18. *A Pirate of the Land*

ONE CROWDED HOUR

THE place was the Eastbourne-Tunbridge road, not very far from the Cross in Hand—a lonely stretch, with a heath running upon either side. The time was half-past eleven upon a Sunday night in the late summer. A motor was passing slowly down the road.

It was a long, lean Rolls-Royce, running smoothly with a gentle purring of the engine. Through the two vivid circles cast by the electric head-lights the waving grass fringes and clumps of heather streamed swiftly like some golden cinematograph, leaving a blacker darkness behind and around them. One ruby-red spot shone upon the road, but no number-plate was visible within the dim ruddy halo of the tail-lamp which cast it. The car was open and of a tourist type, but even in that obscure light, for the night was moonless, an observer could hardly fail to have noticed a curious indefiniteness in its lines. As it slid into and across the broad stream of light from an open cottage door the reason could be seen. The body was hung with a singular loose arrangement of brown holland. Even the long black bonnet was banded with some close-drawn drapery.

The solitary man who drove this curious car was broad and burly. He sat hunched up over his steering-wheel, with the brim of a Tyrolean hat drawn down over his eyes. The red end of a cigarette smouldered under the black shadow thrown by the headgear. A dark ulster of some frieze-like material was turned up in the collar until it covered his ears. His neck was pushed forward from his rounded shoulders, and he seemed, as the car now slid noiselessly down the long sloping road, with the clutch disengaged and the engine running free, to be peering ahead of him through the darkness in search of some eagerly-expected object.

The distant toot of a motor-horn came faintly from some point far to the south of him. On such a night, at such a place, all traffic must be from south to north when the current of London week-enders sweeps back from the watering-place to the capital—from pleasure to duty. The man sat straight and listened intently. Yes, there it was again, and certainly to the south of him. His face was over the wheel and his eyes strained through the darkness. Then suddenly he spat out his cigarette and gave a sharp intake of the breath. Far away down the road two little yellow points had rounded a curve. They vanished into a dip, shot upwards once more, and then vanished again. The inert man in the draped car woke suddenly into intense life. From his pocket he pulled a mask of dark cloth, which he fastened securely across his face, adjusting it carefully that his sight might be unimpeded. For an instant he uncovered an acety-lene hand-lantern, took a hasty glance at his own pre-parations, and laid it beside a Mauser pistol upon the seat alongside him. Then, twitching his hat down lower than ever, he released his clutch and slid downward his gear-lever. With a chuckle and shudder the long, black machine sprang forward, and shot with a soft sigh from her powerful engines down the sloping gradient. The driver stooped and switched off his electric head-lights. Only a dim grey swathe cut through the black heath indicated the line of his road. From in front there came presently a confused puffing and rattling and clanging as the oncoming car breasted the slope. It coughed and spluttered on a powerful, old-fashioned low gear, while its engine throbbed like a weary heart. The yellow, glaring lights dipped for the last time into a switchback curve. When they reappeared over the crest the two cars were within thirty yards of each other. The dark one darted across the road and barred the other's passage, while a warning acetylene lamp was waved in the air. With a jarring of brakes the noisy new-comer was brought to a halt.

" I say," cried an aggrieved voice, " 'pon my soul, you know, we might have had an accident. Why the devil don't you keep your head-lights on ? I never saw you till I nearly burst my radiators on you ! "

The acetylene lamp, held forward, discovered a very angry young man, blue-eyed, yellow-moustached, and florid, sitting alone at the wheel of an antiquated twelve-horse Wolseley. Suddenly the aggrieved look upon his flushed face changed to one of absolute bewilderment. The driver in the dark car had sprung out of the seat, a black, long-barrelled, wicked-looking pistol was poked in the traveller's face, and behind the further sights of it was a circle of black cloth with two deadly eyes looking from as many slits.

" Hands up ! " said a quick, stern voice. " Hands up ! or, by the Lord——"

The young man was as brave as his neighbours, but the hands went up all the same.

" Get down ! " said his assailant, curtly.

The young man stepped forth into the road, followed closely by the covering lantern and pistol. Once he made as if he would drop his hands, but a short, stern word jerked them up again.

" I say, look here, this is rather out o' date, ain't it ? " said the traveller. " I expect you're joking—what ? "

" Your watch," said the man behind the Mauser pistol.

" You can't really mean it ! "

" Your watch, I say ! "

" Well, take it, if you must. It's only plated, anyhow. You're two centuries out in time, or a few thousand miles longitude. The bush is your mark—or America. You don't seem in the picture on a Sussex road."

" Purse," said the man. There was something very compelling in his voice and methods. The purse was handed over.

" Any rings ? "

" Don't wear 'em."

" Stand there ! Don't move ! "

The highwayman passed his victim and threw open the bonnet of the Wolseley. His hand, with a pair of steel pliers, was thrust deep into the works. There was the snap of a parting wire.

" Hang it all, don't crock my car ! " cried the traveller.

He turned, but quick as a flash the pistol was at his head once more. And yet even in that flash, whilst the robber whisked round from the broken circuit, something had caught the young man's eye which made him gasp and start. He opened his mouth as if about to shout some words. Then with an evident effort he restrained himself.

" Get in," said the highwayman.

The traveller climbed back to his seat.

" What is your name ? "

" Ronald Barker. What's yours ? "

The masked man ignored the impertinence.

" Where do you live ? " he asked.

" My cards are in my purse. Take one."

The highwayman sprang into his car, the engine of which had hissed and whispered in gentle accompaniment to the interview. With a clash he threw back his sidebrake, flung in his gears, twirled the wheel hard round, and cleared the motionless Wolseley. A minute later he was gliding swiftly, with all his lights gleaming, some half-mile southward on the road, while Mr. Ronald Barker, a side-lamp in his hand, was rummaging furiously

among the odds and ends of his repair-box for a strand
of wire which would connect up his electricity and set
him on his way once more.

When he had placed a safe distance between himself
and his victim, the adventurer eased up, took his booty
from his pocket, replaced the watch, opened the purse,
and counted out the money. Seven shillings constituted
the miserable spoil. The poor result of his efforts
seemed to amuse rather than annoy him, for he chuckled
as he held the two half-crowns and the florin in the
glare of his lantern. Then suddenly his manner changed.
He thrust the thin purse back into his pocket, released
his brake, and shot onwards with the same tense bearing with which he had started upon his adventure. The
lights of another car were coming down the road.

On this occasion the methods of the highwayman were
less furtive. Experience had clearly given him confidence. With lights still blazing he ran towards the
new-comers, and, halting in the middle of the road,
summoned them to stop. From the point of view of
the astonished travellers the result was sufficiently
impressive. They saw in the glare of their own head-
lights two glowing discs on either side of the long, black-
muzzled snout of a high-power car, and above the masked
face and menacing figure of its solitary driver. In the
golden circle thrown by the rover there stood an elegant,
open-topped, twenty-horse Humber, with an under-
sized and very astonished chauffeur blinking from under
his peaked cap. From behind the wind-screen the veil-
bound hats and wondering faces of two very pretty
young women protruded, one upon either side, and a
little crescendo of frightened squeaks announced the
acute emotion of one of them. The other was cooler
and more critical.

" Don't give it away, Hilda," she whispered. " Do
shut up, and don't be such a silly. It's Bertie or one
of the boys playing it on us."

" No, no ! It's the real thing, Flossie. It's a robber,

sure enough. Oh, my goodness, whatever shall we do?"

"What an ' ad.' ! " cried the other. "Oh, what a glorious ' ad.' ! Too late now for the mornings, but they'll have it in every evening paper, sure."

"What's it going to cost?" groaned the other. "Oh, Flossie, Flossie, I'm sure I'm going to faint! Don't you think if we both screamed together we could do some good? Isn't he too awful with that black thing over his face? Oh, dear, oh, dear! He's killing poor little Alf!"

The proceedings of the robber were indeed somewhat alarming. Springing down from his car, he had pulled the chauffeur out of his seat by the scruff of his neck. The sight of the Mauser had cut short all remonstrance, and under its compulsion the little man had pulled open the bonnet and extracted the sparking plugs. Having thus secured the immobility of his capture, the masked man walked forward, lantern in hand, to the side of the car. He had laid aside the gruff sternness with which he had treated Mr. Ronald Barker, and his voice and manner were gentle, though determined. He even raised his hat as a prelude to his address.

"I am sorry to inconvenience you, ladies," said he, and his voice had gone up several notes since the previous interview. "May I ask who you are?"

Miss Hilda was beyond coherent speech, but Miss Flossie was of a sterner mould.

"This is a pretty business," said she. "What right have you to stop us on the public road, I should like to know?"

"My time is short," said the robber, in a sterner voice. "I must ask you to answer my question."

"Tell him, Flossie! For goodness' sake be nice to him!" cried Hilda.

"Well, we're from the Gaiety Theatre, London, if you want to know," said the young lady. "Perhaps you've heard of Miss Flossie Thornton and Miss Hilda

208

Mannering ? We've been playing a week at the Royal at Eastbourne, and took a Sunday off to ourselves. So now you know ! "

" I must ask you for your purses and for your jewellery."

Both ladies set up shrill expostulations, but they found, as Mr. Ronald Barker had done, that there was something quietly compelling in this man's methods. In a very few minutes they had handed over their purses, and a pile of glittering rings, bangles, brooches and chains was lying upon the front seat of the car. The diamonds glowed and shimmered like little electric points in the light of the lantern. He picked up the glittering tangle and weighed it in his hand.

" Anything you particularly value ? " he asked the ladies ; but Miss Flossie was in no humour for concessions.

" Don't come the Claude Duval over us," said she. " Take the lot or leave the lot. We don't want bits of our own given back to us."

" Except just Billy's necklace ! " cried Hilda, and snatched at a little rope of pearls. The robber bowed, and released his hold of it.

" Anything else ? "

The valiant Flossie began suddenly to cry. Hilda did the same. The effect upon the robber was surprising. He threw the whole heap of jewellery into the nearest lap.

" There ! there ! Take it ! " he said. " It's trumpery stuff, anyhow. It's worth something to you, and nothing to me."

Tears changed in a moment to smiles.

" You're welcome to the purses. The ' ad.' is worth ten times the money. But what a funny way of getting a living nowadays ! Aren't you afraid of being caught ? It's all so wonderful, like a scene from a comedy."

" It may be a tragedy," said the robber.

" Oh, I hope not—I'm sure I hope not ! " cried the two ladies of the drama.

But the robber was in no mood for further conversation. Far away down the road tiny points of light had appeared. Fresh business was coming to him, and he must not mix his cases. Disengaging his machine, he raised his hat, and slipped off to meet this new arrival, while Miss Flossie and Miss Hilda leaned out of their derelict car, still palpitating from their adventure, and watched the red gleam of the tail-light until it merged into the darkness.

This time there was every sign of a rich prize. Behind its four grand lamps set in a broad frame of glittering brasswork the magnificent sixty-horse Daimler breasted the slope with the low, deep, even snore which proclaimed its enormous latent strength. Like some rich-laden, high-pooped Spanish galleon, she kept her course until the prowling craft ahead of her swept across her bows and brought her to a sudden halt. An angry face, red, blotched, and evil, shot out of the open window of the closed limousine. The robber was aware of a high, bald forehead, gross pendulous cheeks, and two little crafty eyes which gleamed between creases of fat.

" Out of my way, sir ! Out of my way this instant ! " cried a rasping voice. " Drive over him, Hearn ! Get down and pull him off the seat. The fellow's drunk —he's drunk, I say ! "

Up to this point the proceedings of the modern highwayman might have passed as gentle. Now they turned in an instant to savagery. The chauffeur, a burly, capable fellow, incited by that raucous voice behind him, sprang from the car and seized the advancing robber by the throat. The latter hit out with the butt-end of his pistol, and the man dropped groaning on the road. Stepping over his prostrate body the adventurer pulled open the door, seized the stout occupant savagely by the ear, and dragged him bellowing on to the highway. Then, very deliberately, he struck him twice across the face with his open hand. The blows rang out like pistol-shots in the silence of the night. The fat traveller turned a ghastly colour and fell back half senseless against the side of the limousine. The robber dragged open his coat, wrenched away the heavy gold watch-chain with all that it held, plucked out the great diamond pin that sparkled in the black satin tie, dragged off four rings—not one of which could have cost less than three figures—and finally tore from his inner pocket a bulky leather note-book. All this property he transferred to his own black overcoat, and added to it the man's pearl cuff-links, and even the golden stud which held his collar. Having made sure that there was nothing else to take, the robber flashed his lantern upon the prostrate chauffeur, and satisfied himself that he was stunned and not dead. Then, returning to the master, he proceeded very deliberately to tear all his clothes from his body with a ferocious energy which set his victim whimpering and writhing in imminent expectation of murder.

Whatever his tormentor's intention may have been, it was very effectually frustrated. A sound made him turn his head, and there, no very great distance off, were the lights of a car coming swiftly from the north. Such a car must have already passed the wreck-age which this pirate had left behind him. It was following his track with a deliberate purpose, and might be crammed with every county constable of the district.

The adventurer had no time to lose. He darted from his bedraggled victim, sprang into his own seat, and with his foot on the accelerator shot swiftly off down the road. Some way down there was a narrow side lane, and into this the fugitive turned, cracking on his high speed and leaving a good five miles between him and any pursuer before he ventured to stop. Then, in a quiet corner, he counted over his booty of the evening —the paltry plunder of Mr. Ronald Barker, the rather better-furnished purses of the actresses, which contained four pounds between them, and, finally, the gorgeous jewellery and well-filled note-book of the plutocrat upon the Daimler. Five notes of fifty pounds, four of ten, fifteen sovereigns, and a number of valuable papers made up a most noble haul. It was clearly enough for one night's work. The adventurer replaced all his ill-gotten gains in his pocket, and, lighting a cigarette, set forth upon his way with the air of a man who has no further care upon his mind.

It was on the Monday morning following upon this eventful evening that Sir Henry Hailworthy, of Walcot Old Place, having finished his breakfast in a leisurely fashion, strolled down to his study with the intention of writing a few letters before setting forth to take his place upon the county bench. Sir Henry was a Deputy-Lieutenant of the county ; he was a baronet of ancient blood ; he was a magistrate of ten years' standing ; and he was famous above all as the breeder of many a good horse and the most desperate rider in all the Weald country. A tall, upstanding man, with a strong clean-shaven face, heavy black eyebrows, and a square, resolute jaw, he was one whom it was better to call friend than foe. Though nearly fifty years of age, he bore no sign of having passed his youth, save that Nature, in one of her freakish moods, had planted one little feather of white hair above his right ear, making the rest of his thick black curls the darker by contrast. He was in thoughtful mood this morning, for having lit his pipe he sat at his desk with his blank note-paper in front of him, lost in a deep reverie.

Suddenly his thoughts were brought back to the present. From behind the laurels of the curving drive there came a low, clanking sound, which swelled into the clatter and jingle of an ancient car. Then from round the corner there swung an old-fashioned Wolseley, with a fresh-complexioned, yellow-moustached young man at the wheel. Sir Henry sprang to his feet at the sight, and then sat down once more. He rose again as a minute later the footman announced Mr. Ronald

Barker. It was an early visit, but Barker was Sir Henry's intimate friend. As each was a fine shot, horseman, and billiard-player, there was much in common between the two men, and the younger (and poorer) was in the habit of spending at least two evenings a week at Walcot Old Place. Therefore, Sir Henry advanced cordially with outstretched hand to welcome him.

" You're an early bird this morning," said he. " What's up ? If you are going over to Lewes we could motor together."

But the younger man's demeanour was peculiar and ungracious. He disregarded the hand which was held out to him, and he stood pulling at his own long moustache and staring with troubled, questioning eyes at the county magistrate.

" Well, what's the matter ? " asked the latter.

Still the young man did not speak. He was clearly on the edge of an interview which he found it most difficult to open. His host grew impatient.

" You don't seem yourself this morning. What on earth is the matter ? Anything upset you ? "

" Yes," said Ronald Barker, with emphasis.

" What has ? "

" *You* have."

Sir Henry smiled. " Sit down, my dear fellow. If you have any grievance against me, let me hear it."

Barker sat down. He seemed to be gathering himself for a reproach. When it did come it was like a bullet from a gun.

" Why did you rob me last night ? "

The magistrate was a man of iron nerve. He showed neither surprise nor resentment. Not a muscle twitched upon his calm, set face.

" Why do you say that I robbed you last night ? "

" A big, tall fellow in a motor-car stopped me on the Mayfield road. He poked a pistol in my face and took my purse and my watch. Sir Henry, that man was you."

The magistrate smiled.

" Am I the only big, tall man in the district ?   Am I the only man with a motor-car ? "

" Do you think I couldn't tell a Rolls-Royce when I see it—I, who spend half my life on a car and the other half under it ?   Who has a Rolls-Royce about here except you ? "

" My dear Barker, don't you think that such a modern highwayman as you describe would be more likely to operate outside his own district ?   How many hundred Rolls-Royces are there in the South of England ? "

" No, it won't do, Sir Henry—it won't do !   Even your voice, though you sunk it a few notes, was familiar enough to me.   But hang it, man !   What did you do it *for* ?   That's what gets over me.   That you should stick up me, one of your closest friends, a man that worked himself to the bone when you stood for the division—and all for the sake of a Brummagem watch and a few shillings—is simply incredible."

" Simply incredible," repeated the magistrate, with a smile.

" And then those actresses, poor little devils, who have to earn all they get.   I followed you down the road, you see.   That was a dirty trick, if ever I heard one.   The City shark was different.   If a chap must go a-robbing, that sort of fellow is fair game.   But your friend, and then the girls—well, I say again, I couldn't have believed it."

" Then why believe it ? "

" Because it *is* so."

" Well, you seem to have persuaded yourself to that effect.   You don't seem to have much evidence to lay before anyone else."

" I could swear to you in a police court.   What put the lid on it was that when you were cutting my wire— and an infernal liberty it was !—I saw that white tuft of yours sticking out from behind your mask."

For the first time an acute observer might have

seen some slight sign of emotion upon the face of the baronet.

" You seem to have a fairly vivid imagination," said he.

His visitor flushed with anger.

" See here, Hailworthy," said he, opening his hand and showing a small, jagged triangle of black cloth. " Do you see that ? It was on the ground near the car of the young women. You must have ripped it off as you jumped out from your seat. Now send for that heavy black driving-coat of yours. If you don't ring the bell I'll ring it myself, and we shall have it in. I'm going to see this thing through, and don't you make any mistake about that."

The baronet's answer was a surprising one. He rose, passed Barker's chair, and, walking over to the door, he locked it and placed the key in his pocket.

" You *are* going to see it through," said he. " I'll lock you in until you do. Now we must have a straight talk, Barker, as man to man, and whether it ends in tragedy or not depends on you."

He had half-opened one of the drawers in his desk as he spoke. His visitor frowned in anger.

" You won't make matters any better by threatening me, Hailworthy. I am going to do my duty, and you won't bluff me out of it."

" I have no wish to bluff you. When I spoke of a tragedy I did not mean to you. What I meant was that there are some turns which this affair cannot be allowed to take. I have neither kith nor kin, but there is the family honour, and some things are impossible."

" It is late to talk like that."

" Well, perhaps it is, but not too late. And now I have a good deal to say to you. First of all, you are quite right, and it was I who held you up last night on the Mayfield road."

" But why on earth——"

"All right. Let me tell it my own way. First I want you to look at these." He unlocked a drawer and he took out two small packages. "These were to be posted in London to-night. This one is addressed to you, and I may as well hand it over to you at once. It contains your watch and your purse. So, you see, bar your cut wire you would have been none the worse for your adventure. This other packet is addressed to the young ladies of the Gaiety Theatre, and their properties are enclosed. I hope I have convinced you that I had intended full reparation in each case before you came to accuse me ? "

"Well ? " asked Barker.

"Well, we will now deal with Sir George Wilde, who is, as you may not know, the senior partner of Wilde and Guggendorf, the founders of the Ludgate Bank of infamous memory. His chauffeur is a case apart. You may take it from me, upon my word of honour, that I had plans for the chauffeur. But it is the master that I want to speak of. You know that I am not a rich man myself. I expect all the county knows that. When Black Tulip lost the Derby I was hard hit. And other things as well. Then I had a legacy of a thousand. This infernal bank was paying 7 per cent. on deposits. I knew Wilde. I saw him. I asked him if it was safe. He said it was. I paid it in, and within forty-eight hours the whole thing went to bits. It came out before the Official Receiver that Wilde had known for three months that nothing could save him. And yet he took all my cargo aboard his sinking vessel. He was all right—confound him ! He had plenty besides. But I had lost all my money and no law could help me. Yet he had robbed me as clearly as one man could rob another, I saw him and he laughed in my face. Told me to stick to Consols, and that the lesson was cheap at the price. So I just swore that, by hook or by crook, I would get level with him. I knew his habits, for I had made it my business to do so. I knew that he came back from

Eastbourne on Sunday nights. I knew that he carried a good sum with him in his pocket-book. Well, it's *my* pocket-book now. Do you mean to tell me that I'm not morally justified in what I have done? By the Lord, I'd have left the devil as bare as he left many a widow and orphan if I'd had the time!"

"That's all very well. But what about me? What about the girls?"

"Have some common sense, Barker. Do you suppose that I could go and stick up this one personal enemy of mine and escape detection? It was impossible. I was bound to make myself out to be just a common robber who had run up against him by accident. So I turned myself loose on the high road and took my chance. As the devil would have it, the first man I met was yourself. I was a fool not to recognize that old ironmonger's store of yours by the row it made coming up the hill. When I saw you I could hardly speak for laughing. But I was bound to carry it through. The same with the actresses. I'm afraid I gave myself away, for I couldn't take their little fal-lals, but I had to keep up a show. Then came my man himself. There was no bluff about that. I was out to skin him, and I did. Now, Barker, what do you think of it all? I had a pistol at your head last night, and, by George! whether you believe it or not, you have one at mine this morning!"

The young man rose slowly, and with a broad smile he wrung the magistrate by the hand.

"Don't do it again. It's too risky," said he. "The swine would score heavily if you were taken."

"You're a good chap, Barker," said the magistrate. "No, I won't do it again. Who's the fellow who talks of ' one crowded hour of glorious life '? By George! it's too fascinating. I had the time of my life! Talk of fox-hunting! No, I'll never touch it again, for it might get a grip of me."

A telephone rang sharply upon the table, and the

baronet put the receiver to his ear. As he listened, he smiled across at his companion.

"I'm rather late this morning," said he, "and they are waiting for me to try some petty larcenies on the county bench."

TALES OF BLUE WATER

19. *The Striped Chest*

"WHAT do you make of her, Allardyce?" I asked.

My second mate was standing beside me upon the poop, with his short, thick legs astretch, for the gale had left a considerable swell behind it, and our two quarter-boats nearly touched the water with every roll. He steadied his glass against the mizzen-shrouds, and he looked long and hard at this disconsolate stranger every time she came reeling up on to the crest of a roller and hung balanced for a few seconds before swooping down upon the other side. She lay so low in the water that I could only catch an occasional glimpse of a pea-green line of bulwark.

She was a brig, but her mainmast had been snapped short off some ten feet above the deck, and no effort seemed to have been made to cut away the wreckage, which floated, sails and yards, like the broken wing of a wounded gull, upon the water beside her. The fore-mast was still standing, but the fore-topsail was flying loose, and the headsails were streaming out in long white pennons in front of her. Never have I seen a vessel which appeared to have gone through rougher handling.

But we could not be surprised at that, for there had been times during the last three days when it was a question whether our own barque would ever see land again. For thirty-six hours we had kept her nose to it, and if the *Mary Sinclair* had not been as good a sea-boat as ever left the Clyde, we could not have gone through. And yet here we were at the end of it with the loss only of our gig and of part of the starboard bulwark. It did not astonish us, however, when the smother had cleared away, to find that others had been less lucky, and that this mutilated brig, staggering about upon a blue sea, and under a cloudless sky, had been left, like a blinded man after a lightning flash, to tell of the terror which is past.

Allardyce, who was a slow and methodical Scotchman, stared long and hard at the little craft, while our seamen lined the bulwark or clustered upon the fore shrouds to have a view of the stranger. In latitude 20° and longitude 10°, which were about our bearings, one becomes a little curious as to whom one meets, for one has left the main lines of Atlantic commerce to the north. For ten days we had been sailing over a solitary sea.

" She's derelict, I'm thinking," said the second mate.

I had come to the same conclusion, for I could see no sign of life upon her deck, and there was no answer to the friendly wavings from our seamen. The crew had probably deserted her under the impression that she was about to founder.

" She can't last long," continued Allardyce, in his measured way. " She may put her nose down and her tail up any minute. The water's lipping up to the edge of her rail."

" What's her flag ? " I asked.

" I'm trying to make out. It's got all twisted and tangled with the halyards. Yes, I've got it now, clear enough. It's the Brazilian flag, but it's wrong side up."

She had hoisted a signal of distress, then, before her people had abandoned her. Perhaps they had only just gone. I took the mate's glass and looked round over the tumultuous face of the deep blue Atlantic, still veined and starred with white lines and spoutings of foam. But nowhere could I see anything human beyond ourselves.

" There may be living men aboard," said I.

" There may be salvage," muttered the second mate.

" Then we will run down upon her lee side, and lie to."

We were not more than a hundred yards from her when we swung our foreyard aback, and there we were, the barque and the brig, ducking and bowing like two clowns in a dance.

" Drop one of the quarter-boats," said I. " Take four men, Mr. Allardyce, and see what you can learn of her."

But just at that moment my first officer, Mr. Armstrong, came on deck, for seven bells had struck, and it was but a few minutes off his watch. It would interest me to go myself to this abandoned vessel and to see what there might be aboard of her. So, with a word to Armstrong, I swung myself over the side, slipped down the falls, and took my place in the sheets of the boat.

It was but a little distance, but it took some time to traverse, and so heavy was the roll, that often, when we were in the trough of the sea, we could not see either the barque which we had left or the brig which we were approaching. The sinking sun did not penetrate down there, and it was cold and dark in the hollows of the waves, but each passing billow heaved us up into the warmth and the sunshine once more. At each of these moments, as we hung upon a white-capped ridge between the two dark valleys, I caught a glimpse of the long, pea-green line, and the nodding foremast of the brig, and I steered so as to come round by her stern, so that we might determine which was the best way of boarding her. As we passed her we saw the name *Nossa Sehnora da Vittoria* painted across her dripping counter.

" The weather side, sir," said the second mate. " Stand by with the boathook, carpenter ! " An instant later we had jumped over the bulwarks, which were hardly higher than our boat, and found ourselves upon the deck of the abandoned vessel.

Our first thought was to provide for our own safety in case—as seemed very probable—the vessel should settle down beneath our feet. With this object two of our men held on to the painter of the boat, and fended her off from the vessel's side, so that she might be ready in case we had to make a hurried retreat. The carpenter was sent to find out how much water there was, and whether it was still gaining, while the other seaman, Allardyce and myself, made a rapid inspection of the vessel and her cargo.

The deck was littered with wreckage and with hencoops, in which the dead birds were washing about. The boats were gone, with the exception of one, the bottom of which had been stove, and it was certain that the crew had abandoned the vessel. The cabin was in a deck house, one side of which had been beaten in by a heavy sea. Allardyce and I entered it, and found the captain's table as he had left it, his books and papers—all Spanish or Portuguese—scattered over it, with piles of cigarette ash everywhere. I looked about for the log, but could not find it.

" As likely as not he never kept one," said Allardyce. " Things are pretty slack aboard a South American trader, and they don't do more than they can help. If there was one it must have been taken away with him in the boat."

" I should like to take all these books and papers," said I. " Ask the carpenter how much time we have."

His report was reassuring. The vessel was full of water, but some of the cargo was buoyant, and there was no immediate danger of her sinking. Probably she would never sink, but would drift about as one of those terrible, unmarked reefs which have sent so many stout vessels to the bottom.

In that case there is no danger in your going below, **Mr. Allardyce**," said I. " See what you can make of her, and find out how much of her cargo may be saved. I'll look through these papers while you are gone."

The bills of lading, and some notes and letters which lay upon the desk, sufficed to inform me that the Brazilian brig *Nossa Sehnora da Vittoria* had cleared from Bahia a month before. The name of the captain was Texeira, but there was no record as to the number of the crew. She was bound for London, and a glance at the bills of lading was sufficient to show me that we were not likely to profit much in the way of salvage. Her cargo consisted of nuts, ginger, and wood, the latter in the shape of great logs of valuable tropical growths. It was these, no doubt, which had prevented the ill-fated vessel from going to the bottom, but they were of such a size as to make it impossible for us to extract them. Besides these, there were a few fancy goods, such as a number of ornamental birds for millinery purposes, and a hundred cases of preserved fruits. And then, as I turned over the papers, I came upon a short note in English, which arrested my attention.

" It is requested," said the note, " that the various old Spanish and Indian curiosities, which came out of the Santarem collection, and which are consigned to Prontfoot and Neuman, of Oxford Street, London, should be put in some place where there may be no danger of these very valuable and unique articles being injured or tampered with. This applies most particularly to the treasure-chest of Don Ramirez di Leyra, which must on no account be placed where anyone can get at it."

The treasure-chest of Don Ramirez! Unique and valuable articles! Here was a chance of salvage after all! I had risen to my feet with the paper in my hand, when my Scotch mate appeared in the doorway.

" I'm thinking all isn't quite as it should be aboard of this ship, sir," said he. He was a hard-faced man, and yet I could see that he had been startled.

" What's the matter ? "

" Murder's the matter, sir. There's a man here with his brains beaten out."

" Killed in the storm ? " said I.

" Maybe so, sir. But I'll be surprised if you think so after you have seen him."

" Where is he, then ? "

" This way, sir ; here in the main-deck house."

There appeared to have been no accommodation below in the brig, for there was the afterhouse for the captain, another by the main hatchway with the cook's galley attached to it, and a third in the forecastle for the men. It was to this middle one that the mate led me. As you entered, the galley, with its litter of tumbled pots and dishes, was upon the right, and upon the left was a small room with two bunks for the officers. Then beyond there was a place about twelve feet square, which was littered with flags and spare canvas. All round the walls were a number of packets done up in coarse cloth and carefully lashed to the woodwork. At the other end was a great box, striped red and white, though the red was so faded and the white so dirty that it was only where the light fell directly upon it that one could see the colouring. The box was, by subsequent measurement, four feet three inches in length, three feet two inches in height, and three feet across—considerably larger than a seaman's chest.

But it was not to the box that my eyes or my thoughts were turned as I entered the store-room. On the floor, lying across the litter of bunting, there was stretched a small, dark man with a short, curling beard. He lay as far as it was possible from the box, with his feet towards it and his head away. A crimson patch was printed upon the white canvas on which his head was resting, and little red ribbons wreathed themselves round his swarthy neck and trailed away on to the floor, but there was no sign of a wound that I could see, and his face was as placid as that of a sleeping child.

It was only when I stooped that I could perceive his

injury, and then I turned away with an exclamation of horror. He had been pole-axed; apparently by some person standing behind him. A frightful blow had smashed in the top of his head and penetrated deeply into his brain. His face might well be placid, for death must have been absolutely instantaneous, and the position of the wound showed that he could never have seen the person who had inflicted it.

"Is that foul play or accident, Captain Barclay?" asked my second mate, demurely.

"You are quite right, Mr. Allardyce. The man has been murdered, struck down from above by a sharp and heavy weapon. But who was he, and why did they murder him?"

"He was a common seaman, sir," said the mate. "You can see that if you look at his fingers." He turned out his pockets as he spoke and brought to light a pack of cards, some tarred string, and a bundle of Brazilian tobacco.

"Hullo, look at this!" said he.

It was a large, open knife with a stiff spring blade which he had picked up from the floor. The steel was shining and bright, so that we could not associate it with the crime, and yet the dead man had apparently held it in his hand when he was struck down, for it still lay within his grasp.

"It looks to me, sir, as if he knew he was in danger, and kept his knife handy," said the mate. "However, we can't help the poor beggar now. I can't make out these things that are lashed to the wall. They seem to be idols and weapons and curios of all sorts done up in old sacking."

"That's right," said I. "They are the only things of value that we are likely to get from the cargo. Hail the barque and tell them to send the other quarter-boat to help us to get the stuff aboard."

While he was away I examined this curious plunder which had come into our possession. The curiosities were so wrapped up that I could only form a general idea as to their nature, but the striped box stood in a good light where I could thoroughly examine it. On the lid, which was clamped and cornered with metal-work, there was engraved a complex coat of arms, and beneath it was a line of Spanish which I was able to decipher as meaning, " The treasure-chest of Don Ramirez di Leyra, Knight of the Order of Saint James, Governor and Captain-General of Terra Firma and of the Province of Veraquas." In one corner was the date 1606, and on the other a large white label, upon which was written in English, " You are earnestly requested, upon no account, to open this box." The same warning was repeated underneath in Spanish. As to the lock, it was a very complex and heavy one of engraved steel, with a Latin motto, which was above a seaman's comprehension.

By the time I had finished this examination of the peculiar box, the other quarter-boat with Mr. Armstrong, the first officer, had come alongside, and we began to carry out and place in her the various curiosities which appeared to be the only objects worth moving from the derelict ship. When she was full I sent her back to the barque, and then Allardyce and I, with a carpenter and one seaman, shifted the striped box, which was the only thing left, to our boat, and lowered it over, balancing it upon the two middle thwarts, for it was so heavy that it would have given the boat a dangerous tilt had we placed it at either end. As to the dead man, we left him where we had found him.

The mate had a theory that, at the moment of the desertion of the ship, this fellow had started plundering, and that the captain in an attempt to preserve discipline, had struck him down with a hatchet or some other heavy weapon. It seemed more probable than any other explanation, and yet it did not entirely satisfy me either. But the ocean is full of mysteries, and we were content to leave the fate of the dead seaman of the Brazilian brig to be added to that long list which every sailor can recall.

The heavy box was slung up by ropes on to the deck of the *Mary Sinclair*, and was carried by four seamen into the cabin, where, between the table and the after-lockers, there was just space for it to stand. There it remained during supper, and after that meal the mates remained with me, and discussed over a glass of grog the event of the day. Mr. Armstrong was a long, thin, vulture-like man, an excellent seaman, but famous for his nearness and cupidity. Our treasure-trove had excited him greatly, and already he had begun with glistening eyes to reckon up how much it might be worth to each of us when the shares of the salvage came to be divided.

" If the paper said that they were unique, Mr. Barclay, then they may be worth anything that you like to name. You wouldn't believe the sums that the rich collectors give. A thousand pounds is nothing to them. We'll have something to show for our voyage, or I am mistaken."

" I don't think that," said I. " As far as I can see they are not very different from any other South American curios."

" Well, sir, I've traded there for fourteen voyages, and I have never seen anything like that chest before. That's worth a pile of money, just as it stands. But it's so heavy, that surely there must be something valuable inside it. Don't you think that we ought to open it and see ? "

" If you break it open you will spoil it, as likely as not," said the second mate.

Armstrong squatted down in front of it, with his head on one side, and his long, thin nose within a few inches of the lock.

" The wood is oak," said he, " and it has shrunk a little with age. If I had a chisel or a strong-bladed knife I could force the lock back without doing any damage at all."

The mention of a strong-bladed knife made me think of the dead seaman upon the brig.

" I wonder if he could have been on the job when someone came to interfere with him," said I.

" I don't know about that, sir, but I am perfectly certain that I could open the box. There's a screw-driver here in the locker. Just hold the lamp, Allardyce, and I'll have it done in a brace of shakes."

"Wait a bit," said I, for already, with eyes which gleamed with curiosity and with avarice, he was stooping over the lid. " I don't see that there is any hurry over this matter. You've read that card which warns us not to open it. It may mean anything or it may mean nothing, but somehow I feel inclined to obey it. After all, whatever is in it will keep, and if it is valuable it will be worth as much if it is opened in the owner's offices as in the cabin of the *Mary Sinclair*."

The first officer seemed bitterly disappointed at my decision.

" Surely, sir, you are not superstitious about it," said he, with a slight sneer upon his thin lips. " If it gets out of our own hands, and we don't see for ourselves what is inside it, we may be done out of our rights ; besides——"

" That's enough, Mr. Armstrong," said I, abruptly. " You may have every confidence that you will get your rights, but I will not have that box opened to-night."

" Why, the label itself shows that the box has been examined by Europeans," Allardyce added. " Because a box is a treasure-box is no reason that it has treasures inside it now. A good many folk have had a peep into it since the days of the old Governor of Terra Firma."

Armstrong threw the screwdriver down upon the table and shrugged his shoulders.

" Just as you like," said he ; but for the rest of the evening, although we spoke upon many subjects, I noticed that his eyes were continually coming round, with the same expression of curiosity and greed, to the old striped box.

And now I come to that portion of my story which fills me even now with a shuddering horror when I think of it. The main cabin had the rooms of the officers round it, but mine was the farthest away from it at the end of the little passage which led to the companion. No regular watch was kept by me, except in cases of emergency, and the three mates divided the watches among them. Armstrong had the middle watch, which ends at four in the morning, and he was relieved by Allardyce. For my part I have always been one of the soundest of sleepers, and it is rare for anything less than a hand upon my shoulder to arouse me.

And yet I was aroused that night, or rather in the early grey of the morning. It was just half-past four by my chronometer when something caused me to sit up in my berth wide awake and with every nerve tingling. It was a sound of some sort, a crash with a human cry at the end of it, which still jarred upon my ears. I sat listening, but all was now silent. And yet it could not have been imagination, that hideous cry, for the echo of it still rang in my head, and it seemed to have come from some place quite close to me. I sprang from my bunk, and, pulling on some clothes, I made my way into the cabin.

At first I saw nothing unusual there. In the cold, grey light I made out the red-clothed table, the six rotating chairs, the walnut lockers, the swinging barometer, and there, at the end, the big striped chest. I was turning away with the intention of going upon deck and asking the second mate if he had heard anything, when my eyes fell suddenly upon something which projected from under the table. It was the leg of a man—a leg with a long sea-boot upon it. I stooped, and there was a figure sprawling upon his face, his arms thrown forward and his body twisted. One glance told me that it was Armstrong, the first officer, and a second

231

that he was a dead man. For a few moments I stood gasping. Then I rushed on to the deck, called Allardyce to my assistance, and came back with him into the cabin.

Together we pulled the unfortunate fellow from under the table, and as we looked at his dripping head we exchanged glances, and I do not know which was the paler of the two.

" The same as the Spanish sailor," said I.

" The very same. God preserve us ! It's that infernal chest ! Look at Armstrong's hand ! " .

He held up the mate's right hand, and there was the screwdriver which he had wished to use the night before.

" He's been at the chest, sir. He knew that I was on deck and you asleep. He knelt down in front of it, and he pushed the lock back with that tool. Then something happened to him, and he cried out so that you heard him."

" Allardyce," I whispered, " what *could* have happened to him ? "

The second mate put his hand upon my sleeve and drew me into his cabin.

" We can talk here, sir, and we don't know who may be listening to us in there. What do you suppose is in that box, Captain Barclay ? "

" I give you my word, Allardyce, that I have no idea."

" Well, I can only find one theory which will fit all the facts. Look at the size of the box. Look at all the carving and metal-work which may conceal any number of holes. Look at the weight of it ; it took four men to carry it. On the top of that, remember that two men have tried to open it, and both have come to their end through it. Now, sir, what can it mean except one thing ? "

" You mean there is a man in it ? "

" Of course there is a man in it. You know how it is in these South American States, sir. A man may be President one week and hunted like a dog the next.

They are for ever flying for their lives. My idea is that there is some fellow in hiding there, who is armed and desperate, and who will fight to the death before he is taken."

"But his food and drink?"

"It's a roomy chest, sir, and he may have some provisions stowed away. As to his drink, he had a friend among the crew upon the brig who saw that he had what he needed."

"You think, then, that the label asking people not to open the box was simply written in his interest?"

"Yes, sir, that is my idea. Have you any other way of explaining the facts?"

I had to confess that I had not.

"The question is what are we to do?" I asked.

"The man's a dangerous ruffian who sticks at nothing. I'm thinking it wouldn't be a bad thing to put a rope round the chest and tow it alongside for half an hour; then we could open it at our ease. Or if we just tied the box up and kept him from getting any water maybe that would do as well. Or the carpenter could put a coat of varnish over it and stop all the blowholes."

"Come, Allardyce," said I, angrily. "You don't seriously mean to say that a whole ship's company are going to be terrorized by a single man in a box. If he's there, I'll engage to fetch him out!" I went to my room and came back with my revolver in my hand. "Now, Allardyce," said I. "Do you open the lock, and I'll stand on guard."

"For God's sake, think what you are doing, sir!" cried the mate. "Two men have lost their lives over it, and the blood of one not yet dry upon the carpet."

"The more reason why we should revenge him."

"Well, sir, at least let me call the carpenter. Three are better than two, and he is a good stout man."

He went off in search of him, and I was left alone with the striped chest in the cabin. I don't think that I'm a nervous man, but I kept the table between me and this solid old relic of the Spanish Main. In the growing light of morning the red and white striping was beginning to appear, and the curious scrolls and wreaths of metal and carving which showed the loving pains which cunning craftsmen had expended upon it. Presently the carpenter and the mate came back together, the former with a hammer in his hand.

" It's a bad business, this, sir," said he, shaking his head, as he looked at the body of the mate. " And you think there's someone hiding in the box ? "

" There's no doubt about it," said Allardyce, picking up the screwdriver and setting his jaw like a man who needs to brace his courage. " I'll drive the lock back if you will both stand by. If he rises let him have it on the head with your hammer, carpenter ! Shoot at once, sir, if he raises his hand. Now ! "

He had knelt down in front of the striped chest, and passed the blade of the tool under the lid. With a sharp snick the lock flew back. " Stand by ! " yelled the mate, and with a heave he threw open the massive top of the box. As it swung up, we all three sprang back, I with my pistol levelled, and the carpenter with the hammer above his head. Then, as nothing happened, we each took a step forward and peeped in. The box was empty.

Not quite empty either, for in one corner was lying an old yellow candlestick, elaborately engraved, which appeared to be as old as the box itself. Its rich yellow tone and artistic shape suggested that it was an object of value. For the rest there was nothing more weighty or valuable than dust in the old striped treasure-chest.

" Well, I'm blessed ! " cried Allardyce, staring blankly into it. " Where does the weight come in, then ? "

" Look at the thickness of the sides and look at the lid. Why, it's five inches through. And see that great metal spring across it."

" That's for holding the lid up," said the mate. " You see, it won't lean back. What's that German printing on the inside ? "

" It means that it was made by Johann Rothstein of Augsburg, in 1606."

" And a solid bit of work, too. But it doesn't throw much light on what has passed, does it, Captain Barclay ? That candlestick looks like gold. We shall have something for our trouble after all."

He leant forward to grasp it, and from that moment I have never doubted as to the reality of inspiration, for on the instant I caught him by the collar and pulled him straight again. It may have been some story of the Middle Ages which had come back to my mind, or it may have been that my eye had caught some red which was not that of rust upon the upper part of the lock, but to him and to me it will always seem an inspiration, so prompt and sudden was my action.

" There's devilry here," said I. " Give me the crooked stick from the corner."

It was an ordinary walking-cane with a hooked top. I passed it over the candlestick and gave it a pull. With a flash a row of polished steel fangs shot out from below the upper lip, and the great striped chest snapped at us like a wild animal. Clang came the huge lid into its place, and the glasses on the swinging rack sang and tinkled with the shock. The mate sat down on the edge of the table and shivered like a frightened horse.

" You've saved my life, Captain Barclay ! " said he.

So this was the secret of the striped treasure-chest of old Don Ramirez di Leyra, and this was how he preserved his ill-gotten gains from the Terra Firma and the Province of Veraquas. Be the thief ever so cunning he could not tell that golden candlestick from the other articles of value, and the instant that he laid hand upon it the terrible spring was unloosed and the murderous steel spikes were driven into his brain, while the shock of the blow sent the victim backwards and enabled the chest to automatically close itself. How many, I wondered, had fallen victims to the ingenuity of the Mechanic of Augsburg. And as I thought of the possible history of that grim striped chest my resolution was very quickly taken.

" Carpenter, bring three men and carry this on deck."

" Going to throw it overboard, sir ? "

" Yes, Mr. Allardyce. I'm not superstitious as a rule, but there are some things which are more than a sailor can be called upon to stand."

" No wonder that brig made heavy weather, Captain Barclay, with such a thing on board. The glass is dropping fast, sir, and we are only just in time."

So we did not even wait for the three sailors, but we carried it out, the mate, the carpenter, and I, and we pushed it with our own hands over the bulwarks. There was a white spout of water, and it was gone. There it lies, the striped chest, a thousand fathoms deep, and if, as they say, the sea will some day be dry land, I grieve for the man who finds that old box and tries to penetrate into its secret.

20. *The Captain of the " Polestar "*

[Being an extract from the singular journal of JOHN M'ALISTER RAY, student of medicine.]

SEPTEMBER 11th.—Lat. 81° 40' N. ; long. 2° E. Still lying-to amid enormous ice-fields. The one which stretches away to the north of us, and to which our ice-anchor is attached, cannot be smaller than an English county. To the right and left unbroken sheets extend to the horizon. This morning the mate reported that there were signs of pack ice to the southward. Should this form of sufficient thickness to bar our return, we shall be in a position of danger, as the food, I hear, is already running somewhat short. It is late in the season, and the nights are beginning to reappear. This morning I saw a star twinkling just over the fore-yard, the first since the beginning of May. There is considerable discontent among the crew, many of whom are anxious to get back home to be in time for the herring season, when labour always commands a high price upon the Scotch coast. As yet their displeasure is only signified by sullen countenances and black looks, but I heard from the second mate this afternoon that they contemplated sending a deputation to the captain to explain their grievance. I much doubt how he will receive it, as he is a man of fierce temper, and very sensitive about anything approaching to an infringement of his rights. I shall venture after dinner to say a few words to him upon the subject. I have always found that he will tolerate from me what he would resent from any other member of the crew. Amsterdam Island, at the north-west corner of Spitzbergen, is visible upon our starboard quarter—a rugged line of volcanic rocks, intersected by white seams, which represent glaciers. It is curious to think that at the present moment there is probably no human being nearer to us than the Danish settlements in the south of Greenland—a good nine hundred miles as the crow flies. A captain takes a great responsibility upon himself when he risks his vessel under such circumstances. No whaler has ever remained in these latitudes till so advanced a period of the year.

9 P.M.—I have spoken to Captain Craigie, and though the result has been hardly satisfactory, I am bound to say that he listened to what I had to say very quietly and even deferentially. When I had finished he put on that air of iron determination which I have frequently observed upon his face, and paced rapidly backwards and forwards across the narrow cabin for some minutes. At first I feared that I had seriously offended him, but he dispelled the idea by sitting down again, and putting his hand upon my arm with a gesture which almost amounted to a caress. There was a depth of tenderness too in his wild dark eyes which surprised me considerably. "Look here, Doctor," he said, "I'm sorry I ever took you—I am indeed—and I would give fifty pounds this

minute to see you standing safe upon the Dundee quay.
It's hit or miss with me this time. There are fish to
the north of us. How dare you shake your head, sir,
when I tell you I saw them blowing from the mast-
head ? "—this in a sudden burst of fury, though I was
not conscious of having shown any signs of doubt.
" Two-and-twenty fish in as many minutes as I am a
living man, and not one under ten foot.[1] Now, Doctor,
do you think I can leave the country when there is only
one infernal strip of ice between me and my fortune ?
If it came on to blow from the north to-morrow we
could fill the ship and be away before the frost could
catch us. If it came on to blow from the south—well,
I suppose the men are paid for risking their lives, and
as for myself it matters but little to me, for I have more
to bind me to the other world than to this one. I confess that I am sorry for *you*, though. I wish I had old
Angus Tait who was with me last voyage, for he was
a man that would never be missed, and you—you said
once that you were engaged, did you not ? "

" Yes," I answered, snapping the spring of the locket
which hung from my watch-chain, and holding up the
little vignette of Flora.

" Curse you ! " he yelled, springing out of his seat,
with his very beard bristling with passion. " What is
your happiness to me ? What have I to do with her
that you must dangle her photograph before my eyes ? "
I almost thought that he was about to strike me in the
frenzy of his rage, but with another imprecation he
dashed open the door of the cabin and rushed out upon
deck, leaving me considerably astonished at his extraordinary violence. It is the first time that he has ever
shown me anything but courtesy and kindness. I can
hear him pacing excitedly up and down overhead as I
write these lines.

I should like to give a sketch of the character of this

[1] A whale is measured among whalers not by the length of
its body, but by the length of its whalebone.

man, but it seems presumptuous to attempt such a thing upon paper, when the idea in my own mind is at best a vague and uncertain one. Several times I have thought that I grasped the clue which might explain it, but only to be disappointed by his presenting himself in some new light which would upset all my conclusions. It may be that no human eye but my own shall ever rest upon these lines, yet as a psychological study I shall attempt to leave some record of Captain Nicholas Craigie.

A man's outer case generally gives some indication of the soul within. The captain is tall and well-formed, with dark, handsome face, and a curious way of twitching his limbs, which may arise from nervousness, or be simply an outcome of his excessive energy. His jaw and whole cast of countenance is manly and resolute, but the eyes are the distinctive feature of his face. They are of the very darkest hazel, bright and eager, with a singular mixture of recklessness in their expression, and of something else which I have sometimes thought was more allied with horror than any other emotion. Generally the former predominated, but on occasions, and more particularly when he was thoughtfully inclined, the look of fear would spread and deepen until it imparted a new character to his whole countenance. It is at these times that he is most subject to tempestuous fits of anger, and he seems to be aware of it, for I have known him lock himself up so that no one might approach him until his dark hour was passed. He sleeps badly, and I have heard him shouting during the night, but his cabin is some little distance from mine, and I could never distinguish the words which he said.

This is one phase of his character, and the most disagreeable one. It is only through my close association with him, thrown together as we are day after day, that I have observed it. Otherwise he is an agreeable companion, well-read and entertaining, and as gallant a seaman as ever trod a deck. I shall not easily forget the way in which he handled the ship when we were caught by a gale among the loose ice at the beginning of April. I have never seen him so cheerful, and even hilarious, as he was that night, as he paced backwards and forwards upon the bridge amid the flashing of the lightning and the howling of the wind. He has told me several times that the thought of death was a pleasant one to him, which is a sad thing for a young man to say ; he cannot be much more than thirty, though his hair and moustache are already slightly grizzled. Some great sorrow must have overtaken him and blighted his whole life. Perhaps I should be the same if I lost my Flora —God knows ! I think if it were not for her that I should care very little whether the wind blew from the north or the south to-morrow. There, I hear him come down the companion, and he has locked himself up in his room, which shows that he is still in an un-amiable mood. And so to bed, as old Pepys would say, for the candle is burning down (we have to use them now since the nights are closing in), and the steward has turned in, so there are no hopes of another one.

September 12th.—Calm, clear day, and still lying in the same position. What wind there is comes from the south-east, but it is very slight. Captain is in a better humour, and apologised to me at breakfast for his rudeness. He still looks somewhat distrait, however, and retains that wild look in his eyes which in a High-lander would mean that he was " fey "—at least so our chief engineer remarked to me, and he has some reputation among the Celtic portion of our crew as a seer and expounder of omens.

It is strange that superstition should have obtained such mastery over this hard-headed and practical race. I could not have believed to what an extent it is carried had I not observed it for myself. We have had a perfect epidemic of it this voyage, until I have felt inclined to serve out rations of sedatives and nerve-tonics with the Saturday allowance of grog. The first symptom of it was that shortly after leaving Shetland the men at the wheel used to complain that they heard plaintive cries and screams in the wake of the ship, as if something were following it and were unable to overtake it. This fiction has been kept up during the whole voyage, and on dark nights at the beginning of the seal-fishing it was only with great difficulty that men could be induced to do their spell. No doubt what they heard was either the creaking of the rudder-chains, or the cry of some passing sea-bird. I have been fetched out of bed several times to listen to it, but I need hardly say that I was never able to distinguish anything unnatural. The men, however, are so absurdly positive upon the subject that it is hopeless to argue with them. I mentioned the matter to the captain once, but to my surprise he took it very gravely, and indeed appeared to be considerably disturbed by what I told him. I should have thought that he at least would have been above such vulgar delusions.

All this disquisition upon superstition leads me up to the fact that Mr. Manson, our second mate, saw a ghost last night—or, at least, says that he did, which of course is the same thing. It is quite refreshing to have some new topic of conversation after the eternal routine of bears and whales which has served us for so many months. Manson swears the ship is haunted; and that he would not stay in her a day if he had any other place to go to. Indeed the fellow is honestly frightened, and I had to give him some chloral and bromide of potassium this morning to steady him down. He seemed quite indignant when I suggested that he had been having an extra glass the night before, and I was obliged to pacify him by keeping as grave a coun- tenance as possible during his story, which he certainly narrated in a very straightforward and matter-of-fact way.

"I was on the bridge," he said, "about four bells in the middle watch, just when the night was at its darkest. There was a bit of a moon, but the clouds were blowing across it so that you couldn't see far from the ship. John M'Leod, the harpooner, came aft from the fo'c'sle-head and reported a strange noise on the starboard bow. I went forrard and we both heard it, sometimes like a bairn crying and sometimes like a wench in pain. I've been seventeen years to the country and I never heard seal, old or young, make a sound like that. As we were standing there on the fo'c'sle-head the moon came out from behind a cloud, and we both saw a sort of white figure moving across the ice-field in the same direction that we had heard the cries. We lost sight of it for a while, but it came back on the port bow, and we could just make it out like a shadow on the ice. I sent a hand aft for the rifles, and M'Leod and I went down on to the pack, thinking that maybe it might be a bear. When we got on the ice I lost sight of M'Leod, but I pushed on in the direction where I could still hear the cries. I followed them for a mile or maybe more, and then running round a hummock I came right on to the top of it standing and waiting for me seemingly. I don't know what it was. It wasn't a bear, anyway. It was tall and white and straight, and if it wasn't a man nor a woman, I'll stake my davy it was something worse. I made for the ship as hard as I could run, and precious glad I was to find myself aboard. I signed articles to do my duty by the ship, and on the ship I'll stay, but you don't catch me on the ice again after sundown."

That is his story, given as far as I can in his own words. I fancy what he saw must, in spite of his denial, have been a young bear erect upon its hind legs, an attitude which they often assume when alarmed. In the uncertain light this would bear a resemblance to a human figure, especially to a man whose nerves were already somewhat shaken. Whatever it may have been, the occurrence is unfortunate, for it has produced a most unpleasant effect upon the crew. Their looks are more sullen than before, and their discontent more open.

The double grievance of being debarred from the herring
fishing and of being detained in what they choose to
call a haunted vessel, may lead them to do something
rash. Even the harpooners, who are the oldest and
steadiest among them, are joining in the general agitation.

Apart from this absurd outbreak of superstition,
things are looking rather more cheerful. The pack
which was forming to the south of us has partly cleared
away, and the water is so warm as to lead me to believe
that we are lying in one of those branches of the gulf-
stream which run up between Greenland and Spitzbergen. There are numerous small Medusæ and
sea-lemons about the ship, with abundance of shrimps,
so that there is every possibility of " fish " being sighted.
Indeed one was seen blowing about dinner-time, but
in such a position that it was impossible for the boats
to follow it.

September 13*th.*—Had an interesting conversation
with the chief mate, Mr. Milne, upon the bridge. It
seems that our captain is as great an enigma to the
seamen, and even to the owners of the vessel, as he
has been to me. Mr. Milne tells me that when the
ship is paid off, upon returning from a voyage, Captain
Craigie disappears, and is not seen again until the approach
of another season, when he walks quietly into the office
of the company, and asks whether his services will be
required. He has no friend in Dundee, nor does anyone pretend to be acquainted with his early history.
His position depends entirely upon his skill as a seaman,
and the name for courage and coolness which he had
earned in the capacity of mate, before being entrusted
with a separate command. The unanimous opinion
seems to be that he is not a Scotchman, and that his
name is an assumed one. Mr. Milne thinks that he
has devoted himself to whaling simply for the reason
that it is the most dangerous occupation which he
could select, and that he courts death in every possible
manner. He mentioned several instances of this, one

of which is rather curious, if true. It seems that on one occasion he did not put in an appearance at the office, and a substitute had to be selected in his place. That was at the time of the last Russian and Turkish War. When he turned up again next spring he had a puckered wound in the side of his neck which he used to endeavour to conceal with his cravat. Whether the mate's inference that he had been engaged in the war is true or not I cannot say. It was certainly a strange coincidence.

The wind is veering round in an easterly direction, but is still very slight. I think the ice is lying closer than it did yesterday. As far as the eye can reach on every side there is one wide expanse of spotless white, only broken by an occasional rift or the dark shadow of a hummock. To the south there is the narrow lane of blue water which is our sole means of escape, and which is closing up every day. The captain is taking a heavy responsibility upon himself. I hear that the tank of potatoes has been finished, and even the biscuits are running short, but he preserves the same impassable countenance, and spends the greater part of the day at the crow's nest, sweeping the horizon with his glass. His manner is very variable, and he seems to avoid my society, but there has been no repetition of the violence which he showed the other night.

7.30 P.M.—My deliberate opinion is that we are commanded by a madman. Nothing else can account for the extraordinary vagaries of Captain Craigie. It is fortunate that I have kept this journal of our voyage, as it will serve to justify us in case we have to put him under any sort of restraint, a step which I should only consent to as a last resource. Curiously enough it was he himself who suggested lunacy and not mere eccentricity as the secret of his strange conduct. He was standing upon the bridge about an hour ago, peering as usual through his glass, while I was walking up and down the quarter-deck. The majority of the men were below at their tea, for the watches have not been regularly kept of late. Tired of walking, I leaned against the bulwarks, and admired the mellow glow cast by the sinking sun upon the great ice-fields which surround us. I was suddenly aroused from the reverie into which I had fallen by a hoarse voice at my elbow, and starting round I found that the captain had descended and was standing by my side. He was staring out over the ice with an expression in which horror, surprise, and something approaching to joy were contending for the mastery. In spite of the cold, great drops of perspiration were coursing down his forehead, and he was evidently fearfully excited. His limbs twitched like those of a man upon the verge of an epileptic fit, and the lines about his mouth were drawn and hard.

" Look ! " he gasped, seizing me by the wrist, but still keeping his eyes upon the distant ice, and moving his head slowly in a horizontal direction, as if following some object which was moving across the field of vision. " Look ! There, man, there ! Between the hummocks ! Now coming out from behind the far one ! You see her—you *must* see her ! There still ! Flying from me, by God, flying from me—and gone ! "

He uttered the last two words in a whisper of concentrated agony which shall never fade from my remembrance. Clinging to the ratlines he endeavoured to climb up upon the top of the bulwarks as if in the hope of obtaining a last glance at the departing object. His strength was not equal to the attempt, however, and he staggered back against the saloon skylights, where he leaned panting and exhausted. His face was so livid that I expected him to become unconscious, so lost no time in leading him down the companion, and stretching him upon one of the sofas in the cabin. I then poured him out some brandy, which I held to his lips, and which had a wonderful effect upon him, bringing the blood back into his white face and steadying his poor shaking limbs. He raised himself up upon his elbow, and looking round to see that we were alone, he beckoned to me to come and sit beside him.

" You saw it, didn't you ? " he asked, still in the same subdued awesome tone so foreign to the nature of the man.

" No, I saw nothing."

His head sank back again upon the cushions. " No, he wouldn't without the glass," he murmured. " He couldn't. It was the glass that showed her to me, and then the eyes of love—the eyes of love. I say, Doc, don't let the steward in ! He'll think I'm mad. Just bolt the door, will you ! "

I rose and did what he had commanded.

He lay quiet for a while, lost in thought apparently, and then raised himself up upon his elbow again, and asked for some more brandy.

" You don't think I am, do you, Doc ? " he asked, as I was putting the bottle back into the after-locker. " Tell me now, as man to man, do you think that I am mad ? "

" I think you have something on your mind," I answered, " which is exciting you and doing you a good deal of harm."

" Right there, lad ! " he cried, his eyes sparkling from the effects of the brandy. " Plenty on my mind— plenty ! But I can work out the latitude and the longitude, and I can handle my sextant and manage my logarithms. You couldn't prove me mad in a court of law, could you, now ? " It was curious to hear the man lying back and coolly arguing out the question of his own sanity.

" Perhaps not," I said ; " but still I think you would be wise to get home as soon as you can, and settle down to a quiet life for a while."

" Get home, eh ? " he muttered, with a sneer upon his face. " One word for me and two for yourself, lad. Settle down with Flora—pretty little Flora. Are bad dreams signs of madness ? "

246

" Sometimes," I answered.

" What else ? What would be the first symptoms ? "

" Pains in the head, noises in the ears, flashes before the eyes, delusions——"

" Ah ! what about them ? " he interrupted. " What would you call a delusion ? "

" Seeing a thing which is not there is a delusion."

" But she *was* there ! " he groaned to himself. " She *was* there ! " and rising, he unbolted the door and walked with slow and uncertain steps to his own cabin, where I have no doubt that he will remain until to-morrow morning. His system seems to have received a terrible shock, whatever it may have been that he imagined himself to have seen. The man becomes a greater mystery every day, though I fear that the solution which he has himself suggested is the correct one, and that his reason is affected. I do not think that a guilty conscience has anything to do with his behaviour. The idea is a popular one among the officers, and, I believe, the crew ; but I have seen nothing to support it. He has not the air of a guilty man, but of one who has had terrible usage at the hands of fortune, and who should be regarded as a martyr rather than a criminal.

The wind is veering round to the south to-night. God help us if it blocks that narrow pass which is our only road to safety ! Situated as we are on the edge of the main Arctic pack, or the " barrier " as it is called by the whalers, any wind from the north has the effect of shredding out the ice around us and allowing our escape, while a wind from the south blows up all the loose ice behind us, and hems us in between two packs. God help us, I say again !

September 14*th*.—Sunday, and a day of rest. My fears have been confirmed, and the thin strip of blue water has disappeared from the southward. Nothing but the great motionless ice-fields around us, with their weird hummocks and fantastic pinnacles. There is a deathly silence over their wide expanse which is horrible.

TALES OF BLUE WATER

No lapping of the waves now, no cries of seagulls or straining of sails, but one deep universal silence in which the murmurs of the seamen, and the creak of their boots upon the white shining deck, seem discordant and out of place. Our only visitor was an Arctic fox, a rare animal upon the pack, though common enough upon the land. He did not come near the ship, however, but after surveying us from a distance fled rapidly across the ice. This was curious conduct, as they generally know nothing of man, and being of an inquisitive nature, become so familiar that they are easily captured. Incredible as it may seem, even this little incident produced a bad effect upon the crew. " Yon puir beastie kens mair, ay, an' sees mair nor you nor me ! " was the comment of one of the leading harpooners, and the others nodded their acquiescence. It is vain to attempt to argue against such puerile superstition. They have made up their minds that there is a curse upon the ship, and nothing will ever persuade them to the contrary.

The captain remained in seclusion all day except for about half an hour in the afternoon, when he came out upon the quarter-deck. I observed that he kept his eye fixed upon the spot where the vision of yesterday had appeared, and was quite prepared for another outburst, but none such came. He did not seem to see me, although I was standing close beside him. Divine service was read as usual by the chief engineer. It is a curious thing that in whaling vessels the Church of England Prayer-book is always employed, although there is never a member of that Church among either officers or crew. Our men are all Roman Catholics or Presbyterians, the former predominating. Since a ritual is used which is foreign to both, neither can complain that the other is preferred to them, and they listen with all attention and devotion, so that the system has something to recommend it.

A glorious sunset, which made the great fields of

ice look like a lake of blood. I have never seen a finer and at the same time more weird effect. Wind is veering round. If it will blow twenty-four hours from the north all will yet be well.

September 15th.—To-day is Flora's birthday. Dear lass ! it is well that she cannot see her boy, as she used to call me, shut up among the ice-fields with a crazy captain and a few weeks' provisions. No doubt she scans the shipping list in the *Scotsman* every morning to see if we are reported from Shetland. I have to set an example to the men and look cheery and unconcerned ; but God knows, my heart is very heavy at times.

The thermometer is at nineteen Fahrenheit to-day. There is but little wind, and what there is comes from an unfavourable quarter. Captain is in an excellent humour ; I think he imagines he has seen some other omen or vision, poor fellow, during the night, for he came into my room early in the morning, and stooping down over my bunk, whispered, " It wasn't a delusion, Doc ; it's all right ! " After breakfast he asked me to find out how much food was left, which the second mate and I proceeded to do. It is even less than we had expected. Forward they have half a tank full of biscuits, three barrels of salt meat, and a very limited supply of coffee beans and sugar. In the after-hold and lockers there are a good many luxuries, such as tinned salmon, soups, haricot mutton, etc., but they will go a very short way among a crew of fifty men. There are two barrels of flour in the store-room, and an unlimited supply of tobacco. Altogether there is about enough to keep the men on half rations for eighteen or twenty days—certainly not more. When we reported the state of things to the captain, he ordered all hands to be piped, and addressed them from the quarter-deck. I never saw him to better advantage. With his tall, well-knit figure, and dark animated face, he seemed a man born to command, and he discussed the situation in a cool sailor-like way which showed that while appreciating the danger he had an eye for every loophole of escape.

"My lads," he said, "no doubt you think I brought you into this fix, if it is a fix, and maybe some of you feel bitter against me on account of it. But you must remember that for many a season no ship that comes to the country has brought in as much oil-money as the old *Polestar*, and every one of you has had his share of it. You can leave your wives behind you in comfort, while other poor fellows come back to find their lassies on the parish. If you have to thank me for the one you have to thank me for the other, and we may call it quits. We've tried a bold venture before this and succeeded, so now that we've tried one and failed we've no cause to cry out about it. If the worst comes to the worse, we can make the land across the ice, and lay in a stock of seals which will keep us alive until the spring. It won't come to that, though, for you'll see the Scotch coast again before three weeks are out. At present every man must go on half rations, share and share alike, and no favour to any. Keep up your hearts and you'll pull through this as you've pulled through many a danger before." These few simple words of his had a wonderful effect upon the crew. His former unpopularity was forgotten, and the old harpooner whom I have already mentioned for his superstition, led off three cheers, which were heartily joined in by all hands.

September 16th.—The wind has veered round to the north during the night, and the ice shows some symptoms of opening out. The men are in a good humour in spite of the short allowance upon which they have been placed. Steam is kept up in the engine-room, that there may be no delay should an opportunity for escape present itself. The captain is in exuberant spirits, though he still retains that wild "fey" expression which I have already remarked upon. This burst of cheerfulness puzzles me more than his former gloom. I cannot understand it. I think I mentioned in an early part of this journal that one of his oddities is that he never permits any person to enter his cabin, but insists upon making his own bed, such as it is, and performing every other office for himself. To my surprise he handed me the key to-day and requested me to go down there and take the time by his chronometer while he measured the altitude of the sun at noon. It is a bare little room, containing a washing-stand and a few books, but little else in the way of luxury, except some pictures upon the walls. The majority of these are small cheap oleographs, but there was one water-colour sketch of the head of a young lady which arrested my attention. It was evidently a portrait, and not one of those fancy types of female beauty which sailors particularly affect. No artist could have evolved from his own mind such a curious mixture of character and weakness. The languid, dreamy eyes, with their drooping lashes, and the broad, low brow, unruffled by thought or care, were in strong contrast with the clean-cut, prominent jaw, and the resolute set of the lower lip. Underneath it in one of the corners was written, " M.B., æt. 19." That anyone in the short space of nineteen years of existence could develop such strength of will as was stamped upon her face seemed to me at the time to be well-nigh incredible. She must have been an extraordinary woman. Her features have thrown such a glamour over me that, though I had but a fleeting glance at them, I could, were I a draughtsman, reproduce them line for line upon this page of the journal. I wonder what part she has played in our captain's life. He has hung her picture at the end of his berth, so that his eyes continually rest upon it. Were he a less reserved man I should make some remark upon the subject. Of the other things in his cabin there was nothing worthy of mention—uniform coats, a camp-stool, small looking-glass, tobacco-box, and numerous pipes, including an oriental hookah—which, by the by, gives some colour to Mr. Milne's story about his participation in the war, though the connection may seem rather a distant one.

11.20 P.M.—Captain just gone to bed after a long and interesting conversation on general topics. When he chooses he can be a most fascinating companion, being remarkably well-read, and having the power of expressing his opinion forcibly without appearing to be dogmatic. I hate to have my intellectual toes trod upon. He spoke about the nature of the soul, and sketched out the views of Aristotle and Plato upon the subject in a masterly manner. He seems to have a leaning for metempsychosis and the doctrines of Pythagoras. In discussing them we touched upon modern spiritualism, and I made some joking allusion to the impostures of Slade, upon which, to my surprise, he warned me most impressively against confusing the innocent with the guilty, and argued that it would be as logical to brand Christianity as an error because Judas, who professed that religion, was a villain. He shortly afterwards bade me good night and retired to his room.

The wind is freshening up, and blows steadily from the north. The nights are as dark now as they are in England. I hope to-morrow may set us free from our frozen fetters.

September 17th.—The Bogie again. Thank Heaven that I have strong nerves! The superstition of these poor fellows, and the circumstantial accounts which they give, with the utmost earnestness and self-conviction, would horrify any man not accustomed to their ways. There are many versions of the matter, but the sum-total of them all is that something uncanny has been flitting round the ship all night, and that Sandie M'Donald of Peterhead and " lang " Peter Williamson of Shetland saw it, as also did Mr. Milne on the bridge —so, having three witnesses, they can make a better case of it than the second mate did. I spoke to Milne after breakfast, and told him that he should be above such nonsense, and that as an officer he ought to set the men a better example. He shook his weather-beaten head ominously, but answered with characteristic caution, " Mebbe, aye, mebbe na, Doctor," he said, " I didna ca' it a ghaist. I canna' say I preen my faith in sea-bogles an' the like, though there's a mony as claims to ha' seen a' that and waur. I'm no easy feared, but maybe your ain bluid would run a bit cauld, mun, if instead o' speerin' aboot it in daylicht ye were wi' me last night, an' seed an awfu' like shape, white an' grue-some, whiles here, whiles there, an' it greetin' and ca'ing in the darkness like a bit lambie that hae lost its mither. Ye would na' be sae ready to put it a' doon to auld wives' clavers then, I'm thinkin'." I saw it was hopeless to reason with him, so contented myself with begging him as a personal favour to call me up the next time the spectre appeared—a request to which he acceded with many ejaculations expressive of his hopes that such an opportunity might never arise.

As I had hoped, the white desert behind us has become broken by many thin streaks of water which intersect it in all directions. Our latitude to-day was 80° 52′ N., which shows that there is a strong southerly drift upon the pack. Should the wind continue favourable it will break up as rapidly as it formed. At present we can do nothing but smoke and wait and hope for the best. I am rapidly becoming a fatalist. When dealing with such uncertain factors as wind and ice a man can be nothing else. Perhaps it was the wind and sand of the Arabian deserts which gave the minds of the original followers of Mahomet their tendency to bow to kismet.

These spectral alarms have a very bad effect upon the captain. I feared that it might excite his sensitive mind, and endeavoured to conceal the absurd story from him, but unfortunately he overheard one of the men making an allusion to it, and insisted upon being informed about it. As I had expected, it brought out all his latent lunacy in an exaggerated form. I can hardly believe that this is the same man who discoursed philosophy last night with the most critical acumen and coolest judgment. He is pacing backwards and forwards upon the quarter-deck like a caged tiger, stopping now and again to throw out his hands with a yearning gesture, and stare impatiently out over the ice. He keeps up a continual mutter to himself, and once he called out, " But a little time, love—but a little time ! " Poor fellow, it is sad to see a gallant seaman and accomplished gentleman reduced to such a pass, and to think that imagination and delusion can cow a mind to which real danger was but the salt of life. Was ever a man in such a position as I, between a demented captain and a ghost-seeing mate ? I sometimes think I am the only really sane man aboard the vessel—except perhaps the second engineer, who is a kind of ruminant, and would care nothing for all the fiends in the Red Sea so long as they would leave him alone and not disarrange his tools.

The ice is still opening rapidly, and there is every probability of our being able to make a start to-morrow morning. They will think I am inventing when I tell them at home all the strange things that have befallen me.

12 P.M.—I have been a good deal startled, though I feel steadier now, thanks to a stiff glass of brandy. I am hardly myself yet, however, as this handwriting will testify. The fact is, that I have gone through a very strange experience, and am beginning to doubt whether I was justified in branding everyone on board as madmen because they professed to have seen things which did not seem reasonable to my understanding. Pshaw ! I am a fool to let such a trifle unnerve me ; and yet, coming as it does after all these alarms, it has an additional significance, for I cannot doubt either Mr. Manson's story or that of the mate, now that I have experienced that which I used formerly to scoff at.

After all it was nothing very alarming—a mere sound, and that was all. I cannot expect that anyone reading this, if anyone ever should read it, will sympathise with my feelings, or realize the effect which it produced upon me at the time. Supper was over, and I had gone on deck to have a quiet pipe before turning in. The night was very dark—so dark that, standing under the quarter-boat, I was unable to see the officer upon the bridge. I think I have already mentioned the extraordinary silence which prevails in these frozen seas. In other parts of the world, be they ever so barren, there is some slight vibration of the air—some faint hum, be it from the distant haunts of men, or from the leaves of the trees, or the wings of the birds, or even the faint rustle of the grass that covers the ground. One may not actively perceive the sound, and yet if it were withdrawn it would be missed. It is only here in these Arctic seas that stark, unfathomable stillness obtrudes itself upon you all in its gruesome reality. You find your tympanum straining to catch some little murmur, and dwelling eagerly upon every accidental sound within the vessel. In this state I was leaning against the bulwarks when there arose from the ice almost directly underneath me a cry, sharp and shrill, upon the silent air of the night, beginning, as it seemed to me, at a note such as prima donna never reached, and mounting from that ever higher and higher until it culminated in a long wail of agony, which might have been the last cry of a lost soul. The ghastly scream is still ringing in my ears. Grief, unutterable grief, seemed to be expressed in it, and a great longing, and yet through it all there was an occasional wild note of exultation. It shrilled out from close beside me, and yet as I glared into the darkness I could discern nothing. I waited some little time, but without hearing any repetition of the sound, so I came below, more shaken than I have ever been in my life before. As I came down the companion I met Mr. Milne coming up to relieve the watch. "Weel, Doctor," he said, " maybe that's auld wives' clavers tae ? Did ye no hear it skirling ? Maybe that's a supersteetion ? What d'ye think o't noo ? " I was obliged to apologise to the honest fellow, and acknowledge that I was as puzzled by it as he was. Perhaps to-morrow things may look different. At present I dare hardly write all that I think. Reading it again in days to come, when I have shaken off all these associations, I should despise myself for having been so weak.

September 18th.—Passed a restless and uneasy night, still haunted by that strange sound. The captain does not look as if he had had much repose either, for his face is haggard and his eyes bloodshot. I have not told him of my adventure of last night, nor shall I. He is already restless and excited, standing up, sitting down, and apparently utterly unable to keep still.

A fine lead appeared in the pack this morning, as I had expected, and we were able to cast off our ice-anchor, and steam about twelve miles in a west-sou'-westerly direction. We were then brought to a halt by a great floe as massive as any which we have left behind us. It bars our progress completely, so we can do nothing but anchor again and wait until it breaks up, which it will probably do within twenty-four hours, if the wind holds. Several bladder-nosed seals were seen swimming in the water, and one was shot, an immense creature more than eleven feet long. They are fierce, pugnacious animals, and are said to be more than a match for a bear. Fortunately they are slow and clumsy in their movements, so that there is little danger in attacking them upon the ice.

The captain evidently does not think we have seen the last of our troubles, though why he should take a gloomy view of the situation is more than I can fathom, since everyone else on board considers that we have had a miraculous escape, and are sure now to reach the open sea.

" I suppose you think it's all right now, Doctor ? " he said, as we sat together after dinner.

" I hope so," I answered.

" We mustn't be too sure—and yet no doubt you are

right. We'll all be in the arms of our own true loves before long, lad, won't we? But we mustn't be too sure—we mustn't be too sure."

He sat silent a little, swinging his leg thoughtfully backwards and forwards. " Look here," he continued ; " it's a dangerous place this, even at its best—a treacherous, dangerous place. I have known men cut off very suddenly in a land like this. A slip would do it sometimes—a single slip, and down you go through a crack, and only a bubble on the green water to show where it was that you sank. It's a queer thing," he continued with a nervous laugh, " but all the years I've been in this country I never once thought of making a will— not that I have anything to leave in particular, but still when a man is exposed to danger he should have everything arranged and ready—don't you think so ? "

" Certainly," I answered, wondering what on earth he was driving at.

" He feels better for knowing it's all settled," he went on. " Now if anything should ever befall me, I hope that you will look after things for me. There is very little in the cabin, but such as it is I should like it to be sold, and the money divided in the same proportion as the oil-money among the crew. The chronometer I wish you to keep yourself as some slight remembrance of our voyage. Of course all this is a mere precaution, but I thought I would take the opportunity of speaking to you about it. I suppose I might rely upon you if there were any necessity ? "

" Most assuredly," I answered ; " and since you are taking this step, I may as well——"

" You ! you ! " he interrupted. " You're all right. What the devil is the matter with you ? There, I didn't mean to be peppery, but I don't like to hear a young fellow, that has hardly began life, speculating about death. Go up on deck and get some fresh air into your lungs instead of talking nonsense in the cabin, and encouraging me to do the same."

The more I think of this conversation of ours the less do I like it. Why should the man be settling his affairs at the very time when we seem to be emerging from all danger ? There must be some method in his madness. Can it be that he contemplates suicide ? I remember that upon one occasion he spoke in a deeply reverent manner of the heinousness of the crime of self-destruction. I shall keep my eye upon him, however, and though I cannot obtrude upon the privacy of his cabin, I shall at least make a point of remaining on deck as long as he stays up.

Mr. Milne pooh-poohs my fears, and says it is only the " skipper's little way." He himself takes a very rosy view of the situation. According to him we shall be out of the ice by the day after to-morrow, pass Jan Meyen two days after that, and sight Shetland in little more than a week. I hope he may not be too sanguine. His opinion may be fairly balanced against the gloomy precautions of the captain, for he is an old and experienced seaman, and weighs his words well before uttering them.

*   *   *   *   *

The long-impending catastrophe has come at last. I hardly know what to write about it. The captain is gone. He may come back to us again alive, but I fear me—I fear me. It is now seven o'clock of the morning of the 19th of September. I have spent the whole night traversing the great ice-floe in front of us with a party of seamen in the hope of coming upon some trace of him, but in vain. I shall try to give some account of the circumstances which attended upon his disappearance. Should anyone ever chance to read the words which I put down, I trust they will remember that I do not write from conjecture or from hearsay, but that I, a sane and educated man, am describing accurately what actually occurred before my very eyes. My inferences are my own, but I shall be answerable for the facts.

The captain remained in excellent spirits after the

conversation which I have recorded. He appeared to be nervous and impatient, however, frequently changing his position, and moving his limbs in an aimless choreic way which is characteristic of him at times. In a quarter of an hour he went upon deck seven times, only to descend after a few hurried paces. I followed him each time, for there was something about his face which confirmed my resolution of not letting him out of my sight. He seemed to observe the effect which his movements had produced, for he endeavoured by an overdone hilarity, laughing boisterously at the very smallest of jokes, to quiet my apprehensions.

After supper he went on to the poop once more, and I with him. The night was dark and very still, save for the melancholy soughing of the wind among the spars. A thick cloud was coming up from the northwest, and the ragged tentacles which it threw out in front of it were drifting across the face of the moon, which only shone now and again through a rift in the wrack. The captain paced rapidly backwards and forwards, and then seeing me still dogging him, he came across and hinted that he thought I should be better below—which, I need hardly say, had the effect of strengthening my resolution to remain on deck.

I think he forgot about my presence after this, for he stood silently leaning over the taffrail and peering out across the great desert of snow, part of which lay in shadow, while part glittered mistily in the moonlight. Several times I could see by his movements that he was referring to his watch, and once he muttered a short sentence, of which I could only catch the one word "ready." I confess to having felt an eerie feeling creeping over me as I watched the loom of his tall figure through the darkness, and noted how completely he fulfilled the idea of a man who is keeping a tryst. A tryst with whom? Some vague perception began to dawn upon me as I pieced one fact with another, but I was utterly unprepared for the sequel.

By the sudden intensity of his attitude I felt that he saw something. I crept up behind him. He was staring with an eager questioning gaze at what seemed to be a wreath of mist, blown swiftly in a line with the ship. It was a dim nebulous body, devoid of shape, sometimes more, sometimes less apparent, as the light fell on it. The moon was dimmed in its brilliancy at the moment by a canopy of thinnest cloud, like the coating of an anemone.

" Coming, lass, coming," cried the skipper, in a voice of unfathomable tenderness and compassion, like one who soothes a beloved one by some favour long looked for, and as pleasant to bestow as to receive.

What followed happened in an instant. I had no power to interfere. He gave one spring to the top of the bulwarks, and another which took him on to the ice, almost to the feet of the pale misty figure. He held out his hands as if to clasp it, and so ran into the darkness with outstretched arms and loving words. I still stood rigid and motionless, straining my eyes after his retreating form, until his voice died away in the distance. I never thought to see him again, but at that moment the moon shone out brilliantly through a chink in the cloudy heaven, and illuminated the great field of ice. Then I saw his dark figure already a very long way off, running with prodigious speed across the frozen plain. That was the last glimpse which we caught of him— perhaps the last we ever shall. A party was organized to follow him, and I accompanied them, but the men's hearts were not in the work, and nothing was found. Another will be formed within a few hours. I can hardly believe I have not been dreaming, or suffering from some hideous nightmare, as I write these things down.

7.30 P.M.—Just returned dead beat and utterly tired out from a second unsuccessful search for the captain. The floe is of enormous extent, for though we have traversed at least twenty miles of its surface, there has been no sign of its coming to an end. The frost has been so severe of late that the overlying snow is frozen as hard as granite, otherwise we might have had the footsteps to guide us. The crew are anxious that we should cast off and steam round the floe and so to the southward, for the ice has opened up during the night, and the sea is visible upon the horizon. They argue that Captain Craigie is certainly dead, and that we are all risking our lives to no purpose by remaining when we have an opportunity of escape. Mr. Milne and I have had the greatest difficulty in persuading them to wait until to-morrow night, and have been compelled to promise that we will not under any circumstances delay our departure longer than that. We propose therefore to take a few hours' sleep, and then to start upon a final search.

September 20th, evening.—I crossed the ice this morning with a party of men exploring the southern part of the floe, while Mr. Milne went off in a northerly direction. We pushed on for ten or twelve miles without seeing a trace of any living thing except a single bird, which fluttered a great way over our heads, and which by its flight I should judge to have been a falcon. The southern extremity of the ice-field tapered away into a long narrow spit which projected out into the sea. When we came to the base of this promontory, the men halted, but I begged them to continue to the extreme end of it, that we might have the satisfaction of knowing that no possible chance had been neglected.

We had hardly gone a hundred yards before M'Donald of Peterhead cried out that he saw something in front of us, and began to run. We all got a glimpse of it and ran too. At first it was only a vague darkness against the white ice, but as we raced along together it took the shape of a man, and eventually of the man of whom we were in search. He was lying face downwards upon a frozen bank. Many little crystals of ice and feathers of snow had drifted on to him as he lay, and sparkled upon his dark seaman's jacket. As we came

up some wandering puff of wind caught these tiny
flakes in its vortex, and they whirled up into the air,
partially descended again, and then, caught once more
in the current, sped rapidly away in the direction of
the sea. To my eyes it seemed but a snow-drift, but
many of my companions averred that it started up in
the shape of a woman, stooped over the corpse and
kissed it, and then hurried away across the floe. I
have learned never to ridicule any man's opinion, however strange it may seem. Sure it is that Captain
Nicholas Craigie had met with no painful end, for there
was a bright smile upon his blue pinched features, and
his hands were still outstretched as though grasping
at the strange visitor which had summoned him away
into the dim world that lies beyond the grave.

We buried him the same afternoon with the ship's
ensign around him, and a thirty-two pound shot at his
feet. I read the burial service, while the rough sailors
wept like children, for there were many who owed much
to his kind heart, and who showed now the affection
which his strange ways had repelled during his lifetime.
He went off the grating with a dull, sullen splash, and
as I looked into the green water I saw him go down,
down, down until he was but a little flickering patch
of white hanging upon the outskirts of eternal darkness.
Then even that faded away, and he was gone. There
he shall lie, with his secret and his sorrows and his
mystery all still buried in his breast, until that great
day when the sea shall give up its dead, and Nicholas
Craigie come out from among the ice with the smile
upon his face, and his stiffened arms outstretched in
greeting. I pray that his lot may be a happier one
in that life than it has been in this.

I shall not continue my journal. Our road to home
lies plain and clear before us, and the great ice-field
will soon be but a remembrance of the past. It will
be some time before I get over the shock produced by
recent events. When I began this record of our voyage

I little thought of how I should be compelled to finish it. I am writing these final words in the lonely cabin, still starting at times and fancying I hear the quick nervous step of the dead man upon the deck above me. I entered his cabin to-night, as was my duty, to make a list of his effects in order that they might be entered in the official log. All was as it had been upon my previous visit, save that the picture which I have described as having hung at the end of his bed had been cut out of its frame, as with a knife, and was gone. With this last link in a strange chain of evidence I close my diary of the voyage of the *Polestar*.

[NOTE by Dr. John M'Alister Ray, senior.—I have read over the strange events connected with the death of the captain of the *Polestar*, as narrated in the journal of my son. That everything occurred exactly as he describes it I have the fullest confidence, and, indeed, the most positive certainty, for I know him to be a strong-nerved and unimaginative man, with the strictest regard for veracity. Still, the story is, on the face of it, so vague and so improbable, that I was long opposed to its publication. Within the last few days, however, I have had independent testimony upon the subject which throws a new light upon it. I had run down to Edinburgh to attend a meeting of the British Medical Association, when I chanced to come across Dr. P——, an old college chum of mine, now practising at Saltash, in Devonshire. Upon my telling him of this experience of my son's, he declared to me that he was familiar with the man, and proceeded, to my no small surprise, to give me a description of him, which tallied remarkably well with that given in the journal, except that he depicted him as a younger man. According to his account, he had been engaged to a young lady of singular beauty residing upon the Cornish coast. During his absence at sea his betrothed had died under circumstances of peculiar horror.]

21. *The Fiend of the Cooperage*

IT was no easy matter to bring the *Gamecock* up to the island, for the river had swept down so much silt that the banks extended for many miles out into the Atlantic. The coast was hardly to be seen

when the first white curl of the breakers warned us of
our danger, and from there onwards we made our way
very carefully under mainsail and jib, keeping the
broken water well to the left, as is indicated on the
chart. More than once her bottom touched the sand
(we were drawing something under six feet at the time),
but we had always way enough and luck enough to carry
us through. Finally, the water shoaled, very rapidly,
but they had sent a canoe from the factory, and the
Krooboy pilot brought us within two hundred yards
of the island. Here we dropped our anchor, for the
gestures of the negro indicated that we could not hope
to get any farther. The blue of the sea had changed
to the brown of the river, and, even under the shelter
of the island, the current was singing and swirling round
our bows. The stream appeared to be in spate, for it
was over the roots of the palm trees, and everywhere
upon its muddy greasy surface we could see logs of
wood and debris of all sorts which had been carried
down by the flood.

When I had assured myself that we swung securely
at our moorings, I thought it best to begin watering
at once, for the place looked as if it reeked with fever.
The heavy river, the muddy, shining banks, the bright
poisonous green of the jungle, the moist steam in the
air, they were all so many danger signals to one who
could read them. I sent the long-boat off, therefore,
with two large hogsheads, which should be sufficient
to last us until we made St. Paul de Loanda. For my
own part I took the dinghy and rowed for the island, for
I could see the Union Jack fluttering above the palms
to mark the position of Armitage and Wilson's trading
station.

When I had cleared the grove, I could see the place,
a long, low, whitewashed building, with a deep verandah
in front, and an immense pile of palm-oil barrels heaped
upon either flank of it. A row of surf boats and canoes
lay along the beach, and a single small jetty projected

into the river. Two men in white suits with red cummer-bunds round their waists were waiting upon the end of it to receive me. One was a large portly fellow with a greyish beard. The other was slender and tall, with a pale pinched face, which was half-concealed by a great mushroom-shaped hat.

" Very glad to see you," said the latter, cordially. " I am Walker, the agent of Armitage and Wilson. Let me introduce Doctor Severall of the same company. It is not often we see a private yacht in these parts."

" She's the *Gamecock*," I explained. " I'm owner and captain—Meldrum is the name."

" Exploring ? " he asked.

" I'm a lepidopterist—a butterfly-catcher. I've been doing the west coast from Senegal downwards."

" Good sport ? " asked the Doctor, turning a slow yellow-shot eye upon me.

" I have forty cases full. We came in here to water, and also to see what you have in my line."

These introductions and explanations had filled up the time whilst my two Krooboys were making the dinghy fast. Then I walked down the jetty with one of my new acquaintances upon either side, each plying me with questions, for they had seen no white man for months.

" What do we do ? " said the Doctor, when I had begun asking questions in my turn. " Our business keeps us pretty busy, and in our leisure time we talk politics."

" Yes, by the special mercy of Providence Severall is a rank Radical, and I am a good stiff Unionist, and we talk Home Rule for two solid hours every evening."

" And drink quinine cocktails," said the Doctor. " We're both pretty well salted now, but our normal temperature was about 103 last year. I shouldn't, as an impartial adviser, recommend you to stay here very long unless you are collecting bacilli as well as butter-flies. The mouth of the Ogowai River will never develop into a health resort."

There is nothing finer than the way in which these outlying pickets of civilization distil a grim humour out of their desolate situation, and turn not only a bold, but a laughing face upon the chances which their lives may bring. Everywhere from Sierra Leone downwards I had found the same reeking swamps, the same isolated fever-racked communities, and the same bad jokes. There is something approaching to the divine in that power of man to rise above his conditions and to use his mind for the purpose of mocking at the miseries of his body.

"Dinner will be ready in about half an hour, Captain Meldrum," said the Doctor. "Walker has gone in to see about it ; he's the housekeeper this week. Meanwhile, if you like, we'll stroll round and I'll show you the sights of the island."

The sun had already sunk beneath the line of palm trees, and the great arch of the heaven above our head was like the inside of a huge shell, shimmering with dainty pinks and delicate iridescence. No one who has not lived in a land where the weight and heat of a napkin become intolerable upon the knees can imagine the blessed relief which the coolness of evening brings along with it. In this sweeter and purer air the Doctor and I walked round the little island, he pointing out the stores, and explaining the routine of his work.

" There's a certain romance about the place," said he, in answer to some remark of mine about the dullness of their lives. " We are living here just upon the edge of the great unknown. Up there," he continued, pointing to the north-east, " Du Chaillu penetrated, and found the home of the gorilla. That is the Gaboon country—the land of the great apes. In this direction," pointing to the south-east, " no one has been very far. The land which is drained by this river is practically unknown to Europeans. Every log which is carried past us by the current has come from an undiscovered country. I've often wished that I was a better botanist

when I have seen the singular orchids and curious-
looking plants which have been cast up on the eastern
end of the island."

The place which the Doctor indicated was a sloping
brown beach, freely littered with the flotsam of the
stream. At each end was a curved point, like a little
natural breakwater, so that a small shallow bay was left
between. This was full of floating vegetation, with a
single huge splintered tree lying stranded in the middle
of it, the current rippling against its high black side.

"These are all from up country," said the Doctor.
"They get caught in our little bay, and then when
some extra freshet comes they are washed out again and
carried out to sea."

"What is the tree?" I asked.

"Oh, some kind of teak, I should imagine, but pretty
rotten by the look of it. We get all sorts of big hard-
wood trees floating past here, to say nothing of the palms.
Just come in here, will you?"

He led the way into a long building with an immense
quantity of barrel staves and iron hoops littered about
in it.

"This is our cooperage," said he. "We have the
staves sent out in bundles, and we put them together
ourselves. Now, you don't see anything particularly
sinister about this building, do you?"

I looked round at the high corrugated iron roof, the
white wooden walls, and the earthen floor. In one
corner lay a mattress and a blanket.

"I see nothing very alarming," said I.

"And yet there's something out of the common, too,"
he remarked. "You see that bed? Well, I intend to
sleep there to-night. I don't want to buck, but I think
it's a bit of a test for nerve."

"Why?"

"Oh, there have been some funny goings on. You
were talking about the monotony of our lives, but I
assure you that they are sometimes quite as exciting as

we wish them to be. You'd better come back to the house now, for after sundown we begin to get the fever-fog up from the marshes. There, you can see it coming across the river."

I looked and saw long tentacles of white vapour writhing out from among the thick green underwood and crawling at us over the broad swirling surface of the brown river. At the same time the air turned suddenly dank and cold.

" There's the dinner gong," said the Doctor. " If this matter interests you I'll tell you about it afterwards."

It did interest me very much, for there was something earnest and subdued in his manner as he stood in the empty cooperage, which appealed very forcibly to my imagination. He was a big, bluff, hearty man, this Doctor, and yet I had detected a curious expression in his eyes as he glanced about him—an expression which I would not describe as one of fear, but rather that of a man who is alert and on his guard.

" By the way," said I, as we returned to the house, " you have shown me the huts of a good many of your native assistants, but I have not seen any of the natives themselves."

" They sleep in the hulk over yonder," the Doctor answered, pointing over to one of the banks.

" Indeed. I should not have thought in that case they would need the huts."

" Oh, they used the huts until quite recently. We've put them on the hulk until they recover their confidence a little. They were all half mad with fright, so we let them go, and nobody sleeps on the island except Walker and myself."

" What frightened them ? " I asked.

" Well, that brings us back to the same story. I suppose Walker has no objection to your hearing all about it. I don't know why we should make any secret about it, though it is certainly a pretty bad business."

He made no further allusion to it during the excellent

dinner which had been prepared in my honour. It appeared that no sooner had the little white topsail of the *Gamecock* shown round Cape Lopez than these kind fellows had begun to prepare their famous pepper-pot —which is the pungent stew peculiar to the West Coast —and to boil their yams and sweet potatoes. We sat down to as good a native dinner as one could wish, served by a smart Sierra Leone waiting boy. I was just remarking to myself that he at least had not shared in the general flight when, having laid the dessert and wine upon the table, he raised his hand to his turban.

" Anyting else I do, Massa Walker ? " he asked.

" No, I think that is all right, Moussa," my host answered. " I am not feeling very well to-night, though, and I should much prefer if you would stay on the island."

I saw a struggle between his fears and his duty upon the swarthy face of the African. His skin had turned of that livid purplish tint which stands for pallor in a negro, and his eyes looked furtively about him.

" No, no, Massa Walker," he cried, at last, " you better come to the hulk with me, sah. Look after you much better in the hulk, sah ! "

" That won't do, Moussa. White men don't run away from the posts where they are placed."

Again I saw the passionate struggle in the negro's face, and again his fears prevailed.

" No use, Massa Walker, sah ! " he cried. " S'elp me, I can't do it. If it was yesterday or if it was to-morrow, but this is the third night, sah, an' it's more than I can face."

Walker shrugged his shoulders.

" Off with you then ! " said he. " When the mail-boat comes you can get back to Sierra Leone, for I'll have no servant who deserts me when I need him most. I suppose this is all mystery to you, or has the Doctor told you, Captain Meldrum ? "

" I showed Captain Meldrum the cooperage, but I did

not tell him anything," said Doctor Severall. "You're looking bad, Walker," he added, glancing at his companion. "You have a strong touch coming on you."

"Yes, I've had the shivers all day, and now my head is like a cannon-ball. I took ten grains of quinine, and my ears are singing like a kettle. But I want to sleep with you in the cooperage to-night."

"No, no, my dear chap. I won't hear of such a thing. You must get to bed at once, and I am sure Meldrum will excuse you. I shall sleep in the cooperage, and I promise you that I'll be round with your medicine before breakfast."

It was evident that Walker had been struck by one of those sudden and violent attacks of remittent fever which are the curse of the West Coast. His sallow cheeks were flushed and his eyes shining with fever, and suddenly as he sat there he began to croon out a song in the high-pitched voice of delirium.

"Come, come, we must get you to bed, old chap," said the Doctor, and with my aid he led his friend into his bedroom. There we undressed him and presently, after taking a strong sedative, he settled down into a deep slumber.

"He's right for the night," said the Doctor, as we sat down and filled our glasses once more. "Sometimes it is my turn and sometimes his, but, fortunately, we have never been down together. I should have been sorry to be out of it to-night, for I have a little mystery to unravel. I told you that I intended to sleep in the cooperage."

"Yes, you said so."

"When I said sleep I meant watch, for there will be no sleep for me. We've had such a scare here that no native will stay after sundown, and I mean to find out to-night what the cause of it all may be. It has always been the custom for a native watchman to sleep in the cooperage, to prevent the barrel hoops being stolen. Well, six days ago the fellow who slept there disappeared, and we have never seen a trace of him since. It was certainly singular, for no canoe had been taken, and these waters are too full of crocodiles for any man to swim to shore. What became of the fellow, or how he could have left the island is a complete mystery. Walker and I were merely surprised, but the blacks were badly scared and queer Voodoo tales began to get about amongst them. But the real stampede broke out three nights ago, when the new watchman in the cooperage also disappeared."

"What became of him ? " I asked.

"Well, we not only don't know, but we can't even give a guess which would fit the facts. The niggers swear there is a fiend in the cooperage who claims a man every third night. They wouldn't stay in the island —nothing could persuade them. Even Moussa, who is a faithful boy enough, would, as you have seen, leave his master in a fever rather than remain for the night. If we are to continue to run this place we must reassure our niggers, and I don't know any better way of doing it than by putting in a night there myself. This is the third night, you see, so I suppose the thing is due, whatever it may be."

"Have you no clue ? " I asked. "Was there no mark of violence, no blood-stain, no footprints, nothing to give a hint as to what kind of danger you may have to meet ? "

"Absolutely nothing. The man was gone and that was all. Last time it was old Ali, who has been wharf-tender here since the place was started. He was always as steady as a rock, and nothing but foul play would take him from his work."

"Well," said I, "I really don't think that this is a one-man job. Your friend is full of laudanum, and come what might he can be of no assistance to you. You must let me stay and put in a night with you at the cooperage."

"Well, now, that's very good of you, Meldrum,"

said he heartily, shaking my hand across the table. " It's not a thing that I should have ventured to propose, for it is asking a good deal of a casual visitor, but if you really mean it——"

" Certainly I mean it. If you will excuse me a moment, I will hail the *Gamecock* and let them know that they need not expect me."

As we came back from the other end of the little jetty we were both struck by the appearance of the night. A huge blue-black pile of clouds had built itself up upon the landward side, and the wind came from it in little hot pants, which beat upon our faces like the draught from a blast furnace. Under the jetty the river was swirling and hissing, tossing little white spurts of spray over the planking.

" Confound it ! " said Doctor Severall. " We are likely to have a flood on the top of all our troubles. That rise in the river means heavy rain up-country, and when it once begins you never know how far it will go. We've had the island nearly covered before now. Well, we'll just go and see that Walker is comfortable, and then if you like we'll settle down in our quarters."

The sick man was sunk in a profound slumber, and we left him with some crushed limes in a glass beside him in case he should awake with the thirst of fever upon him. Then we made our way through the unnatural gloom thrown by that menacing cloud. The river had risen so high that the little bay which I have described at the end of the island had become almost obliterated through the submerging of its flanking peninsula. The great raft of driftwood, with the huge black tree in the middle, was swaying up and down in the swollen current.

" That's one good thing a flood will do for us," said the Doctor. " It carries away all the vegetable stuff which is brought down on to the east end of the island. It came down with the freshet the other day, and here it will stay until a flood sweeps it out into the main stream. Well, here's our room, and here are some books and here is my tobacco pouch, and we must try and put in the night as best we may."

By the light of our single lantern the great lonely room looked very gaunt and dreary. Save for the piles of staves and heaps of hoops there was absolutely nothing in it, with the exception of the mattress for the Doctor, which had been laid in the corner. We made a couple of seats and a table out of the staves, and settled down together for a long vigil. Severall had brought a revolver for me and was himself armed with a double-barrelled shot-gun. We loaded our weapons and laid them cocked within reach of our hands. The little circle of light and the black shadows arching over us were so melancholy that he went off to the house, and returned with two candles. One side of the cooperage was pierced, however, by several open windows, and it was only by screening our lights behind staves that we could prevent them from being extinguished.

The Doctor, who appeared to be a man of iron nerves, had settled down to a book, but I observed that every now and then he laid it upon his knee, and took an earnest look all round him. For my part, although I tried once or twice to read, I found it impossible to concentrate my thoughts upon the book. They would would always wander back to this great empty silent room, and to the sinister mystery which overshadowed it. I racked my brains for some possible theory which would explain the disappearance of these two men. There was the black fact that they were gone, and not the least tittle of evidence as to why or whither. And here we were waiting in the same place—waiting without an idea as to what we were waiting for. I was right in saying that it was not a one-man job. It was trying enough as it was, but no force upon earth would have kept me there without a comrade.

What an endless, tedious night it was ! Outside we

heard the lapping and gurgling of the great river, and
the soughing of the rising wind. Within, save for our
breathing, the turning of the Doctor's pages, and the
high, shrill ping of an occasional mosquito, there was
a heavy silence. Once my heart sprang into my mouth
as Severall's book suddenly fell to the ground and he
sprang to his feet with his eyes on one of the windows.

" Did you see anything, Meldrum ? "

" No, did you ? "

" Well, I had a vague sense of movement outside
that window." He caught up his gun and approached
it. " No, there's nothing to be seen, and yet I could
have sworn that something passed slowly across it."

" A palm leaf, perhaps," said I, for the wind was
growing stronger every instant.

" Very likely," said he, and settled down to his book
again, but his eyes were for ever darting little suspicious
glances up at the window. I watched it also, but all
was quiet outside.

And then suddenly our thoughts were turned into a
new direction by the bursting of the storm. A blinding
flash was followed by a clap which shook the building.
Again and again came the vivid white glare with thunder
at the same instant, like the flash and roar of a monstrous
piece of artillery. And then down came the tropical
rain, crashing and rattling on the corrugated iron roofing
of the cooperage. The big hollow room boomed like
a drum. From the darkness arose a strange mixture
of noises, a gurgling, splashing, tinkling, bubbling,
washing, dripping—every liquid sound that nature can
produce from the thrashing and swishing of the rain
to the deep steady boom of the river. Hour after hour
the uproar grew louder and more sustained.

" My word," said Severall, " we are going to have
the father of all the floods this time. Well, here's the
dawn coming at last and that is a blessing. We've about
exploded the third night superstition, anyhow."

A grey light was stealing through the room, and there

was the day upon us in an instant. The rain had eased off, but the coffee-coloured river was roaring past like a waterfall. Its power made me fear for the anchor of the *Gamecock*.

" I must get aboard," said I. " If she drags she'll never be able to beat up the river again."

" The island is as good as a breakwater," the Doctor answered. " I can give you a cup of coffee if you will come up to the house."

I was chilled and miserable, so the suggestion was a welcome one. We left the ill-omened cooperage with its mystery still unsolved, and we splashed our way up to the house.

" There's the spirit lamp," said Severall. " If you would just put a light to it, I will see how Walker feels this morning."

He left me, but was back in an instant with a dreadful face.

" He's gone ! " he cried hoarsely.

The words sent a thrill of horror through me. I stood with the lamp in my hand, glaring at him.

" Yes, he's gone ! " he repeated. " Come and look ! "

I followed him without a word, and the first thing that I saw as I entered the bedroom was Walker himself lying huddled on his bed in the grey flannel sleeping suit in which I had helped to dress him on the night before.

" Not dead, surely ! " I gasped.

The Doctor was terribly agitated. His hands were shaking like leaves in the wind.

" He's been dead some hours."

" Was it fever ? "

" Fever ! Look at his foot ! "

I glanced down and a cry of horror burst from my lips. One foot was not merely dislocated, but was turned completely round in a most grotesque contortion.

" Good God ! " I cried. " What can have done this ? "

Severall had laid his hand upon the dead man's chest.

" Feel here," he whispered.

I placed my hand at the same spot. There was no resistance. The body was absolutely soft and limp. It was like pressing a sawdust doll.

" The breast-bone is gone," said Severall in the same awed whisper. " He's broken to bits. Thank God that he had the laudanum. You can see by his face that he died in his sleep."

" But who can have done this ? "

" I've had about as much as I can stand," said the Doctor, wiping his forehead. " I don't know that I'm a greater coward than my neighbours, but this gets beyond me. If you're going out to the *Gamecock*——"

" Come on ! " said I, and off we started. If we did not run it was because each of us wished to keep up the last shadow of his self-respect before the other. It was dangerous in a light canoe on that swollen river, but we never paused to give the matter a thought. He bailing and I paddling we kept her above water, and gained the deck of the yacht. There, with two hundred yards of water between us and this cursed island we felt that we were our own men once more.

" We'll go back in an hour or so," said he. " But we need have a little time to steady ourselves. I wouldn't have had the niggers see me as I was just now for a year's salary."

" I've told the steward to prepare breakfast. Then we shall go back," said I. " But in God's name, Doctor Severall, what do you make of it all ? "

" It beats me—beats me clean. I've heard of Voodoo devilry, and I've laughed at it with the others. But that poor old Walker, a decent, God-fearing, nineteenth-century, Primrose-League Englishman should go under like this without a whole bone in his body—it's given me a shake, I won't deny it. But look there, Meldrum, is that hand of yours mad or drunk, or what is it ? "

Old Patterson, the oldest man of my crew, and as steady as the Pyramids, had been stationed in the bows with a boat-hook to fend off the drifting logs which came sweeping down with the current. Now he stood with crooked knees, glaring out in front of him, and one forefinger stabbing furiously at the air.

" Look at it ! " he yelled. " Look at it ! "

And at the same instant we saw it.

A huge black tree trunk was coming down the river, its broad glistening back just lapped by the water. And in front of it—about three feet in front—arching upwards like the figure-head of a ship, there hung a dreadful face, swaying slowly from side to side. It was flattened, malignant, as large as a small beer-barrel, of a faded fungoid colour, but the neck which supported it was mottled with a dull yellow and black. As it flew past the *Gamecock* in the swirl of the waters I saw two immense coils roll up out of some great hollow in the tree, and the villainous head rose suddenly to the height of eight or ten feet, looking with dull, skin-covered eyes at the yacht. An instant later the tree had shot past us and was plunging with its horrible passenger towards the Atlantic.

" What was it ? " I cried.

" It is our fiend of the cooperage," said Doctor Severall, and he had become in an instant the same bluff, self-confident man that he had been before. " Yes, that is the devil who has been haunting our island. It is the great python of the Gaboon."

I thought of the stories which I had heard all down the coast of the monstrous constrictors of the interior, of their periodical appetite, and of the murderous effects of their deadly squeeze. Then it all took shape in my mind. There had been a freshet the week before. It had brought down this huge hollow tree with its hideous occupant. Who knows from what far distant tropical forest it may have come ! It had been stranded on the little east bay of the island. The cooperage had been the nearest house. Twice with the return of its appetite it had carried off the watchman. Last night it had doubtless come again, when Severall had thought he saw something move at the window, but our lights had driven it away. It had writhed onwards and had slain poor Walker in his sleep.

" Why did it not carry him off ? " I asked.

" The thunder and lightning must have scared the brute away. There's your steward, Meldrum. The sooner we have breakfast and get back to the island the better, or some of those niggers might think that we had been frightened."

22. *Jelland's Voyage*

"WELL," said our Anglo-Jap as we all drew up our chairs round the smoking-room fire, " it's an old tale out yonder, and may have spilt over into print for all I know. I don't want to turn this club-room into a chestnut stall, but it is a long way to the Yellow Sea, and it is just as likely that none of you have ever heard of the yawl *Matilda*, and of what happened to Henry Jelland and Willy McEvoy aboard of her.

" The middle of the 'sixties was a stirring time out in Japan. That was just after the Simonosaki bombardment, and before the Daimio affair. There was a Tory party and there was a Liberal party among the natives, and the question that they were wrangling over was whether the throats of the foreigners should be cut or not. I tell you all, politics have been tame to me since then. If you lived in a treaty port, you were bound to wake up and take an interest in them. And to make it better, the outsider had no way of knowing how the game was going. If the opposition won it would not be a newspaper paragraph that would tell him of it, but a good old Tory in a suit of chain mail, with a sword in each hand, would drop in and let him know all about it in a single upper cut.

" Of course it makes men reckless when they are living on the edge of a volcano like that. Just at first they are very jumpy, and then there comes a time when they learn to enjoy life while they have it. I tell you there's nothing makes life so beautiful as when the shadow of death begins to fall across it. Time is too precious to be dawdled away then, and a man lives every minute of it. That was the way with us in Yokohama. There were many European places of business which had to go on running, and the men who worked them made the place lively for seven nights in the week.

" One of the heads of the European colony was Randolph Moore, the big export merchant. His offices were in Yokohama, but he spent a good deal of his time at his house up in Jeddo, which had only just been opened to the trade. In his absence he used to leave his affairs in the hands of his head clerk, Jelland, whom he knew to be a man of great energy and resolution. But energy and resolution are two-edged things, you know, and when they are used against you you don't appreciate them so much.

" It was gambling that set Jelland wrong. He was a little dark-eyed fellow with black curly hair—more than three-quarters Celt, I should imagine. Every night in the week you would see him in the same place, on the left-hand side of the croupier at Matheson's *rouge et noir* table. For a long time he won, and lived in better style than his employer. And then came a turn of luck, and he began to lose so that at the end of a single week his partner and he were stone broke, without a dollar to their names.

" This partner was a clerk in the employ of the same firm—a tall, straw-haired young Englishman called McEvoy. He was a good boy enough at the start, but he was clay in the hands of Jelland, who fashioned him into a kind of weak model of himself. They were for

279

ever on the prowl together, but it was Jelland who led
and McEvoy who followed. Lynch and I and one or
two others tried to show the youngster that he could
come to no good along that line, and when we were
talking to him we could win him round easily enough,
but five minutes of Jelland would swing him back again.
It may have been animal magnetism or what you like,
but the little man could pull the big one along like a
sixty-foot tug in front of a full-rigged ship. Even
when they had lost all their money they would still take
their places at the table and look on with shining eyes
when anyone else was raking in the stamps.

"But one evening they could keep out of it no longer.
Red had turned up sixteen times running, and it was
more than Jelland could bear. He whispered to McEvoy,
and then said a word to the croupier.

"'Certainly, Mr. Jelland; your cheque is as good as
notes,'. said he.

"Jelland scribbled a cheque and threw it on the
black. The card was the king of hearts, and the croupier
raked in the little bit of paper. Jelland grew angry,
and McEvoy white. Another and a heavier cheque
was written and thrown on the table. The card was
the nine of diamonds. McEvoy leaned his head upon
his hands and looked as if he would faint. 'By God!'
growled Jelland, 'I won't be beat,' and he threw on
a cheque that covered the other two. The card was
the deuce of hearts. A few minutes later they were
walking down the Bund, with the cool night-air playing
upon their fevered faces.

"'Of course you know what this means,' said Jelland,
lighting a cheroot; 'we'll have to transfer some of the
office money to our current account. There's no occasion to make a fuss over it. Old Moore won't look
over the books before Easter. If we have any luck,
we can easily replace it before then.'

"'But if we have no luck?' faltered McEvoy.

"'Tut, man, we must take things as they come.

You stick to me, and I'll stick to you, and we'll pull through together. You shall sign the cheques to-morrow night, and we shall see if your luck is better than mine.'

" But if anything it was worse. When the pair rose from the table on the following evening, they had spent over £5,000 of their employer's money. But the resolute Jelland was as sanguine as ever.

" ' We have a good nine weeks before us before the books will be examined,' said he. ' We must play the game out, and it will all come straight.'

" McEvoy returned to his rooms that night in an agony of shame and remorse. When he was with Jelland he borrowed strength from him ; but alone he recognized the full danger of his position, and the vision of his old white-capped mother in England, who had been so proud when he had received his appointment, rose up before him to fill him with loathing and madness. He was still tossing upon his sleepless couch when his Japanese servant entered the bedroom. For an instant McEvoy thought that the long-expected outbreak had come, and plunged for his revolver. Then, with his heart in his mouth, he listened to the message which the servant had brought.

" Jelland was downstairs, and wanted to see him.

" What on earth could he want at that hour of night ? McEvoy dressed hurriedly and rushed downstairs. His companion, with a set smile upon his lips, which was belied by the ghastly pallor of his face, was sitting in the dim light of a solitary candle, with a slip of paper in his hands.

" ' Sorry to knock you up, Willy,' said he. ' No eavesdroppers, I suppose ? '

" McEvoy shook his head. He could not trust himself to speak.

" ' Well, then, our little game is played out. This note was waiting for me at home. It is from Moore, and says that he will be down on Monday morning for an examination of the books. It leaves us in a tight place.'

" ' Monday ! ' gasped McEvoy ; ' tc-day is Friday.'

" ' Saturday, my son, and 3 a.m. We have not much time to turn round in.'

" ' We are lost ! ' screamed McEvoy.

" ' We soon will be, if you make such an infernal row,' said Jelland harshly. ' Now do what I tell you, Willy, and we'll pull through yet.'

" ' I will do anything—anything.'

" ' That's better. Where's your whisky ? It's a beastly time of the day to have to get your back stiff, but there must be no softness with us, or we are gone. First of all, I think there is something due to our relations, don't you ? '

" McEvoy stared.

" ' We must stand or fall together, you know. Now I, for one, don't intend to set my foot inside a felon's dock under any circumstances. D'ye see ? I'm ready to swear to that. Are you ? '

" ' What d'you mean ? ' asked McEvoy, shrinking back.

" ' Why, man, we all have to die, and it's only the pressing of a trigger. I swear that I shall never be taken alive. Will you ? If you don't, I leave you to your fate.'

" ' All right. I'll do whatever you think best.'

" ' You swear it ? '

" ' Yes.'

" ' Well, mind, you must be as good as your word. Now we have two clear days to get off in. The yawl *Matilda* is on sale, and she has all her fixings and plenty of tinned stuff aboard. We'll buy the lot to-morrow morning, and whatever we want, and get away in her. But, first, we'll clear all that is left in the office. There are 5,000 sovereigns in the safe. After dark we'll get them aboard the yawl, and take our chance of reaching California. There's no use hesitating, my son, for we have no ghost of a look-in in any other direction. It's that or nothing.'

" ' I'll do what you advise.'

" ' All right ; and mind you get a bright face on you
to-morrow, for if Moore gets the tip and comes before
Monday, then——' He tapped the side-pocket of his
coat and looked across at his partner with eyes that were
full of a sinister meaning.

" All went well with their plans next day. The
Matilda was bought without difficulty ; and, though
she was a tiny craft for so long a voyage, had she been
larger two men could not have hoped to manage her.
She was stocked with water during the day, and after
dark the two clerks brought down the money from the
office and stowed it in the hold. Before midnight they
had collected all their own possessions without exciting
suspicion, and at two in the morning they left their
moorings and stole quietly out from among the shipping.
They were seen, of course, and were set down as keen
yachtsmen who were on for a good long Sunday cruise ;
but there was no one who dreamed that that cruise would
only end either on the American coast or at the bottom
of the North Pacific Ocean. Straining and hauling,
they got their mainsail up and set their foresail and jib.
There was a slight breeze from the south-east, and the
little craft went dipping along upon her way. Seven
miles from land, however, the wind fell away and they
lay becalmed, rising and falling on the long swell
of a glassy sea. All Sunday they did not make a
mile, and in the evening Yokohama still lay along the
horizon.

" On Monday morning down came Randolph Moore
from Jeddo, and made straight for the offices. He had
had the tip from someone that his clerks had been
spreading themselves a bit, and that had made him
come down out of his usual routine ; but when he reached
his place and found the three juniors waiting in the
street with their hands in their pockets he knew that the
matter was serious.

" ' What's this ? ' he asked. He was a man of action,

and a nasty chap to deal with when he had his topmasts lowered.

" ' We can't get in,' said the clerks.

" ' Where is Mr. Jelland ? '

" ' He has not come to-day.'

" ' And Mr. McEvoy ? '

" ' He has not come either.'

" Randolph Moore looked serious. ' We must have the door down,' said he.

" They don't build houses very solid in that land of earthquakes, and in a brace of shakes they were all in the office. Of course the thing told its own story. The safe was open, the money gone, and the clerks fled. Their employer lost no time in talk.

" ' Where were they seen last ? '

" ' On Saturday they bought the *Matilda* and started for a cruise.'

" Saturday ! The matter seemed hopeless if they had got two days' start. But there was still the shadow of a chance. He rushed to the beach and swept the ocean with his glasses.

" ' My God ! ' he cried. ' There's the *Matilda* out yonder. I know her by the rake of her mast. I have my hand upon the villains after all ! '

" But there was a hitch even then. No boat had steam up, and the eager merchant had not patience to wait. Clouds were banking up along the haunch of the hills, and there was every sign of an approaching change of weather. A police boat was ready with ten armed men in her, and Randolph Moore himself took the tiller as she shot out in pursuit of the becalmed yawl.

" Jelland and McEvoy, waiting wearily for the breeze which never came, saw the dark speck which sprang out from the shadow of the land and grew larger with every swish of the oars. As she drew nearer, they could see also that she was packed with men, and the gleam of weapons told what manner of men they were. Jelland stood leaning against the tiller, and he looked at the threatening sky, the limp sails, and the approaching boat.

" ' It's a case with us, Willy,' said he. ' By the Lord, we are two most unlucky devils, for there's wind in that sky, and another hour would have brought it to us.'

" McEvoy groaned.

" ' There's no good softening over it, my lad,' said Jelland. ' It's the police boat right enough, and there's old Moore driving them to row like hell. It'll be a ten-dollar job for every man of them.'

" Willy McEvoy crouched against the side with his knees on the deck. ' My mother ! my poor old mother ! ' he sobbed.

" ' She'll never hear that you have been in the dock anyway,' said Jelland. ' My people never did much for me, but I will do that much for them. It's no good, Mac. We can chuck our hands. God bless you, old man ! Here's the pistol ! '

" He cocked the revolver, and held the butt towards the youngster. But the other shrank away from it with little gasps and cries. Jelland glanced at the approaching boat. · It was not more than a few hundred yards away.

" ' There's no time for nonsense,' said he. ' Damn it ! man, what's the use of flinching ? You swore it ! '

" ' No, no, Jelland ! '

" ' Well, anyhow, I swore that neither of us should be taken. Will you do it ? '

" ' I can't ! I can't ! '

" ' Then I will for you.'

" The rowers in the boat saw him lean forwards, they heard two pistol shots, they saw him double himself across the tiller, and then, before the smoke had lifted, they found that they had something else to think of.

" For at that instant the storm broke—one of those short sudden squalls which are common in these seas. The *Matilda* heeled over, her sails bellied out, she plunged her lee-rail into a wave, and was off like a frightened deer. Jelland's body had jammed the helm, and

285

she kept a course right before the wind, and fluttered away over the rising sea like a blown piece of paper. The rowers worked frantically, but the yawl still drew ahead, and in five minutes it had plunged into the storm-wrack never to be seen again by mortal eye. The boat put back, and reached Yokohama with the water washing half-way up to the thwarts.

"And that was how it came that the yawl *Matilda*, with a cargo of five thousand pounds and a crew of two dead young men, set sail across the Pacific Ocean. What the end of Jelland's voyage may have been no man knows. He may have foundered in that gale, or he may have been picked up by some canny merchant-man, who stuck to the bullion and kept his mouth shut, or he may still be cruising in that vast waste of waters, blown north to the Behring Sea, or south to the Malay Islands. It's better to leave it unfinished than to spoil a true story by inventing a tag to it."

23. *J. Habakuk Jephson's Statement*

IN the month of December in the year 1873, the British ship *Dei Gratia* steered into Gibraltar, having in tow the derelict brigantine *Marie Celeste*, which had been picked up in latitude 38° 40', longitude 17° 15' W. There were several circumstances in connection with the condition and appearance of this abandoned vessel which excited considerable comment at the time, and aroused a curiosity which has never been satisfied. What these circumstances were was summed up in an able article which appeared in the *Gibraltar Gazette*. The curious can find it in the issue for January 4, 1874, unless my memory deceives me. For the benefit of those, however, who may be unable to refer to the paper in question, I shall subjoin a few extracts which touch upon the leading features of the case.

"We have ourselves," says the anonymous writer in

the *Gazette*, " been over the derelict *Marie Celeste*, and have closely questioned the officers of the *Dei Gratia* on every point which might throw light on the affair. They are of opinion that she had been abandoned several days, or perhaps weeks, before being picked up. The official log, which was found in the cabin, states that the vessel sailed from Boston to Lisbon, starting upon October 16. It is, however, most imperfectly kept, and affords little information. There is no reference to rough weather, and, indeed, the state of the vessel's paint and rigging excludes the idea that she was abandoned for any such reason. She is perfectly watertight. No signs of a struggle or of violence are to be detected, and there is absolutely nothing to account for the disappearance of the crew. There are several indications that a lady was present on board, a sewing-machine being found in the cabin and some articles of female attire. These probably belonged to the captain's wife, who is mentioned in the log as having accompanied her husband. As an instance of the mildness of the weather, it may be remarked that a bobbin of silk was found standing upon the sewing-machine, though the least roll of the vessel would have precipitated it to the floor. The boats were intact and slung upon the davits ; and the cargo, consisting of tallow and American clocks, was untouched. An old-fashioned sword of curious workmanship was discovered among some lumber in the forecastle, and this weapon is said to exhibit a longitudinal striation on the steel, as if it had been recently wiped. It has been placed in the hands of the police, and submitted to Dr. Monaghan, the analyst, for inspection. The result of his examination has not yet been published. We may remark, in conclusion, that Captain Dalton, of the *Dei Gratia*, an able and intelligent seaman, is of opinion that the *Marie Celeste* may have been abandoned a considerable distance from the spot at which she was picked up, since a powerful current runs up in that latitude from the African coast. He confesses his inability, however, to advance any hypothesis which can reconcile all the facts of the case. In the utter absence of a clue or grain of evidence, it is to be feared that the fate of the crew of the *Marie Celeste* will be added to those numerous mysteries of the deep which will never be solved until the great day when the sea shall give up its dead. If crime has been committed, as is much to be suspected, there is little hope of bringing the perpetrators to justice."

I shall supplement this extract from the *Gibraltar Gazette* by quoting a telegram from Boston, which went the round of the English papers, and represented the total amount of information which had been collected about the *Marie Celeste*. " She was," it said, " a brigantine of 170 tons burden, and belonged to White, Russell & White, wine importers, of this city. Captain J. W. Tibbs was an old servant of the firm, and was a man of known ability and tried probity. He was accompanied by his wife, aged thirty-one, and their youngest child, five years old. The crew consisted of seven hands, including two coloured seamen, and a boy. There were three passengers, one of whom was the well-known Brooklyn specialist on consumption, Dr. Habakuk Jephson, who was a distinguished advocate for Abolition in the early days of the movement, and whose pamphlet, entitled ' Where is thy Brother ? ' exercised a strong influence on public opinion before the war. The other passengers were Mr. J. Harton, a writer in the employ of the firm, and Mr. Septimius Goring, a half-caste gentleman, from New Orleans. All investigations have failed to throw any light upon the fate of these fourteen human beings. The loss of Dr. Jephson will be felt both in political and scientific circles."

I have here epitomised, for the benefit of the public, all that has been hitherto known concerning the *Marie Celeste* and her crew, for the past ten years have not in any way helped to elucidate the mystery. I have now taken up my pen with the intention of telling all that I know of the ill-fated voyage. I consider that it is a duty which I owe to society, for symptoms which I am familiar with in others lead me to believe that before many months my tongue and hand may be alike incapable of conveying information. Let me remark, as a preface to my narrative, that I am Joseph Habakuk Jephson, Doctor of Medicine of the University of Harvard, and ex-Consulting Physician of the Samaritan Hospital of Brooklyn.

Many will doubtless wonder why I have not proclaimed myself before, and why I have suffered so many conjectures and surmises to pass unchallenged. Could the ends of justice have been served in any way by my revealing the facts in my possession I should unhesitatingly have done so. It seemed to me, however, that there was no possibility of such a result ; and when I attempted after the occurrence, to state my case to an English official, I was met with such offensive incredulity that I determined never again to expose myself to the chance of such an indignity. I can excuse the discourtesy of the Liverpool magistrate, however, when I reflect upon the treatment which I received at the hands of my own relatives, who, though they knew my unimpeachable character, listened to my statement with an indulgent smile as if humouring the delusion of a monomaniac. This slur upon my veracity led to a quarrel between myself and John Vanburger, the brother of my wife, and confirmed me in my resolution to let the matter sink into oblivion—a determination which I have only altered through my son's solicitations. In order to make my narrative intelligible, I must run lightly over one or two incidents in my former life which throw light upon subsequent events.

My father, William K. Jephson, was a preacher of the sect called Plymouth Brethren, and was one of the most respected citizens of Lowell. Like most of the other Puritans of New England, he was a determined opponent of slavery, and it was from his lips that I received those lessons which tinged every action of my life. While

I was studying medicine at Harvard University, I had already made a mark as an advanced Abolitionist; and when, after taking my degree, I bought a third share of the practice of Dr. Willis, of Brooklyn, I managed, in spite of my professional duties, to devote a considerable time to the cause which I had at heart, my pamphlet, "Where is thy Brother?" (Swarburgh, Lister & Co., 1859) attracting considerable attention.

When the war broke out I left Brooklyn and accompanied the 113th New York Regiment through the campaign. I was present at the second battle of Bull's Run and at the battle of Gettysburg. Finally, I was severely wounded at Antietam, and would probably have perished on the field had it not been for the kindness of a gentleman named Murray, who had me carried to his house and provided me with every comfort. Thanks to his charity, and to the nursing which I received from his black domestics, I was soon able to get about the plantation with the help of a stick. It was during this period of convalescence that an incident occurred which is closely connected with my story.

Among the most assiduous of the negresses who had watched my couch during my illness there was one old crone who appeared to exert considerable authority over the others. She was exceedingly attentive to me, and I gathered from the few words that passed between us that she had heard of me, and that she was grateful to me for championing her oppressed race.

One day as I was sitting alone in the verandah, basking in the sun, and debating whether I should rejoin Grant's army, I was surprised to see this old creature hobbling towards me. After looking cautiously around to see that we were alone, she fumbled in the front of her dress, and produced a small chamois leather bag which was hung round her neck by a white cord.

"Massa," she said, bending down and croaking the words into my ear, "me die soon. Me very old woman. Not stay long on Massa Murray's plantation."

J. HABAKUK JEPHSON'S STATEMENT

"You may live a long time yet, Martha," I answered. "You know I am a doctor. If you feel ill let me know about it, and I will try to cure you."

"No wish to live—wish to die. I'm gwine to join the heavenly host." Here she relapsed into one of those half-heathenish rhapsodies in which negroes indulge. "But, massa, me have one thing must leave behind me when I go. No able to take it with me across the Jordan. That one thing very precious, more precious and more holy than all thing else in the world. Me, a poor old black woman, have this because my people, very great people, 'spose they was back in the old country. But you cannot understand this same as black folk could. My fader give it me, and his fader give it him, but now who shall I give it to? Poor Martha hab no child, no relation, nobody. All round I see black man very bad man. Black woman very stupid woman. Nobody worthy of the stone. And so I say, Here is Massa Jephson who write books and fight for coloured folk—he must be a good man, and he shall have it though he is white man, and nebber can know what it mean or where it came from." Here the old woman fumbled in the chamois leather bag and pulled out a flattish black stone with a hole through the middle of it. "Here, take it," she said, pressing it into my hand; "take it. No harm nebber come from anything good. Keep it safe—nebber lose it!" and with a warning gesture the old crone hobbled away in the same cautious way as she had come, looking from side to side to see if we had been observed.

I was more amused than impressed by the old woman's earnestness, and was only prevented from laughing during her oration by the fear of hurting her feelings. When she was gone I took a good look at the stone which she had given me. It was intensely black, of extreme hardness, and oval in shape—just such a flat stone as one would pick up on the seashore if one wished to throw a long way. It was about three inches long, and an inch and a half broad at the middle, but rounded off at the extremities. The most curious part about it was several well-marked ridges which ran in semicircles over its surface, and gave it exactly the appearance of a human ear. Altogether I was rather interested in my new possession and determined to submit it, as a geological specimen to my friend Professor Shroeder of the New York Institute upon the earliest opportunity. In the meantime I thrust it into my pocket, and rising from my chair started off for a short stroll in the shrubbery, dismissing the incident from my mind.

As my wound had nearly healed by this time, I took my leave of Mr. Murray shortly afterwards. The Union armies were everywhere victorious and converging on Richmond, so that my assistance seemed unnecessary, and I returned to Brooklyn. There I resumed my practice, and married the second daughter of Josiah Vanburger, the well-known wood engraver. In the course of a few years I built up a good connection and acquired considerable reputation in the treatment of pulmonary complaints. I still kept the old black stone in my pocket, and frequently told the story of the dramatic way in which I had become possessed of it. I also kept my resolution of showing it to Professor Shroeder, who was much interested both by the anecdote and the specimen. He pronounced it to be a piece of meteoric stone, and drew my attention to the fact that its resemblance to an ear was not accidental, but that it was most carefully worked into that shape. A dozen little anatomical points showed that the worker had been as accurate as he was skilful. " I should not wonder," said the Professor, " if it were broken off from some larger statue, though how such hard material could be so perfectly worked is more than I can understand. If there is a statue to correspond I should like to see it ! " So I thought at the time, but I have changed my opinion since.

The next seven or eight years of my life were quiet and uneventful. Summer followed spring, and spring followed winter, without any variation in my duties. As the practice increased I admitted J. S. Jackson as partner, he to have one-fourth of the profits. The continued strain had told upon my constitution, however, and I became at last so unwell that my wife insisted upon my consulting Dr. Kavanagh Smith, who was my colleague at the Samaritan Hospital. That gentleman examined me, and pronounced the apex of my left lung to be in a state of consolidation, recommending me at the same time to go through a course of medical treatment and to take a long sea-voyage.

My own disposition, which is naturally restless, predisposed me strongly in favour of the latter piece of advice, and the matter was clinched by my meeting young Russell, of the firm of White, Russell & White, who offered me a passage in one of his father's ships, the *Marie Celeste*, which was just starting from Boston. " She is a snug little ship," he said, " and Tibbs, the captain, is an excellent fellow. There is nothing like a sailing ship for an invalid." I was very much of the same opinion myself, so I closed with the offer on the spot.

My original plan was that my wife should accompany me on my travels. She has always been a very poor sailor, however, and there were strong family reasons against her exposing herself to any risk at the time, so we determined that she should remain at home. I am not a religious or an effusive man ; but oh, thank God for that ! As to leaving my practice, I was easily reconciled to it, as Jackson, my partner, was a reliable and hard-working man.

I arrived in Boston on October 12, 1873, and proceeded immediately to the office of the firm in order to thank them for their courtesy. As I was sitting in the counting-house waiting until they should be at liberty to see me, the words *Marie Celeste* suddenly attracted my attention. I looked round and saw a very tall, gaunt man, who was leaning across the polished mahogany counter asking some questions of the clerk at the other side. His face was turned half towards me, and I could see that he had a strong dash of negro blood in him, being probably a quadroon or even nearer akin to the black. His curved aquiline nose and straight lank hair showed the white strain ; but the dark, restless eye, sensuous mouth, and gleaming teeth all told of his African origin. His complexion was of a sickly, unhealthy yellow, and as his face was deeply pitted with small-pox, the general impression was so unfavourable as to be almost revolting. When he spoke, however, it was in a soft, melodious voice, and in well-chosen words, and he was evidently a man of some education.

"I wished to ask a few questions about the *Marie Celeste*," he repeated, leaning across to the clerk. "She sails the day after to-morrow, does she not?"

"Yes, sir," said the young clerk, awed into unusual politeness by the glimmer of a large diamond in the stranger's shirt front.

"Where is she bound for?"

"Lisbon."

"How many of a crew?"

"Seven, sir."

"Passengers?"

"Yes, two. One of our young gentlemen, and a doctor from New York."

"No gentleman from the South?" asked the stranger eagerly.

"No, none, sir."

"Is there room for another passenger?"

"Accommodation, for three more," answered the clerk.

"I'll go," said the quadroon decisively; "I'll go, I'll engage my passage at once. Put it down, will you— Mr. Septimius Goring, of New Orleans."

The clerk filled up a form and handed it over to the stranger, pointing to a blank space at the bottom. As Mr. Goring stooped over to sign it I was horrified to observe that the fingers of his right hand had been lopped off, and that he was holding the pen between his thumb and the palm. I have seen thousands slain in battle, and assisted at every conceivable surgical operation, but I cannot recall any sight which gave me such a thrill of disgust as that great brown sponge-like hand with the single member protruding from it. He used it skilfully enough, however, for, dashing off his signature, he nodded to the clerk and strolled out of the office just as Mr. White sent out word that he was ready to receive me.

I went down to the *Marie Celeste* that evening, and looked over my berth, which was extremely comfortable considering the small size of the vessel. Mr. Goring, whom I had seen in the morning, was to have the one next mine. Opposite was the captain's cabin and a small berth for Mr. John Harton, a gentleman who was going out in the interests of the firm. These little rooms were arranged on each side of the passage which led from the main-deck to the saloon. The latter was a comfortable room, the panelling tastefully done in oak and mahogany, with a rich Brussels carpet and luxurious settees. I was very much pleased with the accommodation, and also with Tibbs the captain, a bluff, sailor-like fellow, with a loud voice and hearty manner, who welcomed me to the ship with effusion, and insisted upon our splitting a bottle of wine in his cabin. He told me that he intended to take his wife and youngest child with him on the voyage, and that he hoped with good luck to make Lisbon in three weeks. We had a pleasant chat and parted the best of friends, he warning me to make the last of my preparations next morning, as he intended to make a start by the mid-day tide, having now shipped all his cargo. I went back to my hotel, where I found a letter from my wife awaiting me, and, after a refreshing night's sleep, returned to the boat in the morning. From this point I am able to quote from the journal which I kept in order to vary the monotony of the long sea-voyage. If it is somewhat bald in places

I can at least rely upon its accuracy in details, as it was written conscientiously from day to day.

October 16th.—Cast off our warps at half-past two and were towed out into the bay, where the tug left us, and with all sail set we bowled along at about nine knots an hour. I stood upon the poop watching the low land of America sinking gradually upon the horizon until the evening haze hid it from my sight. A single red light, however, continued to blaze balefully behind us, throwing a long track like a trail of blood upon the water, and it is still visible as I write, though reduced to a mere speck. The captain is in a bad humour, for two of his hands disappointed him at the last moment, and he was compelled to ship a couple of negroes who happened to be on the quay. The missing men were steady, reliable fellows, who had been with him several voyages, and their non-appearance puzzled as well as irritated him. Where a crew of seven men have to work a fair-sized ship the loss of two experienced seamen is a serious one, for though the negroes may take a spell at the wheel or swab the decks, they are of little or no use in rough weather. Our cook is also a black man, and Mr. Septimius Goring has a little darkie servant, so that we are rather a piebald community. The accountant, John Harton, promises to be an acquisition, for he is a cheery, amusing young fellow. Strange how little wealth has to do with happiness ! He has all the world before him and is seeking his fortune in a far land, yet he is as transparently happy as a man can be. Goring is rich, if I am not mistaken, and so am I ; but I know that I have a lung, and Goring has some deeper trouble still, to judge by his features. How poorly do we both contrast with the careless, penniless clerk !

October 17th.—Mrs. Tibbs appeared upon the deck for the first time this morning—a cheerful, energetic woman, with a dear little child just able to walk and prattle. Young Harton pounced on it at once, and carried it away to his cabin, where no doubt he will lay

the seeds of future dyspepsia in the child's stomach.
Thus medicine doth make cynics of us all ! The weather
is still all that could be desired, with a fine fresh breeze
from the west-sou'-west. The vessel goes so steadily
that you would hardly know that she was moving were
it not for the creaking of the cordage, the bellying of the
sails, and the long white furrow in our wake. Walked
the quarter-deck all morning with the captain, and I
think the keen fresh air has already done my breathing
good, for the exercise did not fatigue me in any way.
Tibbs is a remarkably intelligent man, and we had an
interesting argument about Maury's observations on
ocean currents, which we terminated by going down
into his cabin to consult the original work. There we
found Goring, rather to the captain's surprise, as it is
not usual for passengers to enter that sanctum unless
specially invited. He apologised for his intrusion,
however, pleading his ignorance of the usages of ship
life ; and the good-natured sailor simply laughed at the
incident, begging him to remain and favour us with his
company. Goring pointed to the chronometers, the
case of which he had opened, and remarked that he had
been admiring them. He has evidently some practical
knowledge of mathematical instruments, as he told at
a glance which was the most trustworthy of the three,
and also named their price within a few dollars. He had
a discussion with the captain too upon the variation of
the compass, and when we came back to the ocean currents he showed a thorough grasp of the subject. Altogether he rather improves upon acquaintance, and is
a man of decided culture and refinement. His voice
harmonises with his conversation, and both are the very
antithesis of his face and figure.

The noonday observation shows that we have run two
hundred and twenty miles. Towards evening the breeze
freshened up, and the first mate ordered reefs to be
taken in the topsails and top-gallant sails in expectation
of a windy night. I observe that the barometer has fallen

to twenty-nine. I trust our voyage will not be a rough one, as I am a poor sailor, and my health would probably derive more harm than good from a stormy trip, though I have the greatest confidence in the captain's seamanship and in the soundness of the vessel. Played cribbage with Mrs. Tibbs after supper, and Harton gave us a couple of tunes on the violin.

October 18*th*.—The gloomy prognostications of last night were not fulfilled, as the wind died away again and we are lying now in a long greasy swell, ruffled here, and there by a fleeting catspaw which is insufficient to fill the sails. The air is colder than it was yesterday, and I have put on one of the thick woollen jerseys which my wife knitted for me. Harton came into my cabin in the morning, and we had a cigar together. He says that he remembers having seen Goring in Cleveland, Ohio, in '69. He was, it appears, a mystery then as now, wandering about without any visible employment, and extremely reticent on his own affairs. The man interests me as a psychological study. At breakfast this morning I suddenly had that vague feeling of uneasiness which comes over some people when closely stared at, and, looking quickly up, I met his eyes bent upon me with an intensity which amounted to ferocity, though their expression instantly softened as he made some conventional remark upon the weather. Curiously enough, Harton says that he had a very similar experience yesterday upon deck. I observe that Goring frequently talks to the coloured seamen as he strolls about—a trait which I rather admire, as it is common to find half-breeds ignore their dark strain and treat their black kinsfolk with greater intolerance than a white man would do. His little page is devoted to him, apparently, which speaks well for his treatment of him. Altogether, the man is a curious mixture of incongruous qualities, and unless I am deceived in him will give me food for observation during the voyage.

The captain is grumbling about his chronometers,

which do not register exactly the same time. He says
it is the first time that they have ever disagreed. We
were unable to get a noonday observation on account
of the haze. By dead reckoning, we have done about a
hundred and seventy miles in the twenty-four hours.
The dark seamen have proved, as the skipper prophesied,
to be very inferior hands, but as they can both manage
the wheel well they are kept steering, and so leave the
more experienced men to work the ship. These details
are trivial enough, but a small thing serves as food for
gossip aboard ship. The appearance of a whale in the
evening caused quite a flutter among us. From its
sharp back and forked tail, I should pronounce it to have
been a rorqual, or " finner," as they are called by the
fishermen.

October 19*th.*—Wind was cold, so I prudently remained
in my cabin all day, only creeping out for dinner. Lying
in my bunk I can, without moving, reach my books,
pipes, or anything else I may want, which is one advantage of a small apartment. My old wound began to
ache a little to-day, probably from the cold. Read
Montaigne's Essays and nursed myself. Harton came in
in the afternoon with Doddy, the captain's child, and
the skipper himself followed, so that I held quite a
reception.

October 20*th and* 21*st.*—Still cold, with a continual
drizzle of rain, and I have not been able to leave the
cabin. This confinement makes me feel weak and
depressed. Goring came in to see me, but his company
did not tend to cheer me up much, as he hardly uttered
a word, but contented himself with staring at me in a
peculiar and rather irritating manner. He then got up
and stole out of the cabin without saying anything. I
am beginning to suspect that the man is a lunatic. I
think I mentioned that his cabin is next to mine. The
two are simply divided by a thin wooden partition which
is cracked in many places, some of the cracks being so
large that I can hardly avoid, as I lie in my bunk, observ-

ing his motions in the adjoining room. Without any wish to play the spy, I see him continually stooping over what appears to be a chart and working with a pencil and compasses. I have remarked the interest he displays in matters connected with navigation, but I am surprised that he should take the trouble to work out the course of the ship. However, it is a harmless amusement enough, and no doubt he verifies his results by those of the captain.

I wish the man did not run in my thoughts so much. I had a nightmare on the night of the 20th, in which I thought my bunk was a coffin, that I was laid out in it, and that Goring was endeavouring to nail up the lid, which I was frantically pushing away. Even when I woke up, I could hardly persuade myself that I was not in a coffin. As a medical man, I know that a nightmare is simply a vascular derangement of the cerebral hemispheres, and yet in my weak state I cannot shake off the morbid impression which it produces.

October 22nd.—A fine day, with hardly a cloud in the sky, and a fresh breeze from the sou'-west which wafts us gaily on our way. There has evidently been some heavy weather near us, as there is a tremendous swell on, and the ship lurches until the end of the fore-yard nearly touches the water. Had a refreshing walk up and down the quarter-deck, though I have hardly found my sea-legs yet. Several small birds—chaffinches, I think—perched in the rigging.

4.40 P.M.—While I was on deck this morning I heard a sudden explosion from the direction of my cabin, and, hurrying down, found that I had very nearly met with a serious accident. Goring was cleaning a revolver, it seems, in his cabin, when one of the barrels which he thought was unloaded went off. The ball passed through the side partition and imbedded itself in the bulwarks in the exact place where my head usually rests. I have been under fire too often to magnify trifles, but there is no doubt that if I had been in the bunk it must have killed me. Goring, poor fellow, did not know that I had gone on deck that day, and must therefore have felt terribly frightened. I never saw such emotion in a man's face as when, on rushing out of his cabin with the smoking pistol in his hand, he met me face to face as I came down from deck. Of course, he was profuse in his apologies, though I simply laughed at the incident.

11 P.M.—A misfortune has occurred so unexpected and so horrible that my little escape of the morning dwindles into insignificance. Mrs. Tibbs and her child have disappeared—utterly and entirely disappeared. I can hardly compose myself to write the sad details. About half-past eight Tibbs rushed into my cabin with a very white face and asked me if I had seen his wife. I answered that I had not. He then ran wildly into the saloon and began groping about for any trace of her, while I followed him, endeavouring vainly to persuade him that his fears were ridiculous. We hunted over the ship for an hour and a half without coming on any sign of the missing woman or child. Poor Tibbs lost his voice completely from calling her name. Even the sailors, who are generally stolid enough, were deeply affected by the sight of him as he roamed bareheaded and dishevelled about the deck, searching with feverish anxiety the most impossible places, and returning to them again and again with a piteous pertinacity. The last time she was seen was about seven o'clock, when she took Doddy on to the poop to give him a breath of fresh air before putting him to bed. There was no one there at the time except the black seaman at the wheel, who denies having seen her at all. The whole affair is wrapped in mystery. My own theory is that while Mrs. Tibbs was holding the child and standing near the bulwarks it gave a spring and fell overboard, and that in her convulsive attempt to catch or save it, she followed it. I cannot account for the double disappearance in any other way. It is quite feasible that such a tragedy should be enacted without the knowledge of the man at the wheel, since it was dark

at the time, and the peaked skylights of the saloon screen
the greater part of the quarter-deck. Whatever the truth
may be it is a terrible catastrophe, and has cast the darkest
gloom upon our voyage. The mate has put the ship
about, but of course there is not the slightest hope of
picking them up. The captain is lying in a state of
stupor in his cabin. I gave him a powerful dose of
opium in his coffee that for a few hours at least his anguish
may be deadened.

October 23rd.—Woke with a vague feeling of heaviness
and misfortune, but it was not until a few moments'
reflection that I was able to recall our loss of the night
before. When I came on deck I saw the poor skipper
standing gazing back at the waste of waters behind us
which contains everything dear to him upon earth. I
attempted to speak to him, but he turned brusquely
away, and began pacing the deck with his head sunk
upon his breast. Even now, when the truth is so clear,
he cannot pass a boat or an unbent sail without peering
under it. He looks ten years older than he did yesterday
morning. Harton is terribly cut up, for he was fond of
little Doddy, and Goring seems sorry too. At least
he has shut himself up in his cabin all day, and when I
got a casual glance at him his head was resting on his
two hands as if in a melancholy reverie. I fear we are
about as dismal a crew as ever sailed. How shocked
my wife will be to hear of our disaster! The swell
has gone down now, and we are doing about eight knots
with all sail set and a nice little breeze. Hyson is practically in command of the ship, as Tibbs, though he does his
best to bear up and keep a brave front, is incapable of
applying himself to serious work.

October 24th.—Is the ship accursed? Was there
ever a voyage which began so fairly and which changed
so disastrously? Tibbs shot himself through the head
during the night. I was awakened about three o'clock
in the morning by an explosion, and immediately sprang
out of bed and rushed into the captain's cabin to find

out the cause, though with a terrible presentiment in my heart. Quickly as I went, Goring went more quickly still, for he was already in the cabin stooping over the dead body of the captain. It was a hideous sight, for the whole front of his face was blown in, and the little room was swimming in blood. The pistol was lying beside him on the floor, just as it had dropped from his hand. He had evidently put it to his mouth before pulling the trigger. Goring and I picked him reverently up and laid him on his bed. The crew had all clustered into his cabin, and the six white men were deeply grieved, for they were old hands who had sailed with him many years. There were dark looks and murmurs among them too, and one of them openly declared that the ship was haunted. Harton helped to lay the poor skipper out, and we did him up in canvas between us. At twelve o'clock the fore-yard was hauled aback, and we committed his body to the deep, Goring reading the Church of England burial service. The breeze has freshened up, and we have done ten knots all day and sometimes twelve. The sooner we reach Lisbon and get away from this accursed ship the better pleased shall I be. I feel as though we were in a floating coffin. Little wonder that the poor sailors are superstitious when I, an educated man, feel it so strongly.

October 25th.—Made a good run all day. Feel listless and depressed.

October 26th.—Goring, Harton, and I had a chat together on deck in the morning. Harton tried to draw Goring out as to his profession, and his object in going to Europe, but the quadroon parried all his questions and gave us no information. Indeed, he seemed to be slightly offended by Harton's pertinacity, and went down into his cabin. I wonder why we should both take such an interest in this man! I suppose it is his striking appearance, coupled with his apparent wealth, which piques our curiosity. Harton has a theory that he is really a detective, that he is after some criminal who has got away to Portugal, and that he chooses this peculiar way of travelling that he may arrive unnoticed and pounce upon his quarry unawares. I think the supposition is rather a far-fetched one, but Harton bases it upon a book which Goring left on deck, and which he picked up and glanced over. It was a sort of scrap-book, it seems, and contained a large number of newspaper cuttings. All these cuttings related to murders which had been committed at various times in the States during the last twenty years or so. The curious thing which Harton observed about them, however, was that they were invariably murders the authors of which had never been brought to justice. They varied in every detail, he says, as to the manner of execution and the social status of the victim, but they uniformly wound up with the same formula that the murderer was still at large, though, of course, the police had every reason to expect his speedy capture. Certainly the incident seems to support Harton's theory, though it may be a mere whim of Goring's, or, as I suggested to Harton, he may be collecting materials for a book which shall outvie De Quincy. In any case it is no business of ours.

October 27th, 28th.—Wind still fair, and we are making good progress. Strange how easily a human unit may drop out of its place and be forgotten ! Tibbs is hardly ever mentioned now ; Hyson has taken possession of his cabin, and all goes on as before. Were it not for Mrs. Tibbs's sewing-machine upon a side-table we might forget that the unfortunate family had ever existed. Another accident occurred on board to-day, though fortunately not a very serious one. One of our white hands had gone down the afterhold to fetch up a spare coil of rope, when one of the hatches which he had removed came crashing down on the top of him. He saved his life by springing out of the way, but one of his feet was terribly crushed, and he will be of little use for the remainder of the voyage. He attributes the accident to the carelessness of his negro companion, who had

helped him to shift the hatches. The latter, however,
puts it down to the roll of the ship. Whatever be the
cause, it reduces our short-handed crew still further.
This run of ill-luck seems to be depressing Harton, for
he has lost his usual good spirits and joviality. Goring
is the only one who preserves his cheerfulness. I see
him still working at his chart in his own cabin. His
nautical knowledge would be useful should anything
happen to Hyson—which God forbid !

October 29*th*, 30*th*.—Still bowling along with a fresh
breeze. All quiet and nothing of note to chronicle.

October 31*st*.—My weak lungs, combined with the
exciting episodes of the voyage, have shaken my nervous
system so much that the most trivial incident affects
me. I can hardly believe that I am the same man who
tied the external iliac artery, an operation requiring the
nicest precision, under a heavy rifle fire at Antietam. I
am as nervous as a child. I was lying half dozing last
night about four bells in the middle watch trying in
vain to drop into a refreshing sleep. There was no
light inside my cabin, but a single ray of moonlight
streamed in through the port-hole, throwing a silvery
flickering circle upon the door. As I lay I kept my drowsy
eyes upon this circle, and was conscious that it was
gradually becoming less well-defined as my senses left
me, when I was suddenly recalled to full wakefulness by
the appearance of a small dark object in the very centre
of the luminous disc. I lay quietly and breathlessly
watching it. Gradually it grew larger and plainer, and
then I perceived that it was a human hand which had
been cautiously inserted through the chink of the half-
closed door—a hand which, as I observed with a thrill
of horror, was not provided with fingers. The door
swung cautiously backwards, and Goring's head followed
his hand. It appeared in the centre of the moonlight,
and was framed as it were in a ghastly uncertain halo,
against which his features showed out plainly. It seemed
to me that I had never seen such an utterly fiendish and

merciless expression upon a human face. His eyes were dilated and glaring, his lips drawn back so as to show his white fangs, and his straight black hair appeared to bristle over his low forehead like the hood of a cobra. The sudden and noiseless apparition had such an effect upon me that I sprang up in bed trembling in every limb, and held out my hand towards my revolver. I was heartily ashamed of my hastiness when he explained the object of his intrusion, as he immediately did in the most courteous language. He had been suffering from tooth-ache, poor fellow ! and had come in to beg some laudanum, knowing that I possessed a medicine chest. As to a sinister expression he is never a beauty, and what with my state of nervous tension and the effect of the shifting moonlight it was easy to conjure up something horrible. I gave him twenty drops, and he went off again, with many expressions of gratitude. I can hardly say how much this trivial incident affected me. I have felt unstrung all day.

A week's record of our voyage is here omitted, as nothing eventful occurred during the time, and my log consists merely of a few pages of unimportant gossip.

November 7th.—Harton and I sat on the poop all the morning, for the weather is becoming very warm as we come into southern latitudes. We reckon that we have done two-thirds of our voyage. How glad we shall be to see the green banks of the Tagus, and leave this unlucky ship for ever ! I was endeavouring to amuse Harton to-day and to while away the time by telling him some of the experiences of my past life. Among others I related to him how I came into the possession of my black stone, and as a finale I rummaged in the side pocket of my old shooting coat and produced the identical object in question. He and I were bending over it together, I pointing out to him the curious ridges upon its surface, when we were conscious of a shadow falling between us and the sun, and looking round saw Goring standing behind us

glaring over our shoulders at the stone. For some
reason or other he appeared to be powerfully excited,
though he was evidently trying to control himself and
to conceal his emotion. He pointed once or twice at
my relic with his stubby thumb before he could recover
himself sufficiently to ask what it was and how I obtained
it—a question put in such a brusque manner that I
should have been offended had I not known the man
to be an eccentric. I told him the story very much
as I had told it to Harton. He listened with the deepest
interest and then asked me if I had any idea what the
stone was. I said I had not, beyond that it was meteoric.
He asked me if I had ever tried its effect upon a negro.
I said I had not. " Come," said he, " we'll see what
our black friend at the wheel thinks of it." He took
the stone in his hand and went across to the sailor,
and the two examined it carefully. I could see the man
gesticulating and nodding his head excitedly as if making
some assertion, while his face betrayed the utmost
astonishment, mixed, I think, with some reverence.
Goring came across the deck to us presently, still holding the stone in his hand. " He says it is a worthless,
useless thing," he said, " and fit only to be chucked
overboard," with which he raised his hand and would
most certainly have made an end of my relic, had the
black sailor behind him not rushed forward and seized
him by the wrist. Finding himself secured Goring
dropped the stone and turned away with a very bad
grace to avoid my angry remonstrances at his breach
of faith. The black picked up the stone and handed
it to me with a low bow and every sign of profound
respect. The whole affair is inexplicable. I am rapidly
coming to the conclusion that Goring is a maniac or
something very near one. When I compare the effect
produced by the stone upon the sailor, however, with
the respect shown to Martha on the plantation, and
the surprise of Goring on its first production, I cannot
but come to the conclusion that I have really got

hold of some powerful talisman which appeals to the whole dark race. I must not trust it in Goring's hands again.

November 8th, 9th.—What splendid weather we are having! Beyond one little blow, we have had nothing but fresh breezes the whole voyage. These two days we have made better runs than any hitherto. It is a pretty thing to watch the spray fly up from our prow as it cuts through the waves. The sun shines through it and breaks it up into a number of miniature rainbows —" sun-dogs," the sailors call them. I stood on the fo'c'sle-head for several hours to-day watching the effect, and surrounded by a halo of prismatic colours. The steersman has evidently told the other blacks about my wonderful stone, for I am treated by them all with the greatest respect. Talking about optical phenomena, we had a curious one yesterday evening which was pointed out to me by Hyson. This was the appearance of a triangular well-defined object high up in the heavens to the north of us. He explained that it was exactly like the Peak of Teneriffe as seen from a great distance —the peak was, however, at that moment at least five hundred miles to the south. It may have been a cloud, or it may have been one of those strange reflections of which one reads. The weather is very warm. The mate says that he never knew it so warm in these latitudes. Played chess with Harton in the evening.

November 10th.—It is getting warmer and warmer. Some land birds came and perched in the rigging to-day, though we are still a considerable way from our destination. The heat is so great that we are too lazy to do anything but lounge about the decks and smoke. Goring came over to me to-day and asked me some more questions about my stone ; but I answered him rather shortly, for I have not quite forgiven him yet for the cool way in which he attempted to deprive me of it.

November 11th, 12th.—Still making good progress. I had no idea Portugal was ever as hot as this, but no doubt it is cooler on land. Hyson himself seemed surprised at it, and so do the men.

November 13th.—A most extraordinary event has happened, so extraordinary as to be almost inexplicable. Either Hyson has blundered wonderfully, or some magnetic influence has disturbed our instruments. Just about daybreak the watch on the fo'c'sle-head shouted out that he heard the sound of surf ahead, and Hyson thought he saw the loom of land. The ship was put about, and, though no lights were seen, none of us doubted that we had struck the Portuguese coast a little sooner than we had expected. What was our surprise to see the scene which was revealed to us at break of day ! As far as we could look on either side was one long line of surf, great, green billows rolling in and breaking into a cloud of foam. But behind the surf what was there ! Not the green banks nor the high cliffs of the shores of Portugal, but a great sandy waste which stretched away and away until it blended with the skyline. To right and left, look where you would, there was nothing but yellow sand, heaped in some places into fantastic mounds, some of them several hundred feet high, while in other parts were long stretches as level apparently as a billiard board. Harton and I, who had come on deck together, looked at each other in astonishment, and Harton burst out laughing. Hyson is exceedingly mortified at the occurrence, and protests that the instruments have been tampered with. There is no doubt that this is the mainland of Africa, and that it was really the Peak of Teneriffe which we saw some days ago upon the northern horizon. At the time when we saw the land birds we must have been passing some of the Canary Islands. If we continued on the same course, we are now to the north of Cape Blanco, near the unexplored country which skirts the great Sahara. All we can do is to rectify our instruments as far as possible and start afresh for our destination.

8.30 P.M.—Have been lying in a calm all day. The

coast is now about a mile and a half from us. Hyson has examined the instruments, but cannot find any reason for their extraordinary deviation.

This is the end of my private journal, and I must make the remainder of my statement from memory. There is little chance of my being mistaken about facts, which have seared themselves into my recollection. That very night the storm which had been brewing so long burst over us, and I came to learn whither all those little incidents were tending which I had recorded so aimlessly. Blind fool that I was not to have seen it sooner ! I shall tell what occurred as precisely as I can.

I had gone into my cabin about half-past eleven, and was preparing to go to bed, when a tap came at my door. On opening it I saw Goring's little black page, who told me that his master would like to have a word with me on deck. I was rather surprised that he should want me at such a late hour, but I went up without hesitation. I had hardly put my foot on the quarter-deck before I was seized from behind, dragged down upon my back, and a handkerchief slipped round my mouth. I struggled as hard as I could, but a coil of rope was rapidly and firmly wound round me, and I found myself lashed to the davit of one of the boats, utterly powerless to do or say anything, while the point of a knife pressed to my throat warned me to cease my struggles. The night was so dark that I had been unable hitherto to recognize my assailants, but as my eyes became accustomed to the gloom, and the moon broke out through the clouds that obscured it, I made out that I was surrounded by the two negro sailors, the black cook, and my fellow-passenger, Goring. Another man was crouching on the deck at my feet, but he was in the shadow and I could not recognize him.

All this occurred so rapidly that a minute could hardly have elapsed from the time I mounted the companion until I found myself gagged and powerless. It was so sudden that I could scarce bring myself to realize it, or to comprehend what it all meant. I heard the gang round me speaking in short, fierce whispers to each other, and some instinct told me that my life was the question at issue. Goring spoke authoritatively and angrily—the others doggedly and all together, as if disputing his commands. Then they moved away in a body to the opposite side of the deck, where I could still hear them whispering, though they were concealed from my view by the saloon skylights.

All this time the voices of the watch on deck chatting and laughing at the other end of the ship were distinctly audible, and I could see them gathered in a group, little dreaming of the dark doings which were going on within thirty yards of them. Oh! That I could have given them one word of warning, even though I had lost my life in doing it! but it was impossible. The moon was shining fitfully through the scattered clouds, and I could see the silvery gleam of the surge, and beyond it the vast weird desert with its fantastic sand-hills. Glancing down, I saw that the man who had been crouching on the deck was still lying there, and as I gazed at him a flickering ray of moonlight fell full upon his upturned face. Great heaven! even now, when more than twelve years have elapsed, my hand trembles as I write that, in spite of distorted features and projecting eyes, I recognized the face of Harton, the cheery young clerk who had been my companion during the voyage. It needed no medical eye to see that he was quite dead, while the twisted handkerchief round the neck, and the gag in his mouth, showed the silent way in which the hell-hounds had done their work. The clue which explained every event of our voyage came upon me like a flash of light as I gazed on poor Harton's corpse. Much was dark and unexplained, but I felt a great dim perception of the truth.

I heard the striking of a match at the other side of the skylights, and then I saw the tall, gaunt figure of

Goring standing up on the bulwarks and holding in his hands what appeared to be a dark lantern. He lowered this for a moment over the side of the ship, and, to my inexpressible astonishment, I saw it answered instantaneously by a flash among the sand-hills on shore, which came and went so rapidly, that unless I had been following the direction of Goring's gaze, I should never have detected it. Again he lowered the lantern, and again it was answered from the shore. He then stepped down from the bulwarks, and in doing so slipped, making such a noise, that for a moment my heart bounded with the thought that the attention of the watch would be directed to his proceedings. It was a vain hope. The night was calm and the ship motionless, so that no idea of duty kept them vigilant. Hyson, who after the death of Tibbs was in command of both watches, had gone below to snatch a few hours' sleep, and the boatswain, who was left in charge, was standing with the other two men at the foot of the foremast. Powerless, speechless, with the cords cutting into my flesh and the murdered man at my feet, I awaited the next act in the tragedy.

The four ruffians were standing up now at the other side of the deck. The cook was armed with some sort of a cleaver, the others had knives, and Goring had a revolver. They were all leaning against the rail and looking out over the water as if watching for something. I saw one of them grasp another's arm and point as if at some object, and following the direction I made out the loom of a large moving mass making towards the ship. As it emerged from the gloom I saw that it was a great canoe crammed with men and propelled by at least a score of paddles. As it shot under our stern the watch caught sight of it also, and raising a cry hurried aft. They were too late, however. A swarm of gigantic negroes clambered over the quarter, and led by Goring swept down the deck in an irresistible torrent. All opposition was overpowered in a moment,

the unarmed watch were knocked over and bound, and
the sleepers dragged out of their bunks and secured in
the same manner. Hyson made an attempt to defend
the narrow passage leading to his cabin, and I heard
a scuffle, and his voice shouting for assistance. There
was none to assist, however, and he was brought on
to the poop with the blood streaming from a deep cut
in his forehead. He was gagged like the others, and
a council was held upon our fate by the negroes. I
saw our black seamen pointing towards me and making
some statement, which was received with murmurs of
astonishment and incredulity by the savages. One of
them then came over to me, and plunging his hand into
my pocket took out my black stone and held it up.
He then handed it to a man who appeared to be a chief,
who examined it as minutely as the light would permit,
and muttering a few words passed it on to the warrior
beside him, who also scrutinized it and passed it on
until it had gone from hand to hand round the whole
circle. The chief then said a few words to Goring in
the native tongue, on which the quadroon addressed
me in English. At this moment I seem to see the scene.
The tall masts of the ship with the moonlight streaming
down, silvering the yards and bringing the network of
cordage into hard relief ; the group of dusky warriors
leaning on their spears ; the dead man at my feet ; the
line of white-faced prisoners, and in front of me the
loathsome half-breed, looking in his white linen and
elegant clothes a strange contrast to his associates.

" You will bear me witness," he said in his softest
accents, " that I am no party to sparing your life. If it
rested with me you would die as these other men are
about to do. I have no personal grudge against either
you or them, but I have devoted my life to the destruction of the white race, and you are the first that has
ever been in my power and has escaped me. You may
thank that stone of yours for your life. These poor
fellows reverence it, and indeed if it really be what they

think it is they have cause. Should it prove when we get ashore that they are mistaken, and that its shape and material is a mere chance, nothing can save your life. In the meantime we wish to treat you well, so if there are any of your possessions which you would like to take with you, you are at liberty to get them." As he finished he gave a sign, and a couple of the negroes unbound me, though without removing the gag. I was led down into the cabin, where I put a few valuables into my pockets, together with a pocket-compass and my journal of the voyage. They then pushed me over the side into a small canoe, which was lying beside the large one, and my guards followed me, and shoving off began paddling for the shore. We had got about a hundred yards or so from the ship when our steersman held up his hand, and the paddlers paused for a moment and listened. Then on the silence of the night I heard a sort of dull, moaning sound, followed by a succession of splashes in the water. That is all I know of the fate of my poor shipmates. Almost immediately afterwards the large canoe followed us, and the deserted ship was left drifting about—a dreary spectre-like hulk. Nothing was taken from her by the savages. The whole fiendish transaction was carried through as decorously and temperately as though it were a religious rite.

The first grey of daylight was visible in the east as we passed through the surge and reached the shore. Leaving half a dozen men with the canoes, the rest of the negroes set off through the sand-hills, leading me with them, but treating me very gently and respectfully. It was difficult walking, as we sank over our ankles into the loose, shifting sand at every step, and I was nearly dead beat by the time we reached the native village, or town rather, for it was a place of considerable dimensions. The houses were conical structures not unlike bee-hives, and were made of compressed seaweed cemented over with a rude form of mortar, there being neither stick nor stone upon the coast nor anywhere within many hundreds of miles. As we entered the town an enormous crowd of both sexes came swarming out to meet us, beating tom-toms and howling and screaming. On seeing me they redoubled their yells and assumed a threatening attitude, which was instantly quelled by a few words shouted by my escort. A buzz of wonder succeeded the war-cries and yells of the moment before, and the whole dense mass proceeded down the broad central street of the town, having my escort and myself in the centre.

My statement hitherto may seem so strange as to excite doubt in the minds of those who do not know me, but it was the fact which I am now about to relate which caused my own brother-in-law to insult me by disbelief. I can but relate the occurrence in the simplest words, and trust to chance and time to prove their truth. In the centre of this main street there was a large building, formed in the same primitive way as the others, but towering high above them ; a stockade of beautifully polished ebony rails was planted all round it, the framework of the door was formed by two magnificent elephant's tusks sunk in the ground on each side and meeting at the top, and the aperture was closed by a screen of native cloth richly embroidered with gold. We made our way to this imposing-looking structure, but on reaching the opening in the stockade, the multitude stopped and squatted down upon their hams, while I was led through into the enclosure by a few of the chiefs and elders of the tribe, Goring accompanying us, and in fact directing the proceedings. On reaching the screen which closed the temple—for such it evidently was—my hat and my shoes were removed, and I was then led in, a venerable old negro leading the way carrying in his hand my stone, which had been taken from my pocket. The building was only lit up by a few long slits in the roof, through which the tropical sun poured, throwing broad golden bars upon the clay floor, alternating with intervals of darkness.

The interior was even larger than one would have imagined from the outside appearance. The walls were hung with native mats, shells, and other ornaments, but the remainder of the great space was quite empty, with the exception of a single object in the centre. This was the figure of a colossal negro, which I at first thought to be some real king or high priest of titanic size, but as I approached it I saw by the way in which the light was reflected from it that it was a statue admirably cut in jet-black stone. I was led up to this idol, for such it seemed to be, and looking at it closer I saw that though it was perfect in every other respect, one of its ears had been broken short off. The grey-haired negro who held my relic mounted upon a small stool, and stretching up his arm fitted Martha's black stone on to the jagged surface on the side of the statue's head. There could not be a doubt that the one had been broken off from the other. The parts dovetailed together so accurately that when the old man removed his hand the ear stuck in its place for a few seconds before dropping into his open palm. The group round me prostrated themselves upon the ground at the sight with a cry of reverence, while the crowd outside, to whom the result was communicated, set up a wild whooping and cheering.

In a moment I found myself converted from a prisoner into a demi-god. I was escorted back through the town in triumph, the people pressing forward to touch my clothing and to gather up the dust on which my foot had trod. One of the largest huts was put at my disposal, and a banquet of every native delicacy was served me. I still felt, however, that I was not a free man, as several spearmen were placed as a guard at the entrance of my hut. All day my mind was occupied with plans of escape, but none seemed in any way feasible. On the one side was the great arid desert stretching away to Timbuctoo, on the other was a sea untraversed by vessels. The more I pondered over the problem the more hopeless did it seem. I little dreamed how near I was to its solution.

J. HABAKUK JEPHSON'S STATEMENT

Night had fallen, and the clamour of the negroes had died gradually away. I was stretched on the couch of skins which had been provided for me, and was still meditating over my future, when Goring walked stealthily into the hut. My first idea was that he had come to complete his murderous holocaust by making away with me, the last survivor, and I sprang up upon my feet, determined to defend myself to the last. He smiled when he saw the action, and motioned me down again while he seated himself upon the other end of the couch.

"What do you think of me?" was the astonishing question with which he commenced our conversation.

"Think of you!" I almost yelled. "I think you the vilest, most unnatural renegade that ever polluted the earth. If we were away from these black devils of yours I would strangle you with my hands!"

"Don't speak so loud," he said, without the slightest appearance of irritation. "I don't want our chat to be cut short. So you would strangle me, would you!" he went on, with an amused smile. "I suppose I am returning good for evil, for I have come to help you to escape."

"You!" I gasped incredulously.

"Yes, I," he continued. "Oh, there is no credit to me in the matter. I am quite consistent. There is no reason why I should not be perfectly candid with you. I wish to be king over these fellows—not a very high ambition, certainly, but you know what Cæsar said about being first in a village in Gaul. Well, this unlucky stone of yours has not only saved your life, but has turned all their heads so that they think you are come down from heaven, and my influence will be gone until you are out of the way. That is why I am going to help you to escape, since I cannot kill you"—this in the most natural and dulcet voice, as if the desire to do so were a matter of course.

"You would give the world to ask me a few questions,"

317

he went on, after a pause ; " but you are too proud to do it. Never mind, I'll tell you one or two things, because I want your fellow white men to know them when you go back—if you are lucky enough to get back. About that cursed stone of yours, for instance. These negroes, or at least so the legend goes, were Mahometans originally. While Mahomet himself was still alive, there was a schism among his followers, and the smaller party moved away from Arabia, and eventually crossed Africa. They took away with them, in their exile, a valuable relic of their old faith in the shape of a large piece of the black stone of Mecca. The stone was a meteoric one, as you may have heard, and in its fall upon the earth it broke into two pieces. One of these pieces is still at Mecca. The larger piece was carried away to Barbary, where a skilful worker modelled it into the fashion which you saw to-day. These men are the descendants of the original seceders from Mahomet, and they have brought their relic safely through all their wanderings until they settled in this strange place, where the desert protects them from their enemies."

" And the ear ? " I asked, almost involuntarily.

" Oh, that was the same story over again. Some of the tribe wandered away to the south a few hundred years ago, and one of them, wishing to have good luck for the enterprise, got into the temple at night and carried off one of the ears. There has been a tradition among the negroes ever since that the ear would come back some day. The fellow who carried it was caught by some slaver, no doubt, and that was how it got into America, and so into your hands—and you have had the honour of fulfilling the prophecy."

He paused for a few minutes, resting his head upon his hands, waiting apparently for me to speak. When he looked up again, the whole expression of his face had changed. His features were firm and set, and he changed the air of half-levity with which he had spoken before for one of sternness and almost ferocity.

" I wish you to carry a message back," he said, " to the white race, the great dominating race whom I hate and defy. Tell them that I have battened on their blood for twenty years, that I have slain them until even I became tired of what had once been a joy, that I did this unnoticed and unsuspected in the face of every precaution which their civilization could suggest. There is no satisfaction in revenge when your enemy does not know who has struck him. I am not sorry, therefore, to have you as a messenger. There is no need why I should tell you how this great hate became born in me. See this," and he held up his mutilated hand ; " that was done by a white man's knife. My father was white, my mother was a slave. When he died she was sold again, and I, a child then, saw her lashed to death to break her of some of the little airs and graces which her late master had encouraged in her. My young wife, too, oh, my young wife ! " a shudder ran through his whole frame. " No matter ! I swore my oath, and I kept it. From Maine to Florida, and from Boston to San Francisco, you could track my steps by sudden deaths which baffled the police. I warred against the whole white race as they for centuries had warred against the black one. At last, as I tell you, I sickened of blood. Still, the sight of a white face was abhorrent to me, and I determined to find some bold free black people and to throw in my lot with them, to cultivate their latent powers and to form a nucleus for a great coloured nation. This idea possessed me, and I travelled over the world for two years seeking for what I desired. At last I almost despaired of finding it. There was no hope of regeneration in the slavedealing Soudanese, the debased Fantee, or the Americanized negroes of Liberia. I was returning from my quest when chance brought me in contact with this magnificent tribe of dwellers in the desert, and I threw in my lot with them. Before doing so, however, my old instinct of revenge prompted me to make one last visit to the United States, and I returned from it in the *Marie Celeste*.

" As to the voyage itself, your intelligence will have told you by this time that, thanks to my manipulation, both compasses and chronometers were entirely untrustworthy. I alone worked out the course with correct instruments of my own, while the steering was done by my black friends under my guidance. I pushed Tibbs's wife overboard. What! You look surprised and shrink away. Surely you had guessed that by this time. I would have shot you that day through the partition, but unfortunately you were not there. I tried again afterwards, but you were awake. I shot Tibbs. I think the idea of suicide was carried out rather neatly. Of course when once we got on the coast the rest was simple. I had bargained that all on board should die ; but that stone of yours upset my plans. I also bargained that there should be no plunder. No one can say we are pirates. We have acted from principle, not from any sordid motive."

I listened in amazement to the summary of his crimes which this strange man gave me, all in the quietest and most composed of voices, as though detailing incidents of every-day occurrence. I still seem to see him sitting like a hideous nightmare at the end of my couch, with the single rude lamp flickering over his cadaverous features.

" And now," he continued, " there is no difficulty about your escape. These stupid adopted children of mine will say that you have gone back to heaven from whence you came. The wind blows off the land. I have a boat all ready for you, well stored with provisions and water. I am anxious to be rid of you, so you may rely that nothing is neglected. Rise up and follow me."

I did what he commanded, and he led me through the door of the hut. The guards had either been withdrawn, or Goring had arranged matters with them. We passed unchallenged through the town and across the sandy plain. Once more I heard the roar of the sea, and saw the long white line of the surge. Two figures were standing upon the shore arranging the gear of a small boat. They were the two sailors who had been with us on the voyage.

" See him safely through the surf," said Goring. The two men sprang in and pushed off, pulling me in after them. With mainsail and jib we ran out from the land and passed safely over the bar. Then my two companions without a word of farewell sprang overboard, and I saw their heads like black dots on the white foam as they made their way back to the shore, while I scudded away into the blackness of the night. Looking back I caught my last glimpse of Goring. He was standing upon the summit of a sand-hill, and the rising moon behind him threw his gaunt angular figure into hard relief. He was waving his arms frantically to and fro ; it may have been to encourage me on my way, but the gestures seemed to me at the time to be threatening ones, and I have often thought that it was more likely that his old savage instinct had returned when he realized that I was out of his power. Be that as it may, it was the last that I ever saw or ever shall see of Septimius Goring.

There is no need for me to dwell upon my solitary voyage. I steered as well as I could for the Canaries, but was picked up upon the fifth day by the British and African Steam Navigation Company's boat *Monrovia*. Let me take this opportunity of tendering my sincerest thanks to Captain Stornoway and his officers for the great kindness which they showed me from that time till they landed me in Liverpool, where I was enabled to take one of the Guion boats to New York.

From the day on which I found myself once more in the bosom of my family I have said little of what I have undergone. The subject is still an intensely painful one to me, and the little which I have dropped has been discredited. I now put the facts before the public as they occurred, careless how far they may be believed, and simply writing them down because my lung is growing weaker, and I feel the responsibility of holding my peace longer. I make no vague statement. Turn to your map of Africa. There above Cape Blanco, where the land trends away north and south from the westernmost point of the continent, there it is that Septimius Goring still reigns over his dark subjects, unless retribution has overtaken him ; and there, where the long green ridges run swiftly in to roar and hiss upon the hot yellow sand, it is there that Harton lies with Hyson and the other poor fellows who were done to death in the *Marie Celeste*.

24. *That Little Square Box*

ALL aboard ? " said the captain.
"All aboard, sir ! " said the mate.
"Then stand by to let her go."
It was nine o'clock on a Wednesday morning. The good ship *Spartan* was lying off Boston Quay with her cargo under hatches, her passengers shipped, and everything prepared for a start. The warning whistle had been sounded twice ; the final bell had been rung. Her bowsprit was turned towards England, and the hiss of escaping steam showed that all was ready for her run of three thousand miles. She strained at the warps that held her like a greyhound at its leash.

I have the misfortune to be a very nervous man. A sedentary literary life has helped to increase the morbid love of solitude which, even in my boyhood, was one of my distinguishing characteristics. As I stood upon the quarter-deck of the Transatlantic steamer, I bitterly cursed the necessity which drove me back to the land of my forefathers. The shouts of the sailors, the rattle of the cordage, the farewells of my fellow-passengers, and the cheers of the mob, each and all jarred upon

TALES OF TERROR

25. *The Horror of the Heights*

THE idea that the extraordinary narrative which
has been called the Joyce-Armstrong Fragment
is an elaborate practical joke evolved by some
unknown person, cursed by a perverted and sinister
sense of humour, has now been abandoned by all who
have examined the matter. The most *macabre* and
imaginative of plotters would hesitate before linking
his morbid fancies with the unquestioned and tragic
facts which reinforce the statement. Though the asser-
tions contained in it are amazing and even monstrous,
it is none the less forcing itself upon the general intelligence that they are true, and that we must readjust our
ideas to the new situation. This world of ours appears
to be separated by a slight and precarious margin of
safety from a most singular and unexpected danger. I
will endeavour in this narrative, which reproduces the
original document in its necessarily somewhat fragmen-
tary form, to lay before the reader the whole of the facts
up to date, prefacing my statement by saying that, if
there be any who doubt the narrative of Joyce-Armstrong,
there can be no question at all as to the facts concerning
Lieutenant Myrtle, R.N., and Mr. Hay Connor, who
undoubtedly met their end in the manner described.

The Joyce-Armstrong Fragment was found in the
field which is called Lower Haycock, lying one mile to
the westward of the village of Withyham, upon the Kent

and Sussex border. It was on the fifteenth of September last that an agricultural labourer, James Flynn, in the employment of Mathew Dodd, farmer, of the Chauntry Farm, Withyham, perceived a briar pipe lying near the footpath which skirts the hedge in Lower Haycock. A few paces farther on he picked up a pair of broken binocular glasses. Finally, among some nettles in the ditch, he caught sight of a flat, canvas-backed book, which proved to be a note-book with detachable leaves, some of which had come loose and were fluttering along the base of the hedge. These he collected, but some, including the first, were never recovered, and leave a deplorable hiatus in this all-important statement. The note-book was taken by the labourer to his master, who in turn showed it to Dr. J. H. Atherton, of Hartfield. This gentleman at once recognized the need for an expert examination, and the manuscript was forwarded to the Aero Club in London, where it now lies.

The first two pages of the manuscript are missing. There is also one torn away at the end of the narrative, though none of these affect the general coherence of the story. It is conjectured that the missing opening is concerned with the record of Mr. Joyce-Armstrong's qualifications as an aeronaut, which can be gathered from other sources and are admitted to be unsurpassed among the air-pilots of England. For many years he has been looked upon as among the most daring and the most intellectual of flying men, a combination which has enabled him to both invent and test several new devices, including the common gyroscopic attachment which is known by his name. The main body of the manuscript is written neatly in ink, but the last few lines are in pencil and are so ragged as to be hardly legible—exactly, in fact, as they might be expected to appear if they were scribbled off hurriedly from the seat of a moving aeroplane. There are, it may be added, several stains, both on the last page and on the outside cover which have been pronounced by the Home Office experts to be blood—probably human and certainly mammalian. The fact that something closely resembling the organism of malaria was discovered in this blood, and that Joyce-Armstrong is known to have suffered from intermittent fever, is a remarkable example of the new weapons which modern science has placed in the hands of our detectives.

And now a word as to the personality of the author of this epoch-making statement. Joyce-Armstrong, according to the few friends who really knew something of the man, was a poet and a dreamer, as well as a mechanic and an inventor. He was a man of considerable wealth, much of which he had spent in the pursuit of his aeronautical hobby. He had four private aeroplanes in his hangars near Devizes, and is said to have made no fewer than one hundred and seventy ascents in the course of last year. He was a retiring man with dark moods, in which he would avoid the society of his fellows. Captain Dangerfield, who knew him better than anyone, says that there were times when his eccentricity threatened to develop into something more serious. His habit of carrying a shot-gun with him in his aeroplane was one manifestation of it.

Another was the morbid effect which the fall of Lieutenant Myrtle had upon his mind. Myrtle, who was attempting the height record, fell from an altitude of something over thirty thousand feet. Horrible to narrate, his head was entirely obliterated, though his body and limbs preserved their configuration. At every gathering of airmen, Joyce-Armstrong, according to Dangerfield, would ask, with an enigmatic smile : " And where, pray, is Myrtle's head ? "

On another occasion after dinner, at the mess of the Flying School on Salisbury Plain, he started a debate as to what will be the most permanent danger which airmen will have to encounter. Having listened to successive opinions as to air-pockets, faulty construction, and over-banking, he ended by shrugging his shoulders and refusing to put forward his own views, though he gave the impression that they differed from any advanced by his companions.

It is worth remarking that after his own complete disappearance it was found that his private affairs were arranged with a precision which may show that he had a strong premonition of disaster. With these essential explanations I will now give the narrative exactly as it stands, beginning at page three of the blood-soaked notebook :—

" Nevertheless, when I dined at Rheims with Coselli and Gustav Raymond I found that neither of them was aware of any particular danger in the higher layers of the atmosphere. I did not actually say what was in my thoughts, but I got so near to it that if they had any corresponding idea they could not have failed to express it. But then they are two empty, vainglorious fellows with no thought beyond seeing their silly names in the newspaper. It is interesting to note that neither of them had ever been much beyond the twenty-thousand-foot level. Of course, men have been higher than this both in balloons and in the ascent of mountains. It must be well above that point that the aeroplane enters the danger zone—always presuming that my premonitions are correct.

" Aeroplaning has been with us now for more than twenty years, and one might well ask : Why should this peril be only revealing itself in our day ? The answer is obvious. In the old days of weak engines, when a hundred horse-power Gnome or Green was considered ample for every need, the flights were very restricted. Now that three hundred horse-power is the rule rather than the exception, visits to the upper layers have become easier and more common. Some of us can remember how, in our youth, Garros made a world-wide reputation by attaining nineteen thousand feet, and it was considered a remarkable achievement to fly over the Alps. Our standard now has been immeasurably raised, and there

are twenty high flights for one in former years. Many
of them have been undertaken with impunity. The
thirty-thousand-foot level has been reached time after
time with no discomfort beyond cold and asthma. What
does this prove ? A visitor might descend upon this
planet a thousand times and never see a tiger. Yet
tigers exist, and if he chanced to come down into a jungle
he might be devoured. There are jungles of the upper
air, and there are worse things than tigers which inhabit
them. I believe in time they will map these jungles
accurately out. Even at the present moment I could
name two of them. One of them lies over the Pau-Biarritz
district of France. Another is just over my head as I
write here in my house in Wiltshire. I rather think
there is a third in the Homburg-Wiesbaden district.

" It was the disappearance of the airmen that first set
me thinking. Of course, everyone said that they had
fallen into the sea, but that did not satisfy me at all.
First, there was Verrier in France ; his machine was
found near Bayonne, but they never got his body.
There was the case of Baxter also, who vanished, though
his engine and some of the iron fixings were found in
a wood in Leicestershire. In that case, Dr. Middleton,
of Amesbury, who was watching the flight with a telescope, declares that just before the clouds obscured the
view he saw the machine, which was at an enormous
height, suddenly rise perpendicularly upwards in a
succession of jerks in a manner that he would have thought
to be impossible. That was the last seen of Baxter.
There was a correspondence in the papers, but it never
led to anything. There were several other similar cases,
and then there was the death of Hay Connor. What a
cackle there was about an unsolved mystery of the air,
and what columns in the halfpenny papers, and yet how
little was ever done to get to the bottom of the business !
He came down in a tremendous vol-plané from an
unknown height. He never got off his machine and
died in his pilot's seat. Died of what ? ' Heart dis-

ease,' said the doctors. Rubbish ! Hay Connor's heart
was as sound as mine is. What did Venables say ?
Venables was the only man who was at his side when he
died. He said that he was shivering and looked like a
man who had been badly scared. ' Died of fright,' said
Venables, but could not imagine what he was frightened
about. Only said one word to Venables, which sounded
like ' Monstrous.' They could make nothing of that at
the inquest. But I could make something of it. Monsters ! That was the last word of poor Harry Hay Connor.
And he *did* die of fright, just as Venables thought.

" And then there was Myrtle's head. Do you really
believe—does anybody really believe—that a man's head
could be driven clean into his body by the force of a
fall ? Well, perhaps it may be possible, but I, for one,
have never believed that it was so with Myrtle. And the
grease upon his clothes—' all slimy with grease,' said
somebody at the inquest. Queer that nobody got thinking after that ! I did—but, then, I had been thinking
for a good long time. I've made three ascents—how
Dangerfield used to chaff me about my shot-gun—but
I've never been high enough. Now, with this new, light
Paul Veroner machine and its one hundred and seventy-
five Robur, I should easily touch the thirty thousand to-
morrow. I'll have a shot at the record. Maybe I shall
have a shot at something else as well. Of course, it's
dangerous. If a fellow wants to avoid danger he had
best keep out of flying altogether and subside finally
into flannel slippers and a dressing-gown. But I'll
visit the air-jungle to-morrow—and if there's anything
there I shall know it. If I return, I'll find myself a bit
of a celebrity. If I don't, this note-book may explain
what I am trying to do, and how I lost my life in doing it.
But no drivel about accidents or mysteries, if *you* please.

" I chose my Paul Veroner monoplane for the job.
There's nothing like a monoplane when real work is to
be done. Beaumont found that out in very early days.
For one thing it doesn't mind damp, and the weather

looks as if we should be in the clouds all the time. It's a bonny little model and answers my hand like a tender-mouthed horse. The engine is a ten-cylinder rotary Robur working up to one hundred and seventy-five. It has all the modern improvements—enclosed fuselage, high-curved landing skids, brakes, gyroscopic steadiers, and three speeds, worked by an alteration of the angle of the planes upon the Venetian-blind principle. I took a shot-gun with me and a dozen cartridges filled with buck-shot. You should have seen the face of Perkins, my old mechanic, when I directed him to put them in. I was dressed like an Arctic explorer, with two jerseys under my overalls, thick socks inside my padded boots, a storm-cap with flaps, and my talc goggles. It was stifling outside the hangars, but I was going for the summit of the Himalayas, and had to dress for the part. Perkins knew there was something on and implored me to take him with me. Perhaps I should if I were using the biplane, but a monoplane is a one-man show—if you want to get the last foot of lift out of it. Of course, I took an oxygen bag ; the man who goes for the altitude record without one will either be frozen or smothered—or both.

" I had a good look at the planes, the rudder-bar, and the elevating lever before I got in. Everything was in order so far as I could see. Then I switched on my engine and found that she was running sweetly. When they let her go she rose almost at once upon the lowest speed. I circled my home field once or twice just to warm her up, and then, with a wave to Perkins and the others, I flattened out my planes and put her on her highest. She skimmed like a swallow down wind for eight or ten miles until I turned her nose up a little and she began to climb in a great spiral for the cloud-bank above me. It's all-important to rise slowly and adapt yourself to the pressure as you go.

" It was a close, warm day for an English September, and there was the hush and heaviness of impending rain.

Now and then there came sudden puffs of wind from the south-west—one of them so gusty and unexpected that it caught me napping and turned me half-round for an instant. I remember the time when gusts and whirls and air-pockets used to be things of danger—before we learned to put an overmastering power into our engines. Just as I reached the cloud-banks, with the altimeter marking three thousand, down came the rain. My word, how it poured ! It drummed upon my wings and lashed against my face, blurring my glasses so that I could hardly see. I got down on to a low speed, for it was painful to travel against it. As I got higher it became hail, and I had to turn tail to it. One of my cylinders was out of action—a dirty plug, I should imagine, but still I was rising steadily with plenty of power. After a bit the trouble passed, whatever it was, and I heard the full, deep-throated purr—the ten singing as one. That's where the beauty of our modern silencers comes in. We can at last control our engines by ear. How they squeal and squeak and sob when they are in trouble ! All those cries for help were wasted in the old days, when every sound was swallowed up by the monstrous racket of the machine. If only the early aviators could come back to see the beauty and perfection of the mechanism which have been bought at the cost of their lives !

" About nine-thirty I was nearing the clouds. Down below me, all blurred and shadowed with rain, lay the vast expense of Salisbury Plain. Half a dozen flying machines were doing hackwork at the thousand-foot level, looking like little black swallows against the green background. I dare say they were wondering what I was doing up in cloud-land. Suddenly a grey curtain drew across beneath me and the wet folds of vapours were swirling round my face. It was clammily cold and miserable. But I was above the hail-storm, and that was something gained. The cloud was as dark and thick as a London fog. In my anxiety to get clear, I cocked her nose up until the automatic alarm-bell rang, and I actually began to slide backwards. My sopped and dripping wings had made me heavier than I thought, but presently I was in lighter cloud, and soon had cleared the first layer. There was a second—opal-coloured and fleecy—at a great height above my head, a white, unbroken ceiling above, and a dark, unbroken floor below, with the monoplane labouring upwards upon a vast spiral between them. It is deadly lonely in these cloud-spaces. Once a great flight of some small water-birds went past me, flying very fast to the westwards. The quick whir of their wings and their musical cry were cheery to my ear. I fancy that they were teal, but I am a wretched zoologist. Now that we humans have become birds we must really learn to know our brethren by sight.

" The wind down beneath me whirled and swayed the broad cloud-plain. Once a great eddy formed in it, a whirlpool of vapour, and through it, as down a funnel, I caught sight of the distant world. A large white biplane was passing at a vast depth beneath me. I fancy it was the morning mail service betwixt Bristol and London. Then the drift swirled inwards again and the great solitude was unbroken.

" Just after ten I touched the lower edge of the upper cloud-stratum. It consisted of fine diaphanous vapour drifting swiftly from the westward. The wind had been steadily rising all this time and it was now blowing a sharp breeze—twenty-eight an hour by my gauge. Already it was very cold, though my altimeter only marked nine thousand. The engines were working beautifully, and we went droning steadily upwards. The cloud-bank was thicker than I had expected, but at last it thinned out into a golden mist before me, and then in an instant I had shot out from it, and there was an unclouded sky and a brilliant sun above my head—all blue and gold above, all shining silver below, one vast, glimmering plain as far as my eyes could reach. It was a quarter past ten o'clock, and the barograph needle pointed to twelve thousand eight hundred. Up I went and up, my ears concentrated upon the deep purring of my motor, my eyes busy always with the watch, the revolution indicator, the petrol lever, and the oil pump. No wonder aviators are said to be a fearless race. With so many things to think of there is no time to trouble about oneself. About this time I noted how unreliable is the compass when above a certain height from earth. At fifteen thousand feet mine was pointing east and a point south. The sun and the wind gave me my true bearings.

" I had hoped to reach an eternal stillness in these high altitudes, but with every thousand feet of ascent the gale grew stronger. My machine groaned and trembled in every joint and rivet as she faced it, and swept away like a sheet of paper when I banked her on the turn, skimming down wind at a greater pace, perhaps, than ever mortal man has moved. Yet I had always to turn again and tack up in the wind's eye, for it was not merely a height record that I was after. By all my calculations it was above little Wiltshire that my air-jungle lay, and all my labour might be lost if I struck the outer layers at some farther point.

" When I reached the nineteen-thousand-foot level, which was about midday, the wind was so severe that I looked with some anxiety to the stays of my wings, expecting momentarily to see them snap or slacken. I even cast loose the parachute behind me, and fastened its hook into the ring of my leathern belt, so as to be ready for the worst. Now was the time when a bit of scamped work by the mechanic is paid for by the life of the aeronaut. But she held together bravely. Every cord and strut was humming and vibrating like so many harp-strings, but it was glorious to see how, for all the beating and the buffeting, she was still the conqueror of Nature and the mistress of the sky. There is surely something divine in man himself that he should rise so superior to the limitations which Creation seemed to impose—rise, too, by such unselfish, heroic devotion as this air-conquest has shown. Talk of human degeneration! When has such a story as this been written in the annals of our race?

"These were the thoughts in my head as I climbed that monstrous, inclined plane with the wind sometimes beating in my face and sometimes whistling behind my ears, while the cloud-land beneath me fell away to such a distance that the folds and hummocks of silver had all smoothed out into one flat, shining plain. But suddenly I had a horrible and unprecedented experience. I have known before what it is to be in what our neighbours have called a *tourbillon*, but never on such a scale as this. That huge, sweeping river of wind of which I have spoken had, as it appears, whirlpools within it which were as monstrous as itself. Without a moment's warning I was dragged suddenly into the heart of one. I spun round for a minute or two with such velocity that I almost lost my senses, and then fell suddenly, left wing foremost, down the vacuum funnel in the centre. I dropped like a stone, and lost nearly a thousand feet. It was only my belt that kept me in my seat, and the shock and breathlessness left me hanging half-insensible over the side of the fuselage. But I am always capable of a supreme effort—it is my one great merit as an aviator. I was conscious that the descent was slower. The whirlpool was a cone rather than a funnel, and I had come to the apex. With a terrific wrench, throwing my weight all to one side, I levelled my planes and brought her head away from the wind. In an instant I had shot out of the eddies and was skimming down the sky. Then, shaken but victorious, I turned her nose up and began once more my steady grind on the upward spiral. I took a large sweep to avoid the danger-spot of the whirlpool, and soon I was safely above it. Just after one o'clock I was twenty-one thousand feet above the sea-level. To my great joy I had topped the gale, and with every hundred feet of ascent the air grew stiller. On the other hand, it was very cold, and I was conscious of that peculiar nausea which goes with rarefaction of the air. For the first time I unscrewed the mouth of my oxygen bag and took an occasional whiff of the glorious gas. I could feel it running like a cordial through my veins, and I was exhilarated almost to the point of drunkenness. I shouted and sang as I soared upwards into the cold, still outer world.

" It is very clear to me that the insensibility which came upon Glaisher, and in a lesser degree upon Coxwell, when, in 1862, they ascended in a balloon to the height of thirty thousand feet, was due to the extreme speed with which a perpendicular ascent is made. Doing it at an easy gradient and accustoming oneself to the lessened barometric pressure by slow degrees, there are no such dreadful symptoms. At the same great height I found that even without my oxygen inhaler I could breathe without undue distress. It was bitterly cold, however, and my thermometer was at zero, Fahrenheit. At one-thirty I was nearly seven miles above the surface of the earth, and still ascending steadily. I found, however, that the rarefied air was giving markedly less support to my planes, and that my angle of ascent had to be considerably lowered in consequence. It was already clear that even with my light weight and strong engine-power there was a point in front of me where I should be held. To make matters worse, one of my sparking-plugs was in trouble again and there was intermittent misfiring in the engine. My heart was heavy with the fear of failure.

" It was about that time that I had a most extraordinary experience. Something whizzed past me in a trail of smoke and exploded with a loud, hissing sound, sending forth a cloud of steam. For the instant I could not imagine what had happened. Then I remembered that the earth is for ever being bombarded by meteor stones, and would be hardly inhabitable were they not in nearly every case turned to vapour in the outer layers of the atmosphere. Here is a new danger for the high-altitude man, for two others passed me when I was nearing the forty-thousand-foot mark. I cannot doubt that at the edge of the earth's envelope the risk would be a very real one.

" My barograph needle marked forty-one thousand three hundred when I became aware that I could go no farther. Physically, the strain was not as yet greater than I could bear, but my machine had reached its limit. The attenuated air gave no firm support to the wings, and the least tilt developed into side-slip, while she seemed sluggish on her controls. Possibly, had the engine been at its best, another thousand feet might have been within our capacity, but it was still misfiring, and two out of the ten cylinders appeared to be out of action. If I had not already reached the zone for which I was searching then I should never see it upon this journey. But was it not possible that I had attained it? Soaring in circles like a monstrous hawk upon the forty-thousand-foot level I let the monoplane guide herself, and with my Mannheim glass I made a careful observation of my surroundings. The heavens were perfectly clear; there was no indication of those dangers which I had imagined.

" I have said that I was soaring in circles. It struck me suddenly that I would do well to take a wider sweep and open up a new air-tract. If the hunter entered an earth-jungle he would drive through it if he wished to find his game. My reasoning had led me to believe that the air-jungle which I had imagined lay somewhere over Wiltshire. This should be to the south and west of me. I took my bearings from the sun, for the compass was hopeless and no trace of earth was to be seen—nothing but the distant, silver cloud-plain. However, I got my direction as best I might and kept her head straight to the mark. I reckoned that my petrol supply would not last for more than another hour or so, but I could afford to use it to the last drop, since a single magnificent vol-plané could at any time take me to the earth.

" Suddenly I was aware of something new. The air

in front of me had lost its crystal clearness. It was full of long, ragged wisps of something which I can only compare to very fine cigarette-smoke. It hung about in wreaths and coils, turning and twisting slowly in the sunlight. As the monoplane shot through it, I was aware of a faint taste of oil upon my lips, and there was a greasy scum upon the woodwork of the machine. Some infinitely fine organic matter appeared to be suspended in the atmosphere. There was no life there. It was inchoate and diffuse, extending for many square acres and then fringing off into the void. No, it was not life. But might it not be the remains of life? Above all, might it not be the food of life, of monstrous life, even as the humble grease of the ocean is the food for the mighty whale? The thought was in my mind when my eyes looked upwards and I saw the most wonderful vision that ever man has seen. Can I hope to convey it to you even as I saw it myself last Thursday?

" Conceive a jelly-fish such as sails in our summer seas, bell-shaped and of enormous size—far larger, I should judge, than the dome of St. Paul's. It was of a light pink colour veined with a delicate green, but the whole huge fabric so tenuous that it was but a fairy outline against the dark blue sky. It pulsated with a delicate and regular rhythm. From it there depended two long, drooping, green tentacles, which swayed slowly backwards and forwards. This gorgeous vision passed gently with noiseless dignity over my head, as light and fragile as a soap-bubble, and drifted upon its stately way.

" I had half-turned my monoplane, that I might look after this beautiful creature, when, in a moment, I found myself amidst a perfect fleet of them, of all sizes, but none so large as the first. Some were quite small, but the majority about as big as an average balloon, and with much the same curvature at the top. There was in them a delicacy of texture and colouring which reminded me of the finest Venetian glass. Pale shades of pink and green were the prevailing tints, but all had a lovely iridescence where the sun shimmered through their dainty forms. Some hundreds of them drifted past me, a wonderful fairy squadron of strange, unknown argosies of the sky—creatures whose forms and substance were so attuned to these pure heights that one could not conceive anything so delicate within actual sight or sound of earth.

" But soon my attention was drawn to a new phenomenon—the serpents of the outer air. These were long, thin, fantastic coils of vapour-like material, which turned and twisted with great speed, flying round and round at such a pace that the eyes could hardly follow them. Some of these ghost-like creatures were twenty or thirty feet long, but it was difficult to tell their girth,, for their outline was so hazy that it seemed to fade away into the air around them. These air-snakes were of a very light grey or smoke colour, with some darker lines within, which gave the impression of a definite organism. One of them whisked past my very face, and I was conscious of a cold, clammy contact, but their composition was so unsubstantial that I could not connect them with any thought of physical danger, any more than the beautiful bell-like creatures which had preceded them. There was no more solidity in their frames than in the floating spume from a broken wave.

" But a more terrible experience was in store for me. Floating downwards from a great height there came a purplish patch of vapour, small as I saw it first, but rapidly enlarging as it approached me, until it appeared to be hundreds of square feet in size. Though fashioned of some transparent, jelly-like substance, it was none the less of much more definite outline and solid consistence than anything which I had seen before. There were more traces, too, of a physical organization, especially two vast, shadowy, circular plates upon either side, which may have been eyes, and a perfectly solid white projection between them which was as curved and cruel as the beak of a vulture.

339

" The whole aspect of this monster was formidable and threatening, and it kept changing its colour from a very light mauve to a dark, angry purple so thick that it cast a shadow as it drifted between my monoplane and the sun. On the upper curve of its huge body there were three great projections which I can only describe as enormous bubbles, and I was convinced as I looked at them that they were charged with some extremely light gas which served to buoy up the misshapen and semi-solid mass in the rarefied air. The creature moved swiftly along, keeping pace easily with the monoplane, and for twenty miles or more it formed my horrible escort, hovering over me like a bird of prey which is waiting to pounce. Its method of progression—done so swiftly that it was not easy to follow—was to throw out a long, glutinous streamer in front of it, which in turn seemed to draw forward the rest of the writhing body. So elastic and gelatinous was it that never for two successive minutes was it the same shape, and yet each change made it more threatening and loathsome than the last.

" I knew that it meant mischief. Every purple flush of its hideous body told me so. The vague, goggling eyes which were turned always upon me were cold and merciless in their viscid hatred. I dipped the nose of my monoplane downwards to escape it. As I did so, as quick as a flash there shot out a long tentacle from this mass of floating blubber, and it fell as light and sinuous as a whip-lash across the front of my machine. There was a loud hiss as it lay for a moment across the hot engine, and it whisked itself into the air again, while the huge, flat body drew itself together as if in sudden pain. I dipped to a vol-piqué, but again a tentacle fell over the monoplane and was shorn off by the propeller as easily as it might have cut through a smoke wreath. A long, gliding, sticky, serpent-like coil came from behind and caught me round the waist, dragging me out of the fuselage. I tore at it, my fingers sinking into the smooth, glue-like surface, and for an instant I disengaged myself, but only to be caught round the boot by another coil, which gave me a jerk that tilted me almost on to my back.

" As I fell over I blazed off both barrels of my gun, though, indeed, it was like attacking an elephant with a pea-shooter to imagine that any human weapon could cripple that mighty bulk. And yet I aimed better than I knew, for, with a loud report, one of the great blisters upon the creature's back exploded with the puncture of the buck-shot. It was very clear that my conjecture was right, and that these vast, clear bladders were distended with some lifting gas, for in an instant the huge, cloud-like body turned sideways, writhing desperately to find its balance, while the white beak snapped and gaped in horrible fury. But already I had shot away on the steepest glide that I dared to attempt, my engine still full on, the flying propeller and the force of gravity shooting me downwards like an aerolite. Far behind me I saw a dull, purplish smudge growing swiftly smaller and merging into the blue sky behind it. I was safe out of the deadly jungle of the outer air.

" Once out of danger I throttled my engine, for nothing tears a machine to pieces quicker than running on full power from a height. It was a glorious, spiral vol-plané from nearly eight miles of altitude—first, to the level of the silver cloud-bank, then to that of the storm-cloud beneath it, and finally, in beating rain, to the surface of the earth. I saw the Bristol Channel beneath me as I broke from the clouds, but, having still some petrol in my tank, I got twenty miles inland before I found myself stranded in a field half a mile from the village of Ash-combe. There I got three tins of petrol from a passing motor-car, and at ten minutes past six that evening I alighted gently in my own home meadow at Devizes, after such a journey as no mortal upon earth has ever yet taken and lived to tell the tale. I have seen the beauty and I have seen the horror of the heights—and greater beauty or greater horror than that is not within the ken of man.

341

" And now it is my plan to go once again before I give my results to the world. My reason for this is that I must surely have something to show by way of proof before I lay such a tale before my fellow-men. It is true that others will soon follow and will confirm what I have said, and yet I should wish to carry conviction from the first. Those lovely iridescent bubbles of the air should not be hard to capture. They drift slowly upon their way, and the swift monoplane could intercept their leisurely course. It is likely enough that they would dissolve in the heavier layers of the atmosphere, and that some small heap of amorphous jelly might be all that I should bring to earth with me. And yet something there would surely be by which I could substantiate my story. Yes, I will go, even if I run a risk by doing so. These purple horrors would not seem to be numerous. It is probable that I shall not see one. If I do I shall dive at once. At the worst there is always the shotgun and my knowledge of . . ."

Here a page of the manuscript is unfortunately missing. On the next page is written, in large, straggling writing :—

" Forty-three thousand feet. I shall never see earth again. They are beneath me, three of them. God help me ; it is a dreadful death to die ! "

Such in its entirety is the Joyce-Armstrong Statement. Of the man nothing has since been seen. Pieces of his shattered monoplane have been picked up in the preserves of Mr. Budd-Lushington upon the borders of Kent and Sussex, within a few miles of the spot where the note-book was discovered. If the unfortunate aviator's theory is correct that this air-jungle, as he called it, existed only over the south-west of England, then it would seem that he had fled from it at the full speed of his monoplane, but had been overtaken and devoured by these horrible creatures at some spot in the outer atmosphere above the place where the grim relics were found. The picture of that monoplane skimming down the sky, with the nameless terrors flying as swiftly beneath it and cutting it off always from the earth while they gradually closed in upon their victim, is one upon which a man who valued his sanity would prefer not to dwell. There are many, as I am aware, who still jeer at the facts which I have here set down, but even they must admit that Joyce-Armstrong has disappeared, and I would commend to them his own words : " This note-book may explain what I am trying to do, and how I lost my life in doing it. But no drivel about accidents or mysteries, if *you* please."

26. *The Leather Funnel*

MY friend, Lionel Dacre, lived in the Avenue de Wagram, Paris. His house was that small one, with the iron railings and grass plot in front of it, on the left-hand side as you pass down from the Arc de Triomphe. I fancy that it had been there long before the avenue was constructed, for the grey tiles were stained with lichens, and the walls were mildewed and discoloured with age. It looked a small house from the street, five windows in front, if I remember right, but it deepened into a single long chamber at the back. It was here that Dacre had that singular library of occult literature, and the fantastic curiosities which served as a hobby for himself, and an amusement for his friends. A wealthy man of refined and eccentric tastes, he had spent much of his life and fortune in gathering together what was said to be a unique private collection of Talmudic, cabalistic, and magical works, many of them of great rarity and value. His tastes leaned toward the marvellous and the monstrous, and I have heard that his experiments in the direction of the unknown have passed all the bounds of civilization and of decorum. To his English friends he never alluded to such matters, and took the tone of the student and *virtuoso*; but a Frenchman whose tastes were of the same nature has assured me that the worst excesses of the black mass have been perpetrated in that large and lofty hall, which is lined with the shelves of his books, and the cases of his museum.

Dacre's appearance was enough to show that his deep interest in these psychic matters was intellectual rather than spiritual. There was no trace of asceticism upon his heavy face, but there was much mental force in his huge, dome-like skull, which curved upward from amongst his thinning locks, like a snow-peak above its fringe of fir trees. His knowledge was greater than his wisdom, and his powers were far superior to his character. The small bright eyes, buried deeply in his fleshy face, twinkled with intelligence and an unabated curiosity of life, but they were the eyes of a sensualist and an egotist. Enough of the man, for he is dead now, poor devil, dead at the very time that he had made sure that he had at last discovered the elixir of life. It is not with his complex character that I have to deal, but with the very strange and inexplicable incident which had its rise in my visit to him in the early spring of the year '82.

I had known Dacre in England, for my researches in the Assyrian Room of the British Museum had been conducted at the time when he was endeavouring to establish a mystic and esoteric meaning in the Babylonian tablets, and this community of interests had brought us together. Chance remarks had led to daily conversation, and that to something verging upon friendship. I had promised him that on my next visit to Paris I would call upon him. At the time when I was able to fulfil my compact I was living in a cottage at Fontainebleau, and as the evening trains were inconvenient, he asked me to spend the night in his house.

" I have only that one spare couch," said he, pointing

to a broad sofa in his large salon ; " I hope that you will manage to be comfortable there."

It was a singular bedroom, with its high walls of brown volumes, but there could be no more agreeable furniture to a bookworm like myself, and there is no scent so pleasant to my nostrils as that faint, subtle reek which comes from an ancient book. I assured him that I could desire no more charming chamber, and no more congenial surroundings.

" If the fittings are neither convenient nor conventional, they are at least costly," said he, looking round at his shelves. " I have expended nearly a quarter of a million of money upon these objects which surround you. Books, weapons, gems, carvings, tapestries, images —there is hardly a thing here which has not its history, and it is generally one worth telling."

He was seated as he spoke at one side of the open fireplace, and I at the other. His reading-table was on his right, and the strong lamp above it ringed it with a very vivid circle of golden light. A half-rolled palimpsest lay in the centre, and around it were many quaint articles of bric-à-brac. One of these was a large funnel, such as is used for filling wine casks. It appeared to be made of black wood, and to be rimmed with discoloured brass.

" That is a curious thing," I remarked. " What is the history of that ? "

" Ah ! " said he, " it is the very question which I have had occasion to ask myself. I would give a good deal to know. Take it in your hands and examine it."

I did so, and found that what I had imagined to be wood was in reality leather, though age had dried it into an extreme hardness. It was a large funnel, and might hold a quart when full. The brass rim encircled the wide end, but the narrow was also tipped with metal.

" What do you make of it ? " asked Dacre.

" I should imagine that it belonged to some vintner or maltster in the Middle Ages," said I. " I have seen in England leathern drinking flagons of the seventeenth century—' black jacks ' as they were called—which were of the same colour and hardness as this filler."

" I dare say the date would be about the same," said Dacre, " and, no doubt, also, it was used for filling a vessel with liquid. If my suspicions are correct, however, it was a queer vintner who used it, and a very singular cask which was filled. Do you observe nothing strange at the spout end of the funnel."

As I held it to the light I observed that at a spot some five inches above the brass tip the narrow neck of the leather funnel was all haggled and scored, as if someone had notched it round with a blunt knife. Only at that point was there any roughening of the dead black surface.

" Someone has tried to cut off the neck."

" Would you call it a cut ? "

" It is torn and lacerated. It must have taken some strength to leave these marks on such tough material, whatever the instrument may have been. But what do you think of it ? I can tell that you know more than you say."

Dacre smiled, and his little eyes twinkled with knowledge.

" Have you included the psychology of dreams among your learned studies ? " he asked.

" I did not even know that there was such a psychology."

" My dear sir, that shelf above the gem case is filled with volumes, from Albertus Magnus onward, which deal with no other subject. It is a science in itself."

" A science of charlatans."

" The charlatan is always the pioneer. From the astrologer came the astronomer, from the alchemist the chemist, from the mesmerist the experimental psychologist. The quack of yesterday is the professor of to-morrow. Even such subtle and elusive things as dreams will in time be reduced to system and order. When that time comes the researches of our friends on the bookshelf yonder will no longer be the amusement of the mystic, but the foundations of a science."

"Supposing that is so, what has the science of dreams to do with a large, black, brass-rimmed funnel?"

"I will tell you. You know that I have an agent who is always on the lookout for rarities and curiosities for my collection. Some days ago he heard of a dealer upon one of the Quais who had acquired some old rubbish found in a cupboard in an ancient house at the back of the Rue Mathurin, in the Quartier Latin. The dining-room of this old house is decorated with a coat of arms, chevrons, and bars rouge upon a field argent, which prove, upon inquiry, to be the shield of Nicholas de la Reynie, a high official of King Louis XIV. There can be no doubt that the other articles in the cupboard date back to the early days of that king. The inference is, therefore, that they were all the property of this Nicholas de la Reynie, who was, as I understand, the gentleman specially concerned with the maintenance and execution of the Draconic laws of that epoch."

"What then?"

"I would ask you now to take the funnel into your hands once more and to examine the upper brass rim. Can you make out any lettering upon it?"

There were certainly some scratches upon it, almost obliterated by time. The general effect was of several letters, the last of which bore some resemblance to a B.

"You make it a B?"

"Yes, I do."

"So do I. In fact, I have no doubt whatever that it is a B."

"But the nobleman you mentioned would have had R for his initial."

"Exactly! That's the beauty of it. He owned this curious object, and yet he had someone else's initials upon it. Why did he do this?"

"I can't imagine; can you?"

"Well, I might, perhaps, guess. Do you observe something drawn a little farther along the rim?"

347

" I should say it was a crown."

" It is undoubtedly a crown ; but if you examine it in a good light, you will convince yourself that it is not an ordinary crown. It is a heraldic crown—a badge of rank, and it consists of an alternation of four pearls and strawberry leaves, the proper badge of a marquis. We may infer, therefore, that the person whose initials end in B was entitled to wear that coronet."

" Then this common leather filler belonged to a marquis ? "

Dacre gave a peculiar smile.

" Or to some member of the family of a marquis," said he. " So much we have clearly gathered from this engraved rim."

" But what has all this to do with dreams ? " I do not know whether it was from a look upon Dacre's face, or from some subtle suggestion in his manner, but a feeling of repulsion, of unreasoning horror, came upon me as I looked at the gnarled old lump of leather.

" I have more than once received important information through my dreams," said my companion in the didactic manner which he loved to affect. " I make it a rule now when I am in doubt upon any material point to place the article in question beside me as I sleep, and to hope for some enlightenment. The process does not appear to me to be very obscure, though it has not yet received the blessing of orthodox science. According to my theory, any object which has been intimately associated with any supreme paroxysm of human emotion, whether it be joy or pain, will retain a certain atmosphere or association which it is capable of communicating to a sensitive mind. By a sensitive mind I do not mean an abnormal one, but such a trained and educated mind as you or I possess."

" You mean, for example, that if I slept beside that old sword upon the wall, I might dream of some bloody incident in which that very sword took part ? "

" An excellent example, for, as a matter of fact, that

348

sword was used in that fashion by me, and I saw in my
sleep the death of its owner, who perished in a brisk
skirmish, which I have been unable to identify, but
which occurred at the time of the wars of the Frondists.
If you think of it, some of our popular observances show
that the fact has already been recognized by our ancestors,
although we, in our wisdom, have classed it among
superstitions."

" For example ? "

" Well, the placing of the bride's cake beneath the
pillow in order that the sleeper may have pleasant dreams.
That is one of several instances which you will find set
forth in a small *brochure* which I am myself writing upon
the subject. But to come back to the point, I slept one
night with this funnel beside me, and I had a dream which
certainly throws a curious light upon its use and origin."

" What did you dream ? "

" I dreamed——" He paused, and an intent look of
interest came over his massive face. " By Jove, that's
well thought of," said he. " This really will be an
exceedingly interesting experiment. You are yourself
a psychic subject—with nerves which respond readily
to any impression."

" I have never tested myself in that direction."

" Then we shall test you to-night. Might I ask you
as a very great favour, when you occupy that couch to-
night, to sleep with this old funnel placed by the side of
your pillow ? "

The request seemed to me a grotesque one ; but I
have myself, in my complex nature, a hunger after all
which is bizarre and fantastic. I had not the faintest
belief in Dacre's theory, nor any hopes for success in
such an experiment ; yet it amused me that the experiment should be made. Dacre, with great gravity, drew a
small stand to the head of my settee, and placed the
funnel upon it. Then, after a short conversation, he
wished me good night and left me.

* * * * *

I sat for some little time smoking by the smouldering fire, and turning over in my mind the curious incident which had occurred, and the strange experience which might lie before me. Sceptical as I was, there was something impressive in the assurance of Dacre's manner, and my extraordinary surroundings, the huge room with the strange and often sinister objects which were hung round it, struck solemnity into my soul. Finally I undressed, and turning out the lamp, I lay down. After long tossing I fell asleep. Let me try to describe as accurately as I can the scene which came to me in my dreams. It stands out now in my memory more clearly than anything which I have seen with my waking eyes.

There was a room which bore the appearance of a vault. Four spandrels from the corners ran up to join a sharp, cup-shaped roof. The architecture was rough, but very strong. It was evidently part of a great building.

Three men in black, with curious, top-heavy, black velvet hats, sat in a line upon a red-carpeted dais. Their faces were very solemn and sad. On the left stood two long-gowned men with portfolios in their hands, which seemed to be stuffed with papers. Upon the right, looking toward me, was a small woman with blonde hair and singular, light-blue eyes—the eyes of a child. She was past her first youth, but could not yet be called middle-aged. Her figure was inclined to stoutness and her bearing was proud and confident. Her face was pale, but serene. It was a curious face, comely and yet feline, with a subtle suggestion of cruelty about the straight, strong little mouth and chubby jaw. She was draped in some sort of loose, white gown. Beside her stood a thin, eager priest, who whispered in her ear, and continually raised a crucifix before her eyes. She turned her head and looked fixedly past the crucifix at the three men in black, who were, I felt, her judges.

As I gazed the three men stood up and said something, but I could distinguish no words, though I was aware that it was the central one who was speaking. They then swept out of the room, followed by the two men with the papers. At the same instant several rough-looking fellows in stout jerkins came bustling in and removed first the red carpet, and then the boards which formed the dais, so as to entirely clear the room. When this screen was removed I saw some singular articles of furniture behind it. One looked like a bed with wooden rollers at each end, and a winch handle to regulate its length. Another was a wooden horse. There were several other curious objects, and a number of swinging cords which played over pulleys. It was not unlike a modern gymnasium.

When the room had been cleared there appeared a new figure upon the scene. This was a tall, thin person clad in black, with a gaunt and austere face. The aspect of the man made me shudder. His clothes were all shining with grease and mottled with stains. He bore himself with a slow and impressive dignity, as if he took command of all things from the instant of his entrance. In spite of his rude appearance and sordid dress, it was now *his* business, *his* room, his to command. He carried a coil of light ropes over his left forearm. The lady looked him up and down with a searching glance, but her expression was unchanged. It was confident—even defiant. But it was very different with the priest. His face was ghastly white, and I saw the moisture glisten and run on his high, sloping forehead. He threw up his hands in prayer and he stooped continually to mutter frantic words in the lady's ear.

The man in black now advanced, and taking one of the cords from his left arm, he bound the woman's hands together. She held them meekly toward him as he did so. Then he took her arm with a rough grip and led her toward the wooden horse, which was little higher than her waist. On to this she was lifted and laid, with her back upon it, and her face to the ceiling, while the priest, quivering with horror, had rushed out of the room. The woman's lips were moving rapidly, and though I could hear nothing I knew that she was praying. Her feet hung down on either side of the horse, and I saw that the rough varlets in attendance had fastened cords to her ankles and secured the other ends to iron rings in the stone floor.

My heart sank within me as I saw these ominous preparations, and yet I was held by the fascination of horror, and I could not take my eyes from the strange spectacle. A man had entered the room with a bucket of water in either hand. Another followed with a third bucket. They were laid beside the wooden horse. The second man had a wooden dipper—a bowl with a straight handle —in his other hand. This he gave to the man in black. At the same moment one of the varlets approached with a dark object in his hand, which even in my dream filled me with a vague feeling of familiarity. It was a leathern filler. With horrible energy he thrust it—but I could stand no more. My hair stood on end with horror. I writhed, I struggled, I broke through the bonds of sleep, and I burst with a shriek into my own life, and found myself lying shivering with terror in the huge library, with the moonlight flooding through the window and throwing strange silver and black traceries upon the opposite wall. Oh, what a blessed relief to feel that I was back in the nineteenth century—back out of that mediæval vault into a world where men had human hearts within their bosoms. I sat up on my couch, trembling in every limb, my mind divided between thankfulness and horror. To think that such things were ever done—that they *could* be done without God striking the villains dead. Was it all a fantasy, or did it really stand for something which had happened in the black, cruel days of the world's history? I sank my throbbing head upon my shaking hands. And then, suddenly, my heart seemed to stand still in my bosom, and I could not even scream, so great was my terror. Something was advancing toward me through the darkness of the room.

It is a horror coming upon a horror which breaks a

man's spirit. I could not reason, I could not pray ; I could only sit like a frozen image, and glare at the dark figure which was coming down the great room. And then it moved out into the white lane of moonlight, and I breathed once more. It was Dacre, and his face showed that he was as frightened as myself.

" Was that you ? For God's sake what's the matter ? " he asked in a husky voice.

" Oh, Dacre, I am glad to see you ! I have been down into hell. It was dreadful."

" Then it was you who screamed ? "

" I dare say it was."

" It rang through the house. The servants are all terrified." He struck a match and lit the lamp. " I think we may get the fire to burn up again," he added, throwing some logs upon the embers. " Good God, my dear chap, how white you are ! You look as if you had seen a ghost."

" So I have—several ghosts."

" The leather funnel has acted, then ? "

" I wouldn't sleep near the infernal thing again for all the money you could offer me."

Dacre chuckled.

" I expected that you would have a lively night of it," said he. " You took it out of me in return, for that scream of yours wasn't a very pleasant sound at two in the morning. I suppose from what you say that you have seen the whole dreadful business."

" What dreadful business ? "

" The torture of the water—the ' Extraordinary Question,' as it was called in the genial days of ' Le Roi Soleil.' Did you stand it out to the end ? "

" No, thank God, I awoke before it really began."

" Ah ! it is just as well for you. I held out till the third bucket. Well, it is an old story, and they are all in their graves now anyhow, so what does it matter how they got there ? I suppose that you have no idea what it was that you have seen ? "

" The torture of some criminal. She must have been
a terrible malefactor indeed if her crimes are in proportion
to her penalty."

" Well, we have that small consolation," said Dacre,
wrapping his dressing-gown round him and crouching
closer to the fire. " They *were* in proportion to her
penalty. That is to say, if I am correct in the lady's
identity."

" How could you possibly know her identity ? "

For answer Dacre took down an old vellum-covered
volume from the shelf.

" Just listen to this," said he ; " it is in the French of
the seventeenth century, but I will give a rough transla-
tion as I go. You will judge for yourself whether I
have solved the riddle or not."

" ' The prisoner was brought before the Grand
Chambers and Tournelles of Parliament, sitting as a
court of justice, charged with the murder of Master
Dreux d'Aubray, her father, and of her two brothers,
MM. d'Aubray, one being civil lieutenant, and the other
a counsellor of Parliament. In person it seemed hard
to believe that she had really done such wicked deeds,
for she was of a mild appearance, and of short stature,
with a fair skin and blue eyes. Yet the Court, having
found her guilty, condemned her to the ordinary and
to the extraordinary question in order that she might be
forced to name her accomplices, after which she should
be carried in a cart to the Place de Grève, there to have
her head cut off, her body being afterwards burned and
her ashes scattered to the winds.'

The date of this entry is July 16, 1676."

" It is interesting," said I, " but not convincing.
How do you prove the two women to be the same ? "

" I am coming to that. The narrative goes on to tell
of the woman's behaviour when questioned. ' When the
executioner approached her she recognized him by the

cords which he held in his hands, and she at once held out her own hands to him, looking at him from head to foot without uttering a word.' How's that ? "

" Yes, it was so."

" ' She gazed without wincing upon the wooden horse and rings which had twisted so many limbs and caused so many shrieks of agony. When her eyes fell upon the three pails of water, which were all ready for her, she said with a smile, " All that water must have been brought here for the purpose of drowning me, Monsieur. You have no idea, I trust, of making a person of my small stature swallow it all." ' Shall I read the details of the torture ? "

" No, for Heaven's sake, don't."

" Here is a sentence which must surely show you that what is here recorded is the very scene which you have gazed upon to-night : ' The good Abbé Pirot, unable to contemplate the agonies which were suffered by his penitent, had hurried from the room.' Does that convince you ? "

" It does entirely. There can be no question that it is indeed the same event. But who, then, is this lady whose appearance was so attractive and whose end was so horrible ? "

For answer Dacre came across to me, and placed the small lamp upon the table which stood by my bed. Lifting up the ill-omened filler, he turned the brass rim so that the light fell full upon it. Seen in this way the engraving seemed clearer than on the night before.

" We have already agreed that this is the badge of a marquis or of a marquise," said he. " We have also settled that the last letter is B."

" It is undoubtedly so."

" I now suggest to you that the other letters from left to right are, M, M, a small d, A, a small d, and then the final B."

" Yes, I am sure that you are right. I can make out the two small d's quite plainly."

"What I have read to you to-night," said Dacre, "is the official record of the trial of Marie Madeleine d'Aubray, Marquise de Brinvilliers, one of the most famous poisoners and murderers of all time."

I sat in silence, overwhelmed at the extraordinary nature of the incident, and at the completeness of the proof with which Dacre had exposed its real meaning. In a vague way I remembered some details of the woman's career, her unbridled debauchery, the cold-blooded and protracted torture of her sick father, the murder of her brothers for motives of petty gain. I recollected also that the bravery of her end had done something to atone for the horror of her life, and that all Paris had sympathised with her last moments, and blessed her as a martyr within a few days of the time when they had cursed her as a murderess. One objection, and one only, occurred to my mind.

"How came her initials and her badge of rank upon the filler ? Surely they did not carry their mediæval homage to the nobility to the point of decorating instruments of torture with their titles ? "

"I was puzzled with the same point," said Dacre, "but it admits of a simple explanation. The case excited extraordinary interest at the time, and nothing could be more natural than that La Reynie, the head of the police, should retain this filler as a grim souvenir. It was not often that a marchioness of France underwent the extraordinary question. That he should engrave her initials upon it for the information of others was surely a very ordinary proceeding upon his part."

"And this ? " I asked, pointing to the marks upon the leathern neck.

"She was a cruel tigress," said Dacre, as he turned away. "I think it is evident that like other tigresses her teeth were both strong and sharp."

27. *The New Catacomb*

"LOOK here, Burger," said Kennedy, "I do wish that you would confide in me."

The two famous students of Roman remains sat together in Kennedy's comfortable room overlooking the Corso. The night was cold, and they had both pulled up their chairs to the unsatisfactory Italian stove which threw out a zone of stuffiness rather than of warmth. Outside under the bright winter stars lay the modern Rome, the long, double chain of the electric lamps, the brilliantly lighted cafés, the rushing carriages, and the dense throng upon the footpaths. But inside, in the sumptuous chamber of the rich young English archæologist, there was only old Rome to be seen. Cracked and timeworn friezes hung upon the walls, grey old busts of senators and soldiers with their fighting heads and their hard, cruel faces peered out from the corners. On the centre table, amidst a litter of inscriptions, fragments, and ornaments, there stood the famous reconstruction by Kennedy of the Baths of Caracalla, which excited such interest and admiration when it was exhibited in Berlin. Amphoræ hung from the ceiling, and a litter of curiosities strewed the rich red Turkey carpet. And of them all there was not one which was not of the most unimpeachable authenticity, and of the utmost rarity and value ; for Kennedy, though little more than thirty, had a European reputation in this particular branch of research, and was, moreover, provided with that long purse which either proves to be a fatal handicap to the student's energies, or, if his mind is still true to its purpose, gives him an enormous advantage in the race for fame. Kennedy had often been seduced by whim and pleasure from his studies, but his mind was an incisive one, capable of long and concentrated efforts which ended in sharp reactions of sensuous languor. His handsome face, with its high, white forehead, its aggressive nose, and its somewhat loose and sensual mouth, was a fair index of the compromise between strength and weakness in his nature.

Of a very different type was his companion, Julius Burger. He came of a curious blend, a German father and an Italian mother, with the robust qualities of the North mingling strangely with the softer graces of the South. Blue Teutonic eyes lightened his sun-browned face, and above them rose a square, massive forehead, with a fringe of close yellow curls lying round it. His strong, firm jaw was clean-shaven, and his companion had frequently remarked how much it suggested those old Roman busts which peered out from the shadows in the corners of his chamber. Under its bluff German strength there lay always a suggestion of Italian subtlety, but the smile was so honest, and the eyes so frank, that one understood that this was only an indication of his ancestry, with no actual bearing upon his character. In age and in reputation, he was on the same level as his English companion, but his life and his work had both been far more arduous. Twelve years before, he had come as a poor student to Rome, and had lived ever since upon some small endowment for research which had been awarded to him by the University of Bonn. Painfully, slowly, and doggedly, with extraordinary tenacity and single-mindedness, he had climbed from rung to rung of the ladder of fame, until now he was a member of the Berlin Academy, and there was every reason to believe that he would shortly be promoted to the Chair of the greatest of German Universities. But the singleness of purpose which had brought him to the same high level as the rich and brilliant Englishman, had caused him in everything outside their work to stand infinitely below him. He had never found a pause in his studies in which to cultivate the social graces. It was only when he spoke of his own subject that his face was filled with life and soul. At other times he was silent and embarrassed, too conscious of his own limitations in larger subjects, and impatient of that small talk which is the conventional refuge of those who have no thoughts to express.

And yet for some years there had been an acquaintanceship which appeared to be slowly ripening into a friendship between these two very different rivals. The base and origin of this lay in the fact that in their own studies each was the only one of the younger men who had knowledge and enthusiasm enough to properly appreciate the other. Their common interests and pursuits had brought them together, and each had been attracted by the other's knowledge. And then gradually something had been added to this. Kennedy had been amused by the frankness and simplicity of his rival, while Burger in turn had been fascinated by the brilliancy and vivacity which had made Kennedy such a favourite in Roman society. I say "had," because just at the moment the young Englishman was somewhat under a cloud. A love-affair, the details of which had never quite come out, had indicated a heartlessness and callousness upon his part which shocked many of his friends. But in the bachelor circles of students and artists in which he preferred to move there is no very rigid code of honour in such matters, and though a head might be shaken or a pair of shoulders shrugged over the flight of two and the return of one, the general sentiment was probably one of curiosity and perhaps of envy rather than of reprobation.

"Look here, Burger," said Kennedy, looking hard at the placid face of his companion, "I do wish that you would confide in me."

As he spoke he waved his hand in the direction of a rug which lay upon the floor. On the rug stood a long, shallow fruit-basket of the light wicker-work which is used in the Campagna, and this was heaped with a litter of objects, inscribed tiles, broken inscriptions, cracked mosaics, torn papyri, rusty metal ornaments, which to the uninitiated might have seemed to have come straight from a dustman's bin, but which a specialist would have speedily recognized as unique of their kind. The pile of odds and ends in the flat wicker-work basket supplied exactly one of those missing links of social development which are of such interest to the student. It was the German who had brought them in, and the Englishman's eyes were hungry as he looked at them.

" I won't interfere with your treasure-trove, but I should very much like to hear about it," he continued, while Burger very deliberately lit a cigar. " It is evidently a discovery of the first importance. These inscriptions will make a sensation throughout Europe."

" For every one here there are a million there ! " said the German. " There are so many that a dozen savants might spend a lifetime over them, and build up a reputation as solid as the Castle of St. Angelo."

Kennedy sat thinking with his fine forehead wrinkled and his fingers playing with his long, fair moustache.

" You have given yourself away, Burger ! " said he at last. " Your words can only apply to one thing. You have discovered a new catacomb."

" I had no doubt that you had already come to that conclusion from an examination of these objects."

" Well, they certainly appeared to indicate it, but your last remarks make it certain. There is no place except a catacomb which could contain so vast a store of relics as you describe."

" Quite so. There is no mystery about that. I *have* discovered a new catacomb."

" Where ? "

" Ah, that is my secret, my dear Kennedy. Suffice it that it is so situated that there is not one chance in a million of anyone else coming upon it. Its date is different from that of any known catacomb, and it has been reserved for the burial of the highest Christians, so that the remains and the relics are quite different from anything which has ever been seen before. If I was not aware of your knowledge and of your energy, my friend,

I would not hesitate, under the pledge of secrecy, to
tell you everything about it. But as it is I think that I
must certainly prepare my own report of the matter
before I expose myself to such formidable competition."

Kennedy loved his subject with a love which was
almost a mania—a love which held him true to it, amidst
all the distractions which come to a wealthy and dissipated
young man. He had ambition, but his ambition was
secondary to his mere abstract joy and interest in everything which concerned the old life and history of the city.
He yearned to see this new underworld which his companion had discovered.

" Look here, Burger," said he, earnestly, " I assure
you that you can trust me most implicitly in the matter.
Nothing would induce me to put pen to paper about
anything which I see until I have your express permission. I quite understand your feeling and I think it
is most natural, but you have really nothing whatever
to fear from me. On the other hand, if you don't tell
me I shall make a systematic search, and I shall most
certainly discover it. In that case, of course, I should
make what use I liked of it, since I should be under no
obligation to you."

Burger smiled thoughtfully over his cigar.

" I have noticed, friend Kennedy," said he, " that when
I want information over any point you are not always so
ready to supply it."

" When did you ever ask me anything that I did not
tell you ? You remember, for example, my giving you
the material for your paper about the temple of the
Vestals."

" Ah, well, that was not a matter of much importance.
If I were to question you upon some intimate thing would
you give me an answer, I wonder ! This new catacomb
is a very intimate thing to me, and I should certainly
expect some sign of confidence in return."

" What you are driving at I cannot imagine," said the
Englishman, " but if you mean that you will answer my

question about the catacomb if I answer any question which you may put to me I can assure you that I will certainly do so."

"Well, then," said Burger, leaning luxuriously back in his settee, and puffing a blue tree of cigar-smoke into the air, "tell me all about your relations with Miss Mary Saunderson."

Kennedy sprang up in his chair and glared angrily at his impassive companion.

"What the devil do you mean ?" he cried. "What sort of a question is this ? You may mean it as a joke, but you never made a worse one."

"No, I don't mean it as a joke," said Burger, simply. "I am really rather interested in the details of the matter. I don't know much about the world and women and social life and that sort of thing, and such an incident has the fascination of the unknown for me. I know you, and I knew her by sight—I had even spoken to her once or twice. I should very much like to hear from your own lips exactly what it was which occurred between you."

"I won't tell you a word."

"That's all right. It was only my whim to see if you would give up a secret as easily as you expected me to give up my secret of the new catacomb. You wouldn't, and I didn't expect you to. But why should you expect otherwise of me ? There's Saint John's clock striking ten. It is quite time that I was going home."

"No ; wait a bit, Burger," said Kennedy ; "this is really a ridiculous caprice of yours to wish to know about an old love-affair which has burned out months ago. You know we look upon a man who kisses and tells as the greatest coward and villain possible."

"Certainly," said the German, gathering up his basket of curiosities, "when he tells anything about a girl which is previously unknown he must be so. But in this case, as you must be aware, it was a public matter which was the common talk of Rome, so that you are not really doing Miss Mary Saunderson any injury by discussing her case with me. But still, I respect your scruples, and so good night!"

"Wait a bit, Burger," said Kennedy, laying his hand upon the other's arm; "I am very keen upon this catacomb business, and I can't let it drop quite so easily. Would you mind asking me something else in return—something not quite so eccentric this time?"

"No, no; you have refused, and there is an end of it," said Burger, with his basket on his arm. "No doubt you are quite right not to answer, and no doubt I am quite right also—and so again, my dear Kennedy, good night!"

The Englishman watched Burger cross the room, and he had his hand on the handle of the door before his host sprang up with the air of a man who is making the best of that which cannot be helped.

"Hold on, old fellow," said he; "I think you are behaving in a most ridiculous fashion; but still, if this is your condition, I suppose that I must submit to it. I hate saying anything about a girl, but, as you say, it is all over Rome, and I don't suppose I can tell you anything which you do not know already. What was it you wanted to know?"

The German came back to the stove, and, laying down his basket, he sank into his chair once more.

"May I have another cigar?" said he. "Thank you very much! I never smoke when I work, but I enjoy a chat much more when I am under the influence of tobacco. Now, as regards this young lady, with whom you had this little adventure. What in the world has become of her?"

"She is at home with her own people."

"Oh, really—in England?"

"Yes."

"What part of England—London?"

"No, Twickenham."

"You must excuse my curiosity, my dear Kennedy, and you must put it down to my ignorance of the world.

No doubt it is quite a simple thing to persuade a young lady to go off with you for three weeks or so, and then to hand her over to her own family at—what did you call the place ? "

" Twickenham."

" Quite so—at Twickenham. But it is something so entirely outside my own experience that I cannot even imagine how you set about it. For example, if you had loved this girl your love could hardly disappear in three weeks, so I presume that you could not have loved her at all. But if you did not love her why should you make this great scandal which has damaged you and ruined her ? "

Kennedy looked moodily into the red eye of the stove.

" That's a logical way of looking at it, certainly," said he. " Love is a big word, and it represents a good many different shades of feeling. I liked her, and—well, you say you've seen her—you know how charming she could look. But still I am willing to admit, looking back, that I could never have really loved her."

" Then, my dear Kennedy, why did you do it ? "

" The adventure of the thing had a great deal to do with it."

" What ! You are so fond of adventures ! "

" Where would the variety of life be without them ? It was for an adventure that I first began to pay my attentions to her. I've chased a good deal of game in my time, but there's no chase like that of a pretty woman. There was the piquant difficulty of it also, for, as she was the companion of Lady Emily Rood, it was almost impossible to see her alone. On the top of all the other obstacles which attracted me, I learned from her own lips very early in the proceedings that she was engaged."

" Mein Gott ! To whom ? "

" She mentioned no names."

" I do not think that anyone knows that. So that made the adventure more alluring, did it ? "

" Well, it did certainly give a spice to it. Don't you think so ? "

" I tell you that I am very ignorant about these things."

" My dear fellow, you can remember that the apple you stole from your neighbour's tree was always sweeter than that which fell from your own. And then I found that she cared for me."

" What—at once ? "

" Oh, no, it took about three months of sapping and mining. But at last I won her over. She understood that my judicial separation from my wife made it impossible for me to do the right thing by her—but she came all the same, and we had a delightful time, as long as it lasted."

" But how about the other man ? "

Kennedy shrugged his shoulders.

" I suppose it is the survival of the fittest," said he. " If he had been the better man she would not have deserted him. Let's drop the subject, for I have had enough of it ! "

" Only one other thing. How did you get rid of her in three weeks ? "

" Well, we had both cooled down a bit, you understand. She absolutely refused, under any circumstances, to come back to face the people she had known in Rome. Now, of course, Rome is necessary to me, and I was already pining to be back at my work—so there was one obvious cause of separation. Then, again, her old father turned up at the hotel in London, and there was a scene, and the whole thing became so unpleasant that really—though I missed her dreadfully at first—I was very glad to slip out of it. Now, I rely upon you not to repeat anything of what I have said."

" My dear Kennedy, I should not dream of repeating it. But all that you say interests me very much, for it gives me an insight into your way of looking at things, which is entirely different from mine, for I have seen so little of life. And now you want to know about my

365

new catacomb. There's no use my trying to describe it, for you would never find it by that. There is only one thing, and that is for me to take you there."

" That would be splendid."

" When would you like to come ? "

" The sooner the better. I am all impatience to see it."

" Well, it is a beautiful night—though a trifle cold. Suppose we start in an hour. We must be very careful to keep the matter to ourselves. If anyone saw us hunting in couples they would suspect that there was something going on."

" We can't be too cautious," said Kennedy. " Is it far ? "

" Some miles."

" Not too far to walk ? "

" Oh, no, we could walk there easily."

" We had better do so, then. A cabman's suspicions would be aroused if he dropped us both at some lonely spot in the dead of the night."

" Quite so. I think it would be best for us to meet at the Gate of the Appian Way at midnight. I must go back to my lodgings for the matches and candles and things."

" All right, Burger ! I think it is very kind of you to let me into this secret, and I promise you that I will write nothing about it until you have published your report. Good-bye for the present ! You will find me at the Gate at twelve."

The cold, clear air was filled with the musical chimes from that city of clocks as Burger, wrapped in an Italian overcoat, with a lantern hanging from his hand, walked up to the rendezvous. Kennedy stepped out of the shadow to meet him.

" You are ardent in work as well as in love ! " said the German, laughing.

" Yes ; I have been waiting here for nearly half an hour."

" I hope you left no clue as to where we were going."

" Not such a fool ! By Jove, I am chilled to the bone ! Come on, Burger, let us warm ourselves by a spurt of hard walking."

Their footsteps sounded loud and crisp upon the rough stone paving of the disappointing road which is all that is left of the most famous highway of the world. A peasant or two going home from the wine-shop, and a few carts of country produce coming up to Rome, were the only things which they met. They swung along, with the huge tombs looming up through the darkness upon each side of them, until they had come as far as the Catacombs of St. Calixtus, and saw against a rising moon the great circular bastion of Cecilia Metella in front of them. Then Burger stopped with his hand to his side.

" Your legs are longer than mine, and you are more accustomed to walking," said he, laughing. " I think that the place where we turn off is somewhere here. Yes, this is it, round the corner of the trattoria. Now, it is a very narrow path, so perhaps I had better go in front and you can follow."

He had lit his lantern, and by its light they were enabled to follow a narrow and devious track which wound across the marshes of the Campagna. The great Aqueduct of old Rome lay like a monstrous caterpillar across the moon-lit landscape, and their road led them under one of its huge arches, and past the circle of crumbling bricks which marks the old arena. At last Burger stopped at a solitary wooden cow-house, and he drew a key from his pocket.

" Surely your catacomb is not inside a house ! " cried Kennedy.

" The entrance to it is. That is just the safeguard which we have against anyone else discovering it."

" Does the proprietor know of it ? "

" Not he. He had found one or two objects which made me almost certain that his house was built on the

entrance to such a place. So I rented it from him, and
did my excavations for myself. Come in, and shut the
door behind you."

It was a long, empty building, with the mangers of the
cows along one wall. Burger put his lantern down on
the ground, and shaded its light in all directions save
one by draping his overcoat round it.

"It might excite remark if anyone saw a light in this
lonely place," said he. "Just help me to move this
boarding."

The flooring was loose in the corner, and plank by
plank the two savants raised it and leaned it against the
wall. Below there was a square aperture and a stair of
old stone steps which led away down into the bowels of
the earth.

"Be careful!" cried Burger, as Kennedy, in his
impatience, hurried down them. "It is a perfect rabbits'-
warren below, and if you were once to lose your way there
the chances would be a hundred to one against your ever
coming out again. Wait until I bring the light."

"How do you find your own way if it is so complicated?"

"I had some very narrow escapes at first, but I have
gradually learned to go about. There is a certain system
to it, but it is one which a lost man, if he were in the dark,
could not possibly find out. Even now I always spin
out a ball of string behind me when I am going far into
the catacomb. You can see for yourself that it is difficult,
but every one of these passages divides and subdivides
a dozen times before you go a hundred yards."

They had descended some twenty feet from the level
of the byre, and they were standing now in a square
chamber cut out of the soft tufa. The lantern cast a
flickering light, bright below and dim above, over the
cracked brown walls. In every direction were the black
openings of passages which radiated from this common
centre.

"I want you to follow me closely, my friend," said

Burger. " Do not loiter to look at anything upon the way, for the place to which I will take you contains all that you can see, and more. It will save time for us to go there direct."

He led the way down one of the corridors, and the Englishman followed closely at his heels. Every now and then the passage bifurcated, but Burger was evidently following some secret marks of his own, for he neither stopped nor hesitated. Everywhere along the walls, packed like the berths upon an emigrant ship, lay the Christians of old Rome. The yellow light flickered over the shrivelled features of the mummies, and gleamed upon rounded skulls and long, white armbones crossed over fleshless chests. And everywhere as he passed Kennedy looked with wistful eyes upon inscriptions, funeral vessels, pictures, vestments, utensils, all lying as pious hands had placed them so many centuries ago. It was apparent to him, even in those hurried, passing glances, that this was the earliest and finest of the catacombs, containing such a storehouse of Roman remains as had never before come at one time under the observation of the student.

" What would happen if the light went out ? " he asked, as they hurried onwards.

" I have a spare candle and a box of matches in my pocket. By the way, Kennedy, have you any matches ? "

" No ; you had better give me some."

" Oh, that is all right. There is no chance of our separating."

" How far are we going ? It seems to me that we have walked at least a quarter of a mile."

" More than that, I think. There is really no limit to the tombs—at least, I have never been able to find any. This is a very difficult place, so I think that I will use our ball of string."

He fastened one end of it to a projecting stone and he carried the coil in the breast of his coat, paying it out as he advanced. Kennedy saw that it was no unnecessary precaution, for the passages had become more complex

and tortuous than ever, with a perfect network of inter-
secting corridors. But these all ended in one large
circular hall with a square pedestal of tufa topped with
a slab of marble at one end of it.

" By Jove ! " cried Kennedy in an ecstasy, as Burger
swung his lantern over the marble. " It is a Christian
altar—probably the first one in existence. Here is the
little consecration cross cut upon the corner of it. No
doubt this circular space was used as a church."

" Precisely," said Burger. " If I had more time I
should like to show you all the bodies which are buried
in these niches upon the walls, for they are the early
popes and bishops of the Church, with their mitres,
their croziers, and full canonicals. Go over to that one
and look at it ! "

Kennedy went across, and stared at the ghastly head
which lay loosely on the shredded and mouldering mitre.

" This is most interesting," said he, and his voice
seemed to boom against the concave vault. " As far
as my experience goes, it is unique. Bring the lantern
over, Burger, for I want to see them all."

But the German had strolled away, and was standing
in the middle of a yellow circle of light at the other side
of the hall.

" Do you know how many wrong turnings there are
between this and the stairs ? " he asked. " There are
over two thousand. No doubt it was one of the means
of protection which the Christians adopted. The odds
are two thousand to one against a man getting out, even
if he had a light ; but if he were in the dark it would, of
course, be far more difficult."

" So I should think."

" And the darkness is something dreadful. I tried it
once for an experiment. Let us try it again ! " He
stooped to the lantern, and in an instant it was as if an
invisible hand was squeezed tightly over each of Kennedy's
eyes. Never had he known what such darkness was. It
seemed to press upon him and to smother him. It was

a solid obstacle against which the body shrank from advancing. He put his hands out to push it back from him.

" That will do, Burger," said he, " let's have the light again."

But his companion began to laugh, and in that circular room the sound seemed to come from every side at once.

" You seem uneasy, friend Kennedy," said he.

" Go on, man, light the candle ! " said Kennedy impatiently.

" It's very strange, Kennedy, but I could not in the least tell by the sound in which direction you stand. Could you tell where I am ? "

" No ; you seem to be on every side of me."

" If it were not for this string which I hold in my hand I should not have a notion which way to go."

" I dare say not. Strike a light, man, and have an end of this nonsense."

" Well, Kennedy, there are two things which I understand that you are very fond of. The one is an adventure, and the other is an obstacle to surmount. The adventure must be the finding of your way out of this catacomb. The obstacle will be the darkness and the two thousand wrong turns which make the way a little difficult to find. But you need not hurry, for you have plenty of time, and when you halt for a rest now and then, I should like you just to think of Miss Mary Saunderson, and whether you treated her quite fairly."

" You devil, what do you mean ? " roared Kennedy. He was running about in little circles and clasping at the solid blackness with both hands.

" Good-bye," said the mocking voice, and it was already at some distance. " I really do not think, Kennedy, even by your own showing that you did the right thing by that girl. There was only one little thing which you appeared not to know, and I can supply it. Miss Saunderson was engaged to a poor ungainly devil of a student, and his name was Julius Burger."

There was a rustle somewhere, the vague sound of a foot striking a stone, and then there fell silence upon that old Christian church—a stagnant, heavy silence which closed round Kennedy and shut him in like water round a drowning man.

* * * * *

Some two months afterwards the following paragraph made the round of the European Press :—

" One of the most interesting discoveries of recent years is that of the new catacomb in Rome, which lies some distance to the east of the well-known vaults of St. Calixtus. The finding of this important burial-place, which is exceeding rich in most interesting early Christian remains, is due to the energy and sagacity of Dr. Julius Burger, the young German specialist, who is rapidly taking the first place as an authority upon ancient Rome. Although the first to publish his discovery, it appears that a less fortunate adventurer had anticipated Dr. Burger. Some months ago Mr. Kennedy, the well-known English student, disappeared suddenly from his rooms in the Corso, and it was conjectured that his association with a recent scandal had driven him to leave Rome. It appears now that he had in reality fallen a victim to that fervid love of archæology which had raised him to a distinguished place among living scholars. His body was discovered in the heart of the new catacomb, and it was evident from the condition of his feet and boots that he had tramped for days through the tortuous corridors which make these subterranean tombs so dangerous to explorers. The deceased gentleman had, with inexplicable rashness, made his way into this labyrinth without, as far as can be discovered, taking with him either candles or matches, so that his sad fate was the natural result of his own temerity. What makes the matter more painful is that Dr. Julius Burger was an intimate friend of the deceased. His joy at the extra-

ordinary find which he has been so fortunate as to make
has been greatly marred by the terrible fate of his comrade
and fellow-worker."

28. *The Case of Lady Sannox*

THE relations between Douglas Stone and the
notorious Lady Sannox were very well known
both among the fashionable circles of which
she was a brilliant member, and the scientific bodies
which numbered him among their most illustrious *con-
frères*. There was naturally, therefore, a very widespread
interest when it was announced one morning that the
lady had absolutely and for ever taken the veil, and that
the world would see her no more. When, at the very
tail of this rumour, there came the assurance that the
celebrated operating surgeon, the man of steel nerves,
had been found in the morning by his valet, seated on
one side of his bed, smiling pleasantly upon the universe,
with both legs jammed into one side of his breeches and
his great brain about as valuable as a cap full of porridge,
the matter was strong enough to give quite a little
thrill of interest to folk who had never hoped that their
jaded nerves were capable of such a sensation.

Douglas Stone in his prime was one of the most
remarkable men in England. Indeed, he could hardly
be said to have ever reached his prime, for he was but
nine-and-thirty at the time of this little incident. Those
who knew him best were aware that famous as he was
as a surgeon, he might have succeeded with even greater
rapidity in any of a dozen lines of life. He could have
cut his way to fame as a soldier, struggled to it as an
explorer, bullied for it in the courts, or built it out of
stone and iron as an engineer. He was born to be great,
for he could plan what another man dare not do, and he
could do what another man dare not plan. In surgery
none could follow him. His nerve, his judgment, his

intuition, were things apart. Again and again his knife cut away death, but grazed the very springs of life in doing it, until his assistants were as white as the patient. His energy, his audacity, his full-blooded self-confidence —does not the memory of them still linger to the south of Marylebone Road and the north of Oxford Street ?

His vices were as magnificent as his virtues, and infinitely more picturesque. Large as was his income, and it was the third largest of all professional men in London, it was far beneath the luxury of his living. Deep in his complex nature lay a rich vein of sensualism, at the sport of which he placed all the prizes of his life. The eye, the ear, the touch, the palate, all were his masters. The bouquet of old vintages, the scent of rare exotics, the curves and tints of the daintiest potteries of Europe, it was to these that the quick-running stream of gold was transformed. And then there came his sudden mad passion for Lady Sannox, when a single interview with two challenging glances and a whispered word set him ablaze. She was the loveliest woman in London and the only one to him. He was one of the handsomest men in London, but not the only one to her. She had a liking for new experiences, and was gracious to most men who wooed her. It may have been cause or it may have been effect that Lord Sannox looked fifty, though he was but six-and-thirty.

He was a quiet, silent, neutral-tinted man, this lord, with thin lips and heavy eyelids, much given to gardening, and full of home-like habits. He had at one time been fond of acting, had even rented a theatre in London, and on its boards had first seen Miss Marion Dawson, to whom he had offered his hand, his title, and the third of a county. Since his marriage this early hobby had become distasteful to him. Even in private theatricals it was no longer possible to persuade him to exercise the talent which he had often shown that he possessed. He was happier with a spud and a watering-can among his orchids and chrysanthemums.

It was quite an interesting problem whether he was absolutely devoid of sense, or miserably wanting in spirit. Did he know his lady's ways and condone them, or was he a mere blind, doting fool ? It was a point to be discussed over the teacups in snug little drawing-rooms, or with the aid of a cigar in the bow windows of clubs. Bitter and plain were the comments among men upon his conduct. There was but one who had a good word to say for him, and he was the most silent member in the smoking-room. He had seen him break in a horse at the University, and it seemed to have left an impression upon his mind.

But when Douglas Stone became the favourite all doubts as to Lord Sannox's knowledge or ignorance were set for ever at rest. There was no subterfuge about Stone. In his high-handed, impetuous fashion, he set all caution and discretion at defiance. The scandal became notorious. A learned body intimated that his name had been struck from the list of its vice-presidents. Two friends implored him to consider his professional credit. He cursed them all three, and spent forty guineas on a bangle to take with him to the lady. He was at her house every evening, and she drove in his carriage in the afternoons. There was not an attempt on either side to conceal their relations ; but there came at last a little incident to interrupt them.

It was a dismal winter's night, very cold and gusty, with the wind whooping in the chimneys and blustering against the window-panes. A thin spatter of rain tinkled on the glass with each fresh sough of the gale, drowning for the instant the dull gurgle and drip from the eaves. Douglas Stone had finished his dinner, and sat by his fire in the study, a glass of rich port upon the malachite table at his elbow. As he raised it to his lips, he held it up against the lamplight, and watched with the eye of a connoisseur the tiny scales of beeswing which floated in its rich ruby depths. The fire, as it spurted up, threw fitful lights upon his bold, clear-cut face, with its widely-opened grey eyes, its thick and yet firm lips, and the deep, square jaw, which had something Roman in its strength and its animalism. He smiled from time to time as he nestled back in his luxurious chair. Indeed, he had a right to feel well pleased, for, against the advice of six colleagues, he had performed an operation that day of which only two cases were on record, and the result had been brilliant beyond all expectation. No other man in London would have had the daring to plan, or the skill to execute, such a heroic measure.

But he had promised Lady Sannox to see her that evening and it was already half-past eight. His hand was outstretched to the bell to order the carriage when he heard the dull thud of the knocker. An instant later there was the shuffling of feet in the hall, and the sharp closing of a door.

" A patient to see you, sir, in the consulting room," said the butler.

" About himself ? "

" No, sir ; I think he wants you to go out."

" It is too late," cried Douglas Stone peevishly. " I won't go."

" This is his card, sir."

The butler presented it upon the gold salver which had been given to his master by the wife of a Prime Minister.

" ' Hamil Ali, Smyrna.' Hum ! The fellow is a Turk, I suppose."

" Yes, sir. He seems as if he came from abroad, sir. And he's in a terrible way."

" Tut, tut ! I have an engagement. I must go somewhere else. But I'll see him. Show him in here, Pim."

A few moments later the butler swung open the door and ushered in a small and decrepit man, who walked with a bent back and with the forward push of the face and blink of the eyes which goes with extreme short sight. His face was swarthy, and his hair and beard of the deepest black. In one hand he held a turban of white muslin striped with red, in the other a small chamois leather bag.

" Good evening," said Douglas Stone, when the butler had closed the door. " You speak English, I presume ? "

" Yes, sir. I am from Asia Minor, but I speak English when I speak slow."

" You wanted me to go out, I understand ? "

" Yes, sir. I wanted very much that you should see my wife."

" I could come in the morning, but I have an engagement which prevents me from seeing your wife to-night."

The Turk's answer was a singular one. He pulled the string which closed the mouth of the chamois leather bag, and poured a flood of gold on to the table.

" There are one hundred pounds there," said he, " and I promise you that it will not take you an hour. I have a cab ready at the door."

Douglas Stone glanced at his watch. An hour would not make it too late to visit Lady Sannox. He had been there later. And the fee was an extraordinarily high one. He had been pressed by his creditors lately, and he could not afford to let such a chance pass. He would go.

" What is the case ? " he asked.

" Oh, it is so sad a one ! So sad a one ! You have not, perhaps, heard of the daggers of the Almohades ? "

" Never."

" Ah, they are Eastern daggers of a great age and of a singular shape, with the hilt like what you call a stirrup. I am a curiosity dealer, you understand, and that is why I have come to England from Smyrna, but next week I go back once more. Many things I brought with me, and I have a few things left, but among them, to my sorrow, is one of these daggers."

" You will remember that I have an appointment, sir," said the surgeon, with some irritation ; " pray confine yourself to the necessary details."

" You will see that it is necessary. To-day my wife fell down in a faint in the room in which I keep my wares, and she cut her lower lip upon this cursed dagger of Almohades."

" I see," said Douglas Stone, rising. " And you wish me to dress the wound ? "

" No, no, it is worse than that."

" What then ? "

" These daggers are poisoned."

" Poisoned ! "

" Yes, and there is no man, East or West, who can tell now what is the poison or what the cure. But all that is known I know, for my father was in this trade before me, and we have had much to do with these poisoned weapons."

" What are the symptoms ? "

" Deep sleep, and death in thirty hours."

" And you say there is no cure. Why then should you pay me this considerable fee ? "

" No drug can cure, but the knife may."

" And how ? "

" The poison is slow of absorption. It remains for hours in the wound."

" Washing, then, might cleanse it ? "

" No more than in a snake bite. It is too subtle and too deadly."

" Excision of the wound, then ? "

" That is it. If it be on the finger, take the finger off. So said my father always. But think of where this wound is, and that it is my wife. It is dreadful ! "

But familiarity with such grim matters may take the finer edge from a man's sympathy. To Douglas Stone this was already an interesting case, and he brushed aside as irrelevant the feeble objections of the husband.

" It appears to be that or nothing," said he brusquely. " It is better to lose a lip than a life."

" Ah, yes, I know that you are right. Well, well, it

is kismet, and it must be faced. I have the cab, and you will come with me and do this thing."

Douglas Stone took his case of bistouries from a drawer, and placed it with a roll of bandage and a compress of lint in his pocket. He must waste no more time if he were to see Lady Sannox.

" I am ready," said he, pulling on his overcoat. " Will you take a glass of wine before you go.out into this cold air ? "

His visitor shrank away, with a protesting hand upraised

" You forget that I am a Mussulman, and a true follower of the Prophet," said he. " But tell me what is the bottle of green glass which you have placed in your pocket ? "

" It is chloroform."

" Ah, that also is forbidden to us. It is a spirit, and we make no use of such things."

" What ! You would allow your wife to go through an operation without an anæsthetic ? "

" Ah ! she will feel nothing, poor soul. The deep sleep has already come on, which is the first working of the poison. And then I have given her of our Smyrna opium. Come, sir, for already an hour has passed."

As they stepped out into the darkness, a sheet of rain was driven in upon their faces, and the hall lamp, which dangled from the arm of a marble Caryatid, went out with a fluff. Pim, the butler, pushed the heavy door to, straining hard with his shoulder against the wind, while the two men groped their way towards the yellow glare which showed where the cab was waiting. An instant later they were rattling upon their journey.

" Is it far ? " asked Douglas Stone.

" Oh, no. We have a very little quiet place off the Euston Road."

The surgeon pressed the spring of his repeater and listened to the little tings which told him the hour. It was a quarter past nine. He calculated the distances,

379

and the short time which it would take him to perform so trivial an operation. He ought to reach Lady Sannox by ten o'clock. Through the fogged windows he saw the blurred gas lamps dancing past, with occasionally the broader glare of a shop front. The rain was pelting and rattling upon the leathern top of the carriage, and the wheels swashed as they rolled through puddle and mud. Opposite to him the white headgear of his companion gleamed faintly through the obscurity. The surgeon felt in his pockets and arranged his needles, his ligatures and his safety-pins, that no time might be wasted when they arrived. He chafed with impatience and drummed his foot upon the floor.

But the cab slowed down at last and pulled up. In an instant Douglas Stone was out, and the Smyrna merchant's toe was at his very heel.

" You can wait," said he to the driver.

It was a mean-looking house in a narrow and sordid street. The surgeon, who knew his London well, cast a swift glance into the shadows, but there was nothing distinctive—no shop, no movement, nothing but a double line of dull, flat-faced houses, a double stretch of wet flagstones which gleamed in the lamplight, and a double rush of water in the gutters which swirled and gurgled towards the sewer gratings. The door which faced them was blotched and discoloured, and a faint light in the fan pane above it served to show the dust and the grime which covered it. Above, in one of the bedroom windows, there was a dull yellow glimmer. The merchant knocked loudly, and, as he turned his dark face towards the light, Douglas Stone could see that it was contracted with anxiety. A bolt was drawn, and an elderly woman with a taper stood in the doorway, shielding the thin flame with her gnarled hand.

" Is all well ? " gasped the merchant.

" She is as you left her, sir."

" She has not spoken ? "

" No, she is in a deep sleep."

The merchant closed the door, and Douglas Stone walked down the narrow passage, glancing about him in some surprise as he did so. There was no oil-cloth, no mat, no hat-rack. Deep grey dust and heavy festoons of cobwebs met his eyes everywhere. Following the old woman up the winding stair, his firm footfall echoed harshly through the silent house. There was no carpet.

The bedroom was on the second landing. Douglas Stone followed the old nurse into it, with the merchant at his heels. Here, at least, there was furniture and to spare. The floor was littered and the corners piled with Turkish cabinets, inlaid tables, coats of chain mail, strange pipes, and grotesque weapons. A single small lamp stood upon a bracket on the wall. Douglas Stone took it down, and picking his way among the lumber, walked over to a couch in the corner, on which lay a woman dressed in the Turkish fashion, with yashmak and veil. The lower part of the face was exposed, and the surgeon saw a jagged cut which zigzagged along the border of the under lip.

" You will forgive the yashmak," said the Turk. " You know our views about woman in the East."

But the surgeon was not thinking about the yashmak. This was no longer a woman to him. It was a case. He stooped and examined the wound carefully.

" There are no signs of irritation," said he. " We might delay the operation until local symptoms develop."

The husband wrung his hands in uncontrollable agitation.

" Oh ! sir, sir," he cried. " Do not trifle. You do not know. It is deadly. I know, and I give you my assurance that an operation is absolutely necessary. Only the knife can save her."

" And yet I am inclined to wait," said Douglas Stone.

" That is enough," the Turk cried, angrily. " Every minute is of importance, and I cannot stand here and see my wife allowed to sink. It only remains for me to give you my thanks for having come, and to call in some other surgeon before it is too late."

Douglas Stone hesitated. To refund that hundred pounds was no pleasant matter. But of course if he left the case he must return the money. And if the Turk were right and the woman died, his position before a coroner might be an embarrassing one.

"You have had personal experience of this poison?" he asked.

"I have."

"And you assure me that an operation is needful."

"I swear it by all that I hold sacred."

"The disfigurement will be frightful."

"I can understand that the mouth will not be a pretty one to kiss."

Douglas Stone turned fiercely upon the man. The speech was a brutal one. But the Turk has his own fashion of talk and of thought, and there was no time for wrangling. Douglas Stone drew a bistoury from his case, opened it and felt the keen straight edge with his forefinger. Then he held the lamp closer to the bed. Two dark eyes were gazing up at him through the slit in the yashmak. They were all iris, and the pupil was hardly to be seen.

"You have given her a very heavy dose of opium."

"Yes, she has had a good dose."

He glanced again at the dark eyes which looked straight at his own. They were dull and lustreless, but, even as he gazed, a little shifting sparkle came into them, and the lips quivered.

"She is not absolutely unconscious," said he.

"Would it not be well to use the knife while it will be painless?"

The same thought had crossed the surgeon's mind. He grasped the wounded lip with his forceps, and with two swift cuts he took out a broad V-shaped piece. The woman sprang up on the couch with a dreadful gurgling scream. Her covering was torn from her face. It was a face that he knew. In spite of that protruding upper lip and that slobber of blood, it was a face that he knew. She kept on putting her hand up to the gap and screaming. Douglas Stone sat down at the foot of the couch with his knife and his forceps. The room was whirling round, and he had felt something go like a ripping seam behind his ear. A bystander would have said that his face was the more ghastly of the two. As in a dream, or as if he had been looking at something at the play, he was conscious that the Turk's hair and beard lay upon the table, and that Lord Sannox was leaning against the wall with his hand to his side, laughing silently. The screams had died away now, and the dreadful head had dropped back again upon the pillow, but Douglas Stone still sat motionless, and Lord Sannox still chuckled quietly to himself.

" It was really very necessary for Marion, this operation," said he, " not physically, but morally, you know, morally."

Douglas Stone stooped forwards and began to play with the fringe of the coverlet. His knife tinkled down upon the ground, but he still held the forceps and something more.

" I had long intended to make a little example," said Lord Sannox, suavely. " Your note of Wednesday miscarried, and I have it here in my pocket-book. I took some pains in carrying out my idea. The wound, by the way, was from nothing more dangerous than my signet ring."

He glanced keenly at his silent companion, and cocked the small revolver which he held in his coat pocket. But Douglas Stone was still picking at the coverlet.

" You see you have kept your appointment after all," said Lord Sannox.

And at that Douglas Stone began to laugh. He laughed long and loudly. But Lord Sannox did not laugh now. Something like fear sharpened and hardened his features. He walked from the room, and he walked on tiptoe. The old woman was waiting outside.

"Attend to your mistress when she awakes," said Lord Sannox.

Then he went down to the street. The cab was at the door, and the driver raised his hand to his hat.

"John," said Lord Sannox, "you will take the doctor home first. He will want leading downstairs, I think. Tell his butler that he has been taken ill at a case."

"Very good, sir."

"Then you can take Lady Sannox home."

"And how about yourself, sir?"

"Oh, my address for the next few months will be Hotel di Roma, Venice. Just see that the letters are sent on. And tell Stevens to exhibit all the purple chrysanthemums next Monday, and to wire me the result."

29. *The Terror of Blue John Gap*

THE following narrative was found among the papers of Dr. James Hardcastle, who died of phthisis on February 4, 1908, at 36, Upper Coventry Flats, South Kensington. Those who knew him best, while refusing to express an opinion upon this particular statement, are unanimous in asserting that he was a man of a sober and scientific turn of mind, absolutely devoid of imagination, and most unlikely to invent any abnormal series of events. The paper was contained in an envelope, which was docketed, "A Short Account of the Circumstances which occurred near Miss Allerton's Farm in North-West Derbyshire in the Spring of Last Year." The envelope was sealed, and on the other side was written in pencil—

"DEAR SEATON,—

"It may interest, and perhaps pain you, to know that the incredulity with which you met my story has prevented me from ever opening my mouth upon the subject again. I leave this record after my death, and perhaps strangers may be found to have more confidence in me than my friend."

Inquiry has failed to elicit who this Seaton may have been. I may add that the visit of the deceased to Allerton's Farm, and the general nature of the alarm there, apart from his particular explanation, have been absolutely established. With this foreword I append his account exactly as he left it. It is in the form of a diary, some entries in which have been expanded, while a few have been erased.

April 17.—Already I feel the benefit of this wonderful upland air. The farm of the Allertons lies fourteen hundred and twenty feet above sea-level, so it may well be a bracing climate. Beyond the usual morning cough I have very little discomfort, and, what with the fresh. milk and the home-grown mutton, I have every chance of putting on weight. I think Saunderson will be pleased.

The two Miss Allertons are charmingly quaint and kind, two dear little hard-working old maids, who are ready to lavish all the heart which might have gone out to husband and to children upon an invalid stranger. Truly, the old maid is a most useful person, one of the reserve forces of the community. They talk of the superfluous woman, but what would the poor superfluous man do without her kindly presence? By the way, in their simplicity they very quickly let out the reason why Saunderson recommended their farm. The Professor rose from the ranks himself, and I believe that in his youth he was not above scaring crows in these very fields.

It is a most lonely spot, and the walks are picturesque in the extreme. The farm consists of grazing land lying at the bottom of an irregular valley. On each side are the fantastic limestone hills, formed of rock so soft that you can break it away with your hands. All this country is hollow. Could you strike it with some gigantic hammer it would boom like a drum, or possibly cave in altogether and expose some huge subterranean sea. A great sea there must surely be, for on all sides the streams run into the mountain itself, never to reappear. There are gaps everywhere amid the rocks, and when you pass through them you find yourself in great caverns, which wind down into the bowels of the earth. I have a small bicycle lamp, and it is a perpetual joy to me to carry it into these weird solitudes, and to see the wonderful silver and black effects when I throw its light upon the stalactites which drape the lofty roofs. Shut off the lamp, and you are in the blackest darkness. Turn it on, and it is a scene from the Arabian Nights.

But there is one of these strange openings in the earth which has a special interest, for it is the handiwork, not of nature, but of man. I had never heard of Blue John when I came to these parts. It is the name given to a peculiar mineral of a beautiful purple shade, which is only found at one or two places in the world. It is so rare that an ordinary vase of Blue John would be valued at a great price. The Romans, with that extraordinary instinct of theirs, discovered that it was to be found in this valley, and sank a horizontal shaft deep into the mountain side. The opening of their mine has been called Blue John Gap, a clean-cut arch in the rock, the mouth all overgrown with bushes. It is a goodly passage which the Roman miners have cut, and it intersects some of the great water-worn caves, so that if you enter Blue John Gap you would do well to mark your steps and to have a good store of candles, or you may never make your way back to the daylight again. I have not yet gone deeply into it, but this very day I stood at the mouth of the arched tunnel, and peering down into the black recesses beyond, I vowed that when my health returned I would devote some holiday to exploring those mysterious depths and finding out for myself how far the Roman had penetrated into the Derbyshire hills.

Strange how superstitious these countrymen are ! I should have thought better of young Armitage, for he is a man of some education and character, and a very fine fellow for his station in life. I was standing at the Blue John Gap when he came across the field to me.

" Well, doctor," said he, " you're not afraid, anyhow."

" Afraid ! " I answered. " Afraid of what ? "

" Of it," said he, with a jerk of his thumb towards the black vault, " of the Terror that lives in the Blue John Cave."

How absurdly easy it is for a legend to arise in a lonely countryside ! I examined him as to the reasons for his weird belief. It seems that from time to time sheep have been missing from the fields, carried bodily away, according to Armitage. That they could have wandered away of their own accord and disappeared among the mountains was an explanation to which he would not listen. On one occasion a pool of blood had been found, and some tufts of wool. That also, I pointed out, could be explained in a perfectly natural way. Further, the nights upon which sheep disappeared were invariably very dark, cloudy nights with no moon. This I met with the obvious retort that those were the nights which a commonplace sheep-stealer would naturally choose for his work. On one occasion a gap had been made in a wall, and some of the stones scattered for a considerable distance. Human agency again, in my opinion. Finally, Armitage clinched all his arguments by telling me that he had actually heard the Creature—indeed, that anyone could hear it who remained long enough at the Gap. It was a distant roaring of an immense volume. I could not but smile at this, knowing, as I do, the strange reverberations which come out of an underground water system running amid the chasms of a limestone formation. My incredulity annoyed Armitage so that he turned and left me with some abruptness.

And now comes the queer point about the whole business. I was still standing near the mouth of the cave turning over in my mind the various statements of Armitage, and reflecting how readily they could be explained away, when suddenly, from the depth of the tunnel beside me, there issued a most extraordinary sound. How shall I describe it ? First of all, it seemed to be a great distance away, far down in the bowels of the earth. Secondly, in spite of this suggestion of distance, it was very loud. Lastly, it was not a boom, nor a crash, such as one would associate with falling water or tumbling rock, but it was a high whine, tremulous and vibrating, almost like the whinnying of a horse. It was certainly a most remarkable experience, and one which for a moment, I must admit, gave a new significance to Armitage's words. I waited by the Blue John Gap for half an hour or more, but there was no return of the sound, so at last I wandered back to the farmhouse, rather mystified by what had occurred. Decidedly I shall explore that cavern when my strength is restored. Of course, Armitage's explanation is too absurd for discussion, and yet that sound was certainly very strange. It still rings in my ears as I write.

April 20.—In the last three days I have made several expeditions to the Blue John Gap, and have even penetrated some short distance, but my bicycle lantern is so small and weak that I dare not trust myself very far. I shall do the thing more systematically. I have heard no sound at all, and could almost believe that I had been the victim of some hallucination suggested, perhaps, by Armitage's conversation. Of course, the whole idea is absurd, and yet I must confess that those bushes at the entrance of the cave do present an appearance as if some heavy creature had forced its way through them. I begin to be keenly interested. I have said nothing to the Miss Allertons, for they are quite superstitious enough already, but I have bought some candles, and mean to investigate for myself.

I observed this morning that among the numerous tufts of sheep's wool which lay among the bushes near the cavern there was one which was smeared with blood. Of course, my reason tells me that if sheep wander into such rocky places they are likely to injure themselves, and yet somehow that splash of crimson gave me a sudden shock, and for a moment I found myself shrinking back in horror from the old Roman arch. A fetid breath seemed to ooze from the black depths into which I peered. Could it indeed be possible that some nameless thing, some dreadful presence, was lurking down yonder ? I should have been incapable of such feelings in the days of my strength, but one grows more nervous and fanciful when one's health is shaken.

For the moment I weakened in my resolution, and was ready to leave the secret of the old mine, if one exists, for ever unsolved. But to-night my interest has returned and my nerves grown more steady. To-morrow I trust that I shall have gone more deeply into this matter.

April 22.—Let me try and set down as accurately as I can my extraordinary experience of yesterday. I started in the afternoon, and made my way to the Blue John Gap. I confess that my misgivings returned as I gazed into its depths, and I wished that I had brought a companion to share my exploration. Finally, with a return of resolution, I lit my candle, pushed my way through the briars, and descended into the rocky shaft.

It went down at an acute angle for some fifty feet, the floor being covered with broken stone. Thence there extended a long, straight passage cut in the solid rock. I am no geologist, but the lining of this corridor was certainly of some harder material than limestone, for there were points where I could actually see the tool-marks which the old miners had left in their excavation, as fresh as if they had been done yesterday. Down this strange, old-world corridor I stumbled, my feeble flame throwing a dim circle of light around me, which made the shadows beyond the more threatening and obscure. Finally, I came to a spot where the Roman tunnel opened into a water-worn cavern—a huge hall, hung with long white icicles of lime deposit. From this central chamber I could dimly perceive that a number of passages worn by the subterranean streams wound away into the depths of the earth. I was standing there wondering whether I had better return, or whether I dare venture farther into this dangerous labyrinth, when my eyes fell upon something at my feet which strongly arrested my attention.

The greater part of the floor of the cavern was covered with boulders of rock or with hard incrustations of lime, but at this particular point there had been a drip from the distant roof, which had left a patch of soft mud. In the very centre of this there was a huge mark—an ill-defined blotch, deep, broad and irregular, as if a great boulder had fallen upon it. No loose stone lay near, however, nor was there anything to account for the impression. It was far too large to be caused by any possible animal, and besides, there was only the one, and the patch of mud was of such a size that no reasonable stride could have covered it. As I rose from the examination of that singular mark and then looked round into the black shadows which hemmed me in, I must confess that I felt for a moment a most unpleasant sinking of my heart, and that, do what I could, the candle trembled in my outstretched hand.

I soon recovered my nerve, however, when I reflected how absurd it was to associate so huge and shapeless a mark with the track of any known animal. Even an elephant could not have produced it. I determined, therefore, that I would not be scared by vague and senseless fears from carrying out my exploration. Before proceeding, I took good note of a curious rock formation in the wall by which I could recognise the entrance of the Roman tunnel. The precaution was very necessary, for the great cave, so far as I could see it, was intersected by passages. Having made sure of my position, and reassured myself by examining my spare candles and my matches, I advanced slowly over the rocky and uneven surface of the cavern.

And now I come to the point where I met with such sudden and desperate disaster. A stream, some twenty feet broad, ran across my path, and I walked for some little distance along the bank to find a spot where I could cross dry-shod. Finally, I came to a place where a single flat boulder lay near the centre, which I could reach in a stride. As it chanced, however, the rock had been cut away and made top-heavy by the rush of the stream, so that it tilted over as I landed on it and shot me into the ice-cold water. My candle went out, and I found myself floundering about in utter and absolute darkness.

I staggered to my feet again, more amused than alarmed by my adventure. The candle had fallen from my hand, and was lost in the stream, but I had two others in my pocket, so that it was of no importance. I got one of them ready, and drew out my box of matches to light it. Only then did I realize my position. The box had been soaked in my fall into the river. It was impossible to strike the matches.

A cold hand seemed to close round my heart as I realized my position. The darkness was opaque and horrible. It was so utter that one put one's hand up to one's face as if to press off something solid. I stood still, and by an effort I steadied myself. I tried to reconstruct in my mind a map of the floor of the cavern as I had last seen it. Alas! the bearings which had impressed themselves upon my mind were high on the wall, and not to be found by touch. Still, I remembered in a general way how the sides were situated, and I hoped that by groping my way along them I should at last come to the opening of the Roman tunnel. Moving very slowly, and continually striking against the rocks, I set out on this desperate quest.

But I very soon realized how impossible it was. In that black, velvety darkness one lost all one's bearings in an instant. Before I had made a dozen paces, I was utterly bewildered as to my whereabouts. The rippling of the stream, which was the one sound audible, showed me where it lay, but the moment that I left its bank I was utterly lost. The idea of finding my way back in absolute darkness through that limestone labyrinth was clearly an impossible one.

I sat down upon a boulder and reflected upon my unfortunate plight. I had not told anyone that I proposed to come to the Blue John mine, and it was unlikely that a search party would come after me. Therefore I must trust to my own resources to get clear of the danger. There was only one hope, and that was that the matches might dry. When I fell into the river, only half of me had got thoroughly wet. My left shoulder had remained above the water. I took the box of matches, therefore, and put it into my left armpit. The moist air of the cavern might possibly be counteracted by the heat of my body, but even so, I knew that I could not hope to get a light for many hours. Meanwhile there was nothing for it but to wait.

By good luck I had slipped several biscuits into my pocket before I left the farm-house. These I now devoured, and washed them down with a draught from that wretched stream which had been the cause of all my misfortunes. Then I felt about for a comfortable seat among the rocks, and, having discovered a place where I could get a support for my back, I stretched out my legs and settled myself down to wait. I was wretchedly damp and cold, but I tried to cheer myself with the reflection that modern science prescribed open windows and walks in all weather for my disease. Gradually, lulled by the monotonous gurgle of the stream, and by the absolute darkness, I sank into an uneasy slumber.

How long this lasted I cannot say. It may have been

for an hour, it may have been for several. Suddenly I sat up on my rock couch, with every nerve thrilling and every sense acutely on the alert. Beyond all doubt I had heard a sound—some sound very distinct from the gurgling of the waters. It had passed, but the reverberation of it still lingered in my ear. Was it a search party ? They would most certainly have shouted, and vague as this sound was which had wakened me, it was very distinct from the human voice. I sat palpitating and hardly daring to breathe. There it was again ! And again ! Now it had become continuous. It was a tread—yes, surely it was the tread of some living creature. But what a tread it was ! It gave one the impression of enormous weight carried upon sponge-like feet, which gave forth a muffled but ear-filling sound. The darkness was as complete as ever, but the tread was regular and decisive. And it was coming beyond all question in my direction.

My skin grew cold, and my hair stood on end as I listened to that steady and ponderous footfall. There was some creature there, and surely by the speed of its advance, it was one which could see in the dark. I crouched low on my rock and tried to blend myself into it. The steps grew nearer still, then stopped, and presently I was aware of a loud lapping and gurgling. The creature was drinking at the stream. Then again there was silence, broken by a succession of long sniffs and snorts of tremendous volume and energy. Had it caught the scent of me ? My own nostrils were filled by a low fetid odour, mephitic and abominable. Then I heard the steps again. They were on my side of the stream now. The stones rattled within a few yards of where I lay. Hardly daring to breathe, I crouched upon my rock. Then the steps drew away. I heard the splash as it returned across the river, and the sound died away into the distance in the direction from which it had come.

For a long time I lay upon the rock, too much horrified

to move. I thought of the sound which I had heard coming from the depths of the cave, of Armitage's fears, of the strange impression in the mud, and now came this final and absolute proof that there was indeed some inconceivable monster, something utterly unearthly and dreadful, which lurked in the hollow of the mountain. Of its nature or form I could frame no conception, save that it was both light-footed and gigantic. The combat between my reason, which told me that such things could not be, and my senses, which told me that they were, raged within me as I lay. Finally, I was almost ready to persuade myself that this experience had been part of some evil dream, and that my abnormal condition might have conjured up an hallucination. But there remained one final experience which removed the last possibility of doubt from my mind.

I had taken my matches from my armpit and felt them. They seemed perfectly hard and dry. Stooping down into a crevice of the rocks, I tried one of them. To my delight it took fire at once. I lit the candle, and, with a terrified backward glance into the obscure depths of the cavern, I hurried in the direction of the Roman passage. As I did so I passed the patch of mud on which I had seen the huge imprint. Now I stood astonished before it, for there were three similar imprints upon its surface, enormous in size, irregular in outline, of a depth which indicated the ponderous weight which had left them. Then a great terror surged over me. Stooping and shading my candle with my hand, I ran in a frenzy of fear to the rocky archway, hastened up it, and never stopped until, with weary feet and panting lungs, I rushed up the final slope of stones, broke through the tangle of briars, and flung myself exhausted upon the soft grass under the peaceful light of the stars. It was three in the morning when I reached the farm-house, and to-day I am all unstrung and quivering after my terrific adventure. As yet I have told no one. I must move warily in the matter. What would the poor lonely women, or the uneducated yokels here think of it if I were to tell them my experience ? Let me go to someone who can understand and advise.

April 25.—I was laid up in bed for two days after my incredible adventure in the cavern. I use the adjective with a very definite meaning, for I have had an experience since which has shocked me almost as much as the other. I have said that I was looking round for someone who could advise me. There is a Dr. Mark Johnson who practises some few miles away, to whom I had a note of recommendation from Professor Saunderson. To him I drove, when I was strong enough to get about, and I recounted to him my whole strange experience. He listened intently, and then carefully examined me, paying special attention to my reflexes and to the pupils of my eyes. When he had finished, he refused to discuss my adventure, saying that it was entirely beyond him, but he gave me the card of a Mr. Picton at Castleton, with the advice that I should instantly go to him and tell him the story exactly as I had done to himself. He was, according to my adviser, the very man who was pre-eminently suited to help me. I went on to the station, therefore, and made my way to the little town, which is some ten miles away. Mr. Picton appeared to be a man of importance, as his brass plate was displayed upon the door of a considerable building on the outskirts of the town. I was about to ring his bell, when some misgiving came into my mind, and, crossing to a neighbouring shop, I asked the man behind the counter if he could tell me anything of Mr. Picton. " Why," said he, " he is the best mad doctor in Derbyshire, and yonder is his asylum." You can imagine that it was not long before I had shaken the dust of Castleton from my feet and returned to the farm, cursing all unimaginative pedants who cannot conceive that there may be things in creation which have never yet chanced to come across their mole's vision. After all, now that I am cooler, I can afford to admit that I have been no more sympathetic to Armitage than Dr. Johnson has been to me.

April 27.—When I was a student I had the reputation of being a man of courage and enterprise. I remember that when there was a ghost-hunt at Coltbridge it was I who sat up in the haunted house. Is it advancing years (after all, I am only thirty-five), or is it this physical malady which has caused degeneration ? Certainly my heart quails when I think of that horrible cavern in the hill, and the certainty that it has some monstrous occupant. What shall I do ? There is not an hour in the day that I do not debate the question. If I say nothing, then the mystery remains unsolved. If I do say anything, then I have the alternative of mad alarm over the whole countryside, or of absolute incredulity which may end in consigning me to an asylum. On the whole, I think that my best course is to wait, and to prepare for some expedition which shall be more deliberate and better thought out than the last. As a first step I have been to Castleton and obtained a few essentials—a large acetylene lantern for one thing, and a good double-barrelled sporting rifle for another. The latter I have hired, but I have bought a dozen heavy game cartridges, which would bring down a rhinoceros. Now I am ready for my troglodyte friend. Give me better health and a little spate of energy, and I shall try conclusions with him yet. But who and what is he ? Ah ! there is the question which stands between me and my sleep. How many theories do I form, only to discard each in turn ! It is all so utterly unthinkable. And yet the cry, the footmark, the tread in the cavern—no reasoning can get past these. I think of the old-world legends of dragons and of other monsters. Were they, perhaps, not such fairy-tales as we have thought ? Can it be that there is some fact which underlies them, and am I, of all mortals, the one who is chosen to expose it ?

May 3.—For several days I have been laid up by the vagaries of an English spring, and during those days there have been developments, the true and sinister meaning of which no one can appreciate save myself. I may say that we have had cloudy and moonless nights of late, which according to my information were the seasons upon which sheep disappeared. Well, sheep *have* disappeared. Two of Miss Allerton's, one of old Pearson's of the Cat Walk, and one of Mrs. Moulton's. Four in all during three nights. No trace is left of them at all, and the countryside is buzzing with rumours of gipsies and of sheep-stealers.

But there is something more serious than that. Young Armitage has disappeared also. He left his moorland cottage early on Wednesday night and has never been heard of since. He was an unattached man, so there is less sensation than would otherwise be the case. The popular explanation is that he owes money, and has found a situation in some other part of the country, whence he will presently write for his belongings. But I have grave misgivings. Is it not much more likely that the recent tragedy of the sheep has caused him to take some steps which may have ended in his own destruction ? He may, for example, have lain in wait for the creature and been carried off by it into the recesses of the mountains. What an inconceivable fate for a civilized Englishman of the twentieth century ! And yet I feel that it is possible and even probable. But in that case, how far am I answerable both for his death and for any other mishap which may occur ? Surely with the knowledge I already possess it must be my duty to see that something is done, or if necessary to do it myself. It must be the latter, for this morning I went down to the local police-station and told my story. The inspector entered it all in a large book and bowed me out with commendable gravity, but I heard a burst of laughter before I had got down his garden path. No doubt he was recounting my adventure to his family.

June 10.—I am writing this, propped up in bed, six

weeks after my last entry in this journal. I have gone
through a terrible shock both to mind and body, arising
from such an experience as has seldom befallen a human
being before. But I have attained my end. The danger
from the Terror which dwells in the Blue John Gap
has passed never to return. Thus much at least I, a
broken invalid, have done for the common good. Let
me now recount what occurred as clearly as I may.

The night of Friday, May 3, was dark and cloudy—
the very night for the monster to walk. About eleven
o'clock I went from the farm-house with my lantern
and my rifle, having first left a note upon the table of
my bedroom in which I said that, if I were missing,
search should be made for me in the direction of the
Gap. I made my way to the mouth of the Roman
shaft, and, having perched myself among the rocks close
to the opening, I shut off my lantern and waited patiently
with my loaded rifle ready to my hand.

It was a melancholy vigil. All down the winding
valley I could see the scattered lights of the farm-houses,
and the church clock of Chapel-le-Dale tolling the hours
came faintly to my ears. These tokens of my fellow-
men served only to make my own position seem the
more lonely, and to call for a greater effort to overcome
the terror which tempted me continually to get back to
the farm, and abandon for ever this dangerous quest.
And yet there lies deep in every man a rooted self-respect
which makes it hard for him to turn back from that
which he has once undertaken. This feeling of personal
pride was my salvation now, and it was that alone which
held me fast when every instinct of my nature was
dragging me away. I am glad now that I had the strength.
In spite of all that it has cost me, my manhood is at least
above reproach.

Twelve o'clock struck in the distant church, then one,
then two. It was the darkest hour of the night. The
clouds were drifting low, and there was not a star in
the sky. An owl was hooting somewhere among the

rocks, but no other sound, save the gentle sough of the wind, came to my ears. And then suddenly I heard it! From far away down the tunnel came those muffled steps, so soft and yet so ponderous. I heard also the rattle of stones as they gave way under that giant tread. They drew nearer. They were close upon me. I heard the crashing of the bushes round the entrance, and then dimly through the darkness I was conscious of the loom of some enormous shape, some monstrous inchoate creature, passing swiftly and very silently out from the tunnel. I was paralysed with fear and amazement. Long as I had waited, now that it had actually come I was unprepared for the shock. I lay motionless and breathless, whilst the great dark mass whisked by me and was swallowed up in the night.

But now I nerved myself for its return. No sound came from the sleeping countryside to tell of the horror which was loose. In no way could I judge how far off it was, what it was doing, or when it might be back. But not a second time should my nerve fail me, not a second time should it pass unchallenged. I swore it between my clenched teeth as I laid my cocked rifle across the rock.

And yet it nearly happened. There was no warning of approach now as the creature passed over the grass. Suddenly, like a dark, drifting shadow, the huge bulk loomed up once more before me, making for the entrance of the cave. Again came that paralysis of volition which held my crooked forefinger impotent upon the trigger. But with a desperate effort I shook it off. Even as the brushwood rustled, and the monstrous beast blended with the shadow of the Gap, I fired at the retreating form. In the blaze of the gun I caught a glimpse of a great shaggy mass, something with rough and bristling hair of a withered grey colour, fading away to white in its lower parts, the huge body supported upon short, thick, curving legs. I had just that glance, and then I heard the rattle of the stones as the creature tore down into its burrow. In an instant, with a triumphant revulsion of feeling, I had cast my fears to the wind, and uncovering my powerful lantern, with my rifle in my hand, I sprang down from my rock and rushed after the monster down the old Roman shaft.

My splendid lamp cast a brilliant flood of vivid light in front of me, very different from the yellow glimmer which had aided me down the same passage only twelve days before. As I ran, I saw the great beast lurching along before me, its huge bulk filling up the whole space from wall to wall. Its hair looked like coarse faded oakum, and hung down in long, dense masses which swayed as it moved. It was like an enormous unclipped sheep in its fleece, but in size it was far larger than the largest elephant, and its breadth seemed to be nearly as great as its height. It fills me with amazement now to think that I should have dared to follow such a horror into the bowels of the earth, but when one's blood is up, and when one's quarry seems to be flying, the old primeval hunting-spirit awakes and prudence is cast to the wind. Rifle in hand, I ran at the top of my speed upon the trail of the monster.

I had seen that the creature was swift. Now I was to find out to my cost that it was also very cunning. I had imagined that it was in panic flight, and that I had only to pursue it. The idea that it might turn upon me never entered my excited brain. I have already explained that the passage down which I was racing opened into a great central cave. Into this I rushed, fearful lest I should lose all trace of the beast. But he had turned upon his own traces, and in a moment we were face to face.

That picture, seen in the brilliant white light of the lantern, is etched for ever upon my brain. He had reared up on his hind legs as a bear would do, and stood above me, enormous, menacing—such a creature as no nightmare had ever brought to my imagination. I have said that he reared like a bear, and there was something bear-like—if one could conceive a bear which was ten-fold the bulk of any bear seen upon earth—in his whole pose and attitude, in his great crooked forelegs with their ivory-white claws, in his rugged skin, and in his red, gaping mouth, fringed with monstrous fangs. Only in one point did he differ from the bear, or from any other creature which walks the earth, and even at that supreme moment a shudder of horror passed over me as I observed that the eyes which glistened in the glow of my lantern were huge, projecting bulbs, white and sightless. For a moment his great paws swung over my head. The next he fell forward upon me, I and my broken lantern crashed to the earth, and I remember no more.

When I came to myself I was back in the farm-house of the Allertons. Two days had passed since my terrible adventure in the Blue John Gap. It seems that I had lain all night in the cave insensible from concussion of the brain, with my left arm and two ribs badly fractured. In the morning my note had been found, a search party of a dozen farmers assembled, and I had been tracked down and carried back to my bedroom, where I had lain in high delirium ever since. There was, it seems, no sign of the creature, and no bloodstain which would· show that my bullet had found him as he passed. Save for my own plight and the marks upon the mud, there was nothing to prove that what I said was true.

Six weeks have now elapsed, and I am able to sit out once more in the sunshine. Just opposite me is the steep hillside, grey with shaly rock, and yonder on its flank is the dark cleft which marks the opening of the Blue John Gap. But it is no longer a source of terror. Never again through that ill-omened tunnel shall any strange shape flit out into the world of men. The educated and the scientific, the Dr. Johnsons and the like, may smile at my narrative, but the poorer folk of the countryside had never a doubt as to its truth. On the day after my recovering consciousness they assembled in their hundreds round the Blue John Gap. As the *Castleton Courier* said :

" It was useless for our correspondent, or for any of the adventurous gentlemen who had come from Matlock, Buxton, and other parts, to offer to descend, to explore the cave to the end, and to finally test the extraordinary narrative of Dr. James Hardcastle. The country people had taken the matter into their own hands, and from an early hour of the morning they had worked hard in stopping up the entrance of the tunnel. There is a sharp slope where the shaft begins, and great boulders, rolled along by many willing hands, were thrust down it until the Gap was absolutely sealed. So ends the episode which has caused such excitement throughout the country. Local opinion is fiercely divided upon the subject. On the one hand are those who point to Dr. Hardcastle's impaired health, and to the possibility of cerebral lesions of tubercular origin giving rise to strange hallucinations. Some *idée fixe*, according to these gentlemen, caused the doctor to wander down the tunnel, and a fall among the rocks was sufficient to account for his injuries. On the other hand, a legend of a strange creature in the Gap has existed for some months back, and the farmers look upon Dr. Hardcastle's narrative and his personal injuries as a final corroboration. So the matter stands, and so the matter will continue to stand, for no definite solution seems to us to be now possible. It transcends human wit to give any scientific explanation which could cover the alleged facts."

Perhaps before the *Courier* published these words they would have been wise to send their representative to me. I have thought the matter out, as no one else has occasion to do, and it is possible that I might have removed some of the more obvious difficulties of the narrative and brought it one degree nearer to scientific acceptance. Let me then write down the only explanation which seems to me to elucidate what I know to my cost to have been a series of facts. My theory may seem to be wildly improbable, but at least no one can venture to say that it is impossible.

My view is—and it was formed, as is shown by my diary, before my personal adventure—that in this part of England there is a vast subterranean lake or sea, which is fed by the great number of streams which pass down through the limestone. Where there is a large collection of water there must also be some evaporation, mists or rain, and a possibility of vegetation. This in turn suggests that there may be animal life, arising, as the vegetable life would also do, from those seeds and types which had been introduced at an early period of the world's history, when communication with the outer air was more easy. This place had then developed a fauna and flora of its own, including such monsters as the one which I had seen, which may well have been the old cave-bear, enormously enlarged and modified by its new environment. For countless æons the internal and the external creation had kept apart, growing steadily away from each other. Then there had come some rift in the depths of the mountain which had enabled one creature to wander up and, by means of the Roman tunnel, to reach the open air. Like all subterranean life, it had lost the power of sight, but this had no doubt been compensated for by nature in other directions. Certainly it had some means of finding its way about, and of hunting down the sheep upon the hillside. As to its choice of dark nights, it is part of my theory that light was painful to those great white eyeballs, and that it was only a pitch-black world which it could tolerate. Perhaps, indeed, it was the glare of my lantern which saved my life at that awful moment when we were face to face. So I read the riddle. I leave these facts behind me, and if you can explain them, do so ; or if you choose to doubt them, do so. Neither your belief nor your incredulity can alter them, nor affect one whose task is nearly over.

So ended the strange narrative of Dr. James Hard castle.

30. *The Brazilian Cat*

IT is hard luck on a young fellow to have expensive tastes, great expectations, aristocratic connections, but no actual money in his pocket, and no profession by which he may earn any. The fact was that my father, a good, sanguine, easy-going man, had such confidence in the wealth and benevolence of his bachelor elder brother, Lord Southerton, that he took it for granted that I, his only son, would never be called upon to earn a living for myself. He imagined that if there were not a vacancy for me on the great Southerton Estates, at least there would be found some post in that diplomatic service which still remains the special preserve of our privileged classes. He died too early to realize how false his calculations had been. Neither my uncle nor the State took the slightest notice of me, or showed any interest in my career. An occasional brace of pheasants, or basket of hares, was all that ever reached me to remind me that I was heir to Otwell House and one of the richest estates in the country. In the meantime, I found myself a bachelor and man about town, living in a suite of apartments in Grosvenor Mansions, with no occupation save that of pigeon-shooting and polo-playing at Hurlingham. Month by month I realized that it was more and more difficult to get the brokers to renew my bills, or to cash any further post-obits upon an unentailed property. Ruin lay right across my path, and every day I saw it clearer, nearer, and more absolutely unavoidable.

What made me feel my own poverty the more was that, apart from the great wealth of Lord Southerton, all my other relations were fairly well-to-do. The nearest of these was Everard King, my father's nephew and my own first cousin, who had spent an adventurous life in Brazil, and had now returned to this country to settle

down on his fortune. We never knew how he made his
money, but he appeared to have plenty of it, for he bought
the estate of Greylands, near Clipton-on-the-Marsh, in
Suffolk. For the first year of his residence in England
he took no more notice of me than my miserly uncle ;
but at last one summer morning, to my very great relief
and joy, I received a letter asking me to come down
that very day and spend a short visit at Greylands Court.
I was expecting a rather long visit to Bankruptcy Court
at the time, and this interruption seemed almost providential. If I could only get on terms with this unknown relative of mine, I might pull through yet. For
the family credit he could not let me go entirely to the
wall. I ordered my valet to pack my valise, and I set
off the same evening for Clipton-on-the-Marsh.

After changing at Ipswich, a little local train deposited
me at a small, deserted station lying amidst a rolling
grassy country, with a sluggish and winding river curving in and out amidst the valleys, between high, silted
banks, which showed that we were within reach of the
tide. No carriage was awaiting me (I found afterwards
that my telegram had been delayed), so I hired a dog-
cart at the local inn. The driver, an excellent fellow,
was full of my relative's praises, and I learned from him
that Mr. Everard King was already a name to conjure
with in that part of the country. He had entertained
the school-children, he had thrown his grounds open to
visitors, he had subscribed to charities—in short, his
benevolence had been so universal that my driver could
only account for it on the supposition that he had Parliamentary ambitions.

My attention was drawn away from my driver's pane-
gyric by the appearance of a very beautiful bird which
settled on a telegraph-post beside the road. At first I
thought that it was a jay, but it was larger, with a brighter
plumage. The driver accounted for its presence at once
by saying that it belonged to the very man whom we
were about to visit. It seems that the acclimatization

of foreign creatures was one of his hobbies, and that he had brought with him from Brazil a number of birds and beasts which he was endeavouring to rear in England. When once we had passed the gates of Greylands Park we had ample evidence of this taste of his. Some small spotted deer, a curious wild pig known, I believe, as a peccary, a gorgeously feathered oriole, some sort of armadillo, and a singular lumbering intoed beast like a very fat badger, were among the creatures which I observed as we drove along the winding avenue.

Mr. Everard King, my unknown cousin, was standing in person upon the steps of his house, for he had seen us in the distance, and guessed that it was I. His appearance was very homely and benevolent, short and stout, forty-five years old, perhaps, with a round, good-humoured face, burned brown with the tropical sun, and shot with a thousand wrinkles. He wore white linen clothes, in true planter style, with a cigar between his lips, and a large Panama hat upon the back of his head. It was such a figure as one associates with a verandahed bungalow, and it looked curiously out of place in front of this broad, stone English mansion, with its solid wings and its Palladio pillars before the doorway.

" My dear ! " he cried, glancing over his shoulder ; " my dear, here is our guest ! Welcome, welcome to Greylands ! I am delighted to make your acquaintance, Cousin Marshall, and I take it as a great compliment that you should honour this sleepy little country place with your presence."

Nothing could be more hearty than his manner, and he set me at my ease in an instant. But it needed all his cordiality to atone for the frigidity and even rudeness of his wife, a tall, haggard woman, who came forward at his summons. She was, I believe, of Brazilian extraction, though she spoke excellent English, and I excused her manners on the score of her ignorance of our customs. She did not attempt to conceal, however, either then or afterwards, that I was no very welcome visitor at Greylands Court. Her actual words were, as a rule, courteous, but she was the possessor of a pair of particularly expressive dark eyes, and I read in them very clearly from the first that she heartily wished me back in London once more.

However, my debts were too pressing and my designs upon my wealthy relative were too vital for me to allow them to be upset by the ill-temper of his wife, so I disregarded her coldness and reciprocated the extreme cordiality of his welcome. No pains had been spared by him to make me comfortable. My room was a charming one. He implored me to tell him anything which could add to my happiness. It was on the tip of my tongue to inform him that a blank cheque would materially help towards that end, but I felt that it might be premature in the present state of our acquaintance. The dinner was excellent, and as we sat together afterwards over his Havanas and coffee, which latter he told me was specially prepared upon his own plantation, it seemed to me that all my driver's eulogies were justified, and that I had never met a more large-hearted and hospitable man.

But, in spite of his cheery good nature, he was a man with a strong will and a fiery temper of his own. Of this I had an example upon the following morning. The curious aversion which Mrs. Everard King had conceived towards me was so strong, that her manner at breakfast was almost offensive. But her meaning became unmistakable when her husband had quitted the room.

"The best train in the day is at twelve fifteen," said she.

"But I was not thinking of going to-day," I answered, frankly—perhaps even defiantly, for I was determined not to be driven out by this woman.

"Oh, if it rests with you——" said she, and stopped with a most insolent expression in her eyes.

" I am sure," I answered, " that Mr. Everard King would tell me if I were outstaying my welcome."

" What's this ? What's this ? " said a voice, and there he was in the room. He had overheard my last words, and a glance at our faces had told him the rest. In an instant his chubby, cheery face set into an expression of absolute ferocity.

" Might I trouble you to walk outside, Marshall," said he ? (I may mention that my own name is Marshall King.)

He closed the door behind me, and then, for an instant, I heard him talking in a low voice of concentrated passion to his wife. This gross breach of hospitality had evidently hit upon his tenderest point. I am no eavesdropper, so I walked out on to the lawn. Presently I heard a hurried step behind me, and there was the lady, her face pale with excitement, and her eyes red with tears.

" My husband has asked me to apologize to you, Mr. Marshall King," said she, standing with downcast eyes before me.

" Please do not say another word, Mrs. King."

Her dark eyes suddenly blazed out at me.

" You fool ! " she hissed, with frantic vehemence, and turning on her heel swept back to the house.

The insult was so outrageous, so insufferable, that I could only stand staring after her in bewilderment. I was still there when my host joined me. He was his cheery, chubby self once more.

" I hope that my wife has apologized for her foolish remarks," said he.

" Oh, yes—yes, certainly ! "

He put his hand through my arm and walked with me up and down the lawn.

" You must not take it seriously," said he. " It would grieve me inexpressibly if you curtailed your visit by one hour. The fact is—there is no reason why there should be any concealment between relatives—that my poor dear wife is incredibly jealous. She hates that any-one—male or female—should for an instant come be-tween us. Her ideal is a desert island and an eternal *tête-à-tête*. That gives you the clue to her actions, which are, I confess, upon this particular point, not very far removed from mania. Tell me that you will think no more of it."

" No, no ; certainly not."

" Then light this cigar and come round with me and see my little menagerie."

The whole afternoon was occupied by this inspection, which included all the birds, beasts, and even reptiles which he had imported. Some were free, some in cages, a few actually in the house. He spoke with enthusiasm of his successes and his failures, his births and his deaths, and he would cry out in his delight, like a schoolboy, when, as we walked, some gaudy bird would flutter up from the grass, or some curious beast slink into the cover. Finally he led me down a corridor which extended from one wing of the house. At the end of this there was a heavy door with a sliding shutter in it, and beside it there projected from the wall an iron handle attached to a wheel and a drum. A line of stout bars extended across the passage.

" I am about to show you the jewel of my collection," said he. " There is only one other specimen in Europe, now that the Rotterdam cub is dead. It is a Brazilian cat."

" But how does that differ from any other cat ? "

" You will soon see that," said he, laughing. " Will you kindly draw that shutter and look through ? "

I did so, and found that I was gazing into a large, empty room, with stone flags, and small, barred windows upon the farther wall. In the centre of this room, lying in the middle of a golden patch of sunlight, there was stretched a huge creature, as large as a tiger, but as black and sleek as ebony. It was simply a very enormous and very well-kept black cat, and it cuddled up and basked in that yellow pool of light exactly as a cat would do. It was so graceful, so sinewy, and so gently and smoothly diabolical, that I could not take my eyes from the opening.

" Isn't he splendid ? " said my host, enthusiastically.

" Glorious ! I never saw such a noble creature."

" Some people call it a black puma, but really it is not a puma at all. That fellow is nearly eleven feet from tail to tip. Four years ago he was a little ball of black fluff, with two yellow eyes staring out of it. He was sold me as a new-born cub up in the wild country at the head-waters of the Rio Negro. They speared his mother to death after she had killed a dozen of them."

" They are ferocious, then ? "

" The most absolutely treacherous and bloodthirsty creatures upon earth. You talk about a Brazilian cat to an up-country Indian, and see him get the jumps. They prefer humans to game. This fellow has never tasted living blood yet, but when he does he will be a terror. At present he won't stand anyone but me in his den. Even Baldwin, the groom, dare not go near him. As to me, I am his mother and father in one."

As he spoke he suddenly, to my astonishment, opened the door and slipped in, closing it instantly behind him. At the sound of his voice the huge, lithe creature rose, yawned and rubbed its round, black head affectionately against his side, while he patted and fondled it.

" Now, Tommy, into your cage ! " said he.

The monstrous cat walked over to one side of the room and coiled itself up under a grating. Everard King came out, and taking the iron handle which I have mentioned, he began to turn it. As he did so the line of bars in the corridor began to pass through a slot in the wall and closed up the front of this grating, so as to make an effective cage. When it was in position he opened the door once more and invited me into the room, which was heavy with the pungent, musty smell peculiar to the great carnivora.

" That's how we work it," said he. " We give him the run of the room for exercise, and then at night we put him in his cage. You can let him out by turning the handle from the passage, or you can, as you have seen, coop him up in the same way. No, no, you should not do that ! "

I had put my hand between the bars to pat the glossy, heaving flank. He pulled it back, with a serious face.

" I assure you that he is not safe. Don't imagine that because I can take liberties with him anyone else can. He is very exclusive in his friends—aren't you, Tommy ? Ah, he hears his lunch coming to him ! Don't you, boy ? "

A step sounded in the stone-flagged passage, and the creature had sprung to his feet, and was pacing up and down the narrow cage, his yellow eyes gleaming, and his scarlet tongue rippling and quivering over the white line of his jagged teeth. A groom entered with a coarse joint upon a tray, and thrust it through the bars to him. He pounced lightly upon it, carried it off to the corner, and there, holding it between his paws, tore and wrenched at it, raising his bloody muzzle every now and then to look at us. It was a malignant and yet fascinating sight.

" You can't wonder that I am fond of him, can you ? " said my host, as we left the room, " especially when you consider that I have had the rearing of him. It was no joke bringing him over from the centre of South America ; but here he is safe and sound—and, as I have said, far the most perfect specimen in Europe. The people at the Zoo are dying to have him, but I really can't part with him. Now, I think that I have inflicted my hobby upon you long enough, so we cannot do better than follow Tommy's example, and go to our lunch."

My South American relative was so engrossed by his grounds and their curious occupants, that I hardly gave him credit at first for having any interests outside them. That he had some, and pressing ones, was soon borne in upon me by the number of telegrams which he received.

They arrived at all hours, and were always opened by him with the utmost eagerness and anxiety upon his face. Sometimes I imagined that it must be the Turf, and sometimes the Stock Exchange, but certainly he had some very urgent business going forwards which was not transacted upon the Downs of Suffolk. During the six days of my visit he had never fewer than three or four telegrams a day, and sometimes as many as seven or eight.

I had occupied these six days so well, that by the end of them I had succeeded in getting upon the most cordial terms with my cousin. Every night we had sat up late in the billiard-room, he telling me the most extraordinary stories of his adventures in America— stories so desperate and reckless, that I could hardly associate them with the brown little, chubby man before me. In return, I ventured upon some of my own re- miniscences of London life, which interested him so much, that he vowed he would come up to Grosvenor Mansions and stay with me. He was anxious to see the faster side of city life, and certainly, though I say it, he could not have chosen a more competent guide. It was not until the last day of my visit that I ventured to approach that which was on my mind. I told him frankly about my pecuniary difficulties and my impend- ing ruin, and I asked his advice—though I hoped for something more solid. He listened attentively, puffing hard at his cigar.

" But surely," said he, " you are the heir of our relative, Lord Southerton ? "

" I have every reason to believe so, but he would never make me any allowance."

" No, no, I have heard of his miserly ways. My poor Marshall, your position has been a very hard one. By the way, have you heard any news of Lord Southerton's health lately ? "

" He has always been in a critical condition ever since my childhood."

" Exactly—a creaking hinge, if ever there was one. Your inheritance may be a long way off. Dear me, how awkwardly situated you are ! "

" I had some hopes, sir, that you, knowing all the facts, might be inclined to advance——"

" Don't say another word, my dear boy," he cried, with the utmost cordiality ; " we shall talk it over to-night, and I give you my word that whatever is in my power shall be done."

I was not sorry that my visit was drawing to a close, for it is unpleasant to feel that there is one person in the house who eagerly desires your departure. Mrs. King's sallow face and forbidding eyes had become more and more hateful to me. She was no longer actively rude —her fear of her husband prevented her—but she pushed her insane jealousy to the extent of ignoring me, never addressing me, and in every way making my stay at Greylands as uncomfortable as she could. So offensive was her manner during that last day, that I should certainly have left had it not been for that interview with my host in the evening which would, I hoped, retrieve my broken fortunes.

It was very late when it occurred, for my relative, who had been receiving even more telegrams than usual during the day, went off to his study after dinner, and only emerged when the household had retired to bed. I heard him go round locking the doors, as his custom was of a night, and finally he joined me in the billiard-room. His stout figure was wrapped in a dressing-gown, and he wore a pair of red Turkish slippers without any heels. Settling down into an arm-chair, he brewed himself a glass of grog, in which I could not help noticing that the whisky considerably predominated over the water.

" My word ! " said he, " what a night ! "

It was, indeed. The wind was howling and screaming round the house, and the latticed windows rattled and shook as if they were coming in. The glow of the yellow lamps and the flavour of our cigars seemed the brighter and more fragrant for the contrast.

" Now, my boy," said my host, " we have the house and the night to ourselves. Let me have an idea of how your affairs stand, and I will see what can be done to set them in order. I wish to hear every detail."

Thus encouraged, I entered into a long exposition, in which all my tradesmen and creditors from my landlord to my valet, figured in turn. I had notes in my pocket-book, and I marshalled my facts, and gave, I flatter myself, a very business-like statement of my own un-businesslike ways and lamentable position. I was depressed, however, to notice that my companion's eyes were vacant and his attention elsewhere. When he did occasionally throw out a remark it was so entirely perfunctory and pointless, that I was sure he had not in the least followed my remarks. Every now and then he roused himself and put on some show of interest, asking me to repeat or to explain more fully, but it was always to sink once more into the same brown study. At last he rose and threw the end of his cigar into the grate.

" I'll tell you what, my boy," said he. " I never had a head for figures, so you will excuse me. You must jot it all down upon paper, and let me have a note of the amount. I'll understand it when I see it in black and white."

The proposal was encouraging. I promised to do so.

" And now it's time we were in bed. By Jove, there's one o'clock striking in the hall."

The tingling of the chiming clock broke through the deep roar of the gale. The wind was sweeping past with the rush of a great river.

" I must see my cat before I go to bed," said my host. " A high wind excites him. Will you come ? "

" Certainly," said I.

" Then tread softly and don't speak, for everyone is asleep."

We passed quietly down the lamp-lit Persian-rugged hall, and through the door at the farther end. All was dark in the stone corridor, but a stable lantern hung on a hook, and my host took it down and lit it. There was no grating visible in the passage, so I knew that the beast was in its cage.

" Come in ! " said my relative, and opened the door.

A deep growling as we entered showed that the storm had really excited the creature. In the flickering light of the lantern, we saw it, a huge black mass coiled in the corner of its den and throwing a squat, uncouth shadow upon the whitewashed wall. Its tail switched angrily among the straw.

" Poor Tommy is not in the best of tempers," said Everard King, holding up the lantern and looking in at him. " What a black devil he looks, doesn't he ? I must give him a little supper to put him in a better humour. Would you mind holding the lantern for a moment ? "

I took it from his hand and he stepped to the door.

" His larder is just outside here," said he. " You will excuse me for an instant, won't you ? " He passed out, and the door shut with a sharp metallic click behind him.

That hard crisp sound made my heart stand still. A sudden wave of terror passed over me. A vague perception of some monstrous treachery turned me cold. I sprang to the door, but there was no handle upon the inner side.

" Here ! " I cried. " Let me out ! "

" All right ! Don't make a row ! " said my host from the passage. " You've got the light all right."

" Yes, but I don't care about being locked in alone like this."

" Don't you ? " I heard his hearty, chuckling laugh. " You won't be alone long."

" Let me out, sir ! " I repeated angrily. " I tell you I don't allow practical jokes of this sort."

415

" Practical is the word," said he, with another hateful chuckle. And then suddenly I heard, amidst the roar of the storm, the creak and whine of the winch-handle turning, and the rattle of the grating as it passed through the slot. Great God, he was letting loose the Brazilian cat !

In the light of the lantern I saw the bars sliding slowly before me. Already there was an opening a foot wide at the farther end. With a scream I seized the last bar with my hands and pulled with the strength of a madman I *was* a madman with rage and horror. For a minute or more I held the thing motionless. I knew that he was straining with all his force upon the handle, and that the leverage was sure to overcome me. I gave inch by inch, my feet sliding along the stones, and all the time I begged and prayed this inhuman monster to save me from this horrible death. I conjured him by his kinship. I reminded him that I was his guest ; I begged to know what harm I had ever done him. His only answers were the tugs and jerks upon the handle, each of which, in spite of all my struggles, pulled another bar through the opening. Clinging and clutching, I was dragged across the whole front of the cage, until at last, with aching wrists and lacerated fingers, I gave up the hopeless struggle. The grating clanged back as I released it, and an instant later I heard the shuffle of the Turkish slippers in the passage, and the slam of the distant door. Then everything was silent.

The creature had never moved during this time. He lay still in the corner, and his tail had ceased switching. This apparition of a man adhering to his bars and dragged screaming across him had apparently filled him with amazement. I saw his great eyes staring steadily at me. I had dropped the lantern when I seized the bars, but it still burned upon the floor, and I made a movement to grasp it, with some idea that its light might protect me. But the instant I moved, the beast gave a deep and menacing growl. I stopped and stood still, quiver-

ing with fear in every limb. The cat (if one may call
so fearful a creature by so homely a name) was not more
than ten feet from me. The eyes glimmered like two
disks of phosphorus in the darkness. They appalled
and yet fascinated me. I could not take my own eyes
from them. Nature plays strange tricks with us at such
moments of intensity, and those glimmering lights waxed
and waned with a steady rise and fall. Sometimes they
seemed to be tiny points of extreme brilliancy—little
electric sparks in the black obscurity—then they would
widen and widen until all that corner of the room was
filled with their shifting and sinister light. And then
suddenly they went out altogether.

The beast had closed its eyes. I do not know whether
there may be any truth in the old idea of the dominance
of the human gaze, or whether the huge cat was simply
drowsy, but the fact remains that, far from showing any
symptom of attacking me, it simply rested its sleek,
black head upon its huge forepaws and seemed to sleep.
I stood, fearing to move lest I should rouse it into malignant life once more. But at least I was able to think
clearly now that the baleful eyes were off me. Here I
was shut up for the night with the ferocious beast. My
own instincts, to say nothing of the words of the plausible
villain who laid this trap for me, warned me that the
animal was as savage as its master. How could I stave
it off until morning ? The door was hopeless, and so
were the narrow, barred windows. There was no shelter
anywhere in the bare, stone-flagged room. To cry for
assistance was absurd. I knew that this den was an
outhouse, and that the corridor which connected it with
the house was at least a hundred feet long. Besides,
with that gale thundering outside, my cries were not
likely to be heard. I had only my own courage and
my own wits to trust to.

And then, with a fresh wave of horror, my eyes fell
upon the lantern. The candle had burned low, and was
already beginning to gutter. In ten minutes it would

be out. I had only ten minutes then in which to do something, for I felt that if I were once left in the dark with that fearful beast I should be incapable of action. The very thought of it paralysed me. I cast my despairing eyes round this chamber of death, and they rested upon one spot which seemed to promise I will not say safety, but less immediate and imminent danger than the open floor.

I have said that the cage had a top as well as a front, and this top was left standing when the front was wound through the slot in the wall. It consisted of bars at a few inches' interval, with stout wire netting between, and it rested upon a strong stanchion at each end. It stood now as a great barred canopy over the crouching figure in the corner. The space between this iron shelf and the roof may have been from two to three feet. If I could only get up there, squeezed in between bars and ceiling, I should have only one vulnerable side. I should be safe from below, from behind, and from each side. Only on the open face of it could I be attacked. There, it is true, I had no protection whatever ; but, at least, I should be out of the brute's path when he began to pace about his den. He would have to come out of his way to reach me. It was now or never, for if once the light were out it would be impossible. With a gulp in my throat I sprang up, seized the iron edge of the top, and swung myself panting on to it. I writhed in face downwards, and found myself looking straight into the terrible eyes and yawning jaws of the cat. Its fetid breath came up into my face like the steam from some foul pot.

It appeared, however, to be rather curious than angry. With a sleek ripple of its long, black back it rose, stretched itself, and then rearing itself on its hind legs, with one forepaw against the wall, it raised the other, and drew its claws across the wire meshes beneath me. One sharp, white hook tore through my trousers—for I may mention that I was still in evening dress—and dug a furrow in my knee. It was not meant as an attack, but rather as an experiment, for upon my giving a sharp cry of pain he dropped down again, and springing lightly into the room, he began walking swiftly round it, looking up every now and again in my direction. For my part I shuffled backwards until I lay with my back against the wall, screwing myself into the smallest space possible. The farther I got the more difficult it was for him to attack me.

He seemed more excited now that he had begun to move about, and he ran swiftly and noiselessly round and round the den, passing continually underneath the iron couch upon which I lay. It was wonderful to see so great a bulk passing like a shadow, with hardly the softest thudding of velvety pads. The candle was burning low—so low that I could hardly see the creature. And then, with a last flare and splutter it went out altogether. I was alone with the cat in the dark!

It helps one to face a danger when one knows that one has done all that possibly can be done. There is nothing for it then but to quietly await the result. In this case, there was no chance of safety anywhere except the precise spot where I was. I stretched myself out, therefore, and lay silently, almost breathlessly, hoping that the beast might forget my presence if I did nothing to remind him. I reckoned that it must already be two o'clock. At four it would be full dawn. I had not more than two hours to wait for daylight.

Outside, the storm was still raging, and the rain lashed continually against the little windows. Inside, the poisonous and fetid air was overpowering. I could neither hear nor see the cat. I tried to think about other things—but only one had power enough to draw my mind from my terrible position. That was the contemplation of my cousin's villainy, his unparalleled hypocrisy, his malignant hatred of me. Beneath that cheerful face there lurked the spirit of a mediæval assassin. And as I thought of it I saw more clearly how cunningly the thing had been arranged. He had apparently gone to bed with the others. No doubt he had his witnesses to prove it. Then, unknown to them, he had slipped down, had lured me into this den and abandoned me. His story would be so simple. He had left me to finish my cigar in the billiard-room. I had gone down on my own account to have a last look at the cat. I had entered the room without observing that the cage was opened, and I had been caught. How could such a crime be brought home to him? Suspicion, perhaps—but proof, never!

How slowly those dreadful two hours went by! Once I heard a low, rasping sound, which I took to be the creature licking its own fur. Several times those greenish eyes gleamed at me through the darkness, but never in a fixed stare, and my hopes grew stronger that my presence had been forgotten or ignored. At last the least faint glimmer of light came through the windows—I first dimly saw them as two grey squares upon the black wall, then grey turned to white, and I could see my terrible companion once more. And he, alas, could see me!

It was evident to me at once that he was in a much more dangerous and aggressive mood than when I had seen him last. The cold of the morning had irritated him, and he was hungry as well. With a continual growl he paced swiftly up and down the side of the room which was farthest from my refuge, his whiskers bristling angrily, and his tail switching and lashing. As he turned at the corners his savage eyes always looked upwards at me with a dreadful menace. I knew then that he meant to kill me. Yet I found myself even at that moment admiring the sinuous grace of the devilish thing, its long, undulating, rippling movements, the gloss of its beautiful flanks, the vivid, palpitating scarlet of the glistening tongue which hung from the jet-black muzzle. And all the time that deep, threatening growl was rising and rising in an unbroken crescendo. I knew that the crisis was at hand.

It was a miserable hour to meet such a death—so

cold, so comfortless, shivering in my light dress clothes
upon this gridiron of torment upon which I was stretched.
I tried to brace myself to it, to raise my soul above it,
and at the same time, with the lucidity which comes
to a perfectly desperate man, I cast round for some
possible means of escape. One thing was clear to me.
If that front of the cage was only back in its position
once more, I could find a sure refuge behind it. Could
I possibly pull it back? I hardly dared to move for
fear of bringing the creature upon me. Slowly, very
slowly, I put my hand forward until it grasped the edge
of the front, the final bar which protruded through the
wall. To my surprise it came quite easily to my jerk.
Of course the difficulty of drawing it out arose from the
fact that I was clinging to it. I pulled again, and three
inches of it came through. It ran apparently on wheels.
I pulled again . . . and then the cat sprang!

It was so quick, so sudden, that I never saw it happen.
I simply heard the savage snarl, and in an instant afterwards the blazing yellow eyes, the flattened black head
with its red tongue and flashing teeth, were within reach
of me. The impact of the creature shook the bars upon
which I lay, until I thought (as far as I could think of
anything at such a moment) that they were coming
down. The cat swayed there for an instant, the head
and front paws quite close to me, the hind paws clawing
to find a grip upon the edge of the grating. I heard
the claws rasping as they clung to the wire-netting, and
the breath of the beast made me sick. But its bound
had been miscalculated. It could not retain its position.
Slowly, grinning with rage, and scratching madly at the
bars, it swung backwards and dropped heavily upon the
floor. With a growl it instantly faced round to me and
crouched for another spring.

I knew that the next few moments would decide
my fate. The creature had learned by experience. It
would not miscalculate again. I must act promptly,
fearlessly, if I were to have a chance for life. In an

instant I had formed my plan. Pulling off my dress-coat, I threw it down over the head of the beast. At the same moment I dropped over the edge, seized the end of the front grating, and pulled it frantically out of the wall.

It came more easily than I could have expected. I rushed across the room, bearing it with me ; but, as I rushed, the accident of my position put me upon the outer side. Had it been the other way, I might have come off scathless. As it was, there was a moment's pause as I stopped it and tried to pass in through the opening which I had left. That moment was enough to give time to the creature to toss off the coat with which I had blinded him and to spring upon me. I hurled myself through the gap and pulled the rails to behind me, but he seized my leg before I could entirely withdraw it. One stroke of that huge paw tore off my calf as a shaving of wood curls off before a plane. The next moment, bleeding and fainting, I was lying among the foul straw with a line of friendly bars between me and the creature which ramped so frantically against them.

Too wounded to move, and too faint to be conscious of fear, I could only lie, more dead than alive, and watch it. It pressed its broad, black chest against the bars and angled for me with its crooked paws as I have seen a kitten do before a mouse-trap. It ripped my clothes, but, stretch as it would, it could not quite reach me. I have heard of the curious numbing effect produced by wounds from the great carnivora, and now I was destined to experience it, for I had lost all sense of personality, and was as interested in the cat's failure or success as if it were some game which I was watching. And then gradually my mind drifted away into strange vague dreams, always with that black face and red tongue coming back into them, and so I lost myself in the nirvana of delirium, the blessed relief of those who are too sorely tried.

Tracing the course of events afterwards, I conclude that I must have been insensible for about two hours. What roused me to consciousness once more was that sharp metallic click which had been the precursor of my terrible experience. It was the shooting back of the spring lock. Then, before my senses were clear enough to entirely apprehend what they saw, I was aware of the round, benevolent face of my cousin peering in through the open door. What he saw evidently amazed him. There was the cat crouching on the floor. I was stretched upon my back in my shirt-sleeves within the cage, my trousers torn to ribbons and a great pool of blood all round me. I can see his amazed face now, with the morning sunlight upon it. He peered at me, and peered again. Then he closed the door behind him, and advanced to the cage to see if I were really dead.

I cannot undertake to say what happened. I was not in a fit state to witness or to chronicle such events. I can only say that I was suddenly conscious that his face was away from me—that he was looking towards the animal.

" Good old Tommy ! " he cried. " Good old Tommy ! "

Then he came near the bars, with his back still towards me.

" Down, you stupid beast ! " he roared. " Down, sir ! Don't you know your master ? "

Suddenly even in my bemuddled brain a remembrance came of those words of his when he had said that the taste of blood would turn the cat into a fiend. My blood had done it, but he was to pay the price.

" Get away ! " he screamed. " Get away, you devil ! Baldwin ! Baldwin ! Oh, my God ! "

And then I heard him fall, and rise, and fall again, with a sound like the ripping of sacking. His screams grew fainter until they were lost in the worrying snarl. And then, after I thought that he was dead, I saw, as in a nightmare, a blinded, tattered, blood-soaked figure running wildly round the room—and that was the last glimpse which I had of him before I fainted once again.

I was many months in my recovery—in fact, I cannot say that I have ever recovered, for to the end of my days I shall carry a stick as a sign of my night with the Brazilian cat. Baldwin, the groom, and the other servants could not tell what had occurred, when, drawn by the death-cries of their master, they found me behind the bars, and his remains—or what they afterwards discovered to be his remains—in the clutch of the creature which he had reared. They stalled him off with hot irons, and afterwards shot him through the loophole of the door before they could finally extricate me. I was carried to my bedroom, and there, under the roof of my would-be murderer, I remained between life and death for several weeks. They had sent for a surgeon from Clipton and a nurse from London, and in a month I was able to be carried to the station, and so conveyed back once more to Grosvenor Mansions.

I have one remembrance of that illness, which might have been part of the ever-changing panorama conjured up by a delirious brain were it not so definitely fixed in my memory. One night, when the nurse was absent, the door of my chamber opened, and a tall woman in blackest mourning slipped into the room. She came across to me, and as she bent her sallow face I saw by the faint gleam of the night-light that it was the Brazilian woman whom my cousin had married. She stared intently into my face, and her expression was more kindly than I had ever seen it.

" Are you conscious ? " she asked.

I feebly nodded—for I was still very weak.

" Well, then, I only wished to say to you that you have yourself to blame. Did I not do all I could for you ? From the beginning I tried to drive you from the house. By every means, short of betraying my husband, I tried to save you from him. I knew that he had a reason for bringing you here. I knew that he would never let you get away again. No one knew him as I knew him, who had suffered from him so often. I did not dare to tell you all this. He would have killed me. But I did my best for you. As things have turned out, you have been the best friend that I have ever had. You have set me free, and I fancied that nothing but death would do that. I am sorry if you are hurt, but I cannot reproach myself. I told you that you were a fool— and a fool you have been." She crept out of the room, the bitter, singular woman, and I was never destined to see her again. With what remained from her husband's property she went back to her native land, and I have heard that she afterwards took the veil at Pernambuco.

It was not until I had been back in London for some time that the doctors pronounced me to be well enough to do business. It was not a very welcome permission to me, for I feared that it would be the signal for an inrush of creditors ; but it was Summers, my lawyer, who first took advantage of it.

" I am very glad to see that your lordship is so much better," said he. " I have been waiting a long time to offer my congratulations."

" What do you mean, Summers ? This is no time for joking."

" I mean what I say," he answered. " You have been Lord Southerton for the last six weeks, but we feared that it would retard your recovery if you were to learn it."

Lord Southerton ! One of the richest peers in England ! I could not believe my ears. And then suddenly I thought of the time which had elapsed, and how it coincided with my injuries.

" Then Lord Southerton must have died about the same time that I was hurt ? "

" His death occurred upon that very day." Summers looked hard at me as I spoke, and I am convinced—for he was a very shrewd fellow—that he had guessed the true state of the case. He paused for a moment as if awaiting a confidence from me, but I could not see what was to be gained by exposing such a family scandal.

"Yes, a very curious coincidence," he continued, with the same knowing look. "Of course, you are aware that your cousin Everard King was the next heir to the estates. Now, if it had been you instead of him who had been torn to pieces by this tiger, or whatever it was, then of course he would have been Lord Souther-ton at the present moment."

"No doubt," said I.

"And he took such an interest in it," said Summers. "I happen to know that the late Lord Southerton's valet was in his pay, and that he used to have telegrams from him every few hours to tell him how he was getting on. That would be about the time when you were down there. Was it not strange that he should wish to be so well informed, since he knew that he was not the direct heir?"

"Very strange," said I. "And now, Summers, if you will bring me my bills and a new cheque-book, we will begin to get things into order."

TALES OF TWILIGHT AND THE UNSEEN

38. *The Brown Hand*

EVERYONE knows that Sir Dominick Holden, the famous Indian surgeon, made me his heir, and that his death changed me in an hour from a hard-working and impecunious medical man to a well-to-do landed proprietor. Many know also that there were at least five people between the inheritance and me, and that Sir Dominick's selection appeared to be altogether arbitrary and whimsical. I can assure them, however, that they are quite mistaken, and that, although I only knew Sir Dominick in the closing years of his life, there were, none the less, very real reasons why he should show his goodwill towards me. As a matter of fact, though I say it myself, no man ever did more for another than I did for my Indian uncle. I cannot expect the story to be believed, but it is so singular that I should feel that it was a breach of duty if I did not put it upon record —so here it is, and your belief or incredulity is your own affair.

Sir Dominick Holden, C.B., K.C.S.I., and I don't know what besides, was the most distinguished Indian surgeon of his day. In the Army originally, he afterwards settled down into civil practice in Bombay, and visited, as a consultant, every part of India. His name is best remembered in connection with the Oriental Hospital which he founded and supported. The time came, however, when his iron constitution began to show signs of the long strain to which he had subjected it, and his brother practitioners (who were not, perhaps, entirely disinterested upon the point) were unanimous in recom-

mending him to return to England. He held on so
long as he could, but at last he developed nervous symptoms of a very pronounced character, and so came back,
a broken man, to his native county of Wiltshire. He
bought a considerable estate with an ancient manor-house
upon the edge of Salisbury Plain, and devoted his old
age to the study of Comparative Pathology, which had
been his learned hobby all his life, and in which he was
a foremost authority.

We of the family were, as may be imagined, much
excited by the news of the return of this rich and childless
uncle to England. On his part, although by no means
exuberant in his hospitality, he showed some sense of his
duty to his relations, and each of us in turn had an
invitation to visit him. From the accounts of my cousins
it appeared to be a melancholy business, and it was with
mixed feelings that I at last received my own summons
to appear at Rodenhurst. My wife was so carefully
excluded in the invitation that my first impulse was to
refuse it, but the interests of the children had to be considered, and so, with her consent, I set out one October
afternoon upon my visit to Wiltshire, with little thought
of what that visit was to entail.

My uncle's estate was situated where the arable land
of the plains begins to swell upwards into the rounded
chalk hills which are characteristic of the county. As I
drove from Dinton Station in the waning light of that
autumn day, I was impressed by the weird nature of the
scenery. The few scattered cottages of the peasants
were so dwarfed by the huge evidences of prehistoric
life, that the present appeared to be a dream and the
past to be the obtrusive and masterful reality. The road
wound through the valleys, formed by a succession of
grassy hills, and the summit of each was cut and carved
into the most elaborate fortifications, some circular, and
some square, but all on a scale which has defied the winds
and the rains of many centuries. Some call them Roman
and some British, but their true origin and the reasons

for this particular tract of country being so interlaced
with entrenchments have never been finally made clear.
Here and there on the long, smooth, olive-coloured slopes
there rose small, rounded barrows or tumuli. Beneath
them lie the cremated ashes of the race which cut so
deeply into the hills, but their graves tell us nothing save
that a jar full of dust represents the man who once
laboured under the sun.

It was through this weird country that I approached
my uncle's residence of Rodenhurst, and the house was,
as I found, in due keeping with its surroundings. Two
broken and weather-stained pillars, each surmounted by
a mutilated heraldic emblem, flanked the entrance to a
neglected drive. A cold wind whistled through the elms
which lined it, and the air was full of the drifting leaves.
At the far end, under the gloomy arch of trees, a single
yellow lamp burned steadily. In the dim half-light of
the coming night I saw a long, low building stretching
out two irregular wings, with deep eaves, a sloping
gambrel roof, and walls which were criss-crossed with
timber balks in the fashion of the Tudors. The cheery
light of a fire flickered in the broad, latticed window to
the left of the low-porched door, and this, as it proved,
marked the study of my uncle, for it was thither that I
was led by his butler in order to make my host's acquaintance.

He was cowering over his fire, for the moist chill of
an English autumn had set him shivering. His lamp
was unlit, and I only saw the red glow of the embers
beating upon a huge, craggy face, with a Red Indian
nose and cheek, and deep furrows and seams from eye to
chin, the sinister marks of hidden volcanic fires. He
sprang up at my entrance with something of an old-
world courtesy and welcomed me warmly to Rodenhurst.
At the same time I was conscious, as the lamp was
carried in, that it was a very critical pair of light-blue
eyes which looked out at me from under shaggy eyebrows,
like scouts beneath a bush, and that this outlandish

431

uncle of mine was carefully reading off my character
with all the ease of a practised observer and an experienced man of the world.

For my part I looked at him, and looked again, for
I had never seen a man whose appearance was more
fitted to hold one's attention. His figure was the framework of a giant, but he had fallen away until his coat
dangled straight down in a shocking fashion from a pair
of broad and bony shoulders. All his limbs were huge
and yet emaciated, and I could not take my gaze from his
knobby wrists, and long, gnarled hands. But his eyes
—those peering, light-blue eyes—they were the most
arrestive of any of his peculiarities. It was not their
colour alone, nor was it the ambush of hair in which
they lurked ; but it was the expression which I read in
them. For the appearance and bearing of the man were
masterful, and one expected a certain corresponding
arrogance in his eyes, but instead of that I read the look
which tells of a spirit cowed and crushed, the furtive,
expectant look of the dog whose master has taken the
whip from the rack. I formed my own medical diagnosis
upon one glance at those critical and yet appealing eyes.
I believed that he was stricken with some mortal ailment,
that he knew himself to be exposed to sudden death,
and that he lived in terror of it. Such was my judgment
—a false one, as the event showed ; but I mention it
that it may help you to realize the look which I read in
his eyes.

My uncle's welcome was, as I have said, a courteous
one, and in an hour or so I found myself seated between
him and his wife at a comfortable dinner, with curious,
pungent delicacies upon the table, and a stealthy, quick-
eyed Oriental waiter behind his chair. The old couple
had come round to that tragic imitation of the dawn of
life when husband and wife, having lost or scattered all
those who were their intimates, find themselves face to
face and alone once more, their work done, and the end
nearing fast. Those who have reached that stage in

sweetness and love, who can change their winter into a gentle, Indian summer, have come as victors through the ordeal of life. Lady Holden was a small, alert woman with a kindly eye, and her expression as she glanced at him was a certificate of character to her husband. And yet, though I read a mutual love in their glances, I read also mutual horror, and recognized in her face some reflection of that stealthy fear which I had detected in his. Their talk was sometimes merry and sometimes sad, but there was a forced note in their merriment and a naturalness in their sadness which told me that a heavy heart beat upon either side of me.

We were sitting over our first glass of wine, and the servants had left the room, when the conversation took a turn which produced a remarkable effect upon my host and hostess. I cannot recall what it was which started the topic of the supernatural, but it ended in my showing them that the abnormal in psychical experiences was a subject to which I had, like many neurologists, devoted a great deal of attention. I concluded by narrating my experiences when, as a member of the Psychical Research Society, I had formed one of a committee of three who spent the night in a haunted house. Our adventures were neither exciting nor convincing, but, such as it was, the story appeared to interest my auditors in a remarkable degree. They listened with an eager silence, and I caught a look of intelligence between them which I could not understand. Lady Holden immediately afterwards rose and left the room.

Sir Dominick pushed the cigar-box over to me, and we smoked for some little time in silence. That huge, bony hand of his was twitching as he raised it with his cheroot to his lips, and I felt that the man's nerves were vibrating like fiddle-strings. My instincts told me that he was on the verge of some intimate confidence, and I feared to speak lest I should interrupt it. At last he turned towards me with a spasmodic gesture like a man who throws his last scruple to the winds.

" From the little that I have seen of you it appears to me, Dr. Hardacre," said he, " that you are the very man I have wanted to meet."

" I am delighted to hear it, sir."

" Your head seems to be cool and steady. You will acquit me of any desire to flatter you, for the circumstances are too serious to permit of insincerities. You have some special knowledge upon these subjects, and you evidently view them from that philosophical standpoint which robs them of all vulgar terror. I presume that the sight of an apparition would not seriously discompose you ? "

" I think not, sir."

" Would even interest you, perhaps ? "

" Most intensely."

" As a psychical observer, you would probably investigate it in as impersonal a fashion as an astronomer investigates a wandering comet ? "

" Precisely."

He gave a heavy sigh.

" Believe me, Dr. Hardacre, there was a time when I could have spoken as you do now. My nerve was a byword in India. Even the Mutiny never shook it for an instant. And yet you see what I am reduced to —the most timorous man, perhaps, in all this county of Wiltshire. Do not speak too bravely upon this subject, or you may find yourself subjected to as long-drawn a test as I am—a test which can only end in the madhouse or the grave."

I waited patiently until he should see fit to go farther in his confidence. His preamble had, I need not say, filled me with interest and expectation.

" For some years, Dr. Hardacre," he continued, " my life and that of my wife have been made miserable by a cause which is so grotesque that it borders upon the ludicrous. And yet familiarity has never made it more easy to bear—on the contrary, as time passes my nerves become more worn and shattered by the constant attrition.

434

If you have no physical fears, Dr. Hardacre, I should very much value your opinion upon this phenomenon which troubles us so."

" For what it is worth my opinion is entirely at your service. May I ask the nature of the phenomenon ? "

" I think that your experiences will have a higher evidential value if you are not told in advance what you may expect to encounter. You are yourself aware of the quibbles of unconscious cerebration and subjective impressions with which a scientific sceptic may throw a doubt upon your statement. It would be as well to guard against them in advance."

" What shall I do, then ? "

" I will tell you. Would you mind following me this way ? " He led me out of the dining-room and down a long passage until we came to a terminal door. Inside there was a large, bare room fitted as a laboratory, with numerous scientific instruments and bottles. A shelf ran along one side, upon which there stood a long line of glass jars containing pathological and anatomical specimens.

" You see that I still dabble in some of my old studies," said Sir Dominick. " These jars are the remains of what was once a most excellent collection, but unfortunately I lost the greater part of them when my house was burned down in Bombay in '92. It was a most unfortunate affair for me—in more ways than one. I had examples of many rare conditions, and my splenic collection was probably unique. These are the survivors."

I glanced over them, and saw that they really were of a very great value and rarity from a pathological point of view : bloated organs, gaping cysts, distorted bones, odious parasites—a singular exhibition of the products of India.

" There is, as you see, a small settee here," said my host. " It was far from our intention to offer a guest so meagre an accommodation, but since affairs have taken this turn, it would be a great kindness upon your part if you would consent to spend the night in this apartment. I beg that you will not hesitate to let me know if the idea should be at all repugnant to you."

" On the contrary," I said, " it is most acceptable."

" My own room is the second on the left, so that if you should feel that you are in need of company a call would always bring me to your side."

" I trust that I shall not be compelled to disturb you."

" It is unlikely that I shall be asleep. I do not sleep much. Do not hesitate to summon me."

And so with this agreement we joined Lady Holden in the drawing-room and talked of lighter things.

It was no affectation upon my part to say that the prospect of my night's adventure was an agreeable one. I have no pretence to greater physical courage than my neighbours, but familiarity with a subject robs it of those vague and undefined terrors which are the most appalling to the imaginative mind. The human brain is capable of only one strong emotion at a time, and if it be filled with curiosity or scientific enthusiasm, there is no room for fear. It is true that I had my uncle's assurance that he had himself originally taken this point of view, but I reflected that the break-down of his nervous system might be due to his forty years in India as much as to any psychical experiences which had befallen him. I at least was sound in nerve and brain, and it was with something of the pleasurable thrill of anticipation with which the sportsman takes his position beside the haunt of his game that I shut the laboratory door behind me, and partially undressing, lay down upon the rug-covered settee.

It was not an ideal atmosphere for a bed-room. The air was heavy with many chemical odours, that of methylated spirit predominating. Nor were the decorations of my chamber very sedative. The odious line of glass jars with their relics of disease and suffering stretched

in front of my very eyes. There was no blind to the
window, and a three-quarter moon streamed its white
light into the room, tracing a silver square with filigree
lattices upon the opposite wall. When I had extinguished
my candle this one bright patch in the midst of the
general gloom had certainly an eerie and discomposing
aspect. A rigid and absolute silence reigned throughout
the old house, so that the low swish of the branches in
the garden came softly and smoothly to my ears. It
may have been the hypnotic lullaby of this gentle susurrus,
or it may have been the result of my tiring day, but after
many dozings and many efforts to regain my clearness of
perception, I fell at last into a deep and dreamless sleep.

I was awakened by some sound in the room, and I
instantly raised myself upon my elbow on the couch.
Some hours had passed, for the square patch upon the
wall had slid downwards and sideways until it lay obliquely
at the end of my bed. The rest of the room was in deep
shadow. At first I could see nothing, presently, as my
eyes became accustomed to the faint light, I was aware,
with a thrill which all my scientific absorption could not
entirely prevent, that something was moving slowly along
the line of the wall. A gentle, shuffling sound, as of soft
slippers, came to my ears, and I dimly discerned a human
figure walking stealthily from the direction of the door.
As it emerged into the patch of moonlight I saw very
clearly what it was and how it was employed. It was
a man, short and squat, dressed in some sort of dark-grey
gown, which hung straight from his shoulders to his
feet. The moon shone upon the side of his face, and
I saw that it was chocolate-brown in colour, with a ball
of black hair like a woman's at the back of his head.
He walked slowly, and his eyes were cast upwards
towards the line of bottles which contained those grue-
some remnants of humanity. He seemed to examine
each jar with attention, and then to pass on to the next.
When he had come to the end of the line, immediately
opposite my bed, he stopped, faced me, threw up his

hands with a gesture of despair, and vanished from my sight.

I have said that he threw up his hands, but I should have said his arms, for as he assumed that attitude of despair I observed a singular peculiarity about his appearance. He had only one hand! As the sleeves drooped down from the upflung arms I saw the left plainly, but the right ended in a knobby and unsightly stump. In every other way his appearance was so natural, and I had both seen and heard him so clearly, that I could easily have believed that he was an Indian servant of Sir Dominick's who had come into my room in search of something. It was only his sudden disappearance which suggested anything more sinister to me. As it was I sprang from my couch, lit a candle, and examined the whole room carefully. There were no signs of my visitor, and I was forced to conclude that there had really been something outside the normal laws of Nature in his appearance. I lay awake for the remainder of the night, but nothing else occurred to disturb me.

I am an early riser, but my uncle was an even earlier one, for I found him pacing up and down the lawn at the side of the house. He ran towards me in his eagerness when he saw me come out from the door.

" Well, well ! " he cried. " Did you see him ? "

" An Indian with one hand ? "

" Precisely."

" Yes, I saw him "—and I told him all that occurred. When I had finished, he led the way into his study.

" We have a little time before breakfast," said he. " It will suffice to give you an explanation of this extraordinary affair—so far as I can explain that which is essentially inexplicable. In the first place, when I tell you that for four years I have never passed one single night, either in Bombay, aboard ship, or here in England without my sleep being broken by this fellow, you will understand why it is that I am a wreck of my former self. His programme is always the same. He appears by my bedside, shakes me roughly by the shoulder, passes from my room into the laboratory, walks slowly along the line of my bottles, and then vanishes. For more than a thousand times he has gone through the same routine."

" What does he want ? "

" He wants his hand."

" His hand ? " ·

" Yes, it came about in this way. I was summoned to Peshawur for a consultation some ten years ago, and while there I was asked to look at the hand of a native who was passing through with an Afghan caravan. The fellow came from some mountain tribe living away at the back of beyond somewhere on the other side of Kaffiristan. He talked a bastard Pushtoo, and it was all I could do to understand him. He was suffering from a soft sarcomatous swelling of one of the metacarpal joints, and I made him realize that it was only by losing his hand that he could hope to save his life. After much persuasion he consented to the operation, and he asked me, when it was over, what fee I demanded. The poor fellow was almost a beggar, so that the idea of a fee was absurd, but I answered in jest that my fee should be his hand, and that I proposed to add it to my pathological collection.

" To my surprise he demurred very much to the suggestion, and he explained that according to his religion it was an all-important matter that the body should be reunited after death, and so make a perfect dwelling for the spirit. The belief is, of course, an old one, and the mummies of the Egyptians arose from an analogous superstition. I answered him that his hand was already off, and asked him how he intended to preserve it. He replied that he would pickle it in salt and carry it about with him. I suggested that it might be safer in my keeping than his, and that I had better means than salt for preserving it. On realizing that I really intended to carefully keep it, his opposition vanished instantly. ' But remember, sahib,' said he, ' I shall want it back when I am dead.' I laughed at the remark, and so the matter ended. I returned to my practice, and he no doubt in the course of time was able to continue his journey to Afghanistan.

"Well, as I told you last night, I had a bad fire in my house at Bombay. Half of it was burned down, and, among other things, my pathological collection was largely destroyed. What you see are the poor remains of it. The hand of the hillman went with the rest, but I gave the matter no particular thought at the time. That was six years ago.

"Four years ago—two years after the fire—I was awakened one night by a furious tugging at my sleeve. I sat up under the impression that my favourite mastiff was trying to arouse me. Instead of this, I saw my Indian patient of long ago, dressed in the long, grey gown which was the badge of his people. He was holding up his stump and looking reproachfully at me. He then went over to my bottles, which at that time I kept in my room, and he examined them carefully, after which he gave a gesture of anger and vanished. I realized that he had just died, and that he had come to claim my promise that I should keep his limb in safety for him.

"Well, there you have it all, Dr. Hardacre. Every night at the same hour for four years this performance has been repeated. It is a simple thing in itself, but it has worn me out like water dropping on a stone. It has brought a vile insomnia with it, for I cannot sleep now for the expectation of his coming. It has poisoned my old age and that of my wife, who has been the sharer in this great trouble. But there is the breakfast gong, and she will be waiting impatiently to know how it fared with you last night. We are both much indebted to you for your gallantry, for it takes something from the weight of our misfortune when we share it, even for a single night, with a friend, and it reassures us to our sanity, which we are sometimes driven to question."

This was the curious narrative which Sir Dominick

confided to me—a story which to many would have
appeared to be a grotesque impossibility, but which,
after my experience of the night before, and my previous
knowledge of such things, I was prepared to accept as
an absolute fact. I thought deeply over the matter,
and brought the whole range of my reading and experience to bear upon it. After breakfast, I surprised my
host and hostess by announcing that I was returning to
London by the next train.

" My dear doctor," cried Sir Dominick in great
distress, " you make me feel that I have been guilty of
a gross breach of hospitality in intruding this unfortunate
matter upon you. I should have borne my own burden."

" It is, indeed, that matter which is taking me to
London," I answered ; " but you are mistaken, I assure
you, if you think that my experience of last night was
an unpleasant one to me. On the contrary, I am about
to ask your permission to return in the evening and spend
one more night in your laboratory. I am very eager to
see this visitor once again."

My uncle was exceedingly anxious to know what I
was about to do, but my fears of raising false hopes
prevented me from telling him. I was back in my own
consulting-room a little after luncheon, and was confirm-
ing my memory of a passage in a recent book upon
occultism which had arrested my attention when I read
it.

" In the case of earth-bound spirits," said my authority,
" some one dominant idea obsessing them at the hour
of death is sufficient to hold them in this material world.
They are the amphibia of this life and of the next, capable
of passing from one to the other as the turtle passes from
land to water. The causes which may bind a soul so
strongly to a life which its body has abandoned are any
violent emotion. Avarice, revenge, anxiety, love and
pity have all been known to have this effect. As a rule
it springs from some unfulfilled wish, and when the wish
has been fulfilled the material bond relaxes. There are

many cases upon record which show the singular persistence of these visitors, and also their disappearance when their wishes have been fulfilled, or in some cases when a reasonable compromise has been effected."

" *A reasonable compromise effected* "—those were the words which I had brooded over all the morning, and which I now verified in the original. No actual atonement could be made here—but a reasonable compromise ! I made my way as fast as a train could take me to the Shadwell Seamen's Hospital, where my old friend Jack Hewett was house-surgeon. Without explaining the situation I made him understand what it was that I wanted.

" A brown man's hand ! " said he, in amazement. " What in the world do you want that for ? "

" Never mind. I'll tell you some day. I know that your wards are full of Indians."

" I should think so. But a hand——" He thought a little and then struck a bell.

" Travers," said he to a student-dresser, " what became of the hands of the Lascar which we took off yesterday ? I mean the fellow from the East India Dock who got caught in the steam winch."

" They are in the *post-mortem* room, sir."

" Just pack one of them in antiseptics and give it to Dr. Hardacre."

And so I found myself back at Rodenhurst before dinner with this curious outcome of my day in town. I still said nothing to Sir Dominick, but I slept that night in the laboratory, and I placed the Lascar's hand in one of the glass jars at the end of my couch.

So interested was I in the result of my experiment that sleep was out of the question. I sat with a shaded lamp beside me and waited patiently for my visitor. This time I saw him clearly from the first. He appeared beside the door, nebulous for an instant, and then hardening into as distinct an outline as any living man. The slippers beneath his grey gown were red and heelless, which accounted for the low, shuffling sound which he made as he walked. As on the previous night he passed slowly along the line of bottles until he paused before that which contained the hand. He reached up to it, his whole figure quivering with expectation, took it down, examined it eagerly, and then, with a face which was convulsed with fury and disappointment, he hurled it down on the floor. There was a crash which resounded through the house, and when I looked up the mutilated Indian had disappeared. A moment later my door flew open and Sir Dominick rushed in.

" You are not hurt ? " he cried.

" No—but deeply disappointed."

He looked in astonishment at the splinters of glass, and the brown hand lying upon the floor.

" Good God ! " he cried. " What is this ? "

I told him my idea and its wretched sequel. He listened intently, but shook his head.

" It was well thought of," said he, " but I fear that there is no such easy end to my sufferings. But one thing I now insist upon. It is that you shall never again upon any pretext occupy this room. My fears that something might have happened to you—when I heard that crash—have been the most acute of all the agonies which I have undergone. I will not expose myself to a repetition of it."

He allowed me, however, to spend the remainder of that night where I was, and I lay there worrying over the problem and lamenting my own failure. With the first light of morning there was the Lascar's hand still lying upon the floor to remind me of my fiasco. I lay looking at it—and as I lay suddenly an idea flew like a bullet through my head and brought me quivering with excitement out of my couch. I raised the grim relic from where it had fallen. Yes, it was indeed so. The hand was the *left* hand of the Lascar.

By the first train I was on my way to town, and hurried at once to the Seamen's Hospital. I remembered that both hands of the Lascar had been amputated, but I was terrified lest the precious organ which I was in search of might have been already consumed in the crematory. My suspense was soon ended. It had still been preserved in the *post-mortem* room. And so I returned to Rodenhurst in the evening with my mission accomplished and the material for a fresh experiment.

But Sir Dominick Holden would not hear of my occupying the laboratory again. To all my entreaties he turned a deaf ear. It offended his sense of hospitality, and he could no longer permit it. I left the hand, therefore, as I had done its fellow the night before, and I occupied a comfortable bedroom in another portion of the house, some distance from the scene of my adventures.

But in spite of that my sleep was not destined to be uninterrupted. In the dead of night my host burst into my room, a lamp in his hand. His huge, gaunt figure was enveloped in a loose dressing-gown, and his whole appearance might certainly have seemed more formidable to a weak-nerved man than that of the Indian of the night before. But it was not his entrance so much as his expression which amazed me. He had turned suddenly younger by twenty years at the least. His eyes were shining, his features radiant, and he waved one hand in triumph over his head. I sat up astounded, staring sleepily at this extraordinary visitor. But his words soon drove the sleep from my eyes.

" We have done it ! We have succeeded ! " he shouted. " My dear Hardacre, how can I ever in this world repay you ? "

" You don't mean to say that it is all right ? "

" Indeed I do. I was sure that you would not mind being awakened to hear such blessed news."

" Mind ! I should think not indeed. But is it really certain ? "

" I have no doubt whatever upon the point. I owe you such a debt, my dear nephew, as I have never owed a man before, and never expected to. What can I

possibly do for you that is commensurate ? Providence
must have sent you to my rescue. You have saved both
my reason and my life, for another six months of this
must have seen me either in a cell or a coffin. And my
wife—it was wearing her out before my eyes. Never
could I have believed that any human being could have
lifted this burden off me." He seized my hand and wrung
it in his bony grip.

" It was only an experiment—a forlorn hope—but I
am delighted from my heart that it has succeeded. But
how do you know that it is all right ? Have you seen
something ? "

He seated himself at the foot of my bed.

" I have seen enough," said he. " It satisfies me that
I shall be troubled no more. What has passed is easily
told. You know that at a certain hour this creature
always comes to me. To-night he arrived at the usual
time, and aroused me with even more violence than is
his custom. I can only surmise that his disappointment
of last night increased the bitterness of his anger against
me. He looked angrily at me, and then went on his
usual round. But in a few minutes I saw him, for the
first time since this persecution began, return to my
chamber. He was smiling. I saw the gleam of his white
teeth through the dim light. He stood facing me at the
end of my bed, and three times he made the low, Eastern
salaam which is their solemn leave-taking. And the
third time that he bowed he raised his arms over his
head, and I saw his *two* hands outstretched in the air.
So he vanished, and, as I believe, for ever."

So that is the curious experience which won me the
affection and the gratitude of my celebrated uncle, the
famous Indian surgeon. His anticipations were realised,
and never again was he disturbed by the visits of the
restless hillman in search of his lost member. Sir
Dominick and Lady Holden spent a very happy old age,
unclouded, so far as I know, by any trouble, and they

finally died during the great influenza epidemic within a few weeks of each other. In his lifetime he always turned to me for advice in everything which concerned that English life of which he knew so little ; and I aided him also in the purchase and development of his estates. It was no great surprise to me, therefore, that I found myself eventually promoted over the heads of five exasperated cousins, and changed in a single day from a hard-working country doctor into the head of an important Wiltshire family. I, at least, have reason to bless the memory of the man with the brown hand, and the day when I was fortunate enough to relieve Rodenhurst of his unwelcome presence.

39. *The Usher of Lea House School*

MR. LUMSDEN, the senior partner of Lumsden and Westmacott, the well-known scholastic and clerical agents, was a small, dapper man, with a sharp, abrupt manner, a critical eye, and an incisive way of speaking.

" Your name, sir ? " said he, sitting, pen in hand, with his long, red-lined folio in front of him.

" Harold Weld."

" Oxford or Cambridge ? "

" Cambridge."

" Honours ? "

" No, sir."

" Athlete ? "

" Nothing remarkable, I am afraid."

" Not a Blue ? "

" Oh no."

Mr. Lumsden shook his head despondently and shrugged his shoulders in a way which sent my hopes down to zero. " There is a very keen competition for masterships, Mr. Weld," said he. " The vacancies are few and the applicants innumerable. A first-class athlete, oar, or cricketer, or a man who has passed very high in his examinations, can usually find a vacancy—I might say always in the case of the cricketer. But the average man—if you will excuse the description, Mr. Weld—has a very great difficulty, almost an insurmountable difficulty. We have already more than a hundred such names upon our lists, and if you think it worth while our adding yours, I dare say that in the course of some years we may possibly be able to find you some opening which——"

He paused on account of a knock at the door. It was a clerk with a note. Mr. Lumsden broke the seal and read it.

" Why, Mr. Weld," said he, " this is really rather an interesting coincidence. I understand you to say that Latin and English are your subjects, and that you would prefer for a time to accept a place in an elementary establishment, where you would have time for private study ? "

" Quite so."

" This note contains a request from an old client of ours, Dr. Phelps McCarthy, of Willow Lea House Academy, West Hampstead, that I should at once send him a young man who should be qualified to teach Latin and English to a small class of boys under fourteen years of age. His vacancy appears to be the very one which you are looking for. The terms are not munificent—sixty pounds, board, lodging, and washing—but the work is not onerous, and you would have the evenings to yourself."

" That would do," I cried, with all the eagerness of the man who sees work at last after weary months of seeking.

" I don't know that it is quite fair to these gentlemen whose names have been so long upon our list," said Mr. Lumsden, glancing down at his open ledger. " But the coincidence is so striking that I feel we must really give you the refusal of it."

" Then I accept it, sir, and I am much obliged to you."

447

" There is one small provision in Dr. McCarthy's better. He stipulates that the applicant must be a man with an imperturbably good temper."

" I am the very man," said I, with conviction.

" Well," said Mr. Lumsden, with some hesitation, " I hope that your temper is really as good as you say, for I rather fancy that you may need it."

" I presume that every elementary schoolmaster does."

" Yes, sir, but it is only fair to you to warn you that there may be some especially trying circumstances in this particular situation. Dr. Phelps McCarthy does not make such a condition without some very good and pressing reason."

There was a certain solemnity in his speech which struck a chill in the delight with which I had welcomed this providential vacancy.

" May I ask the nature of these circumstances ? " I asked.

" We endeavour to hold the balance equally between our clients, and to be perfectly frank with all of them. If I knew of objections to you I should certainly communicate them to Dr. McCarthy, and so I have no hesitation in doing as much for you. I find," he continued, glancing over the pages of his ledger, " that within the last twelve months we have supplied no fewer than seven Latin masters to Willow Lea House Academy, four of them having left so abruptly as to forfeit their month's salary, and none of them having stayed more than eight weeks."

" And the other masters ? Have they stayed ? "

" There is only one other residential master, and he appears to be unchanged. You can understand, Mr. Weld," continued the agent, closing both the ledger and the interview, " that such rapid changes are not desirable from a master's point of view, whatever may be said for them by an agent working on commission. I have no idea why these gentlemen have resigned their situations so early. I can only give you the facts, and advise you

to see Dr. McCarthy at once and to form your own conclusions."

Great is the power of the man who has nothing to lose,
and it was therefore with perfect serenity, but with a good
deal of curiosity, that I rang, early that afternoon, the
heavy, wrought-iron bell of the Willow Lea House
Academy. The building was a massive pile, square and
ugly, standing in its own extensive grounds, with a
broad carriage-sweep curving up to it from the road.
It stood high, and commanded a view on the one side of
the grey roofs and bristling spires of Northern London,
and on the other of the well-wooded and beautiful
country which fringes the great city. The door was
opened by a boy in buttons, and I was shown into a
well-appointed study, where the principal of the academy
presently joined me.

The warnings and insinuations of the agent had prepared me to meet a choleric and overbearing person—
one whose manner was an insupportable provocation
to those who worked under him. Anything further
from the reality cannot be imagined. He was a frail,
gentle creature, clean-shaven and round-shouldered, with
a bearing which was so courteous that it became almost
deprecating. His bushy hair was thickly shot with grey,
and his age I should imagine to verge upon sixty. His
voice was low and suave, and he walked with a certain
mincing delicacy of manner. His whole appearance was
that of a kindly scholar, who was more at home among
his books than in the practical affairs of the world.

" I am sure that we shall be very happy to have your
assistance, Mr. Weld," said he, after a few professional
questions. " Mr. Percival Manners left me yesterday,
and I should be glad if you could take over his duties
to-morrow."

" May I ask if that is Mr. Percival Manners of
Selwyn ? " I asked.

" Precisely. Did you know him ? "

" Yes ; he is a friend of mine."

" An excellent teacher, but a little hasty in his disposition. It was his only fault. Now, in your case, Mr. Weld, is your own temper under good control? Supposing, for argument's sake, that I were to so far forget myself as to be rude to you, or to speak roughly, or to jar your feelings in any way, could you rely upon yourself to control your emotions? "

I smiled at the idea of this courteous, little, mincing creature ruffling my nerves.

" I think that I could answer for it, sir," said I.

" Quarrels are very painful to me," said he. " I wish everyone to live in harmony under my roof. I will not deny Mr. Percival Manners had provocation, but I wish to find a man who can raise himself above provocation, and sacrifice his own feelings for the sake of peace and concord."

" I will do my best, sir."

" You cannot say more, Mr. Weld. In that case I shall expect you to-night, if you can get your things ready so soon."

I not only succeeded in getting my things ready, but I found time to call at the Benedict Club in Piccadilly, where I knew that I should find Manners if he were still in town. There he was, sure enough, in the smoking-room, and I questioned him, over a cigarette, as to his reasons for throwing up his recent situation.

" You don't tell me that you are going to Dr. Phelps McCarthy's Academy? " he cried, staring at me in surprise. " My dear chap, it's no use. You can't possibly remain there."

" But I saw him, and he seemed the most courtly, inoffensive fellow. I never met a man with more gentle manners."

" He! oh, he's all right. There's no vice in him. Have you seen Theophilus St. James? "

" I have never heard the name. Who is he? "

" Your colleague. The other master."

" No, I have not seen him."

" *He's* the terror. If you can stand him, you have either the spirit of a perfect Christian or else you have no spirit at all. A more perfect bounder never bounded."

" But why does McCarthy stand it ? "

My friend looked at me significantly through his cigarette smoke, and shrugged his shoulders.

" You will form your own conclusions about that. Mine were formed very soon, and I never found occasion to alter them."

" It would help me very much if you would tell me them."

" When you see a man in his own house allowing his business to be ruined, his comfort destroyed, and his authority defied by another man in a subordinate position, and calmly submitting to it without so much as a word of protest, what conclusion do you come to ? "

" That the one has a hold over the other."

Percival Manners nodded his head.

" There you are ! You've hit it first barrel. It seems to me that there's no other explanation which will cover the facts. At some period in his life the little Doctor has gone astray. *Humanum est errare.* I have even done it myself. But this was something serious, and the other man got a hold of it and has never let go. That's the truth. Blackmail is at the bottom of it. But he had no hold over me, and there was no reason why *I* should stand his insolence, so I came away—and I very much expect to see you do the same."

For some time he talked over the matter, but he always came to the same conclusion—that I should not retain my new situation very long.

It was with no very pleasant feelings after this preparation that I found myself face to face with the very man of whom I had received so evil an account. Dr. McCarthy introduced us to each other in his study on the evening of that same day immediately after my arrival at the school.

" This is your new colleague, Mr. St. James," said

he, in his genial, courteous fashion. " I trust that you will mutually agree, and that I shall find nothing but good feeling and sympathy beneath this roof."

I shared the good Doctor's hope, but my expectations of it were not increased by the appearance of my *confrère.* He was a young, bull-necked fellow about thirty years of age, dark-eyed and black-haired, with an exceedingly vigorous physique. I have never seen a more strongly built man, though he tended to run to fat in a way which showed that he was in the worst of training. His face was coarse, swollen, and brutal, with a pair of small, black eyes deeply sunken in his head. His heavy jowl, his projecting ears, and his thick, bandy legs all went to make up a personality which was as formidable as it was repellent.

" I hear you've never been out before," said he, in a rude, brusque fashion. " Well, it's a poor life : hard work and starvation pay, as you'll find out for yourself."

" But it has some compensations," said the principal. " Surely you will allow that, Mr. St. James ? "

" Has it ? I never could find them. What do you call compensations ? "

" Even to be in the continual presence of youth is a privilege. It has the effect of keeping youth in one's own soul, for one reflects something of their high spirits and their keen enjoyment of life."

" Little beasts ! " cried my colleague.

" Come, come, Mr. St. James, you are too hard upon them."

" I hate the sight of them ! If I could put them and their blessed copybooks and lexicons and slates into one bonfire I'd do it to-night."

" This is Mr. St. James's way of talking," said the principal, smiling nervously as he glanced at me. " You must not take him too seriously. Now, Mr. Weld, you know where your room is, and no doubt you have your own little arrangements to make. The sooner you make them the sooner you will feel yourself at home."

It seemed to me that he was only too anxious to remove me at once from the influence of this extraordinary colleague, and I was glad to go, for the conversation had become embarrassing.

And so began an epoch which always seems to me as I look back to it to be the most singular in all my experience. The school was in many ways an excellent one. Dr. Phelps McCarthy was an ideal principal. His methods were modern and rational. The management was all that could be desired. And yet in the middle of this well-ordered machine there intruded the incongruous and impossible Mr. St. James, throwing everything into confusion. His duties were to teach English and mathematics, and how he acquitted himself of them I do not know, as our classes were held in separate rooms. I can answer for it, however, that the boys feared him and loathed him, and I know that they had good reason to do so, for frequently my own teaching was interrupted by his bellowings of anger, and even by the sound of his blows. Dr. McCarthy spent most of his time in his class, but it was, I suspect, to watch over the master rather than the boys, and to try to moderate his ferocious temper when it threatened to become dangerous.

It was in his bearing to the head master, however, that my colleague's conduct was most outrageous. The first conversation which I have recorded proved to be typical of their intercourse. He domineered over him openly and brutally. I have heard him contradict him roughly before the whole school. At no time would he show him any mark of respect, and my temper often rose within me when I saw the quiet acquiescence of the old Doctor, and his patient tolerance of this monstrous treatment. And yet the sight of it surrounded the principal also with a certain vague horror in my mind, for, supposing my friend's theory to be correct—and I could devise no better one—how black must have been the story which could be held over his head by this man and, by fear of its publicity, force him to undergo such humiliations. This quiet, gentle Doctor might be a profound hypocrite, a criminal, a forger possibly, or a poisoner. Only such a secret as this could account for the complete power which the young man held over him. Why else should he admit so hateful a presence into his house and so harmful an influence into his school ? Why should he submit to degradations which could not be witnessed, far less endured, without indignation ?

And yet, if it were so, I was forced to confess that my principal carried it off with extraordinary duplicity. Never by word or sign did he show that the young man's presence was distasteful to him. I have seen him look pained, it is true, after some peculiarly outrageous exhibition, but he gave me the impression that it was always on account of the scholars or of me, never on account of himself. He spoke to and of St. James in an indulgent fashion, smiling gently at what made my blood boil within me. In his way of looking at him and addressing him, one could see no trace of resentment, but rather a sort of timid and deprecating good will. His company he certainly courted, and they spent many hours together in the study and the garden.

As to my own relations with Theophilus St. James, I made up my mind from the beginning that I should keep my temper with him, and to that resolution I steadfastly adhered. If Dr. McCarthy chose to permit this disrespect, and to condone these outrages, it was his affair and not mine. It was evident that his one wish was that there should be peace between us, and I felt that I could help him best by respecting this desire. My easiest way to do so was to avoid my colleague, and this I did to the best of my ability. When we were thrown together I was quiet, polite and reserved. He, on his part, showed me no ill will, but met me rather with a coarse joviality, and a rough familiarity which he meant to be ingratiating. He was insistent in his attempts to get me into his room at night, for the purpose of playing euchre and of drinking.

"Old McCarthy doesn't mind," said he. "Don't
you be afraid of him. We'll do what we like, and I'll
answer for it that he won't object." Once only I went,
and when I left, after a dull and gross evening, my host
was stretched dead drunk upon the sofa. After that I
gave the excuse of a course of study, and spent my spare
hours alone in my own room.

One point upon which I was anxious to gain information was as to how long these proceedings had been
going on. When did St. James assert his hold over Dr.
McCarthy? From neither of them could I learn how
long my colleague had been in his present situation.
One or two leading questions upon my part were eluded
or ignored in a manner so marked that it was easy to
see that they were both of them as eager to conceal the
point as I was to know it. But at last, one evening, I
had the chance of a chat with Mrs. Carter, the matron—
for the Doctor was a widower—and from her I got the
information which I wanted. It needed no questioning
to get at her knowledge, for she was so full of indignation
that she shook with passion as she spoke of it, and raised
her hands into the air in the earnestness of her denuncia-
tion, as she described the grievances which she had
against my colleague.

"It was three years ago, Mr. Weld, that he first
darkened this doorstep," she cried. "Three bitter years
they have been to me. The school had fifty boys then.
Now it has twenty-two. That's what he has done for
us in three years. In another three there won't be one.
And the Doctor, that angel of patience, you see how he
treats him, though he is not fit to lace his boots for him.
If it wasn't for the Doctor, you may be sure that I wouldn't
stay for an hour under the same roof with such a man,
and so I told him to his own face, Mr. Weld. If the
Doctor would only pack him about his business—but I
know that I am saying more than I should!" She
stopped herself with an effort, and spoke no more upon
the subject. She had remembered that I was almost a

stranger in the school, and she feared that she had been indiscreet.

There were one or two very singular points about my colleague. The chief one was that he rarely took any exercise. There was a playing-field within the college grounds, and that was his farthest point. If the boys went out, it was I or Dr. McCarthy who accompanied them. St. James gave as a reason for this that he had injured his knee some years before, and that walking was painful to him. For my own part I put it down to pure laziness upon his part, for he was of an obese, heavy temperament. Twice, however, I saw him from my window stealing out of the grounds late at night, and the second time I watched him return in the grey of the morning and slink in through an open window. These furtive excursions were never alluded to, but they exposed the hollowness of his story about his knee, and they increased the dislike and distrust which I had of the man. His nature seemed to be vicious to the core.

Another point, small but suggestive, was that he hardly ever during the months that I was at Willow Lea House received any letters, and on those few occasions they were obviously tradesmen's bills. I am an early riser, and used every morning to pick my own correspondence out of the bundle upon the hall table. I could judge, therefore, how few were ever there for Mr. Theophilus St. James. There seemed to me to be something peculiarly ominous in this. What sort of a man could he be who during thirty years of life had never made a single friend, high or low, who cared to continue to keep in touch with him? And yet the sinister fact remained that the head master not only tolerated, but was even intimate with him. More than once on entering a room I had found them talking confidentially together, and they would walk arm in arm in deep conversation up and down the garden paths. So curious did I become to know what the tie was which bound them, that I found it gradually push out my other interests and become the main purpose of my life. In school and out of school, at meals and at play, I was perpetually engaged in watching Dr. Phelps McCarthy and Mr. Theophilus St. James, and in endeavouring to solve the mystery which surrounded them.

But, unfortunately, my curiosity was a little too open. I had not the art to conceal the suspicions which I felt about the relations which existed between these two men and the nature of the hold which the one appeared to have over the other. It may have been my manner of watching them, it may have been some indiscreet question, but it is certain that I showed too clearly what I felt. One night I was conscious that the eyes of Theophilus St. James were fixed upon me in a surly and menacing stare. I had a foreboding of evil, and I was not surprised when Dr. McCarthy called me, next morning, into his study.

" I am very sorry, Mr. Weld," said he, " but I am afraid that I shall be compelled to dispense with your services."

" Perhaps you would give me some reason for dismissing me," I answered, for I was conscious of having done my duties to the best of my power, and knew well that only one reason could be given.

" I have no fault to find with you," said he, and the colour came to his cheeks.

" You send me away at the suggestion of my colleague."

His eyes turned away from mine.

" We will not discuss the question, Mr. Weld. It is impossible for me to discuss it. In justice to you, I will give you the strongest recommendation for your next situation. I can say no more. I hope that you will continue your duties here until you have found a place elsewhere."

My whole soul rose against the injustice of it, and yet I had no appeal and no redress. I could only bow and leave the room, with a bitter sense of ill-usage at my heart.

457

My first instinct was to pack my boxes and leave the house. But the head master had given me permission to remain until I had found another situation. I was sure that St. James desired me to go, and that was a strong reason why I should stay. If my presence annoyed him, I should give him as much of it as I could. I had begun to hate him and to long to have my revenge upon him. If he had a hold over our principal, might not I in turn obtain one over him ? It was a sign of weakness that he should be so afraid of my curiosity. He would not resent it so much if he had not something to fear from it. I entered my name once more upon the books of the agents, but meanwhile I continued to fulfil my duties at Willow Lea House, and so it came about that I was present at the *dénouement* of this singular situation.

During that week—for it was only a week before the crisis came—I was in the habit of going down each evening, after the work of the day was done, to inquire about my new arrangements. One night, it was a cold and windy evening in March, I had just stepped out from the hall door when a strange sight met my eyes. A man was crouching before one of the windows of the house. His knees were bent and his eyes were fixed upon the small line of light between the curtain and the sash. The window threw a square of brightness in front of it, and in the middle of this the dark shadow of this ominous visitor showed clear and hard. It was but for an instant that I saw him, for he glanced up and was off in a moment through the shrubbery. I could hear the patter of his feet as he ran down the road, until it died away in the distance.

It was evidently my duty to turn back and to tell Dr. McCarthy what I had seen. I found him in his study. I had expected him to be disturbed at such an incident, but I was not prepared for the state of panic into which he fell. He leaned back in his chair, white and gasping, like one who has received a mortal blow.

" Which window, Mr. Weld ? " he asked, wiping his forehead. " Which window was it ? "

" The next to the dining-room—Mr. St. James's window."

" Dear me ! Dear me ! This is, indeed, unfortunate ! A man looking through Mr. St. James's window ! " He wrung his hands like a man who is at his wits' end what to do.

" I shall be passing the police-station, sir. Would you wish me to mention the matter ? "

" No, no," he cried, suddenly, mastering his extreme agitation ; " I have no doubt that it was some poor tramp who intended to beg. I attach no importance to the incident—none at all. Don't let me detain you, Mr. Weld, if you wish to go out."

I left him sitting in his study with reassuring words upon his lips, but with horror upon his face. My heart was heavy for my little employer as I started off once more for town. As I looked back from the gate at the square of light which marked the window of my colleague, I suddenly saw the black outline of Dr. McCarthy's figure passing against the lamp. He had hastened from his study, then, to tell St. James what he had heard. What was the meaning of it all, this atmosphere of mystery, this inexplicable terror, these confidences between two such dissimilar men ? I thought and thought as I walked, but do what I would I could not hit upon any adequate conclusion. I little knew how near I was to the solution of the problem.

It was very late—nearly twelve o'clock—when I returned, and the lights were all out save one in the Doctor's study. The black, gloomy house loomed before me as I walked up the drive, its sombre bulk broken only by the one glimmering point of brightness. I let myself in with my latch-key, and was about to enter my own room when my attention was arrested by a short, sharp cry like that of a man in pain. I stood and listened, my hand upon the handle of my door.

All was silent in the house save for a distant murmur of voices which came, I knew, from the Doctor's room. I stole quietly down the corridor in that direction., The sound resolved itself now into two voices, the rough, bullying tones of St. James and the lower tone of the Doctor, the one apparently insisting and the other arguing and pleading. Four thin lines of light in the blackness showed me the door of the Doctor's room, and step by step I drew nearer to it in the darkness. St. James's voice within rose louder and louder, and his words now came plainly to my ear.

" I'll have every pound of it. If you won't give it me I'll take it. Do you hear ? "

Dr. McCarthy's reply was inaudible, but the angry voice broke in again.

" Leave you destitute ! I leave you this little goldmine of a school, and that's enough for one old man, is it not ? How am I to set up in Australia without money ? Answer me that ! "

Again the Doctor said something in a soothing voice, but his answer only roused his companion to a higher pitch of fury.

" Done for me ! What have you ever done for me except what you couldn't help doing ? It was for your good name, not for my safety, that you cared. But enough cackle ! I must get on my way before morning. Will you open your safe or will you not ? "

" Oh, James, how can you use me so ? " cried a wailing voice, and then there came a sudden little scream of pain. At the sound of that helpless appeal from brutal violence I lost for once that temper upon which I had prided myself. Every bit of manhood in me cried out against any further neutrality. With my walking-cane in my hand I rushed into the study. As I did so I was conscious that the hall-door bell was violently ringing.

" You villain ! " I cried, " let him go ! "

The two men were standing in front of a small safe, which stood against one wall of the Doctor's room.

St. James held the old man by the wrist, and he had twisted his arm round in order to force him to produce the key. My little head master, white but resolute, was struggling furiously in the grip of the burly athlete. The bully glared over his shoulder at me with a mixture of fury and terror upon his brutal features. Then, realizing that I was alone, he dropped his victim and made for me with a horrible curse.

"You infernal spy!" he cried. "I'll do for you anyhow before I leave."

I am not a very strong man, and I realised that I was helpless if once at close quarters. Twice I cut at him with my stick, but he rushed in at me with a murderous growl, and seized me by the throat with both his muscular hands. I fell backwards and he on the top of me, with a grip which was squeezing the life from me. I was conscious of his malignant, yellow-tinged eyes within a few inches of my own, and then, with a beating of pulses in my head and a singing in my ears, my senses slipped away from me. But even in that supreme moment I was aware that the door-bell was still violently ringing.

When I came to myself, I was lying upon the sofa in Dr. McCarthy's study, and the Doctor himself was seated beside me. He appeared to be watching me intently and anxiously, for as I opened my eyes and looked about me he gave a great cry of relief. "Thank God!" he cried. "Thank God!"

"Where is he?" I asked, looking round the room. As I did so, I became aware that the furniture was scattered in every direction, and that there were traces of an even more violent struggle than that in which I had been engaged.

The Doctor sank his face between his hands.

"They have him," he groaned. "After these years of trial they have him again. But how thankful I am that he has not for a second time stained his hands in blood."

As the Doctor spoke I became aware that a man in the

braided jacket of an inspector of police was standing in the doorway.

"Yes, sir," he remarked, "you have had a pretty narrow escape. If we had not got in when we did, you would not be here to tell the tale. I don't know that I ever saw anyone much nearer to the undertaker."

I sat up with my hands to my throbbing head.

"Dr. McCarthy," said I, "this is all a mystery to me. I should be glad if you could explain to me who this man is, and why you have tolerated him so long in your house."

"I owe you an explanation, Mr. Weld—and the more so since you have, in so chivalrous a fashion, almost sacrificed your life in my defence. There is no reason now for secrecy. In a word, Mr. Weld, this unhappy man's real name is James McCarthy, and he is my only son."

"Your son?"

"Alas, yes. What sin have I ever committed that I should have such a punishment? He has made my whole life a misery from the first years of his boyhood. Violent, headstrong, selfish, unprincipled, he has always been the same. At eighteen he was a criminal. At twenty, in a paroxysm of passion, he took the life of a boon companion and was tried for murder. He only just escaped the gallows, and he was condemned to penal servitude. Three years ago he succeeded in escaping, and managed, in face of a thousand obstacles, to reach my house in London. My wife's heart had been broken by his condemnation, and as he had succeeded in getting a suit of ordinary clothes, there was no one here to recognize him. For months he lay concealed in the attics until the first search of the police should be over. Then I gave him employment here, as you have seen, though by his rough and overbearing manners he made my own life miserable, and that of his fellow-masters unbearable. You have been with us for four months, Mr. Weld, but no other master endured him so long. I apologise now for all you have had to submit to, but I ask you what else could I do? For his dead mother's sake I could not let harm come to him as long as it was in my power to fend it off. Only under my roof could he find a refuge —the only spot in all the world—and how could I keep him here without its exciting remark unless I gave him some occupation? I made him English master, therefore, and in that capacity I have protected him here for three years. You have no doubt observed that he never, during the daytime, went beyond the college grounds. You now understand the reason. But when to-night you came to me with your report of a man who was looking through his window, I understood that his retreat was at last discovered. I besought him to fly at once, but he had been drinking, the unhappy fellow, and my words fell upon deaf ears. When at last he made up his mind to go he wished to take from me, in his flight, every shilling which I possessed. It was your entrance which saved me from him, while the police in turn arrived only just in time to rescue you. I have made myself amenable to the law by harbouring an escaped prisoner, and remain here in the custody of the inspector, but a prison has no terrors for me after what I have endured in this house during the last three years."

"It seems to me, Doctor," said the inspector, "that, if you have broken the law, you have had quite enough punishment already."

"God knows I have!" cried Dr. McCarthy, and sank his haggard face upon his hands.

40. *B. 24*

I TOLD my story when I was taken, and no one would listen to me. Then I told it again at the trial— the whole thing absolutely as it happened, without so much as a word added. I set it all out truly, so help me God, all that Lady Mannering said and did, and then all that I had said and done, just as it occurred. And what did I get for it? "The prisoner put forward a rambling and inconsequential statement, incredible in its details, and unsupported by any shred of corroborative evidence." That was what one of the London papers said, and others let it pass as if I had made no defence at all. And yet, with my own eyes I saw Lord Mannering murdered, and I am as guiltless of it as any man on the jury that tried me.

Now, sir, you are there to receive the petitions of prisoners. It all lies with you. All I ask is that you read it—just read it—and then that you make an inquiry or two about the private character of this "lady" Mannering, if she still keeps the name that she had three years ago, when to my sorrow and ruin I came to meet her. You could use a private inquiry agent or a good lawyer, and you would soon learn enough to show you that my story is the true one. Think of the glory it would be to you to have all the papers saying that there would have been a shocking miscarriage of justice if it had not been for your perseverance and intelligence! That must be your reward, since I am a poor man and can offer you nothing. But if you don't do it, may you never lie easy in your bed again! May no night pass that you are not haunted by the thought of the man who rots in gaol because you have not done the duty which you are paid to do! But you will do it, sir, I know. Just make one or two inquiries, and you will soon find which way the wind blows. Remember, also, that the only person who profited by the crime was herself, since it changed her from an unhappy wife to a rich young widow. There's the end of the string in your hand, and you only have to follow it up and see where it leads to.

Mind you, sir, I make no complaint as far as the burglary goes. I don't whine about what I have deserved, and so far I have had no more than I have deserved. Burglary it was, right enough, and my three years have gone to pay for it. It was shown at the trial that I had had a hand in the Merton Cross business, and did a year

for that, so my story had the less attention on that
account. A man with a previous conviction never gets a
really fair trial. I own to the burglary, but when it
comes to the murder which brought me a lifer—any
judge but Sir James might have given me the gallows—
then I tell you that I had nothing to do with it, and that
I am an innocent man. And now I'll take that night,
the 13th of September, 1894, and I'll give you just exactly
what occurred, and may God's hand strike me down if
I go one inch over the truth.

I had been at Bristol in the summer looking for work,
and then I had a notion that I might get something at
Portsmouth, for I was trained as a skilled mechanic, so
I came tramping my way across the south of England,
and doing odd jobs as I went. I was trying all I knew to
keep off the cross, for I had done a year in Exeter Gaol,
and I had had enough of visiting Queen Victoria. But
it's cruel hard to get work when once the black mark is
against your name, and it was all I could do to keep soul
and body together. At last, after ten days of wood-cutting
and stone-breaking on starvation pay, I found myself
near Salisbury with a couple of shillings in my pocket,
and my boots and my patience clean wore out. There's
an ale-house called " The Willing Mind," which stands
on the road between Blandford and Salisbury, and it was
there, that night, I engaged a bed. I was sitting alone
in the tap-room just about closing time, when the inn-
keeper—Allen his name was—came beside me and began
yarning about the neighbours. He was a man that liked
to talk and to have someone to listen to his talk, so I
sat there smoking and drinking a mug of ale which he
had stood me ; and I took no great interest in what he
said until he began to talk (as the devil would have it)
about the riches of Mannering Hall.

" Meaning the large house on the right before I came
to the village ? " said I. " The one that stands in its
own park ? "

" Exactly," said he—and I am giving all our talk so

that you may know that I am telling you the truth and hiding nothing. " The long, white house with the pillars," said he. " At the side of the Blandford Road."

Now I had looked at it as I passed, and it had crossed my mind, as such thoughts will, that it was a very easy house to get into with that great row of grand windows and glass doors. I had put the thought away from me, and now here was this landlord bringing it back with his talk about the riches within. I said nothing, but I listened, and as luck would have it, he would always come back to this one subject.

" He was a miser young, so you can think what he is now in his age," said he. " Well, he's had some good out of his money."

" What good can he have had if he does not spend it ? " said I.

" Well, it bought him the prettiest wife in England, and that was some good that he got out of it. She thought she would have the spending of it, but she knows the difference now."

" Who was she then ? " I asked, just for the sake of something to say.

" She was nobody at all until the old Lord made her his Lady," said he. " She came from up London way, and some said that she had been on the stage there, but nobody knew. The old Lord was away for a year, and when he came home he brought a young wife back with him, and there she has been ever since. Stephens, the butler, did tell me once that she was the light of the house when fust she came, but what with her husband's mean and aggravatin' way, and what with her loneliness—for he hates to see a visitor within his doors ; and what with his bitter words—for he has a tongue like a hornet's sting—her life all went out of her, and she became a white, silent creature, moping about the country lanes. Some say that she loved another man, and that it was just the riches of the old Lord which tempted her to be false to her lover, and that now she is eating her heart out

because she has lost the one without being any nearer
to the other, for she might be the poorest woman in the
parish for all the money that she has the handling of."

Well, sir, you can imagine that it did not interest me
very much to hear about the quarrels between a Lord
and a Lady. What did it matter to me if she hated the
sound of his voice, or if he put every indignity upon her
in the hope of breaking her spirit, and spoke to her as he
would never have dared to speak to one of his servants ?
The landlord told me of these things, and of many more
like them, but they passed out of my mind, for they were
no concern of mine. But what I did want to hear was
the form in which Lord Mannering kept his riches.
Title-deeds and stock certificates are but paper, and more
danger than profit to the man who takes them. But
metal and stones are worth a risk. And then, as if he
were answering my very thoughts, the landlord told me
of Lord Mannering's great collection of gold medals,
that it was the most valuable in the world, and that it
was reckoned that if they were put into a sack the strongest
man in the parish would not be able to raise them. Then
his wife called him, and he and I went to our beds.

I am not arguing to make out a case for myself, but I
beg you, sir, to bear all the facts in your mind, and to
ask yourself whether a man could be more sorely tempted
than I was. I make bold to say that there are few who
could have held out against it. There I lay on my bed
that night, a desperate man without hope or work, and
with my last shilling in my pocket. I had tried to be
honest, and honest folk had turned their backs upon me.
They taunted me for theft ; and yet they pushed me
towards it. I was caught in the stream and could not
get out. And then it was such a chance : the great house
all lined with windows, the golden medals which could
so easily be melted down. It was like putting a loaf
before a starving man and expecting him not to eat it.
I fought against it for a time, but it was no use. At
last I sat up on the side of my bed, and I swore that that

night I should either be a rich man and able to give up crime for ever, or that the irons should be on my wrists once more. Then I slipped on my clothes, and, having put a shilling on the table—for the landlord had treated me well, and I did not wish to cheat him—I passed out through the window into the garden of the inn.

There was a high wall round this garden, and I had a job to get over it, but once on the other side it was all plain sailing. I did not meet a soul upon the road, and the iron gate of the avenue was open. No one was moving at the lodge. The moon was shining, and I could see the great house glimmering white through an archway of trees. I walked up it for a quarter of a mile or so, until I was at the edge of the drive, where it ended in a broad, gravelled space before the main door. There I stood in the shadow and looked at the long building, with a full moon shining in every window and silvering the high, stone front. I crouched there for some time, and I wondered where I should find the easiest entrance. The corner window of the side seemed to be the one which was least overlooked, and a screen of ivy hung heavily over it. My best chance was evidently there. I worked my way under the trees to the back of the house, and then crept along in the black shadow of the building. A dog barked and rattled his chain, but I stood waiting until he was quiet, and then I stole on once more until I came to the window which I had chosen.

It is astonishing how careless they are in the country, in places far removed from large towns, where the thought of burglars never enters their heads. I call it setting temptation in a poor man's way when he puts his hand, meaning no harm, upon a door, and finds it swing open before him. In this case it was not so bad as that, but the window was merely fastened with the ordinary catch, which I opened with a push from the blade of my knife. I pulled up the window as quickly as possible, then I thrust the knife through the slit in the shutter and prized it open. They were folding shutters, and I shoved them before me and walked into the room.

" Good evening, sir ! You are very welcome ! " said a voice.

I've had some starts in my life, but never one to come up to that one. There, in the opening of the shutters, within reach of my arm, was standing a woman with a small coil of wax taper burning in her hand. She was tall and straight and slender, with a beautiful, white face that might have been cut out of clear marble, but her hair and eyes were as black as night. She was dressed in some sort of white dressing-gown which flowed down to her feet, and what with this robe and what with her face, it seemed as if a spirit from above was standing in front of me. My knees knocked together, and I held on to the shutter with one hand to give me support. I should have turned and run away if I had had the strength, but I could only just stand and stare at her.

She soon brought me back to myself once more.

" Don't be frightened ! " said she, and they were strange words for the mistress of a house to have to use to a burglar. " I saw you out of my bedroom window when you were hiding under those trees, so I slipped downstairs, and then I heard you at the window. I should have opened it for you if you had waited, but you managed it yourself just as I came up."

I still held in my hand the long clasp-knife with which I had opened the shutter. I was unshaven and grimed from a week on the roads. Altogether, there are few people who would have cared to face me alone at one in the morning ; but this woman, if I had been her lover meeting her by appointment, could not have looked upon me with a more welcoming eye. She laid her hand upon my sleeve and drew me into the room.

" What's the meaning of this, ma'am ? Don't get trying any little games upon me," said I, in my roughest way—and I can put it on rough when I like. " It'll be the worse for you if you play me any trick," I added, showing her my knife.

" I will play you no trick," said she. " On the contrary, I am your friend, and I wish to help you."

" Excuse me, ma'am, but I find it hard to believe that," said I. " Why should you wish to help me ? "

" I have my own reasons," said she ; and then suddenly with those black eyes blazing out of her white face : " It's because I hate him, hate him, hate him ! Now you understand."

I remembered what the landlord had told me, and I did understand. I looked at her Ladyship's face, and I knew that I could trust her. She wanted to revenge herself upon her husband. She wanted to hit him where it would hurt him most—upon the pocket. She hated him so that she would even lower her pride to take such a man as me into her confidence if she could gain her end by doing so. I've hated some folk in my time, but I don't think I ever understood what hate was until I saw that woman's face in the light of the taper.

" You'll trust me now ? " said she, with another coaxing touch upon my sleeve.

" Yes, your Ladyship."

" You know me, then ? "

" I can guess who you are."

" I dare say my wrongs are the talk of the county. But what does he care for that ? He only cares for one thing in the whole world, and that you can take from him this night. Have you a bag ? "

" No, your Ladyship."

" Shut the shutter behind you. Then no one can see the light. You are quite safe. The servants all sleep in the other wing. I can show you where all the most valuable things are. You cannot carry them all, so we must pick the best."

The room in which I found myself was long and low, with many rugs and skins scattered about on a polished wood floor. Small cases stood here and there, and the walls were decorated with spears and swords and paddles, and other things which find their way into museums. There were some queer clothes, too, which had been brought from savage countries, and the lady took down a large leather sack-bag from among them.

" This sleeping-sack will do," said she. " Now come with me and I will show you where the medals are."

It was like a dream to me to think that this tall, white woman was the lady of the house, and that she was lending me a hand to rob her own home. I could have burst out laughing at the thought of it, and yet there was something in that pale face of hers which stopped my laughter and turned me cold and serious. She swept on in front of me like a spirit, with the green taper in her hand, and I walked behind with my sack until we came to a door at the end of this museum. It was locked, but the key was in it, and she led me through.

The room beyond was a small one, hung all round with curtains which had pictures on them. It was the hunting of a deer that was painted on it, as I remember, and in the flicker of that light you'd have sworn that the dogs and the horses were streaming round the walls. The only other thing in the room was a row of cases made of walnut, with brass ornaments. They had glass tops, and beneath this glass I saw the long lines of those gold medals, some of them as big as a plate and half an inch thick, all resting upon red velvet and glowing and gleaming in the darkness. My fingers were just itching to be at them, and I slipped my knife under the lock of one of the cases to wrench it open.

" Wait a moment," said she, laying her hand upon my arm. " You might do better than this."

" I am very well satisfied, ma'am," said I, " and much obliged to your Ladyship for kind assistance."

" You can do better," she repeated. " Would not golden sovereigns be worth more to you than these things ? "

" Why, yes," said I. " That's best of all."

"Well," said she. "He sleeps just above our head. It is but one short staircase. There is a tin box with money enough to fill this bag under his bed."

"How can I get it without waking him?"

"What matter if he does wake?" She looked very hard at me as she spoke. "You could keep him from calling out."

"No, no, ma'am, I'll have none of that."

"Just as you like," said she. "I thought that you were a stout-hearted sort of man by your appearance, but I see that I made a mistake. If you are afraid to run the risk of one old man, then of course you cannot have the gold which is under his bed. You are the best judge of your own business, but I should think that you would do better at some other trade."

"I'll not have murder on my conscience."

"You could overpower him without harming him. I never said anything about murder. The money lies under the bed. But if you are faint-hearted, it is better that you should not attempt it."

She worked upon me so, partly with her scorn and partly with this money that she held before my eyes, that I believe I should have yielded and taken my chances upstairs, had it not been that I saw her eyes following the struggle within me in such a crafty, malignant fashion, that it was evident she was bent upon making me the tool of her revenge, and that she would leave me no choice but to do the old man an injury or to be captured by him. She felt suddenly that she was giving herself away, and she changed her face to a kindly, friendly smile, but it was too late, for I had had my warning.

"I will not go upstairs," said I. "I have all I want here."

She looked her contempt at me, and there never was a face which could look it plainer.

"Very good. You can take these medals. I should be glad if you would begin at this end. I suppose they will all be the same value when melted down, but these are the ones which are the rarest, and, therefore, the most precious to him. It is not necessary to break the locks. If you press that brass knob you will find that there is a secret spring. So! Take that small one first—it is the very apple of his eye."

She had opened one of the cases, and the beautiful things all lay exposed before me. I had my hand upon the one which she had pointed out, when suddenly a change came over her face, and she held up one finger as a warning. " Hist ! " she whispered. " What is that ? "

Far away in the silence of the house we heard a low, dragging, shuffling sound, and the distant tread of feet. She closed and fastened the case in an instant.

" It's my husband ! " she whispered. " All right. Don't be alarmed. I'll arrange it. Here ! Quick, behind the tapestry ! "

She pushed me behind the painted curtains upon the wall, my empty leather bag still in my hand. Then she took her taper and walked quickly into the room from which we had come. From where I stood I could see her through the open door.

" Is that you, Robert ? " she cried.

The light of a candle shone through the door of the museum, and the shuffling steps came nearer and nearer. Then I saw a face in the doorway, a great, heavy face, all lines and creases, with a huge, curving nose, and a pair of gold glasses fixed across it. He had to throw his head back to see through the glasses, and that great nose thrust out in front of him like the beak of some sort of fowl. He was a big man, very tall and burly, so that in his loose dressing-gown his figure seemed to fill up the whole doorway. He had a pile of grey, curling hair all round his head, but his face was clean-shaven. His mouth was thin and small and prim, hidden away under his long, masterful nose. He stood there, holding the candle in front of him, and looking at his wife with a queer, malicious gleam in his eyes. It only needed that one look to tell me that he was as fond of her as she was of him.

" How's this ? " he asked. " Some new tantrum ? What do you mean by wandering about the house ? Why don't you go to bed ? "

" I could not sleep," she answered. She spoke languidly and wearily. If she was an actress once, she had not forgotten her calling.

" Might I suggest," said he, in the same mocking kind of voice, " that a good conscience is an excellent aid to sleep ? "

" That cannot be true," she answered, " for you sleep very well."

" I have only one thing in my life to be ashamed of," said he, and his hair bristled up with anger until he looked like an old cockatoo. " You know best what that is. It is a mistake which has brought its own punishment with it."

" To me as well as to you. Remember that ! "

" You have very little to whine about. It was I who stooped and you who rose."

" Rose ! "

" Yes, rose. I suppose you do not deny that it is a promotion to exchange the music-hall for Mannering Hall. Fool that I was ever to take you out of your true sphere ! "

" If you think so, why do you not separate ? "

" Because private misery is better than public humiliation. Because it is easier to suffer for a mistake than to own to it. Because also I like to keep you in my sight, and to know that you cannot go back to him."

" You villain ! You cowardly villain ! "

" Yes, yes, my lady. I know your secret ambition, but it shall never be while I live, and if it happens after my death I will at least take care that you go to him as a beggar. You and dear Edward will never have the satisfaction of squandering my savings, and you may make up your mind to that, my lady. Why are those shutters and the window open ? "

"I found the night very close."

"It is not safe. How do you know that some tramp may not be outside ? Are you aware that my collection of medals is worth more than any similar collection in the world ?. You have left the door open also. What is there to prevent anyone from rifling the cases ? "

"I was here."

"I know you were. I heard you moving about in the medal room, and that was why I came down. What were you doing ? "

"Looking at the medals. What else should I be doing ? "

"This curiosity is something new." He looked suspiciously at her and moved on towards the inner room, she walking beside him.

It was at this moment that I saw something which startled. I had laid my clasp-knife open upon the top of one of the cases, and there it lay in full view. She saw it before he did, and with a woman's cunning she held her taper out so that the light of it came between Lord Mannering's eyes and the knife. Then she took it with her left hand and held it against her gown out of his sight. He looked about from case to case—I could have put my hand at one time upon his long nose—but there was nothing to show that the medals had been tampered with, and so, still snarling and grumbling, he shuffled off into the other room once more.

And now I have to speak of what I heard rather than of what I saw, but I swear to you, as I shall stand some day before my Maker, that what I say is the truth.

When they passed into the outer room I saw him lay his candle upon the corner of one of the tables, and he sat himself down, but in such a position that he was just out of my sight. She moved behind him, as I could tell from the fact that the light of her taper threw his long, lumpy shadow upon the floor in front of him. Then he began talking about this man whom he called Edward, and every word that he said was like a blistering drop of vitriol. He spoke low, so that I could not hear it all, but from what I heard I should guess that she would as soon have been lashed with a whip. At first she said some hot words in reply, but then she was silent, and he went on and on in that cold, mocking voice of his, nagging and insulting and tormenting, until I wondered that she could bear to stand there in silence and listen to it. Then suddenly I heard him say in a sharp voice, " Come from behind me ! Leave go of my collar ! What ! would you dare to strike me ? " There was a sound like a blow, just a soft sort of thud, and then I heard him cry out, " My God, it's blood ! " He shuffled with his feet as if he was getting up, and then I heard another blow, and he cried out, " Oh, you she-devil ! " and was quiet, except for a dripping and splashing upon the floor.

I ran out from behind my curtain at that, and rushed into the other room, shaking all over with the horror of it. The old man had slipped down in the chair, and his dressing-gown had rucked up until he looked as if he had a monstrous hump to his back. His head, with the gold glasses still fixed on his nose, was lolling over upon one side, and his little mouth was open just like a dead fish. I could not see where the blood was coming from, but I could still hear it drumming upon the floor. She stood behind him with the candle shining full upon her face. Her lips were pressed together and her eyes shining, and a touch of colour had come into each of her cheeks. It just wanted that to make her the most beautiful woman I had ever seen in my life.

" You've done it now ! " said I.

" Yes," said she, in her quiet way, " I've done it now."

" What are you going to do ? " I asked. " They'll have you for murder as sure as fate."

" Never fear about me. I have nothing to live for, and it does not matter. Give me a hand to set him straight in the chair. It is horrible to see him like this ! "

I did so, though it turned me cold all over to touch him. Some of his blood came on my hand and sickened me.

"Now," said she, "you may as well have the medals as anyone else. Take them and go."

"I don't want them. I only want to get away. I was never mixed up with a business like this before."

"Nonser.se!" said she. "You came for the medals, and here they are at your mercy. Why should you not have them? There is no one to prevent you."

I held the bag still in my hand. She opened the case, and between us we threw a hundred or so of the medals into it. They were all from the one case, but I could not bring myself to wait for any more. Then I made for the window, for the very air of this house seemed to poison me after what I had seen and heard. As I looked back, I saw her standing there, tall and graceful, with the light in her hand, just as I had seen her first. She waved good-bye, and I waved back at her and sprang out into the gravel drive.

I thank God that I can lay my hand upon my heart and say that I have never done a murder, but perhaps it would be different if I had been able to read that woman's mind and thoughts. There might have been two bodies in the room instead of one if I could have seen behind that last smile of hers. But I thought of nothing but of getting safely away, and it never entered my head how she might be fixing the rope round my neck. I had not taken five steps out from the window skirting down the shadow of the house in the way that I had come, when I heard a scream that might have raised the parish, and then another and another.

"Murder!" she cried. "Murder! Murder! Help!" and her voice rang out in the quiet of the night-time and sounded over the whole country-side. It went through my head, that dreadful cry. In an instant lights began to move and windows to fly up, not only in the house behind me, but at the lodge and in the stables in front. Like a frightened rabbit I bolted down the drive, but I heard the clang of the gate being shut before I could reach it. Then I hid my bag of medals under some dry fagots, and I tried to get away across the park, but some-one saw me in the moonlight, and presently I had half a dozen of them with dogs upon my heels. I crouched down among the brambles, but those dogs were too many for me, and I was glad enough when the men came up and prevented me from being torn into pieces. They seized me, and dragged me back to the room from which I had come.

" Is this the man, your Ladyship ? " asked the oldest of them—the same whom I found out afterwards to be the butler.

She had been bending over the body, with her hand-kerchief to her eyes, and now she turned upon me with the face of a fury. Oh, what an actress that woman was !

" Yes, yes, it is the very man," she cried. " Oh, you villain, you cruel villain, to treat an old man so ! "

There was a man there who seemed to be a village constable. He laid his hand upon my shoulder.

" What do you say to that ? " said he.

" It was she who did it," I cried, pointing at the woman, whose eyes never flinched before mine.

" Come ! come ! Try another ! " said the constable, and one of the men-servants struck at me with his fist.

" I tell you that I saw her do it. She stabbed him twice with a knife. She first helped me to rob him, and then she murdered him."

The footman tried to strike me again, but she held up her hand.

" Do not hurt him," said she. " I think that his punishment may safely be left to the law."

" I'll see to that, your Ladyship," said the constable. " Your Ladyship actually saw the crime committed, did you not ? "

" Yes, yes, I saw it with my own eyes. It was horrible. We heard the noise and we came down. My poor husband was in front. The man had one of the cases open, and was filling a black leather bag which he held in his hand. He rushed past us, and my husband seized him. There was a struggle, and he stabbed him twice. There you can see the blood upon his hands. If I am not mistaken, his knife is still in Lord Mannering's body."

"Look at the blood upon her hands!" I cried.

"She has been holding up his Lordship's head, you lying rascal," said the butler.

"And here's the very sack her Ladyship spoke of," said the constable, as a groom came in with the one which I had dropped in my flight. "And here are the medals inside it. That's good enough for me. We will keep him safe here to-night, and to-morrow the inspector and I can take him into Salisbury."

"Poor creature," said the woman. "For my own part, I forgive him any injury which he has done me. Who knows what temptation may have driven him to crime? His conscience and the law will give him punishment enough without any reproach of mine rendering it more bitter."

I could not answer—I tell you, sir, I could not answer, so taken aback was I by the assurance of the woman. And so, seeming by my silence to agree to all that she had said, I was dragged away by the butler and the constable into the cellar, in which they locked me for the night.

There, sir, I have told you the whole story of the events which led up to the murder of Lord Mannering by his wife upon the night of September the 14th, in the year 1894. Perhaps you will put my statement on one side as the constable did at Mannering Towers, or the judge afterwards at the county assizes. Or perhaps you will see that there is the ring of truth in what I say, and you will follow it up, and so make your name for ever as a man who does not grudge personal trouble where justice is to be done. I have only you to look to, sir, and if you will clear my name of this false accusation, then I will worship you as one man never yet worshipped another. But if you fail me, then I give you my solemn promise that I will rope myself up, this day month, to the bar of my window, and from that time on I will come to plague you in your dreams if ever yet one man was able to come back and to haunt another. What I ask you to do is very simple. Make inquiries about this woman, watch her, learn her past history, find out what use she is making of the money which has come to her, and whether there is not a man Edward as I have stated. If from all this you learn anything which shows you her real character, or which seems to you to corroborate the story which I have told you, then I am sure that I can rely upon your goodness of heart to come to the rescue of an innocent man.

41. *The Great Keinplatz Experiment*

OF all the sciences which have puzzled the sons of men, none had such an attraction for the learned Professor von Baumgarten as those which relate to psychology and the ill-defined relations between mind and matter. A celebrated anatomist, a profound chemist, and one of the first physiologists in Europe, it was a relief for him to turn from these subjects and to bring his varied knowledge to bear upon the study of the soul and the mysterious relationship of spirits. At first, when as a young man he began to dip into the secrets of mesmerism, his mind seemed to be wandering in a strange land where all was chaos and darkness, save that here and there some great unexplainable and disconnected fact loomed out in front of him. As the years passed, however, and as the worthy Professor's stock of knowledge increased, for knowledge begets knowledge as money bears interest, much which had seemed strange and unaccountable began to take another shape in his eyes. New trains of reasoning became familiar to him, and he perceived connecting links where all had been incomprehensible and startling. By experiments which extended over twenty years, he obtained a basis of facts upon which it was his ambition to build up a new, exact science which should embrace mesmerism, spiritualism, and all cognate subjects. In this he was much helped by his intimate knowledge of the more intricate parts of animal physiology which treat of nerve currents and the working of the brain ; for Alexis von Baumgarten was Regius Professor of Physiology at the University of Keinplatz, and had all the resources of the laboratory to aid him in his profound researches.

Professor von Baumgarten was tall and thin, with a hatchet face and steel-grey eyes, which were singularly bright and penetrating. Much thought had furrowed his forehead and contracted his heavy eyebrows, so that he appeared to wear a perpetual frown, which often misled people as to his character, for though austere he was tender-hearted. He was popular among the students, who would gather round him after his lectures and listen eagerly to his strange theories. Often he would call for volunteers from amongst them in order to conduct some experiment, so that eventually there was hardly a lad in the class who had not, at one time or another, been thrown into a mesmeric trance by his Professor.

Of all these young devotees of science there was none who equalled in enthusiasm Fritz von Hartmann. It had often seemed strange to his fellow-students that wild, reckless Fritz, as dashing a young fellow as ever hailed from the Rhinelands, should devote the time and trouble which he did in reading up abstruse works and in assisting the Professor in his strange experiments. The fact was, however, that Fritz was a knowing and long-headed fellow. Months before he had lost his heart to young Elise, the blue-eyed, yellow-haired daughter of the lecturer. Although he had succeeded in learning from her lips that she was not indifferent to his suit, he had never dared to announce himself to her family as a formal suitor. Hence he would have found it a difficult matter to see his young lady had he not adopted the expedient of making himself useful to the Professor. By this means he frequently was asked to the old man's house, where he willingly submitted to be experimented upon in any way as long as there was a chance of his receiving one bright glance from the eyes of Elise or one touch of her little hand.

Young Fritz von Hartmann was a handsome lad enough. There were broad acres, too, which would descend to him when his father died. To many he would have seemed an eligible suitor ; but Madame frowned upon his presence in the house, and lectured the Professor at times on his allowing such a wolf to prowl around their lamb. To tell the truth, Fritz had an evil name in Keinplatz. Never was there a riot or a duel, or any other mischief afoot, but the young Rhinelander figured as a ringleader in it. No one used more free and violent language, no one drank more, no one played cards more habitually, no one was more idle, save in the one solitary subject. No wonder, then, that the good Frau Professorin gathered her Fräulein under her wing, and resented the attentions of such a *mauvais sujet*. As to the worthy lecturer, he was too much engrossed by his strange studies to form an opinion upon the subject one way or the other.

For many years there was one question which had continually obtruded itself upon his thoughts. All his experiments and his theories turned upon a single point. A hundred times a day the Professor asked himself whether it was possible for the human spirit to exist apart from the body for a time and then to return to it once again. When the possibility first suggested itself to him his scientific mind had revolted from it. It clashed too violently with preconceived ideas and the prejudices of his early training. Gradually, however, as he proceeded farther and farther along the pathway of

original research, his mind shook off its old fetters and
became ready to face any conclusion which could reconcile the facts. There were many things which made
him believe that it was possible for mind to exist apart
from matter. At last it occurred to him that by a daring
and original experiment the question might be definitely
decided.

" It is evident," he remarked in his celebrated article
upon invisible entities, which appeared in the *Keinplatz
wochenliche Medicalschrift* about this time, and which
surprised the whole scientific world—" it is evident that
under certain conditions the soul or mind does separate
itself from the body. In the case of a mesmerised
person, the body lies in a cataleptic condition, but the
spirit has left it. Perhaps you reply that the soul is
there, but in a dormant condition. I answer that this
is not so, otherwise how can one account for the condition
of clairvoyance, which has fallen into disrepute through
the knavery of certain scoundrels, but which can easily
be shown to be an undoubted fact. I have been able
myself, with a sensitive subject, to obtain an accurate
description of what was going on in another room or
another house. How can such knowledge be accounted
for on any hypothesis save that the soul of the subject
has left the body and is wandering through space ? For
a moment it is recalled by the voice of the operator and
says what it has seen, and then wings its way once more
through the air. Since the spirit is by its very nature
invisible, we cannot see these comings and goings, but
we see their effect in the body of the subject, now rigid
and inert, now struggling to narrate impressions which
could never have come to it by natural means. There
is only one way which I can see by which the fact can
be demonstrated. Although we in the flesh are unable
to see these spirits, yet our own spirits, could we separate
them from the body, would be conscious of the presence
of others. It is my intention, therefore, shortly to mesmerise one of my pupils. I shall then mesmerise myself

in a manner which has become easy to me. After that, if my theory holds good, my spirit will have no difficulty in meeting and communing with the spirit of my pupil, both being separated from the body. I hope to be able to communicate the result of this interesting experiment in an early number of the *Keinplatz wochenliche Medical-schrift*."

When the good Professor finally fulfilled his promise, and published an account of what occurred, the narrative was so extraordinary that it was received with general incredulity. The tone of some of the papers was so offensive in their comments upon the matter that the angry savant declared that he would never open his mouth again or refer to the subject in any way—a promise which he has faithfully kept. This narrative has been compiled, however, from the most authentic sources, and the events cited in it may be relied upon as substantially correct.

It happened, then, that shortly after the time when Professor von Baumgarten conceived the idea of the above-mentioned experiment, he was walking thoughtfully homewards after a long day in the laboratory, when he met a crowd of roistering students who had just streamed out from a beer-house. At the head of them, half-intoxicated and very noisy, was young Fritz von Hartmann. The Professor would have passed them, but his pupil ran across and intercepted him.

" Heh ! my worthy master," he said, taking the old man by the sleeve, and leading him down the road with him. " There is something that I have to say to you, and it is easier for me to say it now, when the good beer is humming in my head, than at another time."

" What is it, then, Fritz ? " the physiologist asked, looking at him in mild surprise.

" I hear, mein herr, that you are about to do some wondrous experiment in which you hope to take a man's soul out of his body, and then to put it back again. Is it not so ? "

" It is true, Fritz."

" And have you considered, my dear sir, that you may have some difficulty in finding someone on whom to try this ? Potztausend ! Suppose that the soul went out and would not come back. That would be a bad business. Who is to take the risk ? "

" But Fritz," the Professor cried, very much startled by this view of the matter, " I had relied upon your assistance in the attempt. Surely you will not desert me. Consider the honour and glory."

" Consider the fiddlesticks ! " the student cried angrily. " Am I to be paid always thus ? Did I not stand two hours upon a glass insulator while you poured electricity into my body ? Have you not stimulated my phrenic nerves, besides ruining my digestion with a galvanic current round my stomach ? Four-and-thirty times you have mesmerised me, and what have I got from all this ? Nothing. And now you wish to take my soul out, as you would take the works from a watch. It is more than flesh and blood can stand."

" Dear, dear ! " the Professor cried in great distress. " That is very true, Fritz. I never thought of it before. If you can but suggest how I can compensate you, you will find me ready and willing."

" Then listen," said Fritz solemnly. " If you will pledge your word that after this experiment I may have the hand of your daughter, then I am willing to assist you ; but if not, I shall have nothing to do with it. These are my only terms."

" And what would my daughter say to this ? " the Professor exclaimed, after a pause of astonishment.

" Elise would welcome it," the young man replied. " We have loved each other long."

" Then she shall be yours," the physiologist said with decision, " for you are a good-hearted young man, and one of the best neurotic subjects that I have ever known —that is when you are not under the influence of alcohol. My experiment is to be performed upon the fourth of next month. You will attend at the physiological laboratory at twelve o'clock. It will be a great occasion, Fritz. Von Gruben is coming from Jena, and Hinterstein from Basle. The chief men of science of all South Germany will be there."

" I shall be punctual," the student said briefly ; and so the two parted. The Professor plodded homeward, thinking of the great coming event, while the young man staggered along after his noisy companions, with his mind full of the blue-eyed Elise, and of the bargain which he had concluded with her father.

The Professor did not exaggerate when he spoke of the widespread interest excited by his novel psychological experiment. Long before the hour had arrived the room was filled by a galaxy of talent. Besides the celebrities whom he had mentioned, there had come from London the great Professor Lurcher, who had just established his reputation by a remarkable treatise upon cerebral centres. Several great lights of the Spiritualistic body had also come a long distance to be present, as had a Swedenborgian minister, who considered that the proceedings might throw some light upon the doctrines of the Rosy Cross.

There was considerable applause from this eminent assembly upon the appearance of Professor von Baumgarten and his subject upon the platform. The lecturer, in a few well-chosen words, explained what his views were, and how he proposed to test them. " I hold," he said, " that when a person is under the influence of mesmerism, his spirit is for the time released from his body, and I challenge anyone to put forward any other hypothesis which will account for the fact of clairvoyance. I therefore hope that upon mesmerising my young friend here, and then putting myself into a trance, our spirits may be able to commune together, though our bodies lie still and inert. After a time nature will resume her sway, our spirits will return into our respective bodies, and all will be as before. With your kind permission, we shall now proceed to attempt the experiment."

The applause was renewed at this speech, and the audience settled down in expectant silence. With a few rapid passes the Professor mesmerised the young man, who sank back in his chair, pale and rigid. He then took a bright globe of glass from his pocket, and by concentrating his gaze upon it and making a strong mental effort, he succeeded in throwing himself into the same condition. It was a strange and impressive sight to see the old man and the young sitting together in the same cataleptic condition. Whither, then, had their souls fled? That was the question which presented itself to each and every one of the spectators.

Five minutes passed, and then ten, and then fifteen, and then fifteen more, while the Professor and his pupil sat stiff and stark upon the platform. During that time not a sound was heard from the assembled savants, but every eye was bent upon the two pale faces, in search of the first signs of returning consciousness. Nearly an hour had elapsed before the patient watchers were rewarded. A faint flush came back to the cheeks of Professor von Baumgarten. The soul was coming back once more to its earthly tenement. Suddenly he stretched out his long, thin arms, as one awaking from sleep, and rubbing his eyes, stood up from his chair and gazed about him as though he hardly realised where he was. " Tausend Teufel ! " he exclaimed, rapping out a tremendous South German oath, to the great astonishment of his audience and to the disgust of the Swedenborgian.

" Where the Henker am I then, and what in thunder has occurred ? Oh yes, I remember now. One of these nonsensical mesmeric experiments. There is no result this time, for I remember nothing at all since I became unconscious ; so you have had all your long journeys for nothing, my learned friends, and a very good joke, too "; at which the Regius Professor of Physiology burst into a roar of laughter and slapped his thigh in a highly indecorous fashion. The audience were so enraged at this unseemly behaviour on the part of their host, that there might have been a considerable disturbance, had it not been for the judicious interference of young Fritz von Hartmann, who had now recovered from his lethargy. Stepping to the front of the platform, the young man apologised for the conduct of his companion. " I am sorry to say," he said, " that he is a harum-scarum sort of fellow, although he appeared so grave at the commencement of this experiment. He is still suffering from mesmeric reaction, and is hardly account-able for his words. As to the experiment itself, I do not consider it to be a failure. It is very possible that our spirits may have been communing in space during this hour ; but, unfortunately, our gross bodily memory is distinct from our spirit, and we cannot recall what has occurred. My energies shall now be devoted to devising some means by which spirits may be able to recollect what occurs to them in their free state, and I trust that when I have worked this out, I may have the pleasure of meeting you all once again in this hall, and demonstrating to you the result." This address, coming from so young a student, caused considerable astonishment among the audience, and some were inclined to be offended, thinking that he assumed rather too much importance. The majority, however, looked upon him as a young man of great promise, and many comparisons were made as they left the hall between his dignified conduct and the levity of his professor, who during the above remarks was laughing heartily in a corner, by no means abashed at the failure of the experiment.

Now although all these learned men were filing out of the lecture-room under the impression that they had seen nothing of note, as a matter of fact one of the most wonderful things in the whole history of the world had just occurred before their very eyes. Professor von Baum-garten had been so far correct in his theory that both his spirit and that of his pupil had been, for a time, absent from the body. But here a strange and unforeseen complication had occurred. In their return the spirit of Fritz von Hartmann had entered into the body of Alexis von Baumgarten, and that of Alexis von Baumgarten had taken up its abode in the frame of Fritz von Hartmann. Hence the slang and scurrility which issued from the lips of the serious Professor, and hence also the weighty words and grave statements which fell from the careless student. It was an unprecedented event, yet no one knew of it, least of all those whom it concerned.

The body of the Professor, feeling conscious suddenly of a great dryness about the back of the throat, sallied out into the street, still chuckling to himself over the result of the experiment, for the soul of Fritz within was reckless at the thought of the bride whom he had won so easily. His first impulse was to go up to the house and see her, but on second thoughts he came to the conclusion that it would be best to stay away until Madame Baumgarten should be informed by her husband of the agreement which had been made. He therefore made his way down to the Grüner Mann, which was one of the favourite trysting-places of the wilder students, and ran, boisterously waving his cane in the air, into the little parlour, where sat Spiegel and Müller and half a dozen other boon companions.

" Ha, ha ! my boys," he shouted. " I knew I should find you here. Drink up, every one of you, and call for what you like, for I'm going to stand treat to-day."

Had the green man who is depicted upon the signpost of that well-known inn suddenly marched into the room and called for a bottle of wine, the students could not have been more amazed than they were by this unexpected entry of their revered professor. They were so astonished that for a minute or two they glared at him in utter bewilderment without being able to make any reply to his hearty invitation.

" Donner und Blitzen ! " shouted the Professor angrily. " What the deuce is the matter with you, then ? You sit there like a set of stuck pigs staring at me. What is it then ? "

" It is the unexpected honour," stammered Spiegel, who was in the chair.

" Honour—rubbish ! " said the Professor testily. " Do you think that just because I happen to have been exhibiting mesmerism to a parcel of old fossils, I am therefore too proud to associate with dear old friends like you ? Come out of that chair, Spiegel, my boy, for I shall preside now. Beer, or wine, or schnapps, my lads—call for what you like, and put it all down to me."

Never was there such an afternoon in the Grüner Mann. The foaming flagons of lager and the green-necked bottles of Rhenish circulated merrily. By degrees the students lost their shyness in the presence of their Professor. As for him, he shouted, he sang, he roared, he balanced a long tobacco-pipe upon his nose, and offered to run a hundred yards against any member of the company. The Kellner and the barmaid whispered to each other outside the door their astonishment at such proceedings on the part of a Regius Professor of the ancient university of Keinplatz. They had still more to whisper about afterwards, for the learned man cracked the Kellner's crown, and kissed the barmaid behind the kitchen door.

" Gentlemen," said the Professor, standing up, albeit somewhat totteringly, at the end of the table, and balancing his high, old-fashioned wine glass in his bony hand, " I must now explain to you what is the cause of this festivity."

" Hear ! hear ! " roared the students, hammering their beer glasses against the table ; " a speech, a speech !— silence for a speech ! "

" The fact is, my friends," said the Professor, beaming through his spectacles, " I hope very soon to be married."

" Married ! " cried a student, bolder than the others. " Is Madame dead, then ? "

" Madame who ? "

" Why, Madame von Baumgarten, of course."

" Ha, ha ! " laughed the Professor ; " I can see, then, that you know all about my former difficulties. No, she is not dead, but I have reason to believe that she will not oppose my marriage."

"That is very accommodating of her," remarked one of the company.

"In fact," said the Professor, "I hope that she will now be induced to aid me in getting a wife. She and I never took to each other very much ; but now I hope all that may be ended, and when I marry she will come and stay with me."

"What a happy family ! " exclaimed some wag.

"Yes, indeed ; and I hope you will come to my wedding, all of you. I won't mention names, but here is to my little bride ! " and the Professor waved his glass in the air.

"Here's to his little bride ! " roared the roisterers, with shouts of laughter. "Here's her health. Sie soll leben—Hoch ! " And so the fun waxed still more fast and furious, while each young fellow followed the Professor's example, and drank a toast to the girl of his heart.

While all this festivity had been going on at the Grüner Mann, a very different scene had been enacted elsewhere. Young Fritz von Hartmann, with a solemn face and a reserved manner, had, after the experiment, consulted and adjusted some mathematical instruments ; after which, with a few peremptory words to the janitor, he had walked out into the street and wended his way slowly in the direction of the house of the Professor. As he walked he saw Von Althaus, the professor of anatomy, in front of him, and, quickening his pace, he overtook him.

"I say, Von Althaus," he exclaimed, tapping him on the sleeve, " you were asking me for some information the other day concerning the middle coat of the cerebral arteries. Now I find——"

"Donnerwetter ! " shouted Von Althaus, who was a peppery old fellow. "What the deuce do you mean by your impertinence ! I'll have you up before the Academical Senate for this, sir "; with which threat he turned on his heel and hurried away. Von Hartmann was much surprised at this reception. " It's on account of this failure of my experiment," he said to himself, and continued moodily on his way.

Fresh surprises were in store for him, however. He was hurrying along when he was overtaken by two students. These youths, instead of raising their caps or showing any other sign of respect, gave a wild whoop of delight the instant that they saw him, and rushing at him seized him by each arm and commenced dragging him along with them.

" Gott in Himmel ! " roared Von Hartmann. " What is the meaning of this unparalleled insult ? Where are you taking me ? "

" To crack a bottle of wine with us," said the two students. " Come along ! That is an invitation which you have never refused."

" I never heard of such insolence in my life ! " cried Von Hartmann. " Let go my arms ! I shall certainly have you rusticated for this. Let me go, I say ! " and he kicked furiously at his captors.

" Oh, if you choose to turn ill-tempered, you may go where you like," the students said, releasing him. " We can do very well without you."

" I know you. I'll pay you out" said Von Hartmann furiously, and continued in the direction which he imagined to be his own home, much incensed at the two episodes which had occurred to him on the way.

Now, Madame von Baumgarten, who was looking out of the window and wondering why her husband was late for dinner, was considerably astonished to see the young student come stalking down the road. As already remarked, she had a great antipathy to him, and if ever he ventured into the house it was on sufferance, and under the protection of the Professor. Still more astonished was she, therefore, when she beheld him undo the wicket-gate and stride up the garden path with the air of one who is master of the situation. She could hardly believe her eyes, and hastened to the door with all her maternal instincts up in arms. From the upper windows the fair Elise had also observed this daring move upon the part of her lover, and her heart beat quick with mingled pride and consternation.

"Good day, sir," Madame Baumgarten remarked to the intruder, as she stood in gloomy majesty in the open doorway.

"A very fine day indeed, Martha," returned the other. "Now, don't stand there like a statue of Juno, but bustle about and get the dinner ready, for I am wellnigh starved."

"Martha! Dinner!" ejaculated the lady, falling back in astonishment.

"Yes, dinner, Martha, dinner!" howled Von Hartmann, who was becoming irritable. "Is there anything wonderful in that request when a man has been out all day? I'll wait in the dining-room. Anything will do. Schinken, and sausage, and prunes—any little thing that happens to be about. There you are, standing staring again. Woman, will you or will you not stir your legs?"

This last address, delivered with a perfect shriek of rage, had the effect of sending good Madame Baumgarten flying along the passage and through the kitchen, where she locked herself up in the scullery and went into violent hysterics. In the meantime Von Hartmann strode into the room and threw himself down upon the sofa in the worst of tempers.

"Elise!" he shouted. "Confound the girl! Elise!"

Thus roughly summoned, the young lady came timidly downstairs and into the presence of her lover. "Dearest!" she cried, throwing her arms round him, "I know this is all done for my sake! It is a *ruse* in order to see me."

Von Hartmann's indignation at this fresh attack upon him was so great that he became speechless for a minute from rage, and could only glare and shake his fists, while he struggled in her embrace. When he at last regained his utterance, he indulged in such a bellow of passion that the young lady dropped back, petrified with fear, into an arm-chair.

"Never have I passed such a day in my life," Von Hartmann cried, stamping upon the floor. "My experiment has failed. Von Althaus has insulted me. Two students have dragged me along the public road. My wife nearly faints when I ask her for dinner, and my daughter flies at me and hugs me like a grizzly bear."

"You are ill, dear," the young lady cried. "Your mind is wandering. You have not even kissed me once."

"No, and I don't intend to either," Von Hartmann said with decision. "You ought to be ashamed of yourself. Why don't you go and fetch my slippers, and help your mother to dish the dinner?"

"And is it for this," Elise cried, burying her face in her handkerchief—"is it for this that I have loved you passionately for upwards of ten months? Is it for this that I have braved my mother's wrath? Oh, you have broken my heart; I am sure you have!" and she sobbed hysterically.

"I can't stand much more of this," roared Von Hartmann furiously. "What the deuce does the girl mean? What did I do ten months ago which inspired you with such a particular affection for me? If you are really so very fond, you would do better to run away down and find the Schinken and some bread, instead of talking all this nonsense."

"Oh, my darling!" cried the unhappy maiden, throwing herself into the arms of what she imagined to be her lover, "you do but joke in order to frighten your little Elise."

Now it chanced that at the moment of this unexpected embrace Von Hartmann was still leaning back against the end of the sofa, which, like much German furniture, was in a somewhat rickety condition. It also chanced that beneath this end of the sofa there stood a tank full of water in which the physiologist was conducting certain experiments upon the ova of fish, and which he kept in his drawing-room in order to ensure an equable temperature. The additional weight of the maiden combined with the impetus with which she hurled herself upon him, caused the precarious piece of furniture to give way, and the body of the unfortunate student was hurled backwards into the tank, in which his head and shoulders were firmly wedged, while his lower extremities flapped helplessly about in the air. This was the last straw. Extricating himself with some difficulty from his unpleasant position, Von Hartmann gave an inarticulate yell of fury, and dashing out of the room, in spite of the entreaties of Elise, he seized his hat and rushed off into the town, all dripping and dishevelled, with the intention of seeking in some inn the food and comfort which he could not find at home.

As the spirit of Von Baumgarten encased in the body of Von Hartmann strode down the winding pathway which led down to the little town, brooding angrily over his many wrongs, he became aware that an elderly man was approaching him who appeared to be in an advanced state of intoxication. Von Hartmann waited by the side of the road and watched this individual, who came stumbling along, reeling from one side of the road to the other, and singing a student song in a very husky and drunken voice. At first his interest was merely excited by the fact of seeing a man of so venerable an appearance in such a disgraceful condition, but as he approached nearer, he became convinced that he knew the other well, though he could not recall when or where he had met him. This impression became so strong with him, that when the stranger came abreast of him he stepped in front of him and took a good look at his features.

" Well, sonny," said the drunken man, surveying Von Hartmann and swaying about in front of him, " where the Henker have I seen you before ? I know you as well as I know myself. Who the deuce are you ? "

" I am Professor von Baumgarten," said the student. " May I ask who you are ? I am strangely familiar with your features."

" You should never tell lies, young man," said the other. " You're certainly not the Professor, for he is an ugly, snuffy old chap, and you are a big, broad-shouldered young fellow. As to myself, I am Fritz von Hartmann at your service."

" That you certainly are not," exclaimed the body of Von Hartmann. " You might very well be his father. But hullo, sir, are you aware that you are wearing my studs and my watch-chain ? "

" Donnerwetter ! " hiccoughed the other. " If those are not the trousers for which my tailor is about to sue me, may I never taste beer again."

Now as Von Hartmann, overwhelmed by the many strange things which had occurred to him that day, passed his hand over his forehead and cast his eyes downwards, he chanced to catch the reflection of his own face in a pool which the rain had left upon the road. To his utter astonishment he perceived that his face was that of a youth, that his dress was that of a fashionable young student, and that in every way he was the antithesis of the grave and scholarly figure in which his mind was wont to dwell. In an instant his active brain ran over the series of events which had occurred and sprang to the conclusion. He fairly reeled under the blow.

" Himmel ! " he cried, " I see it all. Our souls are in the wrong bodies. I am you and you are I. My theory is proved—but at what an expense ! Is the most scholarly mind in Europe to go about with this frivolous exterior ? Oh, the labours of a lifetime are ruined ! " and he smote his breast in his despair.

" I say," remarked the real Von Hartmann from the body of the Professor, " I quite see the force of your remarks, but don't go knocking my body about like that.

You received it in excellent condition, but I perceive that you have wet it and bruised it, and spilled snuff over my ruffled shirt-front."

" It matters little," the other said moodily. " Such as we are so must we stay. My theory is triumphantly proved, but the cost is terrible."

" If I thought so," said the spirit of the student, " it would be hard indeed. What could I do with these stiff old limbs, and how could I woo Elise and persuade her that I was not her father ? No, thank Heaven, in spite of the beer which has upset me more than ever it could upset my real self, I can see a way out of it."

" How ? " gasped the Professor.

" Why, by repeating the experiment. Liberate our souls once more, and the chances are that they will find their way back into their respective bodies."

No drowning man could clutch more eagerly at a straw than did Von Baumgarten's spirit at this suggestion. In feverish haste he dragged his own frame to the side of the road and threw it into a mesmeric trance ; he then extracted the crystal ball from the pocket, and managed to bring himself into the same condition.

Some students and peasants who chanced to pass during the next hour were much astonished to see the worthy Professor of Physiology and his favourite student both sitting upon a very muddy bank and both completely insensible. Before the hour was up quite a crowd had assembled, and they were discussing the advisability of sending for an ambulance to convey the pair to hospital, when the learned savant opened his eyes and gazed vacantly around him. For an instant he seemed to forget how he had come there, but next moment he astonished his audience by waving his skinny arms above his head and crying out in a voice of rapture, " Gott sei gedankt ! I am myself again. I feel I am ! " Nor was the amazement lessened when the student, springing to his feet, burst into the same cry, and the two performed a sort of *pas de joie* in the middle of the road.

For some time after that people had some suspicion of the sanity of both the actors in this strange episode. When the Professor published his experiences in the *Medicalschrift* as he had promised, he was met by an intimation, even from his colleagues, that he would do well to have his mind cared for, and that another such publication would certainly consign him to a madhouse. The student also found by experience that it was wisest to be silent about the matter.

When the worthy lecturer returned home that night he did not receive the cordial welcome which he might have looked for after his strange adventures. On the contrary, he was roundly upbraided by both his female relatives for smelling of drink and tobacco, and also for being absent while a young scapegrace invaded the house and insulted its occupants. It was long before the domestic atmosphere of the lecturer's house resumed its normal quiet, and longer still before the genial face of Von Hartmann was seen beneath its roof. Perseverance, however, conquers every obstacle, and the student eventually succeeded in pacifying the enraged ladies and in establishing himself upon the old footing. He has now no longer any cause to fear the enmity of Madame, for he is Hauptmann von Hartmann of the Emperor's own Uhlans, and his loving wife Elise had already presented him with two little Uhlans as a visible sign and token of her affection.

42. *Cyprian Overbeck Wells*

A LITERARY MOSAIC

FROM my boyhood I have had an intense and overwhelming conviction that my real vocation lay in the direction of literature. I have, however, had a most unaccountable difficulty in getting any responsible person to share my views. It is true that private friends have sometimes, after listening to my effusions,

gone the length of remarking, " Really, Smith, that's
not half bad ! " or, " You take my advice, old boy, and
send that to some magazine ! " but I have never on these
occasions had the moral courage to inform my adviser
that the article in question had been sent to well-nigh
every publisher in London, and had come back again
with a rapidity and precision which spoke well for the
efficiency of our postal arrangements.

Had my manuscripts been paper boomerangs they
could not have returned with greater accuracy to their
'unhappy despatcher. Oh, the vileness and utter degra-
dation of the moment when the stale little cylinder of
closely written pages, which seemed so fresh and full
of promise a few days ago, is handed in by a remorseless
postman ! And what moral depravity shines through
the editor's ridiculous plea of " want of space ! " But
the subject is a painful one, and a digression from the
plain statement of facts which I originally contemplated.

From the age of seventeen to that of three-and-twenty
I was a literary volcano in a constant state of eruption.
Poems and tales, articles and reviews, nothing came amiss
to my pen. From the great sea-serpent to the nebular
hypothesis, I was ready to write on anything or everything,
and I can safely say that I seldom handled a subject without throwing new lights upon it. Poetry and romance,
however, had always the greatest attractions for me. How
I have wept over the pathos of my heroines, and laughed
at the comicalities of my buffoons ! Alas ! I could find
no one to join me in my appreciation, and solitary admiration for one's self, however genuine, becomes satiating
after a time. My father remonstrated with me too on the
score of expense and loss of time, so that I was finally
compelled to relinquish my dreams of literary inde-
pendence and to become a clerk in a wholesale mercantile
firm connected with the West African trade.

Even when condemned to the prosaic duties which
fell to my lot in the office, I continued faithful to my first
love. I have introduced pieces of word-painting into

the most commonplace business letters which have, I
am told, considerably astonished the recipients. My
refined sarcasm has made defaulting creditors writhe and
wince. Occasionally, like the great Silas Wegg, I would
drop into poetry, and so raise the whole tone of the
correspondence. Thus what could be more elegant than
my rendering of the firm's instructions to the captain of
one of their vessels. It ran in this way :—

> " From England, Captain, you must steer a
> Course directly to Madeira,
> Land the casks of salted beef,
> Then away to Teneriffe.
> Pray be careful, cool, and wary
> With the merchants of Canary.
> When you leave them make the most
> Of the trade-winds to the coast.
> Down it you shall sail as far
> As the land of Calabar,
> And from there you'll onward go
> To Bonny and Fernando Po "——

and so on for four pages. The captain, instead of
treasuring up this little gem, called at the office next
day, and demanded with quite unnecessary warmth
what the thing meant, and I was compelled to translate
it all back into prose. On this, as on other similar
occasions, my employer took me severely to task—for
he was, you see, a man entirely devoid of all pretensions
to literary taste !

All this, however, is a mere preamble, and leads up
to the fact that after ten years or so of drudgery I inherited
a legacy which, though small, was sufficient to satisfy
my simple wants. Finding myself independent, I rented
a quiet house removed from the uproar and bustle of
London, and there I settled down with the intention of
producing some great work which should single me out
from the family of the Smiths, and render my name
immortal. To this end I laid in several quires of foolscap,
a box of quill pens, and a sixpenny bottle of ink, and
having given my housekeeper injunctions to deny me

to all visitors, I proceeded to look round for a suitable subject.

I was looking round for some weeks. At the end of that time I found that I had by constant nibbling devoured a large number of the quills, and had spread the ink out to such advantage, what with blots, spills, and abortive commencements, that there appeared to be some everywhere except in the bottle. As to the story itself, however, the facility of my youth had deserted me completely, and my mind remained a complete blank ; nor could I, do what I would, excite my sterile imagination to conjure up a single incident or character.

In this strait I determined to devote my leisure to running rapidly through the works of the leading English novelists, from Daniel Defoe to the present day, in the hope of stimulating my latent ideas and of getting a good grasp of the general tendency of literature. For some time past I had avoided opening any work of fiction because one of the greatest faults of my youth had been that I invariably and unconsciously mimicked the style of the last author whom I had happened to read. Now, however, I made up my mind to seek safety in a multitude, and by consulting *all* the English classics to avoid the danger of imitating any one too closely. I had just accomplished the task of reading through the majority of the standard novels at the time when my narrative commences.

It was, then, about twenty minutes to ten on the night of the fourth of June, eighteen hundred and eighty-six, that, after disposing of a pint of beer and a Welsh rarebit for my supper, I seated myself in my arm-chair, cocked my feet upon a stool, and lit my pipe, as was my custom. Both my pulse and my temperature were, as far as I know, normal at the time. I would give the state of the barometer, but that unlucky instrument had experienced an unprecedented fall of forty-two inches—from a nail to the ground—and was not in a reliable condition. We live in a scientific age, and I flatter myself that I move with the times.

Whilst in that comfortable lethargic condition which accompanies both digestion and poisoning by nicotine, I suddenly became aware of the extraordinary fact that my little drawing-room had elongated into a great *salon*, and that my humble table had increased in proportion. Round this colossal mahogany were seated a great number of people who were talking earnestly together, and the surface in front of them was strewn with books and pamphlets. I could not help observing that these persons were dressed in a most extraordinary mixture of costumes, for those at the end nearest to me wore peruke wigs, swords, and all the fashions of two centuries back ; those about the centre had tight knee-breeches, high cravats, and heavy bunches of seals ; while among those at the far side the majority were dressed in the most modern style, and among them I saw, to my surprise, several eminent men of letters whom I had the honour of knowing. There were two or three women in the company. I should have risen to my feet to greet these unexpected guests, but all power of motion appeared to have deserted me, and I could only lie still and listen to their conversation, which I soon perceived to be all about myself.

" Egad ! " exclaimed a rough, weather-beaten man, who was smoking a long churchwarden pipe at my end of the table, " my heart softens for him. Why, gossips, we've been in the same straits ourselves. Gadzooks, never did mother feel more concern for her eldest born than I when Rory Random went out to make his own way in the world."

" Right, Tobias, right ! " cried another man, seated at my very elbow. " By my troth, I lost more flesh over poor Robin on his island, than had I the sweating sickness twice told. The tale was well-nigh done when in swaggers my Lord of Rochester—a merry gallant, and one whose word in matters literary might make or mar. ' How now, Defoe,' quoth he, ' hast a tale on hand ? ' ' Even so, your lordship,' I returned. ' A right merry one, I trust,' quoth he. 'Discourse unto me concerning thy heroine, a comely lass, Dan, or I mistake.' 'Nay,' I replied, 'there is no heroine in the matter.' 'Split not your phrases,' quoth he; 'thou weighest every word like a scald attorney. Speak to me of thy principal female character, be she heroine or no.' 'My lord,' I answered, 'there is no female character.' 'Then out upon thyself and thy book too!' he cried. 'Thou hadst best burn it!'—and so out in great dudgeon, whilst I fell to mourning over my poor romance, which was thus, as it were, sentenced to death before its birth. Yet there are a thousand now who have heard of Robin and his man Friday, to one who has heard of my Lord of Rochester."

"Very true, Defoe," said a genial-looking man in a red waistcoat, who was sitting at the modern end of the table. "But all this won't help our good friend Smith in making a start at his story, which, I believe, was the reason why we assembled."

"The Dickens it is!" stammered a little man beside him, and everybody laughed, especially the genial man, who cried out, "Charley Lamb, Charley Lamb, you'll never alter. You would make a pun if you were hanged for it."

"That would be a case of haltering," returned the other, on which everybody laughed again.

By this time I had begun to dimly realize in my confused brain the enormous honour which had been done me. The greatest masters of fiction in every age of English letters had apparently made a rendezvous beneath my roof, in order to assist me in my difficulties. There were many faces at the table whom I was unable to identify; but when I looked hard at others I often found them to be very familiar to me, whether from paintings or from mere description. Thus between the first two speakers, who had betrayed themselves as Defoe and Smollett, there sat a dark, saturnine, corpulent old man, with harsh prominent features, who I was sure could

503

be none other than the famous author of Gulliver. There were several others of whom I was not so sure, sitting at the other side of the table, but I conjecture that both Fielding and Richardson were among them, and I could swear to the lantern-jaws and cadaverous visage of Lawrence Sterne. Higher up I could see among the crowd the high forehead of Sir Walter Scott, the masculine features of George Eliott, and the flattened nose of Thackeray ; while amongst the living I recognised James Payn, Walter Besant, the lady known as " Ouida," Robert Louis Stevenson, and several of lesser note. Never before, probably, had such an assemblage of choice spirits gathered under one roof.

" Well," said Sir Walter Scott, speaking with a very pronounced accent, " ye ken the auld proverb, sirs, ' Ower mony cooks,' or as the Border minstrel sang—

> ' Black Johnstone wi' his troopers ten
> Might mak' the heart turn cauld,
> But Johnstone when he's a' alane
> Is waur ten thoosand fauld.'

The Johnstones were one of the Redesdale families, second cousins of the Armstrongs, and connected by marriage to——"

" Perhaps, Sir Walter," interrupted Thackeray, " you would take the responsibility off our hands by yourself dictating the commencement of a story to this young literary aspirant."

" Na, na ! " cried Sir Walter ; " I'll do my share, but there's Chairlie over there as full o' wut as a Radical's full o' treason. He's the laddie to give a cheery opening to it."

Dickens was shaking his head, and apparently about to refuse the honour, when a voice from among the moderns—I could not see who it was for the crowd—said :

" Suppose we begin at the end of the table and work round, anyone contributing a little as the fancy seizes him ? "

" Agreed ! agreed ! " cried the whole company ; and every eye was turned on Defoe, who seemed very uneasy, and filled his pipe from a great tobacco-box in front of him.

" Nay, gossips," he said, " there are others more worthy——"

But he was interrupted by loud cries of " No ! no ! " from the whole table ; and Smollett shouted out, " Stand to it, Dan—stand to it ! You and I and the Dean here will make three short tacks just to fetch her out of harbour, and then she may drift where she pleases." Thus encouraged, Defoe cleared his throat, and began in this way, talking between the puffs of his pipe :—

" My father was a well-to-do yeoman of Cheshire, named Cyprian Overbeck, but, marrying about the year 1617, he assumed the name of his wife's family, which was Wells ; and thus I, their eldest son, was named Cyprian Overbeck Wells. The farm was a very fertile one, and contained some of the best grazing land in those parts, so that my father was enabled to lay by money to the extent of a thousand crowns, which he laid out in an adventure to the Indies with such surprising success that in less than three years it had increased fourfold. Thus encouraged, he bought a part share of the trader, and, fitting her out once more with such commodities as were most in demand (viz. old muskets, hangars and axes, besides glasses, needles, and the like), he placed me on board as supercargo to look after his interests, and dispatched us upon our voyage.

" We had a fair wind as far as Cape de Verde, and there, getting into the north-west trade-winds, made good progress down the African coast. Beyond sighting a Barbary rover once, whereat our mariners were in sad distress, counting themselves already as little better than slaves, we had good luck until we had come within a hundred leagues of the Cape of Good Hope, when the wind veered round to the southward and blew exceeding hard, while the sea rose to such a height that the end of the mainyard dipped into the water, and I heard the master say that though he had been at sea for five-and-thirty years he had never seen the like of it, and that he had little expectation of riding through it. On this I fell to wringing my hands and bewailing myself, until the mast going by the board with a crash, I thought that the ship had struck, and swooned with terror, falling into the scuppers and lying like one dead, which was the saving of me, as will appear in the sequel. For the mariners, giving up all hope of saving the ship, and being in momentary expectation that she would founder, pushed off in the long-boat, whereby I fear that they met the fate which they hoped to avoid, since I have never from that day heard anything of them. For my own part, on recovering from the swoon into which I had fallen, I found that, by the mercy of Providence, the sea had gone down, and that I was alone in the vessel. At which last discovery I was so terror-struck that I could but stand wringing my hands and bewailing my sad fate, until at last taking heart, I fell to comparing my lot with that of my unhappy camerados, on which I became more cheerful, and descending to the cabin, made a meal off such dainties as were in the captain's locker."

Having got so far, Defoe remarked that he thought he had given them a fair start, and handed over the story to Dean Swift, who, after premising that he feared he would find himself as much at sea as Master Cyprian Overbeck Wells, continued in this way :—

" For two days I drifted about in great distress, fearing that there should be a return of the gale, and keeping an eager look-out for my late companions. Upon the third day, towards evening, I observed to my extreme surprise that the ship was under the influence of a very powerful current, which ran to the north-east with such violence that she was carried, now bows on, now stern on, and occasionally drifting sideways like a crab, at a rate which I cannot compute at less than twelve or fifteen knots an hour. For several weeks I was borne away in this

manner, until one morning, to my inexpressible joy, I
sighted an island upon the starboard quarter. The
current would, however, have carried me past it had I
not made shift, though single-handed, to set the flying-
jib so as to turn her bows, and then clapping on the sprit-
sail, studding-sail, and fore-sail, I clewed up the halliards
upon the port side, and put the wheel down hard
a-star-board, the wind being at the time north-east-
half-east."

At the description of this nautical manœuvre I observed
that Smollett grinned, and a gentleman who was sitting
higher up the table in the uniform of the Royal Navy,
and who I guessed to be Captain Marryat, became very
uneasy and fidgeted in his seat.

" By this means I got clear of the current and was able
to steer within a quarter of a mile of the beach, which
indeed I might have approached still nearer by making
another tack, but being an excellent swimmer, I deemed
it best to leave the vessel, which was almost waterlogged,
and to make the best of my way to the shore.

" I had had my doubts hitherto as to whether this
new-found country was inhabited or no, but· as I
approached nearer to it, being on the summit of a great
wave, I perceived a number of figures on the beach,
engaged apparently in watching me and my vessel. My
joy, however, was considerably lessened when on reaching
the land I found that the figures consisted of a vast concourse of animals of various sorts who were standing
about in groups, and who hurried down to the water's
edge to meet me. I had scarce put my foot upon the
sand before I was surrounded by an eager crowd of deer,
dogs, wild boars, buffaloes, and other creatures, none of
whom showed the least fear either of me or of each other,
but, on the contrary, were animated by a common feeling
of curiosity, as well as, it would appear, by some degree
of disgust."

" A second edition," whispered Lawrence Sterne to
his neighbour ; " Gulliver served up cold."

" Did you speak, sir ? " asked the Dean very sternly, having evidently overheard the remark.

" My words were not addressed to you, sir," answered Sterne, looking rather frightened.

" They were none the less insolent," roared the Dean. " Your reverence would fain make a Sentimental Journey of the narrative, I doubt not, and find pathos in a dead donkey—though, faith, no man can blame thee for mourning over thy own kith and kin."

" Better that than to wallow in all the filth of Yahooland," returned Sterne warmly, and a quarrel would certainly have ensued but for the interposition of the remainder of the company. As it was, the Dean refused indignantly to have any further hand in the story, and Sterne also stood out of it, remarking with a sneer that he was loth to fit a good blade on to a poor handle. Under these circumstances some further unpleasantness might have occurred had not Smollett rapidly taken up the narrative, continuing it in the third person instead of the first :—

" Our hero, being considerably alarmed at this strange reception, lost little time in plunging into the sea again and regaining his vessel, being convinced that the worst which might befall him from the elements would be as nothing compared to the dangers of this mysterious island. It was as well that he took this course, for before nightfall his ship was overhauled and he himself picked up by a British man-of-war, the *Lightning* (74), then returning from the West Indies, where it had formed part of the fleet under the command of Admiral Benbow. Young Wells, being a likely lad enough, well-spoken and high-spirited, was at once entered on the books as officer's servant, in which capacity he both gained great popularity on account of the freedom of his manners, and found an opportunity for indulging in those practical pleasantries for which he had all his life been famous.

" Among the quartermasters of the *Lightning* there was one named Jedediah Anchorstock, whose appearance was so remarkable that it quickly attracted the attention of our hero. He was a man of about fifty, dark with exposure to the weather, and so tall that as he came along the 'tween decks he had to bend himself nearly double. The most striking peculiarity of this individual was, however, that in his boyhood some evil-minded person had tattooed eyes all over his countenance with such marvellous skill that it was difficult at a short distance to pick out his real ones among so many counterfeits. On this strange personage Master Cyprian determined to exercise his talents for mischief, the more so as he learned that he was extremely superstitious, and also that he had left behind him in Portsmouth a strong-minded spouse of whom he stood in mortal terror. With this object he secured one of the sheep which were kept on board for the officer's table, and pouring a can of rumbo down its throat, reduced it to a state of utter intoxication. He then conveyed it to Anchorstock's berth, and with the assistance of some other imps, as mischievous as himself, dressed it up in a high nightcap and gown, and covered it over with the bedclothes.

" When the quartermaster came down from his watch our hero met him at the door of his berth with an agitated face. ' Mr. Anchorstock,' said he, ' can it be that your wife is on board ? ' ' Wife ! ' roared the astonished sailor. ' Ye white-faced swab, what d'ye mean ? ' ' If she's not here in the ship it must be her ghost,' said Cyprian, shaking his head gloomily. ' In the ship ! How in thunder could she get into the ship ? Why, master, I believe as how you're weak in the upper works, d'ye see ? to as much as think o' such a thing. My Poll is moored head and starn, behind the point at Portsmouth, more'n two thousand mile away.' ' Upon my word,' said our hero, very earnestly, ' I saw a female look out of your cabin not five minutes ago.' ' Ay, ay, Mr. Anchorstock,' joined in several of the conspirators. ' We all saw her—a spanking-looking craft with a dead-light mounted on one side.' ' Sure enough,' said Anchorstock, staggered by this accumulation of evidence, ' my Polly's starboard eye was doused for ever by long Sue Williams of the Hard. But if so be as she be there I must see her, be she ghost or quick ' ; with which the honest sailor, in much perturbation and trembling in every limb, began to shuffle forward into the cabin, holding the light well in front of him. It chanced, however, that the unhappy sheep, which was quietly engaged in sleeping off the effects of its unusual potations, was awakened by the noise of his approach, and finding herself in such an unusual position, sprang out of bed and rushed furiously for the door, bleating wildly, and rolling about like a brig in a tornado, partly from intoxication and partly from the nightdress which impeded her movements. As Anchorstock saw this extraordinary apparition bearing down upon him, he uttered a yell and fell flat upon his face, convinced that he had to do with a supernatural visitor, the more so as the confederates heightened the effect by a chorus of most ghastly groans and cries. The joke had nearly gone beyond what was originally intended, for the quartermaster lay as one dead, and it was only with the greatest difficulty that he could be brought to his senses. To the end of the voyage he stoutly asserted that he had seen the distant Mrs. Anchorstock, remarking with many oaths that though he was too woundily scared to take much note of the features, there was no mistaking the strong smell of rum which was characteristic of his better half.

" It chanced shortly after this to be the king's birthday, an event which was signalised aboard the *Lightning* by the death of the commander under singular circumstances. This officer, who was a real fair-weather Jack, hardly knowing the ship's keel from her ensign, had obtained his position through parliamentary interest, and used it with such tyranny and cruelty that he was universally execrated. So unpopular was he that when a plot was entered into by the whole crew to punish his misdeeds with death, he had not a single friend among six hundred souls to warn him of his danger. It was the custom on board the king's ships that upon his birthday the entire ship's company should be drawn up upon deck, and that at a signal they should discharge their muskets into the air in honour of his Majesty. On this occasion word had been secretly passed round for every man to slip a slug into his firelock, instead of the blank cartridge provided. On the boatswain blowing his whistle the men mustered upon deck and formed line, whilst the captain, standing well in front of them, delivered a few words to them. 'When I give the word,' he concluded, ' you shall discharge your pieces, and by thunder, if any man is a second before or a second after his fellows I shall trice him up to the weather rigging!' With these words he roared 'Fire!' on which every man levelled his musket straight at his head and pulled the trigger. So accurate was the aim and so short the distance, that more than five hundred bullets struck him simultaneously, blowing away his head and a large portion of his body. There were so many concerned in this matter, and it was so hopeless to trace it to any individual, that the officers were unable to punish anyone for the affair—the more readily as the captain's haughty ways and heartless conduct had made him quite as hateful to them as to the men whom he commanded.

" By his pleasantries and the natural charm of his manners our hero so far won the good wishes of the ship's company that they parted with infinite regret upon their arrival in England. Filial duty, however, urged him to return home and report himself to his father, with which object he posted from Portsmouth to London, intending to proceed thence to Shropshire. As it chanced, however, one of the horses sprained his off foreleg while passing through Chichester, and as no change could be obtained, Cyprian found himself compelled to put up at the Crown and Bull for the night.

" Ods bodikins ! " continued Smollett, laughing, " I never could pass a comfortable hostel without stopping

511

and so, with your permission, I'll e'en stop here, and whoever wills may lead friend Cyprian to his further adventures. Do you, Sir Walter, give us a touch of the Wizard of the North."

With these words Smollett produced a pipe, and filling it at Defoe's tobacco-pot, waited patiently for the continuation of the story.

" If I must, I must," remarked the illustrious Scotchman, taking a pinch of snuff ; " but I must beg leave to put Mr. Wells back a few hundred years, for of all things I love the true mediæval smack. To proceed then :—

" Our hero being anxious to continue his journey, and learning that it would be some time before any conveyance would be ready, determined to push on alone mounted on his gallant grey steed. Travelling was particularly dangerous at that time, for besides the usual perils which beset wayfarers, the southern parts of England were in a lawless and disturbed state which bordered on insurrection. The young man, however, having loosened his sword in his sheath, so as to be ready for every eventuality, galloped cheerily upon his way, guiding himself to the best of his ability by the light of the rising moon.

" He had not gone far before he realised that the cautions which had been impressed upon him by the landlord, and which he had been inclined to look upon as self-interested advice, were only too well justified. At a spot where the road was particularly rough, and ran across some marshland, he perceived a short distance from him a dark shadow, which his practised eye detected at once as a body of crouching men. Reining up his horse within a few yards of the ambuscade, he wrapped his cloak round his bridle-arm and summoned the party to stand forth.

" ' What ho, my masters ! ' he cried. ' Are beds so scarce, then, that ye must hamper the high road of the king with your bodies ? Now, by St. Ursula of Alpuxerra, there be those who might think that birds who fly o' nights were after higher game than the moorhen or the woodcock ! '

" ' Blades and targets, comrades ! ' exclaimed a tall powerful man, springing into the centre of the road with several companions, and standing in front of the frightened horse. ' Who is this swashbuckler who summons his Majesty's lieges from their repose ? A very soldado, o' truth. Hark ye, sir, or my lord, or thy grace, or whatsoever title your honour's honour may be pleased to approve, thou must curb thy tongue play, or by the seven witches of Gambleside thou may find thyself in but a sorry plight.'

" ' I prythee, then, that thou wilt expound to me who and what ye are,' quoth our hero, ' and whether your purpose be such as an honest man may approve of. As to your threats, they turn from my mind as your caitiffly weapons would shiver upon my hauberk from Milan.'

" ' Nay, Allen,' interrupted one of the party, addressing him who seemed to be their leader ; ' this is a lad of mettle, and such a one as our honest Jack longs for. But we lure not hawks with empty hands. Look ye, sir, there is game afoot which it may need such bold hunters as thyself to follow. Come with us and take a firkin of canary, and we will find better work for that glaive of thine than getting its owner into broil and bloodshed ; for, by my troth ! Milan or no Milan, if my curtel axe do but ring against that morion of thine it will be an ill day for thy father's son.'

" For a moment our hero hesitated as to whether it would best become his knightly traditions to hurl himself against his enemies, or whether it might not be better to obey their requests. Prudence, mingled with a large share of curiosity, eventually carried the day, and dismounting from his horse, he intimated that he was ready to follow his captors.

" ' Spoken like a man ! ' cried he whom they addressed as Allen. ' Jack Cade will be right glad of such a recruit. Blood and carrion ! but thou hast the thews of a young ox; and I swear, by the haft of my sword, that it might have gone ill with some of us hadst thou not listened to reason!'

"'Nay, not so, good Allen—not so,' squeaked a very small man, who had remained in the background while there was any prospect of a fray, but who now came pushing to the front. 'Hadst thou been alone it might indeed have been so, perchance, but an expert swordsman can disarm at pleasure such a one as this young knight. Well I remember in the Palatinate how I clove to the chine even such another—the Baron von Slogstaff. He struck at me, look ye, so; but I, with buckler and blade, did, as one might say, deflect it; and then, countering in carte, I returned in tierce, and so—St. Agnes save us! who comes here?'

"The apparition which frightened the loquacious little man was sufficiently strange to cause a qualm even in the bosom of the knight. Through the darkness there loomed a figure which appeared to be of gigantic size, and a hoarse voice, issuing apparently some distance above the heads of the party, broke roughly on the silence of the night.

"'Now out upon thee, Thomas Allen, and foul be thy fate if thou hast abandoned thy post without good and sufficient cause. By St. Anselm of the Holy Grove, thou hadst best have never been born than rouse my spleen this night. Wherefore is it that you and your men are trailing over the moor like a flock of geese when Michaelmas is near?'

"'Good captain,' said Allen, doffing his bonnet, an example followed by others of the band, 'we have captured a goodly youth who was pricking it along the London road. Methought that some word of thanks were meet reward for such service, rather than taunt or threat.'

"'Nay, take it not to heart, bold Allen,' exclaimed their leader, who was none other than the great Jack Cade himself. 'Thou knowest of old that my temper is somewhat choleric, and my tongue not greased with that unguent which oils the mouths of the lip-serving lords of the land. And you,' he continued, turning suddenly upon our hero, ' are you ready to join the great cause which will make England what it was when the learned Alfred reigned in the ' land ? Zounds, man, speak out, and pick not your phrases.'

" ' I am ready to do aught which may become a knight and a gentleman,' said the soldier stoutly.

" ' Taxes shall be swept away ! ' cried Cade excitedly —' the impost and the anpost—the tithe and the hundred-tax. The poor man's salt-box and flour-bin shall be as free as the nobleman's cellar. Ha ! what sayest thou ? '

" ' It is but just,' said our hero.

" ' Ay, but they give us such justice as the falcon gives the leveret ! ' roared the orator. ' Down with them, I say—down with every man of them ! Noble and judge, priest and king, down with them all ! '

" ' Nay,' said Sir Overbeck Wells, drawing himself up to his full height, and laying his hand upon the hilt of his sword, ' there I cannot follow thee, but must rather defy thee as traitor and fainéant, seeing that thou art no true man, but one who would usurp the rights of our master the king, whom may the Virgin protect ! '

" At these bold words, and the defiance which they conveyed, the rebels seemed for a moment utterly bewildered ; but, encouraged by the hoarse shout of their leader they brandished their weapons and prepared to fall upon the knight, who placed himself in a posture for defence and awaited their attack.

" There now ! " cried Sir Walter, rubbing his hands and chuckling, " I've put the chiel in a pretty warm corner, and we'll see which of you moderns can take him oot o't. Ne'er a word more will ye get frae me to help him one way or the other."

" You try your hand, James," cried several voices, and the author in question had got so far as to make an allusion to a solitary horseman who was approaching, when he was interrupted by a tall gentleman a little farther down with a slight stutter and a very nervous manner.

" Excuse me," he said, " but I fancy that I may be able to do something here. Some of my humble productions have been said to excel Sir Walter at his best, and I was undoubtedly stronger all round. I could picture modern society as well as ancient ; and as to my plays, why Shakespeare never came near *The Lady of Lyons* for popularity. There is this little thing——" (Here he rummaged among a great pile of papers in front of him). " Ah ! that's a report of mine, when I was in India ! Here it is. No, this is one of my speeches in the House, and this is my criticism on Tennyson. Didn't I warm him up ? I can't find what I wanted, but of course you have read them all—*Rienzi*, and *Harold*, and *The Last of the Barons*. Every schoolboy knows them by heart, as poor Macaulay would have said. Allow me to give you a sample :—

" In spite of the gallant knight's valiant resistance the combat was too unequal to be sustained. His sword was broken by a slash from a brown bill, and he was borne to the ground. He expected immediate death, but such did not seem to be the intention of the ruffians who had captured him. He was placed upon the back of his own charger and borne, bound hand and foot, over the trackless moor, in the fastnesses of which the rebels secreted themselves.

" In the depths of these wilds there stood a stone building which had once been a farmhouse, but having been for some reason abandoned had fallen into ruin, and had now become the headquarters of Cade and his men. A large cow-house near the farm had been utilised as sleeping quarters, and some rough attempts had been made to shield the principal room of the main building from the weather by stopping up the gaping apertures in the walls. In this apartment was spread out a rough meal for the returning rebels, and our hero was thrown, still bound, into an empty outhouse, there to await his fate."

Sir Walter had been listening with the greatest impatience to Bulwer Lytton's narrative, but when it had reached this point he broke in impatiently.

" We want a touch of your own style, man," he said. "The animal - magnetico - electro - hysterical - biological - mysterious sort of story is all your own, but at present you are just a poor copy of myself, and nothing more."

There was a murmur of assent from the company, and Defoe remarked, " Truly, Master Lytton, there is a plaguey resemblance in the style, which may indeed be but a chance, and yet methinks it is sufficiently marked to warrant such words as our friend hath used."

" Perhaps you will think that this is an imitation also," said Lytton bitterly, and leaning back in his chair with a morose countenance, he continued the narrative in this way :—

" Our unfortunate hero had hardly stretched himself upon the straw with which his dungeon was littered, when a secret door opened in the wall and a venerable old man swept majestically into the apartment. The prisoner gazed upon him with astonishment not unmixed with awe, for on his broad brow was printed the seal of much knowledge—such knowledge as it is not granted to a son of man to know. He was clad in a long white robe, crossed and chequered with mystic devices in the Arabic character, while a high scarlet tiara marked with the square and circle enhanced his venerable appearance. ' My son,' he said, turning his piercing and yet dreamy gaze upon Sir Overbeck, ' all things lead to nothing, and nothing is the foundation of all things. Cosmos is impenetrable. Why then should we exist ? '

" Astounded at this weighty query, and at the philo- sophic demeanour of his visitor, our hero made shift to bid him welcome and to demand his name and quality. As the old man answered him his voice rose and fell in musical cadences, like the sighing of the east wind, while an ethereal and aromatic vapour pervaded the apartment.

" ' I am the eternal non-ego,' he answered. ' I am the concentrated negative—the everlasting essence of nothing. You see in me that which existed before the beginning of matter many years before the commencement of time. I am the algebraic x which represents the infinite divisibility of a finite particle.'

" Sir Overbeck felt a shudder as though an ice-cold hand had been placed upon his brow. ' What is your message ? ' he whispered, falling prostrate before his mysterious visitor.

" ' To tell you that the eternities beget chaos, and that the immensities are at the mercy of the divine ananke. Infinitude crouches before a personality. The mercurial essence is the prime mover in spirituality, and the thinker is powerless before the pulsating inanity. The cosmical procession is terminated only by the unknowable and unpronounceable '——

" May I ask, Mr. Smollett, what you find to laugh at ? "

" Gadzooks, master," cried Smollett, who had been sniggering for some time back. " It seems to me that there is little danger of anyone venturing to dispute that style with you."

" It's all your own," murmured Sir Walter.

" And very pretty, too," quoth Lawrence Sterne, with a malignant grin. " Pray, sir, what language do you call it ? "

Lytton was so enraged at these remarks, and at the favour with which they appeared to be received, that he endeavoured to stutter out some reply, and then, losing control of himself completely, picked up all his loose papers and strode out of the room, dropping pamphlets and speeches at every step. This incident amused the company so much that they laughed for several minutes without cessation. Gradually the sound of their laughter sounded more and more harshly in my ears, the lights on the table grew dim and the company more misty, until they and their symposium vanished away altogether. I was sitting before the embers of what had been a roaring fire, but was now little more than a heap of grey ashes, and the merry laughter of the august company had changed to the recriminations of my wife, who was shaking me violently by the shoulder and exhorting me to choose some more seasonable spot for my slumbers. So ended the wondrous adventures of Master Cyprian Overbeck Wells, but I still live in the hopes that in some future dream the great masters may themselves finish that which they have begun.

43. *Playing with Fire*

I CANNOT pretend to say what occurred on the 14th of April last at No. 17, Badderly Gardens. Put down in black and white, my surmise might seem too crude, too grotesque, for serious consideration. And yet that something did occur, and that it was of a nature which will leave its mark upon every one of us for the rest of our lives, is as certain as the unanimous testimony of five witnesses can make it. I will not enter into any argument or speculation. I will only give a plain statement, which will be submitted to John Moir, Harvey Deacon, and Mrs. Delamere, and withheld from publication . unless they are prepared to corroborate every detail. I cannot obtain the sanction of Paul Le Duc, for he appears to have left the country.

It was John Moir (the well-known senior partner of Moir, Moir, and Sanderson) who had originally turned our attention to occult subjects. He had, like many very hard and practical men of business, a mystic side to his nature, which had led him to the examination, and eventually to the acceptance, of those elusive phenomena which are grouped together with much that is foolish, and much that is fraudulent, under the common heading of spiritualism. His researches, which had begun with an open mind, ended unhappily in dogma, and he became as positive and fanatical as any other bigot. He represented in our little group the body of men who have turned these singular phenomena into a new religion.

Mrs. Delamere, our medium, was his sister, the wife of Delamere, the rising sculptor. Our experience had shown us that to work on these subjects without a medium was as futile as for an astronomer to make observations without a telescope. On the other hand, the introduction of a paid medium was hateful to all of us. Was it not obvious that he or she would feel bound to return some result for money received, and that the temptation to fraud would be an overpowering one? No phenomena could be relied upon which were produced at a guinea an hour. But, fortunately, Moir had discovered that his sister was mediumistic—in other words, that she was a battery of that animal magnetic force which is the only form of energy which is subtle enough to be acted upon from the spiritual plane as well as from our own material one. Of course, when I say this, I do not mean to beg the question; but I am simply indicating the theories upon which we were ourselves, rightly or wrongly, explaining what we saw. The lady came, not altogether with the approval of her husband, and though she never gave indications of any very great psychic force, we were able, at least, to obtain those usual phenomena of message-tilting which are at the same time so puerile and so inexplicable. Every Sunday evening we met in Harvey Deacon's studio at Badderly Gardens, the next house to the corner of Merton Park Road.

Harvey Deacon's imaginative work in art would prepare anyone to find that he was an ardent lover of everything which was *outré* and sensational. A certain picturesqueness in the study of the occult had been the quality which had originally attracted him to it, but his attention was speedily arrested by some of those phenomena to which I have referred, and he was coming rapidly to the conclusion that what he had looked upon as an amusing romance and an after-dinner entertainment was really a very formidable reality. He is a man with a remarkably clear and logical brain—a true descendant of his ancestor, the well-known Scotch professor—and he represented in our small circle the critical element, the man who has no prejudices, is prepared to follow facts as far as he can see them, and refuses to theorise in advance of his data. His caution annoyed Moir as much as the latter's robust faith amused Deacon, but each in his own way was equally keen upon the matter.

And I ? What am I to say that I represented ? I was not the devotee. I was not the scientific critic. Perhaps the best that I can claim for myself is that I was the dilettante man about town, anxious to be in the swim of every fresh movement, thankful for any new sensation which would take me out of myself and open up fresh possibilities of existence. I am not an enthusiast myself, but I like the company of those who are. Moir's talk, which made me feel as if we had a private pass-key through the door of death, filled me with a vague contentment. The soothing atmosphere of the séance with the darkened lights was delightful to me. In a word, the thing amused me, and so I was there.

It was, as I have said, upon the 14th of April last that the very singular event which I am about to put upon record took place. I was the first of the men to arrive at the studio, but Mrs. Delamere was already there, having had afternoon tea with Mrs. Harvey Deacon. The two ladies and Deacon himself were standing in front of an unfinished picture of his upon the easel. I am not an expert in art, and I have never professed to understand what Harvey Deacon meant by his pictures ; but I could see in this instance that it was all very clever and imaginative, fairies and animals and allegorical figures of all sorts. The ladies were loud in their praises, and indeed the colour effect was a remarkable one.

" What do you think of it, Markham ? " he asked.

" Well, it's above me," said I. " These beasts—what are they ? "

" Mythical monsters, imaginary creatures, heraldic emblems—a sort of weird, bizarre procession of them."

" With a white horse in front ! "

" It's not a horse," said he, rather testily—which was surprising, for he was a very good-humoured fellow as a rule, and hardly ever took himself seriously.

" What is it, then ? "

" Can't you see the horn in front ? It's a unicorn. I told you they were heraldic beasts. Can't you recognize one ? "

" Very sorry, Deacon," said I, for he really seemed to be annoyed.

He laughed at his own irritation.

" Excuse me, Markham ! " said he ; " the fact is that I have had an awful job over the beast. All day I have been painting him in and painting him out, and trying to imagine what a real live, ramping unicorn would look like. At last I got him, as I hoped ; so when you failed to recognise it, it took me on the raw."

" Why, of course it's a unicorn," said I, for he was evidently depressed at my obtuseness. " I can see the horn quite plainly, but I never saw a unicorn except beside the Royal Arms, and so I never thought of the creature. And these others are griffins and cockatrices, and dragons of sorts ? "

" Yes, I had no difficulty with them. It was the unicorn which bothered me. However, there's an end of it until to-morrow." He turned the picture round upon the easel, and we all chatted about other subjects.

Moir was late that evening, and when he did arrive he brought with him, rather to our surprise, a small, stout Frenchman, whom he introduced as Monsieur Paul Le Duc. I say to our surprise, for we held a theory that any intrusion into our spiritual circle deranged the conditions, and introduced an element of suspicion. We knew that we could trust each other, but all our results were vitiated by the presence of an outsider. However, Moir soon reconciled us to the innovation. Monsieur Paul Le Duc was a famous student of occultism, a seer, a medium, and a mystic. He was travelling in England with a letter of introduction to Moir from the President of the Parisian brothers of the Rosy Cross. What more natural than that he should bring him to our little séance, or that we should feel honoured by his presence?

He was, as I have said, a small, stout man, undistinguished in appearance, with a broad, smooth, clean-shaven face, remarkable only for a pair of large, brown, velvety eyes, staring vaguely out in front of him. He was well dressed, with the manners of a gentleman, and his curious little turns of English speech set the ladies smiling. Mrs. Deacon had a prejudice against our researches and left the room, upon which we lowered the lights, as was our custom, and drew up our chairs to the square mahogany table which stood in the centre of the studio. The light was subdued, but sufficient to allow us to see each other quite plainly. I remember that I could even observe the curious, podgy little square-topped hands which the Frenchman laid upon the table.

" What a fun ! " said he. " It is many years since I have sat in this fashion, and it is to me amusing. Madame is medium. Does madame make the trance ? "

" Well, hardly that," said Mrs. Delamere. " But I am always conscious of extreme sleepiness."

" It is the first stage. Then you encourage it, and there comes the trance. When the trance comes, then out jumps your little spirit and in jumps another little spirit, and so you have direct talking or writing. You leave your machine to be worked by another. *Hein?* But what have unicorns to do with it ? "

Harvey Deacon started in his chair. The Frenchman was moving his head slowly round and staring into the shadows which draped the walls.

" What a fun ! " said he. " Always unicorns. Who has been thinking so hard upon a subject so bizarre ? "

" This is wonderful ! " cried Deacon. " I have been trying to paint one all day. But how could you know it ? "

" You have been thinking of them in this room."

" Certainly."

" But thoughts are things, my friend. When you imagine a thing you make a thing. You did not know it, *hein?* But I can see your unicorns because it is not only with my eye that I can see."

" Do you mean to say that I create a thing which has never existed by merely thinking of it ? "

" But certainly. It is the fact which lies under all other facts. That is why an evil thought is also a danger."

" They are, I suppose, upon the astral plane ? " said Moir.

" Ah, well, these are but words, my friends. They are there—somewhere—everywhere—I cannot tell myself. I see them. I could touch them."

" You could not make *us* see them."

" It is to materialise them. Hold ! It is an experiment. But the power is wanting. Let us see what power we have, and then arrange what we shall do. May I place you as I wish ? "

" You evidently know a great deal more about it than we do," said Harvey Deacon ; " I wish that you would take complete control."

" It may be that the conditions are not good. But we will try what we can do. Madame will sit where she is, I next, and this gentleman beside me. Meester Moir will sit next to madame, because it is well to have blacks and blondes in turn. So ! And now with your permission I will turn the lights all out."

" What is the advantage of the dark ? " I asked.

" Because the force with which we deal is a vibration of ether and so also is light. We have the wires all for ourselves now—*hein?* You will not be frightened in the darkness, madame ? What a fun is such a séance ! "

At first the darkness appeared to be absolutely pitchy, but in a few minutes our eyes became so far accustomed to it that we could just make out each other's presence—very dimly and vaguely, it is true. I could see nothing else in the room—only the black loom of the motionless figures. We were all taking the matter much more seriously than we had ever done before.

"You will place your hands in front. It is hopeless that we touch, since we are so few round so large a table. You will compose yourself, madame, and if sleep should come to you you will not fight against it. And now we sit in silence and we expect—*hein?*"

So we sat in silence and expected, staring out into the blackness in front of us. A clock ticked in the passage. A dog barked intermittently far away. Once or twice a cab rattled past in the street, and the gleam of its lamps through the chink in the curtains was a cheerful break in that gloomy vigil. I felt those physical symptoms with which previous séances had made me familiar—the coldness of the feet, the tingling in the hands, the glow of the palms, the feeling of a cold wind upon the back. Strange little shooting pains came in my forearms, especially as it seemed to me in my left one, which was nearest to our visitor—due no doubt to disturbance of the vascular system, but worthy of some attention all the same. At the same time I was conscious of a strained feeling of expectancy which was almost painful. From the rigid, absolute silence of my companions I gathered that their nerves were as tense as my own.

And then suddenly a sound came out of the darkness—a low, sibilant sound, the quick, thin breathing of a woman. Quicker and thinner yet it came, as between clenched teeth, to end in a loud gasp with a dull rustle of cloth.

"What's that? Is all right?" someone asked in the darkness.

"Yes, all is right," said the Frenchman. "It is madame. She is in her trance. Now, gentlemen, if you will wait quiet you will see something, I think, which will interest you much."

Still the ticking in the hall. Still the breathing, deeper and fuller now, from the medium. Still the occasional flash, more welcome than ever, of the passing lights of the hansoms. What a gap we were bridging, the half-raised veil of the eternal on the one side and the cabs of London on the other. The table was throbbing with a mighty pulse. It swayed steadily, rhythmically, with an easy swooping, scooping motion under our fingers. Sharp little raps and cracks came from its substance, file-firing, volley-firing, the sounds of a fagot burning briskly on a frosty night.

"There is much power," said the Frenchman. "See it on the table ! "

I had thought it was some delusion of my own, but all could see it now. There was a greenish-yellow phosphorescent light—or I should say a luminous vapour rather than a light—which lay over the surface of the table. It rolled and wreathed and undulated in dim glimmering folds, turning and swirling like clouds of smoke. I could see the white, square-ended hands of the French medium in this baleful light.

"What a fun ! " he cried. "It is splendid ! "

"Shall we call the alphabet ? " asked Moir.

"But no—for we can do much better," said our visitor. "It is but a clumsy thing to tilt the table for every letter of the alphabet, and with such a medium as madame we should do better than that."

"Yes, you will do better," said a voice.

"Who was that ? Who spoke ? Was that you, Markham ? "

"No, I did not speak."

"It was madame who spoke."

"But it was not her voice."

"Is that you, Mrs. Delamere ? "

"It is not the medium, but it is the power which uses the organs of the medium," said the strange, deep voice.

" Where is Mrs. Delamere ? It will not hurt her, I trust."

" The medium is happy in another plane of existence. She has taken my place, as I have taken hers."

" Who are you ? "

" It cannot matter to you who I am. I am one who has lived as you are living, and who has died as you will die."

We heard the creak and grate of a cab pulling up next door. There was an argument about the fare, and the cabman grumbled hoarsely down the street. The green-yellow cloud still swirled faintly over the table, dull elsewhere, but glowing into a dim luminosity in the direction of the medium. It seemed to be piling itself up in front of her. A sense of fear and cold struck into my heart. It seemed to me that lightly and flippantly we had approached the most real and august of sacraments, that communion with the dead of which the fathers of the Church had spoken.

" Don't you think we are going too far ? Should we not break up this séance ? " I cried.

But the others were all earnest to see the end of it. They laughed at my scruples.

" All the powers are made for use," said Harvey Deacon. " If we *can* do this, we *should* do this. Every new departure of knowledge has been called unlawful in its inception. It is right and proper that we should inquire into the nature of death."

" It is right and proper," said the voice.

" There, what more could you ask ? " cried Moir, who was much excited. " Let us have a test. Will you give us a test that you are really there ? "

" What test do you demand ? "

" Well, now—I have some coins in my pocket. Will you tell me how many ? "

" We come back in the hope of teaching and of elevating, and not to guess childish riddles."

" Ha, ha, Meester Moir, you catch it that time," cried

527

the Frenchman. " But surely this is very good sense what the Control is saying."

" It is a religion, not a game," said the cold, hard voice.

" Exactly—the very view I take of it," cried Moir. " I am sure I am very sorry if I have asked a foolish question. You will not tell me who you are ? "

" What does it matter ? "

" Have you been a spirit long ? "

" Yes."

" How long ? "

" We cannot reckon time as you do. Our conditions are different."

" Are you happy ? "

" Yes."

" You would not wish to come back to life ? "

" No—certainly not."

" Are you busy ? "

" We could not be happy if we were not busy."

" What do you do ? "

" I have said that the conditions are entirely different."

" Can you give us no idea of your work ? "

" We labour for our own improvement and for the advancement of others."

" Do you like coming here to-night ? "

" I am glad to come if I can do any good by coming."

" Then to do good is your object ? "

" It is the object of all life on every plane."

" You see, Markham, that should answer your scruples."

It did, for my doubts had passed and only interest remained.

" Have you pain in your life ? " I asked.

" No ; pain is a thing of the body."

" Have you mental pain ? "

" Yes ; one may always be sad or anxious."

" Do you meet the friends whom you have known on earth ? "

" Some of them."

" Why only some of them ? "

" Only those who are sympathetic."

" Do husbands meet wives ? "

" Those who have truly loved."

" And the others ? "

" They are nothing to each other."

" There must be a spiritual connection ? "

" Of course."

" Is what we are doing right ? "

" If done in the right spirit."

" What is the wrong spirit ? "

" Curiosity and levity."

" May harm come of that ? "

" Very serious harm."

" What sort of harm ? "

" You may call up forces over which you have no control."

" Evil forces ? "

" Undeveloped forces."

" You say they are dangerous. Dangerous to body or mind ? "

" Sometimes to both."

There was a pause, and the blackness seemed to grow blacker still, while the yellow-green fog swirled and smoked upon the table.

" Any questions you would like to ask, Moir ? " said Harvey Deacon.

" Only this—do you pray in your world ? "

" One should pray in every world."

" Why ? "

" Because it is the acknowledgment of forces outside ourselves."

" What religion do you hold over there ? "

" We differ exactly as you do."

" You have no certain knowledge ? "

" We have only faith."

" These questions of religion," said the Frenchman,

" they are of interest to you serious English people, but they are not so much fun. It seems to me that with this power here we might be able to have some great experience—*hein?* Something of which we could talk."

" But nothing could be more interesting than this," said Moir.

" Well, if you think so, that is very well," the Frenchman answered, peevishly. " For my part, it seems to me that I have heard all this before, and that to-night I should weesh to try some experiment with all this force which is given to us. But if you have other questions, then ask them, and when you are finish we can try something more." .

But the spell was broken. We asked and asked, but the medium sat silent in her chair. Only her deep, regular breathing showed that she was there. The mist still swirled upon the table.

" You have disturbed the harmony. She will not answer."

" But we have learned already all that she can tell— *hein?* For my part I wish to see something that I have never seen before."

" What then ? "

" You will let me try ? "

" What would you do ? "

" I have said to you that thoughts are things. Now I wish to *prove* it to you, and to show you that which is only a thought. Yes, yes, I can do it and you will see. Now I ask you only to sit still and say nothing, and keep ever your hands quiet upon the table."

The room was blacker and more silent than ever. The same feeling of apprehension which had lain heavily upon me at the beginning of the séance was back at my heart once more. The roots of my hair were tingling.

" It is working ! It is working ! " cried the Frenchman, and there was a crack in his voice as he spoke which told me that he also was strung to his tightest.

The luminous fog drifted slowly off the table, and

wavered and flickered across the room. There in the farther and darkest corner it gathered and glowed, hardening down into a shining core—a strange, shifty, luminous, and yet non-illuminating patch of radiance, bright itself, but throwing no rays into the darkness. It had changed from a greenish-yellow to a dusky sullen red. Then round this centre there coiled a dark, smoky substance, thickening, hardening, growing denser and blacker. And then the light went out, smothered in that which had grown round it.

" It has gone."

" Hush—there's something in the room."

We heard it in the corner where the light had been, something which breathed deeply and fidgeted in the darkness.

" What is it ? Le Duc, what have you done ? "

" It is all right. No harm will come." The Frenchman's voice was treble with agitation.

" Good heavens, Moir, there's a large animal in the room. Here it is, close by my chair ! Go away ! Go away ! "

It was Harvey Deacon's voice, and then came the sound of a blow upon some hard object. And then . . . And then . . . how can I tell you what happened then ?

Some huge thing hurtled against us in the darkness, rearing, stamping, smashing, springing, snorting. The table was splintered. We were scattered in every direction. It clattered and scrambled amongst us, rushing with horrible energy from one corner of the room to another. We were all screaming with fear, grovelling upon our hands and knees to get away from it. Something trod upon my left hand, and I felt the bones splinter under the weight.

" A light ! A light ! " someone yelled.

" Moir, you have matches, matches ! "

" No, I have none. Deacon, where are the matches ? For God's sake, the matches ! "

" I can't find them. Here, you Frenchman, stop it ! "

" It is beyond me. Oh, *mon Dieu*, I cannot stop it. The door ! Where is the door ? "

My hand, by good luck, lit upon the handle as I groped about in the darkness. The hard-breathing, snorting, rushing creature tore past me and butted with a fearful crash against the oaken partition. The instant that it had passed I turned the handle, and next moment we were all outside, and the door shut behind us. From within came a horrible crashing and rending and stamping.

" What is it ? In Heaven's name, what is it ? "

" A horse. I saw it when the door opened. But Mrs. Delamere——? "

" We must fetch her out. Come on, Markham ; the longer we wait the less we shall like it."

He flung open the door and we rushed in. She was there on the ground amidst the splinters of her chair. We seized her and dragged her swiftly out, and as we gained the door I looked over my shoulder into the darkness. There were two strange eyes glowing at us, a rattle of hoofs, and I had just time to slam the door when there came a crash upon it which split it from top to bottom.

" It's coming through ! It's coming ! "

" Run, run for your lives ! " cried the Frenchman.

Another crash, and something shot through the riven door. It was a long white spike, gleaming in the lamp-light. For a moment it shone before us, and then with a snap it disappeared again.

" Quick ! Quick ! This way ! " Harvey Deacon shouted. " Carry her in ! Here ! Quick ! "

We had taken refuge in the dining-room, and shut the heavy oak door. We laid the senseless woman upon the sofa, and as we did so, Moir, the hard man of business, drooped and fainted across the hearthrug. Harvey Deacon was as white as a corpse, jerking and twitching like an epileptic. With a crash we heard the studio door fly to pieces, and the snorting and stamping were in the passage, up and down, up and down, shaking the house with their fury. The Frenchman had sunk his face on his hands, and sobbed like a frightened child.

" What shall we do ? " I shook him roughly by the shoulder. " Is a gun any use ? "

" No, no. The power will pass. Then it will end."

" You might have killed us all—you unspeakable fool —with your infernal experiments."

" I did not know. How could I tell that it would be frightened ? It is mad with terror. It was his fault. He struck it."

Harvey Deacon sprang up. " Good heavens ! " he cried.

A terrible scream sounded through the house.

" It's my wife ! Here, I'm going out. If it's the Evil One himself I am going out ! "

He had thrown open the door and rushed out into the passage. At the end of it, at the foot of the stairs, Mrs. Deacon was lying senseless, struck down by the sight which she had seen. But there was nothing else.

With eyes of horror we looked about us, but all was perfectly quiet and still. I approached the black square of the studio door, expecting with every slow step that some atrocious shape would hurl itself out of it. But nothing came, and all was silent inside the room. Peeping and peering, our hearts in our mouths, we came to the very threshold, and stared into the darkness. There was still no sound, but in one direction there was also no darkness. A luminous, glowing cloud, with an incandescent centre, hovered in the corner of the room. Slowly it dimmed and faded, growing thinner and fainter, until at last the same dense, velvety blackness filled the whole studio. And with the last flickering gleam of that baleful light the Frenchman broke into a shout of joy.

" What a fun ! " he cried. " No one is hurt, and only the door broken, and the ladies frightened. But, my friends, we have done what has never been done before."

" And as far as I can help," said Harvey Deacon, " it will certainly never be done again."

And that was what befell on the 14th of April last at No. 17 Badderly Gardens. I began by saying that it would seem too grotesque to dogmatise as to what it was which actually did occur ; but I give my impressions, *our* impressions (since they are corroborated by Harvey Deacon and John Moir), for what they are worth. You may, if it pleases you, imagine that we were the victims of an elaborate and extraordinary hoax. Or you may think with us that we underwent a very real and a very terrible experience. Or perhaps you may know more than we do of such occult matters, and can inform us of some similar occurrence. In this latter case a letter to William Markham, 146M, The Albany, would help to throw a light upon that which is very dark to us.

44. *The Ring of Thoth*

MR. JOHN VANSITTART SMITH, F.R.S., of 147A Gower Street, was a man whose energy of purpose and clearness of thought might have placed him in the very first rank of scientific observers. He was the victim, however, of a universal ambition which prompted him to aim at distinction in many subjects rather than pre-eminence in one. In his early days he had shown an aptitude for zoology and for botany which caused his friends to look upon him as a second Darwin, but when a professorship was almost within his reach he had suddenly discontinued his studies and turned his whole attention to chemistry. Here his researches upon the spectra of the metals had won him his fellowship in the Royal Society ; but again he played the coquette with his subject, and after a year's absence from the laboratory he joined the Oriental Society, and delivered a paper on the Hieroglyphic and Demotic inscriptions of El Kab, thus giving a crowning example both of the versatility and of the inconstancy of his talents.

534

The most fickle of wooers, however, is apt to be caught at last, and so it was with John Vansittart Smith. The more he burrowed his way into Egyptology the more impressed he became by the vast field which it opened to the inquirer, and by the extreme importance of a subject which promised to throw a light upon the first germs of human civilisation and the origin of the greater part of our arts and sciences. So struck was Mr. Smith that he straightway married an Egyptological young lady who had written upon the sixth dynasty, and having thus secured a sound base of operations he set himself to collect materials for a work which should unite the research of Lepsius and the ingenuity of Champollion. The preparation of this *magnum opus* entailed many hurried visits to the magnificent Egyptian collections of the Louvre, upon the last of which, no longer ago than the middle of last October, he became involved in a most strange and noteworthy adventure.

The trains had been slow and the Channel had been rough, so that the student arrived in Paris in a somewhat befogged and feverish condition. On reaching the Hôtel de France, in the Rue Laffitte, he had thrown himself upon a sofa for a couple of hours, but finding that he was unable to sleep, he determined, in spite of his fatigue, to make his way to the Louvre, settle the point which he had come to decide, and take the evening train back to Dieppe. Having come to his conclusion, he donned his greatcoat, for it was a raw rainy day, and made his way across the Boulevard des Italiens and down the Avenue de l'Opéra. Once in the Louvre he was on familiar ground, and he speedily made his way to the collection of papyri which it was his intention to consult.

The warmest admirers of John Vansittart Smith could hardly claim for him that he was a handsome man. His high-beaked nose and prominent chin had something of the same acute and incisive character which distinguished his intellect. He held his head in a birdlike fashion, and birdlike, too, was the pecking motion with which, in conversation, he threw out his objections and retorts. As he stood, with the high collar of his greatcoat raised to his ears, he might have seen from the reflection in the glass-case before him that his appearance was a singular one. Yet it came upon him as a sudden jar when an English voice behind him exclaimed in very audible tones, " What a queer-looking mortal ! "

The student had a large amount of petty vanity in his composition which manifested itself by an ostentatious and overdone disregard of all personal considerations. He straightened his lips and looked rigidly at the roll of papyrus, while his heart filled with bitterness against the whole race of travelling Britons.

" Yes," said another voice, " he really is an extraordinary fellow."

" Do you know," said the first speaker, " one could almost believe that by the continual contemplation of mummies the chap has become half a mummy himself ? "

" He has certainly an Egyptian cast of countenance," said the other.

John Vansittart Smith spun round upon his heel with the intention of shaming his countrymen by a corrosive remark or two. To his surprise and relief, the two young fellows who had been conversing had their shoulders turned towards him, and were gazing at one of the Louvre attendants who was polishing some brass-work at the other side of the room.

" Carter will be waiting for us at the Palais Royal," said one tourist to the other, glancing at his watch, and they clattered away, leaving the student to his labours.

" I wonder what these chatterers call an Egyptian cast of countenance," thought John Vansittart Smith, and he moved his position slightly in order to catch a glimpse of the man's face. He started as his eyes fell upon it. It was indeed the very face with which his studies had made him familiar. The regular statuesque features, broad brow, well-rounded chin, and dusky complexion were the exact counterpart of the innumerable statues, mummy-cases, and pictures which adorned the walls of the apartment. The thing was beyond all coincidence. The man must be an Egyptian. The national angularity of the shoulders and narrowness of the hips were alone sufficient to identify him.

John Vansittart Smith shuffled towards the attendant with some intention of addressing him. He was not light of touch in conversation, and found it difficult to strike the happy mean between the brusqueness of the superior and the geniality of the equal. As he came nearer, the man presented his side face to him, but kept his gaze still bent upon his work. Vansittart Smith, fixing his eyes upon the fellow's skin, was conscious of a sudden impression that there was something inhuman and preternatural about its appearance. Over the temple and cheek-bone it was as glazed and as shiny as varnished parchment. There was no suggestion of pores. One could not fancy a drop of moisture upon that arid surface. From brow to chin, however, it was cross-hatched by a million delicate wrinkles, which shot and interlaced as though Nature in some Maori mood had tried how wild and intricate a pattern she could devise.

" Où est la collection de Memphis ? " asked the student, with the awkward air of a man who is devising· a question merely for the purpose of opening a conversation.

" C'est là," replied the man brusquely, nodding his head at the other side of the room.

" Vous êtes un Egyptien, n'est-ce pas ? " asked the Englishman.

The attendant looked up and turned his strange dark eyes upon his questioner. They were vitreous, with a misty dry shininess, such as Smith had never seen in a human head before. As he gazed into them he saw some strong emotion gather in their depths, which rose and deepened until it broke into a look of something akin both to horror and to hatred.

" Non, monsieur ; je suis français." The man turned

abruptly and bent low over his polishing. The student gazed at him for a moment in astonishment, and then turning to a chair in a retired corner behind one of the doors he proceeded to make notes of his researches among the papyri. His thoughts, however, refused to return into their natural groove. They would run upon the enigmatical attendant with the sphinx-like face and the parchment skin.

"Where have I seen such eyes?" said Vansittart Smith to himself. "There is something saurian about them, something reptilian. There's the membrana nictitans of the snakes," he mused, bethinking himself of his zoological studies. "It gives a shiny effect. But there was something more here. There was a sense of power, of wisdom—so I read them—and of weariness, utter weariness, and ineffable despair. It may be all imagination, but I never had so strong an impression. By Jove, I must have another look at them!" He rose and paced round the Egyptian rooms, but the man who had excited his curiosity had disappeared.

The student sat down again in his quiet corner, and continued to work at his notes. He had gained the information which he required from the papyri, and it only remained to write it down while it was still fresh in his memory. For a time his pencil travelled rapidly over the paper, but soon the lines became less level, the words more blurred, and finally the pencil tinkled down upon the floor, and the head of the student dropped heavily forward upon his chest. Tired out by his journey, he slept so soundly in his lonely post behind the door that neither the clanking civil guard, nor the footsteps of sightseers, nor even the loud hoarse bell which gives the signal for closing, were sufficient to arouse him.

Twilight deepened into darkness, the bustle from the Rue de Rivoli waxed and then waned, distant Notre Dame clanged out the hour of midnight, and still the dark and lonely figure sat silently in the shadow. It was not until close upon one in the morning that, with a

sudden gasp and an intaking of the breath, Vansittart
Smith returned to consciousness. For a moment it
flashed upon him that he had dropped asleep in his study-
chair at home. The moon was shining fitfully through
the unshuttered window, however, and as his eye ran
along the lines of mummies and the endless array of
polished cases, he remembered clearly where he was and
how he came there. The student was not a nervous man.
He possessed that love of a novel situation which is
peculiar to his race. Stretching out his cramped limbs,
he looked at his watch, and burst into a chuckle as he
observed the hour. The episode would make an admirable anecdote to be introduced into his next paper as a
relief to the graver and heavier speculations. He was a
little cold, but wide awake and much refreshed. It was
no wonder that the guardians had overlooked him, for
the door threw its heavy black shadow right across him.

The complete silence was impressive. Neither outside
nor inside was there a creak or a murmur. He was alone
with the dead men of a dead civilisation. What though
the outer city reeked of the garish nineteenth century !
In all this chamber there was scarce an article, from the
shrivelled ear of wheat to the pigment-box of the painter,
which had not held its own against four thousand years.
Here was the flotsam and jetsam washed up by the great
ocean of time from that far-off empire. From stately
Thebes, from lordly Luxor, from the great temples of
Heliopolis, from a hundred rifled tombs, these relics had
been brought. The student glanced round at the long-
silent figures who flickered vaguely up through the gloom,
at the busy toilers who were now so restful, and he fell
into a reverent and thoughtful mood. An unwonted
sense of his own youth and insignificance came over him.
Leaning back in his chair, he gazed dreamily down the
long vista of rooms, all silvery with the moonshine, which
extend through the whole wing of the widespread building. His eyes fell upon the yellow glare of a distant
lamp.

John Vansittart Smith sat up on his chair with his nerves all on edge. The light was advancing slowly towards him, pausing from time to time, and then coming jerkily onwards. The bearer moved noiselessly. In the utter silence there was no suspicion of the pat of a footfall. An idea of robbers entered the Englishman's head. He snuggled up farther into the corner. The light was two rooms off. Now it was in the next chamber, and still there was no sound. With something approaching to a thrill of fear the student observed a face, floating in the air as it were, behind the flare of the lamp. The figure was wrapped in shadow, but the light fell full upon the strange, eager face. There was no mistaking the metallic, glistening eyes and the cadaverous skin. It was the attendant with whom he had conversed.

Vansittart Smith's first impulse was to come forward and address him. A few words of explanation would set the matter clear, and lead doubtless to his being conducted to some side-door from which he might make his way to his hotel. As the man entered the chamber, however, there was something so stealthy in his movements, and so furtive in his expression, that the Englishman altered his intention. This was clearly no ordinary official walking the rounds. The fellow wore felt-soled slippers, stepped with a rising chest, and glanced quickly from left to right, while his hurried, gasping breathing thrilled the flame of his lamp. Vansittart Smith crouched silently back into the corner and watched him keenly, convinced that his errand was one of secret and probably sinister import.

There was no hesitation in the other's movements. He stepped lightly and swiftly across to one of the great cases, and, drawing a key from his pocket, he unlocked it. From the upper shelf he pulled down a mummy, which he bore away with him, and laid it with much care and solicitude upon the ground. By it he placed his lamp, and then squatting down beside it in Eastern fashion he began with long, quivering fingers to undo the cerecloths

540

and bandages which girt it round. As the crackling rolls of linen peeled off one after the other, a strong aromatic odour filled the chamber, and fragments of scented wood and of spices pattered down upon the marble floor.

It was clear to John Vansittart Smith that this mummy had never been unswathed before. The operation interested him keenly. He thrilled all over with curiosity, and his bird-like head protruded farther and farther from behind the door. When, however, the last roll had been removed from the four-thousand-year-old head, it was all that he could do to stifle an outcry of amazement. First, a cascade of long, black, glossy tresses poured over the workman's hands and arms. A second turn of the bandage revealed a low, white forehead, with a pair of delicately arched eyebrows. A third uncovered a pair of bright, deeply fringed eyes, and a straight, well-cut nose, while a fourth and last showed a sweet, full, sensitive mouth, and a beautifully curved chin. The whole face was one of extraordinary loveliness, save for the one blemish that in the centre of the forehead there was a single irregular, coffee-coloured splotch. It was a triumph of the embalmer's art. Vansittart Smith's eyes grew larger and larger as he gazed upon it, and he chirruped in his throat with satisfaction.

Its effect upon the Egyptologist was as nothing, however, compared with that which it produced upon the strange attendant. He threw his hands up into the air, burst into a harsh clatter of words, and then, hurling himself down upon the ground beside the mummy, he threw his arms round her, and kissed her repeatedly upon the lips and brow. " Ma petite ! " he groaned in French. " Ma pauvre petite ! " His voice broke with emotion, and his innumerable wrinkles quivered and writhed, but the student observed in the lamp-light that his shining eyes were still dry and tearless as two beads of steel. For some minutes he lay, with a twitching face, crooning and moaning over the beautiful head. Then he broke into a sudden smile, said some words in an unknown tongue, and sprang to his feet with the vigorous air of one who has braced himself for an effort.

In the centre of the room there was a large, circular case which contained, as the student had frequently remarked, a magnificent collection of early Egyptian rings and precious stones. To this the attendant strode, and, unlocking it, threw it open. On the ledge at the side he placed his lamp, and beside it a small, earthenware jar which he had drawn from his pocket. He then took a handful of rings from the case, and with a most serious and anxious face he proceeded to smear each in turn with some liquid substance from the earthen pot, holding them to the light as he did so. He was clearly disappointed with the first lot, for he threw them petulantly back into the case and drew out some more. One of these, a massive ring with a large crystal set in it, he seized and eagerly tested with the contents of the jar. Instantly he uttered a cry of joy, and threw out his arms in a wild gesture which upset the pot and set the liquid streaming across the floor to the very feet of the Englishman. The attendant drew a red handkerchief from his bosom, and, mopping up the mess, he followed it into the corner, where in a moment he found himself face to face with his observer.

" Excuse me," said John Vansittart Smith, with all imaginable politeness ; " I have been unfortunate enough to fall asleep behind this door."

" And you have been watching me ? " the other asked in English, with a most venomous look on his corpse-like face.

The student was a man of veracity. " I confess," said he, " that I have noticed your movements, and that they have aroused my curiosity and interest in the highest degree."

The man drew a long, flamboyant-bladed knife from his bosom. " You have had a very narrow escape," he said ; " had I seen you ten minutes ago, I should have driven this through your heart. As it is, if you touch me or interfere with me in any way you are a dead man."

" I have no wish to interfere with you," the student answered. " My presence here is entirely accidental. All I ask is that you will have the extreme kindness to show me out through some side-door." He spoke with great suavity, for the man was still pressing the tip of his dagger against the palm of his left hand, as though to assure himself of its sharpness, while his face preserved its malignant expression.

" If I thought——" said he. " But no, perhaps it is as well. What is your name ? "

The Englishman gave it.

" Vansittart Smith," the other repeated. " Are you the same Vansittart Smith who gave a paper in London upon El Kab ? I saw a report of it. Your knowledge of the subject is contemptible."

" Sir ! " cried the Egyptologist.

" Yet it is superior to that of many who make even greater pretensions. The whole keystone of our old life in Egypt was not the inscriptions or monuments of which you make so much, but was our hermetic philosophy and mystic knowledge of which you say little or nothing."

" Our old life ! " repeated the scholar, wide-eyed ; and then suddenly, " Good God, look at the mummy's face ! "

The strange man turned and flashed his light upon the dead woman, uttering a long, doleful cry as he did so. The action of the air had already undone all the art of the embalmer. The skin had fallen away, the eyes had sunk inwards, the discoloured lips had writhed away from the yellow teeth, and the brown mark upon the forehead alone showed that it was indeed the same face which had shown such youth and beauty a few short minutes before.

The man flapped his hands together in grief and horror.

Then mastering himself by a strong effort he turned his hard eyes once more upon the Englishman.

" It does not matter," he said, in a shaking voice. " It does not really matter. I came here to-night with the fixed determination to do something. It is now done. All else is as nothing. I have found my quest. The old curse is broken. I can rejoin her. What matter about her inanimate shell so long as her spirit is awaiting me at the other side of the veil ! "

" These are wild words," said Vansittart Smith. He was becoming more and more convinced that he had to do with a madman.

" Time presses, and I must go," continued the other. " The moment is at hand for which I have waited this weary time. But I must show you out first. Come with me."

Taking up the lamp, he turned from the disordered chamber, and led the student swiftly through the long series of the Egyptian, Assyrian, and Persian apartments. At the end of the latter he pushed open a small door let into the wall and descended a winding, stone stair. The Englishman felt the cold, fresh air of the night upon his brow. There was a door opposite him which appeared to communicate with the street. To the right of this another door stood ajar, throwing a spurt of yellow light across the passage. " Come in here ! " said the attendant shortly.

Vansittart Smith hesitated. He had hoped that he had come to the end of his adventure. Yet his curiosity was strong within him. He could not leave the matter unsolved, so he followed his strange companion into the lighted chamber.

It was a small room, such as is devoted to a *concierge*. A wood fire sparkled in the grate. At one side stood a truckle bed, and at the other a coarse, wooden chair, with a round table in the centre, which bore the remains of a meal. As the visitor's eye glanced round he could not but remark with an ever-recurring thrill that all the small details of the room were of the most quaint design and antique workmanship. The candlesticks, the vases upon the chimney-piece, the fire-irons, the ornaments upon the walls, were all such as he had been wont to associate with the remote past. The gnarled, heavy-eyed man sat himself down upon the edge of the bed, and motioned his guest into the chair.

" There may be design in this," he said, still speaking excellent English. " It may be decreed that I should leave some account behind as a warning to all rash mortals who would set their wits up against workings of Nature. I leave it with you. Make such use as you will of it. I speak to you now with my feet upon the threshold of the other world.

" I am, as you surmised, an Egyptian—not one of the down-trodden race of slaves who now inhabit the Delta of the Nile, but a survivor of that fiercer and harder people who tamed the Hebrew, drove the Ethiopian back into the southern deserts, and built those mighty works which have been the envy and the wonder of all after generations. It was in the reign of Tuthmosis, sixteen hundred years before the birth of Christ, that I first saw the light. You shrink away from me. Wait, and you will see that I am more to be pitied than to be feared.

" My name was Sosra. My father had been the chief priest of Osiris in the great temple of Abaris, which stood in those days upon the Bubastic branch of the Nile. I was brought up in the temple and was trained in all those mystic arts which are spoken of in your own Bible. I was an apt pupil. Before I was sixteen I had learned all which the wisest priest could teach me. From that time on I studied Nature's secrets for myself, and shared my knowledge with no man.

" Of all the questions which attracted me there were none over which I laboured so long as over those which concern themselves with the nature of life. I probed deeply into the vital principle. The aim of medicine had been to drive away disease when it appeared. It seemed to me that a method might be devised which should so fortify the body as to prevent weakness or death from ever taking hold of it. It is useless that I should recount my researches. You would scarce comprehend them if I did. They were carried out partly upon animals, partly upon slaves, and partly on myself. Suffice it that their result was to furnish me with a substance which, when injected into the blood, would endow the body with strength to resist the effects of time, of violence, or of disease. It would not indeed confer immortality, but its potency would endure for many thousands of years. I used it upon a cat, and afterwards drugged the creature with the most deadly poisons. That cat is alive in Lower Egypt at the present moment. There was nothing of mystery or magic in the matter. It was simply a chemical discovery, which may well be made again.

"Love of life runs high in the young. It seemed to me that I had broken away from all human care now that I had abolished pain and driven death to such a distance. With a light heart I poured the accursed stuff into my veins. Then I looked round for someone whom I could benefit. There was a young priest of Thoth, Parmes by name, who had won my goodwill by his earnest nature and his devotion to his studies. To him I whispered my secret, and at his request I injected him with my elixir. I should now, I reflected, never be without a companion of the same age as myself.

"After this grand discovery I relaxed my studies to some extent, but Parmes continued his with redoubled energy. Every day I could see him working with his flasks and his distiller in the Temple of Thoth, but he said little to me as to the result of his labours. For my own part, I used to walk through the city and look around me with exultation as I reflected that all this was destined to pass away, and that only I should remain. The people would bow to me as they passed me, for the fame of my knowledge had gone abroad.

" There was war at this time, and the Great King had sent down his soldiers to the eastern boundary to drive away the Hyksos. A Governor, too, was sent to Abaris, that he might hold it for the King. I had heard much of the beauty of the daughter of this Governor, but one day as I walked out with Parmes we met her, borne upon the shoulders of her slaves. I was struck with love as with lightning. My heart went out from me. I could have thrown myself beneath the feet of her bearers. This was my woman. Life without her was impossible. I swore by the head of Horus that she should be mine. I swore it to the Priest of Thoth. He turned away from me with a brow which was as black as midnight.

" There is no need to tell you of our wooing. She came to love me even as I loved her. I learned that Parmes had seen her before I did, and had shown her that he, too, loved her, but I could smile at his passion, for I knew that her heart was mine. The white plague had come upon the city and many were stricken, but I laid my hands upon the sick and nursed them without fear or scathe. She marvelled at my daring. Then I told her my secret, and begged her that she would let me use my art upon her.

" ' Your flower shall then be unwithered, Atma,' I said. ' Other things may pass away, but you and I, and our great love for each other, shall outlive the tomb of King Chefru.'

" But she was full of timid, maidenly objections. Was it right ? ' she asked, ' was it not a thwarting of the will of the gods ? If the great Osiris had wished that our years should be so long, would he not himself have brought it about ? '

" With fond and loving words I overcame her doubts, and yet she hesitated. It was a great question, she said. She would think it over for this one night. In the morning I should know of her resolution. Surely one night was not too much to ask. She wished to pray to Isis for help in her decision.

"With a sinking heart and a sad foreboding of evil I left her with her tirewomen. In the morning, when the early sacrifice was over, I hurried to her house. A frightened slave met me upon the steps. Her mistress was ill, she said, very ill. In a frenzy I broke my way through the attendants, and rushed through hall and corridor to my Atma's chamber. She lay upon her couch, her head high upon the pillow, with a pallid face and a glazed eye. On her forehead there blazed a single angry, purple patch. I knew that hell-mark of old. It was the scar of the white plague, the sign-manual of death.

"Why should I speak of that terrible time? For months I was mad, fevered, delirious, and yet I could not die. Never did an Arab thirst after the sweet wells as I longed after death. Could poison or steel have shortened the thread of my existence, I should soon have rejoined my love in the land with the narrow portal. I tried, but it was of no avail. The accursed influence was too strong upon me. One night as I lay upon my couch, weak and weary, Parmes, the priest of Thoth, came to my chamber. He stood in the circle of the lamp-light, and he looked down upon me with eyes which were bright with a mad joy.

"'Why did you let the maiden die?' he asked; 'why did you not strengthen her as you strengthened me?'

"'I was too late,' I answered. 'But I had forgot. You also loved her. You are my fellow in misfortune. Is it not terrible to think of the centuries which must pass ere we look upon her again? Fools, fools, that we were to take death to be our enemy!'

"'You may say that,' he cried with a wild laugh; 'the words come well from your lips. For me they have no meaning.'

"'What mean you?' I cried, raising myself upon my elbow. 'Surely, friend, this grief has turned your brain.' His face was aflame with joy, and he writhed and shook like one who hath a devil.

" ' Do you know whither I go ? ' he asked.

" ' Nay,' I answered, ' I cannot tell.'

" ' I go to her,' said he. ' She lies embalmed in the farther tomb by the double palm-tree beyond the city wall.'

" ' Why do you go there ? ' I asked.

" ' To die ! ' he shrieked, ' to die ! I am not bound by earthen fetters.'

" ' But the elixir is in your blood,' I cried.

" ' I can defy it,' said he ; ' I have found a stronger principle which will destroy it. It is working in my veins at this moment, and in an hour I shall be a dead man. I shall join her, and you shall remain behind.'

" As I looked upon him I could see that he spoke words of truth. The light in his eye told me that he was indeed beyond the power of the elixir.

" ' You will teach me ! ' I cried.

" ' Never ! ' he answered.

" ' I implore you, by the wisdom of Thoth, by the majesty of Anubis ! '

" ' It is useless,' he said coldly.

" ' Then I will find it out,' I cried.

" ' You cannot,' he answered ; ' it came to me by chance. There is one ingredient which you can never get. Save that which is in the ring of Thoth, none will ever more be made.'

" ' In the ring of Thoth ! ' I repeated, ' where then is the ring of Thoth ? '

" ' That also you shall never know,' he answered. ' You won her love. Who has won in the end ? I leave you to your sordid earth life. My chains are broken. I must go ! ' He turned upon his heel and fled from the chamber. In the morning came the news that the Priest of Thoth was dead.

" My days after that were spent in study. I must find this subtle poison which was strong enough to undo the elixir. From early dawn to midnight I bent over the test-tube and the furnace. Above all, I collected the papyri and the chemical flasks of the Priest of Thoth. Alas! they taught me little. Here and there some hint or stray expression would raise hope in my bosom, but no good ever came of it. Still, month after month, I struggled on. When my heart grew faint I would make my way to the tomb by the palm-trees. There, standing by the dead casket from which the jewel had been rifled, I would feel her sweet presence, and would whisper to her that I would rejoin her if mortal wit could solve the riddle.

" Parmes had said that his discovery was connected with the ring of Thoth. I had some remembrance of the trinket. It was a large and weighty circlet, made, not of gold, but of a rarer and heavier metal brought from the mines of Mount Harbal. Platinum, you call it. The ring had, I remembered, a hollow crystal set in it, in which some few drops of liquid might be stored. Now, the secret of Parmes could not have to do with the metal alone, for there were many rings of that metal in the Temple. Was it not more likely that he had stored his precious poison within the cavity of the crystal ? I had scarce come to this conclusion before, in hunting through his papers, I came upon one which told me that it was indeed so, and that there was still some of the liquid unused.

" But how to find the ring ? It was not upon him when he was stripped for the embalmer. Of that I made sure. Neither was it among his private effects. In vain I searched every room that he had entered, every box and vase and chattel that he had owned. I sifted the very sand of the desert in the places where he had been wont to walk ; but, do what I would, I could come upon no traces of the ring of Thoth. Yet it may be that my labours would have overcome all obstacles had it not been for a new and unlooked-for misfortune.

" A great war had been waged against the Hyksos, and the Captains of the Great King had been cut off in the desert, with all their bowmen and horsemen. The shepherd tribes were upon us like the locusts in a dry year. From the wilderness of Shur to the great, bitter lake there was blood by day and fire by night. Abaris was the bulwark of Egypt, but we could not keep the savages back. The city fell. The Governor and the soldiers were put to the sword, and I, with many more, was led away into captivity.

" For years and years I tended cattle in the great plains by the Euphrates. My master died, and his son grew old, but I was still as far from death as ever. At last I escaped upon a swift camel, and made my way back to Egypt. The Hyksos had settled in the land which they had conquered, and their own King ruled over the country. Abaris had been torn down, the city had been burned, and of the great Temple there was nothing left save an unsightly mound. Everywhere the tombs had been rifled and the monuments destroyed. Of my Atma's grave no sign was left. It was buried in the sands of the desert, and the palm-trees which marked the spot had long disappeared. The papers of Parmes and the remains of the Temple of Thoth were either destroyed or scattered far and wide over the deserts of Syria. All search after them was vain.

" From that time I gave up all hope of ever finding the ring or discovering the subtle drug. I set myself to live as patiently as might be until the effect of the elixir should wear away. How can you understand how terrible a thing time is, you who have experience only of the narrow course which lies between the cradle and the grave ! I know it to my cost, I who have floated down the whole stream of history. I was old when Ilium fell. I was very old when Herodotus came to Memphis. I was bowed down with years when the new gospel came upon earth. Yet you see me much as other men are, with the cursed elixir still sweetening my blood, and guarding me against that which I would court. Now, at last, at last I have come to the end of it !

" I have travelled in all lands and I have dwelt with

all nations. Every tongue is the same to me. I learned them all to help pass the weary time. I need not tell you how slowly they drifted by, the long dawn of modern civilization, the dreary middle years, the dark times of barbarism. They are all behind me now. I have never looked with the eyes of love upon another woman. Atma knows that I have been constant to her.

" It was my custom to read all that the scholars had to say upon Ancient Egypt. I have been in many positions, sometimes affluent, sometimes poor, but I have always found enough to enable me to buy the journals which deal with such matters. Some nine months ago I was in San Francisco, when I read an account of some discoveries made in the neighbourhood of Abaris. My heart leapt into my mouth as I read it. It said that the excavator had busied himself in exploring some tombs recently unearthed. In one there had been found an unopened mummy with an inscription upon the outer case setting forth that it contained the body of the daughter of the Governor of the city in the days of Tuthmosis. It added that on removing the outer case there had been exposed a large platinum ring set with a crystal, which had been laid upon the breast of the embalmed woman. This, then, was where Parmes had hid the ring of Thoth. He might well say that it was safe, for no Egyptian would ever stain his soul by moving even the outer case of a buried friend.

" That very night I set off from San Francisco, and in a few weeks I found myself once more at Abaris, if a few sand-heaps and crumbling walls may retain the name of the great city. I hurried to the Frenchmen who were digging there and asked them for the ring. They replied that both the ring and the mummy had been sent to the Boulak Museum at Cairo. To Boulak I went, but only to be told that Mariette Bey had claimed them and had shipped them to the Louvre. I followed them, and there, at last, in the Egyptian chamber, I came, after close upon four thousand years, upon the remains of my Atma, and upon the ring for which I had sought so long.

"But how was I to lay hands upon them? How was I to have them for my very own? It chanced that the office of attendant was vacant. I went to the Director. I convinced him that I knew much about Egypt. In my eagerness I said too much. He remarked that a Professor's chair would suit me better than a seat in the conciergerie. I knew more, he said, than he did. It was only by blundering, and letting him think that he had over-estimated my knowledge, that I prevailed upon him to let me move the few effects which I have retained into this chamber. It is my first and my last night here.

"Such is my story, Mr. Vansittart Smith. I need not say more to a man of your perception. By a strange chance you have this night looked upon the face of the woman whom I loved in those far-off days. There were many rings with crystals in the case, and I had to test for the platinum to be sure of the one which I wanted. A glance at the crystal has shown me that the liquid is indeed within it, and that I shall at last be able to shake off that accursed health which has been worse to me than the foulest disease. I have nothing more to say to you. I have unburdened myself. You may tell my story or you may withhold it at your pleasure. The choice rests with you. I owe you some amends, for you have had a narrow escape of your life this night. I was a desperate man, and not to be baulked in my purpose. Had I seen you before the thing was done, I might have put it beyond your power to oppose me or to raise an alarm. This is the door. It leads into the Rue de Rivoli. Good night."

The Englishman glanced back. For a moment the lean figure of Sosra the Egyptian stood framed in the narrow doorway. The next the door had slammed, and the heavy rasping of a bolt broke on the silent night.

It was on the second day after his return to London

that Mr. John Vansittart Smith saw the following concise narrative in the Paris correspondence of *The Times* :—

" *Curious Occurrence in the Louvre.*—Yesterday morning a strange discovery was made in the principal Eastern chamber. The *ouvriers* who are employed to clean out the rooms in the morning found one of the attendants lying dead upon the floor with his arms round one of the mummies. So close was his embrace that it was only with the utmost difficulty that they were separated. One of the cases containing valuable rings had been opened and rifled. The authorities are of opinion that the man was bearing away the mummy with some idea of selling it to a private collector, but that he was struck down in the very act by long-standing disease of the heart. It is said that he was a man of uncertain age and eccentric habits, without any living relations to mourn over his dramatic and untimely end."

45. *The Los Amigos Fiasco*

I USED to be the leading practitioner of Los Amigos. Of course, every one has heard of the great electrical generating gear there. The town is widespread, and there are dozens of little townlets and villages all around, which receive their supply from the same centre, so that the works are on a very large scale. The Los Amigos folk say that they are the largest upon earth, but then we claim that for everything in Los Amigos except the gaol and the death-rate. Those are said to be the smallest.

Now, with so fine an electrical supply, it seemed to be a sinful waste of hemp that the Los Amigos criminals should perish in the old-fashioned manner. And then came the news of the electrocutions in the East, and how the results had not after all been so instantaneous as had been hoped. The Western engineers raised their eyebrows when they read of the puny shocks by which these men had perished, and they vowed in Los Amigos that when an irreclaimable came their way he should be dealt handsomely by, and have the run of all the big dynamos.

There should be no reserve, said the engineers, but he should have all that they had got. And what the result of that would be none could predict, save that it must be absolutely blasting and deadly. Never before had a man been so charged with electricity as they would charge him. He was to be smitten by the essence of ten thunderbolts. Some prophesied combustion, and some disintegration and disappearance. They were waiting eagerly to settle the question by actual demonstration, and it was just at that moment that Duncan Warner came that way.

Warner had been wanted by the law, and by nobody else, for many years. Desperado, murderer, train robber and road agent, he was a man beyond the pale of human pity. He had deserved a dozen deaths, and the Los Amigos folk grudged him so gaudy a one as that. He seemed to feel himself to be unworthy of it, for he made two frenzied attempts at escape. He was a powerful, muscular man, with a lion head, tangled black locks, and a sweeping beard which covered his broad chest. When he was tried, there was no finer head in all the crowded court. It's no new thing to find the best face looking from the dock. But his good looks could not balance his bad deeds. His advocate did all he knew, but the cards lay against him, and Duncan Warner was handed over to the mercy of the big Los Amigos dynamos.

I was there at the committee meeting when the matter was discussed. The town council had chosen four experts to look after the arrangements. Three of them were admirable. There was Joseph M'Connor, the very man who had designed the dynamos, and there was Joshua Westmacott, the chairman of the Los Amigos Electrical Supply Company, Limited. Then there was myself as the chief medical man, and lastly an old German of the name of Peter Stulpnagel. The Germans were a strong body at Los Amigos, and they all voted for their man. That was how he got on the committee.

It was said that he had been a wonderful electrician at home, and he was eternally working with wires and insulators and Leyden jars ; but, as he never seemed to get any further, or to have any results worth publishing, he came at last to be regarded as a harmless crank, who had made science his hobby. We three practical men smiled when we heard that he had been elected as our colleague, and at the meeting we fixed it all up very nicely among ourselves without much thought of the old fellow who sat with his ears scooped forward in his hands, for he was a trifle hard of hearing, taking no more part in the proceedings than the gentlemen of the press who scribbled their notes on the back benches.

We did not take long to settle it all. In New York a strength of some two thousand volts had been used, and death had not been instantaneous. Evidently their shock had been too weak. Los Amigos should not fall into that error. The charge should be six times greater, and therefore, of course, it would be six times more effective. Nothing could possibly be more logical. The whole concentrated force of the great dynamos should be employed on Duncan Warner.

So we three settled it, and had already risen to break up the meeting, when our silent companion opened his mouth for the first time.

" Gentlemen," said he, " you appear to me to show an extraordinary ignorance upon the subject of electricity. You have not mastered the first principles of its actions upon a human being."

The committee was about to break into an angry reply to this brusque comment, but the chairman of the Electrical Company tapped his forehead to claim its indulgence for the crankiness of the speaker.

" Pray tell us, sir," said he, with an ironical smile, " what is there in our conclusions with which you find fault ? "

" With your assumption that a large dose of electricity will merely increase the effect of a small dose. Do you not think it possible that it might have an entirely different result? Do you know anything, by actual experiment, of the effect of such powerful shocks?"

"We know it by analogy," said the chairman pompously. "All drugs increase their effect when they increase their dose; for example—for example——"

"Whisky," said Joseph M'Connor.

"Quite so. Whisky. You see it there."

Peter Stulpnagel smiled and shook his head.

"Your argument is not very good," said he. "When I used to take whisky, I used to find that one glass would excite me, but that six would send me to sleep, which is just the opposite. Now, suppose that electricity were to act in just the opposite way also, what then?"

We three practical men burst out laughing. We had known that our colleague was queer, but we never had thought that he would be as queer as this.

"What then?" repeated Peter Stulpnagel.

"We'll take our chances," said the chairman.

"Pray consider," said Peter, "that workmen who have touched the wires, and who have received shocks of only a few hundred volts, have died instantly. The fact is well known. And yet when a much greater force was used upon a criminal at New York, the man struggled for some little time. Do you not clearly see that the smaller dose is the more deadly?"

"I think, gentlemen, that this discussion has been carried on quite long enough," said the chairman, rising again. "The point, I take it, has already been decided by the majority of the committee, and Duncan Warner shall be electrocuted on Tuesday by the full strength of the Los Amigos dynamos. Is it not so?"

"I agree," said Joseph M'Connor.

"I agree," said I.

"And I protest," said Peter Stulpnagel.

"Then the motion is carried, and your protest will be duly entered in the minutes," said the chairman, and so the sitting was dissolved.

The attendance at the electrocution was a very small one. We four members of the committee were, of course, present with the executioner, who was to act under their orders. The others were the United States Marshal, the governor of the gaol, the chaplain, and three members of the press. The room was a small, brick chamber, forming an out-house to the Central Electrical station. It had been used as a laundry, and had an oven and copper at one side, but no other furniture save a single chair for the condemned man. A metal plate for his feet was placed in front of it, to which ran a thick, insulated wire. Above, another wire depended from the ceiling, which could be connected with a small, metallic rod projecting from a cap which was to be placed upon his head. When this connection was established Duncan Warner's hour was come.

There was a solemn hush as we waited for the coming of the prisoner. The practical engineers looked a little pale, and fidgeted nervously with the wires. Even the hardened Marshal was ill at ease, for a mere hanging was one thing, and this blasting of flesh and blood a very different one. As to the pressmen, their faces were whiter than the sheets which lay before them. The only man who appeared to feel none of the influence of these preparations was the little German crank, who strolled from one to the other with a smile on his lips and mischief in his eyes. More than once he even went so far as to burst into a shout of laughter, until the chaplain sternly rebuked him for his ill-timed levity.

" How can you so far forget yourself, Mr. Stulpnagel," said he, " as to jest in the presence of death ? "

But the German was quite unabashed.

" If I were in the presence of death I should not jest," said he, " but since I am not I may do what I choose."

This flippant reply was about to draw another and a sterner reproof from the chaplain, when the door was swung open and two warders entered leading Duncan

Warner between them. He glanced round him with a set face, stepped resolutely forward, and seated himself upon the chair.

" Touch her off ! " said he.

It was barbarous to keep him in suspense. The chaplain murmured a few words in his ear, the attendant placed the cap upon his head, and then, while we all held our breath, the wire and the metal were brought in contact.

" Great Scott ! " shouted Duncan Warner.

He had bounded in his chair as the frightful shock crashed through his system. But he was not dead. On the contrary, his eyes gleamed far more brightly than they had done before. There was only one change, but it was a singular one. The black had passed from his hair and beard as the shadow passes from a landscape. They were both as white as snow. And yet there was no other sign of decay. His skin was smooth and plump and lustrous as a child's.

The Marshal looked at the committee with a reproachful eye.

" There seems to be some hitch here, gentlemen," said he.

We three practical men looked at each other.

Peter Stulpnagel smiled pensively.

" I think that another one should do it," said I.

Again the connection was made, and again Duncan Warner sprang in his chair and shouted, but, indeed, were it not that he still remained in the chair none of us would have recognised him. His hair and his beard had shredded off in an instant, and the room looked like a barber's shop on a Saturday night. There he sat, his eyes still shining, his skin radiant with the glow of perfect health, but with a scalp as bald as a Dutch cheese, and a chin without so much as a trace of down. He began to revolve one of his arms, slowly and doubtfully at first, but with more confidence as he went on.

" That jint," said he, " has puzzled half the doctors

559

on the Pacific Slope. It's as good as new, and as limber as a hickory twig."

" You are feeling pretty well ? " asked the old German.

" Never better in my life," said Duncan Warner cheerily.

The situation was a painful one. The Marshal glared at the committee. Peter Stulpnagel grinned and rubbed his hands. The engineers scratched their heads. The bald-headed prisoner revolved his arm and looked pleased.

" I think that one more shock——" began the chairman.

" No, sir," said the Marshal ; " we've had foolery enough for one morning. We are here for an execution, and an execution we'll have."

" What do you propose ? "

" There's a hook handy upon the ceiling. Fetch a rope, and we'll soon set this matter straight."

There was another awkward delay while the warders departed for the cord. Peter Stulpnagel bent over Duncan Warner, and whispered something in his ear. The desperado stared in surprise.

" You don't say ? " he asked.

The German nodded.

" What ! No ways ? "

Peter shook his head, and the two began to laugh as though they shared some huge joke between them.

The rope was brought, and the Marshal himself slipped the noose over the criminal's neck. Then the two warders, the assistant and he swung their victim into the air. For half an hour he hung—a dreadful sight—from the ceiling. Then in solemn silence they lowered him down, and one of the warders went out to order the shell to be brought round. But as he touched ground again what was our amazement when Duncan Warner put his hands up to his neck, loosened the noose, and took a long, deep breath.

" Paul Jefferson's sale is goin' well," he remarked

" I could see the crowd from up yonder," and he nodded at the hook in the ceiling.

"Up with him again!" shouted the Marshal, " we'll get the life out of him somehow."

In an instant the victim was up at the hook once more. They kept him there for an hour, but when he came down he was perfectly garrulous.

" Old man Plunket goes too much to the Arcady Saloon," said he. " Three times he's been there in an hour ; and him with a family. Old man Plunket would do well to swear off."

It was monstrous and incredible, but there it was. There was no getting round it. The man was there talking when he ought to have been dead. We all sat staring in amazement, but United States Marshal Carpenter was not a man to be euchred so easily. He motioned the others to one side, so that the prisoner was left standing alone.

" Duncan Warner," said he slowly, " you are here to play your part, and I am here to play mine. Your game is to live if you can, and my game is to carry out the sentence of the law. You've beat us on electricity. I'll give you one there. And you've beat us on hanging, for you seem to thrive on it. But it's my turn to beat you now, for my duty has to be done."

He pulled a six-shooter from his coat as he spoke, and fired all the shots through the body of the prisoner. The room was so filled with smoke that we could see nothing, but when it cleared the prisoner was still standing there, looking down in disgust at the front of his coat.

" Coats must be cheap where you come from," said he. " Thirty dollars it cost me, and look at it now. The six holes in front are bad enough, but four of the balls have passed out, and a pretty fine state the back must be in."

The Marshal's revolver fell from his hand, and he dropped his arms to his sides, a beaten man.

"Maybe some of you gentlemen can tell me what this means," said he, looking helplessly at the committee.

Peter Stulpnagel took a step forward.

"I'll tell you all about it," said he.

"You seem to be the only person who knows anything."

"I *am* the only person who knows anything. I should have warned these gentlemen; but, as they would not listen to me, I have allowed them to learn by experience. What you have done with your electricity is that you have increased the man's vitality until he can defy death for centuries."

"Centuries!"

"Yes, it will take the wear of hundreds of years to exhaust the enormous nervous energy with which you have drenched him. Electricity is life, and you have charged him with it to the utmost. Perhaps in fifty years you might execute him, but I am not sanguine about it."

"Great Scott! What shall I do with him?" cried the unhappy Marshal.

Peter Stulpnagel shrugged his shoulders.

"It seems to me that it does not much matter what you do with him now," said he.

"Maybe we could drain the electricity out of him again. Suppose we hang him up by the heels?"

"No, no, it's out of the question."

"Well, well, he shall do no more mischief in Los Amigos, anyhow," said the Marshal, with decision. "He shall go into the new gaol. The prison will wear him out."

"On the contrary," said Peter Stulpnagel, "I think that it is much more probable that he will wear out the prison."

It was rather a fiasco, and for years we didn't talk more about it than we could help, but it's no secret now, and I thought you might like to jot down the facts in your case-book.

46. *How it Happened*

S HE was a writing medium. This is what she
wrote :—

I can remember some things upon that evening most
distinctly, and others are like some vague, broken dreams.
That is what makes it so difficult to tell a connected
story. I have no idea now what it was that had taken
me to London and brought me back so late. It just
merges into all my other visits to London. But from
the time that I got out at the little country station everything is extraordinarily clear. I can live it again—every
instant of it.

I remember so well walking down the platform and
looking at the illuminated clock at the end which told
me that it was half-past eleven. I remember also my
wondering whether I could get home before midnight.
Then I remember the big motor, with its glaring head-
lights and glitter of polished brass, waiting for me outside. It was my new thirty-horse-power Robur, which
had only been delivered that day. I remember also
asking Perkins, my chauffeur, how she had gone, and
his saying that he thought she was excellent.

" I'll try her myself," said I, and I climbed into the
driver's seat.

" The gears are not the same," said he. " Perhaps,
sir, I had better drive."

" No ; I should like to try her," said I.

And so we started on the five-mile drive for home.

My old car had the gears as they used always to be
in notches on a bar. In this car you passed the gear-
lever through a gate to get on the higher ones. It was
not difficult to master, and soon I thought that I understood it. It was foolish, no doubt, to begin to learn a
new system in the dark, but one often does foolish things,

563

and one has not always to pay the full price for them. I got along very well until I came to Claystall Hill. It is one of the worst hills in England, a mile and a half long and one in six in places, with three fairly sharp curves. My park gate stands at the very foot of it upon the main London road.

We were just over the brow of this hill, where the grade is steepest, when the trouble began. I had been on the top speed, and wanted to get her on the free ; but she stuck between gears, and I had to get her back on the top again. By this time she was going at a great rate, so I clapped on both brakes, and one after the other they gave way. I didn't mind so much when I felt my footbrake snap, but when I put all my weight on my side-brake, and the lever clanged to its full limit without a catch, it brought a cold sweat out of me. By this time we were fairly tearing down the slope. The lights were brilliant, and I brought her round the first curve all right. Then we did the second one, though it was a close shave for the ditch. There was a mile of straight then with the third curve beneath it, and after that the gate of the park. If I could shoot into that harbour all would be well, for the slope up to the house would bring her to a stand.

Perkins behaved splendidly. I should like that to be known. He was perfectly cool and alert. I had thought at the very beginning of taking the bank, and he read my intention.

" I wouldn't do it, sir," said he. " At this pace it must go over and we should have it on the top of us."

Of course he was right. He got to the electric switch and had it off, so we were in the free ; but we were still running at a fearful pace. He laid his hands on the wheel.

" I'll keep her steady," said he, " if you care to jump and chance it. We can never get round that curve. Better jump, sir."

" No," said I ; " I'll stick it out. You can jump if you like."

" I'll stick it with you, sir," said he.

If it had been the old car I should have jammed the gear-lever into the reverse, and seen what would happen. I expect she would have stripped her gears or smashed up somehow, but it would have been a chance. As it was, I was helpless. Perkins tried to climb across, but you couldn't do it going at that pace. The wheels were whirring like a high wind and the big body creaking and groaning with the strain. But the lights were brilliant, and one could steer to an inch. I remember thinking what an awful and yet majestic sight we should appear to anyone who met us. It was a narrow road, and we were just a great, roaring, golden death to anyone who came in our path.

We got round the corner with one wheel three feet high upon the bank. I thought we were surely over, but after staggering for a moment she righted and darted onwards. That was the third corner and the last one. There was only the park gate now. It was facing us, but, as luck would have it, not facing us directly. It was about twenty yards to the left up the main road into which we ran. Perhaps I could have done it, but I expect that the steering-gear had been jarred when we ran on the bank. The wheel did not turn easily. We shot out of the lane. I saw the open gate on the left. I whirled round my wheel with all the strength of my wrists. Perkins and I threw our bodies across, and then the next instant, going at fifty miles an hour, my right wheel struck full on the right-hand pillar of my own gate. I heard the crash. I was conscious of flying through the air, and then—and then——!

When I became aware of my own existence once more I was among some brushwood in the shadow of the oaks upon the lodge side of the drive. A man was standing beside me. I imagined at first that it was Perkins, but when I looked again I saw that it was Stanley, a man whom I had known at college some years before, and for whom I had a really genuine affection. There was always something peculiarly sympathetic to me in Stanley's personality ; and I was proud to think that I had some similar influence upon him. At the present moment I was surprised to see him, but I was like a man in a dream, giddy and shaken and quite prepared to take things as I found them without questioning them.

" What a smash ! " I said. " Good Lord, what an awful smash ! "

He nodded his head, and even in the gloom I could see that he was smiling the gentle, wistful smile which I connected with him.

I was quite unable to move. Indeed, I had not any desire to try to move. But my senses were exceedingly alert. I saw the wreck of the motor lit up by the moving lanterns. I saw the little group of people and heard the hushed voices. There were the lodge-keeper and his wife, and one or two more. They were taking no notice of me, but were very busy round the car. Then suddenly I heard a cry of pain.

" The weight is on him. Lift it easy," cried a voice.

" It's only my leg ! " said another one, which I recognised as Perkins's. " Where's master ? " he cried.

" Here I am," I answered, but they did not seem to hear me. They were all bending over something which lay in front of the car.

Stanley laid his hand upon my shoulder, and his touch was inexpressibly soothing. I felt light and happy, in spite of all.

" No pain, of course ? " said he.

" None," said I.

" There never is," said he.

And then suddenly a wave of amazement passed over me. Stanley ! Stanley ! Why, Stanley had surely died of enteric at Bloemfontein in the Boer War !

" Stanley ! " I cried, and the words seemed to choke my throat—" Stanley, you are dead."

He looked at me with the same old gentle, wistful smile.

" So are you," he answered.

47. *Lot No. 249*

OF the dealings of Edward Bellingham with William Monkhouse Lee, and of the cause of the great terror of Abercrombie Smith, it may be that no absolute and final judgment will ever be delivered. It is true that we have the full and clear narrative of Smith himself, and such corroboration as he could look for from Thomas Styles the servant, from the Reverend Plumptree Peterson, Fellow of Old's, and from such other people as chanced to gain some passing glance at this or that incident in a singular chain of events. Yet, in the main, the story must rest upon Smith alone, and the most will think that it is more likely that one brain, however outwardly sane, has some subtle warp in its texture, some strange flaw in its workings, than that the path of Nature has been overstepped in open day in so famed a centre of learning and light as the University of Oxford. Yet when we think how narrow and how devious this path of Nature is, how dimly we can trace it, for all our lamps of science, and how from the darkness which girds it round great and terrible possibilities loom ever shadowly upwards, it is a bold and confident man who will put a limit to the strange by-paths into which the human spirit may wander.

In a certain wing of what we will call Old College in Oxford there is a corner turret of an exceeding great age. The heavy arch which spans the open door has bent downwards in the centre under the weight of its years, and the grey, lichen-blotched blocks of stone are bound and knitted together with withes and strands of ivy, as though the old mother had set herself to brace them up against wind and weather. From the door a stone stair curves upward spirally, passing two landings, and terminating in a third one, its steps all shapeless and hollowed by the tread of so many generations of the seekers after knowledge. Life has flowed like water down this winding stair, and, waterlike, has left these smooth-worn grooves behind it. From the long-gowned, pedantic scholars of Plantagenet days down to the young bloods of a later age, how full and strong had been that tide of young, English life. And what was left now of all those hopes, those strivings, those fiery energies, save here and there in some old-world churchyard a few scratches upon a stone, and perchance a handful of dust in a mouldering coffin? Yet here were the silent stair and the grey, old wall, with bend and saltire and many another heraldic device still to be read upon its surface, like grotesque shadows thrown back from the days that had passed.

In the month of May, in the year 1884, three young men occupied the sets of rooms which opened on to the separate landings of the old stair. Each set consisted simply of a sitting-room and of a bedroom, while the two corresponding rooms upon the ground-floor were used, the one as a coal-cellar, and the other as the living-room of the servant, or scout, Thomas Styles, whose duty it was to wait upon the three men above him. To right and to left was a line of lecture-rooms and of offices, so that the dwellers in the old turret enjoyed a certain seclusion, which made the chambers popular among the more studious undergraduates. Such were the three who occupied them now—Abercrombie Smith above, Edward Bellingham beneath him, and William Monkhouse Lee upon the lowest storey.

It was ten o'clock on a bright, spring night, and Abercrombie Smith lay back in his arm-chair, his feet upon the fender, and his briar-root pipe between his lips. In a similar chair, and equally at his ease, there lounged on the other side of the fireplace his old school friend Jephro

Hastie. Both men were in flannels, for they had spent their evening upon the river, but apart from their dress no one could look at their hard-cut, alert faces without seeing that they were open-air men—men whose minds and tastes turned naturally to all that was manly and robust. Hastie, indeed, was stroke of his college boat, and Smith was an even better oar, but a coming examination had already cast its shadow over him and held him to his work, save for the few hours a week which health demanded. A litter of medical books upon the table, with scattered bones, models, and anatomical plates, pointed to the extent as well as the nature of his studies, while a couple of single-sticks and a set of boxing-gloves above the mantelpiece hinted at the means by which, with Hastie's help, he might take his exercise in its most compressed and least-distant form. They knew each other very well—so well that they could sit now in that soothing silence which is the very highest development of companionship.

"Have some whisky," said Abercrombie Smith at last between two cloudbursts. "Scotch in the jug and Irish in the bottle."

"No, thanks. I'm in for the sculls. I don't liquor when I'm training. How about you?"

"I'm reading hard. I think it best to leave it alone."

Hastie nodded, and they relapsed into a contented silence.

"By the way, Smith," asked Hastie, presently, "have you made the acquaintance of either of the fellows on your stair yet?"

"Just a nod when we pass. Nothing more."

"Hum! I should be inclined to let it stand at that. I know something of them both. Not much, but as much as I want. I don't think I should take them to my bosom if I were you. Not that there's much amiss with Monkhouse Lee."

"Meaning the thin one?"

"Precisely. He is a gentlemanly little fellow. I don't

569

think there is any vice in him. But then you can't know him without· knowing Bellingham."

" Meaning the fat one ? "

" Yes, the fat one. And he's a man whom I, for one, would rather not know."

Abercrombie Smith raised his eyebrows and glanced across at his companion.

" What's up, then ? " he asked. " Drink ? Cards ? Cad ? You used not to be censorious."

" Ah ! you evidently don't know the man, or you wouldn't ask. There's something damnable about him —something reptilian. My gorge always rises at him. I should put him down as a man with secret vices—an evil liver. He's no fool, though. They say that he is one of the best men in his line that they have ever had in the college."

" Medicine or classics ? "

" Eastern languages. He's a demon at them. Chillingworth met him somewhere above the second cataract last long, and he told me that he just prattled to the Arabs as if he had been born and nursed and weaned among them. He talked Coptic to the Copts, and Hebrew to the Jews, and Arabic to the Bedouins, and they were all ready to kiss the hem of his frock-coat. There are some old hermit Johnnies up in those parts who sit on rocks and scowl and spit at the casual stranger. Well, when they saw this chap Bellingham, before he had said five words they just lay down on their bellies and wriggled. Chillingworth said that he never saw anything like it. Bellingham seemed to take it as his right, too, and strutted about among them and talked down to them like a Dutch uncle. Pretty good for an undergrad. of Old's, wasn't it ? "

" Why do you say you can't know Lee without knowing Bellingham ? "

" Because Bellingham is engaged to his sister Eveline. Such a bright little girl, Smith ! I know the whole family well. It's disgusting to see that brute with her.

A toad and a dove, that's what they always remind me of."

Abercrombie Smith grinned and knocked his ashes out against the side of the grate.

" You show every card in your hand, old chap," said he. " What a prejudiced, green-eyed, evil-thinking old man it is ! You have really nothing against the fellow except that."

" Well, I've known her ever since she was as long as that cherry-wood pipe, and I don't like to see her taking risks. And it is a risk. He looks beastly. And he has a beastly temper, a venomous temper. You remember his row with Long Norton ? "

" No ; you always forget that I am a freshman."

" Ah, it was last winter. Of course. Well, you know the towpath along by the river. There were several fellows going along it, Bellingham in front, when they came on an old market-woman coming the other way. It had been raining—you know what those fields are like when it has rained—and the path ran between the river and a great puddle that was nearly as broad. Well, what does this swine do but keep the path, and push the old girl into the mud, where she and her marketings came to terrible grief. It was a blackguard thing to do, and Long Norton, who is as gentle a fellow as ever stepped, told him what he thought of it. One word led to another, and it ended in Norton laying his stick across the fellow's shoulders. There was the deuce of a fuss about it, and it's a treat to see the way in which Bellingham looks at Norton when they meet now. By Jove, Smith, it's nearly eleven o'clock ! "

" No hurry. Light your pipe again."

" Not I. I'm supposed to be in training. Here I've been sitting gossiping when I ought to have been safely tucked up. I'll borrow your skull, if you can share it. Williams has had mine for a month. I'll take the little bones of your ear, too, if you are sure you won't need them. Thanks very much. Never mind a bag, I can carry them very well under my arm. Good night, my son, and take my tip as to your neighbour."

When Hastie, bearing his anatomical plunder, had clattered off down the winding stair, Abercrombie Smith hurled his pipe into the wastepaper basket, and drawing his chair nearer to the lamp, plunged into a formidable, green-covered volume, adorned with great, coloured maps of that strange, internal kingdom of which we are the hapless and helpless monarchs. Though a freshman at Oxford, the student was not so in medicine, for he had worked for four years at Glasgow and at Berlin, and this coming examination would place him finally as a member of his profession. With his firm mouth, broad forehead, and clear-cut, somewhat hard-featured face, he was a man who, if he had no brilliant talent, was yet so dogged, so patient, and so strong that he might in the end over-top a more showy genius. A man who can hold his own among Scotchmen and North Germans is not a man to be easily set back. Smith had left a name at Glasgow and at Berlin, and he was bent now upon doing as much at Oxford, if hard work and devotion could accomplish it.

He had sat reading for about an hour, and the hands of the noisy carriage clock upon the side-table were rapidly closing together upon the twelve, when a sudden sound fell upon the student's ear—a sharp, rather shrill sound, like the hissing intake of a man's breath who gasps under some strong emotion. Smith laid down his book and slanted his ear to listen. There was no one on either side or above him, so that the interruption came certainly from the neighbour beneath—the same neighbour of whom Hastie had given so unsavoury an account. Smith knew him only as a flabby, pale-faced man of silent and studious habits, a man whose lamp threw a golden bar from the old turret even after he had extinguished his own. This community in lateness had formed a certain silent bond between them. It was soothing to Smith when the hours stole on towards dawning to feel that there was another so close who set as small a value upon his sleep as he did. Even now, as his thoughts turned towards him, Smith's feelings were kindly. Hastie was a good fellow, but he was rough, strong-fibred, with no imagination or sympathy. He could not tolerate departures from what he looked upon as the model type of manliness. If a man could not be measured by a public-school standard, then he was beyond the pale with Hastie. Like so many who are themselves robust, he was apt to confuse the constitution with the character, to ascribe to want of principle what was really a want of circulation. Smith, with his stronger mind, knew his friend's habit, and made allowance for it now as his thoughts turned towards the man beneath him.

There was no return of the singular sound, and Smith was about to turn to his work once more, when suddenly there broke out in the silence of the night a hoarse cry, a positive scream—the call of a man who is moved and shaken beyond all control. Smith sprang out of his chair and dropped his book. He was a man of fairly firm fibre, but there was something in this sudden, uncontrollable shriek of horror which chilled his blood and pringled in his skin. Coming in such a place and at such an hour, it brought a thousand fantastic possibilities into his head. Should he rush down, or was it better to wait ? He had all the national hatred of making a scene, and he knew so little of his neighbour that he would not lightly intrude upon his affairs. For a moment he stood in doubt and even as he balanced the matter there was a quick rattle of footsteps upon the stairs, and young Monkhouse Lee, half-dressed and as white as ashes, burst into his room.

" Come down ! " he gasped. " Bellingham's ill."

Abercrombie Smith followed him closely downstairs into the sitting-room which was beneath his own, and intent as he was upon the matter in hand, he could not but take an amazed glance around him as he crossed the threshold. It was such a chamber as he had never seen before—a museum rather than a study. Walls and ceiling were thickly covered with a thousand strange relics from Egypt and the East. Tall, angular figures bearing burdens or weapons stalked in an uncouth frieze round the apartments. Above were bull-headed, stork-headed, cat-headed, owl-headed statues, with viper-crowned, almond-eyed monarchs, and strange, beetle-like deities cut out of the blue Egyptian lapis lazuli. Horus and Isis and Osiris peeped down from every niche and shelf, while across the ceiling a true son of Old Nile, a great, hanging-jawed crocodile, was slung in a double noose.

In the centre of this singular chamber was a large, square table, littered with papers, bottles, and the dried leaves of some graceful, palm-like plant. These varied objects had all been heaped together in order to make room for a mummy case, which had been conveyed from the wall, as was evident from the gap there, and laid across the front of the table. The mummy itself, a horrid, black, withered thing, like a charred head on a gnarled bush, was lying half out of the case, with its claw-like hand and bony forearm resting upon the table. Propped up against the sarcophagus was an old, yellow scroll of papyrus, and in front of it, in a wooden arm-chair, sat the owner of the room, his head thrown back, his widely opened eyes directed in a horrified stare to the crocodile above him, and his blue, thick lips puffing loudly with every expiration.

"My God! he's dying!" cried Monkhouse Lee, distractedly.

He was a slim, handsome young fellow, olive-skinned and dark-eyed, of a Spanish rather than of an English type, with a Celtic intensity of manner which contrasted with the Saxon phlegm of Abercrombie Smith.

"Only a faint, I think," said the medical student. "Just give me a hand with him. You take his feet. Now on to the sofa. Can you kick all those little wooden devils off? What a litter it is! Now he will be all rignt if we undo his collar and give him some water. What has he been up to at all ? "

" I don't know. I heard him cry out. I ran up. I know him pretty well, you know. It is very good of you to come down."

" His heart is going like a pair of castanets," sa:d Smith, laying his hand on the breast of the unconscious man. " He seems to me to be frightened all to pieces. Chuck the water over him ! What a face he has got on him ! "

It was indeed a strange and most repellent face, for colour and outline were equally unnatural. It was white, not with the ordinary pallor of fear, but with an absolutely bloodless white, like the under side of a sole. He was very fat, but gave the impression of having at some time been considerably fatter, for his skin hung loosely in creases and folds, and was shot with a meshwork of wrinkles. Short, stubbly brown hair bristled up from his scalp, with a pair of thick, wrinkled ears protruding at the sides. His light-grey eyes were still open, the pupils dilated and the balls projecting in a fixed and horrid stare. It seemed to Smith as he looked down upon him that he had never seen Nature's danger signals flying so plainly upon a man's countenance, and his thoughts turned more seriously to the warning which Hastie had given him an hour before.

" What the deuce can have frightened him so ? " he asked.

" It's the mummy."

" The mummy ? How, then ? "

" I don't know. It's beastly and morbid. I wish he would drop it. It's the second fright he has given me. It was the same last winter. I found him just like this, with that horrid thing in front of him."

" What does he want with the mummy, then ? "

" Oh, he's a crank, you know. It's his hobby. He knows more about these things than any man in England. But I wish he wouldn't ! Ah, he's beginning to come to."

A faint tinge of colour had begun to steal back into Bellingham's ghastly cheeks, and his eyelids shivered like a sail after a calm. He clasped and unclasped his hands, drew a long, thin breath between his teeth, and suddenly jerking up his head, threw a glance of recognition around him. As his eyes fell upon the mummy, he sprang off the sofa, seized the roll of papyrus, thrust it into a drawer, turned the key, and then staggered back on to the sofa.

"What's up?" he asked. "What do you chaps want?"

"You've been shrieking out and making no end of a fuss," said Monkhouse Lee. "If our neighbour here from above hadn't come down, I'm sure I don't know what I should have done with you."

"Ah, it's Abercrombie Smith," said Bellingham, glancing up at him. "How very good of you to come in! What a fool I am! Oh, my God, what a fool I am!"

He sank his head on to his hands, and burst into peal after peal of hysterical laughter.

"Look here! Drop it!" cried Smith, shaking him roughly by the shoulder.

"Your nerves are all in a jangle. You must drop these little midnight games with mummies, or you'll be going off your chump. You're all on wires now."

"I wonder," said Bellingham, "whether you would be as cool as I am if you had seen——"

"What then?"

"Oh, nothing. I meant that I wonder if you could sit up at night with a mummy without trying your nerves. I have no doubt that you are quite right. I dare say that I have been taking it out of myself too much lately. But I am all right now. Please don't go, though. Just wait for a few minutes until I am quite myself."

"The room is very close," remarked Lee, throwing open the window and letting in the cool night air.

"It's balsamic resin," said Bellingham. He lifted

576

up one of the dried palmate leaves from the table and
frizzled it over the chimney of the lamp. It broke away
into heavy smoke wreaths, and a pungent, biting odour
filled the chamber. " It's the sacred plant—the plant
of the priests," he remarked. " Do you know anything
of Eastern languages, Smith ? "

" Nothing at all. Not a word."

The answer seemed to lift a weight from the Egyptologist's mind.

" By the way," he continued, " how long was it from
the time that you ran down, until I came to my senses ? "

" Not long. Some four or five minutes."

" I thought it could not be very long," said he, drawing
a long breath. " But what a strange thing unconsciousness is ! There is no measurement to it. I could not
tell from my own sensations if it were seconds or weeks.
Now that gentleman on the table was packed up in the
days of the eleventh dynasty, some forty centuries ago,
and yet if he could find his tongue, he would tell us that
this lapse of time has been but a closing of the eyes and
a reopening of them. He is a singularly fine mummy,
Smith."

Smith stepped over to the table and looked down with
a professional eye at the black and twisted form in front
of him. The features, though horribly discoloured, were
perfect, and two little nut-like eyes still lurked in the
depths of the black, hollow sockets. The blotched skin
was drawn tightly from bone to bone, and a tangled wrap
of black, coarse hair fell over the ears. Two thin teeth,
like those of a rat, overlay the shrivelled lower lip. In
its crouching position, with bent joints and craned head,
there was a suggestion of energy about the horrid thing
which made Smith's gorge rise. The gaunt ribs, with
their parchment-like covering, were exposed, and the
sunken, leaden-hued abdomen, with the long slit where
the embalmer had left his mark ; but the lower limbs
were wrapped round with coarse, yellow bandages. A
number of little clove-like pieces of myrrh and of cassia

were sprinkled over the body, and lay scattered on the inside of the case.

"I don't know his name," said Bellingham, passing his hand over the shrivelled head. "You see the outer sarcophagus with the inscriptions is missing. Lot 249 is all the title he has now. You see it printed on his case. That was his number in the auction at which I picked him up."

"He has been a very pretty sort of fellow in his day," remarked Abercrombie Smith.

"He has been a giant. His mummy is six feet seven in length, and that would be a giant over there, for they were never a very robust race. Feel these great, knotted bones, too. He would be a nasty fellow to tackle."

"Perhaps these very hands helped to build the stones into the pyramids," suggested Monkhouse Lee, looking down with disgust in his eyes at the crooked, unclean talons.

"No fear. This fellow has been pickled in natron, and looked after in the most approved style. They did not serve hodsmen in that fashion. Salt or bitumen was enough for them. It has been calculated that this sort of thing cost about seven hundred and thirty pounds in our money. Our friend was a noble at the least. What do you make of that small inscription near his feet, Smith?"

"I told you that I know no Eastern tongue."

"Ah, so you did. It is the name of the embalmer, I take it. A very conscientious worker he must have been. I wonder how many modern works will survive four thousand years?"

He kept on speaking lightly and rapidly, but it was evident to Abercrombie Smith that he was still palpitating with fear. His hands shook, his lower lip trembled, and look where he would, his eye always came sliding round to his gruesome companion. Through all his fear, however, there was a suspicion of triumph in his tone and manner. His eyes shone, and his footstep, as he paced the room, was brisk and jaunty. He gave the impression of a man who has gone through an ordeal, the marks of which he still bears upon him, but which has helped him to his end.

" You're not going yet ? " he cried, as Smith rose from the sofa.

At the prospect of solitude, his fears seemed to crowd back upon him, and he stretched out a hand to detain him.

" Yes, I must go. I have my work to do. You are all right now. I think that with your nervous system you should take up some less morbid study."

" Oh, I am not nervous as a rule ; and I have unwrapped mummies before."

" You fainted last time," observed Monkhouse Lee.

" Ah, yes, so I did. Well, I must have a nerve tonic or a course of electricity. You are not going, Lee ? "

" I'll do whatever you wish, Ned."

" Then I'll come down with you and have a shake-down on your sofa. Good night, Smith. I am so sorry to have disturbed you with my foolishness."

They shook hands, and as the medical student stumbled up the spiral and irregular stair he heard a key turn in a door, and the steps of his two new acquaintances as they descended to the lower floor.

In this strange way began the acquaintance between Edward Bellingham and Abercrombie Smith, an acquaintance which the latter, at least, had no desire to push further. Bellingham, however, appeared to have taken a fancy to his rough-spoken neighbour, and made his advances in such a way that he could hardly be repulsed without absolute brutality. Twice he called to thank Smith for his assistance, and many times afterwards he looked in with books, papers and such other civilities as two bachelor neighbours can offer each other. He was, as Smith soon found, a man of wide reading, with catholic tastes and an extraordinary memory. His manner, too, was so pleasing and suave that one came, after a time, to overlook his repellent appearance. For a jaded and wearied man he was no unpleasant companion, and Smith found himself, after a time, looking forward to his visits, and even returning them.

Clever as he undoubtedly was, however, the medical student seemed to detect a dash of insanity in the man. He broke out at times into a high, inflated style of talk which was in contrast with the simplicity of his life.

" It is a wonderful thing," he cried, " to feel that one can command powers of good and of evil—a ministering angel or a demon of vengeance." And again, of Monkhouse Lee, he said,—" Lee is a good fellow, an honest fellow, but he is without strength or ambition. He would not make a fit partner for a man with a great enterprise. He would not make a fit partner for me."

At such hints and innuendoes stolid Smith, puffing solemnly at his pipe, would simply raise his eyebrows and shake his head, with little interjections of medical wisdom as to earlier hours and fresher air.

One habit Bellingham had developed of late which Smith knew to be a frequent herald of a weakening mind. He appeared to be for ever talking to himself. At late hours of the night, when there could be no visitor with him, Smith could still hear his voice beneath him in a low, muffled monologue, sunk almost to a whisper, and yet very audible in the silence. This solitary babbling annoyed and distracted the student, so that he spoke more than once to his neighbour about it. Bellingham, however, flushed up at the charge, and denied curtly that he had uttered a sound ; indeed, he showed more annoyance over the matter than the occasion seemed to demand.

Had Abercrombie Smith had any doubt as to his own ears he had not to go far to find corroboration. Tom Styles, the little wrinkled man-servant who had attended to the wants of the lodgers in the turret for a longer time than any man's memory could carry him, was sorely put to it over the same matter.

" If you please, sir," said he, as he tidied down the top chamber one morning, " do you think Mr. Bellingham is all right, sir ? "

" All right, Styles ? "

" Yes, sir. Right in his head, sir."

" Why should he not be, then ? "

" Well, I don't know, sir. His habits has changed of late. He's not the same man he used to be, though I make free to say that he was never quite one of my gentlemen, like Mr. Hastie or yourself, sir. He's took to talkin' to himself something awful. I wonder it don't disturb you. I don't know what to make of him, sir."

" I don't know what business it is of yours, Styles."

" Well, I takes an interest, Mr. Smith. It may be forward of me, but I can't help it. I feel sometimes as if I was mother and father to my young gentlemen. It all falls on me when things go wrong and the relations come. But Mr. Bellingham, sir. I want to know what it is that walks about his room sometimes when he's out and when the door's locked on the outside."

" Eh ? you're talking nonsense, Styles."

" Maybe so, sir ; but I heard it more'n once with my own ears."

" Rubbish, Styles."

" Very good, sir. You'll ring the bell if you want me."

Abercrombie Smith gave little heed to the gossip of the old man-servant, but a small incident occurred a few days later which left an unpleasant effect upon his mind, and brought the words of Styles forcibly to his memory.

Bellingham had come up to see him late one night, and was entertaining him with an interesting account of the rock tombs of Beni Hassan in Upper Egypt, when Smith, whose hearing was remarkably acute, distinctly heard the sound of a door opening on the landing below.

" There's some fellow gone in or out of your room," he remarked.

Bellingham sprang up and stood helpless for a moment, with the expression of a man who is half-incredulous and half-afraid.

" I surely locked it. I am almost positive that I locked it," he stammered. " No one could have opened it."

" Why, I hear someone coming up the steps now," said Smith.

Bellingham rushed out through the door, slammed it loudly behind him, and hurried down the stairs. About half-way down Smith heard him stop, and thought he caught the sound of whispering. A moment later the door beneath him shut, a key creaked in a lock, and Bellingham, with beads of moisture upon his pale face, ascended the stairs once more, and re-entered the room.

" It's all right," he said, throwing himself down in a chair. " It was that fool of a dog. He had pushed the door open. I don't know how I came to forget to lock it."

" I didn't know you kept a dog," said Smith, looking very thoughtfully at the disturbed face of his companion.

" Yes, I haven't had him long. I must get rid of him. He's a great nuisance."

" He must be, if you find it so hard to shut him up. I should have thought that shutting the door would have been enough, without locking it."

" I want to prevent old Styles from letting him out. He's of some value, you know, and it would be awkward to lose him."

" I am a bit of a dog-fancier myself," said Smith, still gazing hard at his companion from the corner of his eyes. " Perhaps you'll let me have a look at it."

" Certainly. But I am afraid it cannot be to-night ; I have an appointment. Is that clock right ? Then I am a quarter of an hour late already. You'll excuse me, I am sure."

He picked up his cap and hurried from the room. In spite of his appointment, Smith heard him re-enter his own chamber and lock his door upon the inside.

This interview left a disagreeable impression upon the medical student's mind. Bellingham had lied to him, and lied so clumsily that it looked as if he had desperate reasons for concealing the truth. Smith knew that his neighbour had no dog. He knew, also, that the step which he had heard upon the stairs was not the step of an animal. But if it were not, then what could it be? There was old Style's statement about the something which used to pace the room at times when the owner was absent. Could it be a woman? Smith rather inclined to the view. If so, it would mean disgrace and expulsion to Bellingham if it were discovered by the authorities, so that his anxiety and falsehoods might be accounted for. And yet it was inconceivable that an undergraduate could keep a woman in his rooms without being instantly detected. Be the explanation what it might, there was something ugly about it, and Smith determined, as he turned to his books, to discourage all further attempts at intimacy on the part of his soft-spoken and ill-favoured neighbour.

But his work was destined to interruption that night. He had hardly caught up the broken threads when a firm, heavy footfall came three steps at a time from below, and Hastie, in blazer and flannels, burst into the room.

" Still at it ! " said he, plumping down into his wonted arm-chair. " What a chap you are to stew ! I believe an earthquake might come and knock Oxford into a cocked hat, and you would sit perfectly placid with your books among the ruins. However, I won't bore you long. Three whiffs of baccy, and I am off."

"What's the news, then ? " asked Smith, cramming a plug of bird's-eye into his briar with his forefinger.

" Nothing very much. Wilson made 70 for the freshmen against the eleven. They say that they will play him instead of Buddicomb, for Buddicomb is clean off colour. He used to be able to bowl a little, but it's nothing but half-volleys and long hops now."

" Medium right," suggested Smith, with the intense

gravity which comes upon a 'varsity man when he speaks
of athletics.

" Inclining to fast, with a work from leg. Comes with
the arm about three inches or so. He used to be nasty
on a wet wicket. Oh, by the way, have you heard about
Long Norton ? "

" What's that ? "

" He's been attacked."

" Attacked ? "

" Yes, just as he was turning out of the High Street,
and within a hundred yards of the gate of Old's."

" But who——"

" Ah, that's the rub ! If you said ' what,' you would
be more grammatical. Norton swears that it was not
human, and, indeed, from the scratches on his throat,
I should be inclined to agree with him."

" What, then ? Have we come down to spooks ? "
Abercrombie Smith puffed his scientific contempt.

" Well, no ; I don't think that is quite the idea, either.
I am inclined to think that if any showman has lost a
great ape lately, and the brute is in these parts, a jury
would find a true bill against it. Norton passes that
way every night, you know, about the same hour. There's
a tree that hangs low over the path—the big elm from
Rainy's garden. Norton thinks the thing dropped on him
out of the tree. Anyhow, he was nearly strangled by
two arms, which, he says, were as strong and as thin as
steel bands. He saw nothing ; only those beastly arms
that tightened and tightened on him. He yelled his
head nearly off, and a couple of chaps came running,
and the thing went over the wall like a cat. He never
got a fair sight of it the whole time. It gave Norton a
shake up, I can tell you. I tell him it has been as good
as a change at the seaside for him."

" A garrotter, most likely," said Smith.

" Very possibly. Norton says not ; but we don't mind
what he says. The garrotter had long nails, and was
pretty smart at swinging himself over walls. By the way,

your beautiful neighbour would be pleased if he heard about it. He had a grudge against Norton, and he's not a man, from what I know of him, to forget his little debts. But hallo, old chap, what have you got in your noddle ? "

" Nothing," Smith answered curtly.

He had started in his chair, and the look had flashed over his face which comes upon a man who is struck suddenly by some unpleasant idea.

" You looked as if something I had said had taken you on the raw. By the way, you have made the acquaintance of Master B. since I looked in last, have you not ? Young Monkhouse Lee told me something to that effect."

" Yes ; I know him slightly. He has been up here once or twice."

" Well, you're big enough and ugly enough to take care of yourself. He's not what I should call exactly a healthy sort of Johnny, though, no doubt, he's very clever, and all that. But you'll soon find out for yourself. Lee is all right ; he's a very decent little fellow. Well, so long, old chap ! I row Mullins for the Vice-Chancellor's pot on Wednesday week, so mind you come down, in case I don't see you before."

Bovine Smith laid down his pipe and turned stolidly to his books once more. But with all the will in the world, he found it very hard to keep his mind upon his work. It would slip away to brood upon the man beneath him, and upon the little mystery which hung round his chambers. Then his thoughts turned to this singular attack of which Hastie had spoken, and to the grudge which Bellingham was said to owe the object of it. The two ideas would persist in rising together in his mind, as though there were some close and intimate connection between them. And yet the suspicion was so dim and vague that it could not be put down in words.

" Confound the chap ! " cried Smith, as he shied his book on pathology across the room. " He has spoiled my night's reading, and that's reason enough, if there were no other, why I should steer clear of him in the future."

For ten days the medical student confined himself so closely to his studies that he neither saw nor heard anything of either of the men beneath him. At the hours when Bellingham had been accustomed to visit him, he took care to sport his oak, and though he more than once heard a knocking at his outer door, he resolutely refused to answer it. One afternoon, however, he was descending the stairs when, just as he was passing it, Bellingham's door flew open, and young Monkhouse Lee came out with his eyes sparkling and a dark flush of anger upon his olive cheeks. Close at his heels followed Bellingham, his fat, unhealthy face all quivering with malignant passion.

" You fool ! " he hissed. " You'll be sorry."

" Very likely," cried the other. " Mind what I say. It's off ! I won't hear of it ! "

" You've promised, anyhow."

" Oh, I'll keep that ! I won't speak. But I'd rather little Eva was in her grave. Once for all, it's off. She'll do what I say. We don't want to see you again."

So much Smith could not avoid hearing, but he hurried on, for he had no wish to be involved in their dispute. There had been a serious breach between them, that was clear enough, and Lee was going to cause the engagement with his sister to be broken off. Smith thought of Hastie's comparison of the toad and the dove, and was glad to think that the matter was at an end. Bellingham's face when he was in a passion was not pleasant to look upon. He was not a man to whom an innocent girl could be trusted for life. As he walked, Smith wondered languidly what could have caused the quarrel, and what the promise might be which Bellingham had been so anxious that Monkhouse Lee should keep.

It was the day of the sculling match between Hastie and Mullins, and a stream of men were making their way down to the banks of the Isis. A May sun was shining brightly, and the yellow path was barred with the black shadows of the tall elm-trees. On either side the grey colleges lay back from the road, the hoary old mothers of minds looking out from their high, mullioned windows at the tide of young life which swept so merrily past them. Black-clad tutors, prim officials, pale, reading men, brown-faced, straw-hatted young athletes in white sweaters or many-coloured blazers, all were hurrying towards the blue, winding river which curves through the Oxford meadows.

Abercrombie Smith, with the intuition of an old oarsman, chose his position at the point where he knew that the struggle, if there were a struggle, would come. Far off he heard the hum which announced the start, the gathering roar of the approach, the thunder of running feet, and the shouts of the men in the boats beneath him. A spray of half-clad, deep-breathing runners shot past him, and craning over their shoulders, he saw Hastie pulling a steady thirty-six, while his opponent, with a jerky forty, was a good boat's length behind him. Smith gave a cheer for his friend, and pulling out his watch, was starting off again for his chambers, when he felt a touch upon his shoulder, and found that young Monkhouse Lee was beside him.

" I saw you there," he said, in a timid, deprecating way. " I wanted to speak to you, if you could spare me a half-hour. This cottage is mine. I share it with Harrington of King's. Come in and have a cup of tea."

" I must be back presently," said Smith. " I am hard on the grind at present. But I'll come in for a few minutes with pleasure. I wouldn't have come out only Hastie is a friend of mine."

" So he is of mine. Hasn't he a beautiful style? Mullins wasn't in it. But come into the cottage. It's a little den of a place, but it is pleasant to work in during the summer months."

It was a small, square, white building, with green doors and shutters, and a rustic trellis-work porch, standing back some fifty yards from the river's bank. Inside, the main room was roughly fitted up as a study—deal table, unpainted shelves with books, and a few cheap oleographs upon the wall. A kettle sang upon a spirit-stove, and there were tea things upon a tray on the table.

"Try that chair and have a cigarette," said Lee. "Let me pour you out a cup of tea. It's so good of you to come in, for I know that your time is a good deal taken up. I wanted to say to you that, if I were you, I should change my rooms at once."

"Eh ? "

Smith sat staring with a lighted match in one hand and his unlit cigarette in the other.

"Yes ; it must seem very extraordinary, and the worst of it is that I cannot give my reasons, for I am under a solemn promise—a very solemn promise. But I may go so far as to say that I don't think Bellingham is a very safe man to live near. I intend to camp out here as much as I can for a time."

"Not safe ! What do you mean ? "

"Ah, that's what I mustn't say. But do take my advice and move your rooms. We had a grand row to-day. You must have heard us, for you came down the stairs."

"I saw that you had fallen out."

"He's a horrible chap, Smith. That is the only word for him. I have had doubts about him ever since that night when he fainted—you remember, when you came down. I taxed him to-day, and he told me things that made my hair rise, and wanted me to stand in with him. I'm not straight-laced, but I am a clergyman's son, you know, and I think there are some things which are quite beyond the pale. I only thank God that I found him out before it was too late, for he was to have married into my family."

"This is all very fine, Lee," said Abercrombie Smith curtly. "But either you are saying a great deal too much or a great deal too little."

588

" I give you a warning."

" If there is real reason for warning, no promise can bind you. If I see a rascal about to blow a place up with dynamite no pledge will stand in my way of preventing him."

" Ah, but I cannot prevent him, and I can do nothing but warn you."

" Without saying what you warn me against."

" Against Bellingham."

" But that is childish. Why should I fear him, or any man ? "

" I can't tell you. I can only entreat you to change your rooms. You are in danger where you are. I don't even say that Bellingham would wish to injure you. But it might happen, for he is a dangerous neighbour just now."

" Perhaps I know more than you think," said Smith, looking keenly at the young man's boyish, earnest face. " Suppose I tell you that someone else shares Bellingham's rooms."

Monkhouse Lee sprang from his chair in uncontrollable excitement.

" You know, then ? " he gasped.

" A woman."

Lee dropped back again with a groan.

" My lips are sealed," he said. " I must not speak."

" Well, anyhow," said Smith, rising, " it is not likely that I should allow myself to be frightened out of rooms which suit me very nicely. It would be a little too feeble for me to move out all my goods and chattels because you say that Bellingham might in some unexplained way do me an injury. I think that I'll just take my chance, and stay where I am, and as I see that it's nearly five o'clock, I must ask you to excuse me."

He bade the young student adieu in a few curt words, and made his way homeward through the sweet spring evening, feeling half-ruffled, half-amused, as any other

589

strong, unimaginative man might who has been menaced by a vague and shadowy danger.

There was one little indulgence which Abercrombie Smith always allowed himself, however closely his work might press upon him. Twice a week, on the Tuesday and the Friday, it was his invariable custom to walk over to Farlingford, the residence of Doctor Plumptree Peterson, situated about a mile and a half out of Oxford. Peterson had been a close friend of Smith's elder brother, Francis, and as he was a bachelor, fairly well-to-do, with a good cellar and a better library, his house was a pleasant goal for a man who was in need of a brisk walk. Twice a week, then, the medical student would swing out there along the dark country roads and spend a pleasant hour in Peterson's comfortable study, discussing, over a glass of old port, the gossip of the 'varsity or the latest developments of medicine or of surgery.

On the day which followed his interview with Monkhouse Lee, Smith shut up his books at a quarter past eight, the hour when he usually started for his friend's house. As he was leaving his room, however, his eyes chanced to fall upon one of the books which Bellingham had lent him, and his conscience pricked him for not having returned it. However repellent the man might be, he should not be treated with discourtesy. Taking the book, he walked downstairs and knocked at his neighbour's door. There was no answer; but on turning the handle he found that it was unlocked. Pleased at the thought of avoiding an interview, he stepped inside, and placed the book with his card upon the table.

The lamp was turned half down, but Smith could see the details of the room plainly enough. It was all much as he had seen it before—the frieze, the animal-headed gods, the hanging crocodile, and the table littered over with papers and dried leaves. The mummy case stood upright against the wall, but the mummy itself was missing. There was no sign of any second occupant of the room, and he felt as he withdrew that he had probably done Bellingham an injustice. Had he a guilty secret to preserve, he would hardly leave his door open so that all the world might enter.

The spiral stair was as black as pitch, and Smith was slowly making his way down its irregular steps, when he was suddenly conscious that something had passed him in the darkness. There was a faint sound, a whiff of air, a light brushing past his elbow, but so slight that he could scarcely be certain of it. He stopped and listened, but the wind was rustling among the ivy outside, and he could hear nothing else.

" Is that you, Styles ? " he shouted.

. There was no answer, and all was still behind him. It must have been a sudden gust of air, for there were crannies and cracks in the old turret. And yet he could almost have sworn that he heard a footfall by his very side. He had emerged into the quadrangle, still turning the matter over in his head, when a man came running swiftly across the smooth-cropped lawn.

" Is that you, Smith ? "

" Hullo, Hastie ! "

" For God's sake come at once ! Young Lee is drowned ! Here's Harrington of King's with the news. The doctor is out. You'll do, but come along at once. There may be life in him."

" Have you brandy ? "

" No."

" I'll bring some. There's a flask on my table."

Smith bounded up the stairs, taking three at a time, seized the flask, and was rushing down with it, when, as he passed Bellingham's room, his eyes fell upon something which left him gasping and staring upon the landing.

The door, which he had closed behind him, was now open, and right in front of him, with the lamp-light shining upon it, was the mummy case. Three minutes ago it had been empty. He could swear to that. Now it framed the lank body of its horrible occupant, who stood, grim and stark, with his black, shrivelled face towards the door. The form was lifeless and inert, but it seemed to Smith as he gazed that there still lingered a lurid spark of vitality, some faint sign of consciousness in the little eyes which lurked in the depths of the hollow sockets. So astounded and shaken was he that he had forgotten his errand, and was still staring at the lean, sunken figure when the voice of his friend below recalled him to himself.

"Come on, Smith!" he shouted. "It's life and death, you know. Hurry up! Now, then," he added, as the medical student reappeared, "let us do a sprint. It is well under a mile, and we should do it in five minutes. A human life is better worth running for than a pot."

Neck and neck they dashed through the darkness, and did not pull up until panting and spent, they had reached the little cottage by the river. Young Lee, limp and dripping like a broken water-plant, was stretched upon the sofa, the green scum of the river upon his black hair, and a fringe of white foam upon his leaden-hued lips. Beside him knelt his fellow-student, Harrington, endeavouring to chafe some warmth back into his rigid limbs.

"I think there's life in him," said Smith, with his hand to the lad's side. "Put your watch glass to his lips. Yes, there's dimming on it. You take one arm, Hastie. Now work it as I do, and we'll soon pull him round."

For ten minutes they worked in silence, inflating and depressing the chest of the unconscious man. At the end of that time a shiver ran through his body, his lips trembled, and he opened his eyes. The three students burst out into an irrepressible cheer.

"Wake up, old chap. You've frightened us quite enough."

"Have some brandy. Take a sip from the flask."

"He's all right now," said his companion Harrington. "Heavens, what a fright I got! I was reading here, and he had gone out for a stroll as far as the river, when I

heard a scream and a splash. Out I ran, and by the time
I could find him and fish him out, all life seemed to have
gone. Then Simpson couldn't get a doctor, for he has
a game-leg, and I had to run, and I don't know what I'd
have done without you fellows. That's right, old chap.
Sit up."

Monkhouse Lee had raised himself on his hands, and
looked wildly about him.

" What's up ? " he asked. " I've been in the water.
Ah, yes ; I remember."

A look of fear came into his eyes, and he sank his face
into his hands.

" How did you fall in ? "

" I didn't fall in."

" How then ? "

" I was thrown in. I was standing by the bank, and
something from behind picked me up like a feather and
hurled me in. I heard nothing, and I saw nothing. But
I know what it was, for all that."

" And so do I," whispered Smith.

Lee looked up with a quick glance of surprise.

" You've learned, then ? " he said. " You remember
the advice I gave you ? "

" Yes, and I begin to think that I shall take it."

" I don't know what the deuce you fellows are talking
about," said Hastie, " but I think, if I were you, Harrington, I should get Lee to bed at once. It will be time
enough to discuss the why and the wherefore when he is
a little stronger. I think, Smith, you and I can leave
him alone now. I am walking back to college ; if you
are coming in that direction, we can have a chat."

But it was little chat that they had upon their homeward
path. Smith's mind was too full of the incidents of
the evening, the absence of the mummy from his neighbour's rooms, the step that passed him on the stair, the
reappearance—the extraordinary, inexplicable reappearance of the grisly thing—and then this attack upon Lee,
corresponding so closely to the previous outrage upon

another man against whom Bellingham bore a grudge. All this settled in his thoughts, together with the many little incidents which had previously turned him against his neighbour, and the singular circumstances under which he was first called in to him. What had been a dim suspicion, a vague, fantastic conjecture, had suddenly taken form, and stood out in his mind as a grim fact, a thing not to be denied. And yet, how monstrous it was ! how unheard of ! how entirely beyond all bounds of human experience. An impartial judge, or even the friend who walked by his side, would simply tell him that his eyes had deceived him, that the mummy had been there all the time, that young Lee had tumbled into the river as any other man tumbles into a river, and the blue pill was the best thing for a disordered liver. He felt that he would have said as much if the positions had been reversed. And yet he could swear that Bellingham was a murderer at heart, and that he wielded a weapon such as no man had ever used in all the grim history of crime.

Hastie had branched off to his rooms with a few crisp and emphatic comments upon his friend's unsociability, and Abercrombie Smith crossed the quadrangle to his corner turret with a strong feeling of repulsion for his chambers and their associations. He would take Lee's advice, and move his quarters as soon as possible, for how could a man study when his ear was ever straining for every murmur or footstep in the room below ? He observed, as he crossed over the lawn, that the light was still shining in Bellingham's window, and as he passed up the staircase the door opened, and the man himself looked out at him. With his fat, evil face he was like some bloated spider fresh from the weaving of his poisonous web.

" Good evening," said he. " Won't you come in ? "

" No," cried Smith fiercely.

" No ? You are as busy as ever ? I wanted to ask you about Lee. I was sorry to hear that there was a rumour that something was amiss with him."

His features were grave, but there was the gleam of a hidden laugh in his eyes as he spoke. Smith saw it, and he could have knocked him down for it.

" You'll be sorrier still to hear that Monkhouse Lee is doing very well, and is out of all danger," he answered. " Your hellish tricks have not come off this time. Oh, you needn't try to brazen it out. I know all about it."

Bellingham took a step back from the angry student, and half-closed the door as if to protect himself.

" You are mad," he said. " What do you mean ? Do you assert that I had anything to do with Lee's accident ? "

" Yes," thundered Smith. " You and that bag of bones behind you ; you worked it between you. I tell you what it is, Master B., they have given up burning folk like you, but we still keep a hangman, and, by George ! if any man in this college meets his death while you are here, I'll have you up, and if you don't swing for it, it won't be my fault. You'll find that your filthy Egyptian tricks won't answer in England."

" You're a raving lunatic," said Bellingham.

" All right. You just remember what I say, for you'll find that I'll be better than my word."

The door slammed, and Smith went fuming up to his chamber, where he locked the door upon the inside, and spent half the night in smoking his old briar and brooding over the strange events of the evening.

Next morning Abercrombie Smith heard nothing of his neighbour, but Harrington called upon him in the afternoon to say that Lee was almost himself again. All day Smith stuck fast to his work, but in the evening he determined to pay the visit to his friend Doctor Peterson upon which he had started the night before. A good walk and a friendly chat would be welcome to his jangled nerves.

Bellingham's door was shut as he passed, but glancing back when he was some distance from the turret, he saw his neighbour's head at the window outlined against the lamp-light, his face pressed apparently against the glass as he gazed out into the darkness. It was a blessing to be away from all contact with him, if but for a few hours, and Smith stepped out briskly, and breathed the soft spring air into his lungs. The half-moon lay in the west between two Gothic pinnacles, and threw upon the silvered street a dark tracery from the stone-work above. There was a brisk breeze, and light, fleecy clouds drifted swiftly across the sky. Old's was on the very border of the town, and in five minutes Smith found himself beyond the houses and between the hedges of a May-scented, Oxfordshire lane.

It was a lonely and little-frequented road which led to his friend's house. Early as it was, Smith did not meet a single soul upon his way. He walked briskly along until he came to the avenue gate, which opened into the long, gravel drive leading up to Farlingford. In front of him he could see the cosy, red light of the windows glimmering through the foliage. He stood with his hand upon the iron latch of the swinging gate, and he glanced back at the road along which he had come. Something was coming swiftly down it.

It moved in the shadow of the hedge, silently and fur-tively, a dark, crouching figure, dimly visible against the black background. Even as he gazed back at it, it had lessened its distance by twenty paces, and was fast closing upon him. Out of the darkness he had a glimpse of a scraggy neck, and of two eyes that will ever haunt him in his dreams. He turned, and with a cry of terror he ran for his life up the avenue. There were the red lights, the signals of safety, almost within a stone's-throw of him. He was a famous runner, but never had he run as he ran that night.

The heavy gate had swung into place behind him but he heard it dash open again before his pursuer. As he rushed madly and wildly through the night, he could hear a swift, dry patter behind him, and could see, as he threw back a glance, that this horror was bounding like a tiger at his heels, with blazing eyes and one stringy arm out-thrown. Thank God, the door was ajar. He could see the thin bar of light which shot from the lamp in the hall. Nearer yet sounded the clatter from behind. He heard a hoarse gurgling at his very shoulder. With a shriek he flung himself against the door, slammed and bolted it behind him, and sank half-fainting on to the hall chair.

" My goodness, Smith, what's the matter ? " asked Peterson, appearing at the door of his study.

" Give me some brandy."

Peterson disappeared, and came rushing out again with a glass and a decanter.

" You need it," he said, as his visitor drank off what he poured out for him. " Why, man, you are as white as a cheese."

Smith laid down his glass, rose up, and took a deep breath.

" I am my own man again now," said he. " I was never so unmanned before. But, with your leave, Peterson, I will sleep here to-night, for I don't think I could face that road again except by daylight. It's weak, I know, but I can't help it."

Peterson looked at his visitor with a very questioning eye.

" Of course you shall sleep here if you wish. I'll tell Mrs. Burney to make up the spare bed. Where are you off to now ? "

" Come up with me to the window that overlooks the door. I want you to see what I have seen."

They went up to the window of the upper hall whence they could look down upon the approach to the house. The drive and the fields on either side lay quiet and still, bathed in the peaceful moonlight.

" Well, really, Smith," remarked Peterson, " it is well that I know you to be an abstemious man. What in the world can have frightened you ? "

" I'll tell you presently. But where can it have gone ?

Ah, now, look, look! See the curve of the road just beyond your gate."

"Yes, I see; you needn't pinch my arm off. I saw someone pass. I should say a man, rather thin, apparently, and tall, very tall. But what of him? And what of yourself? You are still shaking like an aspen leaf."

"I have been within hand-grip of the devil, that's all. But come down to your study, and I shall tell you the whole story."

He did so. Under the cheery lamp-light with a glass of wine on the table beside him, and the portly form and florid face of his friend in front, he narrated, in their order, all the events, great and small, which had formed so singular a chain, from the night on which he had found Bellingham fainting in front of the mummy case until this horrid experience of an hour ago.

"There now," he said as he concluded, "that's the whole, black business. It is monstrous and incredible, but it is true."

Doctor Plumptree Peterson sat for some time in silence with a very puzzled expression upon his face.

"I never heard of such a thing in my life, never!" he said at last. "You have told me the facts. Now tell me your inferences."

"You can draw your own."

"But I should like to hear yours. You have thought over the matter, and I have not."

"Well, it must be a little vague in detail, but the main points seem to me to be clear enough. This fellow Bellingham, in his Eastern studies, has got hold of some infernal secret by which a mummy—or possibly only this particular mummy—can be temporarily brought to life. He was trying this disgusting business on the night when he fainted. No doubt the sight of the creature moving had shaken his nerve, even though he had expected it. You remember that almost the first words he said were to call out upon himself as a fool. Well, he got more hardened afterwards, and carried the matter through without fainting. The vitality which he could put into it was evidently only a passing thing, for I have seen it continually in its case as dead as this table. He has some elaborate process, I fancy, by which he brings the thing to pass. Having done it, he naturally bethought him that he might use the creature as an agent. It has intelligence and it has strength. For some purpose he took Lee into his confidence ; but Lee, like a decent Christian, would have nothing to do with such a business. Then they had a row, and Lee vowed that he would tell his sister of Bellingham's true character. Bellingham's game was to prevent him, and he nearly managed it, by setting this creature of his on his track. He had already tried its powers upon another man—Norton—towards whom he had a grudge. It is the merest chance that he has not two murders upon his soul. Then, when I taxed him with the matter, he had the strongest reasons for wishing to get me out of the way before I could convey my knowledge to anyone else. He got his chance when I went out, for he knew my habits and where I was bound for. I have had a narrow shave, Peterson, and it is mere luck you didn't find me on your doorstep in the morning. I'm not a nervous man as a rule, and I never thought to have the fear of death put upon me as it was to-night."

" My dear boy, you take the matter too seriously," said his companion. " Your nerves are out of order with your work, and you make too much of it. How could such a thing as this stride about the streets of Oxford, even at night, without being seen ? "

" It has been seen. There is quite a scare in the town about an escaped ape, as they imagine the creature to be. It is the talk of the place."

" Well, it's a striking chain of events. And yet, my dear fellow, you must allow that each incident in itself is capable of a more natural explanation."

" What ! even my adventure of to-night ? "

" Certainly. You come out with your nerves all
599

unstrung, and your head full of this theory of yours. Some gaunt, half-famished tramp steals after you, and seeing you run, is emboldened to pursue you. Your fears and imagination do the rest."

" It won't do, Peterson ; it won't do."

" And again, in the instance of your finding the mummy case empty, and then a few moments later with an occupant, you know that it was lamp-light, that the lamp was half turned down, and that you had no special reason to look hard at the case. It is quite possible that you may have overlooked the creature in the first instance."

" No, no ; it is out of the question."

" And then Lee may have fallen into the river, and Norton been garrotted. It is certainly a formidable indictment that you have against Bellingham ; but if you were to place it before a police magistrate, he would simply laugh in your face."

" I know he would. That is why I mean to take the matter into my own hands."

" Eh ? "

" Yes ; I feel that a public duty rests upon me, and, besides, I must do it for my own safety, unless I choose to allow myself to be hunted by this beast out of the college, and that would be a little too feeble. I have quite made up my mind what I shall do. And first of all, may I use your paper and pens for an hour ? "

" Most certainly. You will find all that you want upon that side-table."

Abercrombie Smith sat down before a sheet of foolscap, and for an hour, and then for a second hour his pen travelled swiftly over it. Page after page was finished and tossed aside while his friend leaned back in his arm-chair, looking across at him with patient curiosity. At last, with an exclamation of satisfaction, Smith sprang to his feet, gathered his papers up into order, and laid the last one upon Peterson's desk.

" Kindly sign this as a witness," he said.

" A witness ? Of what ? "

" Of my signature, and of the date. The date is the most important. Why, Peterson, my life might hang upon it."

" My dear Smith, you are talking wildly. Let me beg you to go to bed."

" On the contrary, I never spoke so deliberately in my life. And I will promise to go to bed the moment you have signed it."

" But what is it ? "

" It is a statement of all that I have been telling you to-night. I wish you to witness it."

" Certainly," said Peterson, signing his name under that of his companion. " There you are ! But what is the idea ? "

" You will kindly retain it, and produce it in case I am arrested."

" Arrested ? For what ? "

" For murder. It is quite on the cards. I wish to be ready for every event. There is only one course open to me, and I am determined to take it."

" For Heaven's sake, don't do anything rash ! "

" Believe me, it would be far more rash to adopt any other course. I hope that we won't need to bother you, but it will ease my mind to know that you have this statement of my motives. And now I am ready to take your advice and to go to roost, for I want to be at my best in the morning."

Abercrombie Smith was not an entirely pleasant man to have as an enemy. Slow and easy-tempered, he was formidable when driven to action. He brought to every purpose in life the same deliberate resoluteness which had distinguished him as a scientific student. He had laid his studies aside for a day, but he intended that the day should not be wasted. Not a word did he say to his host as to his plans, but by nine o'clock he was well on his way to Oxford.

In the High Street he stopped at Clifford's, the gunmaker's, and bought a heavy revolver, with a box of central-fire cartridges. Six of them he slipped into the chambers, and half-cocking the weapon, placed it in the pocket of his coat. He then made his way to Hastie's rooms, where the big oarsman was lounging over his breakfast, with the *Sporting Times* propped up against the coffee-pot.

" Hullo ! What's up ? " he asked. " Have some coffee ? "

" No, thank you. I want you to come with me, Hastie, and do what I ask you."

" Certainly, my boy."

" And bring a heavy stick with you."

" Hullo ! " Hastie stared. " Here's a hunting crop that would fell an ox."

" One other thing. You have a box of amputating knives. Give me the longest of them."

" There you are. You seem to be fairly on the war trail. Anything else ? "

" No ; that will do." Smith placed the knife inside his coat, and led the way to the quadrangle. " We are neither of us chickens, Hastie," said he. " I think I can do this job alone, but I take you as a precaution. I am going to have a little talk with Bellingham. If I have only him to deal with, I won't, of course, need you. If I shout, however, up you come, and lam out with your whip as hard as you can lick. Do you understand ? "

" All right. I'll come if I hear you bellow."

" Stay here, then. I may be a little time, but don't budge until I come down."

" I'm a fixture."

Smith ascended the stairs, opened Bellingham's door and stepped in. Bellingham was seated behind his table, writing. Beside him, among his litter of strange possessions, towered the mummy case, with its sale number 249 still stuck upon its front, and its hideous occupant stiff and stark within it. Smith looked very deliberately round him, closed the door, and then, stepping across to the fireplace, struck a match and set the fire alight. Bellingham sat staring, with amazement and rage upon his bloated face.

"Well, really now, you make yourself at home," he gasped.

Smith sat himself deliberately down, placing his watch upon the table, drew out his pistol, cocked it, and laid it in his lap. Then he took the long amputating knife from his bosom, and threw it down in front of Bellingham.

"Now, then," said he, "just get to work and cut up that mummy."

"Oh, is that it?" said Bellingham with a sneer.

"Yes, that is it. They tell me that the law can't touch you. But I have a law that will set matters straight. If in five minutes you have not set to work, I swear by the God who made me that I will put a bullet through your brain!"

"You would murder me?"

Bellingham had half-risen, and his face was the colour of putty.

"Yes."

"And for what?"

"To stop your mischief. One minute has gone."

"But what have I done?"

"I know and you know."

"This is mere bullying."

"Two minutes are gone."

"But you must give reasons. You are a madman—a dangerous madman. Why should I destroy my own property? It is a valuable mummy."

"You must cut it up, and you must burn it."

"I will do no such thing."

"Four minutes are gone."

Smith took up the pistol and he looked towards Bellingham with an inexorable face. As the second-hand stole round, he raised his hand, and the finger twitched upon the trigger.

" There ! there ! I'll do it ! " screamed Bellingham.

In frantic haste he caught up the knife and hacked at the figure of the mummy, ever glancing round to see the eye and the weapon of his terrible visitor bent upon him. The creature crackled and snapped under every stab of the keen blade. A thick, yellow dust rose up from it. Spices and dried essences rained down upon the floor. Suddenly, with a rending crack, its backbone snapped asunder, and it fell, a brown heap of sprawling limbs, upon the floor.

" Now into the fire ! " said Smith.

The flames leaped and roared as the dried and tinder-like debris was piled upon it. The little room was like the stoke-hole of a steamer and the sweat ran down the faces of the two men ; but still the one stooped and worked, while the other sat watching him with a set face. A thick, fat smoke oozed out from the fire, and a heavy smell of burned resin and singed hair filled the air. In a quarter of an hour a few charred and brittle sticks were all that was left of Lot No. 249.

" Perhaps that will satisfy you," snarled Bellingham, with hate and fear in his little grey eyes as he glanced back at his tormentor.

" No ; I must make a clean sweep of all your materials. We must have no more devil's tricks. In with all these leaves ! They may have something to do with it."

" And what now ? " asked Bellingham, when the leaves also had been added to the blaze.

" Now the roll of papyrus which you had on the table that night. It is in that drawer, I think."

" No, no," shouted Bellingham. " Don't burn that ! Why, man, you don't know what you do. It is unique ; it contains wisdom which is nowhere else to be found."

" Out with it ! "

" But look here, Smith, you can't really mean it. I'll share the knowledge with you. I'll teach you all that is in it. Or, stay, let me only copy it before you burn it ! "

Smith stepped forward and turned the key in the drawer. Taking out the yellow, curled roll of paper, he threw it into the fire, and pressed it down with his heel. Bellingham screamed, and grabbed at it ; but Smith pushed him back and stood over it until it was reduced to a formless, grey ash.

" Now, Master B.," said he, " I think I have pretty well drawn your teeth. You'll hear from me again, if you return to your old tricks. And now good morning, for I must go back to my studies."

And such is the narrative of Abercrombie Smith as to the singular events which occurred in Old College, Oxford, in the spring of '84. As Bellingham left the university immediately afterwards, and was last heard of in the Soudan, there is no one who can contradict his statement. But the wisdom of men is small, and the ways of Nature are strange, and who shall put a bound to the dark things which may be found by those who seek for them ?

48. " De Profundis "

SO long as the oceans are the ligaments which bind together the great, broadcast British Empire, so long will there be a dash of romance in our minds. For the soul is swayed by the waters, as the waters are by the moon, and when the great highways of an empire are along such roads as these, so full of strange sights and sounds, with danger ever running like a hedge on either side of the course, it is a dull mind indeed which does not bear away with it some trace of such a passage. And now, Britain lies far beyond herself, for the three-mile limit of every seaboard is her frontier, which has been won by hammer and loom and pick rather than by arts of war. For it is written in history that neither king nor army can bar the path to the man who, having two-pence in his strong box, and knowing well where he can turn it to threepence, sets his mind to that one end. And as the frontier has broadened, the mind of Britain has broadened, too, spreading out until all men can see that the ways of the island are continental, even as those of the Continent are insular.

But for this a price must be paid, and the price is a grievous one. As the beast of old must have one young, human life as a tribute every year, so to our Empire we throw from day to day the pick and flower of our youth. The engine is world-wide and strong, but the only fuel that will drive it is the lives of British men. Thus it is that in the grey, old cathedrals as we look round upon the brasses on the walls, we see strange names, such names as they who reared those walls had never heard, for it is in Peshawur, and Umballah, and Korti, and Fort Pearson that the youngsters die, leaving only a precedent and a brass behind them. But if every man had his obelisk, even where he lay, then no frontier line need be drawn, for a cordon of British graves would ever show how high the Anglo-Celtic tide had lapped.

This, then, as well as the waters which join us to the world, has done something to tinge us with romance. For when so many have their loved ones over the seas, walking amid hillmen's bullets, or swamp malaria, where death is sudden and distance great, then mind communes with mind, and strange stories arise of dream, presentiment, or vision, where the mother sees her dying son, and is past the first bitterness of her grief ere the message comes which should have broken the news. The learned have of late looked into the matter and have even labelled it with a name ; but what can we know more of it save that a poor, stricken soul, when hard-pressed and driven, can shoot across the earth some ten-thousand-mile-distant picture of its trouble to the mind which is most akin to it. Far be it from me to say that there lies no such power within us, for of all things which the brain will grasp the last will be itself ; but yet it is well to be very cautious over such matters, for once at least I have known that which was within the laws of Nature seem to be far upon the further side of them.

John Vansittart was the younger partner of the firm of Hudson and Vansittart, coffee exporters of the Island of Ceylon, three-quarters Dutchman by descent, but wholly English in his sympathies. For years I had been his agent in London, and when in '72 he came over to England for a three months' holiday, he turned to me for the introductions which would enable him to see something of town and country life. Armed with seven letters he left my offices, and for many weeks scrappy notes from different parts of the country let me know that he had found favour in the eyes of my friends. Then came word of his engagement to Emily Lawson, of a cadet branch of the Hereford Lawsons, and at the very tail of the first flying rumour the news of his absolute marriage, for the wooing of a wanderer must be short, and the days were already crowding on towards the date when he must be upon his homeward journey. They were to return together to Colombo in one of the firm's own thousand-ton, barque-rigged sailing ships, and this was to be their princely honeymoon, at once a necessity and a delight.

Those were the royal days of coffee-planting in Ceylon, before a single season and a rotting fungus drove a whole community through years of despair to one of the greatest commercial victories which pluck and ingenuity ever won. Not often is it that men have the heart when their one great industry is withered to rear up, in a few years, another as rich to take its place, and the tea-fields of Ceylon are as true a monument to courage as is the lion at Waterloo. But in '72 there was no cloud yet above the skyline, and the hopes of the planters were as high and as bright as the hill-sides on which they reared their crops. Vansittart came down to London with his young and beautiful wife. I was introduced, dined with them, and it was finally arranged that I, since business called me also to Ceylon, should be a fellow-passenger with them on the

Eastern Star, which was timed to sail on the following Monday.

It was on the Sunday evening that I saw him again. He was shown up into my rooms about nine o'clock at night, with the air of a man who is bothered and out of sorts. His hand, as I shook it, was hot and dry.

" I wish, Atkinson," said he, " that you could give me a little lime-juice and water. I have a beastly thirst upon me, and the more I take the more I seem to want."

I rang and ordered a caraffe and glasses. " You are flushed," said I. " You don't look the thing."

" No, I'm clean off colour. Got a touch of rheumatism in my back, and don't seem to taste my food. It is this vile London that is choking me. I'm not used to breathing air which has been used up by four million lungs all sucking away on every side of you." He flapped his crooked hands before his face, like a man who really struggles for his breath.

" A touch of the sea will soon set you right."

" Yes, I'm of one mind with you there. That's the thing for me. I want no other doctor. If I don't get to sea to-morrow I'll have an illness. There are no two ways about it." He drank off a tumbler of lime-juice, and clapped his two hands with his knuckles doubled up into the small of his back.

" That seems to ease me," said he, looking at me with a filmy eye. " Now I want your help, Atkinson, for I am rather awkwardly placed."

" As how ? "

" This way. My wife's mother got ill and wired for her. I couldn't go—you know best yourself how tied I have been—so she had to go alone. Now I've had another wire to say that she can't come to-morrow, but that she will pick up the ship at Falmouth on Wednesday. We put in there, you know, though I count it hard, Atkinson, that a man should be asked to believe in a mystery, and cursed if he can't do it. Cursed, mind you, no less." He leaned forward and began to draw a catchy breath like a man who is poised on the very edge of a sob.

Then first it came into my mind that I had heard much of the hard-drinking life of the island, and that from brandy came these wild words and fevered hands. The flushed cheek and the glazing eye were those of one whose drink is strong upon him. Sad it was to see so noble a young man in the grip of that most bestial of all the devils.

"You should lie down," I said, with some severity.

He screwed up his eyes like a man who is striving to wake himself, and looked up with an air of surprise.

"So I shall presently," said he, quite rationally. "I felt quite swimmy just now, but I am my own man again now. Let me see, what was I talking about? Oh ah, of course, about the wife. She joins the ship at Falmouth. Now I want to go round by water. I believe my health depends upon it. I just want a little clean, first-lung air to set me on my feet again. I ask you, like a good fellow, to go to Falmouth by rail, so that in case we should be late you may be there to look after the wife. Put up at the Royal Hotel, and I will wire her that you are there. Her sister will bring her down, so that it will be all plain sailing."

"I'll do it with pleasure," said I. "In fact, I would rather go by rail, for we shall have enough and to spare of the sea before we reach Colombo. I believe, too, that you badly need a change. Now, I should go and turn in, if I were you."

"Yes, I will. I sleep aboard to-night. You know," he continued, as the film settled down again over his eyes, "I've not slept well the last few nights. I've been troubled with theolololog—that is to say, theolological—hang it," with a desperate effort, "with the doubts of theolologicians. Wondering why the Almighty made us, you know, and why He made our heads swimmy, and fixed little pains into the small of our backs. Maybe I'll do better to-night." He rose and steadied himself with an effort against the corner of the chair back.

" Look here, Vansittart," said I gravely, stepping up to him, and laying my hand upon his sleeve, " I can give you a shakedown here. You are not fit to go out. You are all over the place. You've been mixing your drinks."

" Drinks ! " He stared at me stupidly.

" You used to carry your liquor better than this."

" I give you my word, Atkinson, that I have not had a drain for two days. It's not drink. I don't know what it is. I suppose you think this is drink." He took up my hand in his burning grasp, and passed it over his own forehead.

" Great Lord ! " said I.

His skin felt like a thin sheet of velvet beneath which lies a close-packed layer of small shot. It was smooth to the touch at any one place, but to a finger passed along it, rough as a nutmeg-grater.

" It's all right," said he, smiling at my startled face. " I've had the prickly heat nearly as bad."

" But this is never prickly heat."

" No, it's London. It's breathing bad air. But to-morrow it'll be all right. There's a surgeon aboard, so I shall be in safe hands. I must be off now."

" Not you," said I, pushing him back into a chair. " This is past a joke. You don't move from here until a doctor sees you. Just stay where you are."

I caught up my hat, and rushing round to the house of a neighbouring physician, I brought him back with me. The room was empty and Vansittart gone. I rang the bell. The servant said that the gentleman had ordered a cab the instant that I had left, and had gone off in it. He had told the cabman to drive to the docks.

" Did the gentleman seem ill ? " I asked.

" Ill ! " The man smiled. " No, sir, he was singin' his 'ardest all the time."

The information was not as reassuring as my servant seemed to think, but I reflected that he was going straight back to the *Eastern Star*, and that there was a doctor aboard of her, so that there was nothing which I could do in the matter. None the less, when I thought of his thirst, his burning hands, his heavy eye, his tripping speech, and lastly, of that leprous forehead, I carried with me to bed an unpleasant memory of my visitor and his visit.

At eleven o'clock next day I was at the docks, but the *Eastern Star* had already moved down the river, and was nearly at Gravesend. To Gravesend I went by train, but only to see her topmasts far off, with a plume of smoke from a tug in front of her. I would hear no more of my friend until I rejoined him at Falmouth. When I got back to my offices, a telegram was awaiting me from Mrs. Vansittart, asking me to meet her ; and next evening found us both at the Royal Hotel, Falmouth, where we were to wait for the *Eastern Star*. Ten days passed, and there came no news of her.

They were ten days which I am not likely to forget. On the very day that the *Eastern Star* had cleared from the Thames, a furious, easterly gale had sprung up, and blew on from day to day for the greater part of a week without the sign of a lull. Such a screaming, raving, long-drawn storm has never been known on the southern coast. From our hotel windows the sea view was all banked in haze, with a little rain-swept half-circle under our very eyes, churned and lashed into one tossing stretch of foam. So heavy was the wind upon the waves that little sea could rise, for the crest of each billow was torn shrieking from it, and lashed broadcast over the bay. Clouds, wind, sea, all were rushing to the west, and there, looking down at this mad jumble of elements, I waited on day after day, my sole companion a white, silent woman, with terror in her eyes, her forehead pressed ever against the window, her gaze from early morning to the fall of night fixed upon that wall of grey haze through which the loom of a vessel might come. She said nothing, but that face of hers was one long wail of fear.

On the fifth day I took counsel with an old seaman. I should have preferred to have done so alone, but she saw me speak with him, and was at our side in an instant, with parted lips and a prayer in her eyes.

" Seven days out from London," said he, " and five in the gale. ' Well, the Channel's swept clear by this wind. There's three things for it. She may have popped into port on the French side. That's like enough."

" No, no ; he knew we were here. He would have telegraphed."

" Ah, yes, so he would. Well, then, he might have run for it, and if he did that he won't be very far from Madeira by now. That'll be it, marm, you may depend."

" Or else ? You said there was a third chance."

" Did I, marm. No, only two, I think. I don't think I said anything of a third. Your ship's out there, depend upon it, away out in the Atlantic, and you'll hear of it time enough, for the weather is breaking. Now don't you fret, marm, and wait quiet and you'll find a real blue Cornish sky to-morrow."

The old seaman was right in his surmise, for the next day broke calm and bright, with only a low, dwindling cloud in the west to mark the last trailing wreaths of the storm-wrack. But still there came no word from the sea, and no sign of the ship. Three more weary days had passed, the weariest that I have ever spent, when there came a seafaring man to the hotel with a letter. I gave a shout of joy. It was from the captain of the *Eastern Star*. As I read the first lines of it I whisked my hand over it, but she laid her own upon it and drew it away. " I have seen it," said she, in a cold, quiet voice. " I may as well see the rest, too."

" DEAR SIR," said the letter,

·   " Mr. Vansittart is down with the small-pox, and we are blown so far on our course that we don't know what to do, he being off his head and unfit to tell us. By dead reckoning we are but three hundred miles from Funchal, so I take it that it is best that we should push on there, get Mr. V. into hospital, and wait in the Bay until you

come. There's a sailing-ship due from Falmouth to
Funchal in a few days' time, as I understand. This
goes by the brig *Marian* of Falmouth, and five pounds
is due to the master,

" Yours respectfully,
" JNO. HINES."

She was a wonderful woman that, only a chit of a girl
fresh from school, but as quiet and strong as a man. She
said nothing—only pressed her lips together tight, and
put on her bonnet.

" You are going out ? " I asked.

" Yes."

" Can I be of use ? "

" No ; I am going to the doctor's."

" To the doctor's ? "

" Yes. To learn how to nurse a small-pox case."

She was busy at that all the evening, and next morning
we were off with a fine ten-knot breeze in the barque
Rose of Sharon for Madeira. For five days we made
good time, and were no great way from the island ; but
on the sixth there fell a calm, and we lay without motion
on a sea of oil, heaving slowly, but making not a foot of
way.

At ten o'clock that night Emily Vansittart and I stood
leaning on the starboard railing of the poop, with a full
moon shining at our backs, and casting a black shadow
of the barque, and of our own two heads, upon the shining
water. From the shadow a broadening path of moonshine stretched away to the lonely skyline, flickering and
shimmering in the gentle heave of the swell. We were
talking with bent heads, chatting of the calm, of the
chances of wind, of the look of the sky, when there came
a sudden plop, like a rising salmon, and there, in the
clear light, John Vansittart sprang out of the water and
looked up at us.

I never saw anything clearer in my life than I saw that
man. The moon shone full upon him, and he was but

three oars' length away. His face was more puffed than when I had seen him last, mottled here and there with dark scabs, his mouth and eyes open as one who is struck with some overpowering surprise. He had some white stuff streaming from his shoulders, and one hand was raised to his ear, the other crooked across his breast. I saw him leap from the water into the air, and in the dead calm the waves of his coming lapped up against the sides of the vessel. Then his figure sank back into the water again, and I heard a rending, crackling sound like a bundle of brushwood snapping in the fire on a frosty night. There were no signs of him when I looked again, but a swift swirl and eddy on the still sea still marked the spot where he had been. How long I stood there, tingling to my finger-tips, holding up an unconscious woman with one hand, clutching at the rail of the vessel with the other, was more than I could afterwards tell. I had been noted as a man of slow and unresponsive emotions, but this time at least I was shaken to the core. Once and twice I struck my foot upon the deck to be certain that I was indeed the master of my own senses, and that this was not some mad prank of an unruly brain. As I stood, still marvelling, the woman shivered, opened her eyes, gasped, and then standing erect with her hands upon the rail, looked out over the moonlit sea with a face which had aged ten years in a summer night.

" You saw his vision ? " she murmured.

" I saw something."

" It was he ! It was John ! He is dead ! "

I muttered some lame words of doubt.

" Doubtless he died at this hour," she whispered. " In hospital at Madeira. I have read of such things. His thoughts were with me. His vision came to me. Oh, my John, my dear, dear, lost John ! "

She broke out suddenly into a storm of weeping, and I led her down into her cabin, where I left her with her sorrow. That night a brisk breeze blew up from the east, and in the evening of the next day we passed the two islets of Los Desertos, and dropped anchor at sundown in the Bay of Funchal. The *Eastern Star* lay no great distance from us, with the quarantine flag flying from her main, and her Jack half-way up her peak.

" You see," said Mrs. Vansittart quickly. She was dry-eyed now, for she had known how it would be.

That night we received permission from the authorities to move on board the *Eastern Star*. The captain, Hines, was waiting upon deck with confusion and grief contending upon his bluff face as he sought for words with which to break this heavy tidings, but she took the story from his lips.

" I know that my husband is dead," she said. " He died yesterday night, about ten o'clock, in hospital at Madeira, did he not ? "

The seaman stared aghast. " No, marm, he died eight days ago at sea, and we had to bury him out there, for we lay in a belt of calm, and could not say when we might make the land."

Well, those are the main facts about the death of John Vansittart, and his appearance to his wife somewhere about lat. 35 N. and long. 15 W. A clearer case of a wraith has seldom been made out, and since then it has been told as such, and put into print as such, and endorsed by a learned society as such, and so floated off with many others to support the recent theory of telepathy. For myself, I hold telepathy to be proved, but I would snatch this one case from amid the evidence, and say that I do not think that it was the wraith of John Vansittart, but John Vansittart himself whom we saw that night leaping into the moonlight out of the depths of the Atlantic. It has ever been my belief that some strange chance—one of those chances which seem so improbable and yet so constantly occur—had becalmed us over the very spot where the man had been buried a week before. For the rest, the surgeon tells me that the leaden weight was not too firmly fixed, and that seven days bring about changes which fetch a body to the surface. Coming from the depth to which the weight would have sunk it, he explains that it might well attain such a velocity as to carry it clear of the water. Such is my own explanation of the matter, and if you ask me what then became of the body, I must recall to you that snapping, crackling sound, with the swirl in the water. The shark is a surface feeder and is plentiful in those parts.

49. *The Lift*

FLIGHT-COMMANDER STANGATE should have been happy. He had come safely through the war without a hurt, and with a good name in the most heroic of services. He had only just turned thirty, and a great career seemed to lie ahead of him. Above all, beautiful Mary MacLean was walking by his side, and he had her promise that she was there for life. What could a young man ask for more ? And yet there was a heavy load upon his heart.

He could not explain it himself, and endeavoured to reason himself out of it. There was the blue sky above him, the blue sea in front, the beautiful gardens with their throngs of happy pleasure-seekers around. Above all, there was that sweet face turned upon his with questioning concern. Why could he not raise himself to so joyful an environment ? He made effort after effort, but they were not convincing enough to deceive the quick instinct of a loving woman.

" What is it, Tom ? " she asked anxiously. " I can see that something is clouding you. Do tell me if I can help you in any way."

He laughed in shamefaced fashion.

" It is such a sin to spoil our little outing," he said. " I could kick myself round these gardens when I think of it. Don't worry, my darling, for I know the cloud will roll off. I suppose I am a creature of nerves, though I should have got past that by now. The Flying Service is supposed either to break you or to warrant you for life."

" It is nothing definite, then ? "

" No, it is nothing definite. That's the worst of it. You could fight it more easily if it was. It's just a dead, heavy depression here in my chest and across my forehead. But do forgive me, dear girl ! What a brute I am to shadow you like this."

" But I love to share even the smallest trouble."

" Well, it's gone—vamosed—vanished. We will talk about it no more."

She gave him a swift, penetrating glance.

" No, no, Tom ; your brow shows, as well as feels. Tell me, dear, have you often felt like this ? You really look very ill. Sit here, dear, in the shade and tell me of it."

They sat together in the shadow of the great, latticed Tower which reared itself six hundred feet high beside them.

" I have an absurd faculty," said he ; " I don't know that I have ever mentioned it to anyone before. But when imminent danger is threatening me I get these strange forebodings. Of course it is absurd to-day in these peaceful surroundings. It only shows how queerly these things work. But it is the first time that it has deceived me."

" When had you it before ? "

" When I was a lad it seized me one morning. I was nearly drowned that afternoon. I had it when the burglar came to Morton Hall and I got a bullet through my coat. Then twice in the war when I was overmatched and escaped by a miracle, I had this strange feeling before ever I climbed into my machine. Then it lifts quite suddenly, like a mist in the sunshine. Why, it is lifting now. Look at me ! Can't you see that it is so ? "

She could indeed. He had turned in a minute from a haggard man to a laughing boy. She found herself laughing in sympathy. A rush of high spirits and energy had swept away his strange foreboding and filled his whole soul with the vivid, dancing joy of youth.

" Thank goodness ! " he cried. " I think it is your dear eyes that have done it. I could not stand that wistful look in them. What a silly, foolish nightmare it all has been ! There's an end for ever in my belief in presentiments. Now, dear girl, we have just time for one good turn before luncheon. After that the gardens get so crowded that it is hopeless to do anything. Shall we have a side-show, or the great wheel, or the flying boat, or what ? "

" What about the Tower ? " she asked, glancing upwards. " Surely that glorious air and the view from the top would drive the last wisps of cloud out of your mind."

He looked at his watch.

" Well, it's past twelve, but I suppose we could do it all in an hour. But it doesn't seem to be working. What about it, conductor ? "

The man shook his head and pointed to a little knot of people who were assembled at the entrance.

" They've all been waiting, sir. It's hung up, but the gear is being overhauled, and I expect the signal every minute. If you join the others I promise it won't be long."

They had hardly reached the group when the steel face of the lift rolled aside—a sign that there was hope in the future. The motley crowd drifted through the opening and waited expectantly upon the wooden platform. They were not numerous, for the gardens are not crowded until the afternoon, but they were fair samples of the kindly, good-humoured north-country folk who take their annual holiday at Northam. Their faces were all upturned now, and they were watching with keen interest a man who was descending the steel framework. It seemed a dangerous, precarious business, but he came as swiftly as an ordinary mortal upon a staircase.

" My word ! " said the conductor, glancing up. " Jim has got a move on this morning."

"Who is he?" asked Commander Stangate.

"That's Jim Barnes, sir, the best workman that ever went on a scaffold. He fair lives up there. Every bolt and rivet are under his care. He's a wonder, is Jim."

"But don't argue religion with him," said one of the group.

The attendant laughed.

"Ah, you know him, then," said he. "No, don't argue religion with him."

"Why not?" asked the officer.

"Well, he takes it very hard, he does. He's the shining light of his sect."

"It ain't hard to be that," said the knowing one. "I've heard there are only six folk in the fold. He's one of those who picture heaven as the exact size of their own back street conventicle and everyone else left outside it."

"Better not tell him so while he's got that hammer in his hand," said the conductor, in a hurried whisper. "Hallo, Jim, how goes it this morning?"

The man slid swiftly down the last thirty feet, and then balanced himself on a cross-bar while he looked at the little group in the lift. As he stood there, clad in a leather suit, with his pliers and other tools dangling from his brown belt, he was a figure to please the eye of an artist. The man was very tall and gaunt, with great, straggling limbs and every appearance of giant strength. His face was a remarkable one, noble and yet sinister, with dark eyes and hair, a prominent, hooked nose, and a beard which flowed over his chest. He steadied himself with one knotted hand, while the other held a steel hammer dangling by his knee.

"It's all ready aloft," said he. "I'll go up with you if I may." He sprang down from his perch and joined the others in the lift.

"I suppose you are always watching it," said the young lady.

"That is what I am engaged for, miss. From morning

to night, and often from night to morning, I am up here.
There are times when I feel as if I were not a man at all,
but a fowl of the air. They fly round me, the creatures,
as I lie out on the girders, and they cry to me until I
find myself crying back to the poor, soulless things."

" It's a great charge," said the Commander, glancing
up at the wonderful tracery of steel outlined against the
deep blue sky.

" Aye, sir, and there is not a nut nor a screw that is
not in my keeping. Here's my hammer to ring them true
and my spanner to wrench them tight. As the Lord over
the earth, so am I—even I—over the Tower, with power
of life and power of death, aye of death and of life."

The hydraulic machinery had begun to work and the
lift very slowly ascended. As it mounted, the glorious
panorama of the coast and bay gradually unfolded itself.
So engrossing was the view that the passengers hardly
noticed it when the platform stopped abruptly between
stages at the five hundred foot level. Barnes, the workman, muttered that something must be amiss, and springing like a cat across the gap which separated them from
the trellis-work of metal he clambered out of sight. The
motley little party, suspended in mid-air, lost something
of their British shyness under such unwonted conditions
and began to compare notes with each other. One couple,
who addressed each other as Dolly and Billy, announced
to the company that they were the particular stars of the
Hippodrome bill, and kept their neighbours tittering with
their rather obvious wit. A buxom mother, her pre-
cocious son, and two married couples upon holiday
formed an appreciative audience.

" You'd like to be a sailor, would you ? " said Billy
the comedian, in answer to some remark of the boy.
" Look 'ere, my nipper, you'll end up as a blooming
corpse if you ain't careful. See 'im standin' at the edge.
At this hour of the morning I can't bear to watch it."

" What's the hour got to do with it ? " asked a stout
commercial traveller.

" My nerves are worth nothin' before midday. Why, lookin' down there, and seein' those folk like dots, puts me all in a twitter. My family is all alike in the mornin'."

" I expect," said Dolly, a high-coloured young woman, " that they're all alike the evening before."

There was a general laugh, which was led by the comedian.

" You got it across that time, Dolly. It's K.O. for Battling Billy—still senseless when last heard of. If my family is laughed at I'll leave the room."

" It's about time we did," said the commercial traveller, who was a red-faced, choleric person. " It's a disgrace the way they hold us up. I'll write to the company."

" Where's the bell-push ? " said Billy. " I'm goin' to ring."

" What for—the waiter ? " asked the lady.

" For the conductor, the chauffeur, whoever it is that drives the old bus up and down. Have they run out of petrol, or broke the mainspring, or what ? "

" We have a fine view, anyhow," said the Commander.

" Well, I've had that," remarked Billy. " I'm done with it, and I'm for getting on."

" I'm getting nervous," cried the stout mother. " I do hope there is nothing wrong with the lift."

" I say, hold on to the slack of my coat, Dolly. I'm going to look over and chance it. Oh, Lord, it makes me sick and giddy ! There's a horse down under, and it ain't bigger than a mouse. I don't see anyone lookin' after us. Where's old Isaiah the prophet who came up with us ? "

" He shinned out of it mighty quick when he thought trouble was coming."

" Look here," said Dolly, looking very perturbed, " this is a nice thing, I don't think. Here we are five hundred foot up, and stuck for the day as like as not. I'm due for the *matinée* at the Hippodrome. I'm sorry for the company if they don't get me down in time for that. I'm billed all over the town for a new song."

" A new one ! What's that, Dolly ? "

" A real pot o' ginger, I tell you. It's called ' On the Road to Ascot.' I've got a hat four foot across to sing it in."

" Come on, Dolly, let's have a rehearsal while we wait."

" No, no ; the young lady here wouldn't understand."

" I'd be very glad to hear it," cried Mary MacLean. " Please don't let me prevent you."

" The words were written to the hat. I couldn't sing the verses without the hat. But there's a nailin' good chorus to it :

> " ' If you want a little mascot
> When you're on the way to Ascot,
> Try the lady with the cartwheel hat.' "

She had a tuneful voice and a sense of rhythm which set everyone nodding. " Try it now all together," she cried ; and the strange little haphazard company sang it with all their lungs.

" I say," said Billy, " that ought to wake somebody up. What ? Let's try a shout all together."

It was a fine effort, but there was no response. It was clear that the management down below was quite ignorant or impotent. No sound came back to them.

The passengers became alarmed. The commercial traveller was rather less rubicund. Billy still tried to joke, but his efforts were not well received. The officer in his blue uniform at once took his place as rightful leader in a crisis. They all looked to him and appealed to him.

" What would you advise, sir ? You don't think there's any danger of it coming down, do you ? "

" Not the least. But it's awkward to be stuck here all the same. I think I could jump across on to that girder. Then perhaps I could see what is wrong."

" No, no, Tom ; for goodness' sake, don't leave us ! "

" Some people have a nerve," said Billy. " Fancy jumping across a five-hundred-foot drop ! "

"I dare say the gentleman did worse things in the war."

"Well, I wouldn't do it myself—not if they starred me in the bills. It's all very well for old Isaiah. It's his job, and I wouldn't do him out of it."

Three sides of the lift were shut in with wooden partitions, pierced with windows for the view. The fourth side, facing the sea, was clear. Stangate leaned over as far as he could and looked upwards. As he did so there came from above him a peculiar, sonorous, metallic twang, as if a mighty harp-string had been struck. Some distance up—a hundred feet, perhaps—he could see a long, brown, corded arm, which was working furiously among the wire cordage above. The form was beyond his view, but he was fascinated by this bare, sinewy arm which tugged and pulled and sagged and stabbed.

"It's all right," he said, and a general sigh of relief broke from his strange comrades at his words. "There is someone above us setting things right."

"It's old Isaiah," said Billy, stretching his neck round the corner. "I can't see him, but it's his arm for a dollar. What's he got in his hand? Looks like a screwdriver or something. No, by George, it's a file."

As he spoke there came another sonorous twang from above. There was a troubled frown upon the officer's brow.

"I say, dash it all, that's the very sound our steel hawser made when it parted, strand by strand, at Dixmude. What the deuce is the fellow about? Heh, there! what are you trying to do?"

The man had ceased his work and was now slowly descending the iron trellis.

"All right, he's coming," said Stangate to his startled companions. "It's all right, Mary. Don't be frightened, any of you. It's absurd to suppose he would really weaken the cord that holds us."

A pair of high boots appeared from above. Then came the leathern breeches, the belt with its dangling tools, the muscular form, and, finally, the fierce, swarthy, eagle face of the workman. His coat was off and his shirt open showing the hairy chest. As he appeared there came another sharp, snapping vibration from above. The man made his way down in leisurely fashion, and then, balancing himself upon the cross-girder and leaning against the side-piece, he stood with folded arms, looking from under his heavy black brows at the huddled passengers upon the platform.

"Hallo!" said Stangate. "What's the matter?"

The man stood impassive and silent, with something indescribably menacing in his fixed, unwinking stare.

The flying officer grew angry.

"Hallo! Are you deaf?" he cried. "How long do you mean to have us stuck here?"

The man stood silent. There was something devilish in his appearance.

"I'll complain of you, my lad," said Billy, in a quivering voice. "This won't stop here, I can promise you."

"Look here!" cried the officer. "We have ladies here and you are alarming them. Why are we stuck here? Has the machinery gone wrong?"

"You are here," said the man, "because I have put a wedge against the hawser above you."

"You fouled the line! How dared you do such a thing! What right have you to frighten the women and put us all to this inconvenience? Take that wedge out this instant, or it will be the worse for you."

The man was silent.

"Do you hear what I say? Why the devil don't you answer? Is this a joke or what? We've had about enough of it, I tell you."

Mary MacLean had gripped her lover by the arm in an agony of sudden panic.

"Oh, Tom!" she cried. "Look at his eyes—look at his horrible eyes! The man is a maniac."

The workman stirred suddenly into sinister life. His dark face broke into writhing lines of passion, and his

624

fierce eyes glowed like embers, while he shook one long arm in the air.

" Behold," he cried, " those who are mad to the children of this world are in very truth the Lord's anointed and the dwellers in the inner temple. Lo, I am one who is prepared to testify even to the uttermost, for of a verity the day has now come when the humble will be exalted and the wicked will be cut off in their sins ! "

" Mother ! Mother ! " cried the little boy, in terror.

" There, there ! It's all right, Jack," said the buxom woman, and then, in a burst of womanly wrath, " What d'you want to make the child cry for ? You're a pretty man, you are ! "

" Better he should cry now than in the outer darkness. Let him seek safety while there is yet time."

The officer measured the gap with a practised eye. It was a good eight feet across, and the fellow could push him over before he could steady himself. It would be a desperate thing to attempt. He tried soothing words once more.

" See here, my lad, you've carried this joke too far. Why should you wish to injure us ? Just shin up and get that wedge out, and we will agree to say no more about it."

Another rending snap came from above.

" By George, the hawser is going ! " cried Stangate. " Here ! Stand aside ! I'm coming over to see to it."

The workman had plucked the hammer from his belt, and waved it furiously in the air.

" Stand back, young man ! Stand back ! Or come— if you would hasten your end."

" Tom, Tom, for God's sake, don't spring ! Help ! Help ! "

The passengers all joined in the cry for aid. The man smiled malignly as he watched them.

" There is no one to help. They could not come if they would. You would be wiser to turn to your own souls that ye be not cast to the burning. Lo, strand by strand the cable snaps which holds you. There is yet another, and with each that goes there is more strain upon the rest. Five minutes of time, and all eternity beyond."

A moan of fear rose from the prisoners in the lift. Stangate felt a cold sweat upon his brow as he passed his arm round the shrinking girl. If this vindictive devil could only be coaxed away for an instant he would spring across and take his chance in a hand-to-hand fight.

"Look here, my friend! We give you best!" he cried. "We can do nothing. Go up and cut the cable if you wish. Go on—do it now, and get it over!"

"That you may come across unharmed. Having set my hand to the work, I will not draw back from it."

Fury seized the young officer.

"You devil!" he cried. "What do you stand there grinning for? I'll give you something to grin about. Give me a stick, one of you."

The man waved his hammer.

"Come, then! Come to judgment!" he howled.

"He'll murder you, Tom! Oh, for God's sake, don't! If we must die, let us die together."

"I wouldn't try it, sir," cried Billy. "He'll strike you down before you get a footing. Hold up, Dolly, my dear! Faintin' won't 'elp us. You speak to him, miss. Maybe he'll listen to you."

"Why should you wish to hurt us?" said Mary. "What have we ever done to you? Surely you will be sorry afterwards if we are injured. Now do be kind and reasonable and help us to get back to the ground."

For a moment there may have been some softening in the man's fierce eyes as he looked at the sweet face which was upturned to him. Then his features set once more into their grim lines of malice.

"My hand is set to the work, woman. It is not for the servant to look back from his task."

"But why should this be your task?"

"Because there is a voice within me which tells me

so. In the night-time I have heard it, and in the day-time, too, when I have lain out alone upon the girders and seen the wicked dotting the streets beneath me, each busy on his own evil intent. 'John Barnes, John Barnes,' said the voice. 'You are here that you may give a sign to a sinful generation—such a sign as shall show them that the Lord liveth and that there is a judgment upon sin.' Who am I that I should disobey the voice of the Lord?"

"The voice of the devil," said Stangate. "What is the sin of this lady, or of these others, that you should seek their lives?"

"You are as the others, neither better nor worse. All day they pass me, load by load, with foolish cries and empty songs and vain babble of voices. Their thoughts are set upon the things of the flesh. Too long have I stood aside and watched and refused to testify. But now the day of wrath is come and the sacrifice is ready. Think not that a woman's tongue can turn me from my task."

"It is useless!" Mary cried. "Useless! I read death in his eyes."

Another cord had snapped.

"Repent! Repent!" cried the madman. "One more, and it is over!"

Commander Stangate felt as if it were all some extra-ordinary dream—some monstrous nightmare. Could it be possible that he, after all his escapes of death in warfare, was now, in the heart of peaceful England, at the mercy of a homicidal lunatic, and that his dear girl, the one being whom he would shield from the very shadow of danger, was helpless before this horrible man? All his energy and manhood rose up in him for one last effort.

"Here, we won't be killed like sheep in the shambles!" he cried, throwing himself against the wooden wall of the lift and kicking with all his force. "Come on, boys! Kick it! Beat it! It's only match-boarding, and it is giving. Smash it down! Well done! Once more all together ! There she goes ! Now for the side ! Out with it ! Splendid ! "

First the back and then the side of the little compartment had been knocked out, and the splinters dropped down into the abyss. Barnes danced upon his girder, his hammer in the air.

" Strive not ! " he shrieked. " It avails not. The day is surely come."

" It's not two feet from the side-girder," cried the officer. " Get across ! Quick ! Quick ! All of you. I'll hold this devil off ! " He had seized a stout stick from the commercial traveller and faced the madman, daring him to spring across.

" Your turn now, my friend ! " he hissed. " Come on, hammer and all ! I'm ready for you."

Above him he heard another snap, and the frail platform began to rock. Glancing over his shoulder, he saw that his companions were all safe upon the side-girder. A strange line of terrified castaways they appeared as they clung in an ungainly row to the trellis-work of steel. But their feet were on the iron support. With two quick steps and a spring he was at their side. At the same instant the murderer, hammer in hand, jumped the gap. They had one vision of him there—a vision which will haunt their dreams—the convulsed face, the blazing eyes, the wind-tossed, raven locks. For a moment he balanced himself upon the swaying platform. The next, with a rending crash, he and it were gone. There was a long silence and then, far down, the thud and clatter of a mighty fall.

With white faces, the forlorn group clung to the cold steel bars and gazed down into the terrible abyss. It was the Commander who broke the silence.

" They'll send for us now. It's all safe," he cried, wiping his brow. " But, by Jove, it was a close call ! "

TALES OF LONG AGO

65. *The Last of the Legions*

PONTUS, the Roman viceroy, sat in the atrium of his palatial villa by the Thames, and he looked with perplexity at the scroll of papyrus which he had just unrolled. Before him stood the messenger who had brought it, a swarthy little Italian, whose black eyes were glazed with want of sleep, and his olive features darker still from dust and sweat. The viceroy was looking fixedly at him, yet he saw him not, so full was his mind of this sudden and most unexpected order. To him it seemed as if the solid earth had given way beneath his feet. His life and the work of his life had come to irremediable ruin.

" Very good," he said at last in a hard, dry voice, " you can go."

The man saluted and staggered out of the hall. A yellow-haired British major-domo came forward for orders.

" Is the General there ? "

" He is waiting, your excellency."

" Then show him in, and leave us together."

A few minutes later Licinius Crassus, the head of the British military establishment, had joined his chief. He was a large bearded man in a white civilian toga, hemmed with the Patrician purple. His rough, bold features, burned and seamed and lined with the long African wars, were shadowed with anxiety as he looked with questioning eyes at the drawn, haggard face of the viceroy.

" I fear, your excellency, that you have had bad news from Rome."

631

" The worst, Crassus. It is all over with Britain. It is a question whether even Gaul will be held."

" Saint Albus save us ! Are the orders precise ? "

" Here they are, with the Emperor's own seal."

" But why ? I had heard a rumour, but it had seemed too incredible."

" So had I only last week, and had the fellow scourged for having spread it. But here it is as clear as words can make it : ' Bring every man of the Legions by forced marches to the help of the Empire. Leave not a cohort in Britain.' These are my orders."

" But the cause ? "

" They will let the limbs wither so that the heart be stronger. The old German hive is about to swarm once more. There are fresh crowds of Barbarians from Dacia and Scythia. Every sword is needed to hold the Alpine passes. They cannot let three legions lie idle in Britain."

The soldier shrugged his shoulders.

" When the legions go no Roman would feel that his life was safe here. For all that we have done, it is none the less the truth that it is no country of ours, and that we hold it as we won it, by the sword."

" Yes, every man, woman, and child of Latin blood must come with us to Gaul. The galleys are already waiting at Portus Dubris. Get the orders out, Crassus, at once. As the Valerian legion falls back from the Wall of Hadrian it can take the northern colonists with it. The Jovians can bring in the people from the west, and the Batavians can escort the easterns if they will muster at Camboricum. You will see to it." He sank his face for a moment in his hands. " It is a fearsome thing," said he, " to tear up the roots of so goodly a tree."

" To make more space for such a crop of weeds," said the soldier bitterly. " My God, what will be the end of these poor Britons ! From ocean to ocean there is not a tribe which will not be at the throat of its neighbour when the last Roman Lictor has turned his back. With these hot-headed Silures it is hard enough now to keep the swords in their sheaths."

"The kennel might fight as they choose among themselves until the best hound won," said the Roman Governor. "At least the victor would keep the arts and the religion which we have brought them, and Britain would be one land. No, it is the bear from the north and the wolves from oversea, the painted savage from beyond the walls and the Saxon pirate from over the water, who will succeed to our rule. Where we saved, they will slay; where we built, they will burn; where we planted, they will ravage. But the die is cast, Crassus. You will carry out the orders."

"I will send out the messengers within an hour. This very morning there has come news that the Barbarians are through the old gap in the wall, and their outriders as far south as Vinovia."

The Governor shrugged his shoulders.

"These things concern us no longer," said he. Then a bitter smile broke upon his aquiline, clean-shaven face. "Whom think you that I see in audience this morning?"

"Nay, I know not."

"Caradoc and Regnus, and Celticus the Icenian, who, like so many of the richer Britons, have been educated at Rome, and who would lay before me their plans as to the ruling of this country."

"And what is their plan?"

"That they themselves should do it."

The Roman soldier laughed. "Well, they will have their will," said he, as he saluted and turned upon his heel. "Farewell, your excellency. There are hard days coming for you and for me."

An hour later the British deputation was ushered into the presence of the Governor. They were good, steadfast men, men who with a whole heart, and at some risk to themselves, had taken up their country's cause, so far as they could see it. At the same time they well knew that under the mild and beneficent rule of Rome it was only when they passed from words to deeds that their backs or their necks would be in danger. They stood now, earnest and a little abashed, before the throne of the viceroy. Celticus was a swarthy, black-bearded little Iberian. Caradoc and Regnus were tall, middle-aged men of the fair flaxen British type. All three were dressed in the draped, yellow toga after the Latin fashion, instead of in the bracae and tunic which distinguished their more insular fellow-countrymen.

" Well ? " asked the Governor.

" We are here," said Celticus boldly, " as the spokesmen of a great number of our fellow-countrymen, for the purpose of sending our petition through you to the Emperor and to the Roman Senate, that we may urge upon them the policy of allowing us to govern this country after our own ancient fashion." He paused, as if awaiting some outburst as an answer to his own temerity ; but the Governor merely nodded his head as a sign that he should proceed. " We had laws of our own before ever Cæsar set foot in Britain, which have served their purpose since first our forefathers came from the land of Ham. We are not a child among the nations, but our history goes back in our own traditions further even than that of Rome, and we are galled by this yoke which you have laid upon us."

" Are not our laws just ? " asked the Governor.

" The code of Cæsar is just, but it is always the code of Cæsar. Our own laws were made for our own uses and our own circumstances, and we would fain have them again."

" You speak Roman as if you had been bred in the Forum ; you wear a Roman toga ; your hair is filleted in Roman fashion—are not these the gifts of Rome ? "

" We would take all the learning and all the arts that Rome or Greece could give, but we would still be Britain, and ruled by Britons."

The viceroy smiled. " By the rood of Saint Helena," said he, " had you spoken thus to some of my heathen ancestors, there would have been an end to your politics. That you have dared to stand before my face and say as much is a proof for ever of the gentleness of our rule. But I would reason with you for a moment upon this your request. You know well that this land has never been one kingdom, but was always under many chiefs and many tribes, who have made war upon each other. Would you in very truth have it so again ? "

" Those were in the evil pagan days, the days of the Druid and the oak-grove, your excellency. But now we are held together by a gospel of peace."

The viceroy shook his head. " If all the world were of the same way of thinking, then it would be easier," said he. " It may be that this blessed doctrine of peace will be little help to you when you are face to face with strong men who still worship the god of war. What would you do against the Picts of the north ? "

" Your excellency knows that many of the bravest legionaries are of British blood. These are our defence."

" But discipline, man, the power to command, the knowledge of war, the strength to act—it is in these things that you would fail. Too long have you leaned upon the crutch."

" The times may be hard, but when we have gone through them, Britain will be herself again."

" Nay, she will be under a different and a harsher master," said the Roman. " Already the pirates swarm upon the eastern coast. Were it not for our Roman Count of the Saxon shore they would land to-morrow. I see the day when Britain may, indeed, be one ; but that will be because you and your fellows are either dead or are driven into the mountains of the west. All goes into the melting-pot, and if a better Albion should come forth from it, it will be after ages of strife, and neither you nor your people will have part or lot in it."

Regnus, the tall young Celt, smiled. " With the

help of God and our own right arms we should hope for a better end," said he. " Give us but the chance, and we will bear the brunt."

" You are as men that are lost," said the viceroy sadly. " I see this broad land, with its gardens and orchards, its fair villas and its walled towns, its bridges and its roads, all the work of Rome. Surely it will pass even as a dream, and these three hundred years of settled order will leave no trace behind. For learn that it will indeed be as you wish, and that this very day the orders have come to me that the legions are to go."

The three Britons looked at each other in amazement. Their first impulse was towards a wild exultation, but reflection and doubt followed close upon its heels.

" This is indeed wondrous news," said Celticus. " This is a day of days to the motherland. When do the legions go, your excellency, and what troops will remain behind for our protection ? "

" The legions go at once," said the viceroy. " You will doubtless rejoice to hear that within a month there will be no Roman soldier in the island, nor, indeed, a Roman of any sort, age, or sex, if I can take them with me."

The faces of the Britons were shadowed, and Caradoc, a grave and thoughtful man, spoke for the first time.

" But this is over sudden, your excellency," said he. " There is much truth in what you have said about the pirates. From my villa near the fort of Anderida I saw eighty of their galleys only last week, and I know well that they would be on us like ravens on a dying ox. For many years to come it would not be possible for us to hold them off."

The viceroy shrugged his shoulders. " It is your affair now," said he. " Rome must look to herself."

The last traces of joy had passed from the faces of the Britons. Suddenly the future had started up clearly before them, and they quailed at the prospect.

" There is a rumour in the market-place," said Celticus,
" that the northern Barbarians are through the gap in
the wall. Who is to stop their progress ? "

" You and your fellows," said the Roman.

Clearer still grew the future, and there was terror
in the eyes of the spokesmen as they faced it.

" But your excellency, if the legions should go at
once, we should have the wild Scots at York, and the
Northmen in the Thames within the month. We can
build ourselves up under your shield, and in a few years
it would be easier for us ; but not now, your excellency,
not now."

" Tut, man ; for years you have been clamouring
in our ears and raising the people. Now you have
got what you asked. What more would you have ?
Within the month you will be as free as were your
ancestors before Cæsar set foot upon your shore."

" For God's sake, your excellency, put our words
out of your head. The matter had not been well considered. We will send to Rome. We will ride post-
haste ourselves. We will fall at the Emperor's feet.
We will kneel before the Senate and beg that the legions
remain."

The Roman proconsul rose from his chair and motioned
that the audience was at an end.

" You will do what you please," said he. " I and
my men are for Italy."

And even as he said, so was it, for before the spring
had ripened into summer, the troops were clanking down
the via Aurelia on their way to the Ligurian passes,
whilst every road in Gaul was dotted with the carts
and the waggons which bore the Brito-Roman refugees on
their weary journey to their distant country. But ere
another summer had passed Celticus was dead, for
he was flayed alive by the pirates and his skin nailed
upon the door of a church near Caistor. Regnus, too,
was dead, for he was tied to a tree and shot with arrows

when the painted men came to the sacking of Isca. Caradoc only was alive, but he was a slave to Elda the red Caledonian and his wife was mistress to Mordred the wild chief of the western Cymri. From the ruined wall in the north to Vectis in the south blood and ruin and ashes covered the fair land of Britain. And after many days it came out fairer than ever, but, even as the Roman had said, neither the Britons nor any men of their blood came into the heritage of that which had been their own.

66. *The Last Galley*

"Mutato nomine, de te, Britannia, fabula narratur."

IT was a spring morning, one hundred and forty-six years before the coming of Christ. The North African coast, with its broad hem of golden sand, its green belt of feathery palm-trees, and its background of barren, red-scarped hills, shimmered like a dream country in the opal light. Save for a narrow edge of snow-white surf, the Mediterranean lay blue and serene as far as the eye could reach. In all its vast expanse there was no break but for a single galley, which was slowly making its way from the direction of Sicily and heading for the distant harbour of Carthage.

Seen from afar it was a stately and beautiful vessel, deep red in colour, double-banked with scarlet oars, its broad, flapping sail stained with Tyrian purple, its bulwarks gleaming with brass work. A brazen, three-pronged ram projected in front, and a high, golden figure of Baal, the God of the Phœnicians, children of Canaan, shone upon the after-deck. From the single high mast above the huge sail streamed the tiger-striped flag of Carthage. So, like some stately, scarlet bird, with golden beak and wings of purple, she swam upon the face of the waters—a thing of might and of beauty as seen from the distant shore.

But approach and look at her now! What are these dark streaks which foul her white decks and dapple her brazen shields? Why do the long, red oars move out of time, irregular, convulsive? Why are some missing from the staring portholes, some snapped with jagged, yellow edges, some trailing inert against the side? Why are two prongs of the brazen ram twisted and broken? See, even the high image of Baal is battered and disfigured! By every sign this ship has passed through some grievous trial, some day of terror, which has left its heavy marks upon her.

And now stand upon the deck itself, and see more closely the men who man her! There are two decks forward and aft, while in the open waist are the double banks of seats, above and below, where the rowers, two to an oar, tug and bend at their endless task. Down the centre is a narrow platform, along which pace a line of warders, lash in hand, who cut cruelly at the slave who pauses, be it only for an instant, to sweep the sweat from his dripping brow. But these slaves—look at them! Some are captured Romans, some Sicilians, many black Libyans, but all are in the last exhaustion, their weary eyelids drooped over their eyes, their lips thick with black crusts, and pink with bloody froth, their arms and backs moving mechanically to the hoarse chant of the overseer. Their bodies of all tints from ivory to jet, are stripped to the waist, and every glistening back shows the angry stripes of the warders. But it is not from these that the blood comes which reddens the seats and tints the salt water washing beneath their manacled feet. Great gaping wounds, the marks of sword slash and spear stab, show crimson upon their naked chests and shoulders, while many lie huddled and senseless athwart the benches, careless for ever of the whips which still hiss above them. Now we can understand those empty portholes and those trailing oars.

Nor were the crew in better case than their slaves.

The decks were littered with wounded and dying men. It was but a remnant who still remained upon their feet. The most lay exhausted upon the fore-deck, while a few of the more zealous were mending their shattered armour, restringing their bows, or cleaning the deck from the marks of combat. Upon a raised platform at the base of the mast stood the sailing-master who conned the ship, his eyes fixed upon the distant point of Megara which screened the eastern side of the Bay of Carthage. On the after-deck were gathered a number of officers, silent and brooding, glancing from time to time at two of their own class who stood apart deep in conversation. The one, tall, dark, and wiry, with pure, Semitic features, and the limbs of a giant, was Magro, the famous Carthaginian captain, whose name was still a terror on every shore, from Gaul to the Euxine. The other, a white-bearded, swarthy man, with indomitable courage and energy stamped upon every eager line of his keen, aquiline face, was Gisco the politician, a man of the highest Punic blood, a Suffete of the purple robe, and the leader of that party in the state which had watched and striven amid the selfishness and slothfulness of his fellow-countrymen to rouse the public spirit and waken the public conscience to the ever-increasing danger from Rome. As they talked, the two men glanced continually, with earnest, anxious faces, towards the northern skyline.

" It is certain," said the older man, with gloom in his voice and bearing, " none have escaped save ourselves."

" I did not leave the press of the battle whilst I saw one ship which I could succour," Magro answered. " As it was, we came away, as you saw, like a wolf which has a hound hanging on to either haunch. The Roman dogs can show the wolf-bites which prove it. Had any other galley won clear, they would surely be with us by now, since they have no place of safety save Carthage."

The younger warrior glanced keenly ahead to the

distant point which marked his native city. Already
the low, leafy hill could be seen, dotted with the white
villas of the wealthy Phœnician merchants. Above
them, a gleaming dot against the pale blue morning sky,
shone the brazen roof of the citadel of Byrsa, which
capped the sloping town.

" Already they can see us from the watch-towers,"
he remarked. " Even from afar they may know the
galley of Black Magro. But which of all of them will
guess that we alone remain of all that goodly fleet which
sailed out with blare of trumpet and roll of drum but
one short month ago ? "

The patrician smiled bitterly. " If it were not for
our great ancestors and for our beloved country, the
Queen of the Waters," said he, " I could find it in my
heart to be glad at this destruction which has come upon
this vain and feeble generation. 'You have spent your
life upon the seas, Magro. You do not know how it
has been with us on the land. But I have seen this
canker grow upon us which now leads us to our death.
I and others have gone down into the market-place to
plead with the people, and been pelted with mud for
our pains. Many a time have I pointed to Rome, and
said, ' Behold these people, who bear arms themselves,
each man for his own duty and pride. How can you
who hide behind mercenaries hope to stand against
them ? '—a hundred times I have said it."

" And had they no answer ? " asked the Rover.

" Rome was far off and they could not see it, so to
them it was nothing," the old man answered. " Some
thought of trade, and some of votes, and some of profits
from the State, but none would see that the State itself,
the mother of all things, was sinking to her end. So
might the bees debate who should have wax or honey
when the torch was blazing which would bring to ashes
the hive and all therein. ' Are we not rulers of the sea ? '
' Was not Hannibal a great man ? ' Such were their
cries, living ever in the past and blind to the future.

Before that sun sets there will be tearing of hair and rending of garments ; but what will that now avail us ? "

" It is some sad comfort," said Magro, " to know that what Rome holds she cannot keep."

" Why say you that ? When we go down, she is supreme in all the world."

" For a time, and only for a time," Magro answered gravely. " Yet you will smile, perchance, when I tell you how it is that I know it. There was a wise woman who lived in that part of the Tin Islands which juts forth into the sea, and from her lips I have heard many things, but not one which has not come aright. Of the fall of our own country, and even of this battle, from which we now return, she told me clearly. There is much strange lore amongst these savage peoples in the west of the land of Tin."

" What said she of Rome ? "

" That she also would fall, even as we, weakened by her riches and her factions."

Gisco rubbed his hands. " That at least makes our own fall less bitter," said he. " But since we have fallen, and Rome will fall, who in turn may hope to be Queen of the Waters ? "

" That also I asked her," said Magro, " and gave her my Tyrian belt with the golden buckle as a guerdon for her answer. But, indeed, it was too high payment for the tale she told, which must be false if all else she said was true. She would have it that in coming days it was her own land, this fog-girt isle where painted savages can scarce row a wicker coracle from point to point, which shall at last take the trident which Carthage and Rome have dropped."

The smile which flickered upon the old patrician's keen features died away suddenly, and his fingers closed upon his companion's wrist. The other had set rigid, his head advanced, his hawk eyes upon the northern skyline. Its straight, blue horizon was broken by two low, black dots.

" Galleys ! " whispered Gisco.

The whole crew had seen them. They clustered along the starboard bulwarks, pointing and chattering. For a moment the gloom of defeat was lifted, and a buzz of joy ran from group to group at the thought that they were not alone—that someone, had escaped the great carnage as well as themselves.

" By the spirit of Baal," said Black Magro, " I could not have believed that any could have fought clear from such a welter. Could it be young Hamilcar in the *Africa*, or is it Beneva in the blue Syrian ship ? We three, with others, may form a squadron and make head against them yet. If we hold our course, they will join us ere we round the harbour mole."

Slowly the injured galley toiled on her way, and more swiftly the two new-comers swept down from the north. Only a few miles off lay the green point and the white houses which flanked the great African city. Already, upon the headland, could be seen a dark group of waiting townsmen. Gisco and Magro were still watching with puckered gaze the approaching galleys, when the brown Libyan boatswain, with flashing teeth and gleaming eyes, rushed upon the poop, his long, thin arm stabbing to the north.

" Romans ! " he cried. " Romans ! "

A hush had fallen over the great vessel. Only the wash of the water and the measured rattle and beat of the oars broke in upon the silence.

" By the horns of God's altar, I believe the fellow is right ! " cried old Gisco. " See how they swoop upon us like falcons. They are full-manned and full-oared."

" Plain wood, unpainted," said Magro. " See how it gleams yellow where the sun strikes it."

" And yonder thing beneath the mast. Is it not the cursed bridge they use for boarding ? "

" So they grudge us even one," said Magro with a bitter laugh. " Not even one galley shall return to the old sea-mother. Well, for my part, I would as soon

643

have it so. I am of a mind to stop the oars and await them."

" It is a man's thought," answered old Gisco ; " but the city will need us in the days to come. What shall it profit us to make the Roman victory complete ? Nay, Magro, let the slaves row as they never rowed before, not for our own safety, but for the profit of the State."

So the great red ship laboured and lurched onwards, like a weary, panting stag which seeks shelter from his pursuers, while ever swifter and ever nearer sped the two lean, fierce galleys from the north. Already the morning sun shone upon the lines of low Roman helmets above the bulwarks, and glistened on the silver wave where each sharp prow shot through the still, blue water. Every moment the ships drew nearer, and the long, thin scream of the Roman trumpets grew louder upon the ear.

Upon the high bluff of Megara there stood a great concourse of the people of Carthage who had hurried forth from the city upon the news that the galleys were in sight. They stood now, rich and poor, effete and plebeian, white Phœnician and dark Kabyle, gazing with breathless interest at the spectacle before them. Some hundreds of feet beneath them the Punic galley had drawn so close that with their naked eyes they could see those stains of battle which told their dismal tale. The Romans, too, were heading in such a way that it was before their very faces that their ship was about to be cut off ; and yet of all this multitude not one could raise a hand in its defence. Some wept in impotent grief, some cursed with flashing eyes and knotted fists, some on their knees held up appealing hands to Baal ; but neither prayer, tears nor curses could undo the past nor mend the present. That broken, crawling galley meant that their fleet was gone. Those two fierce, darting ships meant that the hands of Rome were already at their throat. Behind them would come others and others, the innumerable trained hosts of the great Republic, long mistress of the land, now dominant also upon the waters.   In a month, two months, three at the most, their armies would be there, and what could all the untrained multitudes of Carthage do to stop them?

" Nay ! " cried one, more hopeful than the rest, " at least we are brave men with arms in our hands."

" Fool ! " said another, " is it not such talk which has brought us to our ruin ?   What is the brave man untrained to the brave man trained ?   When you stand before the sweep and rush of a Roman legion you may learn the difference."

" Then let us train ! "

" Too late !   A full year is needful to turn a man to a soldier.   Where will you—where will your city be within the year ?   Nay, there is but one chance for us.   If we give up our commerce and our colonies, if we strip ourselves of all that made us great, then perchance the Roman conqueror may hold his hand."

And already the last sea-fight of Carthage was coming swiftly to an end before them.   Under their very eyes the two Roman galleys had shot in, one on either side of the vessel of Black Magro.   They had grappled with him, and he, desperate in his despair, had cast the crooked flukes of his anchors over their gunwales, and bound them to him in an iron grip, whilst with hammer and crowbar he burst great holes in his own sheathing.   The last Punic galley should never be rowed into Ostia, a sight for the holiday-makers of Rome.   She would lie in her own waters.   And the fierce, dark soul of her rover captain glowed as he thought that not alone should she sink into the depths of the mother sea.

Too late did the Romans understand the man with whom they had to deal.   Their boarders who had flooded the Punic decks, felt the planking sink and sway beneath them.   They rushed to gain their own vessels ; but they, too, were being drawn downwards, held in the dying grip of the great red galley.   Over they went and ever over. Now the deck of Magro's ship is flush with the water, and the Romans', drawn towards it by the iron bonds which hold them, are tilted downwards, one bulwark upon the waves, one reared high in the air. Madly they strain to cast off the death-grip of the galley. She is under the surface now, and ever swifter, with the greater weight, the Roman ships heel after her. There is a rending crash. The wooden side is torn out of one, and mutilated, dismembered, she rights herself, and lies a helpless thing upon the water. But a last, yellow gleam in the blue water shows where her consort has been dragged to her end in the iron death-grapple of her foeman. The tiger-striped flag of Carthage has sunk beneath the swirling surface, never more to be seen upon the face of the sea.

For in that year a great cloud hung for seventeen days over the African coast, a deep black cloud which was the dark shroud of the burning city. And when the seventeen days were over, Roman ploughs were driven from end to end of the charred ashes, and salt was scattered there as a sign that Carthage should be no more. And far off a huddle of naked, starving folk stood upon the distant mountains, and looked down upon the desolate plain which had once been the fairest and richest upon earth. And they understood too late that it is the law of heaven that the world is given to the hardy and to the self-denying, whilst he who would escape the duties of manhood will soon be stripped of the pride, the wealth, and the power, which are the prizes which manhood brings.

67. *Through the Veil*

HE was a great shock-headed, freckle-faced Borderer, the lineal descendant of a cattle-thieving clan in Liddesdale. In spite of his ancestry he was as solid and sober a citizen as one would

wish to see, a town councillor of Melrose, an elder of
the Church, and the chairman of the local branch of
the Young Men's Christian Association. Brown was
his name—and you saw it printed up as " Brown and
Handiside " over the great grocery stores in the High
Street. His wife, Maggie Brown, was an Armstrong
before her marriage, and came from an old farming
stock in the wilds of Teviothead. She was small, swarthy,
and dark-eyed, with a strangely nervous temperament
for a Scotch woman. No greater contrast could be
found than the big, tawny man and the dark little woman,
but both were of the soil as far back as any memory
could extend.

One day—it was the first anniversary of their wedding
—they had driven over together to see the excavations
of the Roman Fort at Newstead. It was not a particularly picturesque spot. From the northern bank of
the Tweed, just where the river forms a loop, there
extends a gentle slope of arable land. Across it run
the trenches of the excavators, with here and there an
exposure of old stonework to show the foundations of
the ancient walls. It had been a huge place, for the
camp was fifty acres in extent, and the fort fifteen.
However, it was all made easy for them since Mr. Brown
knew the farmer to whom the land belonged. Under
his guidance they spent a long summer evening inspecting
the trenches, the pits, the ramparts and all the strange
variety of objects which were waiting to be transported
to the Edinburgh Museum of Antiquities. The buckle
of a woman's belt had been dug up that very day, and
the farmer was discoursing upon it when his eyes fell
upon Mrs. Brown's face.

" Your good leddy's tired," said he. " Maybe you'd
best rest a wee before we gang further."

Brown looked at his wife. She was certainly very
pale, and her dark eyes were bright and wild.

" What is it, Maggie ? I've wearied you. I'm thinkin'
it's time we went back."

" No, no, John, let us go on. It's wonderful ! It's like a dreamland place. It all seems so close and so near to me. How long were the Romans here, Mr. Cunningham ? "

" A fair time, mam. If you saw the kitchen midden-pits you would guess it took a long time to fill them."

" And why did they leave ? "

" Well, mam, by all accounts they left because they had to. The folk round could thole them no longer, so they just up and burned the fort aboot their lugs. You can see the fire marks on the stanes."

The woman gave a quick little shudder. " A wild night—a fearsome night," said she. " The sky must have been red that night—and these grey stones, they may have been red also."

" Aye, I think they were red," said her husband. " It's a queer thing, Maggie, and it may be your words that have done it ; but I seem to see that business aboot as clear as ever I saw anything in my life. The light shone on the water."

" Aye, the light shone on the water. And the smoke gripped you by the throat. And all the savages were yelling."

The old farmer began to laugh. " The leddy will be writin' a story aboot the old fort," said he. " I've shown many a one ower it, but I never heard it put so clear afore. Some folk have the gift."

They had strolled along the edge of the foss, and a pit yawned upon the right of them.

" That pit was fourteen foot deep," said the farmer. " What d'ye think we dug oot from the bottom o't ? Weel, it was just the skeleton of a man wi' a spear by his side. I'm thinkin' he was grippin' it when he died. Now, how cam' a man wi' a spear doon a hole fourteen foot deep. He wasna' buried there, for they aye burned their dead. What make ye o' that, mam ? "

" He sprang doon to get clear of the savages," said the woman.

" Weel, it's likely enough, and a' the professors from Edinburgh couldna gie a better reason. I wish you were aye here, mam, to answer a' oor deeficulties sae readily. Now, here's the altar that we foond last week. There's an inscreeption. They tell me it's Latin, and it means that the men o' this fort give thanks to God for their safety."

They examined the old worn stone. There was a large, deeply cut " VV " upon the top of it.

" What does ' VV ' stand for ? " asked Brown.

" Naebody kens," the guide answered.

" *Valeria Victrix*," said the lady softly. Her face was paler than ever, her eyes far away, as one who peers down the dim aisles of over-arching centuries.

" What's that ? " asked her husband sharply.

She started as one who wakes from sleep. " What were we talking about ? " she asked.

" About this ' VV ' upon the stone."

" No doubt it was just the name of the Legion which put the altar up."

" Aye, but you gave some special name."

" Did I ? How absurd ! How should I ken what the name was ? "

" You said something—' *Victrix*,' I think."

" I suppose I was guessing. It gives me the queerest feeling, this place, as if I were not myself, but someone else."

" Aye, it's an uncanny place," said her husband, looking round with an expression almost of fear in his bold grey eyes. " I feel it mysel'. I think we'll just be wishin' you good evenin', Mr. Cunningham, and get back to Melrose before the dark sets in."

Neither of them could shake off the strange impression which had been left upon them by their visit to the excavations. It was as if some miasma had risen from those damp trenches and passed into their blood. All the evening they were silent and thoughtful, but such remarks as they did make showed that the same subject was in the mind of each. Brown had a restless night, in which he dreamed a strange, connected dream, so vivid that he woke sweating and shivering like a frightened horse. He tried to convey it all to his wife as they sat together at breakfast in the morning.

" It was the clearest thing, Maggie," said he. " Nothing that has ever come to me in my waking life has been more clear than that. I feel as if these hands were sticky with blood."

" Tell me of it—tell me slow," said she.

" When it began, I was oot on a braeside. I was laying flat on the ground. It was rough, and there were clumps of heather. All round me was just darkness, but I could hear the rustle and the breathin' of men. There seemed a great multitude on every side of me, but I could see no one. There was a low chink of steel sometimes, and then a number of voices would whisper, ' Hush ! ' I had a ragged club in my hand, and it had spikes o' iron near the end of it. My heart was beatin' quickly, and I felt that a moment of great danger and excitement was at hand. Once I dropped my club, and again from all round me the voices in the darkness cried, ' Hush ! ' I put oot my hand, and it touched the foot of another man lying in front of me. There was someone at my very elbow on either side. But they said nothin'.

" Then we all began to move. The whole braeside seemed to be crawlin' downwards. There was a river at the bottom and a high-arched wooden bridge. Beyond the bridge were many lights—torches on a wall. The creepin' men all flowed towards the bridge. There had been no sound of any kind, just a velvet stillness. And then there was a cry in the darkness, the cry of a man who had been stabbed suddenly to the hairt. That one cry swelled out for a moment, and then the roar of a thoosand furious voices. I was runnin'. Everyone was runnin'. A bright red light shone out, and the river was a scarlet streak. I could see my companions now. They were more like devils than men, wild figures clad in skins, with their hair and beards streamin'. They were all mad with rage, jumpin' as they ran, their mouths open, their arms wavin', the red light beatin' on their faces. I ran, too, and yelled out curses like the rest. Then I heard a great cracklin' of wood, and I knew that the palisades were doon. There was a loud whistlin' in my ears, and I was aware that arrows were flying past me. I got to the bottom of a dyke, and I saw a hand stretched doon from above. I took it, and was dragged to the top. We looked doon, and there were silver men beneath us holdin' up their spears. Some of our folk sprang on to the spears. Then we others followed, and we killed the soldiers before they could draw the spears oot again. They shouted loud in some foreign tongue, but no mercy was shown them. We went ower them like a wave, and trampled them doon into the mud, for they were few, and there was no end to our numbers.

"I found myself among buildings, and one of them was on fire. I saw the flames spoutin' through the roof. I ran on, and then I was alone among the buildings. Someone ran across in front o' me. It was a woman. I caught her by the arm, and I took her chin and turned her face so as the light of the fire would strike it. Whom think you that it was, Maggie?"

His wife moistened her dry lips. "It was I," she said.

He looked at her in surprise. "That's a good guess," said he. "Yes, it was just you. Not merely like you, you understand. It was you—you yourself. I saw the same soul in your frightened eyes. You looked white and bonnie and wonderful in the firelight. I had just one thought in my head—to get you awa' with me; to keep you all to mysel' in my own home somewhere beyond the hills. You clawed at my face with your nails. I heaved you over my shoulder, and

651

I tried to find a way oot of the light of the burning hoose and back into the darkness.

"Then came the thing that I mind best of all. You're ill, Maggie. Shall I stop? My God! you have the very look on your face that you had last night in my dream. You screamed. He came runnin' in the fire-light. His head was bare; his hair was black and curled; he had a naked sword in his hand, short and broad, little more than a dagger. He stabbed at me, but he tripped and fell. I held you with one hand, and with the other——"

His wife had sprung to her feet with writhing features. "Marcus!" she cried. "My beautiful Marcus! Oh, you brute! you brute! you brute!" There was a clatter of tea-cups as she fell forward senseless upon the table.

They never talk about that strange, isolated incident in their married life. For an instant the curtain of the past had swung aside, and some strange glimpse of a forgotten life had come to them. But it closed down, never to open again. They live their narrow round—he in his shop, she in her household—and yet new and wider horizons have vaguely formed themselves around them since that summer evening by the crumbling Roman fort.

68. *The Coming of the Huns*

IN the middle of the fourth century the state of the Christian religion was a scandal and a disgrace. Patient, humble, and long-suffering in adversity, it had become positive, aggressive, and unreasonable with success. Paganism was not yet dead, but it was rapidly sinking, finding its most faithful supporters among the conservative aristocrats of the best families on the one hand, and among those benighted villagers on the other who gave their name to the expiring creed. Between these two extremes the great majority of reasonable men had turned from the·conception of many gods to that of one, and had rejected for ever the beliefs of their forefathers. But with the vices of polytheism, they had also abandoned its virtues, among which toleration and religious good humour had been conspicuous. The strenuous earnestness of the Christians had compelled them to examine and define every point of their own theology ; but as they had no central authority by which such definitions could be checked, it was not long before a hundred heresies had put forward their rival views, while the same earnestness of conviction led the stronger bands of schismatics to endeavour, for conscience' sake, to force their views upon the weaker, and thus to cover the Eastern world with confusion and strife.

Alexandria, Antioch, and Constantinople were centres of theological warfare. The whole north of Africa, too, was rent by the strife of the Donatists, who upheld their particular schism by iron flails and the war-cry of " Praise to the Lord ! " But minor local controversies sank to nothing when compared with the huge argument of the Catholic and the Arian, which rent every village in twain, and divided every household from the cottage to the palace. The rival doctrines of the Homoousian and of the Homoiousian, containing metaphysical differences so attenuated that they could hardly be stated, turned bishop against bishop and congregation against congregation. The ink of the theologians and the blood of the fanatics were spilled in floods on either side, and gentle followers of Christ were horrified to find that their faith was responsible for such a state of riot and bloodshed as had never yet disgraced the religious history of the world. Many of the more earnest among them, shocked and scandalised, slipped away to the Libyan Desert, or to the solitude of Pontus, there to await in self-denial and prayer that second coming which was supposed to be at hand. Even in the deserts they could not escape the echo of the distant strife, and the hermits themselves scowled fiercely from their dens at passing travellers who might be contaminated by the doctrines of Athanasius or of Arius.

Such a hermit was Simon Melas, of whom I write. A Trinitarian and a Catholic, he was shocked by the excesses of the persecution of the Arians, which could be only matched by the similar outrages with which these same Arians in the day of their power avenged their treatment on their brother Christians. Weary of the whole strife, and convinced that the end of the world was indeed at hand, he left his home in Constantinople and travelled as far as the Gothic settlements in Dacia beyond the Danube, in search of some spot where he might be free from the never-ending disputes. Still journeying to the north and east, he crossed the river which we now call the Dniester, and there, finding a rocky hill rising from an immense plain, he formed a cell near its summit, and settled himself down to end his life in self-denial and meditation. There were fish in the stream, the country teemed with game, and there was an abundance of wild fruits, so that his spiritual exercises were not unduly interrupted by the search of sustenance for his mortal frame.

In this distant retreat he expected to find absolute solitude, but the hope was in vain. Within a week of his arrival, in an hour of worldly curiosity, he explored the edges of the high, rocky hill upon which he lived. Making his way up to a cleft, which was hung with olives and myrtles, he came upon a cave in the opening of which sat an aged man, white-bearded, white-haired, and infirm—a hermit like himself. So long had this stranger been alone that he had almost forgotten the use of his tongue ; but at last, words coming more freely, he was able to convey the information that his name was Paul of Nicopolis, that he was a Greek citizen, and that he also had come out into the desert for the saving of his soul, and to escape from the contamination of heresy.

" Little I thought, brother Simon," said he, " that I should ever find anyone else who had come so far upon the same holy errand. In all these years, and they are so many that I have lost count of them, I have never seen a man, save indeed one or two wandering shepherds far out upon yonder plain."

From where they sat, the huge steppe, covered with waving grass and gleaming with a vivid green in the sun, stretched away as level and as unbroken as the sea, to the eastern horizon. Simon Melas stared across it with curiosity.

" Tell me, brother Paul," said he, " you who have lived here so long—what lies at the farther side of that plain ? "

The old man shook his head. " There is no farther side to the plain," said he. " It is the earth's boundary, and stretches away to eternity. For all these years I have sat beside it, but never once have I seen anything come across it. It is manifest that if there had been a farther side there would certainly at some time have come some traveller from that direction. Over the great river yonder is the Roman post of Tyras ; but that is a long day's journey from here, and they have never disturbed my meditations."

" On what do you meditate, brother Paul ? "

" At first I meditated on many sacred mysteries ; but now, for twenty years, I have brooded continually on the nature of the Logos. What is your view upon that vital matter, brother Simon ? "

" Surely," said the younger man, " there can be no question as to that. The Logos is assuredly but a name used by St. John to signify the Diety."

The old hermit gave a hoarse cry of fury, and his brown, withered face was convulsed with anger. Seizing the huge cudgel which he kept to beat off the wolves, he shook it murderously at his companion.

" Out with you ! Out of my cell ! " he cried. " Have I lived here so long to have it polluted by a vile Trinitarian

—a follower of the rascal Athanasius ? Wretched idolater, learn once for all, that the Logos is in truth an emanation from the Diety, and in no sense equal or co-eternal with Him ! Out with you, I say, or I will dash out your brains with my staff ! "

It was useless to reason with the furious Arian, and Simon withdrew in sadness and wonder, that at this extreme verge of the known earth the spirit of religious strife should still break upon the peaceful solitude of the wilderness. With hanging head and heavy heart he made his way down the valley, and climbed up once more to his own cell, which lay at the crown of the hill, with the intention of never again exchanging visits with his Arian neighbour.

Here, for a year, dwelt Simon Melas, leading a life of solitude and prayer. Three was no reason why anyone should ever come to this outermost point of human habitation. Once a young Roman officer— Caius Crassus—rode out a day's journey from Tyras, and climbed the hill to have speech with the anchorite. He was of an equestrian family, and still held his belief in the old dispensation. He looked with interest and surprise, but also with some disgust, at the ascetic arrangements of that humble abode.

" Whom do you please by living in such a fashion ? " he asked.

" We show that our spirit is superior to our flesh," Simon answered. " If we fare badly in this world, we believe that we shall reap an advantage in the world to come."

The centurion shrugged his shoulders. " There are philosophers among our people, Stoics and others, who have the same idea. When I was in the Herulian Cohort of the Fourth Legion we were quartered in Rome itself, and I saw much of the Christians, but I could never learn anything from them which I had not heard from my own father, whom you, in your arrogance, would call a Pagan. It is true that we talk of numerous gods ; but for many years we have not taken them very seriously. Our thoughts upon virtue and duty and a noble life are the same as your own."

Simon Melas shook his head.

"If you have not the holy books," said he, "then what guide have you to direct your steps ? "

"If you will read our philosophers, and above all the divine Plato, you will find that there are other guides who may take you to the same end. Have you by chance read the book which was written by our Emperor Marcus Aurelius ? Do you not discover there every virtue which man could have, although he knew nothing of your creed ? Have you considered, also, the words and actions of our late Emperor Julian, with whom I served my first campaign when he went out against the Persians ? Where could you find a more perfect man than he ? "

"Such talk is unprofitable, and I will have no more of it," said Simon sternly. "Take heed while there is time, and embrace the true faith ; for the end of the world is at hand, and when it comes there will be no mercy for those who have shut their eyes to the light." So saying, he turned back once more to his praying-stool and to his crucifix, while the young Roman walked in deep thought down the hill, and mounting his horse, rode off to his distant post. Simon watched him until his brazen helmet was but a bead of light on the western edge of the great plain ; for this was the first human face that he had seen in all this long year, and there were times when his heart yearned for the voices and the faces of his kind.

So another year passed, and save for the change of weather and the slow change of the seasons, one day was as another. Every morning when Simon opened his eyes, he saw the same grey line ripening into red in the farthest east, until the bright rim pushed itself above that far-off horizon across which no living creature had ever been known to come. Slowly the sun swept

across the huge arch of the heavens, and as the shadows
shifted from the black rocks which jutted upward from
above his cell, so did the hermit regulate his terms of
prayer and meditation. There was nothing on earth
to draw his eye, or to distract his mind, for the grassy
plain below was as void from month to month as the
heaven above. So the long hours passed, until the red
rim slipped down on the farther side, and the day ended
in the same pearl-grey shimmer with which it had begun.
Once two ravens circled for some days round the lonely
hill, and once a white fish-eagle came from the Dniester
and screamed above the hermit's head. Sometimes red
dots were seen on the green plain where the antelopes
grazed, and often a wolf howled in the darkness from
the base of the rocks. Such was the uneventful life
of Simon Melas the anchorite, until there came the
day of wrath.

It was in the late spring of the year 375 that Simon
came out from his cell, his gourd in his hand, to draw
water from the spring. Darkness had closed in, the
sun had set, but one last glimmer of rosy light rested
upon a rocky peak, which jutted forth from the hill,
on the farther side from the hermit's dwelling. As
Simon came forth from under his ledge, the gourd dropped
from his hand, and he stood gazing in amazement.

On the opposite peak a man was standing, his outline
black in the fading light. He was a strange, almost a
deformed figure, short-statured, round-backed, with a
large head, no neck, and a long rod jutting out from
between his shoulders. He stood with his face advanced,
and his body bent, peering very intently over the plain
to the westward. In a moment he was gone, and the
lonely, black peak showed up hard and naked against
the faint eastern glimmer. Then the night closed down,
and all was black once more.

Simon Melas stood long in bewilderment, wondering
who this stranger could be. He had heard, as had
every Christian, of those evil spirits which were wont

to haunt the hermits in the Thebaid and on the skirts of the Ethiopian waste. The strange shape of this solitary creature, its dark outline and prowling, intent attitude, suggestive rather of a fierce, rapacious beast than of a man, all helped him to believe that he had at last encountered one of those wanderers from the pit, of whose existence, in those days of robust faith, he had no more doubt than of his own. Much of the night he spent in prayer, his eyes glancing continually at the low arch of his cell door, with its curtain of deep purple wrought with stars. At any instant some crouching monster, some horned abomination, might peer in upon him, and he clung with frenzied appeal to his crucifix, as his human weakness quailed at the thought. But at last his fatigue overcame his fears, and falling upon his couch of dried grass, he slept until the bright daylight brought him to his senses.

It was later than was his wont, and the sun was far above the horizon. As he came forth from his cell, he looked across at the peak of rock, but it stood there bare and silent. Already it seemed to him that that strange, dark figure which had startled him so was some dream, some vision of the twilight. His gourd lay where it had fallen, and he picked it up with the intention of going to the spring. But suddenly he was aware of something new. The whole air was throbbing with sound. From all sides it came, rumbling, indefinite, an inarticulate mutter, low, but thick and strong, rising, falling, reverberating among the rocks, dying away into vague whispers, but always there. He looked round at the blue, cloudless sky in bewilderment. Then he scrambled up the rocky pinnacle above him, and sheltering himself in its shadow, he stared out over the plain. In his wildest dream he had never imagined such a sight.

The whole vast expanse was covered with horsemen, hundreds and thousands and tens of thousands, all riding slowly and in silence, out of the unknown east. It was the multitudinous beat of their horses' hoofs which caused that low throbbing in his ears. Some were so close to him as he looked down upon them that he could see clearly their thin, wiry horses, and the strange, humped figures of their swarthy riders, sitting forward on the withers, shapeless bundles, their short legs hanging stirrupless, their bodies balanced as firmly as though they were part of the beast. In those nearest he could see the bow and the quiver, the long spear and the short sword, with the coiled lasso behind the rider, which told that this was no helpless horde of wanderers, but a formidable army upon the march. His eyes passed on from them and swept farther and farther, but still to the very horizon, which quivered with movement, there was no end to this monstrous cavalry. Already the vanguard was far past the island of rock upon which he dwelt, and he could now understand that in front of this vanguard were single scouts who guided the course of the army and that it was one of these whom he had seen the evening before.

All day, held spellbound by this wonderful sight, the hermit crouched in the shadow of the rocks, and all day the sea of horsemen rolled onward over the plain beneath. Simon had seen the swarming quays of Alexandria, he had watched the mob which blocked the hippodrome of Constantinople, yet never had he imagined such a multitude as now defiled beneath his eyes, coming from that eastern skyline which had been the end of his world. Sometimes the dense streams of horsemen were broken by droves of brood-mares and foals, driven along by mounted guards ; sometimes there were herds of cattle ; sometimes there were lines of waggons with skin canopies above them ; but then once more, after every break, came the horsemen, the horsemen, the hundreds and the thousands and the tens of thousands, slowly, ceaselessly, silently drifting from the east to the west. The long day passed, the light waned, and the shadows fell, but still the great broad stream was flowing by.

But the night brought a new and ever-stranger sight. Simon had marked bundles of faggots upon the backs of many of the led horses, and now he saw their use. All over the great plain, red pin-points gleamed through the darkness, which grew and brightened into flickering columns of flame. So far as he could see both to east and west the fires extended, until they were but points of light in the farthest distance. White stars shone in the vast heavens above, red ones in the great plain below. And from every side rose the low, confused murmur of voices, with the lowing of oxen and the neighing of horses.

Simon had been a soldier and a man of affairs before ever he forsook the world, and the meaning of all that he had seen was clear to him. History told him how the Roman world had ever been assailed by fresh swarms of Barbarians, coming from the outer darkness, and that the eastern Empire had already, in its fifty years of existence since Constantine had moved the capital of the world to the shores of the Bosphorus, been tormented in the same way. Gepidæ and Heruli, Ostrogoths and Sarmatians, he was familiar with them all. What the advanced sentinel of Europe had seen from this lonely outlying hill, was a fresh swarm breaking in upon the Empire, distinguished only from the others by its enormous, incredible size and by the strange aspect of the warriors who composed it. He alone of all civilised men knew of the approach of this dreadful shadow, sweeping like a heavy storm-cloud from the unknown depths of the east. He thought of the little Roman posts along the Dniester, of the ruined Dacian wall of Trajan behind them, and then of the scattered, defenceless villages which lay with no thought of danger over all the open country which stretched down to the Danube. Could he but give them the alarm! Was it not, perhaps, for that very end that God had guided him to the wilderness?

Then suddenly he remembered his Arian neighbour,

who dwelt in the cave beneath him. Once or twice during the last year he had caught a glimpse of his tall, bent figure hobbling round to examine the traps which he laid for quails and partridges. On one occasion they had met at the brook ; but the old theologian waved him away as if he were a leper. What did he think now of this strange happening ? · Surely their differences might be forgotten at such a moment. He stole down the side of the hill, and made his way to his fellow-hermit's cave.

But there was a terrible silence as he approached it. His heart sank at that deadly stillness in the little valley. No glimmer of light came from the cleft in the rocks. He entered and called, but no answer came back. Then, with flint, steel, and the dry grass which he used for tinder, he struck a spark, and blew it into a blaze. The old hermit, his white hair dabbled with crimson, lay sprawling across the floor. The broken crucifix, with which his head had been beaten in, lay in splinters across him. Simon had dropped on his knees beside him, straightening his contorted limbs, and muttering the office for the dead, when the thud of a horse's hoofs was heard ascending the little valley which led to the hermit's cell. The dry grass had burned down, and Simon crouched trembling in the darkness, pattering prayers to the Virgin that his strength might be upheld.

It may have been that the new-comer had seen the gleam of the light, or it may have been that he had heard from his comrades of the old man whom they had murdered, and that his curiosity had led him to the spot. He stopped his horse outside the cave, and Simon, lurking in the shadows within, had a fair view of him in the moonlight. He slipped from his saddle, fastened the bridle to a root, and then stood peering through the opening of the cell. He was a very short, thick man, with a dark face, which was gashed with three cuts upon either side. His small eyes were sunk deep in his head, showing like black holes in the heavy, flat, hairless face. His legs were short and very bandy, so that he waddled uncouthly as he walked.

Simon crouched in the darkest angle, and he gripped in his hand that same knotted cudgel which the dead theologian had once raised against him. As that hideous, stooping head advanced into the darkness of the cell, he brought the staff down upon it with all the strength of his right arm, and then, as the stricken savage fell forward upon his face, he struck madly again and again, until the shapeless figure lay limp and still. One roof covered the first slain of Europe and of Asia.

Simon's veins were throbbing and quivering with the unwonted joy of action. All the energy stored up in those years of repose came in a flood at this moment of need. Standing in the darkness of the cell, he saw, as in a map of fire, the outlines of the great Barbaric host, the line of the river, the position of the settlements, the means by which they might be warned. Silently he waited in the shadow until the moon had sunk. Then he flung himself upon the dead man's horse, guided it down the gorge, and set forth at a gallop across the plain.

There were fires on every side of him, but he kept clear of the rings of light. Round each he could see, as he passed, the circle of sleeping warriors, with the long lines of picketed horses. Mile after mile and league after league stretched that huge encampment. And then, at last, he had reached the open plain which led to the river, and the fires of the invaders were but a dull smoulder against the black eastern sky. Ever faster and faster he sped across the steppe, like a single fluttered leaf which whirls before the storm. Even as the dawn whitened the sky behind him, it gleamed also upon the broad river in front, and he flogged his weary horse through the shallows, until he plunged into its full, yellow tide.

So it was that, as the young Roman centurion—Caius

663

Crassus—made his morning round in the fort of Tyras he saw a single horseman, who rode towards him from the river. Weary and spent, drenched with water and caked with dirt and sweat, both horse and man were at the last stage of their endurance. With amazement the Roman watched their progress, and recognized in the ragged, swaying figure, with flying hair and staring eyes, the hermit of the eastern desert. He ran to meet him, and caught him in his arms as he reeled from the saddle.

"What is it, then?" he asked. "What is your news?"

But the hermit could only point at the rising sun. "To arms!" he croaked. "To arms! The day of wrath is come!" And as he looked, the Roman saw —far across the river—a great dark shadow, which moved slowly over the distant plain.

69. *The Contest*

IN the year of our Lord 66, the Emperor Nero, being at that time in the twenty-ninth year of his life and the thirteenth of his reign, set sail for Greece with the strangest company and the most singular design that any monarch has ever entertained. With ten galleys he went forth from Puteoli, carrying with him great stores of painted scenery and theatrical properties, together with a number of knights and senators, whom he feared to leave behind him at Rome, and who were all marked for death in the course of his wanderings. In his train he took Natus, his singing coach; Cluvius, a man with a monstrous voice, who should bawl out his titles; and a thousand trained youths who had learned to applaud in unison whenever their master sang or played in public. So deftly had they been taught that each had his own rôle to play. Some did no more than give forth a low, deep hum of speechless apprecia-

tion. Some clapped with enthusiasm. Some, rising
from approbation into absolute frenzy, shrieked, stamped
and beat sticks upon the benches. Some—and they
were the most effective—had learned from an Alexandrian
a long, droning musical note which they all uttered together, so that it boomed over the assembly. With
the aid of these mercenary admirers, Nero had every
hope, in spite of his indifferent voice and clumsy execution, to return to Rome, bearing with him the chaplets
for song offered for free competition by the Greek cities.
As his great gilded galley with two tiers of oars passed
down the Mediterranean, the Emperor sat in his cabin
all day, his teacher by his side, rehearsing from morning to night those compositions which he had selected,
whilst every few hours a Nubian slave massaged the
Imperial throat with oil and balsam, that it might be
ready for the great ordeal which lay before it in the land
of poetry and song. His food, his drink, and his exercise
were prescribed for him as for an athlete who trains for
a contest, and the twanging of his lyre, with the strident
notes of his voice, resounded continually from the
Imperial quarters.

Now it chanced that there lived in those days a Grecian
goatherd named Policles, who tended and partly owned
a great flock which grazed upon the long flanks of the
hills near Heræa, which is five miles north of the river
Alpheus, and no great distance from the famous Olympia.
This person was noted over all the country-side as a
man of strange gifts and singular character. He was
a poet who had twice been crowned for his verses, and
he was a musician to whom the use and sound of an
instrument were so natural that one would more easily
meet him without his staff than his harp. Even in his
lonely vigils on the winter hills he would bear it always
slung over his shoulder, and would pass the long hours
by its aid, so that it had come to be part of his very self.
He was beautiful also, swarthy and eager, with a head
like Adonis, and in strength there was no one who could

compete with him. But all was ruined by his disposition, which was so masterful that he would brook no opposition nor contradiction. For this reason he was continually at enmity with all his neighbours, and in his fits of temper he would spend months at a time in his stone hut among the mountains, hearing nothing from the world, and living only for his music and his goats.

One spring morning, in the year of 67, Policles, with the aid of his boy Dorus, had driven his goats over to a new pasturage which overlooked from afar the town of Olympia. Gazing down upon it from the mountain, the shepherd was surprised to see that a portion of the famous amphitheatre had been roofed in, as though some performance was being enacted. Living far from the world and from all news, Policles could not imagine what was afoot, for he was well aware that the Grecian games were not due for two years to come. Surely some poetic or musical contest must be proceeding of which he had heard nothing. If so, there would, perhaps, be some chance of his gaining the votes of the judges; and in any case he loved to hear the compositions and admire the execution of the great minstrels who assembled on such an occasion. Calling to Dorus, therefore, he left the goats to his charge, and strode swiftly away, his harp upon his back, to see what was going forward in the town.

When Policles came into the suburbs, he found them deserted; but he was still more surprised when he reached the main street to see no single human being in the place. He hastened his steps, therefore, and as he approached the theatre he was conscious of a low, sustained hum which announced the concourse of a huge assembly. Never in all his dreams had he imagined any musical competition upon so vast a scale as this. There were some soldiers clustering outside the door; but Policles pushed his way swiftly through them, and found himself upon the outskirts of the multitude who filled the great space formed by roofing over a portion of the national stadium. Looking around him, Policles saw a great number of his neighbours, whom he knew by sight, tightly packed upon the benches, all with their eyes fixed upon the stage. He also observed that there were soldiers round the walls, and that a considerable part of the hall was filled by a body of youths of foreign aspect, with white gowns and long hair. All this he perceived ; but what it meant he could not imagine. He bent over to a neighbour to ask him, but a soldier prodded him at once with the butt end of his spear, and commanded him fiercely to hold his peace. The man whom he had addressed, thinking that Policles had demanded a seat, pressed closer to his neighbour, and so the shepherd found himself sitting at the end of the bench which was nearest to the door. Thence he concentrated himself upon the stage, on which Metas, a well-known minstrel from Corinth and an old friend of Policles, was singing and playing without much encouragement from the audience. To Policles it seemed that Metas was having less than his due, so he applauded loudly, but he was surprised to observe that the soldiers frowned at him, and that all his neighbours regarded him with some surprise. Being a man of strong and obstinate character, he was the more inclined to persevere in his clapping when he perceived that the general sentiment was against him.

But what followed filled the shepherd poet with absolute amazement. When Metas of Corinth had made his bow and withdrawn to half-hearted and perfunctory applause, there appeared upon the stage amid the wildest enthusiasm upon the part of the audience, a most extraordinary figure. He was a short, fat man, neither old nor young, with a bull neck and a round, heavy face, which hung in creases in front like the dewlap of an ox. He was absurdly clad in a short, blue tunic, braced at the waist with a golden belt. His neck and part of his chest were exposed, and his short, fat legs were bare from the buskins below to the middle of his thighs, which was as far as his tunic extended. In his hair were two golden wings, and the same upon his heels, after the fashion of the god Mercury. Behind him walked a negro bearing a harp, and beside him a richly dressed officer who bore rolls of music. This strange creature took the harp from the hands of the attendant, and advanced to the front of the stage, whence he bowed and smiled to the cheering audience. " This is some foppish singer from Athens," thought Policles to himself, but at the same time he understood that only a great master of song could receive such a reception from a Greek audience. This was evidently some wonderful performer whose reputation had preceded him. Policles settled hown, therefore, and prepared to give his soul up to the music.

The blue-clad player struck several chords upon his lyre, and then burst suddenly out into the " Ode of Niobe." Policles sat straight up on his bench and gazed at the stage in amazement. The tune demanded a rapid transition from a low note to a high, and had been purposely chosen for this reason. The low note was a grunting, a rumble, the deep, discordant growling of an ill-conditioned dog. Then suddenly the singer threw up his face, straightened his tubby figure, rose upon his tiptoes, and with wagging head and scarlet cheeks emitted such a howl as the same dog might have given had his growl been checked by a kick from his master. All the while the lyre twanged and thrummed, sometimes in front of and sometimes behind the voice of the singer. But what amazed Policles most of all was the effect of this performance upon the audience. Every Greek was a trained critic, and as unsparing in his hisses as he was lavish in his applause. Many a singer far better than this absurd fop had been driven amid execration and abuse from the platform. But now, as the man stopped and wiped the abundant sweat from his fat face, the whole assembly burst into a delirium of appreciation. The shepherd held his hands to his bursting head, and felt that his reason must be leaving him. It was surely a dreadful musical nightmare, and he would wake soon and laugh at the remembrance. But no ; the figures were real, the faces were those of his neighbours, the cheers which resounded in his ears were indeed from an audience which filled the theatre of Olympia. The whole chorus was in full blast, the hummers humming, the shouters bellowing, the tappers hard at work upon the benches, while every now and then came a musical cyclone of " Incomparable ! Divine ! " from the trained phalanx who intoned their applause, their united voices sweeping over the tumult as the drone of the wind dominates the roar of the sea. It was madness—insufferable madness ! If this were allowed to pass, there was an end of all musical justice in Greece. Policles' conscience would not permit him to be still. Standing upon his bench with waving hands and upraised voice, he protested with all the strength of his lungs against the mad judgment of the audience.

At first, amid the tumult, his action was hardly noticed. His voice was drowned in the universal roar which broke out afresh at each bow and smirk from the fatuous musician. But gradually the folk round Policles ceased clapping, and stared at him in astonishment. The silence grew in ever widening circles, until the whole great assembly sat mute, staring at this wild and magnificent creature who was storming at them from his perch near the door.

" Fools ! " he cried. " What are you clapping at ? What are you cheering ? Is this what you call music ? Is this cat-calling to earn an Olympian prize ? The fellow has not a note in his voice. You are either deaf or mad, and I for one cry shame upon you for your folly."

Soldiers ran to pull him down, and the whole audience was in confusion, some of the bolder cheering the sentiments of the shepherd, and others crying that he should be cast out of the building. Meanwhile the successful singer, having handed his lyre to his negro attendant, was inquiring from those around him on the stage as to the cause of the uproar. Finally a herald with an enormously powerful voice stepped forward to the front, and proclaimed that if the foolish person at the back of the hall, who appeared to differ from the opinion of the rest of the audience, would come forward upon the platform, he might, if he dared, exhibit his own powers, and see if he could outdo the admirable and wonderful exhibition which they had just had the privilege of hearing.

Policles sprang readily to his feet at the challenge, and the great company making way for him to pass, he found himself a minute later standing in his unkempt garb, with his frayed and weather-beaten harp in his hand, before the expectant crowd. He stood for a moment tightening a string here and slackening another there until his chords rang true. Then, amid a murmur of laughter and jeers from the Roman benches immediately before him, he began to sing.

He had prepared no composition, but he had trained himself to improvise, singing out of his heart for the joy of the music. He told of the land of Elis, beloved of Jupiter, in which they were gathered that day, of the great bare mountain slopes, of the swift shadows of the clouds, of the winding, blue river, of the keen air of the uplands, of the chill of the evenings, and the beauties of earth and sky. It was all simple and childlike, but it went to the hearts of the Olympians, for it spoke of the land which they knew and loved. Yet when he at last dropped his hand, few of them dared to applaud, and their feeble voices were drowned by a storm of hisses and groans from his opponents. He shrank back in horror from so unusual a reception, and in an instant his blue-clad rival was in his place. If he had sung badly before, his performance now was inconceivable. His screams, his grunts, his discords, and harsh, jarring cacophanies were an outrage to the very name of music.

And yet every time that he paused for breath or to wipe his streaming forehead a fresh thunder of applause came rolling back from the audience. Policles sank his face in his hands and prayed that he might not be insane. Then, when the dreadful performance ceased, and the uproar of admiration showed that the crown was certainly awarded to this impostor, a horror of the audience, a hatred of this race of fools, and a craving for the peace and silence of the pastures mastered every feeling in his mind. He dashed through the mass of people waiting at the wings, and emerged in the open air. His old rival and friend Metas of Corinth was waiting there with an anxious face.

" Quick, Policles, quick ! " he cried. " My pony is tethered behind yonder grove. A grey he is, with red trappings. Get you gone as hard as hoof will bear you, for if you are taken you will have no easy death."

" No easy death ! What mean you, Metas ? Who is the fellow ? "

" Great Jupiter ! did you not know ? Where have you lived ? It is Nero the Emperor ! Never would he pardon what you have said about his voice. Quick, man, quick, or the guards will be at your heels ! "

An hour later the shepherd was well on his way to his mountain home, and about the same time the Emperor, having received the Chaplet of Olympia for the incomparable excellence of his performance, was making inquiries with a frowning brow as to who the insolent person might be who had dared to utter such contemptuous criticisms.

" Bring him to me here this instant," said he, " and let Marcus with his knife and branding-iron be in attendance."

" If it please you, great Cæsar," said Arsenius Platus, the officer of attendance, " the man cannot be found, and there are some very strange rumours flying about."

" Rumours ! " cried the angry Nero. " What do

you mean, Arsenius ? I tell you that the fellow was an ignorant upstart with the bearing of a boor and the voice of a peacock. I tell you also that there are a good many who are as guilty as he among the people, for I heard them with my own ears raise cheers for him when he had sung his ridiculous ode. I have half a mind to burn their town about their ears, so that they may remember my visit."

" It is not to be wondered at if he won their votes, Cæsar," said the soldier, " for from what I hear it would have been no disgrace had you, even you, been conquered in this contest."

" I conquered ! You are mad, Arsenius. What do you mean ? "

" None know him, great Cæsar ! He came from the mountains, and he disappeared into the mountains. You marked the wildness and strange beauty of his face. It is whispered that for once the great god Pan has condescended to measure himself against a mortal."

The cloud cleared from Nero's brow. " Of course, Arsenius ! You are right ! No man would have dared to brave me so. What a story for Rome ! Let the messenger leave this very night, Arsenius, to tell them how their Emperor has upheld their honour in Olympia this day."

70. *The First Cargo*

" Ex ovo omnia "

WHEN you left Britain with your legion, my dear Crassus, I promised that I would write to you from time to time when a messenger chanced to be going to Rome, and keep you informed as to anything of interest which might occur in this country. Personally, I am very glad that I remained behind when the troops and so many of our citizens left, for though the living is rough and the climate is infernal, still by dint of the three voyages which I have made for amber to the Baltic, and the excellent prices which I obtained for it here, I shall soon be in a position to retire, and to spend my old age under my own fig tree, or even perhaps to buy a small villa at Baiæ or Posuoli, where I could get a good sun-bath after the continued fogs of this accursed island. I picture myself on a little farm, and I read the Georgics as a preparation ; but when I hear the rain falling and the wind howling, Italy seems very far away.

In my previous letter I let you know how things were going in this country. The poor folk, who had given up all soldiering during the centuries that we guarded them, are now perfectly helpless before these Picts and Scots, tattooed Barbarians from the north, who overrun the whole country and do exactly what they please. So long as they kept to the north, the people in the south, who are the most numerous, and also the most civilised of the Britons, took no heed of them ; but now the rascals have come as far as London, and the lazy folk in these parts have had to wake up. Vortigern, the king, is useless for anything but drink or women, so he sent across to the Baltic to get over some of the North Germans, in the hope that they would come and help him. It is bad enough to have a bear in your house, but it does not seem to me to mend matters if you call in a pack of ferocious wolves as well. However, nothing better could be devised, so an invitation was sent and very promptly accepted. And it is here that your humble friend appears upon the scene. In the course of my amber trading I had learned the Saxon speech, and so I was sent down in all haste to the Kentish shore that I might be there when our new allies came. I arrived there on the very day when their first vessel appeared, and it is of my adventures that I wish to tell you. It is perfectly clear to me that the landing of these warlike Germans in England will prove to be an event of historical importance, and so your inquisitive mind will not feel wearied if I treat the matter in some detail.

It was, then, upon the day of Mercury, immediately following the Feast of Our Blessed Lord's Ascension, that I found myself upon the south bank of the river Thames, at the point where it opens into a wide estuary. There is an island there named Thanet, which was the spot chosen for the landfall of our visitors. Sure enough, I had no sooner ridden up than there was a great red ship, the first, as it seems, of three, coming in under full sail. The white horse, which is the ensign of these rovers, was hanging from her topmast, and she appeared to be crowded with men. The sun was shining brightly, and the great scarlet ship, with snow-white sails and a line of gleaming shields slung over her side, made as fair a picture on that blue expanse as one would wish to see.

I pushed off at once in a boat, because it had been arranged that none of the Saxons should land until the king had come down to speak with their leaders. Presently I was under the ship, which had a gilded dragon in the bows, and a tier of oars along either side. As I looked up, there was a row of helmeted heads looking down at me, and among them I saw, to my great surprise and pleasure, that of Eric the Swart, with whom I do business at Venta every year. He greeted me heartily when I reached the deck, and became at once my guide, friend, and counsellor. This helped me greatly with these Barbarians, for it is their nature that they are very cold and aloof unless one of their own number can vouch for you, after which they are very hearty and hospitable. Try as they will, they find it hard, however, to avoid a certain suggestion of condescension, and in the baser sort, of contempt, when they are dealing with a foreigner.

It was a great stroke of luck meeting Eric, for he was able to give me some idea of how things stood before I was shown into the presence of Kenna, the leader of this particular ship. The crew, as I learned from him, was entirely made up of three tribes or families—those of Kenna, of Lanc, and of Hasta. Each of these tribes gets its name by putting the letters " ing " after the name of the chief, so that the people on board would describe themselves as Kennings, Lancings, and Hastings. I observed in the Baltic that the villages were named after the family who lived in them, each keeping to itself, so that I have no doubt that if these fellows get a footing on shore, we shall see settlements with names like these rising up among the British towns.

The greater part of the men were sturdy fellows with red, yellow or brown hair, mostly the latter. To my surprise, I saw several women among them. Eric, in answer to my question, explained that they always take their women with them so far as they can, and that instead of finding them an encumbrance as our Roman dames would be, they look upon them as help-mates and advisers. Of course, I remembered after-wards that our excellent and accurate Tacitus has remarked upon this characteristic of the Germans. All laws in the tribes are decided by votes, and a vote has not yet been given to the women, but many are in favour of it, and it is thought that woman and man may soon have the same power in the State, though many of the women themselves are opposed to such an innovation. I observed to Eric that it was fortunate there were several women on board, as they could keep each other company ; but he answered that the wives of chiefs had no desire to know the wives of the inferior officers, and that both of them combined against the more common women, so that any companionship was out of the question. He pointed as he spoke to Editha, the wife of Kenna, a red-faced, elderly woman, who walked among the others, her chin in the air, taking no more notice than if they did not exist.

Whilst I was talking to my friend Eric a sudden alter-cation broke out upon the deck, and a great number of the men paused in their work, and flocked towards the spot with faces which showed that they were deeply interested in the matter. Eric and I pushed our way among the others, for I was very anxious to see as much as I could of the ways and manners of these Barbarians. A quarrel had broken out about a child, a little blue-eyed fellow with curly, yellow hair, who appeared to be greatly amused by the hubbub of which he was the cause. On one side of him stood a white-bearded old man, of very majestic aspect, who signified by his gestures that he claimed the lad for himself, while on the other was a thin, earnest, anxious person, who strongly objected to the boy being taken from him. Eric whispered in my ear that the old man was the tribal high priest, who was the official sacrificer to their great god, Woden, whilst the other was a man who took somewhat different views, not upon Woden, but upon the means by which he should be worshipped. The majority of the crew were on the side of the old priest ; but a certain number, who liked greater liberty of worship, and to invent their own prayers instead of always repeating the official ones, followed the lead of the younger man. The difference was too deep and too old to be healed among the grown men, but each had a great desire to impress his view upon the children. This was the reason why these two were now so furious with each other, and the argument between them ran so high that several of their followers on either side had drawn the short saxes, or knives from which their name of Saxon is derived, when a burly, red-headed man pushed his way through the throng, and in a voice of thunder brought the controversy to an end.

" You priests, who argue about the things which no man can know, are more trouble aboard this ship than all the dangers of the sea," he cried. " Can you not be content with worshipping Woden, over which we are all agreed, and not make so much of those small points upon which we may differ ? If there is all this

fuss about the teaching of the children, then I shall
forbid either of you to teach them, and they must be
content with as much as they can learn from their
mothers."

The two angry teachers walked away with discontented
faces ; and Kenna—for it was he who spoke—ordered
that a whistle should be sounded, and that the crew
should assemble. I was pleased with the free bearing
of these people, for though this was their greatest chief,
they showed none of the exaggerated respect which
soldiers of a legion might show to the Prætor, but met
him on a respectful equality, which showed how highly
they rated their own manhood.

From our Roman standard, his remarks to his men
would seem very wanting in eloquence, for there were
no graces nor metaphors to be found in them, and
yet they were short, strong and to the point. At any
rate it was very clear that they were to the minds of
his hearers. He began by reminding them that they had
left their own country because the land was all taken
up, and that there was no use returning there, since
there was no place where they could dwell as free and
independent men. This island of Britain was but
sparsely inhabited, and there was a chance that every
one of them would be able to found a home of his
own.

" You, Whitta," he said, addressing some of them by
name, " you will found a Whitting hame, and you,
Bucka, we shall see you in a Bucking hame, where
your children's and your children's children will bless
you for the broad acres which your valour will have
gained for them." There was no word of glory or of
honour in his speech, but he said that he was aware
that they would do their duty, on which they all struck
their swords upon their shields so that the Britons on
the beach could hear the clang. Then, his eyes falling
upon me, he asked me whether I was the messenger
from Vortigern, and on my answering, he bid me follow

him into his cabin, where Lanc and Hasta, the other chiefs, were waiting for a council.

Picture me, then, my dear Crassus, in a very low-roofed cabin, with these three huge Barbarians seated round me. Each was clad in some sort of saffron tunic, with a chain-mail shirt over it, and a helmet with the horns of oxen on the sides, laid upon the table before him. Like most of the Saxon chiefs, their beards were shaved, but they wore their hair long and their huge, light-coloured moustaches drooped down on to their shoulders. They are gentle, slow, and somewhat heavy in their bearing, but I can well fancy that their fury is the more terrible when it does arise.

Their minds seem to be of a very practical and positive nature, for they at once began to ask me a series of questions upon the numbers of the Britons, the resources of the kingdom, the conditions of its trade and other such subjects. They then set to work arguing over the information which I had given, and became so absorbed in their own contention that I believe there were times when they forgot my presence. Everything, after due discussion, was decided between them by the vote, the one who found himself in the minority always submitting, though sometimes with very bad grace. Indeed, on one occasion Lanc, who usually differed from the others, threatened to refer the matter to the general vote of the whole crew. There was a constant conflict in the point of view; for whereas Kenna and Hasta were anxious to extend the Saxon power, and to make it greater in the eyes of the world, Lanc was of opinion that they should give less thought to conquest and more to the comfort and advancement of their followers. At the same time it seemed to me that really Lanc was the most combative of the three; so much so that, even in time of peace, he could not forgo this contest with his own brethren. Neither of the others seemed very fond of him, for they were each, as was easy to see, proud of their chieftainship, and anxious to use their authority, referring continually to those noble ancestors from whom it was derived; while Lanc, though he was equally well born, took the view of the common men upon every occasion, claiming that the interests of the many were superior to the privileges of the few. In a word, Crassus, if you could imagine a free-booting Gracchus on one side, and two piratical Patricians upon the other, you would understand the effect which my companions produced upon me.

There was one peculiarity which I observed in their conversation which soothed me very much. I am fond of these Britons, among whom I have spent so much of my life, and I wish them well. It was very pleasing, therefore, to notice that these men insisted upon it in their conversation that the whole object of their visit was the good of the Islanders. Any prospect of advantage to themselves was pushed into the background. I was not clear that these professions could be made to agree with the speech in which Kenna had promised a hundred hides of land to every man on the ship; but on my making this remark, the three chiefs seemed very surprised and hurt by my suspicions, and explained very plausibly that, as the Britons needed them as a guard, they could not aid them better than by settling on the soil, and so being continually at hand in order to help them. In time, they said, they hoped to raise and train the natives to such a point that they would be able to look after themselves. Lanc spoke with some degree of eloquence upon the nobleness of the mission which they had undertaken, and the others clattered their cups of mead (a jar of that unpleasant drink was on the table) in token of their agreement.

I observed also how much interested, and how very earnest and intolerant these Barbarians were in the matter of religion. Of Christianity they knew nothing, so that although they were aware that the Britons were Christians, they had not a notion of what their creed really was. Yet without examination they started by

taking it for granted that their own worship of Woden
was absolutely right, and that therefore this other creed
must be absolutely wrong. "This vile religion,"
"This sad superstition," and "This grievous error"
were among the phrases which they used towards it.
Instead of expressing pity for anyone who had been
misinformed upon so serious a question, their feelings
were those of anger, and they declared most earnestly
that they would spare no pains to set the matter right,
fingering the hilts of their long broadswords as they
said so.

Well, my dear Crassus, you will have had enough
of me and of my Saxons. I have given you a short
sketch of these people and their ways. Since I began
this letter, I have visited the two other ships which have
come in, and as I find the same characteristics among
the people on board them, I cannot doubt that they lie
deeply in the race. For the rest, they are brave, hardy,
and very pertinacious in all that they undertake ; whereas
the Britons, though a great deal more spirited, have not
the same steadiness of purpose, their quicker imaginations
suggesting always some other course, and their more
fiery passions being succeeded by reaction. When I
looked from the deck of the first Saxon ship, and saw
the swaying, excited multitude of Britons on the beach,
contrasting them with the intent, silent men who stood
beside me, it seemed to me more than ever dangerous
to call in such allies. So strongly did I feel it that I
turned to Kenna, who was also looking towards the
beach.

"You will own this island before you have finished,"
said I.

His eyes sparkled as he gazed. "Perhaps," he cried ;
and then suddenly correcting himself and thinking that
he had said too much, he added—

"A temporary occupation—nothing more."

71. *An Iconoclast*

IT was daybreak of a March morning in the year of
Christ 92. Outside the long Semita Alta was
already thronged with people, with buyers and
sellers, callers and strollers, for the Romans were so
early-rising a people that many a Patrician preferred
to see his clients at six in the morning. Such was the
good republican tradition, still upheld by the more
conservative ; but with more modern habits of luxury,
a night of pleasure and banqueting .was no uncommon
thing. Thus one, who had learned the new and yet
adhered to the old, might find his hours overlap, and
without so much as a pretence of sleep come straight from
his night of debauch into his day of business, turning with
heavy wits and an aching head to that round of formal
duties which consumed the life of a Roman gentleman.

So it was with Emilius Flaccus that March morning.
He and his fellow-senator, Caius Balbus, had passed the
night in one of those gloomy drinking bouts to which
the Emperor Domitian summoned his chosen friends
at the high palace on the Palatine. Now, having reached
the portals of the house of Flaccus, they stood together
under the pomegranate-fringed portico which fronted the
peristyle and, confident in each other's tried discretion,
made up by the freedom of their criticism for the long
self-suppression of that melancholy feast.

" If he would but feed his guests," said Balbus, a
little red-faced, choleric nobleman with yellow-shot,
angry eyes. " What had we ? Upon my life, I have
forgotten. Plovers' eggs, a mess of fish, some bird or
other, and then his eternal apples."

" Of which," said Flaccus, " he ate only the apples.
Do him the justice to confess that he takes even less
than he gives. At least they cannot say of him as of
Vitellius, that his teeth beggared the empire."

" No, nor his thirst either, great as it is. That fiery Sabine wine of his could be had for a few sesterces the amphora. It is the common drink of the carters at every wine-house on the country roads. I longed for a glass of my own rich Falernian or the mellow Coan that was bottled in the year that Titus took Jerusalem. Is it even now too late ? Could we not wash this rasping stuff from our palates ? "

" Nay, better come in with me now and take a bitter draught ere you go upon your way. My Greek physician Stephanos has a rare prescription for a morning head. What ! Your clients await you ? Well, I will see you later at the Senate house."

The Patrician had entered his atrium, bright with rare flowers, and melodious with strange singing birds. At the jaws of the hall, true to his morning duties, stood Lebs, the little Nubian slave, with snow-white tunic and turban, a salver of glasses in one hand, whilst in the other he held a flask of thin, lemon-tinted liquid. The master of the house filled up a bitter aromatic bumper, and was about to drink it off, when his hand was arrested by a sudden perception that something was much amiss in his household. It was to be read all around him—in the frightened eyes of the black boy, in the agitated face of the keeper of the atrium, in the gloom and silence of the little knot of ordinarii, the procurator or major-domo at their head, who had assembled to greet their master. Stephanos the physician Cleios the Alexandrine reader, Promus the steward, each turned his head away to avoid his master's questioning gaze.

" What in the name of Pluto is the matter with you all ? " cried the amazed senator, whose night of potations had left him in no mood for patience. " Why do you stand moping there ? Stephanos, Vacculus, is anything amiss ? Here, Promus, you are the head of my household. What is it, then ? Why do you turn your eyes away from me ? "

The burly steward, whose fat face was haggard and mottled with anxiety, laid his hand upon the sleeve of the domestic beside him.

" Sergius is responsible for the atrium, my lord. It is for him to tell you the terrible thing that has befallen in your absence."

" Nay, it was Datus who did it. Bring him in, and let him explain it himself," said Sergius in a sulky voice.

The patience of the Patrician was at an end. " Speak this instant, you rascal ! " he shouted angrily. " Another minute, and I will have you dragged to the ergastulum, where, with your feet in the stocks and the gyves round your wrists, you may learn quicker obedience. Speak, I say, and without delay."

" It is the Venus," the man stammered ; " the Greek Venus of Praxiteles."

The senator gave a cry of apprehension and rushed to the corner of the atrium, where a little shrine, curtained off by silken drapery, held the precious statue, the greatest art treasure of his collection—perhaps of the whole world. He tore the hangings aside and stood in speechless anger before the outraged goddess. The red, perfumed lamp which always burned before her had been spilled and broken ; her altar fire had been quenched, her chaplet had been dashed aside. But worst of all—insufferable sacrilege !—her own beautiful nude body of glistening Pantelic marble, as white and fair as when the inspired Greek had hewed it out five hundred years before, had been most brutally mishandled. Three fingers of the gracious, outstretched hand had been struck off, and lay upon the pedestal beside her. Above her delicate breast a dark mark showed, where a blow had disfigured the marble. Emilius Flaccus, the most delicate and judicious connoisseur in Rome, stood gasping and croaking, his hand to his throat, as he gazed at his disfigured master-piece. Then he turned upon his slaves, his fury in his convulsed face ; but, to his amazement, they were not

683

looking at him, but had all turned in attitudes of deep respect towards the opening of the peristyle. As he faced round and saw who had just entered his house, his own rage fell away from him in an instant, and his manner became as humble as that of his servants.

The new-comer was a man forty-three years of age, clean shaven, with a massive head, large, engorged eyes, a small, clear-cut nose, and the full bull neck which was the especial mark of his breed. He had entered through the peristyle with a swaggering, rolling gait, as one who walks upon his own ground, and now he stood, his hands upon his hips, looking round him at the bowing slaves, and finally at their master, with a half-humorous expression upon his flushed and brutal face.

"Why, Emilius," said he, "I had understood that your household was the best-ordered in Rome. What is amiss with you this morning?"

"Nothing could be amiss with us now that Cæsar has deigned to come under my roof," said the courtier. "This is indeed a most glad surprise which you have prepared for me."

"It was an afterthought," said Domitian. "When you and the others had left me, I was in no mood for sleep, and so it came into my mind that I would have a breath of morning air by coming down to you, and seeing this Grecian Venus of yours, about which you discoursed so eloquently between the cups. But, indeed, by your appearance and that of your servants, I should judge that my visit was an ill-timed one."

"Nay, dear master; say not so. But, indeed, it is truth that I was in trouble at the moment of your welcome entrance, and this trouble was, as the Fates have willed it, brought forth by that very statue in which you have been graciously pleased to show your interest. There it stands, and you can see for yourself how rudely it has been mishandled."

"By Pluto and all the nether gods, if it were mine

some of you should feed the lampreys," said the Emperor, looking round with his fierce eyes at the shrinking slaves. " You were always overmerciful, Emilius. It is the common talk that your catenæ are rusted for want of use. But surely this is beyond all bounds. Let me see how you handle the matter. Whom do you hold responsible ? "

" The slave Sergius is responsible, since it is his place to tend the atrium," said Flaccus. " Stand forward, Sergius. What have you to say ? "

The trembling slave advanced to his master. " If it please you, sir, the mischief has been done by Datus the Christian."

" Datus ! Who is he ? "

" The matulator, the scavenger, my lord. I did not know that he belonged to these horrible people, or I should not have admitted him. He came with his broom to brush out the litter of the birds. His eyes fell upon the Venus, and in an instant he had rushed upon her and struck her two blows with his wooden besom. Then we fell upon him and dragged him away. But alas ! alas ! it was too late, for already the wretch had dashed off the fingers of the goddess."

The Emperor smiled grimly, while the Patrician's thin face grew pale with anger.

" Where is the fellow ? " he asked.

" In the ergastulum, your honour, with the furca on his neck."

" Bring him hither and summon the household."

A few minutes later the whole back of the atrium was thronged by the motley crowd who ministered to the household needs of a great Roman nobleman. There was the arcarius, or account keeper, with his stylum behind his ear ; the sleek prægustator, who sampled all foods, so as to stand between his master and poison, and beside him his predecessor, now a half-witted idiot through the interception twenty years before of a datura draught from Canidia ; the cellarman, summoned from amongst his amphoræ; the cook, with his basting-ladle in his hand; the pompous nomenclator, who ushered the guests; the cubicularius, who saw to their accommodation; the silentiarius, who kept order in the house; the structor, who set forth the tables; the carptor, who carved the food; the cinerarius, who lit the fires—these and many more, half-curious, half-terrified, came to the judging of Datus. Behind them a chattering, giggling swarm of Lalages, Marias, Cerusas, and Amaryllides, from the laundries and the spinning-rooms, stood upon their tiptoes, and extended their pretty, wondering faces over the shoulders of the men. Through this crowd came two stout varlets leading the culprit between them. He was a small, dark, rough-headed man, with an unkempt beard and wild eyes which shone brightly with strong inward emotion. His hands were bound behind him, and over his neck was the heavy wooden collar or furca which was placed upon refractory slaves. A smear of blood across his cheek showed that he had not come uninjured from the preceding scuffle.

" Are you Datus the scavenger ? " asked the Patrician.

The man drew himself up proudly. " Yes," said he, " I am Datus."

" Did you do this injury to my statue ? "

" Yes, I did."

There was an uncompromising boldness in the man's reply which compelled respect. The wrath of his master became tinged with interest.

" Why did you do this ? " he asked.

" Because it was my duty."

" Why, then, was it your duty to destroy your master's property ? "

" Because I am a Christian." His eyes blazed suddenly out of his dark face. " Because there is no God but the one eternal, and all else are sticks and stones. What has this naked harlot to do with Him to whom the great firmament is but a garment and the earth a footstool ? It was in His service that I have broken your statue."

686

Domitian looked with a smile at the Patrician. " You will make nothing of him," said he. " They speak even so when they stand before the lions in the arena. As to argument, not all the philosophers of Rome can break them down. Before my very face they refuse to sacrifice in my honour. Never were such impossible people to deal with. I should take a short way with him if I were you."

" What would Cæsar advise ? "

" There are the games this afternoon. I am showing the new hunting-leopard which King Juba has sent from Numidia. This slave may give us some sport when he finds the hungry beast sniffing at his heels."

The Patrician considered for a moment. He had always been a father to his servants. It was hateful to him to think of any injury befalling them. Perhaps even now, if this strange fanatic would show his sorrow for what he had done, it might be possible to spare him. At least it was worth trying.

" Your offence deserves death," he said. " What reasons can you give why it should not befall you, since you have injured this statue, which is worth your own price a hundred times over ? "

The slave looked steadfastly at his master. " I do not fear death," he said. " My sister Candida died in the arena, and I am ready to do the same. It is true that I have injured your statue, but I am able to find you something of far greater value in exchange. I will give you the truth and the gospel in exchange for your broken idol."

The Emperor laughed. " You will do nothing with him, Emilius," he said. " I know his breed of old. He is ready to die ; he says so himself. Why save him, then ? "

But the Patrician still hesitated. He would make a last effort.

" Throw off his bonds," he said to the guards. " Now take the furca off his neck. So ! Now, Datus, I have

687

released you to show you that I trust you. I have no wish to do you any hurt if you will but acknowledge your error, and so set a better example to my household here assembled."

" How, then, shall I acknowledge my error ? " the slave asked.

" Bow your head before the goddess, and entreat her forgiveness for the violence you have done her. Then perhaps you may gain my pardon as well."

" Put me, then, before her," said the Christian.

Emilius Flaccus looked triumphantly at Domitian. By kindness and tact he was effecting that which the Emperor had failed to do by violence. Datus walked in front of the mutilated Venus. Then with a sudden spring he tore the baton out of the hand of one of his guardians, leaped upon the pedestal, and showered his blows upon the lovely marble woman. With a crack and a dull thud her right-arm dropped to the ground. Another fierce blow and the left had followed. Flaccus danced and screamed with horror, while his servants dragged the raving iconoclast from his impassive victim. Domitian's brutal laughter echoed through the hall.

" Well, friend, what think you now ? " he cried. " Are you wiser than your Emperor ? Can you indeed tame your Christian with kindness ? "

Emilius Flaccus wiped the sweat from his brow. " He is yours, great Cæsar. Do with him as you will."

" Let him be at the gladiator's entrance of the circus an hour before the games begin," said the Emperor. " Now, Emilius, the night has been a merry one. My Ligurian galley waits by the river quay. Come, cool your head with a spin to Ostia ere the business of State calls you to the Senate."

72. *Giant Maximin*

I—THE COMING OF MAXIMIN

MANY are the strange vicissitudes of history. Greatness has often sunk to the dust, and has tempered itself to its new surrounding. Smallness has risen aloft, has flourished for a time, and then has sunk once more. Rich monarchs have become poor monks, brave conquerors have lost their manhood, eunuchs and women have overthrown armies and kingdoms. Surely there is no situation which the mind of man could invent which has not taken shape and been played out upon the world stage. But of all the strange careers and of all the wondrous happenings, stranger than Charles in his monastery, or Justin on his throne, there stands the case of Giant Maximin, what he attained, and how he attained it. Let me tell the sober facts of history, tinged only by that colouring to which the more austere historians could not condescend. It is a record as well as a story.

In the heart of Thrace some ten miles north of the Rhodope mountains, there is a valley which is named Harpessus, after the stream which runs down it. Through this valley lies the main road from the east to the west, and along the road, returning from an expedition against the Alani, there marched, upon the fifth day of the month of June in the year 210, a small but compact Roman army. It consisted of three legions —the Jovian, the Cappadocian, and the men of Hercules. Ten turmæ of Gallic cavalry led the van, whilst the rear was covered by a regiment of Batavian Horse Guards, the immediate attendants of the Emperor Septimus Severus, who had conducted the campaign in person. The peasants who lined the low hills which fringed the valley looked with indifference upon the long files of dusty, heavily burdened infantry, but they broke into murmurs of delight at the gold-faced cuirasses and high, brazen, horse-hair helmets of the guardsmen, applauding their stalwart figures, their martial bearing, and the stately black chargers which they rode. A soldier might know that it was the little weary men with their short swords, their heavy pikes over their shoulders, and their square shields slung upon their backs, who were the real terror of the enemies of the Empire, but to the eyes of the wondering Thracians it was this troop of glittering Apollos who bore Rome's victory upon their banners, and upheld the throne of the purple-togaed prince who rode before them.

Among the scattered groups of peasants who looked on from a respectful distance at this military pageant, there were two men who attracted much attention from those who stood immediately around them. The one was commonplace enough—a little grey-headed man, with uncouth dress and a frame which was bent and warped by a long life of arduous toil, goat-driving and wood-chopping, among the mountains. It was the appearance of his youthful companion which had drawn the amazed observation of the bystanders. In stature he was such a giant as is seen but once or twice in each generation of mankind. Eight feet and two inches was his measure from his sandalled sole to the topmost curls of his tangled hair. Yet for all his mighty stature there was nothing heavy or clumsy in the man. His huge shoulders bore no redundant flesh, and his figure was straight and hard and supple as a young pine tree. A frayed suit of brown leather clung close to his giant body, and a cloak of undressed sheep-skin was slung from his shoulder. His bold blue eyes, shock of yellow hair and fair skin showed that he was of Gothic or northern blood, and the amazed expression upon his broad, frank face as he stared at the passing troops told of a simple and uneventful life in some back valley of the Macedonian mountains.

" I fear your mother was right when she advised that we keep you at home," said the old man anxiously. " Tree-cutting and wood-carrying will seem but dull work after such a sight as this."

" When I see mother next it will be to put a golden torque round her neck," said the young giant. " And you, daddy ; I will fill your leather pouch with gold pieces before I have done."

The old man looked at his son with startled eyes. " You would not leave us, Theckla ! What could we do without you ? "

" My place is down among yonder men," said the young man. " I was not born to drive goats and carry logs, but to sell this manhood of mine in the best market. There is my market in the Emperor's own Guard. Say nothing, daddy, for my mind is set, and if you weep now it will be to laugh hereafter. I will to great Rome with the soldiers."

The daily march of the heavily laden Roman legionary was fixed at twenty miles ; but on this afternoon, though only half the distance had been accomplished, the silver trumpets blared out their welcome news that a camp was to be formed. As the men broke their ranks, the reason of their light march was announced by the decurions. It was the birthday of Geta, the younger son of the Emperor, and in his honour there would be games and a double ration of wine. But the iron discipline of the Roman army required that under all circumstances certain duties should be performed, and foremost among them that the camp should be made secure. Laying down their arms in the order of their ranks, the soldiers seized their spades and axes, and worked rapidly and joyously until sloping vallum and gaping fossa girdled them round, and gave them safe refuge against a night attack. Then in noisy, laughing, gesticulating crowds they gathered in their thousands round the grassy arena where the sports were to be held. A long, green hillside sloped down to a level plain, and on this gentle incline the army lay watching the strife of the chosen athletes who contended before them. They stretched themselves in the glare of the sunshine, their heavy tunics thrown off, and their naked limbs sprawling, wine-cups and baskets of fruit and cakes circling amongst them, enjoying rest and peace as only those can to whom it comes so rarely.

The five-mile race was over, and had been won as usual by Decurion Brennus, the crack long-distance champion of the Herculians. Amid the yells of the Jovians, Capellus of the corps had carried off both the long and the high jump. Big Brebix the Gaul had out-thrown the long guardsman Serenus with the fifty pound stone. Now, as the sun sank towards the western ridge, and turned the Harpessus to a riband of gold, they had come to the final of the wrestling, where the pliant Greek, whose name is lost in the nickname of "Python," was tried out against the bull-necked Lictor of the military police, a hairy Hercules, whose heavy hand had in the way of duty oppressed many of the spectators.

As the two men, stripped save for their loincloths, approached the wrestling-ring, cheers and counter-cheers burst from their adherents, some favouring the Lictor for his Roman blood, some the Greek from their own private grudge. And then, of a sudden, the cheering died, heads were turned towards the slope away from the arena, men stood up and peered and pointed, until finally, in a strange hush, the whole great assembly had forgotten the athletes, and were watching a single man walking swiftly towards them down the green curve of the hill. This huge, solitary figure, with the oaken club in his hand, the shaggy fleece flapping from his great shoulders, and the setting sun gleaming upon a halo of golden hair, might have been the tutelary god of the fierce and barren mountains from which he had issued. Even the Emperor rose from his chair and gazed with open-eyed amazement at the extraordinary being who approached him.

The man, whom we already know as Theckla the Thracian, paid no heed to the attention which he had aroused, but strode onwards, stepping as lightly as a deer, until he reached the fringe of the soldiers. Amid their open ranks he picked his way, sprang over the ropes which guarded the arena, and advanced towards the Emperor, until a spear at his breast warned him that he must go no nearer. Then he sunk upon his right knee and called out some words in the Gothic speech.

" Great Jupiter ! Whoever saw such a body of a man ! " cried the Emperor. " What says he ? What is amiss with the fellow ? Whence comes he, and what is his name ? "

An interpreter translated the Barbarian's answer. " He says, great Cæsar, that he is of good blood, and sprung by a Gothic father from a woman of the Alani. He says that his name is Theckla, and that he would fain carry a sword in Cæsar's service."

The Emperor smiled. " Some post could surely be found for such a man, were it but as janitor at the Palatine Palace," said he to one of the Prefects. " I would fain see him walk even as he is through the forum. He would turn the heads of half the women in Rome. Talk to him, Crassus. You know his speech."

The Roman officer turned to the giant. " Cæsar says that you are to come with him, and he will make you the servant at his door."

The Barbarian rose, and his fair cheeks flushed with resentment.

" I will serve Cæsar as a soldier," said he, " but I will be house-servant to no man—not even to him. If Cæsar would see what manner of man I am let him put one of his guardsmen up against me."

" By the shade of Milo this is a bold fellow ! " cried

the Emperor. " How say you, Crassus ? Shall he make good his words ? "

" By your leave, Cæsar," said the blunt soldier, " good swordsmen are too rare in these days that we should let them slay each other for sport. Perhaps if the Barbarian would wrestle a fall——"

" Excellent ! " cried the Emperor. " Here is the Python, and here Varus the Lictor, each stripped for the bout. Have a look at them, Barbarian, and see which you would choose. What does he say ? He would take them both ? Nay then he is either the king of wrestlers or the king of boasters, and we shall soon see which. Let him have his way, and he has himself to thank if he comes out with a broken neck."

There was some laughter when the peasant tossed his sheep-skin mantle to the ground and, without troubling to remove his leathern tunic, advanced towards the two wrestlers ; but it became uproarious when with a quick spring he seized the Greek under one arm and the Roman under the other, holding them as in a vice. Then with a terrific effort he tore them both from the ground, carried them writhing and kicking round the arena, and finally walking up to the Emperor's throne, threw his two athletes down in front of him. Then, bowing to Cæsar, the huge Barbarian withdrew, and laid his great bulk down among the ranks of the applauding soldiers, whence he watched with stolid unconcern the conclusion of the sports.

It was still daylight, when the last event had been decided, and the soldiers returned to the camp. The Emperor Severus had ordered his horse, and in the company of Crassus, his favourite Prefect, rode down the winding pathway which skirts the Harpessus, chatting over the future dispersal of the army. They had ridden for some miles when Severus, glancing behind him, was surprised to see a huge figure which trotted lightly along at the very heels of his horse.

" Surely this is Mercury as well as Hercules that

we have found among the Thracian mountains," said
he with a smile. " Let us see how soon our Syrian horses
can out-distance him."

The two Romans broke into a gallop, and did not
draw rein until a good mile had been covered at the full
pace of their splendid chargers. Then they turned
and looked back ; but there, some distance off, still
running with a lightness and a spring which spoke of
iron muscles and inexhaustible endurance, came the
great Barbarian. The Roman Emperor waited until
the athlete had come up to them.

" Why do you follow me ? " he asked.

" It is my hope, Cæsar, that I may always follow you."
His flushed face as he spoke was almost level with that
of the mounted Roman.

" By the god of war, I do not know where in all the
world I could find such a servant ! " cried the Emperor.
" You shall be my own body-guard, the one nearest
to me of all."

The giant fell upon his knee. " My life and strength
are yours," he said. " I ask no more than to spend them
for Cæsar."

Crassus had interpreted this short dialogue. He now
turned to the Emperor.

" If he is indeed to be always at your call, Cæsar, it
would be well to give the poor Barbarian some name
which your lips can frame. Theckla is as uncouth and
craggy a word as one of his native rocks."

The Emperor pondered for a moment. " If I am
to have the naming of him," said he, " then surely I
shall call him Maximus, for there is not such a giant
upon earth."

" Hark you," said the Prefect. " The Emperor
has deigned to give you a Roman name, since you have
come into his service. Henceforth you are no longer
Theckla, but you are Maximus. Can you say it after me ? "

" Maximin," repeated the Barbarian, trying to catch
the Roman word.

The Emperor laughed at the mincing accent. " Yes, yes, Maximin let it be. To all the world you are Maximin, the body-guard of Severus. When we have reached Rome, we will soon see that your dress shall correspond with your office. Meanwhile march with the guard until you have my further orders."

So it came about that as the Roman army resumed its march next day, and left behind it the fair Valley of the Harpessus, a huge recruit, clad in brown leather, with a rude sheep-skin floating from his shoulders, marched beside the Imperial troop. But far away in the wooden farmhouse of a distant Macedonian valley two old country folk wept salt tears, and prayed to the gods for the safety of their boy who had turned his face to Rome.

II—THE RISE OF GIANT MAXIMIN

Exactly twenty-five years had passed since the day that Theckla the huge, Thracian peasant, had turned into Maximin, the Roman guardsman. They had not been good years for Rome. Gone for ever were the great Imperial days of the Hadrians and the Trajans. Gone also the golden age of the two Antonines, when the highest were for once the most worthy and most wise. It had been an epoch of weak and cruel men. Severus, the swarthy African, a stark, grim man had died in far away York, after fighting all the winter with the Caledonian Highlanders—a race who have ever since worn the martial garb of the Romans. His son, known only by his slighting nickname of Caracalla, had reigned during six years of insane lust and cruelty, before the knife of an angry soldier avenged the dignity of the Roman name. The nonentity Macrinus had filled the dangerous throne for a single year before he also met a bloody end, and made room for the most grotesque of all monarchs, the unspeakable Heliogabalus with his foul mind and his painted face. He in turn was cut to pieces by the soldiers ; and Severus Alexander, a gentle youth, scarce seventeen years of age, had been thrust into his place. For thirteen years now he had ruled, striving with some success to put some virtue and stability into the rotting Empire, but raising many fierce enemies as he did so—enemies whom he had not the strength nor the wit to hold in check.

And Giant Maximin—what of him ? He had carried his eight feet of manhood through the lowlands of Scotland and the passes of the Grampians. He had seen Severus pass away, and had soldiered with his son. He had fought in Armenia, in Dacia, and in Germany. They had made him a centurion upon the field when with his hands he plucked out one by one the stockades of a northern village, and so cleared a path for the stormers. His strength had been the jest and the admiration of the soldiers. Legends about him had spread through the army, and were the common gossip round the camp fires—of his duel with the German axeman on the Island of the Rhine, and of the blow with his fist that broke the leg of a Scythian's horse. Gradually he had won his way upwards, until now, after quarter of a century's service, he was tribune of the fourth legion and superintendent of recruits for the whole army. The young soldier who had come under the glare of Maximin's eyes, or had been lifted up with one huge hand while he was cuffed by the other, had his first lesson from him in the discipline of the service.

It was nightfall in the camp of the fourth legion upon the Gallic shore of the Rhine. Across the moonlit water, amid the thick forests which stretched away to the dim horizon, lay the wild, untamed German tribes. Down on the river bank the light gleamed upon the helmets of the Roman sentinels who kept guard along the river. Far away a red point rose and fell in the darkness—a watch-fire of the enemy upon the farther shore. Outside his tent, beside some smouldering logs, Giant Maximin was seated, a dozen of his officers around him. He had changed much since the day when we first met him in the Valley of the Harpessus. His huge frame was as erect as ever, and there was no sign of diminution of his strength. But he had aged none the less. The yellow tangle of hair was gone, worn down by the ever-pressing helmet. The fresh young face was drawn and hardened, with austere lines wrought by trouble and privation. The nose was more hawk-like, the eyes more cunning, the expression more cynical and more sinister. In his youth, a child would have run to his arms. Now it would shrink screaming from his gaze. That was what twenty-five years with the eagles had done for Theckla, the Thracian peasant.

He was listening now—for he was a man of few words—to the chatter of his centurions. One of them, Balbus the Sicilian, had been to the main camp at Mainz, only four miles away, and had seen the Emperor Alexander arrive that very day from Rome. The rest were eager at the news, for it was a time of unrest, and the rumour of great changes was in the air.

"How many had he with him?" asked Labienus, a black-browed veteran from the south of Gaul. "I'll wager a month's pay that he was not so trustful as to come alone among his faithful legions."

"He had no great force," replied Balbus. "Ten or twelve cohorts of the Prætorians and a handful of horse."

"Then indeed his head is in the lion's mouth," cried Sulpicius, a hot-headed youth from the African Pentapolis. "How was he received?"

"Coldly enough. There was scarce a shout as he came down the line."

"They are ripe for mischief," said Labienus. "And who can wonder, when it is we soldiers who uphold the Empire upon our spears, while the lazy citizens at Rome reap all of our sowing. Why cannot a soldier have what the soldier gains? So long as they throw us our denarius a day, they think that they have done with us."

" Aye," croaked a grumbling old greybeard. " Our limbs, our blood, our lives—what do they care so long as the Barbarians are held off, and they are left in peace to their feastings and their circus? Free bread, free wine, free games—everything for the loafer at Rome. For us the frontier guard and a soldier's fare."

Maximin gave a deep laugh. " Old Plancus talks like that," said he ; " but we know that for all the world he would not change his steel plate for a citizen's gown. You've earned the kennel, old hound, if you wish it. Go and gnaw your bone and growl in peace."

" Nay, I am too old for change. I will follow the eagle till I die. And yet I had rather die in serving a soldier master than a long-gowned Syrian who comes of a stock where the women are men and the men are women."

There was a laugh from the circle of soldiers, for sedition and mutiny were rife in the camp, and even the old centurion's outbreak could not draw a protest. Maximin raised his great mastiff head and looked at Balbus.

" Was any name in the mouths of the soldiers ? " he asked in a meaning voice.

There was a hush for the answer. The sigh of the wind among the pines and the low lapping of the river swelled out louder in the silence. Balbus looked hard at his commander.

" Two names were whispered from rank to rank," said he. " One was Ascenius Pollio, the General. The other was——"

The fiery Sulpicius sprang to his feet waving a glowing brand above his head.

" Maximinus ! " he yelled, " Imperator Maximinus Augustus ! "

Who could tell how it came about ? No one had thought of it an hour before. And now it sprang in an instant to full accomplishment. The shout of the frenzied young African had scarcely rung through the darkness when from the tents, from the watch-fires, from the sentries, the answer came pealing back : " Ave Maximinus ! Ave Maximinus Augustus ! " From all sides men came rushing, half-clad, wild-eyed, their eyes staring, their mouths agape, flaming wisps of straw or flaring torches above their heads. The giant was caught up by scores of hands, and sat enthroned upon the bull necks of the legionaries. " To the camp ! " they yelled. " To the camp ! Hail ! Hail to the soldier Cæsar ! "

That same night Severus Alexander, the young Syrian Emperor, walked outside his Prætorian camp, accompanied by his friend Licinius Probus, the Captain of the Guard. They were talking gravely of the gloomy faces and seditious bearing of the soldiers. A great foreboding of evil weighed heavily upon the Emperor's heart, and it was reflected upon the stern, bearded face of his companion.

" I like it not," said he. " It is my counsel, Cæsar, that with the first light of morning we make our way south once more."

" But surely," the Emperor answered, " I could not for shame turn my back upon the danger. What have they against me ? How have I harmed them that they should forget their vows and rise upon me ? "

" They are like children who ask always for something new. You heard the murmur as you rode along the ranks. Nay, Cæsar, fly to-morrow, and your Prætorians will see that you are not pursued. There may be some loyal cohorts among the legions, and if we join forces——"

A distant shout broke in upon their conversation— a low, continued roar, like the swelling tumult of a sweeping wave. Far down the road upon which they stood there twinkled many moving lights, tossing and sinking as they rapidly advanced, whilst the hoarse, tumultuous bellowing broke into articulate words, the same tremendous words, a thousand-fold repeated. Licinius seized the Emperor by the wrist and dragged him under the cover of some bushes.

" Be still, Cæsar ! For your life be still ! " he whispered. " One word and we are lost ! "

Crouching in the darkness, they saw that wild procession pass, the rushing, screaming figures, the tossing arms, the bearded, distorted faces, now scarlet and now grey, as the brandished torches waxed or waned. They heard the rush of many feet, the clamour of hoarse voices, the clang of metal upon metal. And then suddenly, above them all, they saw a vision of a monstrous man, a huge bowed back, a savage face, grim hawk eyes, that looked out over the swaying shields. It was seen for an instant in a smoke-fringed circle of fire, and then it had swept on into the night.

" Who is he ? " stammered the Emperor, clutching at his guardsman's sleeve. " They call him Cæsar."

" It is surely Maximin, the Thracian peasant." In the darkness the Prætorian officer looked with strange eyes at his master.

" It is all over, Cæsar. Let us fly together to your tent."

But even as they went a second shout had broken forth tenfold louder than the first. If the one had been the roar of the oncoming wave, the other was the full turmoil of the tempest. Twenty thousand voices from the camp had broken into one wild shout which echoed through the night, until the distant Germans round their watch-fires listened in wonder and alarm.

" Ave ! " cried the voices. " Ave Maximinus Augustus ! "

High upon their bucklers stood the giant, and looked round him at the great floor of upturned faces below. His own savage soul was stirred by the clamour, but only his gleaming eyes spoke of the fire within. He waved his hand to the shouting soldiers as the huntsman waves to the leaping pack. They passed him up a coronet of oak leaves, and clashed their swords in homage as he placed it on his head. And then there came a swirl in the crowd before him, a little space was cleared, and there knelt an officer in the Prætorian garb, blood upon his face, blood upon his bared forearm, blood upon his naked sword. Licinius, too, had gone with the tide.

"Hail, Cæsar, hail!" he cried, as he bowed his head before the giant. "I come from Alexander. He will trouble you no more."

III—THE FALL OF MAXIMIN

For three years the soldier Emperor had been upon the throne. His palace had been his tent, and his people had been the legionaries. With them he was supreme; away from them he was nothing. He had gone with them from one frontier to the other. He had fought against Dacians, Sarmatians, and once again against the Germans. But Rome knew nothing of him, and all her turbulence rose against a master who cared so little for her or her opinion that he never deigned to set foot within her walls. There were cabals and conspiracies against the absent Cæsar. Then his heavy hand fell upon them, and they were cuffed, even as the young soldiers had been who passed under his discipline. He knew nothing, and cared as much for consuls, senates, and civil laws. His own will and the power of the sword were the only forces which he could understand. Of commerce and the arts he was as ignorant as when he left his Thracian home. The whole vast Empire was to him a huge machine for producing the money by which the legions were to be rewarded. Should he fail to get that money, his fellow-soldiers would bear him a grudge. To watch their interests they had raised him upon their shields that night. If city funds had to be plundered or temples desecrated, still the money must be got. Such was the point of view of Giant Maximin.

But there came resistance, and all the fierce energy of the man, all the hardness which had given him the leadership of hard men, sprang forth to quell it. From his youth he had lived amidst slaughter. Life and death were cheap things to him. He struck savagely at all who stood up to him, and when they hit back, he struck more savagely still. His giant shadow lay black across the Empire from Britain to Syria. A strange, subtle vindictiveness became also apparent in him. Omnipotence ripened every fault and swelled it into crime.

In the old days he had been rebuked for his roughness. Now a sullen, dangerous anger rose against those who had rebuked him. He sat by the hour with his craggy chin between his hands, and his elbows resting on his knees, while he recalled all the misadventures, all the vexations of his early youth, when Roman wits had shot their little satires upon his bulk and his ignorance. He could not write, but his son Verus placed the names upon his tablets, and they were sent to the Governor of Rome. Men who had long forgotten their offence were called suddenly to make most bloody reparation.

A rebellion broke out in Africa, but was quelled by his lieutenant. But the mere rumour of it set Rome in a turmoil. The Senate found something of its ancient spirit. So did the Italian people. They would not be for ever bullied by the legions. As Maximin approached from the frontier, with the sack of rebellious Rome in his mind, he was faced with every sign of a national resistance. The country-side was deserted, the farms abandoned, the fields cleared of crops and cattle. Before him lay the walled town of Aquileia. He flung himself fiercely upon it, but was met by as fierce a resistance. The walls could not be forced, and yet there was no food in the country round for his legions. The men were starving and dissatisfied. What did it matter to them who was Emperor? Maximin was no better than themselves. Why should they call down the curse of the whole Empire upon their heads by upholding him? He saw their sullen faces and their averted eyes, and he knew that the end had come.

That night he sat with his son Verus in his tent, and he spoke softly and gently as the youth had never heard him speak before. He had spoken thus in old days with Paullina, the boy's mother; but she had been dead these many years, and all that was soft and gentle in the big man had passed away with her. Now her spirit seemed very near him, and his own was tempered by its presence.

" I would have you go back to the Thracian mountains," he said. " I have tried both, boy, and I can tell you that there is no pleasure which power can bring which can equal the breath of the wind and the smell of the kine upon a summer morning. Against you they have no quarrel. Why should they mishandle you. Keep far from Rome and the Romans. Old Eudoxus has money, and to spare. He awaits you with two horses outside the camp. Make for the Valley of the Harpessus, lad. It was thence that your father came, and there you will find his kin. Buy and stock a homestead, and keep yourself far from the paths of greatness and of danger. God keep you, Verus, and send you safe to Thrace."

When his son had kissed his hand and had left him, the Emperor drew his robe around him and sat long in thought. In his slow brain he revolved the past—his early, peaceful days, his years with Severus, his memories of Britain, his long campaigns, his strivings and battlings, all leading to that mad night by the Rhine. His fellow-soldiers had loved him then. And now he had read death in their eyes. How had he failed them ? Others he might have wronged, but they at least had no complaint against him. If he had his time again, he would think less of them and more of his people, he would try to win love instead of fear, he would live for peace and not for war. If he had his time again ! But there were shuffling steps, furtive whispers, and the low rattle of arms outside his tent. A bearded face looked in at him, a swarthy African face that he knew well. He laughed, and baring his arm, he took his sword from the table beside him.

" It is you, Sulpicius," said he. " You have not come

to cry ' Ave Imperator Maximin ! ' as once by the camp fire. You are tired of me, and by the gods I am tired of you, and glad to be at the end of it. Come and have done with it, for I am minded to see how many of you I can take with me when I go."

They clustered at the door of the tent, peeping over each other's shoulders, and none wishing to be the first to close with that laughing, mocking giant. But something was pushed forward upon a spear point, and as he saw it, Maximin groaned and his sword sank to the earth.

" You might have spared the boy," he sobbed. " He would not have hurt you. Have done with it then, for I will gladly follow him."

So they closed upon him and cut and stabbed and thrust, until his knees gave way beneath him and he dropped upon the floor.

" The tyrant is dead ! " they cried. " The tyrant is dead," and from all the camp beneath them and from the walls of the beleaguered city the joyous cry came echoing back, " He is dead, Maximin is dead ! "

I sit in my study, and upon the table before me lies a denarius of Maximin, as fresh as when the triumvir of the Temple of Juno Moneta sent it from the mint. Around it are recorded his resounding titles—Imperator Maximinus, Pontifex Maximus, Tribunitia potestate, and the rest. In the centre is the impress of a great craggy head, a massive jaw, a rude fighting face, a contracted forehead. For all the pompous roll of titles it is a peasant's face, and I see him not as the Emperor of Rome, but as the great Thracian boor who strode down the hill-side on that far-distant summer day when first the eagles beckoned him to Rome.

73. *The Red Star*

THE house of Theodosius, the famous eastern merchant, was in the best part of Constantinople at the Sea Point which is near the church of Saint Demetrius. Here he would entertain in so princely a fashion that even the Emperor Maurice had been known to come privately from the neighbouring Bucoleon palace in order to join in the revelry. On the night in question, however, which was the fourth of November in the year of our Lord 630, his numerous guests had retired early, and there remained only two intimates, both of them successful merchants like himself, who sat with him over their wine on the marble verandah of his house whence on the one side they could see the lights of the shipping in the Sea of Marmora, and on the other the beacons which marked out the course of the Bosphorus. Immediately at their feet lay a narrow strait of water, with the low, dark loom of the Asiatic hills beyond. A thin haze hid the heavens, but away to the south a single great red star burned sullenly in the darkness.

The night was cool, the light was soothing, and the three men talked freely, letting their minds drift back into the earlier days when they had staked their capital, and often their lives, on the ventures which had built up their present fortunes. The host spoke of his long journeys in North Africa, the land of the Moors; how he had travelled, keeping the blue sea ever upon his right, until he had passed the ruins of Carthage, and so on and ever on until a great tidal ocean beat upon a yellow strand before him, while on the right he could see the high rock across the waves which marked the Pillars of Hercules. His talk was of dark-skinned, bearded men, of lions, and of monstrous serpents. Then Demetrius, the Cilician, an austere man of sixty, told

how he also had built up his mighty wealth. He spoke
of a journey over the Danube and through the country
of the fierce Huns, until he and his friends had found
themselves in the mighty forest of Germany, on the
shores of the great river which is called the Elbe. His
stories were of huge men, sluggish of mind, but murderous in their cups, of sudden midnight broils and nocturnal
flights, of villages buried in dense woods, of bloody
heathen sacrifices, and of the bears and wolves who
haunted the forest paths. So the two elder men capped
each other's stories and awoke each other's memories,
while Manuel Ducas, the young merchant of gold and
ostrich feathers, whose name was already known all
over the Levant, sat in silence and listened to their
talk. At last, however, they called upon him also
for an anecdote, and leaning his cheek upon his
elbow, with his eyes fixed upon the great red star
which burned in the south, the younger man began to
speak.

"It is the sight of that star which brings a story into
my mind," said he. "I do not know its name. Old
Lascaris the astronomer would tell me if I asked, but I
have no desire to know. Yet at this time of the year
I always look out for it, and I never fail to see it burning
in the same place. But it seems to me that it is redder
and larger than it was.

"It was some ten years ago that I made an expedition
into Abyssinia, where I traded to such good effect that
I set forth on my return with more than a hundred camel-
loads of skins, ivory, gold, spices, and other African
produce. I brought them to the sea-coast at Arsinoe,
and carried them up the Arabian Gulf in five of the small
boats of the country. Finally, I landed near Sava which
is a starting-point for caravans, and, having assembled
my camels and hired a guard of forty men from the
wandering Arabs, I set forth for Macoraba. From this
point, which is the sacred city of the idolaters of those
parts, one can always join the large caravans which go

north twice a year to Jerusalem and the sea-coast of Syria.

" Our route was a long and weary one. On our left hand was the Arabian Gulf, lying like a pool of molten metal under the glare cf day, but changing to blood-red as the sun sank each evening behind the distant African coast. On our right was a monstrous desert which extends, so far as I know, across the whole of Arabia and away to the distant kingdom of the Persians. For many days we saw no sign of life save our own long, straggling line of laden camels with their tattered, swarthy guardians. In these deserts the soft sand deadens the footfall of the animals, so that their silent progress day after day through a scene which never changes, and which is itself noiseless, beccmes at last like a strange dream. Often as I rode behind my caravan, and gazed at the grotesque figures which bore my wares in front of me, I found it hard to believe that it was indeed reality, and that it was I, I, Manuel Ducas, who lived near the Theodosian Gate of Constantinople, and shouted for the Green at the hippodrome every Sunday afternoon, who was there in so strange a land and with such singular comrades.

" Now and then, far out at sea, we caught sight of the white, triangular sails of the boats which these people use, but as they are all pirates, we were very glad to be safely upon shore. Once or twice, too, by the water's edge we saw dwarfish creatures—one could scarcely say if they were men or monkeys—who burrow for homes among the seaweed, drink the pools of brackish water, and eat what they can catch. These are the fish-eaters, the Ichthyophagi, of whom old Herodotus talks—surely the lowest of all the human race. Our Arabs shrank from them with horror, for it is well known that, should you die in the desert, these little people will settle on you like carrion crows, and leave not a bone unpicked. They gibbered and croaked and waved their skinny arms at us as we passed, knowing well that they could swim far out to sea if we attempted to pursue them ; for it is said that even the sharks turn with disgust from their foul bodies.

"We had travelled in this way for ten days, camping every evening at the vile wells which offered a small quantity of abominable water. It was our habit to rise very early and to travel very late, but to halt during the intolerable heat of the afternoon, when, for want of trees, we would crouch in the shadow of a sandhill, or, if that were wanting, behind our own camels and merchandise, in order to escape from the insufferable glare of the sun. On the seventh day we were near the point where one leaves the coast in order to strike inland to Macoraba. We had concluded our midday halt, and were just starting once more, the sun still being so hot that we could hardly bear it, when, looking up, I saw a remarkable sight. Standing on a hillock to our right there was a man about forty feet high, holding in his hand a spear which was the size of the mast of a large ship. You look surprised, my friends, and you can therefore imagine my feelings when I saw such a sight. But my reason soon told me that the object in front of me was really a wandering Arab, whose form had been enormously magnified by the strange distorting effects which the hot air of the desert is able to cause.

"However, the actual apparition caused more alarm to my companions than the imagined one had to me, for with a howl of dismay they shrank together into a frightened group, all pointing and gesticulating as they gazed at the distant figure. I then observed that the man was not alone, but that from all the sandhills a line of turbaned heads was gazing down upon us. The chief of the escort came running to me, and informed me of the cause of their terror, which was that they recognised, by some peculiarity in their headgear, that these men belonged to the tribe of the Dilwas, the most ferocious and unscrupulous of the Bedouin, who had evidently laid an ambuscade for us at this point with the intention

of seizing our caravan. When I thought of all my
efforts in Abyssinia, of the length of my journey and of
the dangers and fatigues which I had endured, I could
not bear to think of this total disaster coming upon me
at the last instant and robbing me not only of my profits,
but also of my original outlay. It was evident, however,
that the robbers were too numerous for us to attempt
to defend ourselves, and that we should be very fortunate
if we escaped with our lives. Sitting upon a packet,
therefore, I commended my soul to our Blessesd Saint
Helena, while I watched with despairing eyes the stealthy
and menacing approach of the Arab robbers.

" It may have been our own good fortune, or it may
have been the handsome offering of beeswax candles—
four to the pound—which I had mentally vowed to the
Blessed Helena, but at that instant I heard a great outcry
of joy from among my own followers. Standing upon
the packet that I might have a better view, I was over-
joyed to see a long caravan—five hundred camels at
least—with a numerous armed guard, coming along the
route from Macoraba. It is, I need not tell you, the
custom of all caravans to combine their forces against
the robbers of the desert, and with the aid of these new-
comers we had become the stronger party. The marauders recognised it at once, for they vanished as if their
native sands had swallowed them. Running up to
the summit of a sandhill, I was just able to catch a glimpse
of a dust-cloud whirling away across the yellow plain,
with the long necks of their camels, the flutter of their
loose garments, and the gleam of their spears breaking
out from the heart of it. So vanished the marauders.

" Presently I found, however, that I had only exchanged
one danger for another. At first I had hoped that this
new caravan might belong to some Roman citizen, or
at least to some Syrian Christian, but I found that it
was entirely Arab. The trading Arabs who are settled
in the numerous towns of Arabia are, of course, very
much more peaceable than the Bedouin of the wilderness,

those sons of Ishmael of whom we read in Holy Writ. But the Arab blood is covetous and lawless, so that when I saw several hundred of them formed in a semicircle round our camels, looking with greedy eyes at my boxes of precious metals and my packets of ostrich feathers, I feared the worst.

" The leader of the new caravan was a man of dignified bearing and remarkable appearance. His age I would judge to be about forty. He had aquiline features, a noble black beard, and eyes so luminous, so searching and so intense that I cannot remember in all my wanderings to have seen any which could be compared with them. To my thanks and salutations he returned a formal bow, and stood stroking his beard and looking in silence at the wealth which had suddenly fallen into his power. A murmur from his followers showed the eagerness with which they awaited the order to fall upon the plunder, and a young ruffian, who seemed to be on intimate terms with the leader, came to his elbow and put the desires of his companions into words.

" ' Surely, O Revered One,' said he, ' these people and their treasure have been delivered into our hands. When we return with it to the holy place, who of all the Koraish will fail to see the finger of God which has led us ? '

" But the leader shook his head. ' Nay, Ali, it may not be,' he answered. ' This man is, as I judge, a citizen of Rome, and we may not treat him as though he were an idolater.'

" ' But he is an unbeliever,' cried the youth, fingering a great knife which hung in his belt. ' Were I to be judge, he would lose not only his merchandise, but his life also, if he did not accept the faith.'

" The older man smiled and shook his head. ' Nay, Ali ; you are too hot-headed,' said he, ' seeing that there are not as yet three hundred faithful in the world, our hands would indeed be full if we were to take the lives and property of all who are not with us. Forget not, dear lad, that charity and honesty are the very nose-ring and halter of the true faith.'

" ' Among the faithful,' said the ferocious youth.

" ' Nay, towards everyone. It is the law of Allah. And yet '—here his countenance darkened, and his eyes shone with a most sinister light—' the day may soon come when the hour of grace is past, and woe, then, to those who have not hearkened ! Then shall the sword of Allah be drawn, and it shall not be sheathed until the harvest is reaped. First it shall strike the idolaters on the day when my own people and kinsmen, the unbelieving Koraish, shall be scattered, and the three hundred and sixty idols of the Caaba thrust out upon the dungheaps of the town. Then shall the Caaba be the home and temple of one God only who brooks no rival on earth or in heaven.'

" The man's followers had gathered round him, their spears in their hands, their ardent eyes fixed upon his face, and their dark features convulsed with such fanatic enthusiasm as showed the hold which he had upon their love and respect.

" ' We shall be patient,' said he ; ' but some time next year, the year after, the day may come when the great angel Gabriel shall bear me the message that the time of words has gone by, and that the hour of the sword has come. We are few and weak, but if it is His will, who can stand against us ? Are you of Jewish faith, stranger ? ' he asked.

" I answered that I was not.

" ' The better for you,' he answered, with the same furious anger in his swarthy face. ' First shall the idolaters fall, and then the Jews, in that they have not known those very prophets whom they had themselves foretold. Then last will come the turn of the Christians, who follow indeed a true Prophet, greater than Moses or Abraham, but who have sinned in that they have confounded a creature with the Creator. To each in turn—idolater, Jew, and Christian—the day of reckoning will come.'

" The ragamuffins behind him all shook their spears as he spoke. There was no doubt about their earnestness, but when I looked at their tattered dresses and simple arms, I could not help smiling to think of their ambitious threats, and to picture what their fate would be upon the day of battle before the battle-axes of our Imperial Guards, or the spears of the heavy cavalry of the Armenian Themes. However, I need not say that I was discreet enough to keep my thoughts to myself, as I had no desire to be the first martyr in this fresh attack upon our blessed faith.

" It was now evening, and it was decided that the two caravans should camp together—an arrangement which was the more welcome as we were by no means sure that we had seen the last of the marauders. I had invited the leader of the Arabs to have supper with me, and after a long exercise of prayer with his followers, he came to join me, but my attempt at hospitality was thrown away, for he would not touch the excellent wine which I had unpacked for him, nor would he eat any of my dainties, contenting himself with stale bread, dried dates, and water. After this meal we sat alone by the smouldering fire, the magnificent arch of the heavens above us of that deep, rich blue with those gleaming, clear-cut stars which can only be seen in that dry desert air. Our camp lay before us, and no sound reached our ears save the dull murmur of the voices of our companions and the occasional shrill cry of a jackal among the sandhills around us. Face to face I sat with this strange man, the glow of the fire beating upon his eager and imperious features and reflecting from his passionate eyes. It was the strangest vigil, and one which will never pass from my recollection. I have spoken with many wise and famous men upon my travels, but never with one who left the impression of this one.

" And yet much of his talk was unintelligible to me, though, as you are aware, I speak Arabian like an Arab. It rose and fell in the strangest way. Sometimes it was the babble of a child,. sometimes the incoherent raving of a fanatic, sometimes the lofty dreams of a prophet and philosopher. There were times when his stories of demons, of miracles, of dreams, and of omens, were such as an old woman might tell to please the children of an evening. There were others when, as he talked with shining face of his converse with angels, of the intentions of the Creator, and the end of the universe, I felt as if I were in the company of someone more than mortal, someone who was indeed the direct messenger of the Most High.

"There were good reasons why he should treat me with such confidence. He saw in me a messenger to Constantinople and to the Roman Empire. Even as Saint Paul had brought Christianity to Europe, so he hoped that I might carry his doctrines to my native city. Alas! be the doctrines what they may, I fear that I am not the stuff of which Pauls are made. Yet he strove with all his heart during that long Arabian night to bring me over to his belief. He had with him a holy book, written, as he said, from the dictation of an angel, which he carried in tablets of bone in the nose-bag of a camel. Some chapters of this he read me; but though the precepts were usually good, the language seemed wild and fanciful. There were times when I could scarce keep my countenance as I listened to him. He planned out his future movements, and indeed, as he spoke, it was hard to remember that he was only the wandering leader of an Arab caravan, and not one of the great ones of the earth.

"'When God has given me sufficient power, which will be within a few years,' said he, 'I will unite all Arabia under my banner. Then I will spread my doctrine over Syria and Egypt. When this has been done, I will turn to Persia, and give them the choice of the true faith or the sword. Having taken Persia, it will be easy then to overrun Asia Minor, and so to make our way to Constantinople.'

" I bit my lip to keep from laughing. ' And how long will it be before your victorious troops have reached the Bosphorus ? ' I asked.

" ' Such things are in the hands of God, whose servants we are,' said he. ' It may be that I shall myself have passed away before these things are accomplished, but before the days of our children are completed, all that I have now told you will come to pass. Look at that star,' he added, pointing to a beautiful clear planet above our heads. ' That is the symbol of Christ. See how serene and peaceful it shines, like His own teaching and the memory of His life. Now,' he added, turning his outstretched hand to a dusky red star upon the horizon—the very one on which we are gazing now— ' that is my star, which tells of wrath, of war, of a scourge upon sinners. And yet both are indeed stars, and each does as Allah may ordain.'

" Well, that was the experience which was called to my mind by the sight of this star to-night. Red and angry, it still broods over the south, even as I saw it that night in the desert. Somewhere down yonder that man is working and striving. He may be stabbed by some brother fanatic or slain in a tribal skirmish. If so, that is the end. But if he lives, there was that in his eyes and in his presence which tells me that Mahomet the son of Abdallah—for that was his name—will testify in some noteworthy fashion to the faith that is in him."

74. *The Silver Mirror*

JAN. 3.—This affair of White and Wotherspoon's accounts proves to be a gigantic task. There are twenty thick ledgers to be examined and checked. Who would be a junior partner ? However, it is the first big bit of business which has been left entirely in my hands. I must justify it. But it has to be finished so that the lawyers may have the result in time for the trial. Johnson said this morning that I should have to get the last figure out before the twentieth of the month. Good Lord! Well, have at it, and if human brain and nerve can stand the strain, I'll win out at the other side. It means office-work from ten to five, and then a second sitting from about eight to one in the morning. There's drama in an accountant's life. When I find myself in the still early hours, while all the world sleeps, hunting through column after column for those missing figures which will turn a respected alderman into a felon, I understand that it is not such a prosaic profession after all.

On Monday I came on the first trace of defalcation. No heavy game hunter ever got a finer thrill when first he caught sight of the trail of his quarry. But I look at the twenty ledgers and think of the jungle through which I have to follow him before I get my kill. Hard work—but rare sport, too, in a way! I saw the fat fellow once at a City dinner, his red face glowing above a white napkin. He looked at the little pale man at the end of the table. He would have been pale, too, if he could have seen the task that would be mine.

Jan. 6.—What perfect nonsense it is for doctors to prescribe rest when rest is out of the question! Asses! They might as well shout to a man who has a pack of wolves at his heels that what he wants is absolute quiet. My figures must be out by a certain date; unless they are so, I shall lose the chance of my lifetime, so how on earth am I to rest? I'll take a week or so after the trial.

Perhaps I was myself a fool to go to the doctor at all. But I get nervous and highly strung when I sit alone at my work at night. It's not a pain—only a sort of fullness of the head with an occasional mist over the eyes. I thought perhaps some bromide, or chloral, or something of the kind might do me good. But stop work? It's absurd to ask such a thing. It's like a long-distance race. You feel queer at first and your heart thumps and your lungs pant, but if you have only the pluck to keep on, you get your second wind. I'll stick to my work and wait for my second wind. If it never comes—all the same, I'll stick to my work. Two ledgers are done, and I am well on in the third. The rascal has covered his tracks well, but I pick them up for all that.

Jan. 9.—I had not meant to go to the doctor again. And yet I have had to. " Straining my nerves, risking a complete breakdown, even endangering my sanity." That's a nice sentence to have fired off at one. Well, I'll stand the strain and I'll take the risk, and so long as I can sit in my chair and move a pen I'll follow the old sinner's slot.

By the way, I may as well set down here the queer experience which drove me this second time to the doctor. I'll keep an exact record of my symptoms and sensations, because they are interesting in themselves —" a curious psycho-physiological study," says the doctor—and also because I am perfectly certain that when I am through with them they will all seem blurred and unreal, like some queer dream betwixt sleeping and waking. So now, while they are fresh, I will just make a note of them if only as a change of thought after the endless figures.

There's an old silver-framed mirror in my room. It was given me by a friend who had a taste for antiquities, and he, as I happen to know, picked it up at a sale and had no notion where it came from. It's a large thing— three feet across and two feet high—and it leans at the back of a side-table on my left as I write. The frame is flat, about three inches across, and very old ; far too old for hall-marks or other methods of determining its age. The glass part projects, with a bevelled edge, and has the magnificent reflecting power which is only, as it seems to me, to be found in very old mirrors. There's a feeling of perspective when you look into it such as no modern glass can ever give.

The mirror is so situated that as I sit at the table I can usually see nothing in it but the reflection of the red window curtains. But a queer thing happened last night. I had been working for some hours, very much against the grain, with continual bouts of that mistiness of which I had complained. Again and again I had to stop and clear my eyes. Well, on one of these occasions I chanced to look at the mirror. It had the oddest appearance. The red curtains which should have been reflected in it were no longer there, but the glass seemed to be clouded and steamy, not on the surface, which glittered like steel, but deep down in the very grain of it. This opacity, when I stared hard at it, appeared to slowly rotate this way and that, until it was a thick, white cloud swirling in heavy wreaths. So real and solid was it, and so reasonable was I, that I remember turning, with the idea that the curtains were on fire. But everything was deadly still in the room—no sound save the ticking of the clock, no movement save the slow gyration of that strange woolly cloud deep in the heart of the old mirror.

Then, as I looked, the mist, or smoke, or cloud, or whatever one may call it, seemed to coalesce and solidify at two points quite close together, and I was aware, with a thrill of interest rather than of fear, that these were two eyes looking out into the room. A vague outline of a head I could see—a woman's by the hair, but this was very shadowy. Only the eyes were quite distinct ; such eyes—dark, luminous, filled with some passionate emotion, fury or horror, I could not say which. Never have I seen eyes which were so full of intense, vivid life. They were not fixed upon me, but stared out into the room. Then as I sat erect, passed my hand over my brow, and made a strong conscious effort to pull myself together, the dim head faded into the general opacity, the mirror slowly cleared, and there were the red curtains once again.

A sceptic would say, no doubt, that I had dropped

asleep over my figures, and that my experience was a
dream. As a matter of fact, I was never more vividly
awake in my life. I was able to argue about it even as
I looked at it, and to tell myself that it was a subjective
impression—a chimera of the nerves—begotten by worry
and insomnia. But why this particular shape ? And
who is the woman, and what is the dreadful emotion
which I read in those wonderful brown eyes ? They
come between me and my work. For the first time I
have done less than the daily tally which I had marked
out. Perhaps that is why I have had no abnormal
sensations to-night. To-morrow I must wake up,
come what may.

Jan. 11.—All well, and good progress with my work.
I wind the net, coil after coil, round that bulky body.
But the last smile may remain with him if my own nerves
break over it. The mirror would seem to be a sort of
barometer which marks my brain pressure. Each night
I have observed that it had clouded before I reached the
end of my task.

Dr. Sinclair (who is, it seems, a bit of a psychologist)
was so interested in my account that he came round this
evening to have a look at the mirror. I had observed
that something was scribbled in crabbed old characters
upon the metal work at the back. He examined this
with a lens, but could make nothing of it. " Sanc. X.
Pal." was his final reading of it, but that did not bring
us any further. He advised me to put it away into
another room ; but, after all, whatever I may see in
it is, by his own account, only a symptom. It is in the
cause that the danger lies. The twenty ledgers—not
the silver mirror—should be packed away if I could only
do it. I'm at the eighth now, so I progress.

Jan 13.—Perhaps it would have been wiser after
all if I had packed away the mirror. I had an extraordinary experience with it last night. And yet I find
it so interesting, so fascinating, that even now I will keep
it in its place. What on earth is the meaning of it all ?

I suppose it was about one in the morning, and I was closing my books preparatory to staggering off to bed, when I saw her there in front of me. The stage of mistiness and development must have passed unobserved, and there she was in all her beauty and passion and distress, as clear-cut as if she were really in the flesh before me. The figure was small, but very distinct —so much so that every feature, and every detail of dress, are stamped in my memory. She is seated on the extreme left of the mirror. A sort of shadowy figure crouches down beside her—I can dimly discern that it is a man—and then behind them is cloud, in which I see figures—figures which move. It is not a mere picture upon which I look. It is a scene in life, an actual episode. She crouches and quivers. The man beside her cowers down. The vague figures make abrupt movements and gestures. All my fears were swallowed up in my interest. It was maddening to see so much and not to see more.

But I can at least describe the woman to the smallest point. She is very beautiful and quite young—not more than five-and-twenty, I should judge. Her hair is of a very rich brown, with a warm chestnut shade fining into gold at the edges. A little flat-pointed cap comes to an angle in front and is made of lace edged with pearls. The forehead is high, too high perhaps for perfect beauty ; but one would not have it otherwise, as it gives a touch of power and strength to what would otherwise be a softly feminine face. The brows are most delicately curved over heavy eyelids, and then come those wonderful eyes—so large, so dark, so full of overmastering emotion, of rage and horror, contending with a pride of self-control which holds her from sheer frenzy ! The cheeks are pale, the lips white with agony, the chin and throat most exquisitely rounded. The figure sits and leans forward in the chair, straining and rigid, cataleptic with horror. The dress is black velvet, a jewel gleams like a flame in the breast, and a golden crucifix smoulders in the shadow of a fold. This is the lady whose image still lives in the old silver mirror. What dire deed could it be which has left its impress there, so that now, in another age, if the spirit of a man be but worn down to it, he may be conscious of its presence?

One other detail: On the left side of the skirt of the black dress was, as I thought at first, a shapeless bunch of white ribbon. Then, as I looked more intently or as the vision defined itself more clearly, I perceived what it was. It was the hand of a man, clenched and knotted in agony, which held on with a convulsive grasp to the fold of the dress. The rest of the crouching figure was a mere vague outline, but that strenuous hand shone clear on the dark background, with a sinister suggestion of tragedy in its frantic clutch. The man is frightened—horribly frightened. That I can clearly discern. What has terrified him so? Why does he grip the woman's dress? The answer lies amongst those moving figures in the background. They have brought danger both to him and to her. The interest of the thing fascinated me. I thought no more of its relation to my own nerves. I stared and stared as if in a theatre. But I could get no further. The mist thinned. There were tumultuous movements in which all the figures were vaguely concerned. Then the mirror was clear once more.

The doctor says I must drop work for a day, and I can afford to do so, for I have made good progress lately. It is quite evident that the visions depend entirely upon my own nervous state, for I sat in front of the mirror for an hour to-night, with no result whatever. My soothing day has chased them away. I wonder whether I shall ever penetrate what they all mean? I examined the mirror this evening under a good light, and besides the mysterious inscription " Sanc. X. Pal.," I was able to discern some signs of heraldic marks, very faintly visible upon the silver. They must be very ancient, as they are almost obliterated. So far as I could make out, they were three spear-heads, two above and one below. I will show them to the doctor when he calls to-morrow.

Jan. 14.—Feel perfectly well again, and I intend that nothing else shall stop me until my task is finished. The doctor was shown the marks on the mirror and agreed that they were armorial bearings. He is deeply interested in all that I have told him, and cross-questioned me closely on the details. It amuses me to notice how he is torn in two by conflicting desires—the one that his patient should lose his symptoms, the other that the medium—for so he regards me—should solve this mystery of the past. He advised continued rest, but did not oppose me too violently when I declared that such a thing was out of the question until the ten remaining ledgers have been checked.

Jan. 17.—For three nights I have had no experiences —my day of rest has borne fruit. Only a quarter of my task is left, but I must make a forced march, for the lawyers are clamouring for their material. I will give them enough and to spare. I have him fast on a hundred counts. When they realise what a slippery, cunning rascal he is, I should gain some credit from the case. False trading accounts, false balance-sheets, dividends drawn from capital, losses written down as profits, suppression of working expenses, manipulation of petty cash—it is a fine record !

Jan. 18.—Headaches, nervous twitches, mistiness, fullness of the temples—all the premonitions of trouble, and the trouble came sure enough. And yet my real sorrow is not so much that the vision should come as that it should cease before all is revealed.

But I saw more to-night. The crouching man was as visible as the lady whose gown he clutched. He is a little swarthy fellow, with a black, pointed beard. He has a loose gown of damask trimmed with fur. The prevailing tints of his dress are red. What a fright the fellow is in, to be sure ! He cowers and shivers and glares back over his shoulder. There is a small knife in his other hand, but he is far too tremulous and cowed to use it. Dimly now I begin to see the figures in the background. Fierce faces, bearded and dark, shape themselves out of the mist. There is one terrible creature, a skeleton of a man, with hollow cheeks and eyes sunk in his head. He also has a knife in his hand. On the right of the woman stands a tall man, very young, with flaxen hair, his face sullen and dour. The beautiful woman looks up at him in appeal. So does the man on the ground. This youth seems to be the arbiter of their fate. The crouching man draws closer and hides himself in the woman's skirts. The tall youth bends and tries to drag her away from him. So much I saw last night before the mirror cleared. Shall I never know what it leads to and whence it comes? It is not a mere imagination, of that I am very sure. Somewhere, some time, this scene has been acted, and this old mirror has reflected it. But when—where?

Jan. 20.—My work draws to a close, and it is time. I feel a tenseness within my brain, a sense of intolerable strain, which warns me that something must give. I have worked myself to the limit. But to-night should be the last night. With a supreme effort I should finish the final ledger and complete the case before I rise from my chair. I will do it. I will.

Feb. 7.—I did. My God, what an experience! I hardly know if I am strong enough yet to set it down.

Let me explain in the first instance that I am writing this in Dr. Sinclair's private hospital some three weeks after the last entry in my diary. On the night of January 20 my nervous system finally gave way, and I remembered nothing afterwards until I found myself, three days ago, in the home of rest. And I can rest with a good conscience. My work was done before I went under. My figures are in the solicitors' hands. The hunt is over.

And now I must describe that last night. I had

sworn to finish my work, and so intently did I stick to it, though my head was bursting, that I would never look up until the last column had been added. And yet it was fine self-restraint, for all the time I knew that wonderful things were happening in the mirror. Every nerve in my body told me so. If I looked up there was an end of my work. So I did not look up till all was finished. Then, when at last with throbbing temples I threw down my pen and raised my eyes, what a sight was there !

The mirror in its silver frame was like a stage, brilliantly lit, in which a drama was in progress. There was no mist now. The oppression of my nerves had wrought this amazing clarity. Every feature, every movement, was as clear-cut as in life. To think that I, a tired accountant, the most prosaic of mankind, with the account-books of a swindling bankrupt before me, should be chosen of all the human race to look upon such a scene !

It was the same scene and the same figures, but the drama had advanced a stage. The tall young man was holding the woman in his arms. She strained away from him and looked up at him with loathing in her face. They had torn the crouching man away from his hold upon the skirt of her dress. A dozen of them were round him—savage men, bearded men. They hacked at him with knives. All seemed to strike him together. Their arms rose and fell. The blood did not flow from him—it squirted. His red dress was dabbled in it. He threw himself this way and that, purple upon crimson, like an over-ripe plum. Still they hacked, and still the jets shot from him. It was horrible—horrible ! They dragged him kicking to the door. The woman looked over her shoulder at him and her mouth gaped. I heard nothing, but I knew that she was screaming. And then whether it was this nerve-racking vision before me, or whether, my task finished, all the overwork of the past weeks came in one crushing weight upon me, the room danced round me, the floor seemed to sink away beneath my feet, and I remembered no more. In the early morning my landlady found me stretched senseless before the silver mirror, but I knew nothing myself until three days ago I awoke in the deep peace of the doctor's nursing home.

Feb. 9.—Only to-day have I told Dr. Sinclair my full experience. He had not allowed me to speak of such matters before. He listened with an absorbed interest. "You don't identify this with any well-known scene in history?" he asked, with suspicion in his eyes. I assured him that I knew nothing of history. "Have you no idea whence that mirror came and to whom it once belonged?" he continued. "Have you?" I asked, for he spoke with meaning. "It's incredible," said he, "and yet how else can one explain it? The scenes which you described before suggested it, but now it has gone beyond all range of coincidence. I will bring you some notes in the evening."

Later.—He has just left me. Let me set down his words as closely as I can recall them. He began by laying several musty volumes upon my bed.

"These you can consult at your leisure," said he. "I have some notes here which you can confirm. There is not a doubt that what you have seen is the murder of Rizzio by the Scottish nobles in the presence of Mary, which occurred in March 1566. Your description of the woman is accurate. The high forehead and heavy eyelids combined with great beauty could hardly apply to two women. The tall young man was her husband, Darnley. Rizzio, says the chronicle, 'was dressed in a loose dressing-gown of furred damask, with hose of russet velvet.' With one hand he clutched Mary's gown, with the other he held a dagger. Your fierce, hollow-eyed man was Ruthven, who was new-risen from a bed of sickness. Every detail is exact."

"But why to me?" I asked, in bewilderment. "Why of all the human race to me?"

" Because you were in the fit mental state to receive the impression. Because you chanced to own the mirror which gave the impression."

" The mirror ! You think, then, that it was Mary's mirror—that it stood in the room where the deed was done ? "

" I am convinced that it was Mary's mirror. She had been Queen of France. Her personal property would be stamped with the Royal arms. What you took to be three spear-heads were really the lilies of France."

" And the inscription ? "

" ' Sanc. X. Pal.' You can expand it into Sanctæ Crucis Palatium. Someone has made a note upon the mirror as to whence it came. It was the Palace of the Holy Cross."

" Holyrood ! " I cried.

" Exactly. Your mirror came from Holyrood. You have had one very singular experience, and have escaped. I trust that you will never put yourself into the way of having such another."

75. *The Home-Coming*

IN the spring of the year 528, a small brig used to run as a passenger boat between Chalcedon on the Asiatic shore and Constantinople. On the morning in question, which was that of the feast of Saint George, the vessel was crowded with excursionists who were bound for the great city in order to take part in the religious and festive celebrations which marked the festival of the Megalo-martyr, one of the most choice occasions in the whole vast hagiology of the Eastern Church. The day was fine and the breeze light, so that the passengers in their holiday mood were able to enjoy without a qualm the many objects of interest which marked the approach to the greatest and most beautiful capital in the world.

On the right, as they sped up the narrow strait, there stretched the Asiatic shore, sprinkled with white villages and with numerous villas peeping out from the woods which adorned it. In front of them, the Prince's Islands, rising as green as emeralds out of the deep sapphire blue of the Sea of Marmora, obscured for the moment the view of the capital. As the brig rounded these, the great city burst suddenly upon their sight, and a murmur of admiration and wonder rose from the crowded deck. Tier above tier it rose, white and glittering, a hundred brazen roofs and gilded statues gleaming in the sun, with high over all the magnificent shining cupola of Saint Sophia. Seen against a cloudless sky, it was the city of a dream—too delicate, too airily lovely for earth.

In the prow of the small vessel were two travellers of singular appearance. The one was a very beautiful boy, ten or twelve years of age, swarthy, clear-cut, with dark, curling hair and vivacious black eyes, full of intelligence and of the joy of living. The other was an elderly man, gaunt-faced and grey-bearded, whose stern features were lit up by a smile as he observed the excitement and interest with which his young companion viewed the beautiful distant city and the many vessels which thronged the narrow strait.

" See ! see ! " cried the lad. " Look at the great red ships which sail out from yonder harbour. Surely, your holiness, they are the greatest of all ships in the world."

The old man, who was the abbot of the Monastery of Saint Nicephorus in Antioch, laid his hand upon the boy's shoulder.

" Be wary, Leon, and speak less loudly, for until we have seen your mother we should keep ourselves secret. As to the red galleys they are indeed as large as any, for they are the Imperial ships of war, which come forth from the harbour of Theodosius. Round yonder green point is the Golden Horn, where the merchant ships are moored. But now, Leon, if you follow the line of buildings past the great church, you will see a long row of pillars fronting the sea. It marks the Palace of the Cæsars."

The boy looked at it with fixed attention. " And my mother is there," he whispered.

" Yes, Leon, your mother the Empress Theodora and her husband the great Justinian dwell in yonder palace."

The boy looked wistfully up into the old man's face. " Are you sure, Father Luke, that my mother will indeed be glad to see me ? "

The abbot turned away his face to avoid those questioning eyes.

" We cannot tell, Leon. We can only try. If it should prove that there is no place for you, then there is always a welcome among the brethren of Saint Nicephorus."

" Why did you not tell my mother that we were coming, Father Luke ? Why did you not wait until you had her command ? "

" At a distance, Leon, it would be easy to refuse you. An Imperial messenger would have stopped us. But when she sees you, Leon—your eyes, so like her own, your face, which carries memories of one whom she loved—then, if there be a woman's heart within her bosom, she will take you into it. They say that the Emperor can refuse her nothing. They have no child of their own. There is a great future before you, Leon. When it comes, do not forget the poor brethren of Saint Nicephorus, who took you in when you had no friend in the world."

The old abbot spoke cheerily, but it was easy to see from his anxious countenance that the nearer he came to the capital the more doubtful did his errand appear. What had seemed easy and natural from the quiet cloisters of Antioch became dubious and dark now that the golden domes of Constantinople glittered so close at hand. Ten years before, a wretched woman, whose very name was an offence throughout the eastern world, where she was as infamous for her dishonour as famous for her beauty, had come to the monastery gate, and had persuaded the monks to take charge of her infant son, the child of her shame. There he had been ever since. But she, Theodora, the harlot, returning to the capital, had by the strangest turn of Fortune's wheel caught the fancy and finally the enduring love of Justinian the heir to the throne. Then on the death of his uncle Justin, the young man had become the greatest monarch upon the earth, and had raised Theodora to be not only his wife and Empress, but to be absolute ruler with powers equal to and independent of his own. And she, the polluted one, had risen to the dignity, had cut herself sternly away from all that related to her past life, and had shown signs already of being a great Queen, stronger and wiser than her husband, but fierce, vindictive, and unbending, a firm support to her friends, but a terror to her foes. This was the woman to whom the Abbot Luke of Antioch was bringing Leon, her forgotten son. If ever her mind strayed back to the days when, abandoned by her lover Ecebolus, the Governor of the African Pentapolis, she had made her way on foot through Asia Minor, and left her infant with the monks, it was only to persuade herself that the brethren cloistered far from the world would never identify Theodora the Empress with Theodora the dissolute wanderer, and that the fruits of her sin would be for ever concealed from her Imperial husband.

The little brig had now rounded the point of the Acropolis, and the long, blue stretch of the Golden Horn lay before it. The high wall of Theodosius lined the whole harbour, but a narrow verge of land had been left between it and the water's edge to serve as a quay. The vessel ran alongside near the Neorion Gate, and the passengers, after a short scrutiny from the group of helmeted guards who lounged beside it, were allowed to pass through into the great city.

The abbot, who had made several visits to Con-

stantinople upon the business of his monastery, walked
with the assured step of one who knows his ground ;
while the boy, alarmed and yet pleased by the rush
of people, the roar and clatter of passing chariots, and
the vista of magnificent buildings, held tightly to the
loose gown of his guide, while staring eagerly about
him in every direction. Passing through the steep and
narrow streets which led up from the water, they emerged
into the open space which surrounds the magnificent
pile of Saint Sophia, the great church begun by Constantine, hallowed by Saint Chrysostom, and now the
seat of the Patriarch, and the very centre of the Eastern
Church. Only with many crossings and genuflections
did the pious abbot succeed in passing the revered
shrine of his religion, and hurried on to his difficult
task.

Having passed Saint Sophia, the two travellers crossed
the marble-paved Augusteum, and saw upon their right
the gilded gates of the hippodrome through which a
vast crowd of people was pressing, for though the morning
had been devoted to the religious ceremony, the afternoon was given over to secular festivities. So great
was the rush of the populace that the two strangers
had some difficulty in disengaging themselves from
the stream and reaching the huge arch of black marble
which formed the outer gate of the palace. Within
they were fiercely ordered to halt by a gold-crested and
magnificent sentinel who laid his shining spear across
their breasts until his superior officer should give them
permission to pass. The abbot had been warned,
however, that all obstacles would give way if he mentioned
the name of Basil the eunuch, who acted as chamberlain
of the palace and also as Parakimomen—a high office
which meant that he slept at the door of the Imperial
bed-chamber. The charm worked wonderfully, for
at the mention of that potent name the Protosphathaire,
or Head of the Palace Guards, who chanced to be upon
the spot, immediately detached one of his soldiers with

instructions to convoy the two strangers into the presence of the chamberlain.

Passing in succession a middle guard and an inner guard, the travellers came at last into the palace proper, and followed their majestic guide from chamber to chamber, each more wonderful than the last. Marbles and gold, velvet and silver, glittering mosaics, wonderful carvings, ivory screens, curtains of Armenian tissue and of Indian silk, damask from Arabia, and amber from the Baltic—all these things merged themselves in the minds of the two simple provincials, until their eyes ached and their senses reeled before the blaze and the glory of this, the most magnificent of the dwellings of man. Finally, a pair of curtains, crusted with gold, were parted, and their guide handed them over to a negro eunuch who stood within. A heavy, fat, brown-skinned man, with a large, flabby, hairless face, was pacing up and down the small apartment, and he turned upon them as they entered with an abominable and threatening smile. His loose lips and pendulous cheeks were those of a gross old woman, but above them there shone a pair of dark, malignant eyes, full of fierce intensity of observation and judgment.

" You have entered the palace by using my name," he said. " It is one of my boasts that any of the populace can approach me in this way. But it is not fortunate for those who take advantage of it without due cause." Again he smiled a smile which made the frightened boy cling tightly to the loose serge skirts of the abbot.

But the ecclesiastic was a man of courage. Undaunted by the sinister appearance of the great chamberlain, or by the threat which lay in his words, he laid his hand upon his young companion's shoulder and faced the eunuch with a confident smile.

" I have no doubt, your excellency," said he, " that the importance of my mission has given me the right to enter the palace. The only thing which troubles

me is whether it may not be so important as to forbid
me from broaching it to you, or indeed, to anybody save
the Empress Theodora, since it is she only whom it
concerns."

The eunuch's thick eyebrows bunched together over
his vicious eyes.

"You must make good those words," he said. " If
my gracious master—the ever-glorious Emperor Justinian
—does not disdain to take me into his most intimate
confidence in all things, it would be strange if there were
any subject within your knowledge which I might not
hear. You are, as I gather from your garb and bearing,
the abbot of some Asiatic monastery ? "

"You are right, your excellency, I am the Abbot of
the Monastery of St. Nicephorus in Antioch. But I
repeat that I am assured that what I have to say is for
the ear of the Empress Theodora only."

The eunuch was evidently puzzled, and his curiosity
aroused by the old man's persistence. He came nearer,
his heavy face thrust forward, his flabby brown hands,
like two sponges, resting upon the table of yellow jasper
before him.

"Old man," said he, " there is no secret which concerns the Empress which may not be told to me. But
if you refuse to speak, it is certain that you will never
see her. Why should I admit you, unless I know your
errand ? How should I know that you are not a Mani-
chean heretic with a poniard in your bosom, longing
for the blood of the mother of the Church ? "

The abbot hesitated no longer. " If there be a mistake in the matter, then on your head be it," said he.
" Know then that this lad Leon is the son of Theodora
the Empress, left by her in our monastery within a month
of his birth ten years ago. This papyrus which I hand
you will show you that what I say is beyond all question
or doubt."

The eunuch Basil took the paper, but his eyes were
fixed upon the boy, and his features showed a mixture

of amazement at the news that he had received, and of cunning speculation as to how he could turn it to profit.

" Indeed, he is the very image of the Empress," he muttered ; and then, with sudden suspicion, " Is it not the chance of this likeness which has put the scheme into your head, old man ? "

" There is but one way to answer that," said the abbot. " It is to ask the Empress herself whether what I say is not true, and to give her the glad tidings that her boy is alive and well."

The tone of confidence, together with the testimony of the papyrus, and the boy's beautiful face, removed the last shadow of doubt from the eunuch's mind. Here was a great fact ; but what use could he make of it ? Above all, what advantage could he draw from it ? He stood with his fat chin in his hand, turning it over in his cunning brain.

" Old man," said he at last, " to how many have you told this secret ? "

" To no one in the whole world," the other answered. " There is Deacon Bardas at the monastery and myself. No one else knows anything."

" You are sure of this ? "

" Absolutely certain."

The eunuch had made up his mind. If he alone of all men in the palace knew of this event, he would have a powerful hold over his masterful mistress. He was certain that Justinian the Emperor knew nothing of this. It would be a shock to him. It might even alienate his affections from his wife. She might care to take precautions to prevent him from knowing. And if he, Basil the eunuch, was her confederate in those precautions, then how very close it must draw him to her. All this flashed through his mind as he stood, the papyrus in his hand, looking at the old man and the boy.

" Stay here," said he. " I will be with you again."

With a swift rustle of his silken robes he swept from the chamber.

A few minutes had elapsed when a curtain at the end of the room was pushed aside, and the eunuch, reappearing, held it back, doubling his unwieldy body into a profound obeisance as he did so. Through the gap came a small, alert woman, clad in golden tissue, with a loose outer mantle and shoes of the Imperial purple. That colour alone showed that she could be none other than the Empress ; but the dignity of her carriage, the fierce authority of her magnificent dark eyes, and the perfect beauty of her haughty face, all proclaimed that it could only be that Theodora who, in spite of her lowly origin, was the most majestic as well as the most maturely lovely of all the women in her kingdom. Gone now were the buffoon tricks which the daughter of Acacius the bearward had learned in the amphitheatre ; gone, too, was the light charm of the wanton, and what was left was the worthy mate of a great king, the measured dignity of one who was every inch an empress.

Disregarding the two men, Theodora walked up to the boy, placed her two white hands upon his shoulders, and looked with a long, questioning gaze, a gaze which began with hard suspicion and ended with tender recognition, into those large, lustrous eyes which were the very reflection of her own. At first the sensitive lad was chilled by the cold, intent question of the look ; but as it softened, his own spirit responded, until suddenly with a cry of " Mother ! Mother ! " he cast himself into her arms, his hands locked round her neck, his face buried in her bosom. Carried away by the sudden natural outburst of emotion, her own arms tightened round the lad's figure, and she strained him for an instant to her heart. Then, the strength of the Empress gaining instant command over the temporary weakness of the mother, she pushed him back from her, and waved that they should leave her to herself. The slaves in attendance hurried the two visitors from the room. Basil the eunuch lingered, looking down at his mistress, who had thrown herself upon a damask couch, her lips white and her bosom heaving with the tumult of her emotion. She glanced up and met the chancellor's crafty gaze, her woman's instinct reading the threat that lurked within it.

" I am in your power," she said. " The Emperor must never know of this."

" I am your slave," said the eunuch, with his ambiguous smile. " I am an instrument in your hand. If it is your will that the Emperor should know nothing, then who is to tell him ? "

" But the monk, the boy ? What are we to do ? "

" There is only one way for safety," said the eunuch.

She looked at him with horrified eyes. His spongy hands were pointing down to the floor. There was an underground world to this beautiful palace, a shadow that was ever close to the light, a region of dimly lit passages, of shadowed corners, of noiseless, tongueless slaves, of sudden sharp screams in the darkness. To this the eunuch was pointing.

A terrible struggle rent her breast. The beautiful boy was hers, flesh of her flesh, bone of her bone. She knew it beyond all question or doubt. It was her one child, and her whole heart went out to him. But Justinian ! She knew the Emperor's strange limitations. Her career in the past was forgotten. He had swept it all aside by special Imperial decree published throughout the Empire, as if she were new-born through the power of his will, and her association with his person. But they were childless, and this sight of one which was not his own would cut him to the quick. He could dismiss her infamous past from his mind, but if it took the concrete shape of this beautiful child, then how could he wave it aside as if it had never been ? All her instincts and intimate knowledge of the man told her that even her charm and her influence might

735

fail under such circumstances to save her from ruin.
Her divorce would be as easy to him as her elevation
had been. She was balanced upon a giddy pinnacle,
the highest in the world, and yet the higher the deeper
the fall. Everything that earth could give was now
at her feet. Was she to risk the losing of it all—for
what ? For a weakness which was unworthy of an
Empress, for a foolish, new-born spasm of love, for that
which had no existence within her in the morning ?
How could she be so foolish as to risk losing such a
substance for such a shadow ?

" Leave it to me," said the brown, watchful face above
her.

" Must it be—death ? "

" There is no real safety outside. But if your
heart is too merciful, then by the loss of sight and
speech——"

She saw in her mind the white-hot iron approaching
those glorious eyes, and she shuddered at the thought.

" No, no ! Better death than that ! "

" Let it be death then. You are wise, great Empress,
for there only is real safety and assurance of silence."

" And the monk ? "

" Him also."

" But the Holy Synod ! He is a tonsured priest.
What would the Patriarch do ? "

" Silence his babbling tongue. Then let them do
what they will. How are we of the palace to know that
this conspirator, taken with a dagger in his sleeve, is
really what he says ? "

Again she shuddered and shrank down among the
cushions.

" Speak not of it, think not of it," said the eunuch.
" Say only that you leave it in my hands. Nay, then,
if you cannot say it, do but nod your head, and I take
it as your signal."

In that moment there flashed before Theodora's mind
a vision of all her enemies, of all those who envied her

rise, of all whose hatred and contempt would rise into a clamour of delight could they see the daughter of the bearward hurled down again into that abyss from which she had been dragged. Her face hardened, her lips tightened, her little hands clenched in the agony of her thought.

" Do it ! " she said.

In an instant, with a terrible smile, the messenger of death hurried from the room. She groaned aloud, and buried herself yet deeper amid the silken cushions, clutching them frantically with convulsed and twitching hands.

The eunuch wasted no time, for this deed, once done, he became—save for some insignificant monk in Asia Minor, whose fate would soon be sealed—the only sharer of Theodora's secret, and therefore the only person who could curb and bend that most imperious nature. Hurrying into the chamber where the visitors were waiting, he gave a sinister signal, only too well known in those iron days. In an instant the black mutes in attendance seized the old man and the boy, pushing them swiftly down a passage and into a meaner portion of the palace, where the heavy smell of luscious cooking proclaimed the neighbourhood of the kitchens. A side corridor led to a heavily barred iron door, and this in turn opened upon a steep flight of stone steps, feebly illuminated by the glimmer of wall lamps. At the head and foot stood a mute sentinel like an ebony statue, and below, along the dusky and forbidding passages from which the cells opened, a succession of niches in the wall were each occupied by a similar guardian. The unfortunate visitors were dragged brutally down a number of stone-flagged and dismal corridors until they descended another long stair which led so deeply into the earth that the damp feeling in the heavy air and the drip of water all round showed that they had come down to the level of the sea. Groans and cries, like those of sick animals, from the various grated doors which they passed showed how many there were who spent their whole lives in this humid and poisonous atmosphere

At the end of this lowest passage was a door which opened into a single large, vaulted room. It was devoid of furniture, but in the centre was a large and heavy wooden board clamped with iron. This lay upon a rude stone parapet, engraved with inscriptions beyond the wit of the eastern scholars, for this old well dated from a time before the Greeks founded Byzantium, when men of Chaldea and Phœnicia built with huge, unmortared blocks, far below the level of the town of Constantine. The door was closed, and the eunuch beckoned to the slaves that they should remove the slab which covered the well of death. The frightened boy screamed and clung to the abbot, who, ashy-pale and trembling, was pleading hard to melt the heart of the ferocious eunuch.

" Surely, surely, you would not slay the innocent boy ! " he cried. " What has he done ? Was it his fault that he came here ? I alone—I and Deacon Bardas —are to blame. Punish us, if someone must indeed be punished. We are old. It is to-day or to-morrow with us. But he is so young and so beautiful, with all his life before him. Oh, sir ! oh, your excellency, you would not have the heart to hurt him ! "

He threw himself down and clutched at the eunuch's knees, while the boy sobbed piteously and cast horror-stricken eyes at the black slaves who were tearing the wooden slab from the ancient parapet beneath. The only answer which the chamberlain gave to the frantic pleadings of the abbot was to take a stone which lay on the coping of the well and toss it in. It could be heard clattering against the old, damp, mildewed walls, until it fell with a hollow boom into some far-distant subterranean pool. Then he again motioned with his hands and the black slaves threw themselves upon the boy and dragged him away from his guardian. So shrill was his clamour that no one heard the approach of the

Empress. With a swift rush she had entered the room, and her arms were round her son.

" It shall not be ! It cannot be ! " she cried. " No, no, my darling ! my darling ! they shall do you no hurt. I was mad to think of it—mad and wicked to dream of it. Oh, my sweet boy ! to think that your mother might have had your blood upon her head ! "

The eunuch's brows were gathered together at this failure of his plans, at this fresh example of feminine caprice.

" Why kill them, great lady, if it pains your gracious heart ? " said he. " With a knife and a branding-iron they can be disarmed for ever."

She paid no attention to his words. " Kiss me, Leon ! " she cried. " Just once let me feel my own child's soft lips rest upon mine. Now again ! No, no more, or I shall weaken for what I have still to say and still to do. Old man, you are very near a natural grave, and I cannot think from your venerable aspect that words of falsehood would come readily to your lips. You have indeed kept my secret all these years, have you not ? "

" I have in very truth, great Empress. I swear to you by Saint Nicephorus, patron of our house, that save old Deacon Bardas, there is none who knows."

" Then let your lips still be sealed. If you have kept faith in the past, I see no reason why you should be a babbler in the future. And you, Leon "—she bent her wonderful eyes with a strange mixture of sternness and of love upon the boy——" can I trust you ? Will you keep a secret which could never help you, but would be the ruin and downfall of your mother ? "

" Oh, mother, I would not hurt you ! I swear that I will be silent."

" Then I trust you both. Such provision will be made for your monastery and for your own personal comforts as will make you bless the day you came to my palace. Now you may go. I wish never to see

739

you again. If I did, you might find me in a softer mood, or in a harder, and the one would lead to my undoing, the other to yours. But if by whisper or rumour I have reason to think that you have failed me, then you and your monks and your monastery will have such an end as will be a lesson for ever to those who would break faith with their Empress."

"I will never speak," said the old abbot; "neither will Deacon Bardas; neither will Leon. For all three I can answer. But there are others—these slaves, the chancellor. We may be punished for another's fault."

"Not so," said the Empress, and her eyes were like flints. "These slaves are voiceless; nor have they any means to tell those secrets which they know. As to you, Basil——" She raised her white hand with the same deadly gesture which he had himself used so short a time before. The black slaves were on him like hounds on a stag.

"Oh, my gracious mistress, dear lady, what is this? What is this? You cannot mean it!" he screamed, in his high, cracked voice. "Oh, what have I done? Why should I die?"

"You have turned me against my own. You have goaded me to slay my own son. You have intended to use my secret against me. I read it in your eyes from the first. Cruel, murderous villain, taste the fate which you have yourself given to so many others. This is your doom. I have spoken."

The old man and the boy hurried in horror from the vault. As they glanced back they saw the erect, inflexible, shimmering, gold-clad figure of the Empress. Beyond they had a glimpse of the green-scummed lining of the well, and of the great red, open mouth of the eunuch, as he screamed and prayed while every tug of the straining slaves brought him one step nearer to the brink. With their hands over their ears they rushed away, but even so they heard that last woman-like shriek, and then the heavy plunge far down in the dark abysses of the earth.

76. *A Point of Contact*

A CURIOUS train of thought is started when one
reflects upon those great figures who have trod
the stage of this earth, and actually played
their parts in the same act, without ever coming face
to face, or even knowing of each other's existence.
Baber, the Great Mogul, was, for example, overrunning
India at the very moment when Hernando Cortez was
overrunning Mexico, and yet the two could never have
heard of each other. Or, to take a more supreme example,
what could the Emperor Augustus Cæsar know of a
certain Carpenter's shop wherein there worked a dreamy-
eyed boy who was destined to change the whole face
of the world ? It may be, however, that sometimes
these great contemporary forces did approach, touch,
and separate—each unaware of the true meaning of
the other. So it was in the instance which is now
narrated.

It was evening in the port of Tyre, some eleven hundred
years before the coming of Christ. The city held, at
that time, about a quarter of a million of inhabitants,
the majority of whom dwelt upon the mainland, where
the buildings of the wealthy merchants, each in its own
tree-girt garden, extended for seven miles along the
coast. The great island, however, from which the town
got its name, lay out some distance from the shore,
and contained within its narrow borders the more
famous of the temples and public buildings. Of these
temples the chief was that of Melmoth, which covered
with its long colonnades the greater part of that side of
the island which looked down upon the Sidonian port,
so called because only twenty miles away the older city
of Sidon maintained a constant stream of traffic with
its rising offshoot.

Inns were not yet in vogue, but the poorer traveller

found his quarters with hospitable citizens, while men of distinction were frequently housed in the annexe of the temples, where the servants of the priests attended to their wants. On that particular evening there stood in the portico of the temple of Melmoth two remarkable figures who were the centre of observation for a considerable fringe of Phœnician idlers. One of these men was clearly by his face and demeanour a great chieftain. His strongly marked features were those of a man who had led an adventurous life, and were suggestive of every virile quality from brave resolve to desperate execution. His broad, high brow and contemplative eyes showed that he was a man of wisdom as well as of valour. He was clad, as became a Greek nobleman of the period, with a pure white linen tunic, a gold-studded belt supporting a short sword, and a purple cloak. The lower legs were bare, and the feet covered by sandals of red leather, while a cap of white cloth was pushed back upon his brown curls, for the heat of the day was past and the evening breeze most welcome.

His companion was a short, thick-set man, bull-necked and swarthy, clad in some dusky cloth which gave him a sombre appearance relieved only by the vivid scarlet of his woollen cap. His manner towards his comrade was one of deference, and yet there was in it also something of that freshness and frankness which go with common dangers and a common interest.

"Be not impatient, sire," he was saying. "Give me two days, or three at the most, and we shall make as brave a show at the muster as any. But indeed, they would smile if they saw us crawl up to Tenedos with ten missing oars and the mainsail blown into rags."

The other frowned and stamped his foot with anger.

"We should have been there now had it not been for this cursed mischance," said he. "Aeolus played us a pretty trick when he sent such a blast out of a cloudless sky."

"Well, sire, two of the Cretan galleys foundered,

and Trophimes, the pilot, swears that one of the Argos ships was in trouble. Pray Zeus that it was not the galley of Menelaus. We shall not be the last at the muster."

" It is well that Troy stands a good ten miles from the sea, for if they came out at us with a fleet they might have us at a disadvantage. We had no choice but to come here and refit, yet I shall have no happy hour until I see the white foam from the lash of our oars once more. Go, Seleucas, and speed them all you may."

The officer bowed and departed, while the chieftain stood with his eyes fixed upon his great dismantled galley over which the riggers and carpenters were swarming. Farther out in the roadstead lay eleven other smaller galleys, waiting until their wounded flagship should be ready for them. The sun, as it shone upon them, gleamed upon hundreds of bronze helmets and breast-plates, telling of the war-like nature of the errand upon which they were engaged. Save for them the port was filled with bustling merchant ships taking in cargoes or disgorging them upon the quays. At the very feet of the Greek chieftain three broad barges were moored, and gangs of labourers with wooden shovels were heaving out the mussels brought from Dor, destined to supply the famous Tyrian dye-works which adorn the most noble of all garments. Beside them was a tin ship from Britain, and the square boxes of that precious metal, so needful for the making of bronze, were being passed from hand to hand to the waiting wagons. The Greek found himself smiling at the uncouth wonder of a Cornishman who had come with his tin, and who was now lost in amazement as he stared at the long colonnades of the Temple of Melmoth and the high front of the Shrine of Ashtaroth behind it. Even as he gazed some of his shipmates passed their hands through his arms and led him along the quay to a wine-shop, as being a building much more within his comprehension. The Greek, still smiling, was turning on his heels to return to the

Temple, when one of the clean-shaven priests of Baal came towards him.

" It is rumoured, sire," said he, " that you are on a very distant and dangerous venture. Indeed, it is well known from the talk of your soldiers what it is that you have on hand."

" It is true," said the Greek, " that we have a hard task before us. But it would have been harder to bide at home and to feel that the honour of a leader of the Argives had been soiled by this dog from Asia."

" I hear that all Greece has taken up the quarrel."

" Yes, there is not a chief from Thessaly to the Malea who has not called out his men, and there were twelve hundred galleys in the harbour of Aulis."

" It is a great host," said the priest. " But have ye any seers or prophets among ye who can tell what will come to pass ? "

" Yes, we had one such, Calchas his name. He has said that for nine years we shall strive, and only on the tenth will the victory come."

" That is but cold comfort," said the priest. " It is, indeed, a great prize which can be worth ten years of a man's life."

" I would give," the Greek answered, " not ten years but all my life if I could but lay proud Ilium in ashes and carry back Helen to her palace on the hill of Argos."

" I pray Baal, whose priest I am, that you may have good fortune," said the Phœnician. " I have heard that these Trojans are stout soldiers, and that Hector, the son of Priam, is a mighty leader."

The Greek smiled proudly.

" They must be stout and well-led also," said he, " if they can stand the brunt against the long-haired Argives with such captains as Agamemnon, the son of Atreus from golden Mycenæ, or Achilles, son of Peleus, with his myrmidons. But these things are on the knees of the Fates. In the meantime, my friend, I would fain know who these strange people are who come down the street, for their chieftain has the air of one who is made for great deeds."

A tall man clad in a long, white robe, with a golden fillet through his flowing auburn hair, was striding down the street with the free, elastic gait of one who has lived an active life in the open. His face was ruddy and noble, with a short, crisp beard covering a strong, square jaw. In his clear blue eyes as he looked at the evening sky and the busy waters beneath him there was something of the exaltation of the poet, while a youth walking beside him and carrying a harp hinted at the graces of music. On the other side of him, however, a second squire bore a brazen shield and a heavy spear, so that his master might never be caught unawares by his enemies. In his train there came a tumultuous rabble of dark, hawk-like men, armed to the teeth, and peering about with covetous eyes at the signs of wealth which lay in profusion around them. They were swarthy as Arabs, and yet they were better clad and better armed than the wild children of the desert.

"They are but barbarians," said the priest. "He is a small king from the mountain parts opposite Philistia, and he comes here because he is building up the town of Jebus, which he means to be his chief city. It is only here that he can find the wood, and stone, and crafts-manship that he desires. The youth with the harp is his son. But I pray you, chief, if you would know what is before you at Troy, to come now into the outer hall of the Temple with me, for we have there a famous seer, the prophetess Alaga who is also the priestess of Ashtar-oth. It may be that she can do for you what she has done for many others, and send you forth from Tyre in your hollow ships with a better heart than you came."

To the Greeks, who by oracles, omens, and auguries were for ever prying into the future, such a suggestion was always welcome. The Greek followed the priest to the inner sanctuary, where sat the famous Pythoness

—a tall, fair woman of middle age, who sat at a stone table upon which was an abacus or tray filled with sand. She held a style of chalcedony, and with this she traced strange lines and curves upon the smooth surface, her chin leaning upon her other hand and her eyes cast down. As the chief and the priest approached her she did not look up, but she quickened the movements of her pencil, so that curve followed curve in quick succession. Then, still with downcast eyes, she spoke in a strange, high, sighing voice like wind amid the trees.

"Who, then, is this who comes to Alaga of Tyre, the handmaiden of great Ashtaroth? Behold I see an island to the west, and an old man who is the father, and the great chief, and his wife, and his son who now waits him at home, being too young for the wars. Is this not true?"

"Yes, maiden, you have said truth," the Greek answered.

"I have had many great ones before me, but none greater than you, for three thousand years from now people will still talk of your bravery and of your wisdom. They will remember also the faithful wife at home, and the name of the old man, your father, and of the boy, your son—all will be remembered when the very stones of noble Sidon and royal Tyre are no more."

"Nay, say not so, Alaga!" cried the priest.

"I speak not what I desire but what it is given to me to say. For ten years you will strive, and then you will win, and victory will bring rest to others, but only new troubles to you. Ah!" The prophetess suddenly started in violent surprise, and her hand made ever faster markings on the sand.

"What is it that ails you, Alaga?" asked the priest. The woman had looked up with wild, inquiring eyes. Her gaze was neither for the priest nor for the chief, but shot past them to the farther door. Looking round the Greek was aware that two new figures had entered the room. They were the ruddy barbarian whom he had marked in the street, together with the youth who bore his harp.

" It is a marvel upon marvels that two such should enter my chamber on the same day," cried the priestess. " Have I not said that you were the greatest that ever came, and yet behold here is already one who is greater. For he and his son—even this youth whom I see before me—will also be in the minds of all men when lands beyond the Pillars of Hercules shall have taken the place of Phœnicia and of Greece. Hail to you, stranger, hail ! Pass on to your work, for it awaits you, and it is great beyond words of mine." Rising from her stool the woman dropped her pencil upon the sand and passed swiftly from the room.

" It is over," said the priest. " Never have I heard her speak such words."

The Greek chief looked with interest at the barbarian. " You speak Greek ? " he asked.

" Indifferently well," said the other. " Yet I should understand it seeing that I spent a long year at Ziklag in the land of the Philistines."

" It would seem," said the Greek, " that the gods have chosen us both to play a part in the world."

" Stranger," the barbarian answered, " there is but one God."

" Say you so ? Well, it is a matter to be argued at some better time. But I would fain have your name and style and what is it you purpose to do, so that we may perchance hear of each other in years to come. For my part I am Odysseus, known also as Ulysses, the King of Ithaca, with the good Laertes as my father and young Telemachus as my son. For my work, it is the taking of Troy."

" And my work," said the barbarian, " is the building of Jebus, which now we call Jerusalem. Our ways lie separate, but it may come back to your memory that you have crossed the path of David, second King of the

Hebrews, together with his young son Solomon, who may follow him upon the throne of Israel."

So he turned and went forth into the darkened streets where his spearmen were awaiting him, while the Greek passed down to his boat that he might see what was still to be done ere he could set forth upon his voyage.